TIME FRAMED

ROGER CHIOCCHI

This is in part a work of fiction. Although somewhat inspired by actual events, the names, persons, places and characters are inventions of the author. Any resemblance to people living or deceased is purely coincidental.

DEDICATION

To the greatest generation, particularly my parents, aunts and uncles - Phil, Joe, Bea, Mike, Kay, Roger, Vi, Adolph, John, Terry, Ren, Doris, Lon, Ace, Nat, Pat, Audrey, Sandy.

You taught us great lessons.

ACKNOWLEDGMENTS

This one was tough.

Perhaps if I was a more skilled writer it would not have been to the same degree. Nonetheless, this one stretched whatever skills I had to their natural limits.

I had this idea of writing a story about the present battling with the future to change the course of the intervening period connecting them, each to its own advantage, a conflict of wills and might.

Perhaps I did it out of stubbornness. One of the nicknames my mom crafted for me as a youth was "testa dura," or "hard head." With that one, she was right on.

Why?

Because I hardly knew all the implications I would have to deal with: parallel universes, grandfather paradoxes, wave-particle duality and the nature of human consciousness, just to begin.

So it was of little surprise when it actually took me 12 years to complete the story.

But now it's done, the result of all the storytelling might I could muster.

Not only was this quest a fantastic journey, but an education — it lead me to question such basic concepts as reality, the nature of time, the relationship between mind and brain, the future of our political society and world and, ultimately, the nature of humankind itself.

I enjoyed the journey immensely.

And, of course, there were those fellow passengers and tour guides who helped me throughout the struggle. First, I have to acknowledge Caron Knauer who was my developmental editor, muse and provocateur. She pulled no punches, sending me back to the drawing board time and time again as I simultaneously cussed her out and was awed by her. Whatever she did was always in defense of a better book.

I hope I didn't let her down.

Then there was Molly O'Donnell — or should I say *Dr. Molly O'Donnell* — who artfully copyedited the final draft while also helping me with some final developmental editing. And, as a Professor of Philosophy, was aptly able to school me on the writings of Spinoza and a few others.

And, of course, my creative partner, Victor DeCastro, who willingly listened to the entire first draft— well, actually, more like the *one hundred and first draft* — as we carpooled to work each day. He also designed the book's wonderful cover. Bravo.

Great people, great collaborators.

Then, there's my daughter Catherine who is a constant source of pride and inspiration, a tremendously talented writer herself. And my many friends who have provided guidance and support, too many to list here, plus I don't want to risk leaving anyone out.

And, lastly, all of those out there who are willing to at very least ponder the possibility that what we see as and call "reality" on an everyday basis is really just the tip of a humongous iceberg.

Peace.

Roger Chiocchi
June 5, 2018
Norwalk, CT

TIME FRAMED

"God does not play dice with the universe."
-Albert Einstein

"Einstein, stop telling God what to do."
-Niels Bohr

1

Greenwich, Connecticut, Indian Harbor, December 22, 1963

The annual family Christmas party at the home of the Percival Pennfields' in Greenwich, Connecticut was as much a marker of the season as the carols heralding from the churches, the twinkling colorful lights strung along Main Street and the lush green wreaths adorning front doors throughout the storied town. Everything about the family event held each Sunday before Christmas was the product of a well-rehearsed script, with only slight details changing from year to year.

This year, however, the serene procession of warm family greetings, clinking tumblers of scotch, Christmas cookies, and festive seasonal garb was abruptly hijacked. Without warning, some unknown force sliced a riptide through their holiday ritual. The incident occurred right behind the Pennfields' grand Dutch colonial, even as a warm glow emanated from its windows, floating into the frosty indigo evening over Indian Harbor.

"SHIP! *SHIPPY!*" Jonathan vigorously shook the shoulders of his younger cousin, who was sitting naked, shivering with goosebumps at the end of the old rickety dock.

"Shippy, what happened?" Jonathan shook the seven year old's shoulders once again.

Breathing heavily, Cousin Lance ran over. "Did you see the glow Jonathan? Did you see it? It was right above the water."

"A glow? What kind of glow?" Jonathan asked, confused.

"Over the water. I saw it. I really saw it."

Jonathan shook Shippy once again.

Nothing.

Shippy remained unresponsive and shivering as his vacant eyes stared out to nowhere.

"Go get Ophie," Jonathan shouted at Lance. "Go get Ophie now!"

OPHELIA PENNFIELD, Shippy's twenty-two-year-old sister, arrived quickly, her older cousin Christopher running beside her, with Lance trailing behind. She looked at her little brother sitting naked and shivering, his bare feet dangling off the dock in mid-winter. The site was so odd— so out of place and unexpected— her mind could not fit together the juxtaposition of images.

"Jesus!" cousin Christopher exclaimed.

"I think he saw something," Lance said. "I'm sure he saw something."

The other two young boys nodded.

When Ophie could fully process it, finally grasp the reality that the boy was sitting naked and unresponsive at the end of the dock on a cold, blustery night, she screamed.

Christopher turned towards her, held her face in both hands and commanded her to run back to the house for help.

"FATHER, FATHER!"

All heads in the library turned towards Ophie shaking in the entranceway. The contrast between her stark-white face and jet-black hair was more extreme than usual.

"Ophie? What's wrong?" Her father rushed over.

"It's Arthur. Little Shippy," she blurted.

"What? What about Arthur?"

"Something's wrong. Outside. Something's terribly wrong!"

SPRINTING OUT THE DOOR, Ophelia dragged her father to the inlet and over the rolling, clacking slats, rushing to the end of the dock. Christopher was looking deep into the boy's eyes, calling his name, as Jonathan, Charles and Lance hovered nearby.

"You see, father, you see," Ophelia began anxiously, "there's something wrong. He's not responding to anyone. We've been calling to him. He hears nothing!"

"There was a glow, a glow, Uncle Perce," Lance said as he tugged at his uncle. "It was strange. And then it went away!"

Ignoring his nephews, Percival Pennfield stared directly at his young son.

Shippy's glazed eyes were penetrating and focused, but only at some vague, obscure point.

The men from the library swarmed onto the dock but stood back.

"Arthur! Arthur! *Talk* to me." Percival Pennfield shook his son vigorously by the shoulders.

The young boy shivered, his arms wrapped around his knees, frost clinging to his soft white skin, oblivious to where he was or whom he was with.

"Arthur. Arthur, it's your father!" Pennfield shook more vigorously.

Nothing.

"Ship. Shippy! What's wrong with you?" This time he shook with a fury.

A series of vacant-eyed shivers.

"Arthur! Shippy! *Answer me, damnit!"* Enraged with frustration— *wham!* — Pennfield slapped his large hand across his son's face.

Nothing.

The young boy wiped his face as if the slap was a minor itch and gazed again out into nothingness.

* * *

2

Greenwich, Connecticut, Indian Harbor, December 22, 1963

Up until that moment, nothing out of the ordinary had occurred at this year's episode of the Pennfield family's party. The fire crackled in the marble fireplace and the player-piano cranked out Christmas tunes as clusters of Pennfield scions from throughout the northeast exchanged holiday greetings in the main vestibule, bunching into a bottleneck of goodwill and cheer.

"Bonjour, mon jeune cousin brilliant," Christopher Pennfield bellowed joyously stepping through the doorway and dusting snow from his coat as he spotted his little seven-year old cousin Shippy galloping down the staircase.

"Et comment vos études à Paris avaient-elles progressé?" little Shippy responded, bounding towards his cousin.

"Stimuler, mais difficile. Et vôtre?" Christopher whirled Shippy around in his arms. Ever since little Arthur Shipkin Pennfield was an infant he had formed a special bond with his cousin Christopher. Although separated by twenty years, the two shared a simpatico that transcended age.

"Très bien. J'apprécie en particulier la géométrie," the young boy answered. The two were widely considered the most brilliant members of the family: Christopher, pursuing post-doctoral work in philosophy at the prestigious École Normale Superiéure, and Arthur, a child prodigy, precocious beyond his years, fluent in French since the age of five and already a master of geometry and algebra. The slight, freckle-faced young boy could hold his

own with his older cousin in discussions of mathematics, science and even politics.

"Tres bon. Tres bon."

"AND HOW'S Paris treating you, Chris?" a familiar, raspy voice interrupted.

"Uncle Perce!" Christopher pivoted to greet his uncle, with little Arthur draped on his shoulders. A distinguished investment banker, Percival Pennfield was tall and striking, his silver hair swept back fashionably across his scalp.

"Paris? Well, the professors are unbearably sadistic, the work is difficult but stimulating, and the women are… well, I think you know…". He winked.

His uncle grinned.

"SO, THE PRODIGAL SON FINALLY RETURNS!"

"Ophie!" Christopher exclaimed the moment he caught a glimpse of little Arthur's older sister.

Ophelia Pennfield, a petite dark-haired beauty with classic features and boundless energy, rushed over to Christopher and hugged both him and her brother. "Chris, how are you? It's been months!"

"Only six, but who's counting," he responded, kissing her on the cheek.

"You must tell me about Paris."

"Indeed."

"Jonathan! Charles! Lance!" little Shippy exclaimed with glee the moment he spotted his young cousins entering the vestibule. He sprang from Christopher's grasp and darted towards them.

"Well, it has to be the most beautiful city in the world," Christopher continued with Ophelia, "the food is beyond heavenly and, of course, the wines are—"

Shippy barreled into the crowd and tugged at his mother's festive green and red dress. "Mother, can we go outside and play?"

Margaret "Bunny" Pennfield shook her head. "No, Shippy. It's getting dark and it's viciously cold."

Shippy looked over towards his sister, Ophelia.

Defenseless against the expressive eyes of her spry, freckle-faced brother, Ophie was an easy mark.

"Oh Mother," Ophelia Pennfield twirled towards her mom, "let them go, they hardly see each other."

"Okay," Bunny answered. "But only for twenty minutes, and bundle up."

THE FOUR YOUNG boys barreled out the front door, caroming off arriving guests and bouncing playfully into the mounds of crusty snow bordering the inlet. The narrow beach was cold and brittle, with bristling water brushing back and forth against its thin shoreline.

"Hey, Shippy!" Jonathan Pennfield's voice cast a frosty echo against the slight whistle of the cold December breeze.

"Yeah?" His little cousin Arthur turned around.

"Heads up!" Jonathan lofted a snowball towards Arthur's face.

"Moron!" Arthur scowled, wiping snowflakes from his cheek.

Embarrassed, Arthur scooped up a pile of snow and ran towards his cousin. Larger and faster, Jonathan easily pulled away from Arthur's chase. Little Shippy was an easy target for his stronger, faster cousins; doted upon by his parents and sister, he was protected as if he were a fragile egg, its shell still too thin to weather the vagaries of the world. He made a half-hearted attempt to heave the snow towards the others before they ran off.

"Hey, Charles," Jonathan called over to his other cousin, "bet you I can throw one across the water."

"Bet you can't," Charles answered.

Alone, Shippy walked off towards the dock in a huff. The rickety gray slats on the lone dock protruded out from the beach to cold, dreary waters. He looked up into the twilight dotted by faint twinkles of early evening stars. The setting sent a chill up little Shippy's spine as the boy's oversized intellect conspired with his small, wiry frame to leave him both in awe and fear of his surroundings. Anxiously, he threw a snowball into the water and then looked up with innocence and wonder. After a moment of sheer elation— marveling at the stars and the deep blue sky— his jaw suddenly dropped. He blinked twice, observing a mysterious, shimmering glow.

When he realized what it might be, he gasped.

A blurry oval hovered over the inlet; it appeared as if it might be some sort of figure, but the colors and shapes were too diffuse. The voice emanating from the odd shape was thunderous. It echoed, audible only to Shippy.

The young boy answered it:

"How do you know who I am? Who are you? Are you a Pennfield?"

"Ship! Shippy! Come over here. We're throwing snowballs!" Jonathan called out to him.

"Ship? Shippy…"

When Ship didn't answer, Jonathan sprinted towards the dock.

* * *

3

Lenox, Massachusetts, Gladwell Sanitarium, January 2, 1964

A neglected ivy-covered brick structure, Gladwell Sanitarium jutted out from the Berkshire countryside with an inflated sense of self-worth. The tired old structure could easily have once been a shining castle, a home to the landed aristocracy, but no longer. That passage of time had sapped away all suggestions of ebullience and color. It stood now like a giant mausoleum, surrounded with acres of crunchy brown grass and a spiked, wrought-iron fence. A melancholy pallor hung like a dark veil from above, as if the elements conspired to assume the disposition of Gladwell's residents.

Percival Pennfield adjusted his omnipresent bowtie as he walked around the Cadillac to open the doors for his wife and daughter. As they approached the portico, he surveyed the old red-brick structure, his eye following a vine of ivy up to a third-floor window. He had serious reservations about entrusting his son to this institution. But his close friend Chuck Edwards, a Yale classmate and renowned internist, assured him this was the very best facility of its kind. So with a degree of hesitation, Pennfield agreed to have Shippy transported to Gladwell for observation several days prior to their visit.

"I'M PERCIVAL PENNFIELD," he announced to a Germanic looking woman with short blonde hair at the front desk. "We're here to see Dr. Hazard about our Arthur."

"Of course," the woman answered with a slight accent, and an awkward squint in one of her eyes. "We've been expecting you, Mr. Pennfield."

PERCIVAL PENNFIELD HAD DEVELOPED a set of keen, uncanny instincts over his years on Wall Street, and his instincts sent unsettling signals the moment he first met Dr. Emilio Hazard.

"A *pleazzzure,* a *pleazzzure*, indeed," Hazard announced in his thick, Swiss-German accent as he offered his hand to Pennfield.

Pennfield clasped firmly. *A dead fish,* he thought, assessing Hazard's flimsy handshake.

"So what the hell's going on with my son?" Pennfield blurted as he disengaged hands with Hazard.

"I certainly can understand your extreme concern, Mr. and Mrs. Pennfield, Ophelia," Hazard nodded and then smirked, exposing his misaligned, yellowed teeth.

" 'Concern' is an understatement, Dr. Hazard," Percival Pennfield answered with his sharp, raspy whisper, looking Hazard right in the eyes, sizing him up: a short, unattractive man with a shock of oily black hair brushed across his balding scalp.

"Excuse me, but it's Ha-*ZAIRD*, eh?" Hazard again smirked and raised his eyes above his glasses.

"Of course, Dr. Ha-*ZAIRD*," Pennfield conveyed his impatience by over-exaggerating the name.

"What can you do for our son, Dr. Ha-*ZAIRD*," Bunny Pennfield asked, almost begging.

"Come with me," Hazard directed, leading them up a flight of stairs to Shippy's room.

UPON ENTERING, their faces turned white. The young boy appeared to be some sort of puppet with flesh, returning nothing but a blank stare, a few incoherent mumbles and some facial twitches. Bald spots dotted his scalp, each a connection point for an EEG sensor. The two bright lights added an eerie illumination to his small, freckled face creating menacing shadows behind him. He sat motionless on a beige, steel-framed bed with a Spartan mattress as the hypnotic rhythm of the heart-monitor pulsed somberly, its green line scrolling endlessly across its screen, leaping with each beat.

"We've examined him quite thoroughly, quite thoroughly, indeed," Dr.

Hazard explained as he approached Shippy's bed and flipped him around allowing his legs to dangle off the side.

"And?"

"Watch," said the doctor.

The doctor struck the young boy's knee with a mallet. No response. He pricked his arm with a pin. No response. He brushed his cheek with a small feather. Nothing.

"What in the name of God are you doing, Dr. Hazard?" Pennfield growled. "What's all this poppycock with pins and mallets and feathers?"

"Be patient, Mr. Pennfield," Hazard continued probing the child.

"But I don't think you're getting it. This is *my* son, my own flesh and blood!"

Bunny Pennfield put her hand on her husband's shoulder. "Perce, please—"

"You have to understand, Mr. Pennfield, this is a very complicated diagnosis," said Hazard.

What do you mean?"

"He has limited motor-nerve response but then the X-rays show no lesions on the brain. So we have neurological symptoms with no neurological etiology, at least none that we've been able to discover."

"So you're saying he has a *psychiatric* disorder?" Ophelia asked.

"The signs are pointing in that direction," Hazard answered. "At first we thought his symptoms were consistent with some sort of delirium, but usually a delirium episode is set off by some external factor like a disease or a traumatic experience."

"The boys did say they saw a glow out on the dock, but we checked, there was nothing we could confirm," Ophelia mentioned.

"So then we thought, perhaps it's what we call catatonic schizophrenia."

"Schizophrenia?" Shocked, Bunny Pennfield covered her mouth.

"Yes, it's a rare form. But some of his symptoms lead in that direction. Watch." The doctor walked over to the young boy, propped up against his pillows, almost to a seated position. He pulled Arthur's right elbow up even with his shoulder and allowed his forearm to hang limp.

"What are you doing?" Percival asked, confused.

"Just watch," Hazard answered.

The doctor let go of young Arthur's elbow.

Pennfield gasped. The arm remained in the exact position, jutting out from the young boy's shoulder, his forearm dangling limp from the elbow.

"Jesus!" Ophelia cried.

"Oh my God," her mother gasped.

"What the hell is that?" Percival barked.

"Catalepsy," Hazard answered. "It's a state of muscular rigidity or what we call *waxy flexibility*. We can place his limbs in any position, even a contortionist's position, and they'll stay there. It's a pretty strong marker for catatonic schizophrenia."

"What are you trying to do, make my son into some sort of a side show?"

"Not at all. We're just trying to hone in on the proper diagnosis."

"And that would be…"

"As I said," Hazard explained, "we are leaning towards it not being a neurological affliction, but rather a psychiatric one, catatonic schizophrenia. That's as close as we can get right now."

"Well, I'm sorry Dr. Ha-ZAIRD," Pennfield barked, exaggerating the pronunciation of the doctor's name, "but that's just not good enough!"

"I understand, but let me ask you this: has there been any history of any traits like this in your immediate family, or your wife's family?" Hazard had an ingratiating habit of nodding his head, half-smiling, and raising his eyes above his glasses as a punctuation each time he spoke. Although the gesture was intended to be deferential, Pennfield took it as patronizing.

Percival Pennfield swallowed hard. "Well, we've had our share of…" he stopped and asked himself how far he should go, "…of what I would call… uh…eccentric characters."

"Eccentric, you're saying?" Hazard raised an eyebrow and flashed that ingratiating smirk, exposing his crooked teeth.

Pennfield swallowed again. "Well, yes, you know, I had um, an Aunt Sarah who was very depressed and ended her life in an institution, if I remember correctly. And there may have been a few others, and of course some alcoholics here and there, but how the hell is this relevant to the health of my son?"

"So, Mr. Pennfield, you do not think that a family history of despondency can have anything to do with your son's condition?" Hazard raised his eyebrow, then wrote something down in a notebook.

"We may have had our share of issues, but no more than any other family."

Hazard looked up again and addressed the family. "The young child has a condition which most closely resembles the symptoms for catatonic schizophrenia, eh? And he has at least one relative— a great aunt— who had to be institutionalized for depression and perhaps some other serious psychological conditions."

"So you're saying Shippy might have inherited this condition?" Bunny asked.

"Perhaps," Hazard responded.

"So, what does this treatment entail?" Pennfield asked.

"Unfortunately, there is no simple answer," Hazard responded with an almost condescending smirk. "We hardly see anything of this sort in more industrialized countries. You can count on your fingers the number of cases we see in North America and Europe. This is a phenomenon which we see mostly in third world countries."

"Then why did it happen to Shippy?" Ophelia asked.

"Very good question. Very good, indeed. At this point we can only ponder upon it."

"Ponder?" Percival growled, "You're supposed to be one of the world's leading psychiatrists and all you can do is ponder?"

Hazard nodded and smiled in deference, "Mr. Pennfield, unfortunately, this is a very, very intriguing malady."

"So when the hell is it going to be over and done with?" Pennfield demanded.

"Hard to tell," Hazard answered, "The symptoms may disappear, moderate, or last forever, quite impossible to determine."

"Goddamnit!" Pennfield punched his fist on his son's bed frame.

Bunny put her arm around her husband. "Please, Perce. Please…"

"I certainly understand, Mr. Pennfield, certainly," Hazard responded. "But there is no established protocol of treatment for your son's condition."

"Then let me ask again," Pennfield rasped, "what are we doing here if you're incapable of treating my son?"

Hazard smiled deferentially. "Quite frankly, Mr. Pennfield, if anyone is capable of treating your son, it would be me."

"Then—"

"I have examined more patients with these symptoms than any psychiatrist in the world. I have several well-developed theories of what treatment regimen might be most successful."

"So let's get going," Ophie responded.

"Unfortunately, Ophelia," Hazard nodded and raised his eyebrows again, "it's not quite that simple. I have applied numerous times for funding for clinical research which— in my humble opinion— would help moderate this condition. But, regretfully, the funding has never materialized. They say the affliction is far too rare."

"Funding, eh?" Percival Pennfield knew the subject of money would come up eventually, his only question had been how Hazard might slip it in.

"Yes, funding." Hazard answered. "For fifty or sixty thousand dollars, we would be able to make serious strides in the treatment of young Arthur's affliction." Hazard nodded at Ophelia. "An unfortunate affliction. Very, very unfortunate."

Inside, Pennfield chuckled. The way Dr. Hazard pandered to Ophelia was so transparent it was almost comical. He looked Hazard in the eyes. "Can I speak with my wife and daughter in private for a moment, Dr. Hazard?"

"Yes, of course. Of course, Mr. Pennfield." Hazard nodded and then backed his way out of the room.

"WHAT DO YOU THINK, PERCE?" Bunny asked.

"I don't know. Frankly," Percival answered, "I expected him to ask for much more."

"Father, does everything in life have to be about *money*? Just give it to him." Ophelia raised her voice.

"Perce, will you do it?" Bunny asked.

"Well, you can't deny it," Pennfield rasped, "the man's credentials are impeccable. Yet there's something about him that bothers me, makes me queasy."

"But he's the best in the world, Father," Ophelia countered. "Doesn't our Shippy deserve the very best?"

Silently, Pennfield focused on the catatonic Ship, then gazed out the window at the rolling countryside. He thought for several moments, and then swallowed hard. "Perhaps it might be worth giving Dr. Ha-*ZAIRD* an opportunity. This place is close enough to visit, but far enough away from the New York riff-raff. Yes, it could work for us."

"Percival, is that your only concern, staying away from the New York riff-raff?" Bunny admonished her husband.

"Whatever you may want to think, it's important, Bunny," Pennfield said, "extremely important."

"DR. HAZARD," Percival Pennfield immediately addressed the doctor as he re-entered the room, "My family and I are in agreement. I'm prepared to fund all of your research personally."

"I see. Of course." Hazard nodded, stunned.

"So, it's settled," Pennfield stood up from his chair and offered his hand. "Arthur will stay here at Gladwell, and you will take steps to begin your research immediately."

"Yes. Of course." Hazard was taken aback by the suddenness of the Pennfields' decision.

Pennfield led Bunny and Ophelia towards the door. "You can expect a check in three days, Dr. Hazard. Certified, of course. Just get our Shippy back to normal."

Hazard saved his largest smirk for last.

4

Lenox, Massachusetts, Gladwell Sanitarium, January – June, 1964

For days, the young boy sat straight up in his hospital bed, comatose and oblivious to his surroundings: his head shaven, his eyes vacant and deep, his face expressing a bland state of indifference. Sensors on his head and chest sent a rhythmic set of beats to the monitors above. Ostensibly, he was a seven-year-old boy sitting up in a hospital bed, nothing radically unusual, but the vacant eeriness of his expression, his hollow unresponsiveness, and the rhythmic expansion and contraction of his chest with each breath —the sole evidence of his existence—formed a jolting, disconcerting sight.

Each moment little Ship endured this condition— this stranglehold on his senses— the affliction matured; what began as a presumed acute attack which would hopefully inflict its damage and then be over and done with, soon deepened into something more chronic, one that might last forever. His family gradually resigned themselves to the unsettling possibility of permanence.

Ship's days were not without minor deviations from the norm. During his second month at Gladwell, Drs. Hazard and Hoq noticed some slight twitching around his nose and eyes. Although hopeful— since this slight response by Ship might be a nascent sign of the efficacy of their care— the doctors cautiously reigned in their enthusiasm, restraining themselves from over-reacting. Anxiously, they waited for a more concrete sign.

Several weeks later, such a sign came.

The young boy's eyes bulged, the veins in his neck quivered, sweat poured down his face as he battled with his faculties. He struggled to move his lips even slightly. Gradually he formed a sound, sapping every ounce of energy his body could muster.

"...Spuh...Spuh...," Ship stuttered in a soft whisper, *"Spuh... Spuh..."* He took a deep breath, held it in for a moment, and let out a sound: *"... Spuh... Spuh...Sparrrrrr..."*

Hazard and Hoq hovered over him, noticing every little movement, hanging onto every little grunt. The young boy struggled once more, white-faced and clammy from his sweat. He was not yet done.

"Ruh... Ruh..." his neck turned red, his veins popping as he struggled, "... *Ruh...Ruh... Rowwwww,"* he blurted.

He took a deep, deep breath. He held it in, then spouted hastily as the air rushed out: *"Spaar-rooowww."*

"What was that he said, *'Sparrow'* like the bird?" Hoq asked Hazard.

"That's what I heard," Hazard responded.

"What do you think it means?" Hoq asked.

"I have no idea."

* * *

GREENWICH, Connecticut
Indian Harbor
Time: Unknown

A SPONGE FOR KNOWLEDGE, Shippy Pennfield loved nature and loved to explore. On weekend days he would spend hours in the nearby woods weaving between the houses on Indian Harbor, even wandering right on to their properties, alone or with friends, climbing trees, playing games, chasing squirrels and all other types of animals. On this clear Spring day in April, he and his friends— Tommy Murphy, Jake Sunderland and Allie Johnson— were deep into a series of games of Hide and Seek. This time, Shippy was "It," his hands over his eyes and his face pressed to a tree trunk as his friends scurried about the woods, rushing to find their hiding places.

"... Seven... Eight... Nine... Ten..." Ship removed his hands from over his eyes and shouted, *"Ready or not, here I come!"*

He listened for rustling sounds. He tried to sense his friends' last-second attempts at camouflage, tried to pick up sounds that would lead him to their hiding places. He heard some rustling, but it sounded much too close; it certainly couldn't be his friends.

He looked down, sensing motion. Something covered in leaves jittered around a small puddle. *Some tiny animal*— he thought. He went down on his knees and observed more closely. Whatever it was didn't seem to be moving properly, as if limping. As he leaned closer in, he could see the feathers: a small bird.

"Hello, Mr. Bird," Ship said, surprised it didn't fly away.

Sadly, the little bird just looked back at him.

Ship could tell something was wrong. The bird hardly struggled when Ship picked it up, lifting it to eye-level. Quickly, Ship could see the problem. The little bird's right wing was broken. When he tried to rub his thumb across it, the little bird chirped.

"What happened to you?" Ship asked.

The bird seemed comfortable in Ship's cupped hands, almost as if in a nest, peaceful and nurtured.

"We have to do something about your wing, don't we?" Ship said to the bird. "I think I have an idea."

Ship began to walk off, the bird securely in his hands.

"Ship! Shippy!" his friends shouted, wondering what had happened to their game. "What's going on?"

"Got something I've got to do," Ship shouted back. "Follow me!"

The four of them traded one adventure for another as they followed Ship down the street to his house. He led them over to a little tool shed in the back. Musty and damp, the shed was full of wooden shelves with all sorts of boxes randomly stacked. Ship's eyes roamed across the shelves until he noticed an old shoebox. He pulled it down. It was greasy and full of screws, nuts and bolts. He dumped the contents onto the floor and then ran outside the shed, picking up leaves, grass and twigs. He placed them in the box, patting them down, creating a comfy home for his little guest.

"You think it's gonna stay in there?" Tommy asked.

"Sure," Ship answered, "he has a broken wing."

"But how's it gonna eat?" Jake asked.

Ship thought for a moment, then said, "good point. I'll be right back."

Ship rushed over to the house, leapt up the back steps and into the kitchen. He opened the refrigerator door and searched for a loaf of bread.

"Shippy, what are you doing?" His mother called out to him from the living room.

"I need a piece of bread to feed a bird we found."

"Be careful, they carry germs you know."

"Don't worry, Mom."

Ship bolted out the door and back over to the shed. Carefully, he pulled the piece of bread apart and crumbled it into little pieces. He spread them in the shoebox. At first, the bird was cautious, then began to peck away.

"Welcome to your new home, Mr. Bird," Ship addressed the little animal.

"Yeah, but what are you going to do about his wing?" Allie Johnson asked.

"Tomorrow at school, I'll go to the library and look it up," Ship answered.

THE NEXT DAY, Ship found a book in the school library titled *All About Birds*. Mostly a picture book, it allowed Ship to identify his little friend as a sparrow. He flipped through the pages until he came to a chapter on Care and Feeding. Several pages into it, he spotted a series of drawings demonstrating how to care for a broken wing. Immediately, Ship took the book over to the librarian and checked it out.

"OPHIE, can you take me to the store?" he asked his big sister when he arrived home.

"For what?"

"I need to get some stuff," he answered. "I want to fix my little sparrow's wing."

His father sat nearby in his leather chair, his face buried in his daily copy of *The Times*, his tumbler of scotch on the side-table. "And what do you want to do that for?" he asked, still shielded behind his newspaper.

"Of course, to help him, Father," Shippy answered.

"He's probably gonna die, you know," his father said tersely. "Why waste the time?"

"Oh, phooey, Father," Ophie admonished him. "Who knows? Perhaps we have a doctor in the making." She looked over towards Shippy. "C'mon Ship, let's go."

THAT EVENING, Ship went to work. He pulled on the chain to the tool shed's overhead light and laid out his supplies. First, he washed the little bird with a special soap they bought at the drug store, then sprinkled him with water. He dried the little sparrow carefully, making sure not to hurt his damaged wing. Ship then cut a twelve-inch length of bandage and methodically placed it over the wing, securing it to the bird's tiny body, but not so secure as to interrupt its breathing. He wrapped the bandage underneath the bird's good wing and made several loops around its body. When he reached the end of the bandage, he fastened it to itself with tape. Then he placed the bird in a brand-new cage they purchased at the pet store.

"There, Mr. Bird," Ship lifted him up and looked in the little creature's eyes. "I know it may be uncomfortable, but soon you'll fly again."

FOR THE NEXT FOUR WEEKS, Shippy nursed his little sparrow back to health, each day visiting the tool shed at least twice, feeding him birdseed and bread crumbs, placing drops of water in a little plastic container and checking on his wing.

Then came the day.

The book said to give the bird four weeks to recover after the wing had been properly wrapped, then another few days for the little creature to regain its bearings once the wrapping was removed. Halfway through the fifth week, the little sparrow seemed to have regained its strength, moving briskly around his cage. Ship decided it was time.

He called Ophie outside to view the event.

Carefully, he cupped his hands and lifted the little sparrow out of its cage. He held out his hands and prepared to release it.

"Aren't you going to say anything to your little friend?" Ophie asked.

"What should I say? Ship answered.

"Tell him… good luck, or, you're going to miss him."

"I am, but," he hesitated, "he'll be happier flying around instead of staying in that old cage."

Ophie smiled, impressed by Ship's maturity for an eight year-old.

Ship looked at the little bird in his hands and whispered, "have a good life, Mr. Bird." In one swift motion, he un-cupped his hands, springing the little sparrow into the air.

When the sparrow flapped its wings and flew over to a nearby tree. Ship giggled. "There you go, Mr. Bird. It was good to know you."

Ophie wiped her eye.

EVEN BEFORE SHIPPY launched his adopted little sparrow back into the wilderness, he had developed an itch. His itchy skin—especially around his hands and arms—hadn't been unbearable. But now, after doctoring his own sparrow, the itch had begun to interrupt his concentration on schoolwork and prolong the time it took him to fall asleep at night. Ship's scratching had increased to such a point that Bunny Pennfield finally took him to see the family doctor.

"Bird mites," Dr. Stevenson explained after a brief examination.

"You see, Ship, I warned you about germs," she reminded him.

"Don't be too hard on him, Mrs. Pennfield," Stevenson said. "He saved a little bird. I'll prescribe some ointment and everything will be fine in a week or so."

THAT EVENING, when Percival Pennfield returned home from his Wall Street office, he was much less forgiving.

"I told you not to fool around with things like that," his father admonished him, pouring his nightly tumbler of scotch, "the damn bird's probably dead already. Was it really worth it?"

"Of course," Ship answered. "Don't you realize he flew again, Father?"

* * *

LENOX, Massachusetts
Gladwell Sanitarium
March 30,1964

"HAS HE DONE IT AGAIN?" Ophie exclaimed as she rushed out of her parents' Cadillac and bolted toward Drs. Hazard and Hoq in the hospital's foyer. "Can we actually *see him* do it?"

"Well," began Dr. Hazard, "we will have to be—"

"He said a word, '*Sparrow,*' he actually said it?" Ophie asked excitedly.

"Yes," Dr. Hoq answered. "We were curious if you could ascribe any significance to it?"

Ophie thought for a moment. "No, not really, he loves the outdoors, though, so it wouldn't be—"

"Dr. Hazard."

Mid-sentence, Ophie was abruptly interrupted.

"Exactly what's going on?" Percival Pennfield continued in whispered, strident tones as he and his wife entered the foyer. From his sour expression, it was obvious he was not happy about driving all the way up to Gladwell based upon a few mere grunts.

"It's true that we shouldn't get too enthusiastic, Mr. Pennfield," Hazard responded, "but certainly we would consider this a positive sign, at least directionally."

"Directionally?" Pennfield scoffed. "Either he's responding or he's not. What's happening, Dr. Hazard?"

"Perhaps we should take a look at him?" Hazard suggested.

THE PENNFIELDS HAD SEEN Ship in this state before, yet the horrific impact did not diminish over time; each time they saw him— their poor little Shippy hovering in some gelatinous semi-state between life and death— it discomforted them even more.

Undaunted, Ophelia rushed over and tried to break through his seemingly impenetrable shell. *"Ship!... Shippy!"* She called out to him hugging him brusquely. "*Talk to me, Ship. It's me, your Ophie!"*

Despite embracing him with all the might she could muster, Ship sat straight up: quiet and undisturbed.

"Ophelia, perhaps you shouldn't disturb him," her mother suggested.

"No, no, Mrs. Pennfield," Dr. Hazard said. "It's quite alright. Something has to eventually break through, disrupt his stupor."

Percival Pennfield scowled. "If a hug from his sister can eventually cure him, what the hell is he doing here?"

"Mr. Pennfield, I'm sorry if I sounded cavalier, but that was not my intent. We are experimenting with different protocols of drug therapy combined with electroconvulsive therapy. It's just a matter of finding the right balance. Perhaps a display of warmth from a loved one in combination with the optimal protocol will be what finally breaks through."

"How's your clinical study coming?" Pennfield asked tersely.

"Through your generous contribution, Mr. Pennfield, we are recruiting more and more patients each day, so we are able to test many different regimens simultaneously."

"The sooner, the better, Dr. Hazard. We want our boy back."

"Of course. Of course."

Throughout it all, Ophie's eyes remained fixed on little Shippy, exploring the contours of his face, searching for some sort of slight movement— his lips, his eyes, his ears, anything—some real sign that he was among the living. She had to believe that he was somehow aware of her presence, yet unable to respond. She gently grazed his forehead with the back of her hand. Could he feel her hand, she wondered, or was his mind in another place altogether, creating his own special world? Was she a part of it?

* * *

GREENWICH, Connecticut
Indian Harbor

Time: Unknown

"*Ophie, Ophie, c'mon, let's go out on the Sound!*" Ship called out from their old rickety backyard dock.

The New England summer day was perfect. The full strength of the sun's rays reflected off the waters of Long Island Sound as the afternoon breezes provided a tranquility accented by the pungent odors of a salty sea.

"Okay, okay," Ophie answered from the back porch.

"Make sure he puts his life jacket on," Bunny Pennfield admonished her daughter.

"Of course, Mother," Ophie shouted back as she ran out towards Shippy.

Tethered to the dock, a wooden Sunfish with a bright blue and white striped sail rocked back and forth to the gentle roll of Indian Harbor's waters. Still not an accomplished swimmer, the nine-year-old Shippy was not allowed to take out the small boat on his own. Ophie's presence was just as necessary as a gentle sea and forgiving winds for Ship to enjoy a jaunt on the family's Sunfish.

"Can I work the tiller?" Ship asked anxiously as he jumped onto the small skiff.

"Watch yourself, Shippy, don't jump like that," Ophie warned him as she removed her robe, revealing a classic blue one-piece bathing suit. "And put on your life jacket."

"Do I have to?" Shippy exclaimed.

"Even if you were Johnny Weissmuller, you'd have to," she answered, stepping carefully onto the boat.

"Tarzan wears a life jacket?" Ship questioned in disbelief.

"Yes, Tarzan wears a life jacket," Ophie answered. "Now man the tiller, Captain."

They shoved off onto glassy waters, Ophie letting out the sail to catch a light breeze crossing from port to starboard.

"Steer to starboard," Ophie instructed him as she let out the sail even more, repositioning the small boat for a smooth ride downwind.

"Should I pull up the centerboard?" Shippy asked.

"Sure," Ophie answered.

Free of its dagger keel, the boat sped up, hydroplaning across Indian Harbor's waters and into Long Island Sound. Ship's cheerful enthusiasm soothed Ophie in a way that would be impossible to match. She loved seeing the slight little Shippy enjoying himself so. And, likewise, she loved that he needed her so.

"Can I work the sail?" Ship asked as they skirted across the water.

"Sure, I'll take the tiller," Ophie answered.

They shared a memorable few hours on the Sound, navigating their way past Mead Point, around Tweed Island, across the Sound to Rocky Neck, dipping in and out of Smith Cove, then downwind to Indian Harbor Point where they set course upwind for their ride home.

"Ready to come about?" Ophie asked.

"Ready, Captain!" Ship reveled in his role as a master of the seas.

"Okay, *hard-a-lee!"* Ophie ordered.

Ship let out the sail, and as Ophie steered the boat into the wind, Ship allowed the sail to backwind. He tugged hard on the sheet, so forcefully that the taut sail stood hardened as a strong puff of wind collided with it, tipping the small boat to port.

"Ship, Shippy, let it out!" Ophie screamed.

Panicking, Shippy grabbed for the sheet.

The tip of the small boat's sail dipped perilously close to the water, the boat bouncing on its side. Ophie and Ship struggled to keep their balance.

Plop!

The small boat fell over, capsized. Its port side and colorful sail dipping in the water. The small vessel dunked both Ship and Ophie into the Sound.

"Help! Help!" Shippy yelled as he floated aimlessly in the waters, kept buoyant by his life jacket. *"Help me, Ophie, help me!"*

"Don't worry, don't worry, just float," she reassured him.

A strong swimmer, Ophie dove towards his legs, got a grip and then worked her hand up his torso. She wrapped one arm around his chest while treading water with the other.

"*Ophie, Ophie*!" Ship exclaimed, hanging on to her.

Clutching Ship, she swam him over to the capsized boat, propelled by a strong scissor kick.

"But what do we do now?" Ship asked shivering.

"I'm going to let go of you for a second."

"No, no, don't!" Ship begged.

"Don't worry. Just float. I'll be right here."

Ophie swam over to the boat, pushed down on its starboard side steadying the small craft, then grabbed the mast, tugging it upright. She lifted herself onto the boat then dipped her hand in the water, propelling the vessel with short strokes, guiding it toward Ship.

She pulled him on board.

Ship breathed heavily, goose-bumped and shivering.

"So why did this happen?" she asked. "What did you forget to do?"

"Ummmm...." Ship began, still shivering, "uhhh... maybe... forgot to put the centerboard back in?"

"That's it." She held up the centerboard, then slid it into its notch. "Lesson learned."

Shipped hugged Ophie, holding on tight.

"I love you, Ophie," he whispered.

"And I love you, too, Shippy." She tightened her grip. "More than anything else in the world."

* * *

Greenwich, Connecticut
Indian Harbor
May 30, 1964

A child of privilege, Ophelia Pennfield had her quirks, a set of indulgences most ordinary folk could never imagine. An Aquarius, she would visit her astrologer twice a week— more when the situation warranted— never undertaking a major venture nor finalizing a critical decision without first consulting Miss Felicia. It was a habit her honors professors at Wellesley would have never guessed she had.

Then there was her Ouija board habit, an almost hourly addiction to conjuring up messages from the netherworld. Her elder cousin Xenobia— an odd sort, but with an incisive intuition rivaled by very few— had taught her to read Tarot at an early age.

Perhaps Ophelia's most interesting quirk was what she called "talking to the window." Almost daily, as twilight darkened into night, she would retreat to her third-floor bedroom, darken the room, place two scented candles on the window sill, look out and converse with the darkness.

At times, it would be a moment of silent contemplation, nothing more than a ritualistic respite from the humdrum of daily existence. At other times she would drift into a trance-like state, conversing with all sorts of people— real or imagined— on the other side of the glass. Occasionally, she would embellish her trance with a puff or two of cannabis.

During these window-sill rituals, she had observed many odd visions on the other side. Her grandfather, Benjamin Pennfield, as well as her aunt Sarah Pennfield Morton, the black sheep of the family, were known to converse with her now and then. She felt sure she had spoken with Joan of Arc, Sir Isaac

Newton, Cleopatra, Abraham Lincoln, a slew of family members and even Jesus Christ.

Tonight she stood at the window searching for solace. Ship's condition had preyed upon her, taken its toll. She was known to be emotional, passionate, but this inexplicable assault upon Ship's very humanity stifled her, dragging her into despondency, then mild depression. She was anxious, obsessive, yearning to help him, her little Shippy. Now, she could not bear that he was several hundred miles away, by himself, sitting upright in a hospital bed, doing nothing, experiencing nothing, and she was here at Indian Harbor, helpless and hopeless, impotent to improve his condition.

She gazed outward, awaiting a sign from somewhere, sometime, someone. Gradually, the scenery framed within window— the trees, the inlet, the twinkling stars— became one and the same. Everything darkened, the elements coalescing into some vast somber grayness, a canvas, perhaps, for a painting yet to emerge. Soon the canvas expressed itself, emanating a mysterious glow in the middle, a white spot, confirming her instincts: fuzzy at first, the blurry white spot grew as it sharpened into clarity.

An egg-shaped face, shoulders, arms: monochromatic, the shades of gray more than just an artist's palette; a spectrum of moods and feelings. Soon she could make out a wall, and a bed.

She gasped as the blur became real.

IT WAS SHIPPY, little Shippy, sitting comatose in his hospital bed, just as she had seen him during her last visit. His face— his sorrowful, vacant face— grew larger, closer. She could feel the pulse of his heartbeat, count his freckles, breathe with him in synchrony. He could see her, too. She was sure of it. He knew she was watching. Very slowly, very deliberately, he spoke, his lips quivering:

"Help me, Ophie, help me."

* * *

LENOX, Massachusetts
Gladwell Sanitarium
June 1–19, 1964

HER VISION at the window left Ophelia with only one alternative. She had to be near Shippy. And it had to be *now!* She needed to watch him, touch him, be there for him, maybe even save him. She had no choice but to go to Gladwell immediately. Undoubtedly, her appearance there on a Monday afternoon came as a complete surprise to Gladwell's Chief Medical officer.

"I'll be staying in the area for several weeks, Dr. Hazard," Ophie announced to the esteemed doctor as he greeted her in Gladwell's lobby. "I want to spend as much time with my little brother as possible."

"Of course, of course." Dr. Hazard muttered. "You are welcome here whenever you desire."

"Thank you," she answered. "Now can someone take me to Ship?"

HAZARD WAS NOT sure how to interpret this development. He could sense the strength of the bond between Ophelia and her little brother— absolute and extreme love and affection— but Hazard had an inherent distrust of Percival Pennfield. To him, Pennfield was a domineering bully and he wouldn't put it past him to have sent Ophelia here as a spy.

"Dalipe, I must talk to you," Hazard announced to his assistant. "Please join me in my office."

"What is it, Emilio," Dr. Hoq asked as he sat across from Hazard.

"It appears that we will have a visitor for several weeks," Hazard said.

"Oh?"

"Yes, Ophelia Pennfield will be staying nearby and I would venture to say she'll be spending a good deal of time here with her brother."

"And why is this?" Dr. Hoq asked.

"Frankly, I don't know and it bothers me."

"So, what should we do?"

"Cooperate with her fully on anything to do with her brother."

Hoq nodded.

"But be careful around her."

"I will."

"And Dalipe?"

"Yes, Emilio."

"Make sure she never gets near the basement," Hazard ordered.

"Surely, Emilio."

OPHIE WATCHED over Ship as if she were his personal caretaker. She learned how to help feed him through his tubes, deal with his catheter and bedpan, monitor his EEG and take his blood pressure. But her caretaking skills were far overshadowed by the warmth and comfort she provided, dividends of a truly deep and undying love. She would sit beside him for hours and talk to him, engage in a one-way conversation with his blank, inert stare, peering into his eyes while always yearning to understand what was going on inside.

She regularly read to him, not children's books, but works reflective of his elevated intellect prior to his incident on the dock. She read him the classics: *Ivanhoe, The Adventures of Huckleberry Finn, Captains Courageous, The Grapes of Wrath* and *The Old Man and the Sea.* Rarely did he respond, but Ophie continued undeterred, convinced that somehow the words would get through and when his inevitable return to normalcy occurred, his intellect would be as fine-tuned as ever.

"Today let's talk about politics, leadership…" she began her conversation with him one morning as she did all others, opening with a daily topic for discussion. "There have been many great leaders of men, those who have liberated thousands of people. But there have also been tyrants, those who use their power and charisma to twist the minds of their people, leading to terrible, terrible things…"

Typically, she would go on and on and on, conversing with the glassy-eyed, unresponsive mannequin. On this day, though, when she mentioned the word *tyrant,* she sensed a stir, or perhaps a slight shiver. She went on, mentioning the names of some of history's most hated tyrants.

"Hitler... Mussolini... Lenin... Stalin... Trotsky..."

She stopped short, sensing something.

His lips quivered, he trembled all over, attempting to muster up greater strength. Silent, Ophie focused, grasping for every little sign of movement: another slight twitch, a blink, a quivering lip.

"Buh…" he grunted out.

Elated, Ophie encouraged him. "Go on. Go on, Shippy."

"Buh…" he strained. "Owwwnnnn…"

"Buh… Owwnnnn," he struggled. "Bonnne."

"*Bone?* Was that what you meant?" Ophie asked.

"So…so…sorrrrrr…," His face reddened as he conjured up the sounds. "Ruh…ruh…eeeeee… Saw-Reeee."

"Sorry?" Ophie translated his grunts into a word. *"Bone? Sorry?"*

"HE SAID SOMETHING, Dr. Hazard, he said something to me!" Ophie spouted the moment she flew through his office door.

"Really?" Hazard looked up, rose his eyes above his glass frames and responded softly, undaunted by her abrupt entrance.

"Yes. Yes." Ophie blurted into his face. "He spoke. He actually spoke. Isn't it wonderful?"

"I suppose so," Hazard mumbled. "Exactly what was it he said?

"Two words," she answered. "'*Bone*' and '*Sorry*'."

"And you believe the significance of this is?" he asked.

"I'm not sure," she responded feebly. "He loved animals, loved the outdoors. Maybe it has something to do with a bone he gave to a dog or something. Or maybe he's... *Sorry*... about taking it away? Who knows?"

"It's hard for me to work with something so vague, Miss Pennfield," Hazard responded. "Can you give me anything more?"

"No, I can't right now. But I'm sure there's something to it. *Something*."

* * *

Lenox, Massachusetts
The Berkshires Country Inn
Twilight
June 19, 1964

Ophelia sustained her ritual of "talking to the window" throughout her stay in the Berkshires. Set on a hill surrounded by a grassy meadow, the Inn where Ophelia lodged offered majestic views of the mountains. Just as she did at Indian Harbor, Ophelia lit two small votive candles and set one on each side of her room's window sill. She placed her hands down on the middle and leaned forward, her eyes shut tight. She concentrated mightily, hoping on this special night— the end of a day when Ship actually displayed signs of life, signs that gave her hope— her time at the window would not be in vain. Tonight, she hoped for some real, concrete insight.

She strained, then opened her eyes and gazed outside. Despite the twilight, the panorama of flattened, languorous mountains extending across her window was a sight to behold. Spring had bequeathed them with such plentiful and robust colors that even the sun's daily departure could not mask their vibrancy.

She struggled to achieve a tranquil state, one which freed her mind and opened it to a higher level of consciousness. Perhaps the adrenaline flowing from her encouraging session with Ship was a deterrent. She would try something else. She stepped away from the window and opened the top door of her dresser. There, in a small pouch, she kept her rolling papers and a supply of marijuana. She carefully rolled a cigarette and began to puff, holding the smoke in her lungs long enough so every cell in her body would be soaked with its calming effects.

She walked back to the window, took another puff and breathed in deep once more. Now she could relax, absorb. She looked out over the landscape. It melted away into something different: visions— provocative, resonant visions.

FIRST, Ship in his hospital bed, unresponsive and comatose.

Then, cousin Christopher, but an older cousin Christopher, his face hardened and aged, sitting in a dark room with large windows, sipping a glass of wine.

Then Ship again. Followed by cousin Christopher again.

The images flipped faster and faster, back and forth, swirling together into one composite picture: a transparent Ship over a transparent image of the aged Christopher.

They flipped more and more rapidly, so rapidly they finally melted away into a plain, homogenous white. She rubbed her eyes. *What was the meaning of it? What was she to do?*

She looked up and savored the vista once again. She couldn't stop now. She needed to find out more. She took another puff of marijuana, breathed in and looked up. This time, the quaint Berkshires panorama melted quickly away, replaced by a more startling vision.

A MAN, perhaps about fifty, sitting in a cell in some sort of jail— but the jail looked old-fashioned, perhaps third-world. The vision focused in on the man's face. It looked oddly familiar. The more Ophelia studied it, she became absolutely convinced it was Ship, an adult Ship. She could see it in his eyes.

Then, suddenly, four armed guards marched into the scene and stood before his cell. One of them spoke:

"It's time."

The man gulped.

They pulled him out of his cell and surrounded him, two guards in back, two in front. They pushed him forward. His ankles shackled, he struggled to keep up. After he fell, they dragged him up the cold, sharp-edged cement stairs, scraping his knees and shins along the way.

They pulled him through the door. The sun shone brightly and the sky was an inviting shade of blue. A retinue of officials stood waiting.

One of them stepped forward and read from some sort of official document:

"Dr. Arthur Shipkin Pennfield: By order of the Apexian government and Prime Minister Izan Bonne-Saari, you are hereby sentenced to death by guillotine on this day of May 30th, 2011."

What!

She breathed deeply, her face went flush, her horrific shock wiping the vision away.

Bone. Sorry.

Did that man say Bone Sorry?

She was sure of it, the man in her vision repeated the exact same words Ship had struggled to blurt out earlier that day. She closed her eyes again, trying to find her way back in, trying to learn more.

SHE HAD SEEN Ship and cousin Chris. They merged into a homogeneous oneness in some cryptic sort of way. And then she saw what had to have been an older Ship, being led to an execution, an execution ordered by someone named *Bone Sorry*. She opened her eyes and took another deep long drag, wondering what it all meant. But why would today's Ship, catatonic and flawed, blurt out that name? How could he possibly know it?

Think, think, concentrate! She goaded herself.

There's today's Ship, flawed and afflicted. And then, perhaps there's some future Ship: ostensibly healthy but in some sort of deep trouble. What does this juxtaposition of Ships mean? Was it some sort of choice? Young or old. Flawed or un-flawed. Sheltered or shamed.

Is a healthy Ship somehow destined to be shamed as an adult?

Yet, if Ship stays afflicted with this mysterious condition, any semblance of a normal life is snatched away from him.

Which is better: *healthy and shamed or sick and sheltered?*

And was there even a choice?

* * *

COUSIN CHRISTOPHER, studying in New York for Spring semester, was a constant phone companion of Ophelia's throughout the ordeal. For years, they had always been there for each other, celebrating each other's accomplishments, salving each other's wounds, sharing each other's thoughts and ideas, even to the point of completing each other's sentences. They shared many traits in common: an exuberant, playful *joie de vivre*, intellectual curiosity, an understated urbane refinement and, of course, a deep love for little Shippy.

After her experience at the window earlier in the evening, there was no one's voice in the world Ophelia would rather hear than that of her cousin Christopher.

"HELLO," the familiar voice answered.

"Christopher?" she whispered.

"Yes, yes, my dear," he answered. "How's everything up in Massachusetts?"

"Nothing's changed really. The doctors still don't have a clue."

"My God. That's criminal!"

"I wish you were here right now," she said with a somber seductiveness.

"I know, I know, sweetheart."

"I need you."

"I know. I know. But right now that would be quite impossible. I'm up to my neck in my dissertation, teaching two sophomore sections at Columbia, and… Elizabeth's here with me."

"I understand," she answered resignedly.

"But I'll get there. I'll be there for you. You know that, don't you?"

"Of course," she answered, then paused for a moment. *"Christopher?"*

"Yes, my dear."

"I want you to know something."

"Yes?"

"No matter what happens. No matter what happens to you or me or Shippy, I love you. I'll always love you."

"And I do you," he whispered. "I will love you forever my darling. Nothing will ever change that."

* * *

TIME FRAME: 20 YEARS LATER

5

Upper Manhattan, Columbia Presbyterian Hospital, November 13, 1984

Columbia Presbyterian Hospital towered over the West Side Highway, keeping watch over the Hudson and the GW Bridge. The day was damp and chilly, as grey as the giant steel stanchions suspending the majestic bridge. A mist, similarly somber, tinged the air with gloomy wretchedness.

If anyone were to choose a day to die, Christopher Pennfield thought as he entered the hospital's reception area, *today would be the kind of day to do it.* He still did not believe he was here, paying a visit to say goodbye to someone whose presence in his life transcended family, transcended love, transcended romance. He felt more like a shell-shocked automaton progressing through a series of pre-determined motions.

If there was any place he didn't want to be, any circumstance he didn't want to face, this was it. But he had to be here, had to see her one last time. It would be both comforting and deeply depressing. He would be there with her, and for her, for her last moments. But the thought of living in a world without her was unbearable. A bright light in his life was to be extinguished forever.

"I'M HERE to see Ophelia Pennfield," Christopher Pennfield announced as he approached the hospital's main reception desk.

The receptionist on duty checked her list. "Are you an immediate family member?"

"Yes, I'm her cousin."

"You do realize the intensive care ward does not have the same visiting hours as the rest of the hospital?"

"Yes, but she's dying. I have to see her."

"I'll call up and see if they can take you. And your name?"

"Christopher Pennfield, *Dr. Christopher Pennfield*." he answered briskly. "I told you, I'm her cousin." Perhaps his academic status would add a little heft to his request, he hoped.

"You may have a seat over there." She nodded towards a couch in the waiting area.

Pennfield fidgeted anxiously. He had little patience for the bureaucratic ways of large institutions, particularly hospitals. Annoyed, he waited, as a knot in his stomach began tightening with each moment. Finally, after what seemed like an hour, he jumped up and marched brusquely to the desk.

"Have they responded *yet*?"

On the phone, the receptionist held up her finger, dropped the mouthpiece, and whispered, "I'll call again in a minute."

Pennfield looked at his watch. Only ten minutes had passed since he walked in the doors. He marched back to the couch.

Finally, the receptionist summoned an orderly who escorted Pennfield up to Intensive Care. Two large doors swung open, exposing a methodical chaos of nurses, doctors and attendants crisscrossing the room, intermittently hovering over one of the ten or so hospital beds draped with an array of tubes, monitors, respirators and IV-bags hooked and connected in all sorts of ways to all sorts of body parts. The orderly lead him over to Ophelia's corner. Pennfield braced himself.

"*Jesus Christ!*" he exclaimed. As much as he had prepared himself, he was shocked. This was not his cousin, not the femme fatale who had broken hundreds of hearts, leaving scores of suitors in her wake: the sassy English Lit major from Wellesley, the Park Avenue socialite.

Pennfield's eyes fixated on her now: a chalky white carcass, the bandage around her forehead rendering her androgynous. Yet, still, as his eyes seeped deeper, he could sense her inner beauty, her inimitable sense of style and spunk, her *essence*; those would never die, couldn't possibly, he assured himself.

"Sir? Your visit will be limited. About 30 minutes."

"Right. Is she coherent?"

"Off and on," answered the nurse.

He pulled up a chair next to her bed and clutched for Ophie's hand. He squeezed it. "Ophie, Ophie, what has this terrible cancer done to you?"

For a moment, she opened her eyes and squeezed back.

"Oph! It's me— God bless you my dear, God bless you," Pennfield whispered, squeezing back.

Her lips made a futile attempt to move.

"Shhhhhh," Pennfield hushed her. "Relax, save your energy."

Still, her lips struggled to form coherent speech. It came slowly and deliberately. *"Pain..."*

"What?" Startled, Pennfield at first did not comprehend her message.

She squeezed his hand and summoned up the strength to speak again. This time her meaning was clear. *"Pain..."*

Pennfield grasped her hand tightly. "I know. I know you're suffering Ophie, sweetheart," he whispered. "And as hard as it is for me to say this, soon your suffering will end, you'll be at peace."

Abruptly, she shook her head, her massive effort resulting in minimal movement. "No..."

"I know. I know, my dear," Pennfield responded. "But always know that I love you. I'll love you always."

"No..." She struggled. "You..."

"Me?" Pennfield answered quizzically.

"Yes... You... Pain..."

"What do you mean?"

"You... Pain..."

Gently, he touched her cheek, rubbing it with the back of his hand. "Don't strain yourself, my dear. I understand. I understand it all."

He stood there, clutching her hand for as long as he was allowed. Her eyes remained closed, she laid silent and still until he traced his finger down her cheek once again, preparing to leave.

Her lips moved sparingly, but deliberately. *"Protect...Shippy...Protect..."*

"Ophie! Wait, '*Shippy?* What do you mean?"

"Protect... Shippy... Protect..."

"From— yes, but, Oph?"

She closed her eyes.

* * *

Various Locations
1995-2007

For eleven years, Christopher repeated Ophie's cryptic omen to himself. He refused to believe it could be a prophecy, and yet he couldn't let go of it, couldn't stop hearing it, repeating it to himself, looking for a sign that would smother his doubt.

It began late one autumn night in 1995 at the family's Newport cottage.

Christopher, by then a highly-respected professor of philosophy at Pennfield College in rural Vermont, an institution founded by his great grandfather and his younger brother Jonathan, the Senior Vice President of a major airline, were both fully inebriated and in the midst of a heated but sloppy exchange when they were silenced by the sight of a man rushing down the main stairwell. Exactly as he had done one memorable evening in the late 1950s, their brother Robin, fully-tuxedoed and yet faded and real, descended the steps, threw a phantom champagne-glass against the wall, then disappeared.

Christopher and Jonathan engaged in a bitter dialogue the next morning; Jonathan, the problem-solver, insisting they must do something about it, and Christopher, in denial, trying to brush it under the rug. As they shouted past each other, they stumbled onto a revelation: the prior night's incident was only one in a series of unexplained psychic incidents affecting both of them. Each had separately experienced other psychic episodes during the prior months. Despite the startling evidence that there was definitely some *psychic something* pestering the Pennfield family, it took several weeks before Jonathan could convince Christopher to enlist the aid of a well-respected psychic investigator, a Mr. Edwin Swann from Spring Lake Heights, New Jersey.

"'Well respected.' 'Psychic.' And *New Jersey*? Spare me," protested Christopher.

"You know what we saw, Chris," Jonathan insisted. "This guy is the best, the best I've heard about, anywhere."

"Fine. Make the call," Christopher obliged reluctantly.

Christopher gave his brother and Mr. Swann ample leeway, keeping a distance from Swann's methodical investigations. Soon, after ruling out all other options, Swann concluded that indeed there was some sort of strange psychic activity in the house and that furthermore, the Pennfield family had a genetic psychic trait that enhanced their ability to perceive such phenomena.

Just as the incident in Newport was starting to feel explainable - though strange, a product of particular minds and genetic predispositions— Christopher experienced another brush with the Pennfields' psychic *gift*.

It happened in a dream. He felt a lifting presence as he awakened late one night. He could observe everything, but he knew— at least thought— he was not awake; he remembered hovering above his bed as if his body were filled with helium, passing effortlessly through the bedroom window, and then floating around the Pennfield College campus, circling around its landmark clock tower and then observing a minor skirmish among several drunken undergrads in the parking lot below. After that, he continued to float, rising far above the campus and the clouds, progressing down the New England coastline. He tried to turn, to rise up higher, but it was not his own energy that moved him. His weight was just a warmth, with real air below. He moved in a direction that seemed like a fiat of his own mind, and yet he knew he was not in control. He could see all the landmarks as he floated by: Boston, the Cape, Nantucket and then westward towards Rhode Island. He moved somehow, by wind, or some mysterious psychic force; it was beautiful and terrifying at once. Suddenly he felt as if he wanted to stop, to turn. He was unable to remove himself from where hovered now. He was within a clear view of the family's Newport cottage, but their giant, old white maple tree by the bird-house was just a sapling, only two feet tall. There were two barrel-chested men— dressed in trousers, suspenders and caps seemingly from an era early in the twentieth century— shoveling. They were burying a casket on the grounds behind the house. And then it was dark.

THE NEXT MORNING as his eyes gazed at his bedroom ceiling, he tapped his chest and paid silent homage to Sir Isaac Newton as he felt the weight of his body again firmly secured to his bed. He smirked a little. He wrote the whole experience off to what he honestly thought it was: a provocative, intriguing dream.

His academic curiosity challenged him, however. He thought this would make a fitting topic for his research assistant, Jennifer Winston, a particularly devoted and industrious art history major. She was beautiful. Her hair was some shade of blonde that seemed filled with light, almost unreal at times. He thought he would have her find some literature on what he had heard referred to as *veridical out of body experiences*. The results of her research proved to be both enlightening and disturbing. He read accounts of episodes eerily similar to the one he had experienced, in which one's consciousness actually left the body and travelled to remote locations. In some of these episodes, the person was able to objectively verify what he or she had "seen" after the fact.

As much as he tried to dissuade himself, something inside him compelled the professor to visit the Campus Security Office the next Saturday. He looked through the log and found the row and column of incidents for the night of what he was still referring to as his "dream." Indeed, there was a minor campus skirmish that night at exactly the location he remembered in the parking lot, and at the precise time he had observed from the clock tower. He turned to leave, his face white and damp.

IMMEDIATELY, he summoned Swann and his brother Jonathan to Newport, insisting they shovel at the exact spot where he saw those two burly men. The three of them shoveled in silence. At one point, Christopher paused and eyed their towering, billowing, old white maple tree, the pace of his breath rising.

It was Swann who first struck something hard under his blade. Christopher's stomach churned. Swann and Jonathan worked to unearth it: an in-tact, centuries-old casket.

"Leave it," whispered Christopher.

"We can't." Jonathan was already working through the seal and cranking the lid. He teamed up with Swann to lift it off, their eyes wide, their hearts pounding. But when they opened it, they found it empty, save for some withered old flowers and a rumpled leather pouch containing several sheets of crackly parchment.

Jonathan tossed the parchment to his brother. The title scrawled across the first page unnerved them: *A HISTORY OF THE MEAN AND MALICIOUS SPIRITE WHICH HAS BEEN THE PLAGUE OF THE PENNFIELD FAMILY FOR FIVE GENERATIONS.* The words were those of Nathaniel Pennfield, a merchant in mid eighteenth-century Newport. He went on to relate the story of the Pennfield family curse— until then passed in extreme secrecy from each generations' elders to the next. He told of a poor servant girl on the Mayflower coerced into a suicidal jump overboard by pilgrim Charles Pennfield, the family patriarch, just as the Mayflower was to approach Cape Cod. The note went on, describing how the girl's spirit returned about every other generation, occupying and subsequently destroying a contemporary agent, and casting shame and derision on another generation of Pennfields.

FROM THE MOMENT Swann and Jonathan closed the casket and buried it again while a shaken Christopher looked on, the three men devoted themselves to investigating every word they had read in the note. Their mission took months of fruitless twists, often wracked by self-doubt until encouraged again by tiny clues. In a small sailboat off the Cape Cod coast commandeered by Captain Conrad Scott, their search took a definitive, terrifying turn. A cranky old salt who knew more about the voyage of the Mayflower than anyone else in New

England, Captain Scott accepted a handsome sum to navigate them to the precise spot where the poor girl jumped.

Together they all saw it clearly: an apparition of the Mayflower and the servant girl, her yellow hair filling with wind as she jumped off the stern, just as it happened in 1620.

Though it momentarily stopped their hearts, it was not yet the worst experience they would have, not the one that would ruin at least one of them. At precisely the same instant of their apparition at sea, Christopher Pennfield's assistant Jennifer jumped off the fringe overhang far above Grand Central Terminal, impaling herself on the knob of the famous four-faced clock. She left a note revealing their affair, and that she was pregnant and then shunned by Professor Pennfield, casting guilt, shame and derision on Christopher and the entire Pennfield family.

DESTROYED, Christopher Pennfield rushed up to the family estate in Boothbay Harbor and shut himself off from the rest of the world. Despite persistent urging from Johnathan, Christopher refused to budge from his bedroom, gulping wine and scotch and gazing glassy-eyed out the large leaded windows overlooking the harbor.

Even a once in a lifetime event celebrating the family's philanthropy could not get Christopher Pennfield to budge.

"C'mon Chris, you have to attend. Just at least show up!" Johnathan exclaimed, staring him right in the face.

"No, I can't leave here. They'll skewer me, Jonathan. I'm shamed, a pariah, I'm *cursed* dammit. Don't you get it!" He banged his fist on his curio. *"Don't you fucking get it!"*

"But you've been so much a part of the college," Johnathan entreated, "you *have to attend it*, it's the 100th Anniversary. A ceremony about us, essentially. Just sit with the trustees, show that we're still here, still the founders. Or just come out of here, God damnit!"

"What, so I can be ridiculed in public? Like I deserve? I'm too much of a coward."

"No. You have to show the world you're stronger than that. That she— that this one… 'incident'— can't bring you down."

"Don't blame it on her!" Christopher barked.

"Why not?

"She was as much a victim of the curse as I."

"C'mon, Chris, snap out of it. You don't have to speak. But just be there. Look, I don't know what the fuck is going on, what we're seeing out there these days, but if you go, you show them, and us how proud you are to be a Pennfield."

"*Proud* is not the word I feel right now," Christopher answered. "No, Johnathan, under no circumstances will I slither out of here and go to that stupid ceremony." With that, he took a swill of his scotch and slammed the door in his brother's face.

FOR MONTHS, Pennfield remained at Boothbay Harbor, partitioning himself from the rest of the world. In a form of self-inflicted punishment, each day he would review the public records to remind himself why he was there, alone and shamed. Although he had committed the words to memory, he forced himself to read the New York Post's lead story of May 26, 1996 every single day. The paper was stored permanently in the top drawer of his curio:

UNDERGRADUATE FALLS FOR PROF: Research Assistant's Affair With Prof Stuns GCT. Jennifer Winston, a 21-year-old student at Pennfield College in Percer, VT, jumped to her death yesterday in Grand Central Terminal. Unnoticed by commuters, MTA and security personnel on the floor, Winston somehow found her way up to the fringe walkway lining the terminal's majestic roof, and at approximately 3:30PM leapt to her death, landing on the ornamental knob atop the well-known clock over the terminal's central information booth. The gruesome suicide was the result of a love affair gone wrong with Professor Christopher Pennfield, Chair of the college's Philosophy Dept. and heir to the Pennfield family that founded the college. Winston had left a note at the Post's main editorial office earlier in the day in which she alleged she was pregnant by the Professor. Pennfield, who was scheduled to be keynote speaker at the College's 100th Anniversary Ceremony in several weeks, apparently fled to a family estate in Maine and is in seclusion…

AFTER A FEW UNCOMFORTABLE minutes with the headline story, Pennfield's bony fingers would flip to Page 6. His daily catharsis was never complete until he had again read *The Note* as he had come to call it, printed prominently on a sidebar for all to see.

FALLEN STUDENT'S NOTE TO POST.

How could he do this to me? How could he expect me to stand for it? Did the mighty Professor Christopher Pennfield think he could get away with it? Did he think he could get me pregnant and then discard me like garbage? Did he think the mighty Pennfield name would protect him? Didn't he realize that all mean spirits are doomed to fall?

To be continued……

Jennifer Winston

Incriminating as it was, *The Note* itself was not what bothered Pennfield the most. That was the past, over and done with. It was those last three words— *To be continued*— which festered in his mind.

He yearned for something to do, to make it all go away, but he knew his desire was futile. There was absolutely nothing he could do, and it would never go away. It would take nothing less than the ability to change the past to make things right again, an impossibility. Persistently bored, he read and re-read the classics in his areas of research— Plato, Camus, Arendt, Ayer and Popper, Husserl on Descartes, and then some— to the point where he could recite them from memory and thus found them all the more glib. He began to drink even more, and yearned for real human interaction.

Three years into his exile, his grief had progressed through shock, pain and guilt to outright anger. He often sat in his large leather chair, gazing out upon the harbor and brooding: *Am I mad— is there something wrong with the Pennfield mind, that we think we see things, should I be examined? But— we did see it. I saw it. I've left my body and I've seen... the past, but why me? Why did the blasted... ghost? the curse? some dark underworld... have to choose me. And why haven't I heard from my former colleagues? Has Johnathan given up? Where are they, now when I need them most?*

Finally, he decided to begin the process of making things right, even if his efforts might prove fruitless. He decided to venture out from Boothbay Harbor and pay a visit to what was once his beloved sanctuary.

In preparation, he grew a beard, hoping it would provide some sort of cover, at least a minor camouflage, to those who barely knew him. Each day as his beard filled in a bit more, he wondered if his new looks would be a sufficient shield for his return to Pennfield College.

He could only hope. The moment he stepped onto the cobblestone path traversing the campus green, he felt like his old self again. Seeing the ivy-covered buildings, watching the students studying and sleeping under the shade of the colossal blaze-red maple tree he knew so well and listening to the chimes from the old clock atop the bell tower soothed him in a way he had not enjoyed in years.

He stopped at one point, noticing something new, a disjointed metallic structure in front of the science building. *How odd,* He thought. *What passes for art today is shocking.* To Pennfield, the structure seemed more like a shiny, giant version of one of those toy mobiles that hangs above an infant's crib than a statue worthy of exposure on the Pennfield College campus. He just hoped that the Board of Trustees had not overspent on this work of *art.*

He took a deep breath of the fresh Vermont September air. The clear blue skies were contrasted by a small group of white, puffy clouds, the wispy, subtle winds rustled through the leaves. The chatter of students almost instantly transported him back to his glory days— *so massively under-appreciated by him at the time.*

He strolled around campus all afternoon. For the most part, he blended into the background, incognito. Several times during his almost three-hour jaunt, as he walked past the academic buildings, the dorms, across the campus green, down Main Street— past his favorite coffee shop, the liquor store, deli and pharmacy— he would notice some junior faculty member or campus worker doing a double-take, or perhaps two or three people in a far-off group huddled in whispered conversation pointing in his direction, but largely, his bright white beard and whiskers provided adequate cover.

Of course, the real test would come that evening.

Pennfield's Court was the given moniker to that vaunted corner of the Faculty Club where Christopher Pennfield once reigned supreme; classically attuned to its function, that corner— with its arching mahogany-framed windows overlooking the campus green and its imposing, leather chairs surrounding a cherry cocktail table, all set before a large stone fireplace— was special to Pennfield. It was in that spot where the old Christopher Pennfield was at his pure unabashed best, his natural habitat, a fitting platform for his wit, wisdom, and sarcasm. Other faculty members— less notable than Pennfield, Vice Provost and Chair of the Philosophy Department— considered it an honor when they were accepted participants in the rarefied discourse emanating from the legendary Pennfield's Court. Now, part of him wanted to remain unrecognized, and yet at the same time, he couldn't deny that it would be an honor simply to be seen, and even welcomed.

George Roche, the club's manager and maître de, a mainstay for over twenty years, focused quizzically on the older-looking man with the white, bushy beard hobbling through the entrance foyer. Upon recognizing him as the exiled Professor Christopher Pennfield, he dropped his tray, recovered quickly and greeted him with his usual respect and propriety.

"Good evening, Professor Pennfield."

"And to you as well, George," Pennfield nodded. And with that, the professor felt he no longer needed to remain alone and unseen. He smiled and walked by as if everything was perfectly normal.

At 5:30, there were only a few patrons scattered around the club. Promptly, Pennfield strode over to his personal corner and took his rightful place in the winged chair next to the window overlooking the campus green, a place once reserved only for him. Across the room, he noticed Roche whispering to one of the waiters, ostensibly giving the young man special instructions on the service for one Professor Christopher Pennfield. The young waiter then walked over to the bar and proceeded towards Pennfield.

"Your scotch, sir. Compliments of the house." The white-gloved young man placed a tumbler on the table before Pennfield.

"Thank you," Pennfield responded. "Tell George that was very kind of him."

"Certainly, sir."

Sipping his scotch, Pennfield's eyes roamed around the club as it filled up with guests, mostly faculty members, weary, eager to decompress and enjoy some camaraderie. He thought he recognized a group of three or four more junior members as they strode briskly in his direction, intent on laying claim to the best seats in what was once his personal domain. When they saw him sitting there, they halted.

Pennfield lifted his glass towards them and nodded.

They looked curiously at each other, unsure of what to do next. For several seconds they mumbled amongst themselves, then, avoiding any eye contact with Pennfield, drifted away and took seats at a table far across the room.

So is this what's in store for me, the subtle brush-off? Pennfield wondered.

He scoured the room, seeking out a familiar face.

He spotted Kevin Nordstrom, an Associate Professor of Chemistry, absent-mindedly navigating around the tables. As if by rote, his mind in the clouds, Nordstrom took his usual seat in Pennfield's Court. When Pennfield addressed him, he recoiled.

"Good afternoon, Kevin," Pennfield stated.

Shocked, Nordstrom shook his head, then blinked.

"Christopher?" Nordstrom shuddered. *"Dr. Pennfield?"*

"Yes, that would be me," Pennfield answered. " '*Rumors of my demise have been greatly exaggerated.*' "

"Clemens. Of course. Buh… wow, …excuse me, I don't know what to say," Nordstrom stuttered.

"Then don't. Just drink." Pennfield hailed the young man sipping his drink.

"I'm sorry… I'm very sorry… I mean, for everything that happened."

"I am in no need of your sympathy, Kevin," Pennfield stated, "just your company."

Nordstrom sweat as he guzzled awkwardly from his tumbler. He began to gather his bag when Professors Philip Wentworth and Susan Petty, both old friends of Pennfield's, entered the area.

Wentworth, a venerable professor of the classics, stared quizzically at the bearded man in the corner. After several instants, he recognized the face beneath the beard. "Why *Christopher,* you old dog you. Welcome back!" He shook his hand heartily.

Petty quickly followed up. "Well Chris Pennfield, as I live and breathe!"

Pennfield lifted his hands and motioned downward. "Please, please sit down my friends."

Sensing an opportunity, Nordstrom choked down the rest of his drink. "Excuse me, but I have to be home early tonight. Gotta watch the kids, you know. Just came for a quick one."

Pennfield stood up and extended his hand. "Well, Kevin, it was great to see you, even if only for a few, far too brief moments."

Relieved, Nordstrom strode out of the club.

"I'll tell you something, Philip, Susan." Pennfield huddled over the table and whispered to his old friends. "That man may be a brilliant chemist, but he has absolutely no social skills and can't handle even one glass of scotch."

The three shared a laugh.

"Well how's retirement treating you in lovely, bucolic Maine?" Petty asked politely.

"Let's not sugarcoat it, Susan. It's not a retirement, it's a banishment."

"Christopher, don't you think you're being very hard on—"

"No, I never had an appetite for bullshit or equivocation," said Pennfield. "It is what it is."

"So be it," Wentworth stated. "So how is life in Boothbay?"

"Well, if you had…" Pennfield forced an exaggerated cough, "…umm, wrote me or, God forbid, given me a call, you would know already, now wouldn't you?"

"Oh, please, Christopher, you know all too well the rigors of academic life. And we weren't sure, we just didn't know if you wanted..."

Petty cut in. "It's sad the whole thing happened, Christopher, I know you know that now, too. But if there's ever a chance that you can move forward and continue to be one of our most esteemed and gifted scholars, then, we'll have lost one and not two."

"There's much more to it than that," Pennfield stated.

"Oh..."

"It's a family thing," Pennfield answered.

"What? Affairs?" Wentworth exclaimed.

"*Phil*," Petty protested.

"No, not that. It's not worth getting into," Pennfield responded. "But it's a family thing that did me in."

"Christopher, please," Wentworth broke in, "you need not make up excuses for us. We all realize you're as human as anyone else. We all have our soft spots."

Pennfield thought deliberatively for a moment, then decided to let it out: "Like the time you were fixated on that sophomore boy from Massachusetts, Phil?"

Stunned, Wentworth scowled. "Oh god, that was centuries ago, Chris."

"Or how about your little tryst, Susan, with our visiting scholar who moved here with his wife, from, where was it, Israel?" Pennfield followed.

"Okay Chris… you're angry."

"And who brushed that one under the rug for you?"

"Of course, you, Chris," she answered. "You had tremendous sway at the college back then and of course I am eternally—"

"And neither of you had the decency to write or phone me?"

"Chris," said Wentworth, "you know how much Susan and I respect you and hold you in extremely high regard."

"I have to admit," Pennfield responded, "I'm not so sure."

"Please, Chris," Harris followed up, "you know we do. It's just that, given everything that happened, it's not politically—" He stopped abruptly.

"*Correct?*" Pennfield retorted. "Not so *politically correct* to consort with the formerly revered college luminary, now a pariah, who put his neck on the line for both of you?"

"Chris, I suggest we not go there," Wentworth exclaimed. "For our friendship if not for anything else."

"Ah, friendship." Pennfield giggled.

Pennfield's words proved smothering, cloaking the air with a blanket of awkward silence.

Fidgety and uncomfortable, Wentworth gazed down at his watch. "You know I told Catherine I'd be home by seven. She hasn't seen me since exams a week ago. I should go."

"Yes, yes," Petty followed. "I still have a meeting with a student tonight."

"Christopher," Wentworth said. "So nice to see you."

"Christopher, take care of yourself." Petty repeated.

"Yes, cheers!" Pennfield raised his glass.

Abandoned, he sipped his scotch, sitting alone in *Pennfield's Court.*

PENNFIELD'S VISIT to the Faculty Club sealed his fate. He had tried, perhaps not with the kindest words or sense of fellowship, but had tried to coerce Wentworth and Petty to embrace him, to welcome him back to the community. He had failed. There was nothing else he could do. His future was now cast in stone.

As he withered away, day by day, drinking himself to oblivion, watching time go by from the 8-foot high leaded window in his bedroom overlooking the harbor, his mind would frequently meander to thoughts of one single person, a very special person: his darling Ophie. He replayed that final visit to her hospital bed over and over again, remembering each exact detail and always wondering what she meant by her final words to him: *protect Shippy.* If only he could talk to Ophie, hold her, lay with her and tell her everything they had seen, what they had dug up, what he had dreamed, maybe she would know. *Maybe she does know.*

Just thinking of her made him want to try again to clear his head, to sort it out. On its face, her words about Shippy didn't make any sense to him. Shippy was a cataton, had been, ever since that horrific event in 1963. Fortunately, the trust fund established by Uncle Perce afforded Ship the very best care possible.

What could he possibly do, exiled and shamed, to *protect Shippy?* And from what? It was a question, he feared, that would remain forever unanswered.

* * *

TIME FRAME: 2007

6

Boothbay Harbor, Maine, Night, March 8, 2007

Jolted awake in a cold sweat, Christopher Pennfield brusquely grabbed at his night table and yanked open the drawer. His bony, arthritic fingers rummaged around like spider legs until he found it: a small bottle of scotch set aside for just such an occasion. He sat at the edge of the bed and took a quick swig. His heart raced.

Thank God, it was over.

Sleep paralysis: he hadn't suffered an episode in years yet the symptoms were exactly the same as he remembered: he wakes up, his mind clear as a bell, conscious of everything around him, the room bathed in shades of night-time gray, the trees outside wafting to pleasant breezes, the surf breaking upon the rocks. Tranquil normalcy.

But, then…

He tries to move. Nothing: every cell in every muscle of his body dormant. He strains to grunt, his mind sending violent, raging signals throughout his nerves urging— *no, commanding*— his muscles to move. Nothing, not even a millimeter, an iota. He tries again.

Again, nothing.

Move damnit! He orders them as if they'll really listen. Then he hears it. A recurrent sound, a buzzing, as if a bumblebee is buzzing around him, threatening to sting, taunting him in his paralysis. But there's no bee, never is— just the sound.

His eyeballs force themselves to the edge of their sockets straining to see his phantom tormenter, but he can't. Maybe, just maybe, a hint of an odd shape on the outermost periphery. He strains to swivel his head. Not possible: only his pupils straining, stretching, struggling to reveal just one more inch.

Then, of course, the most dreaded part: that damn pounding. Something pummels his chest, banging on it as if it's a drum.

Each time, at first, he fears it's from the inside; his heart tearing itself from its cavity. But he knows better. Some external demon, he's sure, is elevating his torment from an irritating buzz to a terrifying attack. Toying with him, it was.

Shit!

Why me? he asks himself. He thought these episodes were done with, gone forever.

He remembered once praying to God for mercy when the pummeling began, but it only fueled his tormentor's fury, propelling it to strike with more intensity and rapidity, as if it could read his very thoughts, suck energy from his mind. He had learned his lesson, he would not repeat his mistake.

But, still, there was a speck of doubt: was this merely another irritating episode or was this *the time*? Was this the time his heart or brain or nervous system was finally rebelling against years of abuse? Or, perhaps this time it wouldn't follow the script of his many previous episodes, maybe there was something more, something shocking, something grotesquely haunting yet to come. He shuddered in his cold sweat.

Like every other time, he would endure the pummeling until it ceased, learning just to take the pain and breathe, until it was done. He struggled to wiggle, to readjust himself on his mattress, but his enormous efforts resulted only in miniscule movement, if at all. He had no idea why he even attempted to move, but still some inner instinct compelled him to try.

Soon, it came, following the script. Out of the corner of his eye— a blur, a streak, a hazy *suggestion* of a person. A true apparition, or a mere invention of a mind overtaxed by anxiety and stress and a multitude of other undetermined psychological afflictions?

Yet, it needled at him, this apparition or whatever it was. Like the buzzing bee that initiated the episode, it only crept into his outermost periphery, never entering into full view. And, doubly taunting, Pennfield was incapable of turning his head. But it was there, he was sure: a tall radiating presence, shimmering on the edge.

It ended as it always ended. He drifted into a hazy slumber, his sweat evaporating into thin air along with the remnants of the episode.

AND, now he was awake, sitting on the edge of his bed, in full control of his faculties, swigging his scotch as he did ritualistically after each of these episodes, the Grandfather's clock resonating ten distinct chimes. *Well at least these blasted episodes gave him something, even if it was a convoluted rationale for a drink,* he thought, sipping along, soothed by the swishes of the surf beneath his window.

Thankfully, it was over; he had endured another one of these frightening incidents. He was proud— he was still man enough to endure it— but he had hoped these incidents were over, done with forever, years ago.

A PLEASANT BREEZE ambled in through the window, seducing the curtains into a slow graceful waltz. He smiled, watching the shimmering velvet curtains sway delightfully to and fro, conspiring with the breeze and shades of gray to tease him into a relaxing, meditative calm.

It was almost worth it, he convinced himself, *almost worth enduring the paralyzing, stultifying taunting and buzzing and pummeling and straining, just to appreciate a few moments of calm.*

He reached over to his night table for a Rothmans, but his hand stopped halfway.

His eyes focused on the curtains.

He squinted.

In the curtains, a sort of Rorschach: the folds in the velvet, the shades of darkness, the whims of the breeze painting a picture.

Was it a person? No, no it was just his mind filling in the blanks, like seeing faces in clouds.

He told himself to look away, reach again for his Rothmans and be done with it. But he could not.

With each moment, the image became clearer, focusing into a crisp, unambiguous form, a ghastly realism. A man, middle-aged, sitting in a chair: a shaven head, a hospital gown, in some sort of stupor. Until –

His lips moved: "*Le père m'épargne s'il vous plaît de mon sort.*"

Pennfield crumbled onto the floor.

* * *

7

Boothbay Harbor, Maine, Early Morning, March 9, 2007

So shaken by the vision at the window, Pennfield struggled throughout the night, a prisoner in his own bedroom, sleeping intermittently yet never fully relaxing. His eyes would grow heavy, a drowsy veil lulling him into a light sleep, yet his apprehension would prevent him from drifting into anything deeper. He would awaken, sweaty and restless, twisting and turning, struggling without relief.

Finally, he decided to sit up and pour another glass of scotch. He sat there, the room dark and hazy, counting the ticks of his grandfather's clock, waiting for the sun to cast its morning beams into his room.

My darling Christopher, it's been so long since we last spoke.

He shivered, then stiffened in his chair.

Silence.

In a sudden jolt, he grabbed for his scotch and chugged a gulp directly from the bottle. He settled back and relaxed, the scotch soothing his innards.

He reached across for a Rothmans, put it in his mouth, then clutched for his lighter. He lit the cigarette, sucking hard, allowing the inhaled fumes to commingle with the scotch. As he exhaled, he looked up. "Oh… my god."

He rubbed his eyes. *Was he seeing who he thought he was seeing?* He shivered, then began to feel faint. Sweat moistened his forehead. He breathed deeply. His instincts compelled him to scream, but he whispered,

"Ophie, what's happening? What's wrong with me? Is it you?"

Sorry I sprang upon you without notice, she answered. *But I sensed you might need me, we might need each other.*

His eyes locked upon her. He absorbed her, gazing all around her. In a microscopic segment of time, he convinced himself there was nothing to be scared of, nothing to be alarmed about. This was his beloved Ophie, here—somehow *here*.

"That goes without saying," he said." "Since the first day I set eyes upon you, I've needed you."

But are you happy to see me?

"Delighted, elated." He wiped his forehead with a handkerchief, recovering adroitly from his instant of terror.

Are you sure?

"Well, you just sort of appeared after all these years. You're asking me to process shock and glee at the very same moment. Of course, I'm a bit confounded. Wouldn't you be?"

Absolutely, my love.

He gazed upon her reverently. She looked splendid. Her mysteriously seductive glow, radiantly clear, set against the dark shadows enhanced her allure even more so than the morning Newport sun beaming on her fair young skin during their summers as teens.

"Now here's the Ophie I grew to love and cherish."

As I did you.

She drifted over towards his chair, a seductive gleam in her eyes. Her face was ageless, expressing all the facets of her charm across a lifetime: a composite Ophelia. Amazing, how one vision, one pure glowing vision, could express so many aspects of one individual being.

You've been suffering, I can tell.

"My dear, sweetheart Ophie, that's the understatement of the century. A lot has happened since you left us."

All at once, Christopher could see his beloved teenage Ophelia—her flowing black hair and naughty spunk— the thirty-year-old Ophelia — a beautiful woman with the class and élan of a young Jackie O—and her everlasting spirit, that powerful combination of propriety and wisdom.

The curse?

"Yes, I was the lucky one destined to take the bullet for an entire generation of Pennfields."

Perhaps you were chosen for a reason, said the insouciant, nubile Ophie of her Wellesley years.

"I've yet to think of one."

Perhaps only you had the strength...

"Strength? I crumbled like a Christmas cookie."

You underestimate yourself, responded the piquant Ophelia, the thirty-one-year-old socialite, dragging on a cigarette in her Fifth Avenue apartment in her Pierre Cardin dress.

"Doubt it. If anything, I grossly *overrated* myself over the years. That's what got me into trouble. False hubris and an overblown sense of entitlement."

Some would just call that confidence, no?

"Doubt it," he answered, then bit his lip. Silent, he contorted his face into a painful grimace and covered it with his hand. He whimpered.

What's wrong, my love?

"For the past eleven years, I've sat in this chair, watching that damn harbor day after day after day as my very spirit withers away. God knows I've done wrong, but haven't I suffered enough, Ophie? I want my life back." A small tear rolled down his cheek.

But is that even possible my dear?

"I don't know. But I'm stubborn enough to try."

That you are, my love, that you are. You don't realize how much I regret— deeply regret— that I was not around for you during your darkest hours.

"Listen, Ophie, I know damn well that it can never be the way that it was. But I've thought a lot since I've been sitting here and drowning my sorrows. I was a victim, of the curse, but not an innocent one. The spirit behind the Penn-field family curse used my weaknesses to entrap me. My own bullshit, Ophie, that's what I mean, it put me there, made me an easy mark."

So what are you suggesting?

"I need to do something Ophie; I need to show the world that I'm better than that. There's a soul inside this old body."

And what were you thinking?

"Perhaps I should be the one to warn future generations of Pennfields."

A laudable task, but that's not your purpose. Your calling is much higher I would suspect.

"Exactly what are you trying to say?" he asked, perplexed.

It should be quite obvious.

"Oh?"

You had another visitor earlier this evening, did you not?

"Yes, indeed."

Ship?

"Yes, who else?"

And how do you know that?

"He was sitting right over there." His shaking finger pointed towards the flowing velvet curtains. "Or perhaps hovering is the more correct term. Then he went on to speak to me in French. It had to be him."

A sort of lingua franca for the two of you... And what did he say, my dear?

"Le père m'épargne s'il vous plaît de mon sort."

Father please save me from my fate?

"Yes. I'm still trying to decipher its significance."

Shouldn't that be obvious?

Glassy-eyed, Pennfield stared across the room, silent.

I tried to tell you, but couldn't.

"Tell me what? When?"

Right before I passed...

"Protect Shippy?"

You remembered?

"Of course, that moment is etched forever in my memory."

And have you?

"Protected Shippy? He has the best care possible. Your father saw to that."

And you?

"What can I possibly do?"

Quite a lot, I would think.

"And how can I achieve something that all your father's money cannot?"

For a very good reason.

"Is your intent to perplex me?"

No. Though perhaps a bit of a surprise, it really shouldn't be.

"Then, get on with it, Ophie!"

You're his father.

"What!!" He bounced up off his chair.

It was that summer in Newport. You had just finished your sophomore year at Yale and I was all of fifteen.

Silence. Complete dead silence. Pennfield shrank back in his enormous chair as white as a corpse.

My darling Christopher, are you really that surprised?

He mumbled, barely moving his lips. "I don't know."

You should feel good. We did something together. We left a mark.

"Although a flawed one," Pennfield practically whispered. "I mean, there were always rumors, unsubstantiated of course, that you were his mother..."

Yes, I suppose anyone with an ounce of savvy would've seen through me being sent off to France for finishing school and then returning just after my little brother was born...

"Yes, but the whole world feared the wrath of your father. Your secret was secure."

Perhaps tonight's episode was meant to send a message. To me it's obvious. Now it's time to help poor Shippy.

"But, Ophie, he's a fifty-year-old cataton."

He called out to you, did he not?

"Yes, if you take my so-called 'experience' last night at face value, Ophie — I don't know what these are, I—"

So then perhaps he wants something from you.

"I have no supernatural powers. I can't revive him from his stupor."

Perhaps you're equating reviving him with saving him.

"Isn't that the point, to revive him?" he questioned.

Maybe, maybe not.

"But we've already ruined him. It's our fault he is as he is."

Perhaps. But the world will never know.

"Yes, but I do. And that's not good for a man in my current state."

Believe me, you'll soon be relieved of your morbid existence.

Christopher sat up straight and let it sink in for a moment. "Actually, I find that enlightening."

But first, you must take care of Ship. Your time is running out. You must do it now.

"But I can't possibly..."

You're selling yourself short, my dear cousin. After all, it was you who discovered the family curse after, how many generations?

"That was dumb luck. And, of course we had Swann..."

Say that again.

"What? Dumb luck? Swann?"

There's your answer, my dear.

"Swann?" Pennfield shrugged.

She nodded, smiling, floating before the window.

"But Swann, he opened the whole Pandora's Box— started nosing around, got connected to that curmudgeon, Captain Scott— perhaps we would all be better off today if I had never met the man."

Ignorance is bliss, eh?

"In this case, it's the lesser of two evils."

Shippy needs your help. Make me proud, Christopher, make me proud.

He dragged on his Rothmans and then giggled vigorously.

"Proud? Really?" He shook his head. "I don't think anyone's been proud of me for decades. Don't you realize? I am the mad fornicator, I caused a young woman to leap to her death, and now, the father of a bed-ridden man— a catatonic man— my son. Aren't I such a convenient vessel to fill with the sum total of the world's anger?"

My poor dear Christopher, she chided him, *drowning in a sea of self-pity, are we?*

"At this stage of my life, I find it quite uplifting." He raised his glass. "Cheers!"

Take the step, my love. Do something. Her skin was thinning, her appearance was losing its warmth and its weight. For a moment he saw her as the withered hospital patient, bound by bandages and tubes, and his heart sank.

"I want to, Ophie. But I can't. I'll torture you and myself even more."

You can make a difference, Christopher. You can. Don't let time run out.

"But, wait. Swann? I mean the man's a ghost hunter, how could he possibly…"

"You can make a difference, Christopher. Redeem yourself. Time is running out."

Her likeness, in the last moment young and gorgeous again, faded as she rose toward the window and whispered, one last time before she vanished,

Redeem yourself.

PENNFIELD WOKE AT MID-DAY, a brilliant sun beaming through the windows. Dizzily, he shook his head, wondering: was what he saw last night worth interpreting, was it in some way real, or just some product of this tendency of his, some contrivance of an aging, overtaxed mind? He stumbled, righting himself on his bed, summoning his housekeeper Nora, to bring him coffee. After gaining his bearings, he grasped for the phone. Slowly and deliberately, his trembling finger punched the numbers.

"Hello," a familiar voice answered.

"Mr. Swann?"

"Yes."

"This is Christopher Pennfield. I think I may have a little project for you."

* * *

8

Boothbay Harbor, Maine, Mid-day, March 15, 2007

Apprehension taunted Ed Swann as his old Chevy pick-up puttered along Route 27 winding its way around the Maine coastline. The craggy rocks abutting the brisk deep-blue waters, every now and then punctuated by a lighthouse jutting out from a rocky point, provoked his mind to wonder. *After all these years, what in the name of bejesus could Christopher Pennfield, of all people, ever want out of me?* To Pennfield, he figured, he would be about as welcome as heartburn. Swann smirked: no, Pennfield would accept heartburn much more readily than he would ever welcome Ed Swann again, he was sure.

Of course, the moment he heard that resonant aristocratic voice on his cell phone— *Mr. Swann, I think I may have a little project for you*— Swann knew it could be no one other than Christopher Pennfield. But the question pestered him: *why?* So, with more than a fair degree of curiosity, he accepted the invitation. The once proud, philandering professor and heir to the Pennfield family fortune had been brought down to earth at the hands of a restless spirit from the 1620s. He couldn't deny that he was interested to see how far the high and mighty could fall.

An aromatic breeze freshened by the surf wafted across Swann's ruddy-red face as Nora Murphy, Pennfield's housekeeper, met him at the door.

"A pleasure to see you, Mr. Swann." Her bright green eyes sparkled.

"And you as well," Swann tipped his trademark hound's-tooth hat with a wink.

"Mr. Pennfield will see you up in his study." She led him toward the stairs. "Can I get you anything, Mr. Swann?"

"No, I'm fine, Nora. This beautiful day is enough for me." He sniffed the fine air.

Swann followed Nora up several half-flights of wooden stairs which eventually bent their way upward to a rather large hallway. At the far end of the hallway, a set of classic French doors led into Christopher Pennfield's study— a combination study-bedroom— an old, weathered room with a beamed cathedral-ceiling and a set of tall, leaded windows overlooking the harbor.

A barrage of sunlight blinded Swann as he entered the room. He squinted to see the bony figure of Christopher Pennfield sitting regally in a leather Victorian chair, a shimmering bright corona lining his silhouette.

"CAN I offer you a nice sauterne, Mr. Swann," Pennfield pointed with his long bony finger, "or perhaps a single malt Scotch?"

"No. No," Swann nodded, "too early in the day for me. But I see you haven't changed." Swann winked as he noticed the tumbler of Scotch at Pennfield's side.

"Yes, old habits die hard I'm afraid," Pennfield gulped his scotch.

"Well, you look…uh…." Swann stopped himself.

Pennfield held up his hand and barked, "Don't bother searching for a euphemism to assuage me. I know I look like shit."

"Oh?" Swann nodded.

Indeed, the Christopher Pennfield who sat gulping scotch in his parlor overlooking Boothbay Harbor on this sunny March afternoon was a much different person than the one Swann first met in the mid-1990s. Swann remembered the old Christopher Pennfield as a man who swaggered through life, a deep reservoir of pride pumping him up far more than he deserved. Impeccably groomed, the old Christopher Pennfield could charm anyone he pleased with his quick wit, refined demeanor and unbridled confidence. A considerably vain man, Pennfield— in those days— had a sculpted jaw and cheekbones, sparkling teeth, perfectly tweezed eyebrows and his full shock of silver hair.

The Christopher Pennfield of today, now sitting directly across from Swann, was a very old-looking seventy-one, and could have passed for being in his late-eighties. He was a bony stick-figure, wrapped incongruously in a royal-blue, silk smoking-jacket and emerald ascot; he had a face that was gaunt and white with dry skin deeply cracked and creviced, stretched tightly across a sharply defined facial skeleton. That famous shock of hair was now dry and thin, strewn haphazardly around his flaking pate.

"Well, it's been a while, eh?" Swann suggested.

"Of course," Pennfield muttered, "but what's time anyway, other than a backdrop for our human frailties."

"A little pessimistic wouldn't you say?" Swann responded. "If I remember, the very last time I saw you we were out on the sea with that old salt Captain Scott, seeing an apparition of the Mayflower, and…" Swann's voice suddenly trailed off as he caught himself.

"That's an area where we need not tread, Mr. Swann." Pennfield briskly lit a cigarette.

Nodding, Swann obliged.

An arsenal of objects— more akin to a set of *tools* that defined and sustained his current lifestyle— surrounded Pennfield and his big leather chair. To his right, on an octagonal cherry curio, three packs of Rothmans Royals and a silver ashtray, smeared with ashes and crumpled butts. To his left, on a round mahogany lodge table, a bar's worth of liquor surrounding an ice bucket chilling an uncorked bottle of chardonnay. His left leg was elevated on a deep burgundy leather ottoman, his foot heavily bandaged, his cane resting at his side. *The Complete Works of Friedrich Nietzsche, The Collected Essays of Albert Camus* and Hannah Arendt's *The Human Condition* stood prominently on a bookcase off to the side. Books and magazines— open and unopen, pieces of sticky-pads protruding from some— were strewn around him.

"So after all these years you trust me with another project?" Swann changed the subject.

"Yes, Swann. Indeed, I do." Pennfield answered. "It concerns a relative of mine. Arthur Pennfield."

"Seems the world is full of Pennfields." Swann winked.

"Yes, Ship Pennfield. A victim of unfortunate circumstance."

"Ship?"

"Arthur Shipkin Pennfield is his full name, a young lad with so much potential. Youngest son of my father's older brother."

"Go on…"

"He was born in 1956 and even at a young age showed tremendous potential. He was quite precocious. It may have been that there was a fifteen-year separation between him and his next oldest sibling. Had his IQ measured at age six and it was off the chart, literally off the chart."

Swann smiled. "Unexpected pregnancy, huh?"

"I would assume so." Pennfield fidgeted in his chair.

"And today…"

"Catatonic." Pennfield sat back and took a healthy gulp of scotch. "Has been so for just over forty years."

"And he was normal before?"

"Quite."

"So what happened?" Swann asked.

"Don't really know," Pennfield lit a cigarette. "But I fear it has something to do with our family problem."

"The ghosts?

"I'd prefer the term *psychic gift*, Mr. Swann." Pennfield took another long drag on his Rothmans. "But there's more to it than that."

Swann smiled. "Oh?"

"My dear cousin Ophelia passed away in 1984. Cancer. Much too early, much too early." Pennfield's vacant eyes wandered towards the large window as he shook his head.

"Ophelia Pennfield?" Swann scratched his head, pondering. "I vaguely remember the name… wasn't she a big part of the New York social scene in the 1970s?"

"Indeed so," Pennfield mused, sipping his scotch. "She was at the center of it all. Good friends with Capote, Warhol, Jackie O, all the icons of the time...".

"The two of us were close, quite close." Pennfield puffed on his cigarette, wiped his brow and offered Swann a somewhat compromised version of the facts. "Of course I visited her frequently during her stay in the hospital. On one of my last visits, just before she passed, she informed me that Ship was not my cousin, but instead the result of a playful summer tryst between her and myself."

Swann cracked a half-smile.

Christopher glanced off towards the window. "Mr. Swann, you must realize I'm not shameful of the fact that I had a rather healthy sex-life in my youth."

"So let me guess," Swann pointed at Pennfield, "you have a catatonic son and now, for some odd reason, you're feeling guilty over it?"

"*I'm* not Catholic, Mr. Swann."

"Oh, so then…"

"Well, if indeed as my cousin informed me— and remember the chemo had done a job on her, quite a job, so who knows if she was even lucid or had any memory left whatsoever— if indeed, I am the father of Ship, then I figured that if our family has a psychic gift, and a Pennfield mated with another Pennfield…"

"You might have created a master race?" Swann retorted. "Oh boy."

"Quit goading me, Mr. Swann," Pennfield said, "my concern is… wouldn't the offspring have that um… *psychic gift* to a much, much greater degree?"

"You're thinking that the double whammy of Pennfield genes shocked him into a catatonic state?"

"Could be." Pennfield slithered back in his seat.

"But I'm missing something here," Swann scratched his head. "So for almost twenty years up until Ophelia's death, you had no clue you were Ship's father?"

"No. None at all. Her parents sent Ophie off to give birth, claiming she was studying in Europe for a semester, and then raised Ship as if he was their own."

"Her parents— did they know it was you?"

"No, never," Pennfield answered. "Ophie was quite cunning. She told her family that the father was a cousin of the Kupermans, one of Newport's most prominent families. He was visiting for the summer, a young lad from Harvard. She knew her father would have never pressed the issue. Would have caused too much of a ruckus. Uncle Perce was quite deft at those matters."

"Okay, so then explain something to me," Swann said. "If you've known you were his father for over twenty years, why haven't you visited him in all that time?"

Pennfield took a deep breath, wiped a drop of sweat from his brow, and offered the best answer he could come up with. "It's hard to say. Perhaps I was in denial. Perhaps I was afraid of seeing what the years in that state had done to him. And then, of course, after the incident with Jennifer…".

."So exactly what is it you want me to do for you?" Swann asked.

"I want you to go see him. I want to know what he's like today, how he's being cared for, what his treatment is," he paused, then swiveled his head across the room as if to make sure no one would hear, "and I want to know if this has anything to do with that curse."

"But I don't understand," Swann asked. "Can't you do that all yourself? Why me? I'm a ghost hunter, an investigator of the paranormal. And why have you waited almost 25 years since Ophelia told you?"

After a long pause, Pennfield lit another Rothmans.

"Good question, Mr. Swann. Several nights ago, I had one of those dastardly sleep paralysis attacks."

"Sorry to hear that, but you, of all people, should know they're practically harmless."

"Harmless?" Pennfield lifted his eyebrows. "They're only harmless to someone who's not having one, Mr. Swann."

"Good point."

"Well I hadn't had one in years," Pennfield continued. "And at the end of it, after I thought the whole horrid episode was over, I saw an image of Ship, an adult Ship, and he spoke to me."

"But slow down, if you hadn't seen him since he was what, seven years old, how can you recognize an adult Ship after all these years?"

"I had a very strong, let's call it *intuitive* feeling that it must be him."

"But that's not..."

"True, but then something happened that made it indisputably clear to me."

"And that was?"

"He spoke to me in French. We used to speak to each other in French when he was a child. A definite sign that it was him."

"Okay. So what did he say?"

"It translated to, *'Father, please save me from my fate.'*"

"Oh I see. But, still, you had just had a bout with sleep paralysis. You could have thought you were awake, but actually dreaming. That's pretty common."

"Could be," Pennfield puffed. "I started trying to look into that, but... but then as I thought back, the day little Shippy was first afflicted with his condition out at the dock at the family estate at Indian Harbor, his cousins thought he might have seen a ghost. So now, in retrospect, weaving it all together..."

"I get it, between your family's psychic powers, the ghost he might have seen that shocked him into his condition and now the apparent apparition in your room the other night, it may be the beginning of another chapter in the Pennfield family curse."

"Precisely, Mr. Swann."

"Hmm... an interesting— a very *difficult*— combination of events..." Swann pondered.

"What are you thinking, Mr. Swann?" Pennfield asked anxiously.

"Actually, about the dream specifically, something like that happened to me once," Swann answered. "When I was in college, I woke up one night, and saw the face of my uncle hovering over my bed."

"Really? And? What did you conclude?"

"Scared the bejesus out of me."

"Well, I can't say what happened that night exactly warmed my cockles, either" Pennfield retorted. "But what do you make of it, I mean, what's your point, Mr. Swann?"

"I'm getting there," Swann answered. "The next morning, the morning after I saw my Uncle's face, I received a call."

"Yes?"

"It was my mother. She told me my Uncle had passed away the previous night, right about the time I saw him."

"Oh God!" Pennfield shuddered. "That doesn't mean something could have happened to poor Shippy, do you think?"

"You're listed as the next of kin, aren't you?" Swann interrupted

"Yes, of course," answered Pennfield. "Ever since Aunt Bunny passed in '96, it's been me. I'm the closest relative left."

"So if you haven't received a call by now, I'd take that as a positive sign, wouldn't you?"

"I suppose. But still, we must follow up immediately!" Pennfield demanded.

"Of course, we will," Swann answered. "And I'd be glad to look into all of this for you, Chris, but, still, it might be best if you visited him first, confirm that the image you saw that night was actually him."

"I just can't fathom that yet," Pennfield mumbled, and then reached for his glass of Scotch. He saw his hand quivering, and pulled it back, his face flush. "I've not been in good sorts lately, Mr. Swann. I fear I'm losing control. After many years of normalcy— at least normalcy relative to myself— these psychic attacks have come back to torture me once again."

"I am sorry to hear that." Swann responded. "But why me? Aren't there others?"

"You're the only person outside my family to ever know about the curse. And now you're the only person other than me to know I may be Ship's father. And, of course, it goes without saying, I'll make it worth your while."

Swann chuckled. "I'm delighted you're willing to underwrite my next deep-sea fishing expedition to Florida, but I want you to realize I don't do this for the money."

"Then why do you?"

"Keeps me young," the eighty-two-year-old Swann winked.

"Well, cheers." Pennfield lifted his scotch chugged a gulp, then winced.

"So where is he?" Swann asked.

"In western Massachusetts. When do you think you can be there?"

"Day after tomorrow?" Swann answered. "I've got nothing but time on my hands these days."

"Excellent. I'll make the necessary arrangements immediately." Pennfield crushed the cigarette in an ashtray.

"And exactly where is he in western Mass?" Swann asked.

"He's at the Gladwell Institute of Mental Health Sciences in the Berkshires."

* * *

9

Boothbay Harbor, Maine, Morning, March 16, 2007

Christopher Pennfield rubbed his eyes and surveyed his blurry study. His daily headache stung more than usual this morning. Perhaps having Swann over yesterday had reminded him of his past and stirred the emotional pot. Perhaps he should have fessed up and told Swann that he actually learned that he was Ship's father from an *apparition* of Ophelia, not from her on her deathbed twenty-three years earlier. But that would have gotten him nowhere, compromising his already comprised credibility, even with Swann.

The bright rays of the sun pierced through his eyes and drilled into his brain. He surmised he must have fallen asleep in his drunkenness without drawing the curtains. Pain clamored at his temples. He summoned his housekeeper.

"Can you bring me some breakfast Nora?"

"Certainly, Professor Pennfield."

Fifteen minutes later, Nora returned with her specialty: beans, white pudding and a boiled egg. But for the hangover specifically, only his usual remedy would do. He mixed a shot of vodka into a glass of tomato juice, stirring rapidly.

"Anything else I can get you Mr. Pennfield?"

"No, thank you. That's quite fine, Nora."

DURING HIS YEARS in exile at Boothbay Harbor, Pennfield had settled into a daily routine. After his breakfast and Bloody Marys, he would read yesterday's mail and respond to any letters, if appropriate, spelling everything out precisely in his fine cursive script, finishing several cups of coffee. Usually around 11:30 he would eat again. Afterwards, he would check his email then read, online and off— newsmagazines, academic journals, the classics, whatever pleased his fancy— followed by a short nap. Nora had often tried to cajole him into some kind of afternoon walk, growing increasingly worried about his health. Walk or no walk, he greeted 4 o'clock by opening a bottle of chardonnay and enjoying the sweeping vista out his window to an eclectic mix of music, from Beethoven to Gershwin to the Beatles; he was particularly fond of the White Album. By dinnertime, he would graduate to red— a Pinot Noir, a garnet-red Burgundy or a fine Barolo. His after-dinner time revolved around his Scotch and Rothmans Royals.

But now it was morning, both a blessing and a curse. He could still live to appreciate another day— the sun flowing bountifully through his large bay windows and the sea caressing the harbor with its soothing ripples. Meanwhile, he would have to tolerate his legacy, stew in his own guilt, and accept the limitations fate had imposed upon his once abundant potential.

As familiar to his daily routine as Bloody Marys and Chardonnay, was writing. Beyond the usual business and correspondence, he wrote off and on throughout the day. Sometimes, it was for mere indulgence in melancholy, other times, it was a genuine but short-lived attempt to reconnect with his research. Today his mission was much more critical than either of these. It was time. He had been avoiding the inevitable for years, but Ophie's... *visitation,* had made it perfectly clear to him: there were some things he must do before his mortality swept him away. Step one had been to engage Swann to help with Shippy. And now that Swann was on the case, it was time to embark upon step two.

His bony fingers grasped for the curio's small drawer and reached for the parchments he kept there beside the articles from the Post documenting his downfall. He hadn't looked at it in years, had avoided it at all costs. But now he opened it, slowly and deliberately. Time's passage could not take the chill out of the words: *A HISTORY OF THE MEAN AND MALICIOUS SPIRITE WHICH HAS BEEN THE PLAGUE OF THE PENNFIELD FAMILY FOR FIVE GENERATIONS.*

Pennfield flicked his lighter, and then took a deep drag on his Rothmans. He looked long and hard at his lap-top's screen, and winced in the glaring, artificial light. He slammed it shut. He grasped for his fountain pen, pulled a piece of stationery from the drawer and began to write:

March 16, 2007

TO FUTURE GENERATIONS OF PENNFIELDS:

I am writing to my family's descendants sometime in the future— anonymous as you are to me today— to warn you of the source of the terrible tragedy that led to my personal downfall in 1996.

The intent of this note is in no way to exonerate myself. Although I was trapped in the claws of a restless, otherworldly, and vengeful curse, I brought it on myself. It was I who shaped the person that I am today. It was I who allowed alcohol and philandering to define my life. And by the time it— she— set the trap, it was I who had created her perfect victim.

Yet, she rendered me powerless.

My wife left me long ago. I hardly see my two sons except for a rare obligatory holiday. I am a stranger to my grandchildren, a pariah to the Pennfield family, all because I was the one chosen to be stricken by the curse. But that is over and done with, irreversible.

For the record, let me make it perfectly clear: there is a curse haunting the Pennfield family. It goes back to a rather untoward incident on the Mayflower involving our family patriarch, Charles Pennfield and some anonymous servant girl. The details are in the attached parchments, spelled out eloquently by our ancestor Nathaniel Pennfield in the eighteenth century.

Her spirit returns somewhat regularly to haunt further generations of Pennfields, rubbing salt in the wound, occupying the physical presence of a contemporary agent and then luring some unfortunate Pennfield into a sickening trap— it not only takes the life of the agent, but it casts shame upon an entire generation of Pennfields.

When I was first recovering from the ravages of the curse, I became obsessed with its history, studying numerous family documents and records. As far as I could determine, the curse had struck a member of the Pennfield family every sixty, seventy years or so, sometimes eighty, approximately every other generation. And I was the one for my generation. Several centuries-worth of rage rendered me impotent to pursue the life I had intended.

But in my waning years, that loss of power seems to have finally lost its hold on me. Having nothing left to lose, what was once my liability now becomes an asset. I cannot save myself, but I can save my descendants.

It was 1996 when she struck. And by my calculation she will strike again in the 2050s.

Who will be that generation's unfortunate member of the Pennfield family, I often wonder...

* * *

TIME FRAME: 2052

10

Lower Manhattan, NYCGAB, Evening, November 10, 2052

Rapidly, the footsteps of Jimmy Mashimoto-Pennfield pounded against the pavement, ricocheting snappy echoes, galloping down Fourth Street, propelling him farther and farther away. From her. And that putrid fifth-floor apartment smelling of rat shit.

Mashimoto-Pennfield had no idea why he had put himself at such risk. He knew only that he couldn't resist the rush of it all, placing his neck squarely on the guillotine and then snapping it back just in the nick of time.

He hustled over to the corner of Fourth and Avenue A and hailed a netcab. He flashed his e-let at the cab's sensor, instructing it to take him back to the Pennfield Technologies Tower.

As he zipped along on a sheet of air, he cursed himself for leaving the security of his office and sinking into such a bastion of licentiousness, chock-full of sub-100s. What good was all of his power if he couldn't even prevent himself from coming face-to-face with *her*?

Up until the moment he had left for that hell-hole, the day had been a fine one, a successful one: a morning meeting of the Consortium for Electromagnetic Trans-Substantiation Technologies in London, a quick tube back to New York, a briefing on several new MagLev projects, and then significant progress on the Penn Tech cryonics investment. Yet, as he lounged in his upper office on the 127th floor of the Penn Tech Towers— twinkling lights dotting the megascape and laser blurs zooming across Manhattan's three layers of elevated v-ways— he became outright bored.

THE PENNFIELD TECHNOLOGIES Towers sprouted majestically from a landfill created between E. 20th and E. 23rd St in a small crook where Manhattan Island jutted eastward into the river. The base section of the complex was formed by the massive glass and steel structure folding upon itself into a fifty-story isosceles trapezoid. V-way A, the lowest and most local of virtual highways on the east side of Manhattan, passed through the empty center-space formed by the trapezoidal loop.

The top section of the trapezoid— the *bridge* as it was referred to— served as a three-story tall atrium where visitors could walk on its glass floor over fifty stories of empty space and enjoy views spanning from central Long Island to the east, Sandy Hook to the south, and the Hoboken Trans-Hub and the rolling hills of Jersey to the west.

Two spiral towers rose from atop the bridge: the eastern tower seventy-five stories high, and the western tower, seventy-seven. An airavator passed through the stem of each tower, surrounded by narrowing circular floors. The top two floors of the western tower, the highest point in the entire structure, comprised Jimmy Mashimoto-Pennfield's personal sanctuary.

Made entirely of glass and metal, Mashimoto-Pennfield's office was about forty feet in diameter. His glass desk, his ergonomically-engineered glass chair, his glass conference table, all levitated steadily over the glass floor, its opacity adjustable by voice commands that could only come from Mashimoto-Pennfield, referred to as JMP by his business colleagues. In the center of this private retreat, a series of levitating glass steps spiraled their way upwards to JMP's most personal space.

Only twenty feet in diameter, Mashimoto-Pennfield's upper office, the seventy-seventh floor of the West Tower, or, the hundred and twenty-seventh floor counting the complex's trapezoidal base, was JMP's innermost chamber. The roof spiraled upward in perfect geometric symmetry, its top point— like a mariner's bowsprit— pointing stridently upward, grasping towards the heavens, capturing the mid-day sun at its apex. A multitude of mirrors within the tight spiral magnified and re-magnified the sun's bright rays into a flowing cascade of natural luminescence. Photovoltaic cells embedded with nano-precision in the glass panels converted the excess daytime sunlight into mystical glowing phosphorescence that sustained the aura during the evening and nighttime.

This was the space that Jimmy Mashimoto-Pennfield reserved for his most private moments. After an anxious day, he would sit back in his levitating chair, allowing natural aromatherapy to soothe his pores and gentle electric pulses to massage his muscles as he gazed at the holoscreen hovering above.

IT WAS about 6pm when the compulsion struck. Mashimoto-Pennfield tapped his fingers on his armrest and asked himself the question. He checked to assure all entrances to his private office and sanctuary were locked.

"*JMP Personal Files,*" he spoke authoritatively into the holoscreen floating above his reclined chair and summoned up a document from the Pennfield Technologies QTrove, a private firewalled segment of the QNet, the all-encompassing global quantum computing network.

A warning sign flashed across the screen: *Authorization Required.*

He held his right index finger up to the screen, unlocking the file.

TO FUTURE GENERATIONS OF PENNFIELDS:

I am writing to my family's descendants sometime in the future— anonymous as you are to me today— to warn you of the source of the terrible tragedy that led to my personal downfall in 1996...

THE ONLY EXISTING hardcopy of the note— written by his Great-Uncle Christopher Pennfield in 2007, as the old man wallowed away in shame and ill-health at a family estate on the Maine Coast— had been bequeathed to JMP by his Aunt Winnie. Immediately, it had been locked away in a safe for future consumption once he became of age. Three levels of cyber-security protected the digital copy from any unintended consumption.

The note had always baffled Mashimoto-Pennfield. At first he wrote it off to his Great-Uncle Christopher, apparently a rapscallion posing as an academic with more than his fair share of peccadilloes, in his dying moments attempting to blame his downfall on someone or something other than himself. But then there was always that parchment—included in the same large gray envelope— faint and barely legible, written by Nathaniel Pennfield in the late 18th century. If it wasn't for that, he would have dismissed Great-Uncle Christopher's note in a nanosecond.

Then, of course, there was his Ganzfeld session last week at his refuge in St. John's. He nodded at the holoscreen hovering above his desk, pointed towards a directory, flipping until he found it: a hologram of the Ganzfeld session.

"Play holofile," he told the screen.

INSTANTLY, the playback began: his naked body suspended on a curtain of air in his Ganzfeld chamber, his eyes covered with plain white half-spheres, his ears with noise-canceling headphones, pumping monotonous white noise.

The Ganzfeld Chamber was one of Mashimoto-Pennfield's marketplace triumphs, the forward evolution of what used to be called a sensory deprivation tank. Behind Mashimoto-Pennfield's brilliant marketing strategy, Ganzfelding had become a favorite form of escape and meditation for affluent professionals worldwide.

Mashimoto-Pennfield gazed at the holoscreen and focused on the image of himself: lying still in the Ganzfeld chamber, his lips moving deliberately:

"What? Who are you? Where are you?"

The mysterious woman repeated the words: *She's back.*

"Who? Who's back?" Mashimoto-Pennfield had trained himself to verbally repeat any critical sensations that streamed through his consciousness during a Ganzfeld session. The holofile saved them automatically.

"Soon we will meet? When? Why November 10, 2052?"

He played it back several times, absorbing everything.

"She'll seduce me? Why?"

Tapping his fingers on his desk, his mind wavered back and forth.

He remembered the session vividly: as he had melted from sensory deprivation into a deep, intense psychic awareness, he had heard a voice, a woman.

"Who are you?" he asked.

"Jennifer."

"Where are you from?

"Somewhere, sometime. Is that important?"

"Why are you contacting me?"

"To warn you."

At first, he didn't know how to interpret Jennifer's message. But then, he stiffened, his heart beating rapidly: *could this have something to do with Great-Uncle Christopher's curse?*

He quickly figured why today of all days he had compelled himself to open the folder containing the note and his hologram file:

Today was the day: November 10, 2052.

ABRUPTLY, he swiveled in his seat and pointed at the lower right corner of the holoscreen.

"Narc!" he shouted. *"Narc. Come here. I need you. Right now, this instant."*

Immediately, a holographic clone of Mashimoto-Pennfield materialized.

"Yes, my brilliant cohort, what can I do for you today?" the holographic Narc responded.

"Cut the patronizing bullshit," JMP ordered. "I need your help."

"Of course. Of course," Narc replied obligingly.

THERE WAS ONLY ONE NARC, yet another creation of JMP's fertile mind. The technology underlying him was so advanced it would not be ready for commercial introduction for at least a decade. A perfect holographic clone of JMP, Narc's memory was filled with exabytes of data, thought-patterns, predispositions, value systems, attitudes and behaviors extracted from numerous brain scans of JMP. Then a battery of state-of-the-art Artificial Intelligence algorithms, processing simultaneously at teraflop speeds, were programmed to replicate JMP's manner of thinking so that Narc would respond to any given situation as would JMP with 99.99999% accuracy. Distributed holotronics— an array of micro-sized holographic projection devices that were immanent throughout the world and connected via the worldwide Qnet — allowed Narc to materialize virtually anywhere. With Narc, JMP would always be discussing his most critical issues with someone of equal intelligence: *himself.*

"SO THIS VOICE from the future, presumably— and that's a big assumption— wants you to meet for a drink this evening?" Narc asked.

"Not exactly. But she seems to imply that I inevitably will." JMP spun around in his chair and observed a MagLev, the superfast Magnetic Levitation trains that had dramatically altered 21st-century commuting and lifestyle patterns, zoom out of Hoboken-Hudson terminal and down the East Coast.

"But you hardly ever go to taverns, except for some sporadic trolling now and then, correct?" Narc responded.

"Yes, correct," JMP answered tersely. "And you need not remind me of my eccentricities. I am well aware of them."

THE NAME WAS a combination of the urban street term *Narc*— a betrayer (in this case, Narc only squealed about JMP *to* JMP)— and Narcissus, proving that even JMP had a sense of humor about his own self-adulation.

"Got it." Narc answered. "So wouldn't you think twice before going off to a place that's virtually taboo for anyone with a QA over 100?"

JMP grit his teeth. "Why do you think I summoned you?"

NARC'S ABILITY TO reduce himself to strings of billions of qubits— or quantum bits— allowed him to infiltrate the QNet at will; in fact, the QNet was his home, the only place he actually existed, his discernable holographic presence a mere illusion created by the qubits and processors and the immanent network of holotronic-projectors.

Quantum by definition, the particles defining him could be everywhere and nowhere at once, superimposed or not, probability waves spanning the universe or collapsed particles occupying billions upon billions of precisely-defined points. Narc could slither through the QNet at will, splitting and recomposing himself infinitely, visiting venues, eluding security algorithms, gathering data far beyond the ability of any mere human.

"I'VE GOT IT." Narc snapped his fingers. "It's your age-old compulsion to short-circuit rationality, to roll the dice, tempt fate. Your high level of intelligence makes you excessively bored and you yearn for excitement. Quite simply, there's no risk out there that can possibly challenge your abundant mind. Ergo, you contrive your own."

"Risk?" JMP asked.

"Yes, what did you think I meant?" Narc answered. "Of course, this one's quite a dandy."

"In what way?"

"It should be obvious, my dear JMP," Narc answered. "After all, if this voice of Jennifer was indeed from the future, wasn't she merely recounting her understanding of her recollected past which is now your immediate future?"

"So by definition, it would be impossible for me to alter the outcome of my rendezvous this evening…"

"Aha, but here's the conundrum." Narc raised his index finger. "Your future lay before you; a font of possibilities, but her past has already transpired and, therefore, is unalterable."

"Yeah, but if the past from this Jennifer's perspective is unalterable, then I effectively have no choice. Whatever I do tonight, the string of events that define this evening will inevitably put me face to face with this girl no matter what my intent."

"Yes, correct," Narc answered.

"But," JMP snapped his fingers briskly, "if the future— or the past, as perceived by Jennifer's present— is alterable, then yes I *can* avoid the girl."

"So, it leads us to a quandary, my dear JMP," Narc countered, "is space-time set in stone or is it merely an artifact of overlapping subjective realities? Or perhaps…."

"What?" JMP snapped.

"You're just in the mood for a date. A hook-up, I mean. Perhaps a little tryst with a sub-100 will feed your enormous... ego."

"I'm not sure…. just not sure…." JMP calculated and strategized, tapping his fingers on his levitating glass desk; *the future, the past, alterable, unalterable.* A quandary, indeed. His repartee with Narc resulted in exactly what he had intended, stretching the limits of his thinking. He glanced over for a response from Narc, but was rebuffed.

"I've already helped you as much as I can," the holographic self-clone responded.

JMP strained, fraught with indecision. In a burst of compulsion, he snapped up out of his chair and bolted for the door.

Jimmy Mashimoto-Pennfield was the recipient of both favorable fortune and favorable genes. His grandfather, Jonathan Pennfield, once Chairman of the now-defunct GlobalAir, had also served briefly as U.S. Senator from Connecticut. His father, Alex Pennfield, a boy genius, entered MIT at sixteen and graduated with a PhD at twenty-one. His mother was a world-renowned psychiatrist from Japan. Not only did he benefit from privileged genealogy but also from the bountiful Pennfield family fortune, built up over generations.

But Jimmy Mashimoto-Pennfield had much more than good breeding. His finger always on the pulse of the marketplace, he had keen antennae with an almost psychic comprehension of where the market was going. Mashimoto-Pennfield's mind spanned science, technology, finance, operations and marketing with an uncanny ability to attack an opportunity from all perspectives simultaneously. He made trillions on investments in MagLev technology and deployment, parlayed it into further success in Ganzfeld chambers, brain stimulation therapies, DNA nano-design, and most recently expanded his empire into cryonics.

Mashimoto-Pennfield had always been the perpetual alpha male, the pursuer, not the pursued; the dominator, not the dominated. He had never been the partner abandoned, had never been the partner shamed, had never been the submissive one.

Except once. And he vowed that would never happen again.

MASHIMOTO-PENNFIELD WAS a loyal member of the Apexian nation, the world's most exclusive government with only forty thousand citizens. It had been over forty years since global banker Izan Bonne-Saari used his financial might to carve the world into 15 layers of stratified virtual governments. Governments were no longer defined by geography, but by similarities among its citizens. Though it had not come about without a fight, each global citizen or family was now tested and given a Quality Algorithm or "QA" score— based upon a combination of intelligence, lineage, wealth and other factors — and then assigned to one of 15 PGUs or Para-Geographic Governmental Units as they were commonly referred to. As an Apexian, Jimmy Mashimoto-Pennfield was entitled to privileges and indulgences denied to most others. Resentment from "the lower PGUs" — as they were called— festered, and was kept as far away from the Apexians as possible.

AS HE NETCABBED from his headquarters over to the East Village, he looked back at Penn Tech: the glass cut the air with perfect lines. His own life was reflected in organized, protected, powerful shapes and glimmers of sun. And yet, the netcab obeyed his own command, zooming toward some obscure, shadowy risk, turning away from those secure walls.

JMP shuddered as he was driven on, knowing that part of his motivation was intellectual— an attempt to become a player in the classic contest between destiny and free will— but some, maybe most of his motivation, was not about that. His sexual appetite was voracious and omnivorous. It all depended on his mood, and the individual who intrigued him most at any given point in time. Every once in a while, he would go trolling in a hangout patronized by sub-100s, pick up an attractive subject— male or female— then impose his will on them in a marathon of indulgence with all the impunity of his privileged status.

Various subjects— some anonymous to him, some not— became the objects of his revenge, a revenge impossible to extract from his original perpetrator, as much as he would like to. He had a lover, Hector, stashed away in a luxury apartment in London. Another, his mistress Sophia, a dark-haired Italian beauty, had free reign of his villa on Lake Como. He had dated supermodels, the most beautiful women in the world, enjoyed rough sex with closeted homosexual business partners, exploiting it to his advantage, and had participated in all sorts of exclusive kinky rituals in exotic venues around the world.

Jimmy Mashimoto-Pennfield's lust for domination stretched far beyond the sexual. Brilliant, he loved to mind-fuck his employees, back them into intellectual corners and slap them around a bit. No one in the organization had proven able to outsmart him. Sometimes it was just too easy, no challenge.

SUDDENLY, he stopped, repeating the thought: *Sometimes it was just too easy, no challenge.*

Yes, that's it! He snapped his fingers.

It's for the challenge: him against this mysterious woman and this alleged Pennfield family curse, in a high-stakes match. And as he overpowered this agent of the curse with his prowess, his intellect, his voraciousness, he would also be taking it out on *him*: that hateful, synthetic, vacuous tyrant who had shamed him so. He pushed his chips onto the table with no intention of losing.

THE TAVERN FULFILLED HIS EXPECTATIONS: smelly, earthy, noisy and infested with sub-100s, supposedly the vermin of society. Aside from a few sniffs of his expensive clothes and raised eyebrows, no one paid attention to him, no one had any idea who he was. As he quickly guzzled two beers, reveling in the cheap and fizzy feel of the stuff in his mouth, his eyes scanned the room.

He wondered who it would be, who was the one who would attempt to bring him down? He spotted a short brunette with a cute face and voluptuous curves. He observed her as she engaged in conversation with those around her. When she opened her mouth, he recoiled: her teeth were terribly misaligned. Then standing in a corner near the bar, he spotted a tall blonde in a sleeveless dress with a firm jaw and bony shoulders. *No, not her,* he thought. *A tranny, definitely.* His attention wandered over to a subdued corner of the room, where a short black woman with curly auburn hair and classic cheekbones piqued his interest. He was hoping it would be her. He drifted closer and tried to catch her attention. She glanced in his direction, but then her eyes continued right past him. *Not interested.*

HIS SWIVELED BACK towards the bar. He wanted, needed another drink. He stepped forward, attempting to gingerly navigate through the packs of rollicking, sweaty bodies— what he had been taught to think of as Neanderthals— five deep, crowding the bar.

A tap on his shoulder interrupted him.

"You'll get what you want quicker if you let me order for you."

HE WAS SURPRISED how naturally it happened. She shone against the tavern's sepia tones, sparkling like a fine, polished jewel against a pile of junk.

She was cute, beautiful, even, with long, golden-blonde hair down to her shoulders. Not one touch of make-up was detectable on her perfectly sculpted face. Her lithe, athletic figure was rendered almost naked by her tight-fitting jeans. Even her high-top sneakers, shoelaces loose and untied, drew out his craving to feel casual, free, and careless.

But it was somehow frightening. Their exchange was so perfunctory, it seemed rehearsed— their movements, actions and words— bereft of free will.

"What's your pleasure?" she asked.

"Scotch. Scotch 'n water."

She seeped effortlessly through rows of giants and mere wage-laborers, hovering around the bar.

"Bobby. Bobby!" she waved at the bartender.

Immediately, he stopped serving his other customers and swiveled right over to her. His actions, too, seemed pre-destined. She returned with the glass of scotch. JMP took a sip.

"So what brings a captain of industry to a place like this?" she asked.

"Captain of industry?" he answered, fearing for his anonymity.

"Ah come on Mr. Mashimoto-Pennfield, I know who you are," she answered, as she fingered the expensive buttons of his jacket. He locked his eyes onto hers.

"So my instincts were correct," she winked.

"Got me. Cheers." He held up his scotch.

"But you haven't answered my question." She insisted.

"What question?"

"What's an important person like you doing in a place like this?"

He paused, and then answered. "Looking for you."

"Why me?" Her eyes twinkled.

"It's a long story I suppose. But someone predicted I would run into a beautiful woman here this evening. And you?"

"Bullshit." She rolled her eyes.

"Why did you say that?" he asked.

"Ha! *'Someone predicted...'* I bet they did. Gimme a break."

"You never know." He shrugged. "Now what about *my* question, what are you doing here?"

"Well, I don't know," she answered. "I just had this feeling. That I should come here. Something inside told me that I would meet an attractive, powerful man here tonight."

"Ah, so you're applying a double standard?"

"Maybe." She shrugged.

"Well, have you?" Mashimoto Pennfield asked.

"What?"

"Met an attractive, powerful man?"

"I should say so." Smiling, she placed her hand on his shoulder, taking in the soft texture of the leather jacket as she traced her fingers down the sleeve from his shoulders to his watch. "And you?"

"Have I run into a beautiful woman?"

She nodded.

"I should say so." He scanned her body.

"Now what is it you might want from this here beautiful, low-class girl?" She slid her hand down to his crotch and rubbed.

"Perhaps just a little aesthetic stimulation, or perhaps…"

"More?" She pecked a kiss on his cheek.

"I would hope that might be a possibility…"

"I think I might be able to predict that." She enwrapped her arm completely around him.

"Predictions are working in my favor today, I guess." Mashimoto-Pennfield sipped more scotch.

"Your lucky day?"

"I would hope. So, tell me, what's your name?"

"Robyn."

"Hmmm... Robyn...," he mumbled, sipping on his drink, "So, Robyn, I think the planets are beginning to align, don't you?"

She giggled. "Well I would say…" she blushed, "I would say… if not already, they're getting mighty close, don't you think?"

"I would at very least hope so," he answered, then placed his arm around her waist.

"Me too."

"Perhaps we should leave and find a place to…" he hesitated, grasping for the best possible word, *"…chill?"*

"Works for me," she answered curtly.

He held out his hand and she grasped it, following him as they wove their way around the sub-100s clumped together between the bar and the door.

"WHERE CAN WE GO?" JMP grunted as they emerged up the steps from the subterranean tavern. Normally, he would prefer a hotel, but had no desire to be seen with a sub-100.

"I have a place," she answered. "A friend of mine works late, lets me crash."

The streets— graffiti-smeared and infused with malodorous fumes of strewn refuse— were dark and quiet, as electric consumption was severely restricted in this part of the city. The two walked silently and separately, clearly understanding what was about to transpire. Their mixed feelings of arousal and guilt blended together into a bland dispassion.

They crossed East 4th Street. Then she led him to an old, weathered row-house, its tan paint flaking off in rusted chips, bird-droppings spattered on its front steps.

She pointed her e-let towards the entrance, tapping on it. The door's retro-buzz irritated him.

They stepped into the front hallway. A big dark lump blocked the stairs. JMP looked down on it: an unpleasant, albeit common, site amongst the lower classes ever since the advancement of Bonne-Saari's new government— it was an old bearded man, passed out, his bare toenails infected with orange-yellowish fungus. The old man snored in harsh, irregular cackles.

JMP stepped over him, covering his nose as he followed Robyn. He could not remember the last time he ascended five flights of stairs under his own power. It wasn't the physical challenge that irked him, he was in perfect shape, but that it smelled of rats, mold, and aged— even outlawed— paints and sealants all the way up, blending with other dank, musty scents.

She creaked open an old door, scratched and graffiti-strewn. The apartment was dark and bleak, hardly four-hundred square feet, a lone toilet in the corner, an old-fashioned microwave on a counter next to an old retro-sink and a small electric range. The bed was at the far end, underneath a window with rusted metal bars guarding its outside. The smell was the same as the stair-well, the rat shit permeating through.

And yet, being inside the dimly lit room, alone with her, narrowed all his thoughts and desires down to one.

"Take off your clothes, *everything,*" he commanded.

She obliged. Her skin was soft and pure. Her goose-bumped nipples, tones of tan and mauve, capped her dangling milk-white breasts. Her blonde hair draped sensuously over her perfect shoulders, strands of the same golden hue blanketing her vagina. Mashimoto-Pennfield's eyes sparkled, his libido inflated, it became saturated with anger, even against his own will.

"Now suck me," JMP ordered. "*Suck me hard.*"

She undid his leather belt, and then unzipped his fly. She rolled his leather pants down to his knees then began to lick his crotch, her head nodding as her tongue caressed his pubic hairs.

He stood emotionless— bent at the knees, his tubular thighs spread apart — his pulse steady and even, his breath calm and regular.

Then, sucking vehemently, she made him shuffle backwards towards the bed, attempting to push him down prone. He resisted.

"No. No. On your knees. Stay there," he pronounced.

Rage from the past continued to encroach upon his present. It propelled him on, even while he tried to resist it: an inner voice that approved his aggression—*yes, do to her exactly what that tyrant did to you.*

She sucked, sucked harder, caressing his penis with her tongue, enveloping it with her lips. He still couldn't be sure if she was in it for money, or if she had been serious about her fated prediction, or what.

With barely a grunt, he ejaculated. She pulled away, about to spit.

"No," he ordered. "Swallow."

She gulped, clutched her chest, and then gulped once more, coughing as she choked down his semen. Breathing heavily, she looked up at him.

"Now let's fuck," he said, oblivious to her condition.

Obediently, she walked to the bed and lied down prone on her back.

"No. Doggie style," he said, indicating that she flip over.

The cruel tyrant had no mercy on him, now he would have no mercy on her.

He barreled into her, his penis even harder than before. Her expression seemed to him a contortion of disorientation, desire, fear. He grunted, and then came once again. He pulled out, then stood up and took a deep breath. She began to get up as well.

"No, stay," he ordered.

"Huh?"

"Stay. Stay right there." He hovered over her.

He loved it, being in charge, submitting someone to his will: now, if only it was him, the vapid tyrant.

She obliged, appearing puzzled, unsure of his intent. She twisted her head, looking up at him.

"I need to give you something to remember me by..."

He moved back closer to the edge of the bed. The dark, shadowy room blunted her ability to clearly see what he was doing.

He grabbed for her ass, his once-again swelled penis about to burst through its skin. As he prepared to mount her, a glint of light spread across her buttocks. His eyes darted over and caught sight of it: the one thing he least expected to see. There it was, small and round, but undeniably *it,* tattooed clearly onto her right butt-cheek:

He stopped, catching his breath. *"What!!!"*

"Huh?" she answered, confused.

He paused, his mind spinning furiously, and then barked:

"Oh *fuck.* Fuck *me. You fucking—* you mean to tell me you're one of *them, a radical?! a subversive?"*

"That? Let me…" she gasped, trying to explain.

Ignoring her, his face red, he picked his belt up from the floor, and doubled it around his hand.

"No! I'm *not* really—" she mumbled.

He took a deep breath, rage in his eyes, and snapped the belt on her butt— *once, twice, three times—* right across the tattoo, each time with increased fury.

"*Why you—* you set me up, didn't you?" He looked frantically at the corners of the ceiling for cameras, recorders, anything to indicate he'd been seen, then put down the belt, and grabbed her by her hair, bending her head back.

"Trying to lure me into all this so you could disrepute me? Bomb me? Take us down? Tell me *now.*"

She tried to grunt out a response, but could not.

"Now listen to me." He stuffed his other hand under her chin and forced her jaw upwards, twisting her neck unnaturally so she could look right into his eyes. "Tell your impoverished cronies to fuck off, fuck *off* or I will ruin you, do you understand?" She gurgled softly.

He growled. "Your entire life, your whole existence, is meaningless, get it? I will destroy you. I will destroy you if you ever mention one fucking word about this. Get it? Get it, you little whore…"

On and on and on he punished her, his anger whipping him into a barbaric frenzy.

He fucked her once again— rapidly, panting like a dog. Finished, he took his clothes, his jacket, and disappeared, refusing to listen to her last attempt to explain.

HE BOLTED OFF, crashing through the door, bounding down the stairs, hurdling over the old man in the lobby, and then sprinted down the street, intending to forever distance himself from her and the whole incident.

He didn't stop for several blocks, until he felt adequately far away from that nasty place and that little traitor, little terrorist, out to ruin everything he was and stood for. He hailed a netcab.

Catching his breath, he rested as the cab moved on. *Did he really do it, allow himself to be seduced by someone out to destroy him?* For all his greatness, only two beers, a scotch, his throbbing libido, and a proclivity for attractive blondes had conspired against him. Had he been played?

He rested his head back on the seat and took a breath. Why did this strange encounter with a sub-100 occur? And why a member of the *Apexinators,* a splinter insurrectionist group intent on destruction of the Apexian way of life? But, did he really do it, allow himself to be cruel, to go too far, to hurt someone… badly?

The challenge overwhelmed him, flummoxed his brain. He hated it, absolutely hated it, when his finely tuned mind couldn't solve a puzzle immediately. The hint of emotion— the creeping concern— was the worst, the most foreign to his personality. He suppressed it immediately. The question of the curse, or of the Apexinators, or both, *that* complexity couldn't wait. He needed to figure that out, figure it out now. He wouldn't go back to the office, he'd go to his refuge where he could grapple with his thoughts.

Zaappp! He pointed his e-let at the netcab's console and re-adjusted his location: The MagLev terminal in Hoboken.

* * *

11

NJNY GAB, Night, November 10, 2052

Droves of commuters trudged across the main floor of the Hoboken-Hudson MagLev terminal jutting out over the Hudson: sub-100s from Greenland, professionals from Honduras, Wall-Streeters from Bermuda. Above the fray in his private balcony, Jimmy Mashimoto-Pennfield observed them all. His personal MagLev capsule would be fit onto the track between the 8:42 to Atlanta and the 8:56 Trans-Caribbean. At 8:44 he stepped into the airavator and descended to track level.

An attendant, a sub-100, escorted him inside the capsule. He settled into his recliner and reached for the virtual reality console. As he breezed up through New England to his Newfoundland refuge, he thought it might be calming to spend the time relaxing on the Thai coast. Then, his watchband vibrated.

Shit! "What the hell is this?" he barked.

"Mr. Nimura and his associates would like to talk to you about the cryonics project," Renee Boustard, his New York assistant answered.

"Tell him I can't right now," Mashimoto-Pennfield announced. "Tell him I'm in the middle of another meeting. I'll get back to him tomorrow."

"You sure?" Renee countered, one of six assistants JMP had stationed around the world— in NY, LA, Tokyo, Shanghai, Sydney and Mumbai— so as to have continuous overlapping, around-the-clock coverage.

"Yes, very sure," Mashimoto-Pennfield responded.

JIMMY MASHIMOTO-PENNFIELD WAS NOT HANDSOME per se, but he had an alluringly seductive persona. His shaven scalp exaggerated the roundness of his face, while his odd-shaped ears, somewhat pointy on top, accentuated his unconventionality. Yet, the fascination expressed in the traces of his mother's Japanese eyes, his strong cheekbones and dimpled chin, conveyed an abundantly evident enthusiasm for his life and work. At forty-two, Mashimoto-Pennfield kept himself in perfect shape through an almost obsessive adherence to strict exercise and diet standards. He had a personal nutritionist, an on-call physical trainer, had dabbled in yoga and other Eastern rituals, Ganzfelded regularly, and was experimenting in the relatively new discipline of brain stimulation therapy.

His signature wardrobe was black. An Italian-designer's tightly-fitted black T-shirt hugged his muscular arms, nourished by an anabolic-steroid variant he had commissioned in one of his biotech labs. Black leather pants snugged tightly around his tubular rubber thighs and a black alligator belt tapered his thin well-conditioned waist. Together, his dress, his perfectly-engineered frame, his shaven head, his mother's facial features, created an impression of mind over matter; he, himself, one of his own creations forged by the sheer determination of his will and the power of his intellect.

YAWNING, Mashimoto-Pennfield stretched.

So comfortable in his quiet moments of solitude, he was chagrined to feel the capsule decelerating for its arrival in St John's much more quickly than he would have preferred. From the station, he netcabbed to his glass-and-steel circular island retreat on Placentia Bay.

As his plaything, the retreat catered to his sense of wonderment with the cosmos and provided him a place of refuge to wrestle with his innermost thoughts. The centerpiece of this bold, circular edifice surrounded by the cold frothy waters of the bay, was the observatory. Here, JMP would satiate his appetite for the heavens, gazing at the universe from a telescope far more powerful than those in even the largest observatories only several decades earlier.

But this evening, his lifelong preoccupation with the cosmos would not be the focal point of his attention; tonight, his focus would be on the inner recesses of the human mind. Tonight, he would visit with his psyche. He had a problem, a potentially huge problem. He may have actually encountered the contemporary agent of an age-old family curse. *Had he opened Pandora's Box?*

Paranoid in his obsessiveness to never allow anyone or anything get in the way of his vision for Pennfield Technologies, he had to find out whatever he could about this woman in the tavern. Was she truly a contemporary agent of the curse taking form as an Apexinator and a spy, or simply a random sub-100, eager to be seen with someone of his stature?

His mind snapped to a quick conclusion: he could not risk the possibility that she *wasn't* involved with curse. He must do whatever he can— delve into the past— to pull up the curse by its roots so he could destroy it before it destroyed him, particularly now at a time when the cryonics initiative could bring him and his company unprecedented riches.

AS HE DESCENDED into the underwater basement of his Placentia Bay refuge, he immediately called for help.

"Narc!" he shouted out, looking up.

"Yes, my dear other." Narc materialized immediately.

"I need your assistance."

"A bit of a sticky wicket you got yourself into, eh?" Narc answered, almost mockingly.

"Correction," JMP responded. "*We* got ourselves into."

"Yes, indeed, but under similar circumstances I believe I would have had the perspicacity to display a bit more…"

"Bullshit." JMP cut him off. "We're one and the same."

"Indeed." Narc answered smugly.

"Okay. So then proceed."

"Let's review the facts," Narc began. "Fact number one: you've been known to have a certain amount of psychic ability."

"Correct." JMP nodded.

"Fact number two," Narc continued, "your family, as well, is known to have a genetic predisposition to psychic ability."

"Yes. Well documented."

"Number three: according to your great-uncle Christopher, the entire Pennfield clan is on the receiving end of some restless, unhappy spirit's recurrent curse."

"Yes," JMP responded, "at least I believe that great-uncle Christopher *believed* so."

"Which, of course, may be related to the family's psychic trait."

"Plausible." JMP paced across the room. "Yes, quite plausible."

"Fact number four: some Jennifer, presumably from the future, contacted you and warned you that *she* – whomever she was – was coming back, whatever that meant, correct?"

"Yes, indeed," JMP nodded.

"Fact number five," Narc proceeded, "after our discussion you proceeded to a tavern on the exact date upon which Jennifer predicted you would meet this *she*."

"Why are we repeating all this?" JMP blurted. "You know it and I know it."

"Don't let your emotions get the best of you, my dear other," Narc responded, "There's a method to my approach. Let logic dictate."

"If you must..."

"Fact number six," Narc continued, "you meet the young woman, her name turns out to be *Robyn,* and proceed to have sex with her— if that's what you would call it."

"Be careful, my friend," JMP warned, his face reddening.

"Then you see the young girl's tattoo. What do those barbarians call themselves, *Apexinators?* That freaks you out, and you immediately burst off."

"I would say 'freak me out' is a gross overstatement, Narc. I merely realized that I was potentially getting myself into a compromising situation."

"I stand corrected," Narc answered. "Let's say um... you extracted yourself from a potentially compromising situation, agreed?"

"Agreed."

"Well, then the solution is very simple," Narc stated.

"And that is?"

"Since Ganzfelding lead you into this situation, you must Ganzfeld again to further explore its roots."

"Yes, that was always my intention, that's why I'm here," JMP answered tersely. "That's not the issue."

"And the issue is?" Narc asked.

"You should know it already, shouldn't you?"

"Of course, the issue is *exactly who it is* should you be trying to connect with?"

"Precisely." JMP nodded. "So answer the question, Narc. Who is it that I should be trying to connect with?"

"Do you think I can solve everything, my dear other?" Narc answered. "As much as you despise it, some things are simply a matter of fate."

A ROUND BLACK room with two bright lights hanging overhead, the Ganzfeld

Chamber was simple and stark: positioned in its center, the actual device consisted of a black metallic five-foot high cylindrical post at the head and another at the foot connected together by a seven-foot-long levitation cradle along the floor.

JMP carefully removed his pants, shirt, shoes and socks. He had found that the clearest, purest connections were only possible without any exterior stimulants, without any clothes. He grabbed the headset resting on top of the post at the head and placed it over his ears. Then, he placed the mask — two hollow half-spheres— over his eyes. He laid his naked body on the air-levitation cradle, the cold metal tickling his backside. When he twisted the levitation dial, his body slowly rose, until it floated about four feet off the ground.

Finally, he rested, devoid of any outside stimulation.

SILENT, motionless blandness. His mind played games. *Was he right side up or upside down? For that matter, what was really 'up' and what was really 'down'? How much time had passed?* After all the disorientation— in part because of it— his mind would become so crystal clear it transcended space and time.

Slowly, he lapsed into a trance.

He was there, at that point: his mind clairvoyantly clear, skirting along the dips and curves of spacetime at quantum speed. *But could he make a connection?*

Floating in a chamber, devoid of his senses— but so granularly in touch with every breathing cell and synapse of his brain and every idea and thought that ever touched upon his mind— he focused, the trance deepening.

Then—

Strange sounds echoed through his brain. *No, don't. I don't want to. Let me free. Go away. I want to play. I don't want to know. Please no. No!*

Either this was some hallucinatory dream, a repressed thought from his past, or a real connection with someone, somewhere at some time.

Mashimoto-Pennfield focused and thought hard. *Tell me! Tell me who you are.*

PLEASE DON'T. No. No. I want to go.

AGAIN, Mashimoto-Pennfield reached out: *Who are you? Don't worry. I'm here to help.*

The answer: *Didn't you hear me? I don't understand. I want to play.*

Still, no connection.

Mashimoto-Pennfield tried once again: *Please. Please. Tell me who you are.*

A long hollow silence. And then—

I'm Shippy.

* * *

12

NEWF GAB: St. John's, Newfoundland, Late Night, November 10, 2052

As Mashimoto-Pennfield wavered through different stages of consciousness, he saw an image: a little boy, sitting by himself. A fuzzy image, but he could see white, lots of white, and water, bluish-green chilling water. In some cloudy semi-state between blurred and focused, the image faded. He asked himself: *Was that him? Was that Shippy?*

Halfway between drowsiness and sleep, he heard it: a vacant distant echo funneling out of the darkness.

Stop. Go away. I don't want to talk to you.

The voice twanged like a trombone, in and out, out and in. Soft, then loud. Loud, then soft.

I don't want to talk to you. Leave. Leave me alone.

The black turned to gray and then a faint white. In disjointed blotches, the picture appeared in cubellated images, wavering on edge somewhere between haziness and clarity.

Please. Please. Go away. I'm scared.

In the upper right, a jagged piece of image, almost clear. In the lower left, another jagged piece, more blurred. In the middle, a piece wavering between dark and light. He strained to complete the jigsaw puzzle floating in his mind. Or was it his mind floating in the jigsaw puzzle?

I'm scared. Very scared. Go away.

Though it remained blotchy and blurred, the image began cubellating towards relative clarity: a little boy, sitting at the edge of a dock with a large house in the background, shivering in the cold, his arms around his knees in a semi-fetal position, cold brisk water all around him, an expression of outright fear leaping off his face.

Mashimoto-Pennfield strained to talk with his mind: *Are you Shippy?*

How do you know who I am? Who are you? the little boy answered, almost angrily.

I don't, Mashimoto-Pennfield answered. *I can only guess.*

Yes, I am, the little boy answered.

Are you a Pennfield? Mashimoto-Pennfield asked.

How did you know that?

I am, too, Mashimoto-Pennfield answered.

Really? Then why aren't you at my house?

Why should I be?

Because all my family's at my house. It's Christmas.

I may not be of your time.

I don't understand, Arthur responded.

So quiet and peaceful, Jimmy Mashimoto-Pennfield floated on columns of air, levitating between the Ganzfeld chamber's head and foot pieces. Cold, white, light focused down on him from two overhead lamps. His eyes were covered with goggles, his ears encased in headphones: an extreme state of relaxation in a clean, somberly lit room. But on the inside, inside the recesses of his mind, was a vibrant exchange between present and past— or present and future.

You're scaring me, crackled from Arthur's nervous voice.

That's not what I'm here for. I think we can help each other.

Please. Please don't scare me.

I'm not. Listen to me. You're my only gateway.

I'm not a gate. I'm scared. Go away.

The image began to blur, and then fade, the voice degrading into a long incoherent echo.

Stop. Pleeeeezzzz. Pleeeezzzzz. Gooooo awwaaaaaaaayyyyyy...

There was nothing more.

* * *

13

Pennfield Technology Towers, Manhattan NYCGAB, Mid-afternoon, November 14, 2052

Jimmy Mashimoto-Pennfield had to figure out who this *Shippy* actually was, and it gnawed at him, tugged at him incessantly. So much so, it interrupted his concentration. He blew off a cryonics meeting and even the quarterly financial review with his CFO just to ponder the issue: *Was that really the psychic vibrations of some Shippy Pennfield he was communicating with, or was it merely a creation of his own mind enhanced by the Ganzfeld chamber? Suppose it really was another living entity from another time, was it real or a fraud? Could it perhaps be another manifestation of the mysterious woman in the tavern? Or perhaps the Jennifer from the future?*

He fidgeted at his desk. The sweet aroma of 'Patagonia Evergreen' misted his office as soft vibrations from his chair massaged his muscles. He tapped his fingers as his eyes scanned the holoscreen.

"Pennfield family files." JMP requested softly.

When prompted for authorization, he held up his finger to unlock the files.

"Forward," he commanded.

Simulated files flipped before him until he found what he was looking for. It was titled *Recent Pennfield Lineage.*

"Open."

He carefully scanned the chart he had assembled:

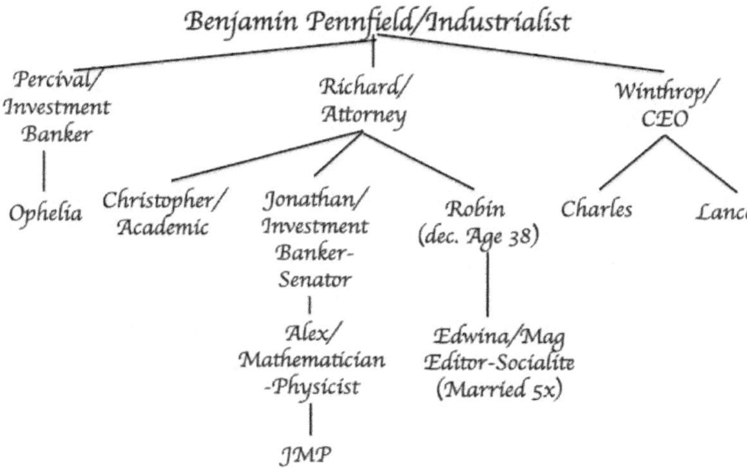

CONSPICUOUS BY ABSENCE, a *Shippy* or *Ship Pennfield* was nowhere to be found. *Could he be further back*? Or could *Shippy* or *Ship* be a nickname for someone already on the chart? This Shippy— at least in his few utterances and images during the Ganzfeld sessions— sounded and looked somewhat modern, definitely mid-twentieth century. JMP was relying merely on his instincts and it bothered him. Although his instincts were unusually keen, they were instincts, nonetheless.

JMP'S WRISTWATCH BUZZED, snapping him out of his trance.

"Yes, Bryan," he sat straight up as a holoscreen materialized.

"*Jimmy MP!*" quipped Bryan McPherson, Pennfield Technologies Director of Security. "How's life in the executive suite today?"

"You tell me. You'd know before I would," Pennfield answered.

"Very good, Mr. MP. Very good," McPherson chuckled.

"So what's up?" Pennfield asked.

McPherson's voice softened to a whisper. "Got a little *situation* I need to fill you in on."

"Sure, come on up."

Ex-NYPD, Bryan McPherson was a cop's cop, and later a detective's detective, an expert in nano-surveillance and digital security. Born in the Riverdale section of the Bronx, McPherson attended Peter Stuyvesant High, then earned a degree in criminal justice at Fordham before joining the force. After an impressive twenty-five-year career as one of New York's top detectives, he filed his retirement papers with the force and applied for a job in security at Pennfield Technologies. He rose quickly to Director of Security Operations for the entire corporation— a critical role given the confidential nature of most of Penn Tech's projects— reporting directly to CEO and Chairman, Jimmy Mashimoto-Pennfield. McPherson was a key cog in the design and implementation of security procedures for Pennfield Technologies biggest project yet: The Cryonics Initiative.

To JMP, McPherson was a throwback. If you could time-transport him back to the golden days of the force— *the Giuliani-Kerik days*— he would fit right in, even wardrobe-wise. He had a square face with a jutting jaw, thinning slicked-back black hair, broad shoulders, a stout frame, and a suit that never fit quite right.

"One of my buddies in the force clued me in on, how should I say this, a little …uh… situation we might need to be aware of." McPherson sat down across from JMP and sniffed the air. "Smells like Christmas in here. You still into that?"

"It's called 'Patagonia Evergreen'. Want some to bring home?"

"Nah," McPherson nodded. "You know me; more into meat and potatoes, through and through."

"Your life, not mine." JMP giggled. "Okay, so fill me in on this situation of yours."

"If I may, let me run a little v-file for you, Mr. MP."

"Sure."

McPherson tapped on the holoscreen floating over JMP's desk and pulled up a file from his library. They watched.

A dusty street in the East Village, darkly lit. Two figures emerge from the darkness, man and woman. Although the image is fuzzy, the man is clearly Jimmy Mashimoto-Pennfield. The woman follows him up the stairs to a row-house. Together they walk through the front door. Fast Forward. The time code indicates thirty-seven minutes have passed. The man— JMP— bolts through the front door of the row house, gallops down the steps and then dashes down the street, separating himself from the location as quickly as possible.

"HOW THE *HELL* did you get this?" JMP asked, only slightly agitated.

"Gnat cams," McPherson held out his finger, revealing a little black dot about the size of a period, a nano-camera that could fly around like a gnat. "Amazing little things, aren't they?"

"I thought they were illegal," JMP responded.

"Not in any area frequented by sub-100s. You know the rules. How else could we keep an eye on things?"

"Okay, so *mea culpa*," JMP answered, "I had a rough day and needed to chill. So yeah, she took me inside, as they say. Understood?"

"Sure, Mr. MP. I can understand that, understand it easily. We all need a little action now and then." McPherson winked. "Although," he cleared his throat, "I wouldn't be doing my job if I didn't tell you that you can probably find… let me say… a better class of person…to hang with than her."

"Okay. Okay. I hear you. I'll back off. Thanks for the warning." JMP swiveled around in his chair, about to begin some other task.

"But, Mr. MP, there's something more."

"Oh?"

"Well, it seems as if that young girl who entered the row-house with you… well, she showed up on a missing person's report. Your little encounter with her is the last time anyone reports seeing her."

"Bullshit! Look, I saw she had a tattoo with the Apexinator symbol and I immediately ran off. That's it. The whole story. Didn't the gnat cam stay there? Don't you have a record of her leaving?"

"Well, yeah sort of. We have another hour or two of surveillance, but no record of the girl leaving."

"That's just silly," JMP answered, "maybe she crashed there for a week. Maybe she drained some SMARF after I left and needed to chill."

"No, I'm sorry, Mr. MP. She's not there. No one's seen her. Hasn't shown up for work."

"Where did you say you got this file?" JMP snapped.

"A friend on the force."

JMP's mind spun: then it *was* a set-up.

"So what do we need to do?" JMP asked.

"I wouldn't really get too worked up over it. Let's just see how it plays out. Who knows, maybe she'll turn up." McPherson shrugged his shoulders.

"And if not?"

"Aaaahh, someone on the force will want to talk to you, take a statement, ask a few questions, usual bureaucratic BS," McPherson looked directly at JMP. "But just to be prepared, you should try to reconstruct what you did later that evening, just to have evidence that you weren't with her."

Quickly, JMP thought: there was definitely evidence that he went up to St. John's that evening. *Could someone try to construe that he was escaping from something?* His stomach churned.

"Can you get Apexian Polcom to keep it under wraps?" JMP asked.

"Shouldn't be a problem, Mr. MP," McPherson answered. "I'm sure I can get the communications folks to keep a lid on it."

"That would be much appreciated, Bryan."

"Yeah I wouldn't worry," McPherson added. "I could probably pull a few other strings and make the whole thing go away, Mr. MP."

BUT WORRY JMP DID. Nervously, he tapped his anxious finger on the desk. *Why is this happening? How did he allow himself to be lured into such an obvious trap?*

* * *

TIME FRAME: 2007

14

Western Massachusetts, Early afternoon, March 17, 2007

An endless black-tar treadmill, the Mass Pike rolled along under Swann's pickup truck, swerving and pitching a little now and then, but mostly rambling along a path of hypnotizing monotony. The scenery changed ever so slightly, mostly highway greenery broken up every once in a while by a city— Worcester or Springfield— or a major rest stop.

As his truck rumbled onward, Swan wondered why he would even work with someone like Christopher Pennfield. The two of them were polar opposites: the upper-crust, erudite, ivory-tower Republican born with a silver spoon in his mouth and a life-long sense of ethical ambiguity, versus the stickball playing son of a construction worker and FDR-Democrat who saved his family's construction company from bankruptcy by getting his hands dirty each and every day of his adult life.

Despite the stunning polarity, he had to admit he probably knew exactly why he was working with Christopher Pennfield: it was the sense of excitement the whole project brought to his life. Looking back, those days with the Pennfields in the mid-1990s were truly monumental for Swann— discovering their psychic powers, finding ghosts in the family Newport home— and ultimately uncovering the Pennfield family curse.

Swann's apple-red cheeks rose up on his face as he tightened his grip on the wheel. *Who would have guessed that his love of ghost stories as a youth would have resulted in such an avocation during his golden years?* As a young kid, he was absolutely mesmerized by stories of apparitions, hauntings and poltergeists. It probably began in church of all places. He remembered hearing about the apparitions of the Blessed Virgin at Lourdes and Fatima as an eight-year-old boy and becoming outright obsessed— and actually scared. For many sleepless nights, he would turn and toss in his bed, burying his face in the pillows, pulling the covers over his head, fearing a visitation right there at the foot of his bed.

Something inside compelled him to learn more. *Can't be explained, not even worth trying, it's a miracle, and it's a sin to even question the ways of our Lord,* Father O'Malley had told him in the confessional one day. *But is there a chance she might visit me in my bedroom, Father?* the shy young boy asked the priest. *The Blessed Virgin in Jersey City?* The priest laughed out loud in his thick brogue. *Don't you think she'd have better sense than that? C'mon now Eddie.*

WHEN SWANN TURNED off the Pike, the monotonous highway greenery quickly morphed into a visual pollution of fast food franchises, gas stations and truck-stop diners. Soon, Swann turned off the main access road and onto a side-street that led into a quaint New England village. Classic Berkshires: serendipitous antique shops, gourmet food stores, tantalizing art galleries and a few upscale restaurants nestled in wood-paned country storefronts all running up a slight hill with a cobblestone street and narrow sidewalks.

The village lasted for all of two blocks then segued into a residential street canopied by a family of large maple trees. After passing several well-restored wrap-around Victorians and a small cobblestone cottage, Swann took a sharp right. The narrow country road climbed a steep hill bordered by a horse farm and several larger homes. The road curved back and forth as it scaled the hill, swerved by an old red barn, then settled on top at an intersection. There, Swann saw it: *Gladwell Institute of Mental Health Sciences.*

THE LARGE, red, brick ivy-covered structure stood out like a well-preserved antique, its old-world craftsmanship gentrified by new-world affluence. Bright green, manicured lawns shimmered in the sunlight. A shiny, spiked, wrought-iron fence framed the sparkling lawns in a perfect square, its precise corners standing guard at strict angular attention. *Reminiscent of Switzerland*— Swann thought— everything so precise and pristine, no blemishes to be found, obsessive in its purity.

Swann's heels clicked on the marble floor as he entered the building's main vestibule: stark and pristine. The foyer's decorative tall pillars supported the ceiling far above the polished marble. Two portraits in ornate gold frames peered mischievously over the receptionist's short, trimmed hair and square-shouldered suit.

Before speaking, Swann gazed up at each portrait. The title of the first was inscribed in a brass plate underneath the frame: "Dr. Emilio Hazard, Medical Director, 1959–1972." And the second read: "Percival Pennfield, Benefactor and Chairman of the Board of Directors, 1964–1989."

"I'm Ed Swann. I'm here to see Dr. Shankar concerning Arthur Pennfield," Swann announced to the receptionist.

"Of course, he's expecting you," she answered.

"PLEASED TO MEET YOU, MR. SWANN." Dr. Fareed Shankar, his bright white teeth shining brilliantly, offered Swann his hand.

"Wonderful place you have here," Swann responded as his eyes scanned the exquisite marble workmanship in the Institute's main vestibule.

"We've been extremely fortunate to have very generous benefactors, particularly the Pennfields." Shankar, a slight man with rich brown skin and thick curly hair, answered in his deliberate, perfectly-enunciated King's English.

"Well I suppose it's time to get to business," Swann responded.

"Certainly…" Shankar nodded once again, "…but are you positive you're ready for it?"

"Why shouldn't I be?" Swann asked.

"Arthur Pennfield suffers from a very rare condition," Shankar explained. "And sometimes when a person first sees him in this state, it can be quite alarming."

"With all due respect, Dr. Shankar, these eyes have seen a lot of alarming things in my eighty-two years. One more isn't going to hurt."

"Certainly. Follow me."

"READY?" Shankar asked Swann as they stood outside Arthur Pennfield's room.

"Ready as I'll ever be," Swann responded.

Slowly, Shankar opened the door.

Swann may have thought he was ready, but he had thought wrong.

His face went flush.

In his entire lifetime, he would never forget that first impression: the bright glare from the light overhead, the puffy white face, the vacant glassy eyes, the frozen expression, the limp jaw hanging in some sort of suspended animation, the scalp dotted with shaven splotches, electrodes patched on. Macabre, indeed: Arthur Shipkin Pennfield as he existed today, an ominous, waxy replica of a fifty-one-year-old man.

"Over the years, we've gone back and forth on our diagnosis," Dr. Shankar explained to Swann. "Delirium, psychosis, paranoia, among others. It's been a quandary because different symptoms come and go. At times, the symptoms point in one direction and then another. But, on the whole, we still basically concur with Dr. Hazard's initial diagnosis, Catatonic Schizophrenia."

"Dr. *Emilio* Hazard?" Swann answered, almost as an afterthought as he first set his eyes on Arthur Shipkin Pennfield.

"Yes. You're familiar with his work?" Shankar asked.

"No."

Swann again carefully studied Arthur Shipkin Pennfield: draped in a standard-issue hospital gown, a rubbery, almost lifeless figure slumped into a chair next to his bed, an expressionless face, a slight chattering to his teeth. To Swann, Arthur resembled a strung-out, middle-aged drug addict, his brain fried, suffering from one too many bad trips.

"So how do you know of Dr. Hazard?" Shankar interrupted.

"I caught a glimpse of his picture in the entrance," Swann answered tersely, his eyes still fixed on Pennfield.

"Yes, Dr. Hazard wrote several landmark papers based on his treatment regimen for Arthur," Shankar offered.

"Oh?"

"For a while, he was able to increase his responsiveness through a combination of ECT and mescaline."

"ECT?" Swann asked.

"Electro Convulsive Therapy."

"Shock treatment?"

"Yes, shock treatment," Shankar answered.

"Ouch!" Swann winced.

"Through intensive and frequent ECT combined with high dosages of mescaline," Shankar continued, "Dr. Hazard was able to increase the patient's responsiveness to external stimuli and even increase his mumblings to an extent where they became semi-coherent."

"Do you have any records of what Arthur did, what he said?"

"Of course," Shankar answered, "we keep impeccable records here at Gladwell."

"Mind if I take a look?" Swann asked.

"Certainly," Shankar answered without hesitation. "Though we'll have to obtain authorization from the Pennfield family."

"No problem. I can wait," Swann answered.

Shankar hesitated, then responded, "I'm afraid the process may not proceed as quickly as you might like. According to our policy, we need to obtain approval from at least two family members."

"That's only a couple of phone calls," said Swann. "And I'm sure Christopher will cooperate, so that's one down."

"It may take several hours," Shankar glanced at his watch, "and it's already past four."

"Tell you what," Swann smiled, his apple-red cheeks rising on his face. "I'm going to find a B&B and then enjoy a good meal at one of those restaurants I saw in that nice little village down the road. I'll be back in the morning."

"Certainly," Shankar answered.

* * *

BY MID-AFTERNOON THE NEXT DAY, Swann received the go-ahead from Pennfield. As he journeyed up the hill towards Gladwell, Swann focused on the stark mid-day sky. A black velvet awning hung from the north, enveloping most of the landscape in a morbid shadow that ended abruptly, slicing a sharp-edged crease in the sky with bright beams sneaking underneath from the south, spraying half the landscape with fresh morning sunlight. Bleak darkness abutted by fresh flowing brightness: a tragicomedy in the heavens.

He stared once again, baffled.

A study in contrasts, he thought: yesterday Gladwell sparkled, like a meticulously well-kept museum or palace nobly showcasing its prowess, but today, nothing more than a musty, weathered monument ineptly grasping back to days of glory gone. He wondered which was the real Gladwell.

"A pleasure to see you again, Mr. Swann," Dr. Shankar greeted his visitor, a strange squint in one of his eyes.

"I understand Chris Pennfield called you," Swann answered. "Everything should be in order I would hope."

"Of course. Of course," Shankar answered in saccharine, deferential tones, "we are so sorry to have made you extend your stay, but we are obligated to enforce a family's wishes, particularly the Pennfields'. I'm sure you understand."

"No problem," Swann stopped short. He heard a strange shimmering sound, like a muffled cymbal. He jerked his head, quickly surveying Shankar's office.

"Are you okay, Mr. Swann?" Shankar asked.

"Sure. Sure," Swann shook his head slightly. Confused, he could not easily locate the source of the sound. *Could it be from inside his head?*

"Fine, then follow me," Shankar motioned towards the door, "I'll take you down to our archives."

Shankar lead Swann deep within the bowels of the sanitarium to a gray, cinderblock room, barely-lit, housing rows of metal shelves stuffed with boxes upon boxes of patient records spanning decades. The heavily painted cinderblock could not mask the stench that reeked from the sweaty walls. With the trained ear of a former contractor, Swann could detect the pitter-patter of mice scurrying throughout the foundation's crevices.

"We've set aside all the boxes with Arthur's records over here," Shankar nodded towards an old, parochial-school desk with about a dozen boxes stacked around it in a corner at the end of a long, narrow row of shelving. "Here, let me give you a little light." He pulled the small metal chain from a lone light bulb hanging overhead.

Geeeez, Swan thought, eyeing the spartan wooden desk, the old boxes and the uncovered ceramic light-socket. *They really go out of their way to encourage investigation, don't they?*

"Something the matter, Mr. Swann?" Shankar asked.

Swann perked up, "No… no… not at all. I assume you have a copier I can use?"

Shankar shook his head. "Mr. Swann, I'm so sorry, I thought you knew, but we do not allow copying of any of our records. It's strictly against Gladwell regulations."

Swann smiled, somehow not surprised. "Well then I guess I'll just have to do it the old-fashioned way. Got a pad and pen?"

"Surely." Shankar nodded.

Swann's rosy cheeks sparkled, "These old fingers aren't as nimble as they used to be," he gripped the pen, "but I guess they'll have to do."

"Well, then, I hope you have everything you need.," Shankar began after what seemed like a long pause.

"Yes. Fine. These should keep me busy for quite some time." Swann nodded, eyeing the stacks of corrugated boxes surrounding the plain, hardwood desk.

"Wonderful," Shankar smiled, turning abruptly towards the exit, "should you have any questions, I'm at—"

A sharp, snapping sound, almost like a like a twig breaking in two followed by a flurry of rapidly ruffling papers interrupted Dr. Shankar.

"What's that?" Swann asked.

Shankar turned back. "Perhaps a slight draft. These old structures are full of eccentricities, don't you think?"

"Eccentricities," Swann shrugged, "I guess."

"Well, anyway, I'm at extension forty-six should you need me," Shankar walked down an aisle and turned towards the exit.

FOR HOURS, Swann pored over the records, focusing on the years Arthur was treated by the esteemed Dr. Hazard. At first, Swann skimmed through the files, painting an overall picture, a broad overview. 1972, then 1968, then back to 1975, then 1966. He scribbled down numerous records of drugs Dr. Hazard had administered on various dates in combination with varying levels of shock therapy.

Finally, Swann went back to Dr. Hazard's very first scribblings:

January 3, 1964. Conducted comprehensive MSE. Eight-year-old male, height 52 inches, weight 64 lbs. Catatonic stupor, no conscious speech, infrequent audible thoughts appear to be delusional. Symptoms consistent with catatonic schiz. Sporadic ruminations. Complete disorientation. Derealization?

INTERESTING, Swann thought. Dr. Hazard had quickly observed the symptoms and began his diagnosis of catatonic schizophrenia, a diagnosis that did not substantively change for the next four decades. *Could Hazard have possibly rushed to judgment?* The thought flickered as Swann flipped through to the next page in the file folder, his adrenaline flowing, the entry dated January 5, 1964:

Patient observed for 48 hours post MSE. Shows definite signs of stupor, mutism, catalepsy, and infrequent/sporadic audible thoughts. Possible hallucinatory symptoms, vegetative symptoms.

SWANN STOPPED, interrupted by a constant, muffled, irritating sound. *Was it that same ruffling noise from before?* Whatever it was, it was a pain in the butt. Just like the *drip, drip, drip* of a leaky faucet, it chipped away at his concentration. Tuning everything else out, he focused:

EEG substantially in theta range (5.6-6.8Hz), several sporadic K-complex and BETS, less sporadic trending up to beta. No visible signs of consciousness.

THETA WAVES? Could there be some underlying psychic phenomena? But, again, the ruffling— *that damn ruffling!*— interrupted, subverting his train of thought. *Damnit*, Swann thought, *that has to stop, that damn sound!* Sweat beaded on his forehead.

March 26, 1964: 16th day in catatonic state, observed coherent verbal activity for the first time. "Sparrow."

SPARROW? The sweat dripped from his forehead. He could feel his heart pounding. His hands shook.

May 23, 1964: Second occurrence of coherent verbal activity. One word: "Yale."

WHY WAS an eight-year-old kid muttering something about a college? But then, suddenly, Swann became quite aware of his heart pounding against his chest. He sensed he was losing control. He focused on the task at hand, straining to ignore the sweating and pulsing:

June 19, 1964: Third occurrence of coherent verbal activity. "Bone" and "Sorry."

MORE RUFFLING, more of that irritating ruffling sound. *Yale? Bone? Sorry? What did they mean? What was the poor boy trying to say?* His heart accelerated.

November 20, 1964: Patient is observed mumbling "Lori." Fourth sign of coherent verbal activity.

SWEAT DRENCHED SWANN, oozing from his collar, splotching his shirt. *Damnit, what's happening? Why am I losing control?* He focused, gasping for breath.

Suddenly—

A rolling, flipping sound, like a giant deck of cards being shuffled.

He looked over to his left. Papers flipping out of a box, as if on their own, falling to the floor.

He rushed over and picked one up. *Patient records*. Not Arthur Pennfield's, but others. For some reason, he was compelled to scribble. Furiously, he wrote away.

Patient #1053: Jan-Mar, 1965 -- Strychnine 10 mg, ECT 240 joules

Patient #1054: Feb-April: 1965 -- Mescaline 400 mg, ECT 160 joules

FASTER AND FASTER, he scribbled, determined to record as many of these patients as possible. There was something here, he was sure of it. The records were speaking to him, reaching out to him, maybe even more.

But the faster he wrote, the weaker he came to feel. He began to feel dizzy. Then, darkness. The lights flashed off and on, off and on, off and on, strobing rapidly.

He scanned the room. *What was that he just saw? Figures, prone figures on stretchers, beds, whatever, flickering between flashes of light and darkness?* Dark, then light. Dark, then light. There, not there. There, not there. Dizzier and dizzier.

Slow down, slow down, please! What's happening to me?

He concentrated, concentrated as best he could, then his breathing exercises: long, long, long exhales, soothing exhales.

Again and again, soothing exhales.

Time slowed down

Now each and every millisecond became crisply clear, etching a sharp image in his mind. Stretchers. Beds. Dark. Light. Dark. Light. Patients lying prone, stacked three to a bunk.

Once again: Stretchers. Beds. Patients stacked.

Shaking rapidly, Swann felt a tap on his shoulder. He turned.

A strange man in a lab coat, his hair brushed sloppily across his scalp, raised his eyes above his glasses and nodded with a slight smirk revealing his crooked yellow teeth.

The flickering ceased.

* * *

15

Western Massachusetts, Evening, March 18, 2007

"B*ren, we need to talk,"* Swann blurted into his phone, still sweating as he sat in his car just down the hill from Gladwell.

"What's up, Ed?" the friendly voice of Dr. Brenda Altieri answered.

"I just had the weirdest experience of my life," Swann answered, catching his breath.

"For you, that's saying a lot," Altieri chuckled. "Where are you?"

"In Massachusetts, the Berkshires," Swann replied.

"On vacation?"

"Uh…no…" Swann answered tersely.

"Don't tell me you're ghost-hunting again?" Altieri admonished him.

"Sort of." Swann answered feebly.

"Oh, Ed," she moaned.

"I know. I know," he stammered.

"I thought we had this conversation before."

"Yeah, I know, but," he hesitated, "but if I don't have anything useful to do I just might as well kick the bucket, Bren."

"Maybe you can find something a little less… taxing." Altieri suggested.

"Then it wouldn't be any fun." Swann quipped.

"What happened?"

"Well, I was researching some records and the room gets blurry on me, the lights start flickering, and I think I see…" Swann paused, his breath rising.

"Did it seem like a panic attack? Are you okay now?" Altieri asked.

Swann hesitated. "Well, uh, maybe a bit. I mean—"

"Do you have your Xanax with you?"

"Yep."

"Why don't you take one just to be safe?"

"Sure. Sure." Swan wiped his brow. "And Bren…"

"Yeah?"

"I need to talk to you about something else." Swann almost whispered.

"And what would that be?" Altieri answered.

"I need your help with this project."

"Oh, geeeeeezz, trying to draw me into the pseudo-science of parapsychology again?"

"Actually, this time it might be psychology without the *'para'* in front, the pure unadulterated kind."

"Really?" Altieri responded, her interest piqued.

"Are you around tomorrow?"

"Sure." Altieri flipped through her calendar. "How about three?"

"See you then," Swann answered with a twinkle in his eyes, his experience all but forgotten.

"And Ed,"

"Yeah?"

"Drive safely, will you?"

* * *

SWANN ARRIVED home that night around 10pm. He tried to sleep, but couldn't. He could not get the haunting, flipping-sounds of those papers out of his head. It tortured him, stifling all pretense of relaxation. At midnight, he got up, turned on his Vivaldi, sat in his comfy old rocker and sipped pinot grigio. It relaxed him for a while, but when he went back to bed, its effectiveness waned. He tossed and turned through the night, haunted by that irritating ruffling sound and the image of that man in the lab coat, with the crooked, yellow teeth.

SHORTLY AFTER NOON the next day, Swann was back in his pickup, this time rumbling across Jersey along I-195. About an hour later, he made a left turn from US-1 onto Washington Avenue in Princeton. Canopied by trees lush with greenery, the avenue was akin to a yellow brick road, leading visitors along a bucolic pathway to some revered seat of enlightenment, with the university's quaint boathouse on the left, and the gymnasium and lacrosse field on the right.

Swann crossed Nassau Street, the demarcation line between the university and the town, and wiggled his pickup along the side streets until he came upon a plain, two-story house, circa 1920, with a sign hanging in the front yard: *Dr. Brenda Altieri, MD.*

"Bren!" Swann beamed when she opened the door.

"Ed, how are you?" She hugged him and patted his back. "I've been worried about you."

Seeing Altieri always brought a smile to Swann's face. Ever since that day he first met her in 1997, she had been a special person to him, very special.

He remembered their very first meeting vividly:

"So Father McDermott referred you to me?" Altieri looked up from the paperwork on her desk, her eyes peering above her small wireframe glasses.

"Yep, he's the culprit." Swann answered with a smirk.

"So what can I do for you, Mr. Swann?" Altieri was an elegantly handsome woman. In her mid-forties back then, thin, fit and standing about five-foot-five, she had smooth, olive skin and a mane of thick gray hair that flowed down to her shoulders.

"Well, let me see," Swann wiggled in his seat, "...how do I start...well, you see, I have this hobby."

"Okay. That's a good place to start." Altieri looked at him directly.

Silence. Swann blushed.

"Do you want to say more about the hobby?" Altieri asked, confused.

"Uh, yeah, okay. I ...ummm... like to hunt ghosts." Swann answered feebly. "Is that, weird? No, I mean, does that bother you?"

"No."

"Really?" Swann asked, surprised.

"You know," she giggled, "we get all types in this business, comes with the territory. I've had a patient with a compulsion to eat worms, one with a phobia of shrubbery, a schizophrenic who hears the voice of Fred Astaire. So I'd say ghost hunting is relatively tame."

"Oh." Swann answered, rendered almost speechless by Altieri's comment. *Did she think he was a real nut job?*

"Well, let's see... how do I start?" Swann pondered for a moment. "Well, when I was a kid, about eight or nine, I saw these movies about apparitions of the Blessed Virgin at Lourdes and Fatima. For some reason I was fascinated by them, totally captivated.

"I see."

"But it's more than that. I think it's fair to say that I became obsessed. Found every book I could read about the subject. Talked to my parish priest in Jersey City for hours about it. Then, something happened."

"Go on."

"For some reason, I became scared. I thought that I would have an apparition right in my bedroom and it scared the bejesus out of me. Couldn't sleep at night. Really drove me crazy. Drove my parents crazy, too, I mean my mom was thrilled to know her boy was consulting a priest about Fatima and stuff, but I was nuts at night, just would not sleep. A mess during the day, you know."

"So how did the situation resolve itself?" Altieri asked. *"Or didn't it?"*

"After a while, it just went away. Took several years though."

"And so you're here today because..." Altieri's discerning eyes peered over her glasses once again.

"Well, good question," Swann answered, "I'm getting there. So a few months ago I just finished this assignment up in Newport. Helped this family at least partially solve a problem they've had with ghosts and spirits for years. Yeah. Okay. So I get back to my life on the Jersey shore, and all of a sudden I have these dreams. I'm a little kid again, eight or nine, and I see the Blessed Virgin at the foot my bed. Wakes me up in a cold sweat."

"I see." Altieri scribbled some notes on her pad.

DR. ALTIERI soon discovered that much more plagued Ed Swann than his childhood fear of religious apparitions. Lonely, he had suffered from sporadic bouts with depression ever since his beloved wife Marie succumbed to cancer. A tear came to Altieri's eye when Swann described how he went out in Arnie Smith's fishing boat one misty March day in 1984 and sprinkled his wife's ashes in the waters off their beloved Sea Girt beach. He and Marie used to stroll that stretch of boardwalk daily, continually enthralled by the changing moods and rhythms of the sea. Each day the Atlantic talked to them.

Instinctively, Altieri realized it was more than therapy that Swann needed. He was close to his children, but only saw them sporadically. His son, Edward Jr., was an engineer in California and his daughter, Allison, an attorney in Chicago. Dr. Altieri— an only child whose parents had passed in the 1980s— lost her husband, Anthony, to a sudden heart attack about a year and a half before her first meeting with Swan. Alone with her seven-year-old daughter,

Pamela, Altieri soon realized they needed someone in their lives just as much as Swann did in his. From there, a relationship was spawned. "Uncle Ed" would see them every several weeks or so, sometimes more. Together they'd spend a day at the beach, go to a Yankees game, fish off the Jersey coast, or enjoy a game of chess and a simple dinner.

"SO HOW DO you know Father McDermott?" Swann asked Altieri as he was leaving after one of their initial sessions.

"John?" Altieri answered. "We worked together."

"Really? Where?"

"At a small parish, upstate in Bergen County," Altieri answered.

"Let me guess, you were a lay teacher in the school?"

"No. Not exactly." She held back a smile.

"An administrator in the rectory?"

"Uh...no" She shook her head.

"A housekeeper or cook?"

"Nope."

Suddenly, Swann got it. *"Jesus, Joseph and Mary."* He blessed himself. *"Were you a nun?"*

"Yep, Benedictine Order, habit and all," Altieri responded, motioning with her hands over her flowing grey hair to indicate the position of a nun's traditional head garb.

"Let me guess, couldn't handle the vow of celibacy?" Swann winked, eyeing the picture sitting on her bookshelf of her, Pamela and her deceased husband, Anthony, at a Red Sox game at Fenway Park.

"Nope, poverty." Altieri winked back.

* * *

16

Princeton, New Jersey, Mid-afternoon, March 19, 2007

"Catatonic Schizophrenia? Really?" Altieri asked, bewildered, after Swann brought her up to speed on the details regarding Arthur Shipkin Pennfield.

"Yep, that's what they call it. Who am I to challenge the doctors at Gladwell?"

"Hardly see it around here anymore." She shrugged.

"Well, it's difficult to believe that someone in that state could communicate— even psychically— with someone miles away," Swann remarked.

"Okay, let's take a look at your notes."

"Here they are, ripe for the pickin'." Swann pulled three yellow legal pads out of his briefcase and spread them out across her desk.

Quickly, Altieri ruffled through Swann's scribbled notes and focused on what appeared to be Dr. Hazard's initial treatment regimens for young Arthur:

Jan, 3-24, 1964: Chlorpromazine 400 mg/day, ECT 10j 2x/wk, limited response.

May 14th- June 15, 1964: Haloperidol 20mg/day, ECT 30j 2x/wk, moderate response, limited voluntary motor activity.

"INTERESTING," Altieri pushed her glasses up and blinked her eyes, "relatively standard levels of anti-psychotics in combination with relatively standard levels of ECT. Although I don't believe Haloperidol was an approved drug in 1964."

"So that means?" Swann began.

Deeply immersed in Swann's scribblings, Altieri flipped through the pages of the yellow-lined pad, stopping on some entries several pages back— the entries from the box that had mysteriously flipped its papers out during his episode in the Gladwell basement:

Patient #1064, Feb-March, 1965: Mescaline 300mg/day; ECT 3x/wk 100j, semi-coherent verbal activity, limited voluntary motor response.

Patient #1078: March-April, 1965: Strychnine 100mg/day; ECT 3x/wk 200j, coherent verbal motor activity, marked involuntary motor response.

Patient #1093, March-April, 1965: LSD 500ug/day, ECT 3x/wk, 1000j, uncontrollable seizure, hallucinatory episodes.

"YOU SURE THAT last one was a thousand joules, not a hundred?" She winced.

"Sure as any vibrant, eighty-two-year-old mind can be," Swann answered, chuckling. "Why?"

"Well, a thousand joules is way beyond the threshold-level of Electro Convulsive Therapy. It only takes three hundred to defibrillate a heart," Altieri answered. "And that was before they used sedation."

"Egads!" Swann shuddered. "No, but I'm quite sure, I wrote it down just as I saw it: *100j, 200j* and *1000j*."

"And then you're sure that on the first patient, it was only 10j, 20j and 30j?" Altieri asked.

"On Arthur Pennfield? Absolutely."

"Okay… okay…" Altieri looked up from Swann's scribbled notes, "…interesting."

"You going to let the rest of the world in on what you're thinking, doc?" Swann teased his friend.

"Well, as I said, on Arthur, Dr. Hazard used relatively standard doses of anti-psychotics in combination with pretty much standard levels of ECT. But with these other patients, in his clinical studies in 1965, he used much more aggressive dosages of a riskier drug class."

"You mean the LSD?" asked Swann.

"Yeah, and Mescaline and Strychnine, other hallucinogenics." Altieri answered.

"Okay, but that was a clinical study. So you would expect—"

"Sure. But the records for Pennfield's treatment were from 1964, correct?" Altieri asked.

"Yep."

"So wouldn't it be interesting to look at Pennfield's records post the clinicals?" Altieri raised an eyebrow.

"Well, they certainly didn't make it easy on me, I got as much as I could under what I would call trying circumstances."

"Well, either Pennfield was one of the numbered patients in the clinical study or, more likely, his treatment was adjusted based on the results from Dr. Hazard's studies."

Perplexed, Swann responded. "So what could that mean?"

"Lots of things. But let's not jump to any conclusions. Can you get back into Gladwell and look at more of Pennfield's records."

"I wouldn't be opposed, but…" he answered slyly.

"But what?"

"I think this ole bloke could be more effective if accompanied by a certain Doctor of Psychiatry."

"Oh wow…," she hesitated, "…I don't know, Ed."

"It'd be fun, don't you think?" He winked at her.

"Yeah, but time every time I get drawn into one of these things…" she paused as she led him out of her office.

"I know, I know it's like a bottomless pit. But will you at least think about it?" he begged.

"Sure, yes, I'll think about it." She smiled.

Swann paused, then asked, "And isn't there something you need to tell me?"

"What?" Altieri exclaimed.

"Well, a little birdie told me something."

"Something like what?"

"Well, perhaps you have a new…friend?"

"And might that little birdie be named Pamela?" she retorted playfully.

"Could be." Swann grinned.

"So I guess that means you'd like to meet him?"

"Why not? Without my approval how could you ever…"

"Okay. Okay. Follow me." She strode out the front door.

* * *

17

Princeton, New Jersey, Late afternoon, March 19, 2007

Swann followed Altieri out to the driveway and into the doctor's Volvo. Altieri scooted the vehicle onto the street, puttered down the avenue and turned right on Nassau Street. They wove through late-afternoon traffic, passing many fashionable shops and college hangouts, until Altieri made a left and entered campus. They drove down Washington Road, passing the venerable Firestone Library, the University Chapel, and Dickinson Hall, all gothic structures reminiscent of the mythical Hogwarts of Harry Potter fame. As they progressed down the road, the architecture morphed from classic gothic to modern contemporary.

Altieri pulled a quick U-turn and squeezed her Volvo into a parking space just across from Jadwin Hall, a modern, angular structure with a stone courtyard hovered over by a large, black, metallic sculpture. She led Swann through the entrance up to the second floor, and then down a long corridor. She stopped outside the office of Dr. Julian Weisman, Professor of Physics.

Perhaps the tattered, yellowing sign above his door— *Abandon all hope, ye who enter!* —was an omen, Swann thought. The office was literally a mess, papers strewn over academic journals strewn over notes strewn over books. Weisman, who looked every bit the part of the absent-minded physics professor with a salt and pepper goatee, bald scalp and professorial spectacles, was swung around towards the wall in his black leather swivel-chair, his sneakered feet up on a filing cabinet, chattering into his phone:

"Of course, Enrique, it's the conjugate metric tensor. You need the conjugate metric tensor to calculate the curvature, and then you can perform the reverse relativistic transformation..."

Altieri cleared her throat and tapped on the doorframe.

Weisman swung back around towards the door. He was wearing a Baltimore Orioles practice jersey and a pair of tattered jeans. His eyes lit up when he saw Altieri. *"Hey Bren,"* he held the phone away from his face and covered it, whispering "... a colleague of mine in Prague, hasn't slept in a day and a half trying to solve some crazy theoretical puzzle... be right with you."

As Weisman chattered away, Swann scoped out the professor's office. Not only was it a mess, Swann thought, it was an *eclectic mess.* The first thing he noticed was that famous picture of Einstein, sticking out his tongue in irreverent glee at some over-zealous photographer. Next to that was a framed autographed picture of Cal Ripken, Jr. The autograph read: *To Jules. Your equations may be far-fetched, but they certainly helped. I owe you one. Cal.* On a shelf to the side, there was Weisman's collection of beer bottles from around the world – *Johnny Courage, Tubourg, Sapporo, Einbecker Dunkel Ur-bock, Dinkel Acker Lager* and a whole array of esoteric brews. A replica of Rodin's *The Thinker* squatted on the john, next to a three-inch-diameter ball of rubber bands. Hanging on the wall above was a concert poster: *Watkins Glen. Summer Jam. The Allman Brothers Band. The Grateful Dead. July 28th 1973.*

When Weisman clicked off his phone, he swung around and rose from his chair, kissed Altieri, and shook hands with Swann— a stranger to him— while beginning a conversation mid-stream and gesticulating around the room.

"You know, I was thinking about this paradox, or maybe quasi-paradox, I don't know, whatever. Suppose your car was a time machine. You get in the driver's side, slide across the seat, and when you get out the passenger side, it's yesterday. Now suppose you're standing outside the driver side and the you from yesterday comes from around the car and shakes your hand. Then, of course, you're now obligated to go through the car, out the passenger side, wait a day so you can walk around to the driver's side and shake your own hand. Then you need to do it again and again. Might you be caught in an infinite time-loop from which you can never escape?"

"And, Jules, the relevance of this is?" Altieri asked grinning.

"Don't know." Weisman shrugged, and then smiled. "Just thought it was interesting."

"Jules, I'd like you to meet a friend of mine, Ed Swann," Altieri interrupted.

Weisman lit up. "The famous Uncle Ed, ghost-hunter extraordinaire?

"Well, sort of." Swann chuckled.

"Interesting. I once reviewed a paper on the physics underlying Random Spontaneous Psychokinesis." Weisman nodded at Swann. "That's 'poltergeists' to you."

"Believe me, I know, Dr. Weisman," Swann answered.

"Fascinating paper. Couldn't recommend it for publication though." Weisman shook his head. "Way too weird."

Swann chuckled. "And how did you two meet?

"Bren and I?" Weisman answered. "We share a mutual passion for rotisserie baseball, and skiing large bumps." He pointed to a photograph on the wall of himself and Altieri atop some foreboding ski slope. "From there, it was just fate."

"Actually," Altieri interrupted, "we had the unfortunate judgment to collaborate on a paper."

"And then nature took its course." Weisman giggled.

"So what was that paper about?" Swann asked.

"Its working title is *'Physics, Consciousness and the Human Psyche,'*" Weisman answered. "Sorta cool, huh? Not even done yet. May take years to finish, but it'll be a real game-changer if we nail it."

"Interesting." Swann pondered for a moment, "So you're relating physics to psychology."

"Why not?" Weisman answered matter-of-factly.

"Well," Swann hesitated, "have to confess, to a layman like me it sounds like a bit of a stretch."

Weisman chuckled, then picked up his ball of rubber bands and squeezed it, fidgeting as he spoke. "Well, let me see…how do I start? Let's put it this way: science is…well, it's sorta magic."

"Huh?" Swann looked at him bewildered. "But you're a scientist, not a magician."

"Bear with me for a second," Weisman said. "I'll explain."

"Okay, shoot," Swann answered.

"The more we learn," Weisman continued, passing his rubber-band ball from hand to hand, "the more we begin to realize that everything we take for granted— our concepts of space, time, matter, energy, gravity, everything— is just a very, very unique special case that really only holds together on a planet composed of crustaceous rock and water on an orbit with a radius of approximately 93-million miles around an average sized G2-class white star, at a time about thirteen-and-a-half billion years after the massive explosion that formed both that planet and the star, and the rest of their universe for that matter, all viewed from the perspective of moderately-intelligent homo-sapiens." He looked up at Swann. "Follow?"

"Lost me the minute you picked up that ball." Swann grinned.

"Okay. Let me try again," Weisman answered. "Take this ball." He held it out before him. "You perceive it as solid and stable, yet at a quantum microscopic level it's anything but. In fact, it's quite unstable and chaotic, mostly empty space with billions of particles floating around in probability functions, wavering between states of energy and matter, trying to decide what positions and momenta to assume. It's only from our blunt macro-perspective that it seems solid."

"Okay?" Swann responded tentatively.

"Now here's a doozey..." Weisman rolled his shoulders back, straightened his spine, and paused.

"We're waiting Jules..." Altieri chided him.

"I'm trying to figure out how to say it." He took a deep breath, cracking his knuckles. "Well, so. Those particles occupying that empty space. They're not there until someone observes them. At least, according to Bohr."

"Huh?"

"Remember that story teachers used tell in grammar-school science? If a tree falls in the forest and no one's there to hear it..."

"... it makes no noise." Swann finished his thought.

"Exactly." Weisman snapped his fingers. "A particle only exists as a wave of probability until someone actually observes it. Then it becomes real."

"So you're saying that our minds create the universe?"

"Sort of."

Swann scratched his head. "That's hard to believe."

"Of course it is," Weisman answered, "we've tricked ourselves into believing just the opposite, because with our limited perceptual abilities that's how it appears." He grinned and waved his finger. "So think about the implications."

"You're way beyond my pay-grade now, professor," Swann responded.

"Nah, let's go there. Check it out: consciousness and the universe are intimately intertwined. The universe as we know it is, at least in some way, observer-dependent. Particles become waves and vice-versa, wave-particle duality, as we call it."

"Is he speaking English, Bren?"

"Not sure anymore," she answered.

"So this fellow Erwin Schrodinger posits this thought experiment. Put a cat into a box with a sealed vile of poisonous gas. Set up an unobserved Geiger counter next to an unobserved piece of radioactive material in the box as well. If the material emits a particle within a given interval of time, the Geiger counter trips a switch which breaks the vial of gas and kills the cat. If the particle is not emitted, the Geiger counter does nothing, and the cat survives."

"Okay?" Swann responded in suspense.

"Now, one school of quantum physics would say that the particle exists in both states – emitted and not emitted—until observed. So, since neither the Geiger counter nor the radioactive material is observed until the box is opened, by definition, the particle is simultaneously existent and non-existent. But when the observer opens the box, the cat is either dead or alive."

"Huh?"

"So the interesting question becomes, at the instant immediately before he opens the box, what is the nature of the cat? Since the particle had not been observed until then, it only exists as a wave of probabilities until the box is opened. Was the cat dead or alive prior to the opening of the box? Was it in some state of suspended animation— half dead, half alive— entangled in the waves of a probability function?"

Dumbfounded, Swann silently watched as Weisman paced across the room.

"Or…," Weisman broke the silence, "…does the cat exist in both states, each in a separate universe, observed both dead and alive by two different versions of the observer."

"A doppelganger?"

Weisman tweaked his beard. "Yeah sort of. So, you see, at the very least, consciousness plays a vital role in the physics of space and time. Reality is all in the eyes of the beholder, at least according to some."

"Never thought of it that way," said Swann.

"Now here's where it gets interesting," Weisman continued streaming. Ed got comfortable in one of the spare wooden chairs in front of the professor's desk, and nodded at Altieri. She put down her bag and sat down. "Suppose some people's perceptual abilities are more finely tuned than others. Well," he corrected himself, "that doesn't even have to be the case. Suppose their perceptual abilities are tuned *slightly different* than others, like a radio tuned to a different station."

"A different station from *what*?" Swann asked.

"From what we would consider our normal state of reality." Weisman paused again, and looked out the window.

"So where are you going with this?" Swann asked.

"If so, that could possibly explain many weird phenomena we observe today but don't fully understand. Suppose a schizophrenic isn't really crazy, but the voices he hears are those from another universe, a universe that exists right here in this space and time— between the lines, so to speak—

but one most of us can't perceive because our normal minds are incapable of it. Suppose when someone sees a ghost, it's merely a result of that person's ability to perceive other dimensions across space and time. Suppose—"

"Slow down for a minute, professor," Swann chided him, then turned to Altieri. "Bren, so this *psychic gift* that we've always talked about with the Pennfields, it could just be that?"

"Watch out, Ed. Jules loves to push the edge of the envelope, but this stuff is all highly speculative."

"What's this all about?" Weisman cut in, his face lighting up.

"Ed has a client—" Altieri began, "Ed, may I?" Ed nodded. "— who recently found out that a relative of his, who has been institutionalized in a catatonic stupor for years, is not his nephew, as he thought, but his biological son. The other night, this client thought he saw his catatonic son floating in his bedroom, speaking to him in French."

"And the significance of the French is?" Weisman asked.

"They used to speak to each other in French before the young boy became catatonic."

"And this client of yours, Ed, you said he had psychic— proclivities?"

"Well, um yeah, I first met the Pennfields when they thought they had ghosts in their family cottage. Among their clan, they've had many paranormal experiences. Yeah, I would say the entire family might be psychically gifted to an extent… or as you would say, their minds may be tuned to *a different station*."

"Cool," Weisman said.

"And when I worked with them, back in 1996, we discovered some papers, from the 1800s where a family member, a wealthy merchant from Newport, claimed the family had a curse, dating back to when their ancestors came over on the Mayflower."

"Wow, no shit?" Weisman responded.

"For sure," Swann answered.

"So what are you doing about this *alleged* visitation from his *alleged* son?" Weisman asked.

"Well, I wanted Bren to come with me to visit with Chris, try to figure it out, but she seems a bit hesitant."

"Bren…" Weisman whispered, then suddenly a surge of enthusiasm overwhelmed him as his eyes widened, "*Bren… BREN…?*"

"That would be me," she answered.

"Are you f—…are you *crazy*?" Weisman blurted. "This is right up our alley. We have a potential test case of consciousness-transcending-space-and-time physics and you don't want to see it for yourself? What *are* you thinking, hon?"

"Well, I never quite thought of it that way, and I'm sort of busy, Jules."

"But you can never be too busy for something like this, Bren. If there's anything to it, this could literally represent a quantum leap in our research, our paper. You *must* go. You *have to* go."

Swann had a wide bellowing grin across his face.

"Don't look at me like that, Ed," Altieri retorted.

"Can't say I disagree with the good professor," Swann announced.

Altieri looked at Swann and then Weisman. They both looked back at her with snarky grins.

Resigned, she mumbled, "Okay, let me think about it."

"I'm sure Chris Pennfield would be delighted to meet you, Bren," Swann said.

"Did you say Chris Pennfield?" Weisman asked, bewildered.

"Yep."

"As in *Professor* Christopher Pennfield?"

"Know him?" Swann asked.

"I certainly do," Weisman responded. "I spent four years at Pennfield College as an associate professor early in my career."

"So what do you think?" Swann asked mischievously.

"Huh, wow… Christopher Pennfield, eh?" Weisman almost giggled. "Imperiously dogmatic. Supercilious snob. Flamboyant womanizer. And… a first-class mind."

* * *

TIME FRAME: 2052

18

Manhattan, NYCGAB, Pennfield Technologies Tower, Mid-day, November 25, 2052

Employees at Pennfield Technologies had coined a term for Jimmy Mashimoto-Pennfield's obsessive approach to work: *multi-matrixing.* Multi-tasking was nothing at all to JMP, mere child's play, only one single "matrix" in his multi-layered world. Virtuality had changed the dynamic, *exponentialized it*, as Mashimoto-Pennfield would commonly say.

He fidgeted this morning, jerking himself around his office in a series of sudden deliberate movements, rocking back and forth in his chair, pointing and flipping through his multiple holoscreens, simultaneously summoning the company barber to come up for a quick trim and commanding his assistant in London to retrieve a report from one of his financial execs. *Perhaps he should schedule an electro-massage simultaneously as well?*

Indeed, his employees knew JMP well; whatever anxiety he experienced wasn't fueled by *too much* work, it was fueled by *too little.* To JMP, being overworked was stress reduction therapy.

"Just a reminder. Bobby O'D will be here in a few minutes, boss." McPherson stuck his head into JMP's office as the barber rolled a laser-prong over his bald scalp, dissolving minute hairs.

McPherson convinced his friends on the force to assign Robert O' Donnell, known to his NYGABPD brethren as *Bobby O'D*, to conduct the interview of JMP. They agreed upon ground rules up front: the interview would take place in JMP's office; the session would last no longer than forty-five minutes; JMP had the right to refuse answering any question; and, of course, there would be absolutely no leaks to the press. Should a leak occur, all inquiries would be directed to Apexia PolCom which would nip them in the bud.

AT THAT INSTANT, a holoscreen materialized: "Mr. Mashimoto-Pennfield?" the receptionist announced. "A Robert O'Donnell is here to see you, sir."

"Fine, let him in," he answered.

"HEY, BRY MAC!" Smiling, Bobby O'Donnell reached for McPherson's hand and gave him a hug as he bounded through the door.

"Bobby O'D, been awhile, huh?"

"Yeah, sometimes life gets in the way. You know the story."

"Hey," McPherson swiveled towards his boss, "meet Mr. Mashimoto-Pennfield. Mr. MP, this is Bobby O'D, one of New York GAB's finest."

Without looking up, JMP extended a tentative hand. "I'm sure he is," he mumbled.

"Well," McPherson began, "we all know why we're here. Might as well get started. Don't want to waste anyone's time."

"Thank you for that." JMP responded

"Ummm, yeah," O'Donnell began, "Mr. Mashimoto-Pennfield, I'd like to use a gnat cam to record our interview with your permission. Is that okay?"

"We'll get a copy, Mr. MP," McPherson followed up. "Already arranged for it with the PD. And for good measure, we'll be recording on our own gnat cam as well."

"Okay," O'Donnell followed, "so then let's get started."

"Do it," JMP said tersely, as if he were about to take a revolting dose of medicine.

O'Donnell pulled out his e-let and summoned up his notes. He cleared his throat. "Mr. Pennfield, tell me about your activities on the night of November 10th."

"I was at work, like almost every other night," he said.

"But what about *after* work? Did you do anything after work?"

"Yes, I went to a tavern in the East Village." He shifted anxiously in his seat. "But you already know that, don't you?"

"Yeah, sure do," O'Donnell answered. "But, for the record, was the name of the establishment *'Undertaker'*?"

"I believe so."

"So tell me, Mr. Mashimoto-Pennfield, why would a prestigious guy like you, an Apexian, choose a tavern that's almost exclusively patronized by sub-100s. Strange, don't you think?"

"Perhaps, but," JMP wiggled anxiously in his chair and paused.

"*But,* was there any particular reason you might've gone there, Mr. Mashimoto-Pennfield?"

"No, not really." He wrung his hands. "It was just an impulsive thing. Every now and then I need to blow off some steam."

"With sub-100s?"

"Why not?"

O'Donnell pointed and whipped up an image on the holoscreen. "You know this woman?"

"Well, I wouldn't say I *know her,* but yes, she approached me when I was in the tavern and offered to get the bartender's attention for me."

"Nice lookin' girl." O'Donnell gazed at the picture of the woman.

"I suppose so," JMP answered, seething.

"Come on, Mr. Mashimoto-Pennfield," Detective O'Donnell chided him, "she's hot, am I right?"

"I don't know if I would describe her as..."

"Rumor has it you have a very healthy sexual appetite," O'Donnell cut him off.

JMP's face reddened. "Which, of course, is none of your business, Detective O'Donnell."

"With all due respect, Mr. Mashimoto-Pennfield, we're talking about a missing person."

Sternly, JMP glared at him. "Detective O'Donnell, if I were you, I would think for a moment before you ask certain questions. You do realize I am very well connected."

"Don't doubt it. Just doing my job." O'Donnell scratched a note on the screen of his e-let. "Let's get back to your sexual appetite."

"Fuck off, why don't you?" JMP blurted.

"A bit of a strong response, wouldn't you say?" Not lifting his head, O'Donnell continued to scratch away on his e-let. "Perhaps you have something to hide."

"My sex life is my own business."

McPherson intervened. "Come on Mr. MP, be respectful."

"Of that?" He pointed at his interrogator.

Unfazed, O'Donnell summoned up another holoscreen. "Let's see, this fellow here is a Hector Dominguez-Hasegawa. Did he not have to be rushed to the hospital in Nice because he was performing oral sex on you with his neck simultaneously in a noose?"

JMP clenched his teeth and tightened his fist.

"And, then, we have this young fellow here," O'Donnell again pointed at the holoscreen, "Suke Nagasaki, did you not engage in sexual activities with him when he was a minor?"

"Bullshit!" JMP pounded his fist on his desk. "I'm an Apexian. He was ninth PGU. Apexian privilege."

"Well, good for you, I suppose," O'Donnell answered. "But you do realize there is no Apexian privilege for kidnapping or murder?"

"How dare you!"

"And now here," O'Donnell pointed at another image, "we have Sophia Zignorelli, an Apexian herself I believe."

"Yes, by virtue of a very fortunate marriage." JMP scowled. "Talk about oral sex…"

"Did she not call the local police in Cernobbio complaining of domestic abuse?"

Boldly, he folded his arms across his chest. "It was a misunderstanding. If you examine the record thoroughly, you'll see she withdrew the charges the very next day, or don't you examine things thoroughly?"

O'Donnell glared at JMP then cleared his throat, "I always do. But wouldn't you say that all of this represents a pattern?"

"Of what?"

"Well at the very least you have a sexual appetite that borders on the aggressive… and you did leave the tavern with the young lady…umm Robyn Viega…and proceed to a nearby apartment where presumably…"

"*We had sex?* Is that what you were going to say?"

"Well, it certainly isn't inconsistent with your history, Mr. Mashimoto-Pennfield."

"Okay, suppose we did. I saw the Apexinator tattoo on her and I fled as quickly as my legs could carry me."

"That's not disputed. The question is, *where's the girl?"*

"How the fuck do you expect me to know. I left. It's very clear. It's on your own v-file, is it not?"

"Sure," O'Donnell responded. "But suppose the sex got a little rough. Maybe you put a noose around her neck like that poor fellow in Nice, who knows? Maybe to the point where you suffocated her, unintentionally, of course."

"But if that were the case," JMP countered, "someone would have found the body."

"Yeah," McPherson answered. "But, as you know, the surveillance v-file ends after an hour. Maybe you had someone remove the body after the surveillance ended?"

"Oh, pleeeeezzzzzz..."

"Or whatever. A man with your resources and technological expertise could have, let's say, *arranged* many ways to dispose of the body. And you did flee off to St. Johns rather abruptly thereafter."

"I go there frequently, it's my getaway. Bryan can confirm that."

Silent, McPherson nodded his head.

"But isn't it unusual, that you just scooted up there on a weeknight, unplanned, as far as we can gather? Don't you usually go there on weekends or for a holiday?"

"True. But I sporadically go there on the spur of the moment. Just like that night."

"That's not what your MagLev records say."

"Listen," JMP pounded his fist, "you can weave together the facts however you want and come up with a myriad of fictional hypotheses. I grant you that. But I am telling you, when I left that putrid apartment the girl was alive and well. I'm sure she'll show up somewhere eventually."

Straight-faced, O'Donnell countered: "Mr. Mashimoto-Pennfield, did you have rough sex with Ms. Viega to the point that it caused asphyxiation and death and then have her body removed from the premises sometime thereafter?"

"That's it!" JMP barked abruptly, his fuse spent. "Bryan, get him out of here. Right now. This instant. This interview is officially over. I think I'm going to have a conversation with Commissioner Newkirk about the interrogation style of this friend of yours."

* * *

HALFWAY ACROSS THE WORLD, a tall man with flowing blonde hair took delight in watching Jimmy Mashimoto-Pennfield sweat as O'Donnell pummeled him with embarrassing questions. Prime Minister Ibu Bonne-Saari, in his office atop the Apexian Capital Pinnacle in the Bonne-Saari Capital District on the island of Sri Lanka, had Mashimoto-Pennfield exactly where he wanted him, vulnerable and apprehensive.

Submission would come next.

* * *

19

Manhattan, NYCGAB, Pennfield Technologies Tower, Mid-day, November 25, 2052

nxiously, JMP tapped his fingers on his desk. He hated uncertainty, hated losing control. It bothered him, made him anxious.

Damnit! He banged his fist on the desk.

He had never been the type to wait for closure. He had to exonerate himself from this police bullshit so he could get on with his work.

He banged his fist on his desk once again and barked: *"Narc! Narc! I need you. Come here! Now!"*

Instantly, his holographic virtual clone materialized.

"So the plot thickens?" Narc greeted him.

"Yes, it does. But you needn't be so cavalier about it."

"My dear other," Narc responded, "if you had no issues, my value to you would be negligible. I would have little reason to exist."

Mashimoto-Pennfield thought for a moment then said, "Granted. So let's get on with it."

"That O'Donnell fellow must've put the fear of God in you."

"No, not really," JMP answered. "I am absolutely certain I did nothing wrong."

"Except… *exploit* a young woman," Narc interjected.

"And *what* do you mean by that?" JMP challenged back.

"Exactly what I said," Narc answered.

"Will you please stop mind-fucking me," JMP censured his alter ego. "As much as my current situation may amuse you, I can assure you, everything that transpired between myself and that woman was perfectly legal."

"Perhaps. But was it *proper*?"

"Proper?"

"Yes, *proper. Legal* and *proper* are two different things."

"Enough of that. Let's move on."

"Whatever you say," Narc responded. "So what's on your mind?"

"This young Shippy," JMP answered. "I'm perplexed by him."

"How so?"

"My instincts tell me our connection was no random occurrence, not at all," said JMP.

"So there was a reason you stumbled upon his psychic presence?"

"Perhaps."

"Then what was it?" Narc asked.

"I'm not sure," JMP whispered.

"That's a rarity, you being unsure of yourself," Narc commented. "Take a deep breath and relax for a moment, will you please? Clear your mind, expunge all other thoughts, think freely."

"Okay. Okay." JMP breathed in deeply, then clenched his teeth and touched his temples.

"Come on. It should be obvious, my dear JMP," Narc prodded him.

"Okay," JMP finally answered. "Suppose, indeed, the Jennifer from my Ganzfeld session, the one who warned me about the woman in the tavern, suppose she was, in fact, from the future. And suppose, taking Shippy at his word, he was a Pennfield, most likely from the past. Could the Jennifer from the future also be a Pennfield? Is there some sort of family influence operating here?"

"Stellar," Narc congratulated his other. "Now let's try this. Suppose the whole event, everything about it, was a set-up. Suppose this Jennifer from the future lured you into that tavern for a reason. The disappearance of Robyn, the one you had sex with, was pre-planned, or *post-planned* depending upon your perspective. As we had speculated, could it be that the Jennifer from the future was attempting to re-create a past that she already knew transpired, or conversely, trying to reverse that very same past?"

"Or...," JMP snapped his fingers, "perhaps the Jennifer from my Ganzfeld session was of the present, not the future: an agent for some contemporary rival intent on bringing me down."

"Could be. Could be. Very interesting."

"But whatever the scenario, they all point in one direction."

"Of course. Of course, my dear other," Narc indulged him.

"They all have something to do with the Pennfield family curse," JMP continued, "embracing the past, present and future."

"I think you've nailed it, JMP. Absolutely nailed it."

Quickly, JMP's mind ruminated through the implications. "So the curse is about to strike a prominent member of the Pennfield family once again. And—"

Abruptly, JMP paused, realizing where this train of thought would take him.

"And, unfortunately, that prominent member of the Pennfield family would be you, my dear other."

"You mean us," JMP interrupted him.

"Indeed, us," Narc responded. "And this alleged curse is primed to occur at the worst possible time. Just as your company is about to launch its most significant initiative of all time."

"No! No! No!" JMPs face turned bright red. "We cannot let anything, *anything*, get in the way of the Cryonics Initiative." He banged his fist on his desk. "This curse is done, it stops *now*. We *have* to defeat it!"

"Remember, JMP, this curse and its agents have proven to be masterfully cunning over the generations."

"Understood. But they've never been up against the likes of me… and, of course, you."

"Agreed, a formidable duo," Narc answered. "But how do you suggest we defeat it?"

* * *

20

Manhattan, NYCGAB, Pennfield Technologies Tower, Afternoon, November 25, 2052

Timidly, McPherson poked his head into JMP's office. As much as he desired to erase all memory of the morning's meeting between Bobby O'D and JMP, he concluded it would be better to go back in and smooth things over.

"Arrogant little snot, isn't he?" JMP grumbled the moment McPherson stepped into his office.

"O'D?" McPherson answered. "He's good at what he does, you gotta give him that."

"I thought it was all pre-arranged, he was going to take it easy on me," said JMP.

"I thought so too," McPherson responded.

"You *thought?"*

"Don't know. Honestly, Mr. MP. Maybe he was grandstanding or something. I can't put words in his mouth, you know."

For the first time, JMP lifted his head from his desk and leaned forward, teeth clenched. "Bryan, I worked very hard to get to where I am. I may have been born into money, but I took what good fortune I had and grew it beyond anyone's wildest expectations. I created scores of innovations that make life better for millions and created hundreds of thousands of jobs. My reward for that should be the right not to be bothered by trivial shit like this. Do I make myself clear?" His eyes drilled into McPherson's.

Nervously, McPherson nodded.

"And it's your job to keep it that way, understood?"

"Yessir, Mr. MP."

"So when are we gonna find this little whore?"

"Yeah, the force is all over it. I'm cooperating with—"

"Fuck the *force*, Bryan!" Abruptly, JMP stood up and screamed at his SVP of Security. "Come *on*. A bunch of incompetent morons if you ask me. I trust them about as much as I trust my worst enemy. Find that fucking girl or it will be your job!"

* * *

21

V-Way 3: en route to MANH GAB, Evening, November 26, 2052

"Frankie D… What's up?" McPherson blurted into his speaker as his hover-jet auto-piloted north from Manhattan to New Hampshire.

"Bryan Mac? Is that you?" Frank DeVito responded.

"None other."

"What's going on?" asked DeVito, one of four Deputy Chiefs of the NYGAB PD and a lifelong friend of McPherson's. "How's life in that rarefied air of yours?"

"Stop shittin' me, Frankie."

"Let's see," DeVito chided him. "SVP at one of the world's leading companies. Fifth PGU, practically a Diamid. I'd say you're doing pretty well for yourself, Mac."

"As will you, the minute you put in your time with the force, Frankie. All in due time," McPherson answered as he watched the colorful rolling hills of Massachusetts fly by below.

"So what's up?" Frankie asked.

"The guy is going bonkers on me."

"Mashimoto-Pennfield?"

"None other."

"So what you need?" DeVito asked.

"I need to know more about the girl."

"Bry, you know me like you know your brother. I'm not shittin' ya. We're making every effort to find her. But when she's a sub-100, Twelfth PGU, it's not easy."

"Believe me, Frankie, I know you ain't pulling any punches, but I gotta do what the boss man says," McPherson answered. "So I'd appreciate a little help if you don't mind."

"I'll do it for *you,* Bry, but not for that scumbag boss of yours."

"So what do you got on her?"

"Off the top of my head, aside from the stuff you already know, her name's Robyn, uh, Robyn Viega."

"Yep, that's what JMP said she called herself."

DeVito pointed briskly at his holoscreen and flipped through several files. "She's employed as a V-way monitor, usually stationed on the east side, not far from you guys, actually." DeVito flipped through a few more files until he found a set of pictures. "Nice looking babe, good buns, too bad she's dumb as shit like all the others in the *12th.* Could see why the ole man went for her, though."

"Alright, alright, Mr. MP has his… needs. So what."

"From what I hear those needs are a little indiscriminate, if you know what I mean," DeVito quipped.

"Stop fuckin' around, Frankie, who the fuck cares." McPherson answered. "It's a well-known item that Mr. MP goes both ways. Tell me something I don't know."

"Okay. Okay. Born in TEXMEX right near the old border. Her mother was always Twelfth PGU; her dad was Tenth until he lost a job as a supply clerk in NORCAL. Lives in a PHA in ARTEX, used to MagLev there almost every night, unless she was shacking up with this guy in PAWVA."

"Did you talk to her neighbors?

"Yeah," DeVito answered. "No one's seen her since that day she met your boss in the tavern."

"How 'bout the guy she shacks up with?"

"Clueless, another dumb fuck. Major druggie."

"Why don't you give me his name and contact info? It's as good a place as any to start."

For a moment, De Vito was silent.

"Ah *come* on!" Said McPherson. "Frank, it's for *me.* It's just contact info."

"Alright Bry. Alright. Lemme take a look. I'll at least get you his GAB."

McPHERSON WOULD HAVE to navigate through an intricate maze of GABs—*Geographic Administrative Bureaus,* local bureaus which provided basic services— and *Para-geographic Governmental Units* or PGU's—virtual governments which traversed the globe— in his pursuit of this Robyn Viega. As a member of the Twelfth PGU, she had very little governmental protection, a plus for McPherson. Even if she cried foul— trying to claim that in his pursuit of her McPherson was somehow violating her rights— she would be subject to the laws and courts of McPherson's PGU, the Fifth.

Instituted by financier Izan Bonne-Saari in the second decade of the twenty-first century, the governmental pecking order was quite precise and transcended all previously existing geographic boundaries. The highest echelon was composed of the *Named PGUs* — Apexia, Betamil, Chrysalix and Diamid. Tremendously exclusive, the Apexia PGU had only 40,000 worldwide members, including Jimmy Mashimoto-Pennfield. Its government was presided over by Prime Minister Ibu Bonne-Saari, the son of the deceased Izan Bonne-Sari. Apexians tended to reside in the most sparkling, sophisticated global cities — New York, San Francisco, Sydney, Kuala Lumpur, Hong Kong, Shanghai, Dubai, Paris, London, Milan, and Capetown. The cities were jewels, overfunded by ridiculous amounts of Apexian revenues, supplemented by proportionate funding from the other named PGUs.

Membership in Apexia required an initiation fee of ten billion GCUs — Global Currency Units, the worldwide currency — and ninety percent approval among existing members. Apexian law was paramount within the echelons of PGUs; in a dispute, either criminal or civil, between members of Apexia and any other PGU, the Apexian law was always binding. Apexians paid minimal taxes; the interest and dividends generated by the cumulative initiation-fee-fund spun off tremendous amounts of revenue to provide for PGU services.

The second most exclusive PGU, Betamil was composed predominantly of large families of multigenerational wealth. Residing mostly in beautiful scenic areas of the world — the rural horse country and coastlines of what used to be the Northeast US, the Swiss Alps, the Maldives, the South African coast, Patagonia, the Canadian Rockies, Betamilians were very conservative, their laws placing stringent restrictions upon religious and social practices, medicine and miscegenation.

Chrysalix was the most liberal of the PGUs, allowing all sorts of experimental behavior in drugs, and social, sexual and medical practices. Most global celebrities from entertainment, music, fashion, and journalism as well as highly renowned artists and the influential literati were Chrysalixians. While there was a fair degree of geographic overlap with Apexia, Chrysalixians tended to reside in Los Angeles, London, Paris, Amsterdam, Rio de

Janeiro, Tokyo and Antsiranana, the beautiful resort city on the northern coast of Madagascar.

Diamid was the most centrist PGU, consisting mostly of global corporate executives and affluent professionals — and the most personally appealing to Bryan McPherson. Diamids either resided in major metropolitan areas or in the commutable scenic rural areas. Diamids enjoyed lower taxes, better social services and guaranteed retirement funds. However, it was access to affordable education in the world's leading colleges and universities that appealed most to McPherson. He had two teenagers at home and needed to think of their futures. Pleasing Jimmy Mashimoto-Pennfield quickly in this endeavor could only help McPherson in that pursuit.

The Fifth PGU— to which McPherson currently belonged— was considered the most prestigious of the mid-level PGUs. Taxes were significant but not unbearable, services were excellent, laws were pretty much straightforward, and the jurisprudence system was fair. Most members of the Fifth PGU resided in the same, mostly scenic, commutable areas as Diamids or in less expensive housing in the major metropolitan areas worldwide. The five other mid-level PGUs, the Sixth through the Tenth, were characterized mostly by differences in income and occupation. The Seventh was considered more Bohemian in nature, with very liberal social standards, and the Eighth was reserved for religious fundamentalists, with different geocentric sects and laws, for Christians, Muslims, Jews, and Buddhists.

The Eleventh through Fifteenth PGUs were reserved for the sub-100s, citizens with a Quality Algorithm or QA score of less than 100. Anyone registered in one of the "Lower PGUs" was subject to strict controls on procreation; while each member of the Lower PGUs was required to produce one offspring— to keep the population stable insuring a sufficient labor pool for menial tasks— if they went beyond this quota they were subject to severe punishment. Limits were placed on energy consumption, both fossil and non-fossil fuels. Advancements in public transportation had allowed members of the lower PGUs to be "transitioned" out of blighted urban areas— now gentrified for the higher PGUs— and relocated to GABs hundreds of miles away from the great cities, but still within a commutable distance due to the speeds achieved via MagLev technology. They were restricted to bicycles in their PHAs, Public Housing Areas, and ownership of energy-consuming personal transportation devices of any kind was prohibited. Access to medical services was strictly rationed and public education ceased at age twelve.

Complicating the whole process for McPherson were the GABs, those geographically-based bureaus responsible for local law enforcement, roads, v-ways, title and property, and other similar administrative functions. Each GAB was funded proportionately by the relevant PGUs based upon the number of PGU members residing within that geography. Law enforcement was selective by PGU membership. Since the geographic area where Robyn Viega was reported to have lived, "ARTEX"— composed of pieces of what were formerly Arkansas and Texas— was inhabited mostly by members of Lower PGUs, the local GAB was grossly underfunded. McPherson grimaced at the thought of cajoling cooperation from a group of moronic Sub-100 bureaucrats.

McPHERSON RUBBED his eyes as the autopilot decelerated his hover jet. In the distance he could see his A-frame nestled within two nicely landscaped acres of evergreen-laced MANH real estate, the GAB which used to be parts of Massachusetts and New Hampshire. Just as the hover jet positioned itself over the circular pad-port about twenty yards from his house—

"Bry?"

"Frankie?"

"Yep, me again," DeVito answered. "Got more info on that druggie our girl shacks up with now and then."

"Shoot."

"Name's 'Fane'. Derek Fane. Lives in a PHA in southwest PAWVA?"

"Know what number?"

"Yep, PHA Number 432B"

"Geeeez, one of those strip mine deals?"

"Think so."

"Thanks, Frankie, I owe you one."

"No prob, Bry."

McPherson scowled. He hated visiting PHAs.

* * *

22

PAWVA GAB: PHA 432B, Afternoon, November 28, 2052

McPherson's hover jet veered over the northern PAWVA landscape, banking towards a maze of PHAs crisscrossing the vestiges of the Appalachians. The chilly, grey late afternoon November sky exacerbated his drab disposition and the tightness of the knot in his stomach; this was one of the last places he ever wanted to be.

A series of flattened mountaintops scattered with sparse brown grass and rows upon rows of flat, angular, one-story cinderblock structures with numbers painted on the roofs punctured the landscape. McPherson looked down upon a pool of dark liquid lying stagnant behind a dam between the cinderblock rows: a coal slurry impoundment with sludge from the coal deposits stripped from the mountains. The sight of it depressed him.

He counted the numbers on the roofs below: *389C, 390A, 390B, 390C* and so on and so on. His auto-navigator indicated that 432B should be about a dozen miles to the southwest. His eyes followed a string of electrical transmission lines stretching out to the horizon, drooping between an endless series of stark metal towers intruding upon the countryside.

The auto-navigator directed his hover jet to follow the transmission lines to a mountain. Unlike the others, this one wasn't flattened from the effects of strip-mining performed decades ago. This one looked normal, appearing just as a typical southwestern-Pennsylvania mountaintop would have at the turn of the century, replete with bulging boulders, dotted with splotches of ferns and moss.

As he swerved over the mountaintop, everything changed: a sudden cliff. It was as if the mountain had been sliced in half, literally. The far side of the mountain was not a mountain at all; abruptly, it fell off into a pit, man-made through years of excavation. The layers of red-clay terraces sloping down its side housed hundreds of large, rusty oil-drums, garbage dumpsters, gigantic steel spools of electrical wire, and piles of rusted, abandoned hover jets and cars.

At the bottom, the pit flattened: a maze of more rusty old junk. And then off to the side, he saw it, Public Housing Area #432B; like the others, a flat, rectangular, windowless cinderblock structure, but unlike the others, it was situated next to a transformer sub-station, the high-voltage transmission lines leading first to what resembled a large, steel capital letter "H" and then through a series of intimidating coils and transformers.

McPherson clicked off the autopilot and took control. He circled around the large open pit, eyeing rows upon rows of garbage dumpsters, gigantic oil cans, plastic outhouses, and people — Sub-100s— strewn all over the pit as if it were a neighborhood park. And then, at the far end: a gigantic piece of machinery, a tremendously large bucket-wheel excavator, the footprint of its rust-red base covering at least a hundred square yards, its long, 90-foot crane stretching across the pit, held aloft by steel-wire rigging.

As he searched for a good place to land—

ZZZzzzzzoooooooommmmm! ZZZZZiiiiiiiizzzzzzzzzz!!

He buckled in his cockpit. Two rotorocks whizzed by, almost slicing off his right wing. He grit his teeth. *Assholes!* Nothing pissed him off more than jerk-off teenagers with high-powered toys. Circling, he looked for a flat place to land, away from where most of the sub-100s were gathered.

He spotted an area behind a large boulder at the far end of the pit, near the transformer station, flat with reddish brown dirt. Hovering above, he scoped out the spot as best he could, and then piloted a perfectly soft vertical descent.

Slowly, he opened the door, and then gulped. *Twenty years on the force and he had seen a lot of shit, but he still hated having to come to a place like this.*

As he jumped out the side, he thought he saw the stir of movement behind the boulder.

Instinctively, he grabbed for his G-pen, a highly powerful Gamma Ray stick, only allowed to be carried by law enforcement and licensed security professionals.

"Who's there?" he barked.

A shy little kid peered out from behind the rock. As McPherson slowly put his G-Penn back in his pocket, the kid stepped out. The child, with tannish skin, bright white teeth, dark curly hair and tattered clothes, eyed McPherson's hover jet with awe. McPherson looked him in the eyes.

"You ain't no chino boy!" the kid cried out to McPherson.

"Chino boy?" McPherson squinted at him. "What's a chino boy?"

"Chino boys on rotorocks." The kid pointed upwards. "Diamids. They buzz us."

"No." McPherson smiled. "I'm no chino boy. Who are you?"

"Min," the kid responded.

The kid was cute, McPherson thought. About nine or ten, Min was understandably shy and untrusting of this intruder who sprang out of the sky from a fancy hover jet. McPherson leaned over, looked Min in the eyes and smiled at him. Reflexively, the little boy stepped back.

"Min, can you help me out with something?" McPherson asked.

"What?"

"You know anyone named Derek, Derek Fane?"

"Yeah, I know Derek. He drains."

"Can you take me to him?

The kid hesitated.

"I can give you some GCUs." McPherson pointed at his e-let.

"How much?" The little kid asked feebly.

"A thousand."

The kid hesitated once again. "Okay. I'll take you. But, Derek, he's fucked," the little boy pointed to his temple, "fucked in the head."

As twilight deadened, the lights strung up on the old wooden telephone poles cast splotchy shadows on the rusted equipment and red clay earth. Silently, McPherson and Min traversed the pit, navigating between oil drums, small cinderblock structures, outhouses and rows of debris. McPherson tried to avoid looking into the eyes of the sub-100s. Nonetheless, they looked at him. As he moved through each cluster of them— sitting on the ground, on rusted oil drums, iron beams and abandoned machinery— they all went silent, their eyes glued to him, following his every step. He wasn't quite sure what to make of it. He surmised it was something like, *you don't fuck with us and we won't fuck with you.*

Min lead McPherson to some odd rusted yellow structure. Once they turned its corner, he could tell what it was: a huge, extinct, excavation bucket, used years ago to scrape earth and coal from the face of the mountain. It was massive, forged together from large beams of steel, about twelve-feet high and twenty-feet across, festooned at the front and back with giant chains of four-foot long steel links and a set of six, ominous steel teeth protruding from its front.

About twenty sub-100s sat in small groups on the bucket's cold metal bottom. The worlds *FARSNEPPEL SHIT*, BONNE-SAARI SWALLOWS BITCH SCUM, *KING SMARF*, *FUCK BONNE-SAARI* sprayed in bright red paint defiled the bucket's inside back wall. McPherson and Min entered cautiously. Min pointed to a dark corner; there were five of them there, draining SMARF. Sitting in a tight, intense circle, each had an IV open in their arm. The bag of SMARF hung on a pipe from above. They passed the tube around, each inserting it into their IV for up to a minute.

A time-phased combination of downer, stimulant and hallucinogenic, SMARF— SiMethadone Amyl Ribophosphate— was a designer drug popularized originally by Chrysalixians. Available in several forms depending upon the desired length and strength of the experience, intravenous SMARF was by far the strongest, and potentially most lethal, form of the drug.

"Derek!" Min yelled out.

One of them in the intense circle jolted his head. *"Huh?"*

"Man wants to talk to Derek." Min pointed at McPherson. "Fifth PGU."

"Fifth-Fuck, huh?" one of them answered, then shook Fane. "Derek, Fifth-Fuck wants to see yah."

Min motioned McPherson to step forward.

Fane looked up at him.

"What? What you want? I'm draining. Draining big time." Unlike most of the others, Derek Fane had bland white skin, his facial features almost flattened, and long, fine, stringy black hair that hung halfway to his shoulders. Dark blue veins popped from his milky white arms.

"My name's McPherson, Bryan McPherson. I'm looking for someone you might know."

"Know? Who do I know? Who might I know?" He accelerated his words, randomly rattling them off. "Do you know who I know? Knowing is believing, don't you know? Or wouldn't you like to know?" He giggled, and then winked.

McPherson sighed. "Do you know a Robyn Viega?"

"Robyn? *Aaaahhhh, senorita, mi amore, seiteki.*" Stimulated by the SMARF, he rattled on, "Yeah I know her, pumped her, fucked her, violated her, spanked her, ate her, SMARFed her. What else you want?"

“Didn’t you two live together for a while?”

“Live?” He giggled again, racing from the SMARF. “Live. Sleep. Fuck. Shit. Piss. Eat. What else? Used to be. No more.”

“So how long’s it been since you’ve seen her?” McPherson asked as the young woman sitting next to Fane— bright red and blue hair spiking from her scalp— disconnected the tube from her IV and passed it on to him.

“Cool off. Slow down, Fifth-fuck,” Fane answered. “Gotta drain.” He twisted the tube into his IV.

Fane took a deep breath, holding it in, stiffening his abdomen as the SMARF flowed through his veins. His face turned from white to gray. His eyes squinted shut and his forehead furled. He held it in for nearly a minute. Then he pulled out the tube.

“Aaaahhh. Yesss.” He gasped, smiling. *“Down. Coming down. Very Nice. Nirvanarama...”* He looked up at McPherson. “Why you look at me like that? You judging me?”

“No, who am I to judge. But, I mean you gotta know what that stuff does to you.” McPherson answered, caught off guard.

“Sure you are!” Fane answered, his voice deeper and slower. “Positive. You’re *judging.* Without a doubt. And you know what I say to you?”

“What?”

“Shrivel snot!” Fane giggled. “Think this stuff does something to us. How about your people, Fifth-fuck? What do *they* do to us?

“Uh…” McPherson muttered.

“Look where you are,” Fane answered slowly, deliberately, a glow across his face. “Look around. Look real good. Twelfth PGU. PHA 432B. See it? Smell it? Feel it? People scrounging for anything in a place that smells like shit and looks even worse. You think there’s a… healthy fucking way out?”

“Well…” McPherson did look around. *Yeah, this is terrible,* he thought, *how can we let people live like this?*

“Lemme tell you something. There ain’t no way out, ‘cept this.” Fane pointed at his IV. “What do we got to look forward to, Fifth-fuck? Busting our balls so guys like you can live the way you want? Fuck it all. This shit keeps me sane, makes me wanna live.”

“So. You have any idea where Robyn is?”

“If I did, why should I tell *you?*”

“I guess if I were you I might say the same thing,” McPherson answered.

“You could never be me,” Fane said with a placid smile. “Don’t have the balls.”

“But maybe I can make it worth your while.”

"The almighty GCU, eh?" Fane giggled again. "The Upper PGUs' ultimate solution."

"Yeah, I guess that's the only thing I have that might be of interest to you."

"How much you thinkin'?" Fane almost whispered.

"Ten thousand."

"Twenty-five," Fane countered briskly. "And I don't even know exactly where she is, but can get you close."

"Done." McPherson reached into his pocket. "Got an e-let?"

"Yeah, somewhere." Fane wiggled his hand into the pocket of his faded, tattered jeans. "Yeah, got it. Here it is." Fane held up a one-inch square chip.

McPherson tapped on his e-let and pointed it toward Fane's, allowing the two devices to correspond, exchanging currency.

Fane stared at his e-let, and then looked up. "Man of your word, huh?"

"I mean what I say."

Fane looked up at him, and then giggled, "I have no fucking clue where she is, Fifth Fuck!"

* * *

23

Manhattan, NYCGAB, Pennfield Technologies Tower, Morning, November 29, 2052

"I think we may be onto something, Mr. MP," McPherson announced the next morning, standing in the entrance to JMP's private office.

Stoically, JMP raised his eyebrows. "Oh?"

"Yeah, I made contact with the girl's lover, or ex-lover, whatever. His name's Fane, Derek Fane. Druggie. The guy was incoherent, draining SMARF the entire time I was with him."

"That must have been abundantly productive." JMP replied.

"You're right. But I ran a report on him. In the past, the guy was high up in the Apexinators. That's probably why the girl had the tattoo. So, let's figure, he's practically brain-dead and she's still an Apexinator. So, I—"

"A brain-dead lead, is that the best you can do?" JMP scoffed.

"But wait a minute—"

Before JMP could respond, the voice of Suke Nagaguchi, JMP's assistant in Tokyo, flowed through the nano-transistor in his ear. *"JMP-san, Prime Minister Bonne-Saari would like to v-conf with you!"*

"The *Prime Minister?"* JMP stiffened in his seat. "When?"

"In exactly thirty minutes," she answered.

Immediately he began to sweat.

"I'm afraid you'll have to scoot, Bryan." JMP motioned towards the door.

"Got it, Mr. MP." McPherson rushed out of the office.

For a moment, JMP sat silent at his desk, breathing rapidly.

"Caught you off guard, didn't he?" Narc materialized and took a swift verbal jab at his other.

"What are you doing here, piling on?" JMP answered.

"Oh, I just thought we could have a little fun."

"What do you think he wants?" JMP asked.

"Perhaps he wants to try again." Narc winked. "Now wouldn't that be… ummm… *delicious?*" Narc touched his forefinger to his mouth and licked it.

"No, no, no." JMP scowled. "I will never engage in anything again with that self-aggrandizing wind-bag."

"Oh, come now." Narc giggled. "You were oh so close to the seat of ultimate power. And I do mean *close*. And I do mean *seat*."

"Stop it. Stop it right now," JMP ordered. "I think it's time for you to leave."

"Oh, dear other, you're such a bore." Narc dematerialized.

JMP simply could not believe Ibu Bonne-Saari would contact him, not after all their baggage. He could not even speculate what the subject might be, only increasing his anxiety. Was it something to do with their "thing" in college?

"Suke!" he barked out.

"Yes, Mr. MP," his assistant in Tokyo answered through his nano-transistor.

"Did the Prime Minister's office tell you the subject he wished to discuss?"

"No, but I can try to find out."

"Yes, please do."

JMP waited and waited, but nothing came from Suke. He was sure Bonne-Saari was withholding the subject intentionally, extracting pleasure from needling him so. Sitting alone in his office, speculating and fretting over the reason Bonne-Saari had requested the meeting, could not help but bring up distant, discomforting memories for JMP.

* * *

24

Sri Lanka: Bonne-Saari Capital District, The Apexia Institute, March–December 2029

Jimmy Mashimoto-Pennfield and Ibu Bonne-Saari first met as students at the Apexia Institute. A very exclusive university in the Bonne-Saari Capital District of Sri Lanka, the Apexia Institute was cobbled together by Izan Bonne-Saari shortly after his new global governmental structure was established. With his voracious appetite to have anything he touched be the uncompromised, absolute best, Bonne-Saari raided the very best academic talent from top universities worldwide to create his own institution, superior to all others.

Not only did students have to be highly intelligent to gain admission to the Apexia Institute— or *AI,* as students would refer to it— but they were also required to be a member of one of the named PGUs, *Apexia, Betamil, Chrysalix* or *Diamid.* Even the most brilliant students would be denied admission if they resided within the lower PGUs: flawed genes, even with a small glimmer of intellectual capacity, would never be tolerated at the Institute.

An architectural wonderland, the Institute's campus was the most beautiful, streamlined, intuitively-ergonomic testament to academic achievement ever imagined. Three crystalline 60-story spires, resembling flames grasping upward— each named for one of the Institute's core values: *Truth, Discovery, Experimentation*— surrounded the outer circumference of the Institute's circular courtyard. Across the campus, each building surpassed the other in aesthetic brilliance and functional elegance: the Arts and Humanities building, designed as a giant, layered bust of William Shakespeare, each layer a separate floor constantly rotating at different speeds and in different directions forming a bevy of interesting shapes until they rotated back to once again form Shakespeare's bust; the Life Sciences Building, a pure glass replica of a human heart seven stories tall, at night pulsing with a reddish phosphorescent glow seventy-two times per minute.

THE FIRST MEETING between Jimmy and Ibu Bonne-Saari occurred sometime in their freshman year at one of their astronomy lab sessions in the science building— a giant half-sphere dome of glass tilted at a forty-five-degree angle to the ground. While most of their classmates were simply amazed by the technology and ergonomics of the 200-inch reflector telescope sprouting out on demand from the building's glass exterior, both Jimmy and Bonne-Saari were pre-occupied with other things.

Initially, it was merely mutual intrigue: Jimmy Mashimoto-Pennfield, a scion of one of the world's wealthiest families, smart as a whip, his badgering questions forcing even the most gifted professors at times to strain for an answer. And Ibu Bonne-Saari, "heir to the throne," so to speak; continuously surrounded by a retinue of bodyguards, the young man was strikingly handsome, standing just over six feet tall with long blonde hair and blue eyes. Both Jimmy and Ibu saw something in the other they desired for themselves. For Ibu, it was Jimmy's intellectual might and cocksure confidence. For Jimmy, it was Ibu's power and fame and seductively attractive good looks. If only he could borrow those traits, those advantages, Jimmy figured, he could rule the world.

Soon they began to converse with one another, at first casually— an involuntary 'Hello' or 'How're you doing?' as their paths crossed on campus— until one day Bonne-Saari took it slightly further:

"Tennis player?" he asked as Jimmy strode by him one day on the marble walkway circling the Apexian Institute's central courtyard.

Jimmy stopped: "Huh?"

"You have the gait of a tennis player," the Prime Minister's son answered.

"The gait?"

"Sure. Of course."

"Well, I hardly ever play, but..."

"Don't worry, I'll teach you," Ibu Bonne-Saari answered.

THEIR FIRST DATE took place at the Institute's tennis courts with Ibu's three bodyguards keeping close watch. Jimmy was embarrassingly awkward as his volleys alternately sliced, skidded and orbited around the court. Luckily, his utter lack of ability in the sport did not seem to overwhelmingly impact Ibu's opinion of him. Actually, the son of the world's most powerful man derived a sort of thrill watching Jimmy— a person for whom he had feelings which he could not quite understand— struggle to impress him.

"Okay, so I suck," Jimmy said to Bonne-Saari as their court time mercifully ended.

"Oh, not to worry," Bonne-Saari answered, "everyone sucks at something."

"And what do you suck at?" Jimmy asked.

Silent, Bonne-Saari pondered for a moment. "I'll let you know as soon as I find out."

The young men shared a laugh.

THE TWO OF them grew closer by the day, latently sharing the desire for private time together, but not quite sure how to express or handle it. This mutual desire, however, faced three major obstacles: Ibu's bodyguards. Major Frank Marsh, Colonel Devon Koenig-Pastille and Lieutenant Ali Hernandez-Reposto; an American, a French woman and a Sri-Lankan national, the three had been assigned to Ibu since he was a young child and were considered a vital part of the Bonne-Saari household, their membership in the 5th PGU the only impediment keeping them from being considered a true part of the Bonne-Saari family.

It was Colonel Koenig-Pastille, the middle-aged French woman— matronly, with jet black hair and a perpetual smile that contradicted her world-class mastery of firearms— who first tuned into their vibes. She broached the subject with Ibu over breakfast one morning.

"So, you're quite fond of this Mashimoto-Pennfield, Ibu?"

Caught off-guard, Ibu's skin crawled up his back. "I think so, I mean um…," he proceeded cautiously, "…he's the only one who can relate to me as *me*, not the 'son of Izan Bonne-Saari'."

"And why do you think that is?" she queried him.

"I'm not sure," he answered pondering. "Maybe because he's from such a wealthy family, maybe because he's so brilliant and confident that me being me is no big deal to him."

"I think you may be correct," she said. "Perhaps you should spend more time with him, explore that idea?"

Defensively, Ibu shrugged. "Maybe."

DURING AN EVENING when she was on solitary shift, Koenig-Pastille allowed Ibu and Jimmy to spend time alone together in Ibu's off-campus quarters. Standing guard outside Ibu's door, she had no idea what might have transpired, but retrospectively could intuit their bond had grown stronger that evening. In the ensuing weeks they opted to take frequent advantage of her latitude.

Within several weeks, the two young men were inseparable. They fed off each other: Bonne-Saari's friendship elevated Jimmy's popularity on campus by mere association; Jimmy's intellectual capacity prodded Bonne-Saari to greater academic achievement than he ever could accomplish on his own. Yet there were times when Bonne-Saari, although bright, could not keep pace with Jimmy and other classmates. He struggled particularly hard in Plasma Astrophysics, falling behind most of the other students. He feared the class might be his downfall.

"I'm going to get my ass reamed," Ibu confided to Jimmy.

"Why's that?"

"I'm gonna be lucky to pull a C in that damn class and my old man, well, anything below an A and I get this blank, cold stare for a couple of months."

"So what'll he do if you get a C?"

"Don't know. I never have." Bonne-Saari answered. "But it's not going to be pretty, I can assure you. He may cut off my allowance."

"Ouch!"

"Have you talked to Professor Umtrick?" Jimmy asked. "Maybe you can persuade him to give you the benefit of the doubt."

"That's not going to work," Bonne-Saari answered. "He's not the type to do anything special for me just because I am who I am."

"Academic Integrity." Jimmy shook his head smiling. "So what do you need help with? How can we solve this?"

"My term-paper. I don't have a fucking clue what to write about or how to do it."

"No problem, I'll help you out."

WITH JIMMY'S AID, Bonne-Saari earned an A- in the class, not enough to spark all-out enthusiasm from the Prime Minister, but at least enough to keep him off his son's back. Indeed, the two young men had grown closer by the day. As the school year came to a close, neither Ibu nor Jimmy had any desire to be separated by ten-thousand miles of geography.

"Stay here for the summer," Bonne-Saari suggested.

"I'd like to, but I can't," Jimmy answered. "I have friends, family to see."

"Okay, how about this?" Ibu's mind churned. "Stay for a month. I'll arrange to get some no-show jobs through my dad and—"

"Then you can come with me to New York for the next month?"

"Exactly." Ibu extended his hand. *"Deal?"*

"Deal." Jimmy responded.

They shook on it.

FOR THE MOST PART, the two young men were left alone in Ibu's private quarters near a beautiful beach with a secluded cove on the northern tip of Sri Lanka. Ostensibly they were employed by the Apexian government as aides to diplomatic officials, however no one in the department had the courage to require them to report for work, nor were they expected to.

The boys spent the majority of their time on the beach during the day and at night cruising the evolving Sri Lankan nighttime scene: clubs catering to all types of music, lifestyle, sexual, and stimulation preferences. While not carousing around the hot spots of Sri Lanka, the two spent a fair amount of time discussing the world, and in effect— the universe. Jimmy's influence on Ibu during that summer helped mold him into a more introspective person, creating a lust for a deeper level of understanding of the world and a capacity to view issues from multiple points of view.

Jimmy saw very little of Ibu's parents. His mother, Jaqueline de Souza Bonne-Saari, was an ex-model and actress, still stunningly beautiful in her late fifties. Her marriage to Ibu's father was more a contractual relationship than a pairing of two people deeply in love. They began seeing each other as Izan Bonne-Saari first ascended to power. As the world's most powerful man, Bonne-Saari, although far from attractive, demanded the world's most beautiful woman as his prize.

Ibu was born six months before the wedding— a spectacle of unmitigated ostentation and grandeur— and was brought up by a series of nannies and bodyguards as Izan and Jaqueline rarely cared to occupy the same hemisphere after their first three years of marriage. Per their nuptial agreement, Jaqueline had her own residences in the south of France, in Antsiranana— the emerging resort for the rich and famous on Madagascar's northern coast— and Rio De Janeiro.

Jacqueline stopped by once, having jetted into Sri Lanka for a quick visit.

Jimmy found her quite civil and warm and was awed by her charm and beauty. It was quite different with Ibu's father.

"So, you're a member of the Pennfield family, eh?" the Prime Minister asked, his eyes buried in some document as he sat behind his large, regal desk, the first time Ibu introduced Jimmy to his father.

"Yes, indeed." Jimmy nodded respectfully.

"And what are those rapscallions up to now?" Izan Bonne-Saari asked.

"Excuse me." Jimmy cleared his throat. "*Rapscallions*, Sir?"

Ibu's face turned red out of embarrassment.

"Well, of course, your family's run roughshod over the rules for generations, have they not?" the Prime Minister countered. "Their arrogance in business is well known. And I speak from personal experience."

"I'm not sure where you're going with this, sir, but my family has done nothing you wouldn't have. I can assure you of that."

For the first time, Izan Bonne-Saari looked up from the document he was reading and nodded. "Well, so be it."

DURING THEIR NEXT month together in New York, the boys did just about everything they did in Sri Lanka except with an urban, cosmopolitan twist. With Jimmy's divorced parents in Japan and India, his Aunt Winnie assumed the role of host, lending them her Park Avenue apartment as a base of operations. Here, unlike Sri Lanka, the young men could gallivant from club to club without ever having to visit the same one twice. On the weekends, they would helicopter out to the eastern end of Long Island where Apexians, Betamilians and Chrysalixians would indulge themselves in the bounties of nature, the sea, and psychotropic pharmaceuticals. Having Ibu Bonne-Saari as part of the pair conferred a sense of spectacle and curiosity upon the two, opening doors that even the Pennfield name could not.

UPON THEIR ARRIVAL back on campus for fall semester, Ibu was summoned to his father's quarters. The room where his father conducted affairs of state was enormous and ostentatious, combining elements of old world classicism with a contemporary opulent flair: Greek columns and sparkling marble floors accented by terraced waterfalls provided the backdrop for shiny metallic sculptures, smooth wooden contours and a giant infinity pool jutting from a balcony. The Prime Minister's desk, a giant slab of semi-finished marble, shiny on top, rough on the edges and bottom, levitated three feet off the floor in front of a large panoramic curving glass wall with a breathtaking view of the ocean below.

"So I take it you enjoyed New York," Izan Bonne-Saari commented to his son.

"Yes, indeed, father."

"And this Pennfield boy?"

"It's Mashimoto-Pennfield, actually," Ibu answered.

"It'll always be Pennfield to me," Izan Bone-Saari countered. "And I've never trusted anyone from that family. They're no good, bad people. They once bankrupted a small bank I owned early in my career. Almost wiped me out."

"But we had a great time together, a fantastic time."

"So you like him, spend a great deal of time with him?"

"Yes, father." Ibu nodded.

"That's what worries me," his father stated vacantly.

Ibu flushed. "And by that you would mean—"

"Exactly what you think I mean," Izan stated. "I'm no fool. I'm no fool at all. I know what's been going on."

Shaking, Ibu gasped. "But father I— " He braced himself for an outburst.

"And I'm willing to look beyond it."

"You *what*?" Ibu responded, confused.

"Sometimes these things are part of life, growing pains, things one must get out of their systems before they mature into full adults. Sometimes these experiences can benefit one in later years."

Silent, Ibu nodded.

"And sometimes, they can come back to disgrace one's self," his father continued. "Understood?"

"Yes, sir." Ibu answered, half-stuttering.

"Which is why you must end this relationship now."

"What!" Ibu exclaimed, his face reddening.

"This relationship must end," his father commanded. "It has run its course."

"But, father—"

"No buts," his father answered. "It's over, do you hear me?"

Shaking all over, Ibu nodded.

"Over and done with, understood?"

Ibu nodded once again.

"I know this will be difficult for you," Izan Bonne-Saari said to his son, "but you must be strong. You will be Prime Minister one day. You must be strong."

Ibu's eyes welled with tears.

BY INTUITION OR PERHAPS APPREHENSION, Jimmy sensed something was not right. There were no concrete clues, somehow Jimmy just felt it. When he walked over to Ibu's quarters after class the first day of the new semester, he was not completely surprised by the reception.

After a few sharp taps at the door, Major Marsh, the senior bodyguard in Ibu's detail, opened the door.

"Uh, hi, Frank, I'm here to see Ibu." Jimmy proceeded through the doorway.

Marsh, a tall, thick man, thrust his arm across the opening between the door and its frame. "Ibu can't see you right now."

"Really?" Jimmy answered, confused. "Well, tell him I'll be back at—"

"He can't see you at all today."

"Are you sure about that?" Jimmy asked.

"Sure as I could ever be," Frank answered.

"What the fuck?" Jimmy's face drooped. "What's happening?"

"He just can't see you," Marsh answered tersely.

"Tomorrow?" Jimmy asked.

"I don't think that'll work either," Marsh responded.

"Huh?"

"He just can't see you right now. That's all I can say."

AT FIRST, Jimmy tried to be optimistic. Perhaps something was going on with Ibu's father. Perhaps security was temporarily tightened. After all, Prime Minister Izan Bonne-Saari obsessed over tight security, at times to the point of paranoia. Jimmy tried to phone and message Ibu several times and received no response. But that could just be part of the heightened security, he surmised. Perhaps all means of communication were being blocked. He waited two days and then tapped at Ibu's door once again.

Again, Marsh answered.

Steadfastly, Jimmy announced, "I'm here to see—"

"He still can't see you." Marsh interrupted him.

"So then when?"

"I have no idea," Marsh answered. "Maybe never."

"But—"

"That's all I can say."

INSTANTLY, Jimmy's stomach tightened into a burning knot. As he walked back to his dorm room, he obsessed over it. *It certainly could not be true*, he thought. *Certainly, there was an explanation.* But to be thrust from the embrace of a deep and meaningful relationship into this— some sort of weird zone of uncertainty, even if only temporarily— placed him in a dark, unanchored place, somewhere he never anticipated being. The abruptness of it, the unexpectedness of it, the unfathomableness of it, sapped the vitality from his spirit, stripping him of any enthusiasm.

The next day was a struggle. He battled long and hard to push himself up from bed. He struggled to dress himself. He sleepwalked around campus, devoid of emotion, barely attentive in his classes. Gone was his appetite, his thirst for knowledge and his desire for any form of human interaction. There was only one thing in the universe that could repel this dark shadow and he— one who prided himself as always being in control— could not control it, not one bit. His mind, hijacked from normalcy, could only focus on one singular subject, his soulmate, Ibu Bonne-Saari.

Two days later, they finally connected.

The incident occurred near the university's central courtyard. Surrounded by all three bodyguards, Ibu proceeded cross-campus en route to his next class. Passing right by, Jimmy stopped short and called out to him. From that point everything happened so quickly, a blur. Jimmy was sure, absolutely sure, he saw Ibu nod and take a half step in his direction. But before that half step became a full step, Marsh yanked him back then pushed him forward assuring he would not break ranks. The entourage continued onward.

Jimmy hoped, desperately hoped, that small nod in his direction was some sort of sign, an indication that Ibu's affections for him had not waned. Yet, that was not enough, just a tease. Jimmy wanted more.

He *had* to re-connect with Ibu, just had to. He obsessed over it. His persistence— his single-minded focus on one thing, that one sole object of his affection— brought him to a place he didn't want to be; a place, in retrospect, he would never want to go again. He could not get Ibu out of his mind. His usual strict focus on academics evaporated, replaced by an insistence to always be near, forever to be in, the presence of Ibu Bonne-Saari.

Jimmy would camp himself outside Ibu's classrooms, drawing stares from Marsh and the other bodyguards. He would walk by Ibu's quarters whenever he could, slowing himself to a snail's pace as approached the building, his eyes darting from window to window as he hoped to catch a short glimpse of his dear Ibu. Whenever Jimmy did get a chance to see him, their interaction was limited to awkward stares at a distance. Somehow, Jimmy sensed Ibu wanted to be back together with him as well. Yet, there was nothing concrete to support Jimmy's feelings, just wisps of pure hope.

Until one day.

He had parked himself in the hallway outside the lecture hall where Ibu was attending class. As the door creaked open, Major Marsh stuck his head out, scoping the area. Marsh's face turned stern and hard when he spotted Jimmy. As the class let out, Marsh yanked at Ibu's arm, pulling him in a direction away from the spot where Jimmy was waiting. Ibu pulled back and said something to Marsh. They went back and forth for almost a minute, deliberating over something, then Ibu walked towards Jimmy, Marsh's eyes focused sharply on his every step.

Jimmy's heart pumped when it became apparent that Ibu was walking straight towards him. He went flush.

"Ibu, how…"

"You've got to stop, Jimmy," Ibu said.

"*What?* What do you mean?"

"You've got to stop stalking me," Ibu continued.

"Stalking? But I'm not…"

"Yes, you are," Ibu interrupted. "And you can get yourself in trouble, big trouble, if you continue."

Shaking Jimmy answered: "But you and I, we were—"

"That's in the past, over," said Ibu. "And it will never happen again. So accept it, will you?"

"Ibu…"

Abruptly, Ibu walked away.

THAT EVENING, Jimmy sought out Devon Koenig-Pastille, the bodyguard who had first encouraged their relationship. If anyone would talk to him, give him insight, it would be her. He caught up to her as she was walking towards the bodyguard's quarters.

"I shouldn't be talking to you," she said, walking brusquely.

"I know but this is important, really important," he responded. "Ibu and I, we had something. You saw it. You know it. And now—"

She stopped and turned towards him. "Jimmy, I know. This is part of life. It hurts, you wish you could make it go away, but it's beyond your control."

"But we were so, so close."

"Yes, you were."

"We *have* to get back together again. We just *have* to..."

She looked him in the eyes. "I can assure you that will never be."

"But why?" He struggled to keep his composure.

"I can't say much," she said. "But it's beyond your control, beyond his control."

"The Prime Minister?"

"I can't say anything more." She walked away.

THE FINALITY of it pierced Jimmy's heart.

His depression and blind hope now turned to anger and disgust. He was mad at everyone, mad at the world, but especially mad at Ibu Bonne-Saari and that pompous-ass father of his. Jimmy's lust for Ibu's affection now turned into a lust for revenge. He was Jimmy Mashimoto-Pennfield, heir to one of the world's greatest and wealthiest families, a genius, bound for greatness. He would not allow that scum of a son of a bogus Prime Minister to fuck up his life, not now, not ever.

He mulled over it for days, going through possibility after possibility, until he came upon it: that one thing, one action he could take that would knock Ibu Bonne-Saari off his faux pedestal, expose him for what he was.

Three weeks before the end of fall semester, he took action.

JIMMY WALKED into the university administration building and announced himself to the receptionist: "I have a two o'clock with Chancellor Espinoza."

The receptionist examined his screen. "Yes, of course. Jimmy Mashimoto-Pennfield, correct?"

"Yes, that's me."

"Let me check with him."

"YOU DO REALIZE what you're saying is a very, very serious charge," the Chancellor, a stately man with dark eyes, an olive complexion and a pointy goatee, stared at Jimmy from across his desk.

"One hundred percent true," Jimmy answered.

"Accusing someone of academic fraud carries with it very serious consequences."

"I'm aware of that, sir."

"If true, Ibu Bonne-Saari could be expelled from the university. And for you, that would mean probation."

"I understand completely. I've thought long and hard about it, Chancellor, and I know I'm doing the right thing."

"So you said you have proof?"

"Yes, I have a time-coded file from my computer with my encrypted FRP scan."

"And why didn't you first go to Professor Umtrick?" the Chancellor asked.

"You have to understand, sir," Jimmy began, "this was very difficult for me. And, well, his father is…"

"You do realize that means nothing. The academic integrity of this institution will not be compromised for anyone."

"I understand that, sir." Jimmy nodded.

"And this file you say you have?"

"Here," Jimmy fingered his e-let, "I'll send it to you."

The chancellor looked over to his screen and scanned its contents. "Yes, I just received it."

"Take a look, the evidence is all there."

"That I will." Chancellor Espinoza responded slowly, pondering. "That I will."

ONCE CHANCELLOR ESPINOZA determined the veracity of Jimmy's file, Ibu was summoned to his office. The young man sweat as Espinoza confronted him with the evidence. He was told his case would be brought up before an Academic Standards Board and that he would have the opportunity to defend himself. Although great effort was put into keeping the charges confidential, leaks soon got out. Two days after the meeting between Ibu and Chancellor Espinoza, the AI student newspaper ran a damning headline:

IBU BONNE-SAARI ACCUSED OF ACADEMIC FRAUD

The moment the news reached the Prime Minister, his reaction was swift and predictable. *"Get me that God-damned Chancellor on the phone. Right now,"* he screamed to his assistants in the Apexian Tower.

Immediately, the Chancellor's face appeared on a holoscreen.

"Yes, Mr. Prime Minister," Espinoza looked up, apparently unsurprised.

"Tell me what the hell is going on over there," Izan Bonne-Saari shouted.

"Well, unfortunately, sir, there appears to be evidence that your son broke our standards of academic integrity," the Chancellor answered calmly.

"And you're taking that Pennfield kid's words over his?"

"We've analyzed the evidence quite thoroughly," Espinoza said. "If you'd like to see it?"

"No! Just do something about it!" Bonne-Saari demanded.

"We are. We will be holding a hearing with our Academic Standards Board—"

"What!" Bonne-Saari blasted. "Let me tell you one thing, Mr. Espinoza, there will be no hearing with your academic standards board."

"But Mr. Prime Minister," Espinoza countered, "academic integrity is our must cherished asset. We simply cannot—"

"Bullshit!" Bonne-Saari interrupted. "You most certainly can."

"But think of how it would make us look? Valuing family status over true academic achievement."

"I don't care *how* it makes you look," Bonne-Saari stated. "Make something up. Just make it go away."

Espinoza paused momentarily, then answered softly, "I don't think I'll be able to do that."

"Is that so."

"Yes, sir."

"Then I'm afraid, my friend," Bonne-Saari said smoothly, "we'll have to find someone who will."

With that, their conversation ended.

ALMOST INSTANTANEOUSLY, the story got out to the major global media. For several days, boosted by an otherwise slow news cycle, the story dominated all media outlets. Paparazzi camped out across the street from Ibu's quarters feasting on any opportunity to get video of him as he proceeded back and forth from class. One news organization bribed a student who worked in the Registrar's office with quite a hefty payoff to provide a copy of Ibu's class schedule. It became so overwhelming that Marsh ordered Ibu to stay isolated in his quarters until the controversy blew over.

ISOLATION TOOK its toll on Ibu, but it was nothing compared to the wrath of his father.

"You see? You see," Izan Bonne-Saari blasted at his son. "I told you to stay away from that Pennfield kid. Those people have a long history of no good."

"But father—"

"No buts!" the Prime Minister exclaimed. "We can take solace in the fact

that I stopped it before he could do further damage. At least this one I can control."

"How?" Ibu asked his father.

"There will be no academic standards hearing. The charges will be dismissed. They will be attributed to a misunderstanding between two former friends. That's it, over and done with!"

"How will you, or how *did* you do that?"

"I have my methods," Izan Bonne-Saari said. "Now make me one pledge."

"Yes, father?"

"Someday you'll get back at that Pennfield kid. Not now. It wouldn't hurt enough. Wait until he does something to distinguish himself— and he will, I'm sure of it— and then bring him down a very steep slope. Very slowly and very painfully. He damn near ruined your reputation and, by association, mine as well. He deserves to become an example, he deserves to suffer."

Ibu nodded. "Yes, father."

THE NEXT DAY the communications office of The Apexia Institute made two announcements. The first regarded Ibu Bonne-Saari. In a few brief sentences, the office announced that charges of academic fraud against Ibu Bonne-Saari would be dropped, the Chancellor's Office having determined that the incident was the result of a feud between Bonne-Saari and his former friend, Jimmy Mashimoto-Pennfield. As a result of attempting to perpetuate the hoax, Mashimoto-Pennfield would be placed on academic probation for a year. The second announcement was the unexpected "retirement" of Chancellor Humberto Espinoza at the rather early age of fifty-five.

Three months later, Espinoza was found dead at his home as a result of some mysterious sudden illness.

UPON IZAN BONNE-SAARI'S death in 2042, Ibu was immediately installed as the second Prime Minister of the Apexia nation, a succession carefully orchestrated by his father. The challenges Ibu Bonne-Saari faced in terms of maintaining the governmental structure were dwarfed by the accomplishments of his father in establishing the PGU system.

By the time Ibu took over, the job was pretty much perfunctory: his nation consisted of only 40,000 citizens, yet they were the wealthiest people on earth and at times, could be both petty and eccentric; there were no taxes as the needs of Apexia were financed by earnings on the exorbitant entrance fees citizens had to pay. Furthermore, Ibu Bonne-Saari's government had so much power— including an unconquerable robotic army and control of the GCU, the worldwide currency— the lower PGUs were not about to challenge Apexia's pre-eminent global position.

Yet there were whispers, and Ibu Bonne-Saari could hear them at times. Constantly compared to his father, he always came up short. He was relatively intelligent, but his father was absolutely brilliant. In hushed circles he was sometimes referred to as the "Mannequin Prime Minister" both reflective of his attractive appearance— inherited without doubt from his mother— and his lack of the panache, brainpower and exuberance of his father.

* * *

25

Manhattan, NYCGAB, Pennfield Technologies Tower, Morning, November 29, 2052

It was time.

JMP tensed up. He flicked a button on the side of his watch, activating his contact lenses. Immediately, the contacts shut out all external light and placed him in the v-conf, a virtual conference room where the body, face and gestures of himself and his fellow conferee would be simulated as if they were occupying the same room. The figure of Ibu Bonne-Saari, Prime Minister of the Apexia PGU, immediately materialized before him.

"Mr. Prime Minister, how are you today?" JMP nodded towards Bonne-Saari.

"Please, please…" Bonne-Saari raised his hand, "We go back way too far. Call me Ibu."

"Sure." JMP answered, still suspicious of the motive behind Bonne-Saari's informality.

"Jimmy, it's been awhile since those days back at AI."

"That's an understatement." JMP answered, making every effort to avoid his eyes.

"Indeed, it does *feel* like centuries ago." Bonne-Saari's tone momentarily derailed JMP's focus. He let himself lock eyes with Ibu, who held his gaze and smiled wryly as he twisted the knife. "And, yes, while our days there might not have ended as we would like, let's put that behind us, shall we?"

"Sure." JMP mumbled. For a moment, Ibu said nothing. Now JMP's mind began to spin at hyper-speeds, growing skeptical again, speculating over what Bonne-Saari wanted from him. "So, what is it you'd like to discuss today?" JMP deftly changed the direction of their conversation.

"I've been very intrigued about what I've been hearing about your cryonics initiative."

"Really."

JMP was relieved. At least this subject of interest was something other than their past relationship. But a new fear was rising in its place; the cryonics initiative was Pennfield Technologies' landmark project, its most important ever. Over one thousand virtually-dead but nonetheless wealthy Apexians and Betamilians had paid mightily to put their bodies in long-term frozen storage with the hope of reconstitution in the years to come— a form of virtual immortality. The revenue potential was enormous. The project was a highly sensitive, ambitious undertaking. Government intrigue could spell disaster if it signified forced allegiances or goals JMP was loath to support. And it wasn't just government, it was *him, Ibu.*

"So, you're ready to be frozen, are you?" JMP quipped.

"Not quite yet," the Prime Minister bantered back. "But I'm always intrigued by the ingenuity of geniuses like yourself. People like you are Apexia's greatest natural resource."

JMP understood that in some sense, the Prime Minister was not exaggerating. The one final piece— the key that would unlock the treasure trove of fame and riches for JMP and his company, as well as affirm Bonne-Saari's pet phrase: *Apexian Exceptionalism*— was the development of the self-replicating, molecule-sized nano-machines, a form of microorganism which would infiltrate all the billions of cells of the preserved bodies. One-by-one, these nano-machines would methodically repair tissue-damage caused either by disease prior to death, or by the freezing process.

"You're much too kind, Ibu." JMP responded. He feigned modesty as his mind again slipped, ruminating in thoughts of their summer together— in its moments of intimacy— before things got ugly. "So," he said, attempting to shake it off. "What would you like to know?"

"Everything," Bonne-Saari answered. "Give me a topline and we'll take it from there."

"Well, as I'm sure you know, we have been freezing human bodies prior to the instant of death and storing them in our facility for two years now."

"The Egg?"

"Yes."

"I hear that's a marvelous structure, one of the finest architectural and engineering feats of all time."

"Why thank you." Now, JMP worried that Bonne-Saari was being much too nice, overly flattering, even. *He must really want something badly.* "Here, let me show it to you."

JMP flicked his wrist and a holosphere materialized.

Its shape was perfectly oval, its gold color majestically reflecting the mid-day sun as it levitated peacefully 300 feet above the countryside. An engineering and architectural marvel, the Egg hovered over the landscape like a modern-day Sphinx, though only a select few knew its real purpose as the holding tank for several thousand preserved human bodies.

Usually un-impressionable, Bonne-Saari gazed at the image in awe. "That's marvelous, Jimmy. If there's a better testament to Apexian Exceptionalism I haven't seen it."

"Thanks, Ibu," Jimmy tried to repress a blush while maintaining a curt, even disinterested expression. "Its state-of-the-art technology was specifically designed to store and revive thousands of canisters of preserved bodies all based upon Dr. Li-Pin's latest research. And, of course, the security is also truly state-of-the-art. I have a holovid of a recent de-levitation procedure. Would you like to see?"

"Please," Bonne-Saari answered.

"The reason the Egg is levitated at all is to restrict access to the facility other than by authorized PT personnel. As you can see, any sub-100 workers must enter by boarding a levi-jet outside the security perimeter, and then they must be jetted up to the entrance-hole in the northeast quadrant."

"De-levitation is a precautionary maintenance procedure performed monthly," JMP continued. "The bottom third of the Egg is filled with millions of gallons of water acting as a diamagnet which is repelled by moderate-temperature superconductors imbedded in the structure's giant marble platform. In order to achieve de-levitation, water is slowly drained, gradually lessening the repulsion by the superconductors. Let's watch." JMP pointed to the holoscreen hovering over the v-conf table.

The Prime Minister watched in awe as fine sprays of water fell from micro-holes in the Egg's golden exterior and the giant structure slowly descended to its resting platform.

"What can I say?" Bonne-Saari stated. "I must see it one day."

"That can definitely be arranged," said JMP. He noticed a smug glint in Ibu's eyes and corrected himself, "it *probably* can, I mean." There was nothing that JMP wanted less than to escort Prime Minister Ibu Bonne-Saari on a private tour of the Egg. The project was too critical, and Ibu had lost JMP's trust long ago. He hoped that Bonne-Saari's comment was just conversational palaver.

"Now I can understand why you're extracting such an extremely high price point for the privilege of immortality."

"Yes, we charge 7.5 million GCUs up front to be preserved and put in storage."

"Congratulations."

"Yeah, it's a high price, but still not enough to cover our investment in R&D."

"I understand."

"We've had Dr. Stavros Li-Pin conducting our research in an undisclosed location for several years."

"That would have been on the Island of Belkoskiy, correct?

"Yes, correct." Inside, JMP growled: Bonne-Saari flaunting his knowledge of the undisclosed location in the Siberian Arctic was an unabashed proclamation of his all-encompassing power, the total omniscience of his reign, an attempt to keep JMP in his place.

"And what a coup it was to lure the great Dr. Li-Pin away from his prestigious chair at the University of Belgrade."

"He's being rewarded handsomely."

"I would hope so," Bonne-Saari responded. "The value of his expertise in nano-biotechnology is incapable of being measured by money."

"I would agree."

"And how is his research progressing?"

"We recently moved his laboratory to the Egg because we believe he is getting quite close to a breakthrough."

"When?"

JMP could detect a hint of excitement in the way Bonne-Saari sat up straight in his chair.

"It could be tomorrow, it could be in three years," JMP answered. He hesitated, then divulged more. "He has already developed a strain of self-replicating nano-microorganism machines that can repair tissue and cell damage. Now it just comes down to achieving sufficient velocity of self-replication."

"How interesting."

"Yes, we think he's very, very close."

"Are you sure your financial projections will cover your vast investment?"

"Well to put it simply, we're already generating north of 5 billion GCUs per year from revenues of the bodies previously frozen and stored in the Egg. Admittedly, that's a very high price point, but eminently affordable by all Apexians and most Betamilians."

"Betamilians?" Ibu Bonne-Saari raised his eyebrow.

"Yes, the whole project depends upon having a broad marketplace. That's why we're experimenting with partial preservation."

"And what would that be?"

"Quite simply, we no longer have to preserve an entire body; it works by just freezing someone's head. Amazing, isn't it?"

"I don't understand," Bonne-Saari shifted in his seat, pursed his lips and stared at the virtual ceiling in deep thought.

"Basically," JMP interjected, "within the next several years, Dr. Li-Pin's cloning technology will allow us to reconstitute the brain and facilitate its growth of a new body. Or, we can even digitize the neuronal content, upload it to a storage device, and then download it back into a completely new body altogether. Think about it. Suppose a physically gifted sub-100 suffers from some incurable disease, but his or her body remains basically intact. We can freeze the sub-100's body, cure the disease that caused its death and then download a frail Apexian's neuronal content into the body. That not only gives our Apexian a second lease on life, but a second lease on a better life."

"Intriguing…" Bonne-Saari tweaked his chin.

"And, most significantly, it opens up the door for re-annuitization pricing,"

"Are you trying to baffle me with your arcane business terms, Jimmy?"

"Sorry about that," JMP continued. "Right now we charge a lucrative premium up front for cryonic preservation, a service charge for each year the canister is in storage."

"Yes, but by definition, your market is extremely limited, correct?"

"You're right, and that's a good point," JMP answered. "When reconstitution becomes possible— and as I said, we think it will be, be soon— that will trigger the back-end fees, which will be our first windfall."

"You mean, there's more?"

"Yes," JMP answered curtly. "After we prove to the world that we can restore whole bodies, that's when partial preservation will kick in. It'll save us money, lower the price-point, and grow the market substantially. Then with re-annuitization we can exponentialize the business model."

"Very impressive, JMP. But, re-annuitization?"

"Re-annuitization boils down to charging substantially less up front— thereby increasing the size of the market significantly— in return for a percentage of a person's income or assets for all years lived post re-constitution. When the market develops we can even offer full or partial preservation for free in return for a larger percentage of post re-constitution earnings. The market would explode."

"You mean you'll allow *anyone* to be preserved?" Bonne-Saari leaned in towards JMP.

"Well," JMP began, "at current price-points the market is de-facto restricted to Apexians and Betamilians. With partial preservation, we can open it up to Chrysalixians and Diamids and, perhaps even— " he caught himself too late, "—um…5th PGUs…"

Bonne-Saari's bronze face turned sour. "Fifth PGUs? Isn't that stretching it a bit?"

"Well they'd be paying us just to *live*, not a bad idea, don't you think?"

Suddenly, Bonne-Saari's reason for the v-conf was becoming very clear.

Bonne-Saari leaned in once again. "Jimmy, your business acumen is without peer. But I must say, people around me who have heard rumblings about your project have questioned exactly how wide your market should be. We certainly don't want to perpetuate mediocrity beyond its natural lifespan, do we?"

"Well we certainly wouldn't allow sub-100s to—"

Bonne-Saari's scowl cut him off mid-sentence.

"I see your point," JMP recovered quickly. He knew all too well that behind Bonne-Saari's apparent civility and politeness, he held a very sharp dagger. Arguing with him would only be detrimental to the cryonics initiative. "When we get to that point, I will consult with you and your advisors before we do anything. I will always welcome your counsel, Ibu."

"I certainly appreciate that." Bonne-Saari looked away for a moment, then turned directly to JMP. "But,"

"There's something more you'd like to discuss?"

Silently, Bonne-Saari nodded.

After another long pause, the Prime Minister leaned across the virtual conference table. His face turned harsh and angular. "My friend,"

"Yes?" JMP shivered inside.

"I have something very important to discuss with you."

"Of course. Of course," JMP obliged.

"This is an extremely sensitive matter and any leaks of the information I am about to disclose will lead to severe consequences."

JMP swallowed hard. "I understand."

"I am only divulging this to you because I hold you in such high regard.

You are one of Apexia's very best. I have seen what I needed to see and I am certain of my path going forward."

"Why thank you. So…"

Bonne-Saari leaned in and softened his whisper even more: "My father's death was reported ten years ago…"

"Of course, his funeral was a massive event."

"Indeed it was," Bonne-Saari responded. "But sometimes perception defies reality."

"I'm not sure what you mean, Ibu."

Bonne-Saari whispered again, "The body disposed of in his coffin was a wax replica."

"What!? No. A *wax rep*—".

"Per my father's wishes, his body was cryonically frozen at the moment just before death," Bonne-Saari said. "He was a man who had everything he ever wanted except immortality."

"But— his *legacy,* how he built Apexia, and this whole system of government, this world, *that's* immortal."

"You need not patronize me, Jimmy," Bonne-Saari responded curtly. "My father wanted real immortality, in the flesh."

"Okay."

"As I said, the freezing of his corpse was highly secretive. We commissioned some specialists to do it under threat of death if anything got out. They used what was considered state-of-the-art procedures at the time, but I would suspect that you, Dr. Li-Pin and your group are eons ahead with your technology."

"I would hope so." JMP smirked.

"So. I would like to move his remains to the Egg and have him cared for under the direct supervision of Dr. Li-Pin and successfully revived at the proper time."

Mashimoto-Pennfield hesitated.

"What? Are you not comfortable with the idea?" Bonne-Saari asked.

"It's just that… that it might put undue pressure on us so early in our development," JMP answered.

"So, are you daring to say 'no'?" Bonne-Saari scowled.

"No. It's just that you sprung this on me from out of nowhere. It's shocking news and I just have to process…"

"I can tell you this. I will help you in any way possible if you do me this favor."

"That would be very nice, but—"

"We need not mince words, Jimmy," Bonne-Saari stated. "My intelligence team is superb. And I did hear you may have a little issue to take care of. Am I correct?

"I'm not sure if it's at that point yet," JMP answered.

"Well what if it was? Wouldn't my help be valuable?"

"Yes, yes, indeed, Ibu," JMP answered.

"Then it's a deal."

Reluctantly, JMP nodded.

"So when can we make the transfer?" Bonne-Saari asked.

"Whenever you're ready, Mr. Prime Minister."

"My aides will be in touch." With that, the Prime Minister's figure dematerialized.

JMP SAT at his desk gazing across the skyline, his heart pounding. The stakes were already sky-high for the successful execution of the cryonics initiative.

Now they were even higher.

* * *

26

Location Unknown, November 29, 2052

Robyn Viega rubbed her eyes and drowsily pushed herself up from her prone position on the giant bed. Although she had been in this hidden sanctuary several weeks, each morning as she awakened she was still surprised by her surroundings. Years of waking up in a cold flat on the lower east side, or in a cement cube in PHA432B, or wherever she could scrounge a place to stay had lowered her morning expectations.

In some ways, she reveled in her new environs, a marble guest house on a beautifully landscaped hillside in some remote, undisclosed location. Her room was spacious and elegant: marble floors, mahogany furniture, large French doors overlooking a terrace leading out to an alluring storybook garden. The emerald green grass sparkled in the morning sun, vibrant red and yellow roses clung to their pristine white trellises, tall perfectly trimmed hunter-green hedges draped the secret garden in seclusion, and the beautifully sparkling pool radiated with a buoyant shade of reflective blue, water gurgling down its rocky wall.

To her, the last few weeks were a blur. Something happened that night in the East Village. Something compelled her to show up at *that* tavern, at *that* time and approach *that* man. Usually adept at self-restraint, all shackles of resistance melted away as she allowed him to seduce her. *Or did she seduce him?* The scene in that disheveled smelly apartment soon turned into a nightmare. That man— what was it, *a Captain of Industry* she called him?—

brutalized her, mistook her for an Apexinator, whipped her, made her submit. Then just as quickly as he had appeared earlier, he fled— appearing shocked by his own rage and fear— and abandoned her, near-lifeless, bruised and humiliated.

She had first woken up here— whisked away, somehow— to this wonderful, secluded cottage overlooking the gardens. But she was isolated. A man, tan-skinned, dressed in white, his chest muscles gleaming and firm under his shirt, his feet in leather sandals, and his jet-black hair cut neatly, would show up now and then and ask her what she needed. He called himself Pascal. She never asked for much. Something to eat, some fruit maybe. Pascal would then leave and return with an abundant basket of pineapple, oranges, kiwis, bananas, cashews, almonds and other exotic fruits and nuts, leave them on a table out on the terrace and, then, swiftly depart. She had no way to summon him, but he always seemed to appear at the right time, even anticipating her need before she realized it.

She loved her new-found sanctuary, but even several weeks in paradise could not make up for her isolation. Soon, she began to long for her previous surroundings, her previous friends. It bothered her. Here, after all these years she lands in paradise and after a few weeks wishes she was back in her own earthly hell. She constantly challenged herself: *How did she get here? Why couldn't she remember?*

Alone, in her secluded paradise, she had nothing more to do than dwell upon it minute after minute, hour after hour, day after day. *If only she could contact Derek.* He had always been a constant source of comfort and advice. When things were good between them, they were *really good.* She smiled, remembering the day they got high together and dared themselves to get matching Apexinator tattoos on their butt-cheeks. For a while, she wore it like a badge. But then, it became a curse, a trigger for a raving madman who had his way with her. And now this— caught in some neverland somewhere south of heaven and north of hell. Derek would be able to help her, she was sure— *the old Derek,* the one before SMARF replaced her as his one true love. If only she could have the old Derek back. Right here, right now. She sighed, realizing her wish was empty and barren.

* * *

27

PAWVA GAB: PHA 432B, December 2, 2052

His eyes opened to a kaleidoscopic rendering of reality. The shapes and colors were there, sort of, but their clarity had degraded into patchy, fuzzy blotches. His throat was dry and scratchy, his lips encrusted, his body clammy. Without expending an ounce of energy, he sweat uncontrollably. Derek Fane's six-day SMARF bender had ended; his abrupt landing back into the harsh world of reality resulted in a sharp, clamoring thud.

His head stung, his ears throbbed, his eyes burned. He wiggled awkwardly, pushing against the steel floor with both arms, then flipped up on his knees. The large excavation bucket swirled around him, abetting his dizziness. He struggled to steady himself, to regain his balance, but his surroundings continued to swirl and swirl.

"Derek! *Derek!*" Lola, his SMARF-mate with her strange orange skin, blue and red spiked hair and in-your-face brusqueness, tugged on his shoulder.

"Huh?" he responded, unanchored.

"Get up, will ya?" She yanked again with a firmer tug.

Finally, the swirling of his surroundings slowed, no longer tilting, righting themselves into sync with himself and his faculties as he queasily regained his bearings.

Slowly, he recovered. Leaning over, he clutched his stomach, then looked up. *"Lo?"* Recognizing Lola, he reached out to her, then smiled broadly and giggled. *"What the fuck? Was that good or what? Got more uh that shit?"*

"Slow down, big boy."

"Huh?"

"You fucked up. Fucked up bad. Goin' off blabberin' to that fifth fuck?"

"Fifth fuck?"

"You was so fucked up, you tole him all sortsa shit."

"What? What did I tell?"

"All your disgustin' behind-the-door sex shit with Robyn."

"Robyn?"

"And lotsa more shit, too."

His head shook as he tried to focus. "Wha- wha- what he wanna know about Robyn?"

"She missin'. He was trying to find her."

"Was he a cop?"

"Kiddin' me. Ain't no cops that're fifth fucks. Seventh, sixth best."

"Anyone know?"

"Not a soul. No one's seen her in months."

"Something wrong?"

"Who knows? All I know is some fifth fuck with GCUs is lookin' fer her so somethin' must be up. Gave you 20K."

"20K of what?"

"GCUs, dumb-ass. Check your e-let."

He wiggled his hand into his pocket and pulled out the small device. He clicked a small button on its side and his still fuzzy eyes attempted to focus. His head gyrated as he tried to lock onto the number. "Holy shit!" he exclaimed. "Where'd this come from."

"Like I told you, from the fifth fuck."

"Why they want *her* so bad? She okay?"

"Who the fuck knows."

Fane stared out to the bright sunlight beaming in from outside the large excavation bucket. His head shook as he thought things through. Then, abruptly, he looked up and turned towards Lola:

"Gotta find her."

"Now that's something I wanna see."

"Why you laughing?" he asked.

"You ain't gonna find shit."

* * *

TIME FRAME: 2007

28

Boothbay Harbor, Maine, Afternoon, March 30, 2007

Ed Swann poked his head through the doorway of Pennfield's bedroom-study. "Chris, I want you to meet someone."

"And who is this lovely creature I would have the pleasure of meeting?" Pennfield eyed the attractive, middle-aged woman with long shapely legs and rich, flowing gray hair standing behind Swann.

"Chris Pennfield, meet Dr. Brenda Altieri."

"A pleasure. A pleasure indeed." Pennfield smiled broadly. "Can I offer you something to drink?"

"No. No. I'm fine Dr. Pennfield. But I'd prefer being referred to as a *woman*, 'Doctor,' or even a *person.* Certainly not a *creature.*"

"Indeed, my *faux pas*." Pennfield tipped his glass in her direction. "And please, call me Chris." Altieri's presence seemed to bring out the inner Christopher, reviving the remnants of his flirtatious former self. "And what do you specialize in my dear?"

" *'Doctor.'* Of Psychiatry," she answered matter-of-factly.

"So you're here to analyze me?" Pennfield asked.

"No, I'm here to help you," she answered back.

"Well if anyone were capable of helping me I would certainly hope it would be you." He sipped his sauterne, as they entered his study and sat down.

"I don't know how to take that."

"Take it as it was intended, my dear Doctor, as an extreme and gracious compliment." Pennfield raised his glass in her direction once more.

"Thanks."

"So tell us what happened that night you think you saw Ship, Chris." Swann quickly changed the subject.

"Well, as I told you, it began with one of those dastardly paralysis attacks," Pennfield announced.

"Sleep paralysis?" Altieri asked.

"Yes, precisely. And after I thought I had recovered and it was over and done with, I saw an apparition of Ship right near my window and he spoke to me in French."

"Sleep paralysis is not uncommon, not uncommon at all. In fact, it's just the opposite of somnambulism, sleep-walking, except in this case the mind is awake and the body asleep. And it's not unusual for a victim to experience some sort of apparition during these episodes."

"And how do you explain that?" Pennfield asked her.

She shrugged. "Could be many things. Your mind could be drifting in and out of sleep and what you perceive as real is simply a dream."

"And then there's the possibility of a real psychic connection," Swann broke in.

"Dr. Altieri?" Pennfield looked over in her direction.

"I love my friend Ed," she smirked, "but I'll plead the Fifth. And you said this person—this apparition— or whatever it was, spoke to you in French?"

"Yes, that's what was so eerie about it," Pennfield answered. "Ship was fluent at a young age, went to a French preschool and elementary school. Of course, Uncle Perce and Aunt Bunny always believed in a very classic education. So whenever I returned from my studies in Paris, Shippy and I, we used to speak to each other in French. It's a sign, I'm sure."

"Could be." Said Swann. "Or the whole episode could have been a… fabrication, of your very gifted mind."

"Mr. Swann, please! Aren't we way beyond that?" Pennfield censured him. "I'd appreciate it if you didn't pander."

"There are a lot of strange coincidences here, granted," Altieri cut in, "but let's not leap to any conclusions."

"So what is it you propose, my dear Doctor?" Pennfield queried her.

She thought for a moment, and then answered, "Perhaps we *should* go there."

"And where is there?" Pennfield asked.

"Gladwell, of course," Altieri answered.

"And by *we*, I presume you are proposing that all three of us go?" Pennfield asked.

"I can't see how we can truly learn anything any other way," she answered.

"Impossible!" Pennfield blared. "Quite impossible!"

"I understand that it's…" Altieri began.

"I am much too weak, my body much too frail." Pennfield interrupted her.

"I think I can be the judge of that," Altieri answered.

"If I were a conjecturing fellow," Swann slipped in, "and I'm not saying I am— I'd say this is really about your fear of seeing Arthur, isn't it?"

"And I thought Dr. Altieri was the psychiatrist, Swann!"

"I am," Altieri answered, "and I think Ed may be right."

"Me, afraid of Shippy?" Pennfield answered, somewhat embarrassed. "Why of course I would feel a bit tepid about seeing him in that compromised state, but I certainly wouldn't characterize it as *fear.*"

"But then we have a slight problem," Altieri said. "If we can't get you there, it might be impossible for us to help you."

"Am I detecting the malodorous scent of a *threat*?" Pennfield asked in his most condescending tone.

"Not a threat, I just don't know where else to go with this, Chris," Altieri answered. "If what you say is— well— if it has any weight, we need to get the two of you together. If not, we may come up empty."

* * *

"WHAT DO YOU THINK?" Swann asked Altieri as they drove back to their hotel.

"The man has a profundity of issues," she answered.

"Well, that's pretty obvious."

"Let's see. Alcoholism, a slew of phobias, probably a touch of paranoia, numerous anxiety disorders. Need anything else?"

"So what are you saying, Bren?"

"I'm saying the man has no credibility. These paranormal experiences he describes can be nothing more than vivid hallucinations."

"Yeah, but you're forgetting. I saw everything he saw in 1994. I saw the ghosts. I saw the evidence of the curse, Bren, I swear to you."

"That was then. This is now," she answered. "He might have been credible before the incident with the young girl, but I would say the trauma caused by that combined with his alcoholism have left him a mess, unreliable."

"So that's your diagnosis, doc?"

"Well you won't find it in the DSM, but yeah, he's a '*mess*'."

"How about his psychic gift, the family's 'psychic gift'?

"Again, what you call a 'psychic gift,' I can call a predisposition to hallucinatory episodes."

Swann pursed his lips and pondered for a second. "Yeah, and what you call obsessive compulsive disorder, I can call superstitions. What you call phobias, I can call fears and what you call paranoia I can call distrust. Different names for the same things, right?"

"So now you're playing a semantics game with me?" she asked.

"Perhaps we all see what we want to see."

"Interesting point," Altieri responded, then paused. "Think he'll do it?"

"Do what?"

"Go to Gladwell."

Swann grinned. "He's an ornery old bastard at times, but, yep, he'll go."

* * *

29

Lenox, Massachusetts, Gladwell Sanitarium, Afternoon, March 31, 2007

Pennfield fidgeted for the entire six-hour ride to Gladwell. Draped across the back seat of a stretch limousine like an aging king on his throne, by noon he had already drank three Bloody Marys and two Mimosas. After the nurse served him a light lunch, he napped for two hours, woke, and immediately demanded a glass of Chardonnay.

As they turned off the Main Street in Lenox towards the sanitarium, Pennfield untwisted the cap to his bottle of scotch. "Ice. Ice, please." He ordered, thrusting his glass toward the nurse.

As the nurse plunked two cubes into the glass, Pennfield gazed upon Gladwell's front portico with its long white pillars standing strident watch, and the vines of ivy crawling up its red brick exterior.

There was something strange and eerie about the place, Pennfield thought. But there was something even more than that. Slowly, his eyes widened until he realized what it was: *hadn't he been here once before?*

"It is such a great honor and pleasure to finally meet you, Dr. Pennfield." Dr. Shankar, dressed in a blue pinstripe suit, stood at attention in the main foyer surrounded by his staff as Pennfield was wheeled through the front doors.

"Where's Swann and Altieri?" Pennfield grunted.

"I'm sure they'll be here soon, Mr. Pennfield."

Pennfield eyed his watch and grumbled. "Don't they realize I'm on a tight schedule?"

THE TENSION in the foyer was soon eased by the growling engine of Swann's pick-up rumbling along the sanitarium's long U-shaped driveway. Shankar whispered orders to his staff while keeping an eye on Pennfield. The eccentricities of this leading member of his institution's most important family of benefactors were many, but the staff appeared determined to assure that things ran smoothly. When Swann walked through the front door with a distinguished-looking, middle-aged woman, Shankar was predictably relieved.

"Mr. Swann, so nice to see you again." Shankar nodded. "And who is accompanying you today?"

"Dr. Brenda Altieri," Swann answered, "a friend of mine from Princeton."

"Dr. Altieri, so nice to meet you," Shankar nodded again. "And what is your field of study, may I ask?"

"Psychiatry."

Shankar's face tensed. "Oh?... Quite interesting."

"Thought she could help me decipher some of those old notes," Swann added.

"Of course." Shankar clenched his teeth.

THE NURSE WHEELED Pennfield down the stairs behind Swann and Altieri. The crusty old man eyed every crack in the wall, every cobweb, and all the stacks of files as they navigated the dimly lit basement.

"The humidity down here is terrible for my arthritis," Pennfield snapped at the nurse, reaching into his pocket for a Rothmans with his long bony fingers.

"I'm sorry, Mr. Pennfield," Shankar interrupted politely, "but Gladwell is a smoke-free facility."

"Bullshit!" Pennfield barked and lit his cigarette. "If it wasn't for my family, there wouldn't be a Gladwell." He turned to the nurse. "Now can you kindly bring me a glass of port?"

PENNFIELD SIPPED his port as Altieri and Swann pored over the records. Altieri jotted some notes now and then, but mostly focused on Dr. Hazard's scribblings from over forty years ago.

"This doesn't make sense…" Altieri mumbled.

"What? What have you found?" Pennfield asked anxiously, fidgeting in his wheelchair.

"Seems as if Dr. Hazard was conducting a pretty extensive clinical study on patients suffering from catatonic schizophrenia in the years right after Arthur was first brought here," Altieri answered.

"We already knew that, didn't we?" Pennfield asked.

"Yes, sure," Altieri answered. "Except for a few things..."

"Such as?" Pennfield asked.

"Well, first of all, for a study of this magnitude I have to wonder where he found the patients. It's not like catatonic schizophrenia is a common affliction, particularly in North America."

"What else?"

"Whoever his patients were, Dr. Hazard seemed to have been shooting them up with high levels of anti-psychotics and hallucinogens, and administering levels of ECT that he would have known to be near-lethal in some instances."

"Really?" Pennfield lurched. "Could he have been experimenting on animals possibly?"

"Mr. Pennfield, with all due respect," Altieri began, "I've yet to come across a catatonic schizophrenic sheep or dog."

"Touché." Pennfield answered.

"So what do you make of it, Bren?" Swann asked.

"I would say it's quite possible, once Arthur was brought here, someone in your family may have funded Dr. Hazard's research in hope that he might find a cure for Arthur," Altieri answered.

"But Uncle Perce would *never* have tolerated lethal dosages." Pennfield sucked hard on his Rothmans. "He just wasn't that type of person. It must've been this Dr. Hazard fellow. Tell me, could his experiments possibly have made Arthur even worse?"

"Don't know," Altieri answered. "It's certainly possible, should he have tried to apply some of the more aggressive protocols on Arthur, but it would be hard to verify." She paused for a moment, and then looked down again at Dr. Hazard's notes. "There is one way we may be able to a get a small hint."

"And what would that be?" Pennfield shuddered.

"I think it's about time we take a look at Arthur."

Pennfield bit down hard. His ashen face turned stark white as his heart rattled in his chest. He wasn't sure if he was ready— or ever would be— to see the fifty-two-year-old catatonic schizophrenic whom he last saw as his presumed seven-year-old cousin, and could very well be his own son.

"My scotch, please!" He barked at his attendant, after a long moment of silence.

OBTUSE BEAMS of somber afternoon light snuck in between the blinds, draping the room in a series of dark, foreboding shadows. The figure of Arthur Shipkin Pennfield, some sort of rubbery, lifeless mannequin propped up in his hospital bed, the light streaming in over his shoulders, disturbed even Altieri as she and Shankar walked through the door. Over his bed, the cardio monitor beeped rhythmically and a wavy green line danced across the EEG monitor.

"Mostly theta range," Altieri said to Shankar as she observed the EEG output.

"Correct," Shankar answered. "Typically, his EEG exhibits theta range waves sometimes wavering into delta."

"And the mumblings?" Altieri lifted Arthur's right arm and held it high over his head. "When's the last time he's said something?"

"I'd have to double-check," Shankar answered. "But I would say about ten weeks ago. The mumblings have been much less frequent lately. Maybe two or three times a year. At times, he's gone years without anything at all."

Altieri released Arthur's right hand. It remained rigid and erect, extended straight above Arthur's head. A macabre image, the man's hair in flaky disarray, an expressionless face and glassy eyes, with his arm extended as if he was a schoolchild in class raising his hand for some teacher.

"Interesting…" Altieri commented, "well, he certainly demonstrates waxy flexibility."

"Of course," Shankar answered, "Dr. Hazard was very deliberate in his diagnosis."

"You worked with him?" Altieri asked as she placed Arthur's arm back down at his side.

"Who?"

"Dr. Hazard," Altieri responded.

"Yes indeed. I had the privilege of studying and interning under the esteemed Dr. Ha-*zaird*."

"And where is he now?"

"Dr. Hazard retired to Switzerland in the early seventies. Unfortunately, the good doctor passed away about ten years ago."

"So you owe a lot to him, don't you?"

Shankar stiffened. "And what would you mean by that, Dr. Altieri?"

"Nothing," Altieri shrugged. "Just stating the obvious." Again, Altieri shone a light in Arthur's eyes. "And how often do you administer ECT?"

"About once a week," Shankar answered tersely.

"How many joules?"

"Usually about 60."

"Ever go much higher?"

Shankar paused for a quick moment. "Sporadically."

"No, I can't do it. I'm just not sure I could take it," Christopher Pennfield scowled as he sat outside the hospital room waiting for Altieri and Shankar to finish their examination.

"Do you think you have a choice?" Swann asked.

"Indeed I do." Pennfield folded his arms tightly across his chest. "Why, may I ask, should I do something that might traumatize me for the rest of my natural life?"

"Wouldn't it be a shame to come so close and never set eyes upon the man who most likely is your very own son, your own flesh and blood? Don't you think you at very least owe it to Ship and Ophie?"

"So now you're tugging at my sense of guilt, are you?" Pennfield gulped some scotch. "Great, bring in the violins. Let's make a real spectacle of it."

Swann ignored Pennfield's comment. "And, of course, if his condition has anything to do with the curse…"

"Don't you ever stop? You're dangling pure speculation in my face," Pennfield lit a Rothmans.

"Perhaps. But sometimes speculation can lead to a windfall."

Pennfield dragged on his Rothmans, then muttered, "Or a downfall."

At that moment, the hospital room door swung open and Dr. Shankar walked out. "Would you like to come in now, Mr. Pennfield?"

PENNFIELD STIFFENED in his wheelchair and grabbed tightly onto the armrests, gulping a deep sudden breath. Instinctively, he reached for his scotch and took a quick sip. He clenched his teeth. "Ready as I'll ever be," he whispered.

Slowly Swann wheeled him into the room, rolling across the cold linoleum floor. At first Pennfield shut his eyes, buying a few more precious moments before he would have to cast his sight on his own flawed flesh and blood. The beeping of the cardio monitor and the antiseptic hospital room smell irritated him. He wiped his lips, licking scotch off his fingers.

Then, trembling all over, slowly, deliberately, cautiously, he opened his eyes.

For a moment, their eyes locked onto one another's from across the room

— Pennfield's bulging and angry— Ship's glassy and vacant. Pennfield to Pennfield. Father to son.

"Jesus! Oh my God!" Pennfield shot straight up. *"What have they done to you, little Shippy?"*

Pennfield's eyes welled up: the seven-year-old, active, vibrant young boy, precociously intelligent, wonderfully fluent in French, now reduced to a lifeless mass of adult flesh.

"What have they done! What have they done!" Pennfield wailed as he stood erect. *"Oh Jesus, what have they done!"*

In the ruckus, Altieri glanced over at the EEG monitor, and then tapped Shankar on the shoulder. The normal theta waves were accelerating to the beta range, indicating increased brain activity.

Swann put his arm around Pennfield, consoling him. *"Take me to him!"* He begged Swann, *"Lord, please take me to him!"*

Awkwardly, Swann walked Pennfield across the room, his bandaged foot dragging across the floor. *"Oh, dear Shippy. Dear, dear Shippy. Why did this have to happen? Who did this to you?"* Pennfield cried out, tears rolling down his face.

Again, Altieri and Shankar glanced at the EEG. The beta waves accelerated to alpha.

"If only I had known! If I had *known!"* Pennfield cried as he drew closer. "What could I have done? *What should I have done?"*

The alpha waves increased in frequency, approaching a level where Ship might suffer a seizure.

"Please! Please! If I had anything to do with this, *please, please forgive me! Dear Lord, forgive me!"*

Pennfield dropped to his knees and extended his long bony fingers towards the lifeless Ship. Ever so gently, he tapped on the fifty-two-year-old's arm.

The alpha waves raced across the EEG monitor.

Curiously, Ship's lips seemed to wobble a bit.

They all gasped, even Shankar. Swann's eyes widened markedly.

Then there was actual deliberate movement. Straining, Ship mumbled: "*Le père m'épargne s'il vous plaît de mon sort."*

Jesus! Altieri bit her lip as Swann squeezed her hand.

Pennfield dropped to the floor. The waves on the monitor decelerated.

* * *

30

Lenox, Massachusetts, Gladwell Sanitarium, Afternoon, March 31, 2007

"Wow, this is almost as good as Woodstock!" Jules Weisman exclaimed the moment Swann and Altieri told him about their trip to Gladwell.

"*Almost* as good, Jules?" Altieri paced across Weisman's office.

"Yeah, you're forgetting one thing." Weisman tossed his rubber band ball back and forth, his legs draped on his credenza.

"What's that?"

"At Woodstock we were naked." Weisman giggled.

Weisman's enthusiasm was infectious. It seemed as if he was just as interested in the goings-on in the Pennfield case as he was in some new spin on string theory or cosmology. He was a little kid in his exuberance.

"Wow, we got a whole lotta shit going on here," Weisman exclaimed. "So let's sort this all out. Pennfield has this apparition of his presumed biological son. He thinks he sees a fifty-something-year-old catatonic Ship hovering over his bed speaking to him in French. Then when you go to the sanitarium, the catatonic son, this Ship fellow, repeats the exact same statement from the apparition in perfect, fluent French, word for word, adding evidence that what happened to Pennfield was, indeed, a real apparition and not an errant dream."

"But we have to remember that Dr. Shankar may have filled up Ship with high doses of hallucinogens and anti-psychotics and jolted him with high levels of ECT," Altieri said. "Add to that the Pennfield family's alleged psychic tendencies, generally, and those of Christopher—most likely his biological father— specifically, and we open up a whole spectrum of possibilities."

"*Alleged*, Bren?" Swann lifted an eyebrow.

"*Alleged* until proven otherwise," Altieri retorted.

Swann looked at Weisman, "So what do you think, Prof?"

"Tell me a little bit more about Chris Pennfield's *alleged* psychic abilities," Weisman spun around once more.

"Well, when I first met him back in 1994," Swann began, "he was suffering from sleep paralysis and seeing all sorts of apparitions at the family's Newport cottage. All this led me to believe, naturally, that he was psychically gifted, and more so that the entire family might be psychically gifted."

"Makes sense." Weisman nodded. "Anything else?"

"Sure, tons," Swann answered.

"Tell me the very most outrageous, fascinating thing you can think of." Weisman put his feet up on his desk and leaned back in his chair.

Swann stopped and thought for a moment, "Well, there were a few, but probably the most fascinating was when we parked my van at a spot in Newport where a famous murder in the 1920s involving a Pennfield family member took place. We induced a Ganzfeld state on Chris Penfield and—"

"Ganzfeld state?" Altieri asked.

Weisman giggled. "It's a parapsychology thing, Bren. They put ping-pong ball halves over your eyes and pump white noise into your ears to create a state of sensory deprivation. It supposedly heightens your psychic sensitivities."

"Hey, you're pretty good." Swann smiled at Weisman. "You know a lot about parapsychology for a physicist."

"One and the same." Weisman winked. "It'll all come together at some point."

"Well," Swann continued, "we induced the Ganzfeld State on Chris and lo and behold, he conjures up an apparition of that murder that took place in the 1920s. Helped us solve a slew of problems."

Weisman spun in his chair and zoned for a moment. He pulled his rubber band ball back off the shelf and began squeezing it.

"What are you thinking, Jules?" Altieri asked.

He spun around back towards Swann and Altieri. "A rather crude hypothesis, but a hypothesis, nonetheless."

"Okay, go on," Altieri prompted him.

"As I understand it, ECT increases brain activity, inducing a controlled seizure, correct?"

"Yep," Altieri answered.

"And then, Ed, you said, if I remember correctly, that Christopher had just suffered a bout of sleep paralysis prior to the crisis apparition?"

"That's right." Swann nodded.

"And the theory is that sleep paralysis— just like a Ganzfeld state— can cause heightened sensitivity which would make one more prone to psychic events."

"Right again," Swann answered.

Weisman spun around in his chair and squeezed his rubber ball. "Hmm.... now wouldn't it be interesting to see if Ship were undergoing ECT when Christopher had his crisis apparition?"

Altieri peered at her colleague raising her bright blue eyes over her wire-frames. "Jules, you just may be onto something."

* * *

IT TOOK little time for Swann and Dr. Altieri to gather the facts. They agreed to divide and conquer: Altieri would contact Dr. Shankar and Swann would talk to Pennfield.

"Didn't I call you the next morning for goodness sakes, Mr. Swann?" Pennfield barked into the phone. "Don't you keep good records?"

"That's not the issue," Swann answered back. "We know the date, it was Thursday March 8. I just need to know the approximate time. Can you help me with that?"

"I guess I can try," Pennfield said begrudgingly.

"What time did you go to bed that evening?" Swann asked.

"The same as always, about 9 o' clock. I'm no spring chicken, Mr. Swann."

"Neither am I." Swann chuckled. "So, do you fall asleep quickly or toss and turn for hours like me?"

"Depends what I drink before bed," Pennfield answered.

"Can you remember what you drank that evening?" Swann asked.

"Most nights I retire right after a nice tumbler of Ardmore single malt, neat, a more-than-effective soporific."

"So you probably fell asleep quickly, within ten or fifteen minutes?"

"Plausible, yes," Pennfield responded.

"And you said you awakened and sat on the side of your bed right after your bout with sleep paralysis and just before the apparition," Swann continued.

"Correct."

"Any clues to about what time that was?" Swann asked.

"Well it's hard to..." he began, "...but perhaps...no, I can't say that...but..."

"I know it's not easy, but think," Swann prodded.

"Well...again, it's difficult...but..." He stopped speaking for a moment.

"Chris? You still there?"

"You know, I think... I think I just may remember my Grandfather's clock chiming. And if I remember correctly, don't ask me why, but for some odd reason I recall it chiming *ten*."

AFTER SEVERAL ATTEMPTS Altieri reached Dr. Shankar on the phone. Guarded as usual, Shankar at first waffled.

"And why is this of importance, Dr. Altieri?"

"Very simple. We're just trying to establish a sequence of events."

"I see. Is Christopher Pennfield aware of this?"

"I wouldn't be calling you if he wasn't. Would you like to talk to him?"

"No, that won't be necessary," Shankar answered softly. "To answer your question, we have consistently administered ECT to Arthur Pennfield each Thursday evening at approximately 10pm."

"And, for the record, on Thursday, March 8, you followed this schedule as usual?"

"Of course."

* * *

31

Princeton, New Jersey, Early evening, April 2, 2007

"Bingo, yahtzee, touchdown, hotel-on-*Boardwalk!"* Jules Weisman sprang up off his chair when the three of them reconvened in his office.

"This is absolutely *phenomenal!* Christopher Pennfield has a bout of sleep paralysis and sees a crisis apparition of Ship Pennfield at the exact same time when Ship is undergoing electro-shock-therapy. 10pm on Thursday, March 22. *Absolutely phenomenal.*" Weisman beamed.

"So your hypothesis is confirmed," Swann offered.

"Not quite yet." Weisman answered, swinging around in his chair.

"I sense a devilish look in your eyes, Jules." Altieri grinned at her friend.

"Of course." Weisman grinned, staring at the far wall.

"Are you going to let us in on what you're thinking?" Altieri chided him.

"As soon as my mind slows down." Weisman leaned back, rested his black-sneakered feet up on his bookshelf and grabbed for his rubber band ball, squeezing it. "Sometimes my words can't keep up with my thoughts."

"Scary." Altieri winked at Swann.

Weisman jolted around in his seat and faced his visitors. He clapped his hands once, sharply. "Okay, here it is. We have preliminary anecdotal evidence that when Ship Pennfield is undergoing ECT and Christopher Pennfield is simultaneously in a sensitized state, such as one induced by sleep paralysis, that the two of them can and actually do make some sort of psychic connection. So, sticking to true scientific method, we must attempt to replicate the phenomenon under laboratory conditions."

"Okay. So far, so good." Altieri responded.

"On the surface, it seems simple," Weisman began. "We get both of our subjects in the same location and while we're administering shock therapy to Ship we simultaneously induce a Ganzfeld state on Christopher. But here's the twist." Once again, he crisply clapped his hands, then looked around as if to figure out one final piece.

"Well, don't keep us waiting," Swann insisted.

"It all has to do with the setting, the laboratory," Weisman answered. "The real issue here is to determine what caused Ship to become catatonic in the first place. So how about this…" he pointed at them and cracked a wide grin. "What if we conduct our experiment— *i.e. set up our laboratory*— at the site where Ship was first afflicted with his condition?"

"At Indian Harbor?" Swann exclaimed.

TIME FRAME: 2052

32

NY GAB: Manhattan, Pennfield Technologies Tower, Early evening, December 2, 2052

It took several days for JMP to fully absorb the ramifications of his v-conf with Bonne-Saari. Once he had a plan of action, he summoned McPherson back to his office.

"A v-conf with the big guy, eh?" McPherson blurted as he burst into the office.

"Shhhh…," JMP shushed him, "let's keep that quiet for now."

"Okay. Okay. Got it," McPherson replied feebly. "So you want the scoop on this Fane guy?"

"No. That will have to wait, Bryan," JMP responded. "I need your help with a personal matter. A very critical and sensitive personal matter."

"No problem, Mr. MP."

"I was Ganzfelding the other day and seem to have connected with some young fellow who purports to be a Pennfield."

"Up to your old habits again, huh?" McPherson smiled.

"Need I remind you that revenues we acquire from Ganzfeld Chambers pay your salary, Bryan?"

"Yeah, I know. I know Mr. MP," McPherson stuttered his response.

"You should try it sometime, it's quite relaxing."

"Uh… I don't think that's my kinda thing, Mr. MP. But how can I help you?"

"Like I said, I think I came in touch with an ancestor from my past..."

McPherson smirked.

"Okay," JMP continued, "I know why you're looking at me like that, but bear with me."

"Will do. Of course, Mr. MP. Wouldn't want to be disrespectful," McPherson answered.

"Well, if I can somehow identify this ancestor of mine, it may help me deal with a problem, help me immensely. Believe it or not, it may even help us find that girl from the tavern."

"I see."

"Yeah."

"So what you got on him— the ancestor— Mr. MP?" McPherson licked his finger and scribbled on his e-let.

"Not much," JMP swiveled in his chair and flipped through his holoscreen as he spoke. "All I can say is he's a young kid and he's sitting on this dock, on some sort of inlet."

"I gotta ask, you think this picture you're seeing, is it something your mind conjured up, or do you think it's real?"

"Real, of course." JMP stopped flipping and swiveled again. "I don't deal in fantasy, Bryan, you should know that by now."

"Got it, Mr. MP. Young kid sitting on dock. An *inlet*." McPherson scribbled again. "So if the image is real and if we could possibly identify the location— wherever this young kid was sitting— would that help you identify him?"

"Yeah, that could help, help quite a bit."

McPherson scratched his head then briskly snapped his fingers. "Okay, got it. Intelligent Robotic Holography."

"What's that?"

"Pretty new tech for us. Some PDs are experimenting with it to ID perps. It's a robotic-based technology that reconstructs pictures qubit by qubit based upon the witnesses' brainwaves. Sorta like the sketch artist in those old detective movies 'cept it comes directly from the brain and its supplemented by AI and a ton of databases and you could manipulate it and look at it from any possible angle."

"Nice." JMP said approvingly. McPherson beamed.

"So if we can get an accurate picture of what's in your head," McPherson said, "we may be able to identify the place and—"

"When can you get one here?" JMP asked as he swiveled back toward his holoscreen.

"An IRH device?" McPherson asked. "Depends. Let me call around."

"Good. Do it."

* * *

33

Manhattan, NYCGAB, Pennfield Technologies Tower, Afternoon, December 3, 2052

The device was small and elegant: a compact, rectangular, white plastic box, about eight-by-four and two inches deep, with smooth, rounded corners, several small non-descript dials, and a miniature set of holographic lenses. Two wireless electrodes fit neatly into slots on top.

"There it is. State of the art, Mr. MP," McPherson announced proudly as he set the device on JMP's desk.

"Interesting… interesting…" JMP scanned the device with all the enthusiasm of a grown man who relished high tech toys. "So how's this thing work?"

"Pretty simple, Mr. MP," McPherson answered. "We put those electrodes on your temples. Then you start thinking about the location we're trying to recreate. The device will prompt you, and then it will begin building a holographic image right in front of your eyes."

"That's a solid combination of technologies," JMP commented. "But how are we going to match the image to the actual site?"

"Good question, Mr. MP," McPherson smiled. "That's what I got these little buggers for." He opened his hand, revealing five little black dots.

"Gnat cams?" JMP asked.

"Yes, indeed. But these buggers are the best you can get. Holographic, built-in nav systems, and they travel at 0.1C."

"Eighteen-thousand miles-a-second. Very impressive, Bryan." JMP patted his Chief Security Officer on the back. "Amazing what nanotechnology can do these days."

"So after we're done creating the image here, I'll send these little buggers to locations all around the world that have to do with Pennfield family history. We'll have them scope out sites near water and they'll project holographic images back to us. Then we'll compare them to our image until we find the actual location."

"Bryan, you never cease to amaze."

"OK, Mr. MP. This is going to be easy," McPherson announced as he placed two small electrodes on JMP's temples.

"So you just want me to concentrate on that site I observed in my mind during the Ganzfelding?"

"That's it," McPherson answered. "Go ahead. You're on, Mr. MP."

JMP squinched his eyes shut. The lines in his face hardened, veins almost popping from his shiny, bald scalp. His concentration was so intense, it appeared painful to McPherson.

"Take it easy, Mr —" McPherson stopped mid-sentence.

Smack in the middle of JMP's office, a holographic image materialized. At first, it was heavily cubelated. But as JMP strained— the lines in his face and veins on his scalp becoming more and more pronounced— the cubes became less and less granular, shrinking and then multiplying into finer and finer degrees of specificity.

"Does this image correspond with your memory?" a voice asked from the small white box.

"What?" JMP answered, startled.

"The IRH box is prompting you, Mr. MP," McPherson answered. "Open your eyes and take a look."

When JMP first looked, a deep sense of intrigue tinted his expression. As he studied the picture, his intrigue morphed into a wide, exuberant grin.

"Shit! This is pretty cool, Bryan." JMP reacted, agog. "Amazing. Amazingly close."

"Okay. So prompt it. Give it some direction," said McPherson.

JMP stared at the image. Still amazed by the accuracy, he studied the details. The perspective was from that of one hovering over a small body of water. Plainly he saw a rickety old dock extending from a very thin shoreline, about three to five feet across, which ended abruptly at about a three-foot high embankment. Beyond that were the grounds of a rather good-sized Dutch

Colonial house with a wrap-around porch and large bay windows on either side of the front entrance. At the end of the rickety dock sat a small figure of a child, dark and in silhouette.

"The grounds above the embankment should be covered with snow," JMP announced to the IRH unit.

"Processing," the machine answered.

The grounds— a mixture of muddy brown interspersed with patches of crunchy green grass on the original image— turned white with snow.

"No! No!" JMP reacted. "Not a fluffy snow, a crunchy snow."

The image of fresh fluffy snow dissolved into one of harder, frozen snow.

"How 'bout the kid on the dock?" McPherson asked.

"Of course. Of course." JMP then spoke directly to the machine. "Can you zoom into the figure at the end of the dock?"

"Certainly. Please indicate when I am close enough," the machine responded.

The image panned across the landscape, centering on the rickety dock and then zooming into the figure at the end. The image was fuzzy, diffuse and gray, indicating that JMP was not focusing sufficiently on this aspect of the image in his initial phase of concentration.

"Kindly concentrate on the exposed object."

JMP strained to remember.

After several series of adjustments, the image was indeed that of a young boy, approximately five to seven years old, with a round, freckled face and dirty-blonde hair with bangs.

"Yes. Yes. Very, very close," JMP reacted. "But the eyes, the eyes are all wrong."

Indeed, the eyes lacked any specificity, black almond shapes with no detail whatsoever.

"Kindly concentrate."

"Okay. Okay." Again, JMP squeezed his eyes tightly shut and concentrated as hard as he possibly could. "How am I doing?" he asked the IRH machine.

"Processing," the machine responded. *"Please observe."*

"Hmmm…" JMP leaned in closer to the image. "Pretty good. Pretty good. The color's right, but what's that in the center. It looks strange."

The machine zoomed in on the child's eyes. Indeed, there was a fuzzy, bright horizontal image over the area where the pupil should be.

"Can you go in closer?" JMP asked.

The machine zoomed in until the eyes filled the entire expanse of the holographic image.

"Still closer, please," JMP commanded.

This time the machine zoomed in on a single eye. The strange fuzzy horizontal image filled the setting, but the image was now unstable, cubelating and even degrading into indistinct blotches of gray.

"I guess that's the best we can do. Let's move on," JMP ordered the machine.

"Would you like to perform a three-hundred-and-sixty-degree extrapolation?"

"What's that?" JMP asked, quizzically.

"Do it, Mr. MP," McPherson answered. "You'll get a kick out of it, I bet."

"Okay. Go ahead."

"Extrapolating. Please wait."

The image panned over to its periphery on the left side and then began extending the scene beyond its boundary by sketching lines which were extensions of the images at the scene's border.

"Pretty cool, eh, Mr. MP." McPherson smirked. "The machine extrapolates based upon the peripheral regions of the image and then applies over a million data sources to complete a full, virtual, three-sixty-degree image."

"Exactly what *kind* of data sources?" JMP asked imperiously.

"All sorts," McPherson answered. "The machine scans a database of millions of images of similar scenes and then fills in the missing parts based upon those which most directly match our image. Then, of course, it picks up every bit of information it can from the known image. Ground conditions, weather, reflections, everything. Add a little AI to that and it gets interesting, huh?"

"I suppose." JMP stretched back in his chair as the image built itself, the perspective rotating and building— at first the scene would extend via black lines against white background, and then color and texture would fill in—revealing the inlet of muddy water, and then the opposite shoreline dotted with evergreens and several large houses.

"How did it come up with those houses?" JMP pointed. "That's more than just extrapolation."

"Like I said, Mr. MP," McPherson answered. "It picks up every bit of information that it can from the known image. Probably the reflections off those bay windows." McPherson pointed to the original image of the house drawn from JMP's memory. Indeed, examined closely, the bay windows shimmered a faint reflection of the houses from across the inlet.

"Nice little toy." JMP smiled.

For a moment, JMP stared at the image and concentrated. Then, slowly, he stood up, and squinted. "What's that?"

"Huh?" McPherson asked, startled.

"That thing." He pointed. "That thing hovering over the water."

McPherson scratched his head. "Not quite sure. Let's zoom in."

As the perspective moved in closer and closer to the white amorphous object hovering over the water, JMP first strained his eyes to study the details. Then he beamed, his eyes sparkling. *"Holy Shit, Bryan. That's me. That's me Ganzfelding."*

"What?"

"The machine must've picked up the reflection from the boy's eyes and translated it into what it thought he was seeing." JMP pointed excitedly, "Look. Look."

The image of a transparent, naked, levitating body hovered over the water. From the headphones over the figure's ears and the goggles over its eyes, Pennfield could tell with certainty that the image was of him during his Ganzfeld session.

"Whoa." McPherson dropped his jaw. "And probably the machine filled in the missing details from your memory."

"Holy shit this is a *fantastic* technology." JMP beamed.

"OKAY, now let's get to the *really* fun part," McPherson suggested. "Time for these little buggers." He pulled a small envelope out of his pocket and poured the tiny gnat cams into his hand.

"And where will you send them?" JMP asked.

"Well," McPherson answered and then threw up his cupped hands, releasing the gnat-cams. "I did a little check on your family history over the last hundred years or so, and pulled a list of ten cold-weather locations near bodies of water where members of the Pennfield family once lived."

"And when will we be able to observe these locations?"

McPherson giggled. "Well at 0.1C, they arrived almost immediately. So let's look, shall we?" He pointed up to the holoscreen.

THEY EXAMINED images from Vancouver Island, Boothbay Harbor, Aquebogue, New York and rejected them quickly, none of them displaying any of the prominent features of the image generated by the IRH machine.

The next image beamed from the gnat cams was from Greenwich, Connecticut.

"What a monstrosity!" JMP exclaimed as he studied a very sprawling, boxy structure composed almost entirely of glass. "It looks like someone from

2010 or so made a very flat-footed attempt to predict the architectural trends of the future. *Yeccch....*"

"Wait a minute. Wait just one minute," McPherson interrupted, squinting at the image.

"But the structure, that monstrosity, it bears no resemblance whatsoever to—"

"Don't worry about that, just look." McPherson interrupted him.

Pennfield scowled, and then directed his eyes towards the hovering images.

"Let's rotate the gnat cam," McPherson continued, twisting a dial on the gnat cam controls, "then look at the opposite bank of the inlet from the extrapolated RH image." He pointed at the Greenwich image with his finger and then directed it to superimpose itself over the RH image. He adjusted the size of the image until it was just right. "Voila, Mr. MP, we have our culprit." McPherson pointed to the superimposed images. The inlet and two shorelines coincided exactly.

"Yes, but that's a bit of a cheap parlor trick, wouldn't you say?" JMP responded, unimpressed.

"How so?"

"The IRH machine itself created the image across the inlet, so it's a virtual match, not a real match and that's not good enough for me."

"Bear with me, Mr. MP. Just bear with me for a second." McPherson directed both images to pan simultaneously across the inlet until the glass house overlapped the Dutch Colonial. "I mean we're talking about two different houses, but the grounds around them jibe pretty nicely..."

Silently, JMP studied the superimposed images. Indeed, the shoreline, the embankment and the grounds seemed to coincide nicely, and while the houses were situated in generally the same position relative to the rest of the property, that's where the congruity ended: the newer structure was an angular collection of what appeared to be stacked glass boxes connected together by a series of white and pastel adobe-style walls, while the older house was Dutch Colonial in the most classic sense. "Close. Pretty close, Bryan. But no cigar. I'm not convinced."

"Okay. Let me try one more little trick, Mr. MP."

"And what's that?"

"I told you those gnat cams were state-of-the-art," McPherson answered as he strutted across the room. "It just so happens, the little buggers could generate virtual seismic waves which, of course, can give us an idea of the foundation underneath the glass house."

McPherson twisted some dials and the ground underneath the glass house glowed green as the gnat cam drew a schematic of the structure's foundation. "Now, all we have to do is have the IRH machine make a similar drawing of the foundation under the old Dutch Colonial…" McPherson adjusted the RH machine's settings, "…and we can compare the two." McPherson pointed at the image of the old Victorian house. "Take a gander, Mr. MP."

As McPherson superimposed the glass house image over the Victorian, JMP observed closely. The two foundations coincided exactly.

"You see," McPherson gloated, "just like I thought. Someone tore down the Victorian and built the glass house on its old foundation."

"Architectural defecation if you ask me," JMP quipped.

"So what do you think, Mr. MP?"

"Very good, Bryan, very good."

"So?"

JMP lounged back in his chair. "Greenwich it is."

* * *

TIME FRAME: 2007/2052

34

Spring Lake Heights, NJ / Boothbay Harbor, ME, Mid-day, April 6, 2007

"Jesus, Swann, I'm just not sure we should do it!" Christopher Pennfield barked through his telephone.

"You seemed pretty sure last time we talked," Swann answered.

"Yes, indeed, but sometimes inner reflection unearths our better judgment."

"Or our deepest fears." Swann commented.

"Mr. Swann, *fear* has nothing to do with this," Pennfield snapped.

"So are you really trying to back out of this or are you just blowing off some steam?" Swann asked.

Begrudgingly, Pennfield responded, "As usual, I suppose it's the latter."

"Okay, then, first things first," Swann said. "I've done a little digging and it seems the Indian Harbor property is still owned by a member of the Pennfield family: a Winston Pennfield, a grand-nephew of yours."

"Yes," Pennfield answered, "and my grand-nephew Winston is a raging homosexual."

"So what's wrong with that?" Swann asked.

"Mr. Swann!" Pennfield scowled.

"Well, couldn't it be said that you're a raging *heterosexual*?" Swann winked.

"Here, here." Pennfield grinned. "You have more wit than I give you credit for, Swann. But, I understand that our dear Winston tore down Uncle Perce's beautiful home and replaced it with some post-modern eyesore."

"And it also seems that your grand-nephew maintains a lifestyle way beyond his means."

"That little deviant never worked an honest day in his life," Pennfield commented.

"And when I told him that his Great Uncle Christopher would like to spend a few days of relaxation in one of the cherished spots from his youth, Winston was more than receptive to the idea."

"For how much?" Pennfield asked immediately.

"Ten thousand."

"Done."

* * *

Manhattan, NYCGAB
Pennfield Technologies Tower
Morning
November 30, 2052

"Okay I got the scoop on that funky house in Greenwich, Mr. MP," Bryan McPherson bolted into JMP's office.

"Yes, Bryan." JMP looked up from his desk. "Please excuse me for a moment," he announced to no one in particular, while looking out his glass wall and punching a button on a small controller device.

"Ooops! Sorry, Mr. MP. I didn't realize—"

"I'm on a v-conf with Zurich," he whispered. "What's up?"

"Like I said, I have some info on that house in Greenwich."

"One sec." Mashimoto-Pennfield swiveled in his chair and pressed the button on his controller once again. He looked out into space and announced: "Gentlemen, can we kindly take a five-minute break?" Then he looked back at McPherson. "Okay, shoot."

"Just like we thought, the place is a white elephant. No one's lived there for years. It's owned by some Brazilian holofilm director. Rarely uses it. Get this, mostly he rents it out for parties. Seems as if it's so retro-ugly, it makes an interesting venue."

JMP scowled. "I swear some people's aesthetics are up their asses."

"We can rent it for a weekend for thirty-five thousand."

"Fine." JMP swiveled in his chair, clicked the button, and re-joined his v-conf.

"And… ummm… I'm thinking we should bring a portable Ganzfeld chamber."

JMP thought for a moment. "Good idea, Bryan. *Very* good!"

* * *

Greenwich, CT
Indian Harbor
April 14, 2007

"What a monstrosity!" Pennfield sneered as he first laid eyes on the house. "Jesus, not only did my grand-nephew Winston lose his sense of masculinity, he lost his sense of taste as well!"

"I'm afraid there's not much we can do about that, let me take you around back."

Pennfield had a nauseous scowl on his face as Swann wheeled him into and through the house. "Oh god, it's just a giant set of glass blocks, looks like he spewed them haphazardly onto a foundation of ugly stone, or, just pure ugliness, adulterated by gaudy tones of pastels," Pennfield uttered under his breath.

When they emerged from the house onto the deck, Weisman was there waiting.

"Dr. Pennfield, I presume!" Weisman beamed, offering a hand to his former colleague.

Pennfield winced, and then scanned Weisman from head to toe: his black and white Keds, his tattered jeans, ripped at the knee, his bristly salt and pepper beard, his spectacles, slightly askew, and his shiny bald pate.

"You haven't aged particularly well, Julian."

"And it's wonderful to see you again, too, Chris."

Not particularly paying attention to Weisman's comment, Pennfield gazed upon the inlet he knew as a youth. "Jesus Christ, to think how that little twerp Winston defiled such a cherished estate." Then he stared at the drab, yellow, stone deck. "I didn't realize that *Stale Urine* was a shade available in that type of stone."

* * *

NYCT GAB: Greenwich
Indian Harbor
Afternoon
December 4, 2052

"GOD, Bryan, the place looks worse in person than it did on your gnat cam!" Jimmy Mashimoto-Pennfield turned to McPherson as they first stepped out of their hover jet and eyed the landscape. "I didn't think it could get any worse."

"Yeah, I don't think that Brazilian guy invests much in upkeep," McPherson commented as they toured the grounds.

"Hardly," JMP answered as he observed the muddied grounds covered with brown, crunchy grass and an array of barely-alive, entangled plants and trees. "What year did you say this was built?"

"Two thousand and three, two thousand four, somewhere around there…" McPherson answered.

"And now this unarticulated pile of glass and stone stands as a monument to the poor taste of an entire generation," JMP harrumphed. "It certainly hasn't aged well in the last five decades. I really can't believe anyone would ever want to rent the place, and for a party no less!"

"Heck, you know," McPherson snickered, "some of those artsy-fartsy types get off on this stuff."

"I suppose."

"C'mon, let's go around the back and scope out the dock." McPherson motioned towards the side of the house.

THE MOMENT JMP saw the dock, he froze.

"What's the matter, Mr. MP?" McPherson asked, concerned.

"Oh my God…" JMP pointed at the dock, his finger quivering.

"What? What?" McPherson begged, excitedly.

"That's it. That's exactly it," JMP answered, his finger still quivering.

"You sure?" McPherson responded. "I mean, after the gnat cam images, you were still a little—"

"No this is different," JMP's voice vibrated unnaturally. "It's beyond rationality. It's a feeling. An eerie feeling, like returning to the scene of a crime or something."

"So you up for a little Ganzfelding, Mr. MP?"

JMP giggled. "I can't believe *you're* inviting *me* to Ganzfeld, Bryan."

* * *

Greenwich, CT
Indian Harbor
Afternoon
April 14, 2007

THE MEDICAL VAN rolled into the driveway at Indian Harbor in the early afternoon. Altieri was the first to hop out, scuffing up pebbles as she approached the entrance.

"How's Ship?" Swann asked as he greeted her.

"About the same," Altieri answered. "The ride didn't seem to affect him much either way."

"I suppose that's good news," Swann replied.

"So where do we set up the equipment?" Altieri asked as they entered the front doorway.

"Your friend *Jules* has scoped out a couple of spots on the deck out back. Follow me."

ENTHUSED, Weisman jumped right in when Altieri emerged from the back door. "Okay. I figured we would set up the ECT equipment here." Weisman pointed to a corner of the long, covered deck. "Right in that corner."

"Outside?" Altieri responded, a bit startled.

"Why not?" Weisman shrugged. "It's covered."

Altieri grinned. "Well, it might be the very first time anyone's ever conducted electro-convulsive therapy outdoors."

"You see, you'll be making history." Weisman grinned. "Then I thought we would induce the Ganzfeld state on Christopher right over there." He pointed to the opposite end of the same deck. "So now we have Ship and Christopher in relatively close proximity to each other so that they can be observed simultaneously, and also in proximity to the dock where Ship originally became catatonic in 1963." He pointed out to the rickety dock extending from the shoreline.

"Very good, Jules. Very good." Altieri nodded, scanning the property.

"AND HOW ARE YOU, MR. PENNFIELD?" Altieri walked over to Pennfield and extended her hand as soon as she spotted him.

"Oh, just peachy." He scowled.

"Why the long face?"

Pennfield snapped back. "Believe me, you'd have one, too, if you had just been subject to the care of some sub-human eunuch on a six-hour drive from Maine, were about to see your presumed illegitimate catatonic son for only the second time in over forty years, and were then allowing yourself to be induced into this pseudo-scientific Ganzfeld *nonsense.*"

"I see your point." Altieri nodded. "Speaking of Ship, I think it's about time we got him settled."

"*Mr. Swann!*" Ignoring Altieri, Pennfield shouted across the deck.

"Yes, Chris?" Swann approached him.

"Can you be a prince and do me a majestically important favor?" he asked.

"Sure. What do you want?"

"In the back seat of the limousine is a chilled bottle of Pouilly Fumé 1998. Can you kindly bring it to me?" Pennfield asked.

"Certainly."

"Don't drop it, thank you," Pennfield added, and then looked over at Altieri. "And Dr. Altieri,"

"Yes?" Altieri obliged.

"Be a saint and please do not bring Ship back here until Mr. Swann returns."

BRISKLY, Swann returned with the bottle and placed it in Pennfield's lap. Grasping it with his long bony fingers, Pennfield examined it and scowled.

"Well I can't exactly drink it corked, now can I, Mr. Swann?" Pennfield muttered.

"Oh is *that* what you want to do with it?" Swann winked.

"You can spare us the humor." Pennfield reached under his wheel chair. "Here, make yourself useful." He handed a corkscrew to Swann.

As Swann uncorked the bottle, Pennfield addressed Altieri: "Now you may bring in Ship." He took a small sip directly from the bottle.

PENNFIELD BRACED HIMSELF, his back stiffening against his wheelchair. He took a deep breath, holding it inside, a tight knot beneath his sternum. He squirmed, nervously shifting in his seat, listening carefully to the rumblings from out front.

"Steady, hold him steady."

"Bring him around the side."

"No through the house. Through the house is easier."

Pennfield's heart pounded against his ribcage. He felt dizzy, weak. Prickles pitter-pattered up his spine. He clenched his teeth as if bracing himself for a sharp blow.

"Okay, get the doors."

"Nice and easy. Watch the sides"

His eyes shot over to the large glass doors leading from the house to the deck. Two stout men in white clutched the wheelchair, tilting it back. An eerie first view: the bottom of the chair, metal and canvas, Ship's feet dangling from above. Pennfield gasped. Carefully, they worked the chair through the doors.

As they set the chair upright on the deck, Ship's chalky face tilted eerily forward. Almost magically, his vacant eyes shot over towards his father.

Again, Pennfield gasped.

"Holy Mother of God!" Christopher Pennfield exclaimed, then grabbed his bottle of wine, raised it to his lips and chugged vigorously.

* * *

NYCT GAB: Greenwich
Indian Harbor
Afternoon
December 19, 2052

"DON'T you think you're going a little overboard, Mr. MP?" Bryan McPherson questioned his boss. "I mean, like we're both guys and that, but..."

"I always Ganzfeld naked, it's essential." JMP pronounced brusquely, stepping out of his black leather pants.

"In the buff, huh?" McPherson muttered.

"If that's what you call it." JMP scoffed, removing his black underpants and shirt, hardly chilled at all by the atypically warm 60-degree December day.

"Well, at least the weather's cooperating." McPherson covered his eyes and looked away.

THE TWO OF them had set the Ganzfeld machine up right before the embankment at the base of the dock. JMP carefully draped his clothes over a rusted piece of deck furniture and walked over towards the machine, but then abruptly stopped.

"Anything the matter, Mr. MP?" McPherson asked.

"Uh, no, not really…except I usually record my Ganzfeld sessions."

"Not a prob." McPherson dug into his right pocket. "Always carry a few spare gnat cams around just in case."

"Always prepared, aren't you?" JMP grinned. "Must've been a boy scout, eh?"

"Of course," McPherson responded. "So how's this thing work?"

"Just watch," JMP responded, shivering. He carefully picked the tiny earphones and mask off the machine, and then settled himself down on the cool metal base between the posts at the head and the foot.

"You gonna start?"

"In just one moment." JMP adjusted the tiny earphones and then placed the mask over his eyes.

"Okay, I'll let 'er fly." McPherson released the tiny gnat came into the air.

"Bryan?" JMP called out, blinded by the mask.

"Yep?"

"Once I turn on the earphones I'll no longer be able to hear you," JMP continued, "So I trust you'll observe keenly."

"Of course, Mr. MP, that's my business."

JMP clicked a micro-button on one of his earphones and then laid himself down prone on the machine's platform. Soon, he began to levitate between the two metal posts.

McPherson's eyes widened as he observed.

* * *

35

Greenwich, CT, Indian Harbor, Twilight, April 14, 2007

NYCT GAB, Twilight , December 4, 2052

To Jules Weisman— teenage wonk turned college hippie revolutionary turned theoretical physicist PhD— the scene evoked his fondest adolescent memories of a compelling sci-fi flick, his jaw dropping just like it did before the large silver screen at the Starlite Drive-in off the Sunrise Highway in his native Long Island. Except this time, there were no cheesy special effects, no over-affectations from B-movie actors, no paper mâché aliens. This time it was real.

Much like those monochromatic double features, the scene glimmered in the burgeoning twilight. A makeshift operating table was set up on the far left side of the deck. IV-bags dangled from metal poles, wide straps straddled the table and an array of monitors and medical devices lined each side. On the opposite end of the deck, about twenty feet away, a much simpler set-up was assembled: another hospital cot, but only accompanied by an EEG machine and a heart monitor. Here, Christopher Pennfield would be induced into his Ganzfeld state.

Weisman continued to survey the materials for their experiment. But for a moment, he allowed himself the luxury of observing the actual air surrounding the dock; salted, somehow clean, but unmistakably filled with the scent of raw earth, dirt, and stone.

"When are we going to get this over with?" the irascible Pennfield barked from his wheel chair.

Weisman snapped back into focus as he listened to his colleagues make a few final adjustments; the attendants strapping Ship in as the anesthesiologist adjusted the bags on her IV pole.

"Soon. Soon." Swann said to Pennfield. "We just have to prepare Ship."

"Mr. Swann?" Pennfield asked feebly.

"Yes, Chris."

"For many reasons which I am sure you can understand, I'd rather not see Ship when they bring him out again," Pennfield stated. "Can we put those blasted ping-pong balls over my eyes *now*?"

"Sure, why not?" Swann walked over to the bed and grabbed a pair of half ping-pong balls connected by an elastic loop and handed them to Pennfield.

Pennfield scowled, shriveling his nose, as he dangled the strange apparatus in front of his face with his thumb and forefinger. Grudgingly, he slipped the elastic around his head and positioned the half-balls over his eyes.

"Okay, bring him out." Swann nodded at Altieri across the deck.

WEISMAN COULD EASILY UNDERSTAND why Christopher Pennfield hesitated to set eyes upon Ship once again. It wasn't the shock of seeing a human being in a catatonic stupor, it was the pity of potential never realized; the enormous chasm between what is versus what could have been.

The vacant, woozy appearance of Ship's face belied his anxious wiggling in the tight, constraining straightjacket. Although he remained expressionless, Ship's vacant eyes seemed to roam around setting as he flailed his arms and legs. He grunted as they lifted him off his wheelchair, placed him on the table and quickly fastened the straps. Methodically, the anesthesiologist took Ship's right arm and began to open an IV.

"YOUR TURN NOW, CHRIS," Altieri announced.

"Oh, if I *must!"* the cantankerous old man snapped back, blinded by the ping-pong balls.

"Okay, you know the drill," Swann stated. "Lay down on the cot and we'll attach a few monitors, then I'll give you the headsets and crank up the white noise. After that, all you have to do is relax."

"It's that simple, eh?" Pennfield answered sardonically as Swann guided him onto the cot. Weisman and Altieri quickly taped EEG monitors to several spots on his head and then Swann placed the headsets over Pennfield's ears.

"Okay. Relax." Swann tried to soothe him.

"Easier said than done," Pennfield snapped, twiddling his fingers on his belly.

Swann clicked on the sound.

The monotonic hum of white noise commingled with the grey monochrome shade cast by the ping-pong balls to create a bland sensory environment. Soon, it would lull Pennfield into a deep state of relaxation.

* * *

TWILIGHT SHADED the inlet as Jimmy Mashimoto-Pennfield levitated peacefully above his Ganzfeld machine. His mind whirled, spinning rapidly. Alternately, it accelerated and decelerated before settling into a boundless zone of comfort and tranquility. JMP relished these moments: when *up* overlapped with *down* and *right* crisscrossed *left.*

BORED, McPherson fidgeted: watching his boss stark-naked and levitating above a Ganzfeld machine at the base of a rickety dock in Greenwich was not his idea of exciting, but, as a dutiful employee, he obliged. He crossed his arms and scratched his triceps.

JMP's skin effervesced, pins and needles pricking each and every cell. Soon, he began to melt, the boundary between body, spirit and surroundings blurring into some mystical vapor wafting through the universe.

McPherson strained to focus solely on JMP's face, avoiding his lower extremities at all costs.

IT NEVER CEASED to amaze JMP how what began as this heterogeneous blur eventually focused everything into such deep sharp clarity: how sooner or later the cloud of probabilities collapsed into a hard-edged reality. The inner recesses of JMP's mind intersected with the infinite possibilities of the universe to conjure up a distinct image as the focus sharpened. Surprisingly, of the multitude of all possible images, this one perplexed him most.

Tranquil, he forced himself to focus: *he was here, a familiar sight.*

The eyes within his mind explored: *the dock, the inlet, Indian Harbor.*

He questioned himself: *place established, but what about time?*

Responding, his vision shifted: *the house, glass cubes and stucco.*

Perplexed even more: *of all the possible destinations, why here, why now?*

His inner eyes shifted to the inlet: *himself Ganzfelding over the water, floating, a mirror image.*

Then to the dock: *the little boy sitting on the edge, Arthur?*

He focused: *they connected, his Ganzfelding presence hovering over the water and the little boy.*

His mind had never been so lucid: spinning in all directions, weighing possibilities, testing hypotheses. He was Ganzfelding now, observing himself Ganzfelding in the past, connecting with Arthur on the dock, all set in the here and now.

But why?

* * *

"STILL ALPHA, BREN," Weisman read from the EEG machine, "getting lower, though. Wavering between eight and ten hertz."

"Okay. We're getting there," Dr. Brenda Altieri responded to Weisman.

"We've decelerated a bit," Weisman called out, "hovering between eight and nine."

"Almost… almost…" Altieri nodded.

"Okay, we've just passed under seven. On the high end of theta." The excitement pumped Weisman's pitch up an octave.

"Just a few more seconds. Just a few more…" Altieri called back.

They waited.

After an eternity which amounted to no more than ten seconds, Weisman announced: "We're wavering between five-and-a-half and six…."

All eyes shot over to Christopher Pennfield.

He appeared placid and rested, his brainwaves smack in the middle of theta range. If he were ever going to reach the exalted Ganzfeld State, it would be now, his mind maximally sensitized to whatever psychic vibrations lurked within the air.

On the opposite side of the deck, Altieri looked up at her anesthesiologist: "Okay, administer the sedative."

The anesthesiologist twisted the valve on the IV, allowing the sedative to enter Ship's bloodstream, then counted down:

Five Four Three Two One.

After a short pause, the anesthesiologist nodded at Altieri. Although she had administered ECT many times before, this time Altieri shook slightly. Altieri took a deep breath and pushed the button: *eighty joules.*

The electricity zapped Ship's brain, excited his neurons. He shook: suddenly and violently, rattling the table, challenging the strength of its straps.

Silently, they waited.

Nothing.

Altieri, Swann, and Weisman: they all scanned the area looking for something magical.

Only stillness and silence.

"WELL?" Weisman shrugged after a long pause.

"All we can do is wait." Altieri nodded.

A soft breeze caressed the April twilight. The inlet's water, frothy and silver, shimmered in harmony with the winds. But, still, nothing else.

Weisman glanced over at Christopher. Outwardly, he seemed relaxed, the EEG still indicating theta range activity. For some odd reason, Weisman sympathized with him for the moment. True, he had been a lecherous, condescending rapscallion for most of his years, but the guilt and humiliation from the Jennifer Winston episode and his downfall at the College had weighed heavily upon him. Perhaps even Christopher Pennfield deserved a moment of peace and tranquility, he thought.

Vigilantly, they all scanned the area, waiting for something. Anything.

Nothing. Only graying shades of twilight.

Weisman looked up, took a deep breath, and relished in his own moment of peace and tranquility, courtesy of the shimmering water and the inlet's salty air. As he surveyed the soothing scene, Weisman thought he caught a glimpse of movement out of the corner of his eye.

He squinted, silent and still.

"Jules?" Swann tugged at his shoulder.

"Shhhhh!" Weisman focused intently upon the shoreline.

"Wha...what's up?" Swann whispered anxiously.

He shushed him again. A hunter stalking his prey, Weisman motioned for Swann to remain still.

Weisman smiled, a gleam in his eye.

Yes, there was movement.

Weisman was sure he could see several small wispy figures skirmishing around near the embankment overlooking the inlet. Silently, he pointed, directing Swann to observe. Then there were sounds. Soft and distant echoes, as if muffled by time's weary passage:

"Hey, Arthur!"

"Yeah?"

"Heads up!"

"Moron!"

Weisman gasped. Swann and Altieri huddled behind him. Together, they observed. Two of the figures ran off. The third, smaller and slighter than the others, appeared to heave something towards them, and then walked over to the end of the dock.

Weisman turned and winked at his two colleagues.

Upon arriving at the end of the dock, the smaller figure tossed something into the water. After that, he just sat there. Silently, Weisman, Swann and Altieri strained to observe every possible detail. The apparition— the boy, or whatever it was— sat motionless at the dock's edge.

Then, almost as an afterthought, Weisman turned to his colleagues and pointed.

"Wha…?" Altieri answered, dumbfounded.

"Look," Weisman whispered. "Up there." He pointed to a spot about ten feet over the water, above the apparition.

A body, a naked body of what appeared to a middle-aged man, hovered over the water.

"Holy Shit!" Altieri shuddered.

* * *

The twilight shimmered, playing mind-games with McPherson. By instinct, he would scan the area every half minute or so, assuring that no unwelcomed guests trespassed on their privacy. When his eyes landed again on the dock, he scratched his temple and squinted.

The mind-games intensified.

At dock's edge, the murky gray of evening seduced his mind: a burgeoning image flirted with his imagination.

McPherson stared, shook his head vigorously, and then stared again.

Huh?

Strange enough that he was watching his naked boss levitating over a Ganzfeld device, but stranger even more that he was convinced— *convinced beyond a doubt*— that he saw a small kid sitting on the edge of the dock, and then a carbon-copy of Mr. MP floating naked above the inlet.

Certainly, the twilight was playing games with him, an optical illusion.

He rubbed his eyes and looked again.

They were both still there. The little kid at the end of the dock— *God knows where he came from!* — and then the mirror-image of his nude boss floating above the inlet.

Jesus! Was he going nuts? Or was it that he tossed down too many cold-ones last night with his old buddies from the NYGABPD?

As he strained his eyes to observe even the most minute detail of this strange occurrence, McPherson's ears rang. Through this empty vacant ringing, he thought he could hear something hollow, distant, as if escaping from the bottom of a deep well, but still they were words, real words.

Tell me! Tell me who you are. A distant, yet thunderous voice rattled the heavens.

"Please don't. No. No. I want to go." Shivering, the young boy pleaded, gazing at this body hovering above him.

Who are you? The voice echoed around the inlet.

Fear evidently infested the young boy. *"Didn't you hear me? I don't want to. I want to play."*

Please. Please. Tell me who you are. The voice was unrelenting.

A long shivering silence, then, a soft whisper:

"I'm Shippy."

Dumbfounded and shocked, McPherson concentrated on the scene unfolding before him. The little figure at the end of the dock was conversing with JMP, had to be. *But was he conversing with the JMP on the Ganzfeld machine at the base of the dock or the JMP floating above the water? Or both?*

McPherson scratched his temple.

* * *

Huddled together as if in a foxhole, Weisman, Swann and Altieri watched silently, their jaws hanging in awe. The scene played out clearly before them: the young boy, alone, at the dock's edge somehow conversing with a supine, naked body floating mysteriously above the inlet.

They remained silent and still, both not to disturb the psychic harmony of the moment and to allow their straining ears to detect the scene's hollow, distant chatter.

Shippy? The distant voice from the heavens questioned.

"Yes, I'm Shippy." The young boy nodded.

Are you a Pennfield? The imperious tone of the voice demanded an immediate answer.

"How did you know that?" Startled, the young boy snapped back.

In the still darkness of the early evening, Weisman clutched the hands of his two colleagues.

I am, too. The voice answered.

"Really? Then why aren't you at my house?" the boy asked sheepishly.

His mind churning, the scientist inside Weisman forced him to question everything. Was this a group hallucination? Why was the naked body hovering over the inlet? Why did the words of the young boy seem to be coming directly from his lips, while the words of the other floating body were coming from the atmosphere, as if from the voice of God?

Why should I be? The voice challenged him.

"Because all my family's at my house. It's Christmas." The young boy explained.

I may not be of your time. The shimmering words rippled through the twilight.

Holy Shit! Weisman thought. *No, Holy Einstein, Newton, Bohr and Kuhn!* If this whole thing they're observing can be taken at face value— *not that it should be* —he may just be witness to the very first credible proof of human beings transcending the boundary of time.

He shook.

* * *

The trained, discerning senses of McPherson could still not determine who the little figure at the end of the dock was conversing with: the ghost-like JMP floating over the inlet, or the real JMP levitating above the Ganzfeld machine. Intently, he listened.

Why should I be?

"Because all my family's at my house. It's Christmas."

I may not be of your time.

"I don't understand."

McPherson shook his head, blinked, and looked again, cupping his ear with his hand. It wasn't the nature of what they were discussing that confounded him so— although shocking, in and of its own right — it was the source of JMP's voice that perplexed him. It seemed to just emanate from the atmosphere, coming from nowhere, but then everywhere.

"You're scaring me."

That's not what I'm here for. I think we can help each other.

"Please. Please don't scare me."

I'm not. Listen to me. You're my only gateway.

"I'm not a gate. I'm scared. Go away."

* * *

Weisman's euphoria over the human race's possible conquest of trans-temporal contact was abruptly interrupted by something even more baffling. He was so intent on focusing on the small figure at the end of the dock and the larger naked figure floating above the inlet, he had neglected to spot something right before his eyes: another naked figure, almost an exact carbon copy of the first, levitating a few feet off the ground at the base of the dock.

Weisman blinked. *Yes*, it was really there. He scratched his bald head. As his mind rummaged, he listened.

"You're scaring me."

That's not what I'm here for. I think we can help each other.

What a disjointed scene, Weisman thought. A kid— presumably the young Ship— at the edge of a dock, a naked body levitating over the water, the voice of God or whomever emanating from above or wherever, and a clone of the naked body levitating at the base of the dock. And now—

Oh my God!

He squinted. Did he see yet another figure standing upright at the dock's base?

"Please. Please don't scare me." The young boy's teeth rattled.

I'm not. Listen to me. You're my only gateway. The amorphous voice countered.

Gateway? Weisman's mind churned. *Could it be? Could this possibly mean what he thinks it means?* That would be remarkable. More than remarkable, actually, that would be—

"I'm not a gate. I'm scared. Go away."

* * *

Adhering to his strict training as a cop, McPherson carefully swiveled around, surveying the scene for any other possible source of the voices. First the stone embankment: nothing, shoreline clear to the point. Then the grounds: only shimmering grass. Then he turned towards the dock.

He froze.

A foggy image. Shaded by the twilight, but there was something there. He squinted, sharpening his focus. Wispy and faint, as if shaded by a large gray translucent curtain…

* * *

This time Weisman was sure he saw it: another figure at the base of the dock.

He interrupted his mental musings and observed, focusing.

Definitely, he was sure of it now.

This one stout and burly, standing adjacent to the body levitating near the dock's base.

Was the figure looking at them?

Somehow, someway, Weisman felt strange, violated.

Was the past merging with the present merging with the future?

* * *

McPherson strained his eyes, focusing on the dock.

Very indistinct, very diffuse, but he could swear he saw something.

Machines possibly? Technicians working?

As his eyes scanned the deck, he sensed movement in the foreground.

Quickly, he redirected his focus.

Some figures, huddled, on the grass, in front of the deck.

Instinctively, he pointed.

* * *

Weisman tapped his two colleagues.

They looked up and saw him, stout and burly.

Holy Shit!

Weisman whispered very softly, "I think he's aware of us."

"Can't be," Swann whispered back tersely.

"Just look. Just look."

Silence. Then—

They gasped.

The mysterious figure was pointing, pointing right at them!

Reflexively, they bristled, overcome with nervous energy.

* * *

McPherson braced himself, standing stout, staring at the strange shadows in the twilight.

What the hell were they doing here? He thought just like a cop would think.

A sudden jerk.

He sensed movement, slight movement: the three huddled in the foreground.

His spine shivered.

Again, he pointed.

* * *

Now, Weisman was sure.

The stout, burly figure saw them, reacted to their movement, pointing right at them.

Weisman motioned his colleagues forward to get a closer look.
Quietly, they shuffled.
Fear flowed through their veins. Curiosity spurred them on.

* * *

SUSPICIOUS, McPherson reached for his G-pen.
He stood motionless. Until—
The three huddled figures shifted, moving towards him.

* * *

THEY WATCHED.
The stout, burly man pulled something out of his belt.
A gun?

* * *

MCPHERSON FIRED.
Zap! A bright streak of light flashed across the grounds.

* * *

36

Greenwich, Connecticut, Indian Harbor, Evening, April 14, 2007

"Just think about it Bren, Ed, Chris," Weisman jabbered, his arms flapping, "this might have been… could have been… very well was… one of the most significant events in the history of…"

"Slow down, Jules," Altieri interrupted. "Let's not put the cart before the horse."

"Yeah, but I think you're underestimating the significance of what we all just saw," Weisman entreated.

They sat around a big bronze fire-pit set in the glass house's center atrium, assessing the consequences of what they had just collectively experienced, or *thought* they had experienced. Their moods ranged from somber— Pennfield stretched out in a lounge chair, quietly sipping champagne, a warm washcloth draped over his forehead— to reserved: Swann and Altieri sitting contemplatively on the atrium's large, canvas-upholstered couch. And then there was the wild enthusiasm of Weisman.

"Before we jump to any conclusions," Altieri warned them, "why don't we review the details of what we *think* we all just experienced? Then we can corroborate with the tapes. Agreed?" She looked over at Swann. "Ed?"

"OK. Sure," Swann agreed. "Once the ECT was administered we eventually saw an apparent apparition of three or four small kids scampering around near the water. Everyone agree?"

They nodded.

"Yes, but there's a key question here." Weisman flapped his arms again, standing up. "Was it an apparition or was it something else?"

"And just what would you propose it was, Jules?" Altieri asked.

"Could've been a number of things," Weisman answered excitedly. "For instance, a discontinuity in the space-time fabric or maybe an uncovering of a quasi-parallel facet of the multiverse or…"

"Whoa!" Altieri held up her hand, placing a brake on her partner's enthusiasm. "Slow down, hon. Slow down."

"Okay," Swann went on, "so the kids are playing. We hear some mumbling and chattering. The two bigger ones look like they throw something at the small one. They run off towards the shoreline, the smaller one walks off slowly towards the dock. Concur?"

Again, they nodded.

"So that raises a question," Swann stated. "Chris, is that the way you remembered it happening the evening of your family Christmas party in 1963?"

PENNFIELD SAT ALL the way up, sipped champagne from his fluted glass, and then pursed his lips. "Well, I must say, I wasn't outside at the time, but I do specifically remember after I exchanged some trivial pleasantries with Shippy in French, he asked Aunt Bun if he could go outside and play with his cousins. Her initial response was 'no,' but then Ophelia intervened."

"So it's not infeasible to think the three kids were outside playing in the snow, maybe even throwing snowballs?" Swann asked.

"Perhaps." Pennfield shrugged.

"Okay." Swann paced across the atrium, "let's assume that for some reason after they throw a few snowballs Ship goes off by himself to the end of the dock. He throws something into the water— maybe another snowball?— and then just sits there. So that was about when Jules pointed at us and we see what appears to be a naked body hovering about ten feet over the inlet. Correct?"

Altieri paused for a moment, then answered, "As much as I want to deny it, as strange as it seems, I can't. Yes, I saw the body of a naked middle-aged man hovering over the inlet."

"Then the little boy seems to be conversing with this naked man, but the voice isn't really coming from the man, it's just there." Swann pointed upward.

"Exactly. Exactly." Still enthused, Weisman answered.

"Then here's when it got crazy," Swann interjected.

"As if it wasn't already?" Pennfield muttered.

"So we hear a conversation between the young kid and what seems to be the body floating above the inlet," Swann continued. "This voice from above asks who he is and he answers, *Shippy.* So far, so good. Then they get into a conversation about if he's a Pennfield or not."

"That's it!" Weisman sprang up off the couch and snapped his fingers. *"Don't you see? It's so, so obvious!* The vision, the connections involved, caused the young kid to go *nutso, bonkers.* I mean, the voice scared him, but the collision of times, the talking across time, pushed his brain, I think, into a catatonic state."

"My dear Jules," Pennfield broke in, "I would think, out of respect alone, your vocabulary is rich enough to come up with something superior to *nutso* or *bonkers*."

"Okay. Okay." Weisman paced across the marble floor and jabbered animatedly. "But then the whole scene goes weird on us, goes 'incredulous.' *That okay, Chris?* We see another naked body levitating at the base of the dock. Then some stocky, burly guy standing next to the second levitating body. Then, this stocky guy seems to be aware of our presence. He points at us twice and then reaches for what appears to be some sort of weapon…"

"Which begs the question," Altieri interjected, "just *what was it* that we saw?"

Weisman smiled at her. "What do you think, Bren?"

"Possibly…" Altieri began tentatively, "… just possibly, we can hypothesize that the combination of Chris and Ship in sensitized states induced an apparition of Ship being *visited*—for a lack of a better term— by this body hovering over the inlet."

"Which begs the question, where did the naked body hovering over the inlet come from?" Weisman addressed the group. "Which begs the further question, where did the carbon copy of the naked body hovering off the ground at the base of the dock and the burly figure standing next to it come from?"

"Ed? Chris?" Altieri nodded at his colleagues.

Swann shook his head. "I don't know. And…why was it, he, *naked…* I'm at a total loss."

"Okay, here's a theory." Weisman sprung up from his seat again. "Suppose, just suppose now, that the two figures at the base of the dock, were doing the exact same thing that we were doing?"

"What do you mean by that?" Altieri asked.

"Suppose for some reason, they were trying to conjure up an apparition of that very same event, an apparition of the day Ship went catatonic. Except they were doing it from another point in time," Weisman answered.

"But why?" Swann asked.

Weisman shrugged. "Could be a variety of reasons. But suppose somehow the two events *overlapped* for lack of a better term. We both sort of tuned into the same apparition."

"Interesting…" Swann interjected, pacing the perimeter of the atrium.

"Ed?" Altieri responded. They all looked at him.

"I've heard stories, never experienced it myself, mind you, but I've heard stories of similar occurrences," said Swann. "There's this famous one, about the owners of an old farm house somewhere in Pennsylvania. One night, they're in the living room watching TV, and, lo and behold, they see an apparition of a guy taking a bath in one of those old-fashioned tubs, smack in the middle of their living room. Funny thing is, the guy taking the bath was just as scared of them as they were of him."

"You see! You see!" Weisman jumped up off the couch. "Just as I thought, two moments in time occupying the same space. That's what it was, had to be."

"Jules?" Altieri spoke softly.

"Yes, darling?" He answered teasingly.

"We all appreciate your enthusiasm, but let's slow down a bit."

"Okay, but here's a thought." Weisman snapped his fingers. "Suppose the body levitating at the base of the dock is the same person who is hovering over the water. Reasonable, huh?" He scanned the group.

Altieri nodded. "I suppose, but…"

"Okay, then suppose this," Weisman interrupted. "Suppose somehow previously he made contact with Ship and wanted to make contact again."

"Interesting speculation, Jules, but—"

"We heard something. We all heard it, I think." Weisman interrupted his mate Altieri. "The voice from above said something to the effect of, *'You're my only gateway'* and the young boy answered back, *'I don't want to be a gate.'* Agreed?"

They all nodded.

"So he's trying to contact Ship again, and by so doing inadvertently connects with us as well. The apparition of Ship at the end of the dock is acting as a kind of bridge between us and them, between two different points in time, actually three. Then the stocky guy sees us, points at us, and fires some sort of weapon."

Altieri squinted, concentrating. "So, we have two apparitions occurring simultaneously?"

"Not really," Weisman answered. "Ship on the dock and the body over the water could very well have been an apparition. But, to me, the body at the base of the dock and the stout man next to him would have to have been the result of a discontinuity in the space-time fabric. They were here as much as we were, just like incident at the farmhouse Ed described."

"Whoa! Slow down, Jules." Altieri interrupted him. "Are you actually claiming that both ourselves as well as the other two people, presumably from somewhere between 1963 and now, observed the apparition – and each other – simultaneously?"

"Yep, mostly right."

"I think you need some *serious* therapy."

"You psychiatrists," Weisman chided her. "To you everything new and different is some sort of psychiatric disorder. Geez, I'm glad you weren't around to analyze Galileo, Bren. You would've had him locked up just like the rest of them. But to answer your question, I really think the two at the base of the dock *were not* from between 1963 and now…."

"Then where were they from?" Swann asked.

Weisman paused, and then smiled. "The future."

"Huh?" Altieri gasped.

"I think they were from the future."

"That's preposterous!" Pennfield shot up from the couch. "The future hasn't happened yet."

"Oh yes it has."

* * *

TIME FRAME: 2052

37

NEWQUE GAB: St. Johns, Newfoundland, Placentia Bay, December 5, 2052

The session at Indian Harbor had prompted JMP to intensify both his alacrity and focus. His escapes to Placentia Bay became more frequent, squeezed in between all his myriad obligations. His sole purpose was to Ganzfeld his way into some sort of breakthrough, some clue that would at least begin to peel away the skin of the onion, moving him even the tiniest bit closer to the discovery of his holy grail— *who is this Shippy and how might he possibly be of help with Jennifer and the Pennfield family curse?*

The sessions were hit or miss. Sometimes his mind would tune into events somewhat related— perhaps a visitation to a family member in the 1880s or 1920s— or completely off course— a soothsayer from the future or some Ouija-board practitioner from the 1980s. But every once in a while, JMP's psychic sensitivities would tune into something compelling, an insight that would free him to single-mindedly focus his gifted mind on the strange mysteries of Arthur, and the woman in the tavern. It took almost twenty sessions before JMP discovered what he believed to be a breakthrough.

Strange, he thought as his mind whirled through a fusillade of visions, ideas, time and space. Levitating over his Ganzfeld machine deep in the recesses of his Placentia Bay refuge, sheltered from all outside stimuli, he enwrapped himself in an array of different worlds, unfolding randomly within his mind or, perhaps, as part of some deeper collective mind.

The visions perplexed him.

He saw a young boy— tall, blonde and handsome— lounging on a courtyard on a college campus, his face buried in a book. As JMP's psyche hovered in closer, he could almost read the fine print. A biology book, some sort of advanced biology textbook. JMP's psyche swirled around, up and above. A bird's eye view. The gothic structures around were so familiar. Could it be? Yale. Yes, it was Yale. Practically a Pennfield family tradition...

Swallowed up by some sort of fog, the vision melted. JMP floated in the whiteness, disoriented, until the fog cleared once more. Then another vision:

A jungle. Africa! Or perhaps a Brazilian rain forest. Hard to place. He swooped into a dilapidated poverty-stricken village. On the outskirts he saw large white tents with a large red cross painted on it. People emerged in what looked like white, hooded space-suits. One of them walked into another, smaller tent. JMP followed. There, the person carefully removed the suit, piece by piece, following some sort of protocol. When he removed his hood, JMP was surprised. Was this the same person he saw at Yale, but about a decade or so older?

The vision blurred away, returning JMP's psyche to white blandness. He was consumed by the nothingness for what seemed quite a while, or perhaps not, floating in through a cloud until a new vision peeked through.

This time he saw the same man again, perhaps aged another decade. Imprisoned somewhere, his hands and feet shackled, under heavy guard. He was about to be taken out of his cell. Large men in military garb escorted him, one on each side, three in front, three in back. They escorted him to some sort of public square. It was filled with people. They paraded him up to a guillotine...

Upon awakening, JMP proceeded through his usual post-Ganzfeld ritual. First, he would enter his nearby steam bath for ten or fifteen minutes, allowing a healthy sweat to drench his skin, as if expurgating himself of any toxic thoughts or concepts experienced during the session. The time for emotion and intuition was over, now rationality would prevail. Next, he showered himself quickly in cold water, draining the toxic sweat beads forever away. Enwrapping himself in a lush terrycloth robe, he would then sit in his underwater glass chamber lined with teak— the deep waters of Placentia Bay illuminated by powerful arc-lights— and sip green tea imported from Thailand as he contemplated the meaning of his session.

Placid and calm, he attempted to interpret his experience.

His mind raced through the possibilities: Could that person possibly be Shippy? Hard to tell. Yet, something told him, some instinctive impulse, that whatever and whomever it was had something to do with his current predicament.

With a sudden jerk, he pointed at the ceiling. A hologram materialized.

"Mr. MP? That you?" A tired Bryan McPherson rubbed his eyes as he lifted himself off the couch in his distant home.

"Who else would bother you at this time of night?"

McPherson pulled out his e-let and focused his fuzzy eyes. "It's only eleven. No big deal. What's up?"

"In my latest Ganzfeld session, I saw certain images that I would like to further explore, I was wondering if we could try to reconstruct them with that IRH machine of yours?"

"Sure, when would you like to do it?" McPherson responded.

"Tomorrow morning, my office"

"Done."

* * *

38

Manhattan, NYCGAB, Pennfield Technologies Tower, Morning, December 6, 2052

"You ready?" McPherson meticulously applied the IRH device's sensors to JMP's bald skull.

"Whenever you are." JMP sat back, relaxed in his comfortable levitating glass chair.

"Okay, same as last time," McPherson began. "I want you to think of those scenes that you experienced during your Ganzfeld session. The machine'll create a hologram and then you can have it adjust to your own specs. Once we get a few of them, I'll run them through a database of images from all over the world from the last hundred years or so and see if we can get a few matches. If we can get a fix on the general locations and time frame, we should be able to find out who this character is you've been dreaming about."

"I'm not *dreaming* about anyone," JMP retorted. "It's more like this fellow has been *trespassing* upon my tranquility."

"Oh, I see," McPherson commented as he adjusted the dials on the IRH machine. "Now relax and concentrate, Mr. MP."

GRADUALLY, the image appeared: as it cubellated into clarity, its identity became evident. A jungle, apparently Africa or South America. Big white tents with a red cross emblazoned on their sides. Two figures in spaceman-like suits walk out and into a smaller tent. They remove the protective clothing. One of them is blonde and appears to be in his early to mid-thirties.

"Does the image correspond with your memory?" the RH machine asked.

"Yes. Yes. Very close. Almost exactly," Mashimoto-Pennfield answered.

"Okay, that's one. Wanna move on, Mr. MP?

"Sure Bryan."

IN THE NEXT FORTY-FIVE MINUTES, the RH machine generated five more images from the mind of Jimmy Mashimoto-Pennfield, all displaying different times and places, but with a common thread: that blonde young man.

* * *

TIME FRAME: 2007

39

Boothbay Harbor, Maine, Early Morning, May 3, 2007

Christopher Pennfield's bouts with the paranormal accelerated over the next several weeks. It reached the point where he was almost embarrassed to tell Swann, Altieri and Weisman. He feared losing whatever credibility he had left. Each time another of these nighttime episodes transpired— as real as they were to him— he wondered if he was slowly losing his mind.

It happened again on a Wednesday night. Pennfield slowly rubbed his eyes as the blurry bedroom morphed into clarity. He surveyed the fuzzy room, settling on the clock: 3:15am. As always, the alcohol was toying with his rest-time, tranquilizing him into what he thought was peaceful sleep and then rudely awakening him with a sudden jolt. *Oh well, the price we pay for our petty indulgences!*

As he prepared to flip back over, he saw her glimmering outside his window.

"Ophie?"

Silent, she nodded.

There was something playful about her, almost pixie-ish, as she waved from beyond the window, beckoning him to join her.

"What? But how could I possibly..." Pennfield asked as he sat up and adjusted his glasses.

Silent, she smiled suggestively and motioned for him to come.

Her presence energized him. Was she teasing him, flirting with him, seducing him, inviting him, or all of the above? Kaleidoscopic, she flipped through a range of ages and dispositions, all of them sparkling.

He yearned to go with her: *but how?*

She looked so inviting out there, so soothing, so unencumbered.

Yes, it would be wonderful to join her.

Marvelous, splendid, ethereal…

Then, a sudden gasp.

Was she here to take him away?

Was this it?

As in forever?

He sweat, cool beads trickling down his clammy face.

But, as his eyes settled on her again, the sweat evaporated, dissipating into thin air; she had a marvelous capacity to soothe him, always did.

As she floated, smiling in that most deliciously seductive way of hers, he felt himself being pulled to her— some mystical, magical force lifting him from his bed.

A strong, prickling narcotic filled his lungs, bubbling effervescently, delightfully warming his heart, his mind, his soul, with an uplifting, euphoric, calming sensation.

Buoyant, he rose from the bed like a helium balloon and bounced up against the ceiling. It had happened once before— this funny, uplifting, buoyant sensation— many years earlier, and this time was just as delightful, maybe more so.

He looked out at Ophelia, she motioned for him to come.

He smiled with boyish glee, giggling as he floated towards the large leaded window. As he looked back, he noticed himself— literally, his own flesh and blood, or his remains —still stretched out on his grand, four-poster bed.

But, for some odd reason, he hardly cared. He had no worries now. He was bonding with the infinite. He slipped effortlessly through the windowpanes, feeling nothing at all.

A hummingbird, Ophelia hovered before him— a mystical, seductive figure, sparkling like a jewel. She waved for him to follow.

She was toying with him, her salaciously engaging smirk, her soft skin, her full red lips doing all her talking.

He floated towards her, following her into the mist hovering above the harbor.

THEY RODE a pillow of air along the New England coast— floating and rising above the craggy Maine coastline, the frothy waters of Boston Harbor, the sandy fishhook at the Cape's north end, the Sankaty Head Light on the eastern tip of Nantucket, then over to the twinkling lights of Montauk. They rose higher and higher, floating effortlessly across Long Island Sound, over small islands dotting the Connecticut coast. Then the lights grew more dense and brighter—New Haven, Bridgeport, Stamford. Now over the grand waterfront homes of Fairfield and Westchester counties; he could even make out the glass and stucco eyesore that was once Uncle' Perce's legendary Dutch Colonial.

The Sound narrowed, siphoning them ever closer to its endpoint. He followed Ophie above the Throggs Neck and then the Whitestone bridges. The lights of Manhattan twinkled against the deep indigo sky, rivaling the stars above.

Then, a sudden shift.

Misty. It grew very, very misty— a deep cloud of fog enveloping them both, masking the twinkling city beyond. He lost all perspective, floating along in this homogenized soup: no up, no down, no left, no right. He wondered: *was this a passageway, a bridge to some other, better place?*

But why here— at Hell's Gate, where the Sound funnels into the East River?

What was the significance?

Just as suddenly as it had appeared, the fog lifted.

But where was Ophie?

Pennfield rubbed his imaginary eyes and looked left, right, up, down.

Still no Ophie.

What's this? No guide, no muse, no inspiration?

Then, he noticed it: a brilliant, shimmering city glistening on the horizon.

Manhattan, for sure, but it was different, raised to some higher sort of level.

BLINDED BY THE BRILLIANCE, Pennfield scanned the panorama. Cleary, the city had evolved. Columns of small aircraft zoomed up, down, and above the city as if following some predetermined skyway. He recognized the Triborough and 59th Street Bridges. The Roosevelt Island Tramway was no longer there, apparently replaced by a series of small aircraft hovering back and forth across the East River. He looked farther downtown, recognizing the Empire State Building.

Clearly, a mixture of classic New York skyline with some wonderfully innovative structures: a shiny glass corkscrew of a skyscraper towering well above the Empire State, and a completely spherical structure, about thirty stories tall, perched prominently upon a shiny, gold, ten-story pedestal where the UN used to stand, and at midtown, giant glass arches spanning from the East Side to the West Side— glowing majestically in the night— tubes for a series of small, cylindrical capsules transporting people crosstown.

He looked over towards Jersey and saw a giant terminal extending out over the Hudson—a tremendously massive structure of glass and steel stretching halfway across the river— an apparent embarkation point for an astonishingly fast train zooming southward. He followed one as it streamed on giant tracks built above the river— hugging the Jersey coast— past rows upon rows of massive solar panels where there used to be only hideous round oil tanks.

Then, momentarily, he looked up, and saw a marvelous sight.

Hanging in the southwestern sky was a brilliant sliver of a moon, a sharp edge to its thinness, the sun's light reflecting magically from below. And across from this magnificent sliver shone two tremendously bright stars, almost as if honoring it with their presence.

Enraptured by it all, Pennfield floated onward, down Manhattan's eastern contour. Rows and columns of those small aircraft— resembling cars with jet engines— flew above the path of the FDR. He looked down: small, yellow, round devices— somewhat reminiscent of cabs— were the only vehicles at street level. The Lower East Side bulged exaggeratedly into the river, definitely not how he remembered it.

In the thick of this unnatural revision of his own memories, something caught his eye: a brilliant, unusual structure sprouting from the bulge. Built on what he presumed must be some sort of landfill, the structure rose majestically, bending upon itself, forming a trapezoidal loop—those small aircraft streaming right through it— and then two towers rising from the top section, one slightly taller than the other.

Magnetically, this structure attracted him. He flew onward: past all sorts of unusual structures, closer and closer to that magnificent building. Finally he could read the inscription emblazoned across the side of the trapezoid's top plank: *Pennfield Technologies.*

His chest swelled. Another tribute to his family's greatness, obviously. But what was the meaning of it all? Was this just a dream, his mind projecting his family's prowess into future generations? Or was he trapped in some neverland, halfway between life and death, his spirit straying in some sort of time warp?

Or was it something else?

HE PONDERED every possibility as he flew closer and closer to the structure— towards the upper plank of the trapezoid and then, suddenly, he felt a jolting rush as he rose up the taller of the two towers, his imaginary stomach struggling to keep up with his spirit. Faster and faster and faster, he rose.

And just as suddenly, he slowed, now gliding effortlessly, rising to the top like a lazy ember hovering above a glowing fire. And what a stunning view— a three-hundred-and-sixty-degree panorama of brilliant lights, streaming airborne vehicles, and a spectacular nighttime sky.

He looked inside the glass structure— a huge round office, a floating desk and a floating spiral staircase leading up to some sort of sanctuary above, at the very peak of the tower.

He saw two men talking: one burly and stocky, wearing a traditional business suit— two sizes two small— the other taut and muscular, with a bald head and slightly pointed ears, wearing black leather pants and a tight black silk shirt, hugging his bulging arms.

As he studied the man in black, he barely noticed he had floated through the building's thick glass wall right into the office. He was intrigued by the fellow's face. Yes, his head was shaven bald. Yes, he seemed to have some Asian features, particularly around the brow and eyes. But, in a way, he had a distinctively Pennfield look— a straight, non-descript nose, a dimpled chin and relatively high cheekbones; in fact, Christopher would say, from the nose down the man was definitely a Pennfield.

Mesmerized by the man's face, Christopher was jolted when the man suddenly pointed to a spot above his desk and a series of three-dimensional images appeared. This man— this taut, muscular man bearing at least a modest Pennfield family resemblance— pointed at the images and apparently was discussing them with the stocky, burly man. But, he couldn't hear a single word of it. The bald fellow poked and pointed at the images, jabbering away with his colleague. Pennfield floated closer and then settled behind the two of them, giving himself a clear view of the images.

Pennfield's heart began to race as he made out images of that night at his nephew Winston's house at Indian Harbor. Clearly, he could make out a picture of the dock area in the twilight. Then, muddy gray pictures of Swann, Weisman and Dr. Altieri, crouching near the shoreline. And then a blurry picture of him on the cot with those ping-pong balls over his eyes.

Then the stocky fellow talked and pointed across the room: more images materialized. This time they were actual, clear pictures.

Oh My God, Pennfield thought.

Pictures of Swann, Dr. Altieri, Weisman and himself. Like mug shots. The stocky man pointed at each one apparently explaining who the characters were in the first set of blurry, grey images likely recorded that night out at Indian Harbor.

Then, the stocky man pointed to another section of the vast round office and another row of images materialized.

A young, blonde man lounging with a textbook on a college courtyard.

A jungle, the same blonde young man, a bit older perhaps, removing some sort of weird protective suit.

Older yet, the same man in prison, being lead to a guillotine.

He studied the pictures, and then suddenly gasped.

Could that young man be Ship?

* * *

"MR. SWANN, ED," Christopher Pennfield blurted into the phone first thing the next morning, "I've had another one of those...what do you call them? OBEs?"

"Out-of-Body Experiences?" Swann responded groggily, awakened by the call.

"Out-of-body, yes, and an experience, definitely," Pennfield answered.

"And where did you go? What did you see?" Swann asked, slipping into his shoes.

"Well, last time I had one of these... um... experiences, I observed the past. I think this time I may have stumbled upon the future."

"Really?" Swann scratched his head. "Okay. I think we should get Brenda and Jules on the phone. Don't you?"

"So be it."

* * *

TIME FRAME: 2052

40

Manhattan, NYCGAB, Pennfield Technologies Tower, Evening, December 7, 2052

Deep in contemplation, Jimmy Mashimoto-Pennfield gazed out his office window, his soul filled with wanderlust. Surrounded by the city's vibrant twinkling lights, the smooth contemporary architecture of his office blended skillfully with New York's more classic structures. The brightly illuminated vista stretching westward to the Hudson and eastward and southward to the Atlantic, kept JMP in perpetual awe.

Yet tonight it was nothing human-made that struck Mashimoto-Pennfield's fancy. Tonight, he focused on the celestial. He gazed upon the sliver moon— ever so thin and delicate— forming an elegant triangle with Venus and Jupiter. It seemed a piece of delicate jewelry, a dainty sliver of white gold designed by a master craftsman, its luster enhanced by two elegant diamonds, sparkling against a rich indigo sky.

Despite his urbanity, JMP was constantly amazed by the workings of the cosmos: at how the universe's fabric of space and time— encompassing billions of galaxies, trillions of stars, comets, quasars, planets, black holes, dark matter and all sorts of yet undiscovered phenomena—responded to the rhythms of some higher-order force. He was astounded by the replication of this special phenomena— this magical triangle of Venus, Jupiter and the sliver moon over the New York skyline— every forty-five years. Yet as stunning as it was, it was only a small residue of much greater forces acting upon one another.

"Mr. MP?"

Mashimoto-Pennfield grimaced. It was McPherson. His momentary high came to an abrupt end.

He turned around. "Yes Bryan?"

"Got some stuff to share with you." Somewhat disheveled, a tight raincoat twisted around his stocky frame, McPherson stood huffing in JMP's doorway. "Got a few minutes?"

"If it's what I think it is, absolutely," JMP answered.

"So here." McPherson briskly pointed his finger to a spot about four feet above JMP's desk.

Immediately, four virtual screens materialized, projecting four side-by-side holograms.

"Okay, here are some pictures my gnat-cams recorded at Indian Harbor," McPherson began, pointing to the screen furthest to the left. "So over here we have the dock. That's you hovering over the Ganzfeld chamber at the base and the… uh… *other* you, hovering about twenty feet above the water. Then, of course, there's the kid, and me."

"Yes… Yes…" JMP nodded, waiting for more.

"Then, there's the three people sorta huddled on the grounds about halfway between the dock and the shoreline," he continued, pointing at the second screen, "then next to that is all of the medical paraphernalia and the hospital bed and then far over to the right, we have some elderly guy laying down on a cot with some sort of mask or something over his eyes."

"Fine," JMP answered briskly. "But what does it all mean?"

"I'm getting there," McPherson answered anxiously. "Let's start with the three figures huddled together on the grounds." He pointed at the image and directed it to zoom in. "I know it gets really fuzzy, but here's our first guy. I matched these images with over a hundred million databases and I think I got an ID on him."

McPherson pointed to another section of the office and another virtual screen appeared, showcasing a flat, two-dimensional picture of an older man — bald with a round face and rosy red cheeks. "The guy's name is Swann, Ed Swann. Born 1927, deceased May 23, 2008. Graduated from Columbia University with a degree in English, took over his family's construction business and retired at age sixty-three. His wife, Marie, died in 1984 from cancer. Born in Jersey City, lived most of his adult life in Montclair, New Jersey then retired to Spring Lake, New Jersey."

"And how does that help us, Bryan?" JMP snapped.

"Hold on. Hold on." McPherson pointed at his boss. "Seems as if after he retired from the construction business, the guy wasn't satisfied with just playing a few rounds of golf a week."

"Oh?"

"Seems as if he took up a second career, or maybe a hobby is more like it..."

"Like what?"

"So, get this," McPherson giggled, "seems as if the guy was a *ghost hunter*. Actually, he had a pretty good rep. Written up in the newspapers. Apparently helped solve a few people's problems." He paused. "Mr. MP?"

JMP grinned gleefully. "Oh, this is too cute, too precious." He giggled. "So they hired a *ghost hunter* to come to the house because they thought it was haunted." He giggled again.

"Apparently so," McPherson answered. "Okay, so let's move on." He pointed again to the fuzzy image of the three figures huddled on the grounds of Indian Harbor. "Now this fellow here," the holographic image zoomed in. "This fellow here is a Dr. Julian Weisman." He again pointed across the room, and another two-dimensional image— a picture of Weisman with scraggly hair and his salt and pepper beard— materialized. "Grew up in Long Island. Great student. Went to Carnegie Mellon where he became a student-radical during the late sixties and early seventies. Had a few drug arrests. Marijuana, LSD, nothing big. Then got his PhD from MIT, spent a stint at Pennfield College, actually. Went on to Princeton where he specialized in theoretical physics, then on to MIT where he became head of the department. Wrote a pretty highly-regarded paper in 2019 which tried to combine human consciousness with... relativistic something... physics?... is that it?"

"Yes," JMP nodded, "relativistic physics. Keep going."

"Yeah, okay, so that, and quantum mechanics. Was on the short list for the Nobel Prize, but never got it. Deceased September 4, 2025."

JMP wrung his hands. "Interesting. Very interesting. Pseudo-science and science, side by side."

"Okay, now this one over here," McPherson continued, pointing at the monitor, "well, this one, her name is Dr. Brenda Altieri." Again, he pointed across the room and a two-dimensional picture of Dr. Altieri materialized. "Interesting background. She started out as a nun, taught at several parochial schools in New Jersey then left the order and pursued her MD at Johns Hopkins. Became one of the leading psychiatrists in the northeast specializing in depression and anxiety disorders. Deceased October 8, 2027."

JMP grinned once more. "So, let's see. Parapsychology. Physics. Theology, Psychiatry. They've got all their bases covered, don't they?"

"Looks that way, Mr. MP." McPherson nodded. "Certainly looks that way." He turned towards the holographic monitor, and pointed again. "Now this one, the old fellow with these weird things covering his eyes, well, this one, is your Great Uncle Christopher Pennfield."

"My—" JMP paused, taking it in.

"A renowned scholar," McPherson continued, "he was a professor and Vice Provost at Pennfield College until a scandal with an undergraduate student effectively ended his career."

"Yeah, I know all about that…"

"Well, okay, the interesting thing is, of course, the objects over his eyes. Now if you zoom in," the holographic image expanded into an extreme close-up, "you can see that what's covering his eyes appear to be, like, ping-pong balls sliced in half. Now if you look at his ears," McPherson pointed as the monitor panned across Pennfield's face, "it's almost a no-brainer that he has some sort of headset on."

"An early form of a Ganzfeld state?" JMP asked imperiously.

"Exactly, Mr. MP."

"Interesting. Very, very interesting," JMP grinned, "for sure, a man ahead of his time."

"Um… let's see what else I got on 'em…" McPherson looked down at his notepad. "Deceased 2007."

"Don't you think I already know that, Bryan?" JMP answered brusquely. "The date of his death isn't what's important. What's important is the Ganzfeld state."

"Really?" McPherson shrugged.

"Of course. I was in a Ganzfeld state. He was in a Ganzfeld state. Both at the same location. Through our dual Ganzfeld states we transcended time and connected. Our collective consciousness must have created some sort of bridge. That's what enabled that whole bizarre scene to take place."

McPherson scratched his head. "Very good, Mr. MP. Very good."

"*Good?* It's intuitively obvious," JMP snapped.

"Okay, okay. But just look at the fellow on the hospital bed." McPherson pointed to one of the holograms hovering over JMP's desk. "A couple of interesting things. First, I did a little following up on the devices around him. I may be wrong on this, but based upon the configuration of equipment, I'd bet my house they were administering shock therapy."

JMP grimaced. *"Barbaric!"*

"Okay, now," McPherson continued, "let's take a look at the fellow's face." He zoomed in on the hologram. Ship's face appeared pasty and weathered, his hair flaky and dry. "From what I can see, rough guess, I'd say he's about fifty."

JMP nodded.

"Now let's look at this set of pictures generated by the IRH machine, the images representing your dream of the blonde young man."

McPherson pointed across the room and several more holographic images materialized: the young blonde man lounging on the college courtyard, an apparently older version of that same man in the jungle wearing some sort of bulky protective suit and, finally, an even slightly older version of the man, shackled and being lead to a guillotine for a public beheading.

"So now back to the fellow that night at Greenwich, the one who looks about fifty and like he's getting shock therapy, I scanned the image and had a program de-age the face by year."

"De-age?"

"Now, if you notice at age twenty-two…" McPherson pointed at the hologram and suddenly Ship's cheekbones hardened, his skin became smoother, his hair fuller with more sheen and luster, "…. we have an almost exact match on this scene here." McPherson pointed across the room to the scene of the young man lounging on the grass at a college campus.

"I age it forward a few more years, age thirty-five…" He pointed again and the face aged ever so slightly, Ship's hairline slightly higher, his skin slightly more weathered. "And now we have an almost exact match with the fellow in the jungle."

He pointed across the room once more and the image of an older Ship removing the protective clothing in the jungle appeared. "Now I took the images of the background and matched the location. West Africa. Cameroon.

JMP sat still, staring at the image. "Very interesting, Bryan."

"So you see, this is a big deal, Mr. MP," McPherson announced proudly. "The fellow on the hospital bed at Indian Harbor is the exact same person you dreamed about during your Ganzfeld session."

JMP did not respond. Instead, his head glanced nervously around the room.

"Mr. MP? Something the matter?"

"I'm not sure," JMP answered.

"How so?"

"Call me crazy, Bryan. But I have a strange feeling we're being watched."

"Impossible," McPherson answered proudly. "This is one of the most secure offices in the world. Geez, I don't think a ghost, an angel, nothing, could get in here."

McPherson's nervous giggles were not appreciated by Mashimoto-Pennfield.

"Yep," McPherson continued "You have absolutely nothing to worry about, Mr. MP."

JMP wiped his brow. "That's all well and good and I appreciate it, Bryan. Appreciate it immensely. But something is still making me jittery."

For a moment, JMP blanked. He felt faint, but not as if he was going to pass out. He felt prickles on the back of his neck and an almost magnetic pull tugging at him, but not in any particular direction. It was a pleasant feeling, a feeling of oneness…

But with what? Or whom?

"Umm…Mr. MP?" McPherson interrupted Mashimoto-Pennfield's momentary lapse. "Can I get you a glass of water?"

"No. No." JMP waved him off. "I'll be fine. Go on."

"OKAY. So now it came down to putting a time frame on all this. So I started with the college image. Like you said, Yale University. Davenport College." He overlayed a picture of the Davenport College courtyard circa 1980 over the image generated from JMP's memory. Almost a perfect match. Then he zoomed in on JMP's image. On the walkway behind where the young blonde man was lounging, he focused on a student carrying a textbook. He zoomed in closer and closer to an extreme, cubellated close up. "See that textbook?"

JMP nodded.

"Samuelson Economics. Ninth edition. Published 1976. So that puts a time frame on it."

"Excellent clue," JMP said. "So the young fellow must have been in his early twenties in the mid-1970s."

"Exactly, Mr. MP."

"Which would have placed his birth date in the mid-1950s. Which means …"

"He would have been anywhere from seven to ten years old in the early 1960s," McPherson finished JMP's thought.

"Okay. So, now that brings us back to the kid at the dock." He pointed at the hologram and zoomed close in on the young boy's face. "Okay, now watch this." He pointed again to the hologram of the man on the hospital bed from the night at Indian Harbor. "Let me de-age him again, this time way, way back." The face morphed from middle-aged, to young adult, to teenager, until finally it became the small, innocent, freckled face of a seven-year-old.

"Now you're gonna like this, Mr. MP." McPherson pointed at the de-aged face and tapped his finger towards the hologram. Then he whisked his finger across the room, dragging the image with it and superimposed it over the picture of the boy on the dock: a perfect fit. "There you go. One and the same. The guy on the hospital bed that night is the grown up Shippy."

JMP stared intently at the superimposed holograms, scratching his head. He paused, and then grinned, "Brilliant, Bryan, brilliant."

"Maybe," McPherson answered. "But there's a little problem."

"What's that?"

"Well, I checked the birth records in Greenwich around that time and it seems as if Percival Pennfield and his wife Margaret did have a son named Arthur Shipkin Pennfield in 1956."

"Go on,"

"But damned if I can find any record of his existence past 1963. I checked out the Yale University alumni files, every prestigious private school in the northeast... no Arthur Pennfield. I couldn't find a single record."

"So we have record of him as a child, and then we have this image of him being administered shock therapy on that bizarre night at Indian Harbor. But, nothing else. Only the images of him as an adult from my Ganzfeld session, correct?"

"Just like you said, Mr. MP."

"So the question now becomes," he gazed out again at the sliver moon, "what happened to Arthur Shipkin Pennfield between 1963 and that night at Indian Harbor?"

* * *

TIME FRAME: 2007

41

Princeton, New Jersey, Early morning, May 10, 2007

Jules Weisman did his best thinking when he least expected it. He could be jogging the streets of Princeton, taking his morning shower, strolling behind a carriage in the supermarket, and all of a sudden, some sort of new and exciting idea would pounce upon his mind.

Today it occurred while he was waiting for a traffic light on Route 1.

All of a sudden, it struck: an idea, one that could help him determine the veracity of Christopher Pennfield's OBE.

He pulled a U-turn on the highway and sped off towards his office.

Weisman raced through the entranceway, up the stairs to his office and grabbed his phone: "Chris I have an idea. I have a boffo idea, but I need your help," Weisman blurted.

"Julian, I've always considered your intellectual curiosity and enthusiasm major strengths, but must you be so curious and enthusiastic so early in the morning." Squinting in pain, Pennfield removed a cold compress from his forehead.

"But it's eight-fifteen. I've already run seven miles."

"And I've already suffered from seven headaches, so there!"

"Headaches, huh?"

"Nothing I can't handle," Pennfield harrumphed back. "So what is it you need from me?"

"I want to try to get a better fix on that OBE you had," Weisman answered.

"What exactly is it you want, Jules? And *boffo*, I haven't heard that since…"

"About 1973, I'd guess," Weisman chuckled, "but, seriously, I need detail, more detail, as much as you can remember… I figure if you could describe the technology that you observed, particularly in context of existing landmarks, we maybe be able to get a fix on the time frame. Think. Think hard."

Pennfield shriveled his nose and crinkled his forehead, straining to pull some specificity from his brain. "Well, I saw lots of things. Fabulous architecture. Interesting vehicles. A whole new skyline…"

"Was it really all new? Or was it a mixed skyline?"

"As I remember, yes, it was a mixture. But I was sort of fixated on the new structures. Marvelous. Absolutely marvelous."

"But how about the old stuff? Grand Central? The Empire State Building? Were they still there?"

Pennfield thought for a moment, and then nodded his head. "Definitely, I remember the Empire State Building. And if I'm not mistaken, I pretty much remember Grand Central as well."

"Good. Good." Weisman bounced around his office enthusiastically. "Tell me more. Tell me about the technology."

"Well, the cars – or whatever they were – flew by. But there seemed to be sort of organized pathways for them, highways in the sky. I think one of them more or less followed the path of the FDR Drive."

"Anything else?"

"Well, perhaps the most amazing thing I saw was this ultra high-speed train. There was a terminal on the Jersey side of the Hudson, which literally hung out over the river. The train tracks were elevated, and the train zoomed by at such high speeds, it was almost unsettling."

"Hmm… a MagLev."

"A what?"

"A MagLev. It's a Magnetic Levitation train which levitates above the track so there's no friction to slow it down. The technology exists today. But they're very expensive to build."

"Interesting…"

More than interesting, Weisman thought. His mind churned at the speed of light. So the mixture of new structures and old structures means that the future New York City which Pennfield visited during his OBE couldn't be *too far* into the future. And he hasn't described any technology which is out of the realm of possibility in the near-to-intermediate future.

"Anything else, Chris? Think. Think hard."

Befuddled, Pennfield scratched his forehead. "I'm thinking. I'm thinking."

"Whatever. No matter how minor or trivial. Anything at all."

"Well, I suppose compared to everything else, it's minor," Pennfield spoke softly, straining to remember. "But it was very poignant."

"*What* was poignant."

"Well, this might sound silly, but I saw a very, very thin slice of the moon, just the very slightest, thinnest edge. And the rest of it had a very magical glow, but subtle. And then there were two very bright stars almost forming a triangle with it. Very, very stunning sight. Very, very stunning. It struck me for the moment, but I suppose it's not that unusual."

Silence.

"Jules? Jules? Are you still there?"

"Yeah I'm still here," Weisman answered, beaming like a Cheshire cat.

"So what do you think?"

"What do I think?" Weisman grinned even wider. "I think we may have just struck gold my friend."

WITHIN MINUTES, Weisman was tapping away at his computer. He pulled up an interactive map of the nighttime sky for the New York City area and feverishly entered times and dates.

Soon, he found what he was looking for.

The date: December 1, 2008.

And yet, that wasn't it, Weisman thought. No way the New York City skyline makes that quantum leap in only one year. Not to mention the construction of a massive transportation terminal that hovers over the Hudson and the deployment of an elevated MagLev line.

No, it's further into the future. But not *that far*.

Weisman tapped away, changing the date onward and onward. 2012. 2019. 2032. 2043....

So engrossed he was with this exploration of the nighttime sky, he neglected to show up for his Senior Physics seminar at 10:00. But listening to a few over-pumped seniors spouting on about their senior theses was nothing, he thought. What he was doing here could be monumental.

He tapped and tapped and tapped, his eyes fixated on the screen.

Finally, a big grin.

Yes, he had it!

* * *

42

Princeton, New Jersey, Afternoon, May 10, 2007

"I *think I've cracked the code, guys!"* Weisman exclaimed, barking into the speakerphone in his office.

"Huh?" Swann answered from his cell phone as he strolled along the Sea Girt boardwalk.

"What?" Brenda Altieri responded from her office only about ten or so blocks way.

"I hope this isn't another one of those cockamamie theories of yours, Jules!" Pennfield answered bitterly, gazing upon Boothbay Harbor, the afternoon sun shimmering across the choppy water.

"It's not a 'cockamamie' theory; not at all, Chris," Weisman spoke as he paced animatedly across his office.

"Physicists!" Pennfield scowled. "Always trying to justify the irrational or counterintuitive."

"But there's nothing irrational or counterintuitive about this," Weisman answered, "it's pure science."

"So what is it, Jules?" Dr. Altieri asked, sitting calmly at her desk.

"I've calculated the date— *to the exact day, practically*— of the future world that Chris visited during his OBE."

"Phooey!" Pennfield gulped Chardonnay from a wine glass in his left hand as he held the telephone in his right. *"How can you possibly do that?"*

"The stars."

"Oh so now you're resorting to astrology, a pseudo-science," Pennfield barked.

"No astronomy, a real science," Weisman retorted.

"Poppycock."

"Let him talk, Chris," Dr. Altieri interrupted. "Go ahead, Jules."

"So I had an inkling when I was driving to the pharmacy this morning that if we could isolate the date of Chris's OBE, we might be able to more fully understand what's going on."

"And so...?" Pennfield's gulp of wine was audible to everyone on the call.

"And *so*, I called him this morning and had him again describe to me— in as much detail as he possibly could— what he actually saw. Based upon his description of the skyline and technology, I guestimated that it would have to be within the next hundred years or so."

"Yes, but that's not anywhere near as precise as you promised," Pennfield countered.

"Hold on," Weisman continued. "But then as I probed and probed and probed, he gave me an unexpected little gem."

"What was that?" Swann asked from his cell phone, as he gazed upon the Atlantic.

"He described something he saw in the night-time sky."

"Go on. Go on." Swann prompted him.

"He told me that he saw a sliver moon with two bright stars beneath it. So that conjured up something, something I vaguely remembered hearing about during my undergraduate astronomy days. So I looked it up. It's an astronomical event— the sliver moon with the conjunction of Venus and Jupiter. Only occurs every forty-four years in this hemisphere."

"Really?" Altieri twiddled the cord of her desk-phone as she sat back in her office.

"It's going to occur next year, 2008. But the time after that, the next time it occurs, is the date of Christopher Pennfield's OBE sojourn into the future."

"What? What is it?" Pennfield demanded.

Weisman grinned broadly. "December 8, 2052. Give or take a day or two."

* * *

43

Princeton, NJ / Spring Lake Heights, NJ / Boothbay Harbor, ME, Afternoon, May 10, 2007

Weisman's certitude over the date stunned the three of them into silence. It was almost a non-sequitur. He had taken something that might have merely been a very vivid dream and tried to analyze it down to a level of detail and precision that was, at best, incongruous with the proposition or, at worst, nonsensical. It was like trying to count the number of angels on the head of a pin, calculating the very day that King Arthur first met Guinevere, or discovering the exact location of the Emerald City— the intermingling of the mythic and fantastical with the scientific.

"So..." Weisman broke the silence, seeking praise or at very least affirmation.

"I'm a bit flabbergasted, I have to say," Swann answered, "but aren't you mixing apples and oranges?"

"No, not at all, I'm not." Weisman announced back.

"Come on. How can you deny that?" Dr. Altieri asked.

"Yes, *can* you?" Pennfield punctuated her comment.

"Simple. Either it was an OBE or it wasn't. If it was an OBE, I feel overwhelmingly confident that the future world Chris visited was on or around December 8, 2052. If it wasn't an OBE, we're barking up the wrong tree anyway, aren't we?"

"Alright, okay... maybe..." Altieri said cautiously.

"So, here's my hypothesis," Weisman announced.

"Should we wait for a drum roll?" Pennfield interjected wryly.

"Very funny," Weisman chided back. "Let's say someone in the Pennfield clan has a child in the next few years. By 2052, this kid becomes a titan of industry. Somehow, perhaps because of the Pennfield family's genetic psychic trait, he makes contact with the young Ship in 1963, and stuns him into a catatonic state. So at a certain point, this future Pennfield in 2052 realizes he shocked the young Ship into a state of catatonic schizophrenia. He's there at Indian Harbor observing the same thing we're observing. Using mid-twenty first century technology, he identifies us and learns about us through historical records."

"But *why,* Julian?" Pennfield challenged him.

"I'm not quite sure. Maybe he wants to undo the damage he's done to Ship."

"But, again I ask, *why, Julian?"*

"I said, maybe he feels guilty, wants to make it right."

"Maybe. But then you'd be leaving out one key factor, Jules," Pennfield retorted.

"What's that?"

"*Guilt* is not, nor has ever been, a Pennfield family trait."

AS HE SIPPED CHAMPAGNE, Pennfield's mind drifted. How little they understood. He gazed upon the windows overlooking the harbor. He thought of his past, then he thought of his visitations by Ophelia. Momentarily, he smiled. She always brightened him, inspired him. *One of the few reasons to keep on living, those precious visitations, whether real or not,* he thought to himself. Until—

Something struck him, something profound.

Ophie had said it in her own words.

We're equating reviving him with saving him.

She had challenged him, practically handed him the answer. *Think. Think about the Ship that might have been but never was...*

Suddenly everything fell into place.

His heart pounded.

But it was so weird, so irrational, so counterintuitive.

"WHO KNOWS..." Weisman continued preaching into his office speakerphone, "... perhaps they know something we don't. What do you think, Chris?"

Weisman's comment jolted Pennfield out of his daze.

"Huh?"

"Perhaps they know something we don't."

"Perhaps. I'm just not sure yet…" Pennfield mumbled.

"My gut tells me they want to undo the past. For some reason, some important reason, they want to. But I don't know why."

"But what happens if they're successful?" Swann asked. "Is it a good thing or a bad thing?"

"I don't know," Weisman answered, "I just don't know."

* * *

TIME FRAME: 2052

44

Transatlantic Tube, Mid-day, December 21, 2052

JMP's personal MagLev capsule slid its way through the Transatlantic Tube. He much preferred The Tube to the supersonic jet. It was at once both relaxing and stimulating. Stretched out in his reclining chair, JMP could lose himself, deep in thought, his senses delighted by the beautiful and exotic underwater scenery passing by. The experience was JMP's tonic— uplifting his spirits and sharpening his focus to the point where he could easily take on the big issues of the day.

Somewhere between the Laurentian Abyss and the Mid-Atlantic Ridge, McPherson interrupted JMP's reverie.

"Mr. MP! Mr. MP!" McPherson's excited face flashed up in a holoscreen before him.

"Yes, Bryan?" Mashimoto-Pennfield answered, almost bored, watching the underwater terrain whisk rapidly by.

"Got a lot of interesting stuff for you."

"Go on…"

"OK. Lemme lay it on you." McPherson continued.

"Shoot."

"Seems as if starting in the mid-1960s your Great Great Uncle Percival— Shippy's father — was a major benefactor of the *Gladwell Institute of Mental Health Sciences.*"

"Never heard of it," JMP answered.

"That's because it no longer exists, Mr. MP. But, get this," he continued, "I was able to access some of the records from the Central Health Authority database. It wasn't easy, but I pulled a few strings, used your name."

"And you found?" JMP answered, growing impatient.

"Well," McPherson smiled broadly, "listed on the patient logs is an S. Pennington."

"So?"

"His date of admission was December 29, 1963. And guess how old he was?"

"Seven?"

"So you're assuming that's Shippy?"

"You got it, Mr. MP. The name was just a cover. And at almost the exact same time your Great-Great-Uncle Percival makes a sixty-thousand-dollar donation to the Institute. Actually, back then it was called *Gladwell Sanitarium*, they changed the name to *Gladwell Institute of Mental Health Sciences* the next year. Guess ole Uncle Perce didn't want his son associated with anything called a sanitarium."

Mashimoto-Pennfield cracked a small smile. "Well that explains a lot."

"It gets even better." McPherson followed.

"Oh?"

"It seems as if the Director of the Institute, a Dr. Emilio Hazard, got booted by the Institution in 1972 for questionable practices."

"A psychiatrist I presume?" JMP interrupted.

"Yep, at one time he was regarded as the world's top expert on something called *catatonic schizophrenia.*"

"And why did they let him go?"

"Well, from what I can piece together, it seems as if this condition, this catatonic schizophrenia, was very rare in the US and mostly afflicted people in what they used to call the Third World countries, mostly Africa. So, in order to do his research, he has his lackeys go around to clinics and villages throughout Africa to find people with the condition. Then he has his representative *pay* their families to take the patient back to Hazard's clinic for the rest of their lives."

"Hmmm..." JMP stretched back. "So he bought his own lab specimens, did he?"

"Yeah, you got it, Mr. MP. He experimented with all sorts of drugs and fried them up with all sorts of volts of shock therapy. Lost quite a few of them, from what I could gather. So finally the state medical board figures it all out. He claims he's doing it in the name of science to cure a terrible psychiatric condition. They claim otherwise."

"And what ultimately happened to this Dr. Hazard?"

"I had to make a few assumptions and a couple of leaps of logic to piece together a theory. So take it as you may, Mr. MP."

"For sure. For sure." Contemplatively, JMP swiveled around in his seat and absorbed the depths of the Atlantic.

"This is how I think it went down," McPherson began. "They find him out. But the whole thing's sort of under the radar. I'm sure Percival Pennfield had something to do about that. My hunch is they suspended his license and agreed not to press charges if he quietly returned to Switzerland."

"So then those other scenes I've observed, later in life when Ship's quite normal, how do they fit into this puzzle?"

"They don't. At least not yet. Haven't found anything yet."

THE MOMENT THE HOLOSPHERE DISAPPEARED, JMP shouted out. *"NARC!"*

"Yes, my dear other?" Narc promptly materialized across from JMP in the underwater capsule. "An interesting riddle I would say, wouldn't you?"

"McPherson's very good at tracking stuff down, don't you think?" JMP mentioned.

Tentatively, Narc answered. "I suppose he's okay for what he is. But let's get to the important part."

"Which is?"

"Why of course, the analysis. Only gifted beings like us can actually do that."

"Then let's do it," JMP said, as he observed a series of bubbles in the murky water outside the tube. They were coming up from some deep-water geysers, he presumed. "The answer is critical, life-defining," he added.

"So let's hypothesize," Narc suggested. "It's been well established that there is, indeed, a Pennfield family curse, correct?"

JMP nodded.

"And your great uncle Christopher Pennfield was involved in a catastrophic incident with a young girl in 1996 that resulted in her death, and him being guilty, grieved and shamed for the rest of his life, an incident that was most likely a manifestation of the curse."

"As best we can tell," JMP answered.

"You then received a message during a Ganzfeld session which implied the curse was about to strike again and the victim would be none other than yourself."

"Yes," JMP answered.

"And then after a nefarious rendezvous with a young girl named Robyn, you Ganzfelded again and came upon the young boy Shippy at Indian Harbor."

"Why are you repeating this?" JMP barked. "Of course I did."

"And not only is this little tryst with Robyn causing you problems, but your intervention with Shippy caused him to become a cataton, presumably for the rest of his natural life."

"Yes, but then why did I see images of Ship as a normal adult in subsequent Ganzfeld sessions?"

"So here's a thought." Narc snapped his virtual fingers. "Didn't you observe in one of your sessions a normal adult Ship being lead to his execution, betrayed, shamed and shackled?"

"Yes." JMP nodded.

"So let's hypothesize."

"Go ahead."

"Suppose you didn't proceed to the tavern that night," Narc continued, "you didn't meet the girl, you didn't flee to St. John's, you didn't Ganzfeld and connect with young Shippy, and he didn't become a cataton."

Slowly, the look of confusion on JMP's face turned into a smile. He raised his finger and pointed at his other. *"Narc, you're a genius, a fucking genius."*

"Any outstanding qualities I have come from you, my dear other."

"So the adult Arthur Shipkin Pennfield I've been observing is the *alternative* person he would have grown into had he not become catatonic?"

"Indeed," Narc answered, "and your observation of this other Ship being walked to the guillotine is strong evidence that he would ultimately have been victimized by the curse."

"So if I hadn't caused Shippy to be inflicted with that condition, he would have become the victim of the curse instead of Christopher Pennfield, most likely. And, possibly, its time frame would have been reset and, consequently, would avoid striking me at this time and place…"

"Stellar!"

"So there's a way out. An escape-hatch." JMP giggled.

"Yes, all you need is some sort of corroboration, my dear other."

* * *

45

Placentia Bay, St. Johns NEWQUE GAB, Evening, December 21, 2052

Immediately upon return from his sub-Transatlantic journey, JMP rushed up to his Placentia Bay refuge, not even bothering to leave the Hoboken-Hudson MagLev terminal. It wasn't that time was of the essence; it was not, this whole matter transcended time, it allowed him to actually intervene in the very passage of time. It was his obsessiveness and anxiousness to take control of his destiny that propelled him onward.

So anxious was JMP that he found it unusually difficult to achieve a Ganzfeld state. Despite the white noise being pumped in his ears, despite the bland grayness of his vision, despite the soothing caress of levitating on thin air, he found it difficult to let go.

He was trying way too hard.

He lost track of time, laying there suspended in mid-air, growing increasingly bored by his bland sensory environment.

Finally, it happened, sneaking up on him.

His corporeal existence melted into the atmosphere, freeing him to experience pure spirit.

But how can he get where he wanted to go? Should he just allow the soothing mellowness of his Ganzfeld state to randomly whisk him there? Or would he need to take more control?

He concentrated. Despite the soothing numbness, he forced himself to focus.

All sorts of images spiraled around in his head.

He concentrated on family, on the Pennfields, on their legacy.

He focused on his target— the one person who could help him in his mission.

He clenched his teeth, his jaw hardened, his brow furled.

Concentrate! Concentrate!

Soon, a budding response: a fog, its shades and puffs of grayness slowly texturing itself into something.

Now: some fuzzy, muffled light breaking through the mist.

Now some more.

He floated through the mist, towards the lights.

He was over water; he was sure. *Was he back at Indian Harbor? Was that where this meeting of the minds was to take place?*

No it looked different, smelled different.

He could hear the clanking of boats against their pilings.

Soon he was at a large, leaded window overlooking the harbor. He slipped right through, floating towards a large, four-poster bed.

He hovered at the foot of the bed.

The man sleeping beneath its covers tossed jerkily, tangling himself within the sheets. He rubbed his eyes, tossed again, and looked up.

His face turned ash white.

"Uncle Christopher, I presume?" JMP's thoughts reverberated through the large bedroom. *"I'm your Grandnephew. It's a pleasure to finally meet you."*

The man shook vigorously, rattling the bed.

TIME FRAME: 2007

46

Boothbay Harbor, Maine, Night, May 15, 2007

"Jesus Christ!" Christopher Pennfield exclaimed, his bed rattling, the apparition of a horizontal, naked man hovering before him.

"No. Jimmy Mashimoto-Pennfield, actually." A disembodied voice reverberated throughout the bedroom.

Pennfield rubbed his eyes and reached for the flask of Scotch he kept on his night table. "This is absurd. This is…"

"All true," the voice answered.

"What the hell are you doing here and where are you from?" Pennfield gulped some Scotch.

"I told you. I'm your Grandnephew Jimmy Mashimoto Pennfield, I'm— I guess— 'channeling' with you from the year 2052."

"Poppycock!" Pennfield took another gulp. "You're just another figment of my warped imagination."

"You have a gift, you know. We all do."

"I would hardly call it a gift," Pennfield chuckled. "And we have a curse as well, too, you know. That is, if you are who you say you are."

"Yes, that's well documented, thanks partially to you."

"What do you mean by that?" Pennfield snapped.

"You left some pretty interesting notes…"

"What are you implying, that you've read my diaries? That's an invasion of privacy."

"Trust me. You were long gone by the time I got my hands on them."

"Thank goodness."

"You see, your privacy has not been violated, at least during your lifetime."

"No, that's not what I'm thanking goodness for. I meant thank goodness that I finally die, get the vestiges of this horrific burden off my shoulders."

"You're referring to the incident, the incident with the young girl?"

"Must you bring that up?"

"That's why I'm here, actually."

"Oh, God," Pennfield shuddered and sipped more Scotch. "I have no appetite for it. None at all! The past is past. There's no reason to rehash it, not with you at least."

"But I might be able to make it all go away."

"Hah!" Pennfield chuckled. "As I said, the past is past."

"But it's true; I might be able to make it all go away."

"Poppy*cock* I said! And when I close my eyes again I dare say I can make you go away."

"But then you would never have the opportunity to undo the curse."

"But, don't you see, young man, the curse has already undone me."

"I'm telling you I might be able to give you your past back."

"But that's impossible, absurd. It's all over, done with, cast in the mold of time."

"Time is relative. Time isn't even sequential."

"Oh, spare me, please!" Pennfield sat up and took a healthy chug of scotch. "I suppose you're some over-hyped physics student from the future trying to use me as the subject of your thesis or something. Poppy, *cock*." He chugged again.

"I'm no student. I run one of the largest companies in the world. You'd be proud."

"You're trying to toy with me and you're not going to get anywhere."

"Ask your friends Weisman or Altieri then."

Stunned, Pennfield stopped short. "How do you know about them?"

"They wrote a pretty interesting paper a few years after you passed. Should have won a prize, actually."

"About what?" Pennfield asked curiously.

"About physics, consciousness and alternate possibilities."

"Hmph, really," he chugged again, "sounds just like Jules, him and his convoluted theories. Add a psychiatrist to the mix and you have no idea what you'll get. Never ever trusted physicists, you know. And I trust psychiatrists even less."

"But they trust you."

"How so?"

"I'm a physicist by training. I trust you."

"Well then I'd have to question your judgment, young man. Nobody should trust me. I haven't been trustworthy in years."

"You sell yourself short."

"Yes, I do, and for good reason. So what will it take to make you go away?"

"Tell me about your cousin Arthur."

"Catatonic. Has been that way for years."

"As I thought. Would you be interested in helping him?"

"Yes, of course. He's my own flesh and blood."

"I think I can reverse his condition, and it will benefit both of us, believe me."

"And how do you propose to do that?" Pennfield quipped.

"I have my methods."

"I'm sure you do."

"So would you help?"

Confused, Pennfield stopped and thought for a moment. "I suppose, if there was anything… But how?"

"Soon, I will tell you."

"What, you haven't figured it out yet?"

"Just a few details to be ironed out."

"Poppycock! You have no idea at all."

"Soon, I will return."

"What? When you finally have it figured out?"

"Of course."

"I won't hold my breath."

* * *

47

Boothbay Harbor, Maine, Morning, May 16, 2007

Pennfield winced when he awakened. *Another one of these blasted experiences.* He pounded his fist on the mattress. *Who would believe him? Why should they believe him? Maybe he is going nuts, or bonkers, as Weisman would say.* He wanted to call them, needed to call them. Yet the more of these experiences he admitted to them, the more they might discredit him altogether. *Had he passed his tipping point?* Frowning, he ruminated for several moments, and then dialed.

"So wait a minute, calm down," Weisman shouted through the speakerphone.

"I'm sorry, but it was quite shocking," Pennfield answered, shaking nervously as he sat on the side of his bed.

"C'mon, Chris," Swann commented from his phone in NJ, "how can *anything* shock you? Or *us* for that matter?"

"Well, this did!" Pennfield answered brusquely. "It certainly did. It wasn't about seeing an apparition— or whatever it was, seen dozens of those— it was the eeriness of its voice and then, how it knew everything it did about me… and us. The blasted voice even mentioned some great academic paper that Jules and Brenda will write someday in the future. It was like a violation of my space."

"And time…" Weisman added. "But at least he had the prescience to predict our success."

"There's a flaw in your logic, Jules," Pennfield interjected, "that wouldn't be his *prescience,* it would be his *hindsight."*

"Well good for him!" Weisman beamed from his bedroom in Princeton.

"Self-flattery will get you nowhere, Jules," Pennfield answered. "Let's move on!"

"Okay. So he told you he was from the year 2052?" Weisman asked.

"Yes, indeed."

"So, you see, I was right." Weisman beamed.

"As I said, Jules, self-flattery will get you nowhere," Pennfield retorted.

"But that's not what's important," Weisman announced. "This fellow, this Pennfield from the future, he's telling you that he could do something to reverse Arthur's condition."

"Yes, indeed, that's how I heard it," Pennfield scowled.

"And he's telling you that by so doing he could also help you. Correct?"

"Yes. Correct again." Pennfield nodded.

"Okay, so let's put two and two together, here."

"Please!" Pennfield ordered.

"Based upon what you know about the Pennfield family curse, it occurs on a regular basis. Did anyone ever calculate the number of years between each occurrence?"

"Between the *returns of the locusts?"* Pennfield commented wittily. "It's not precise, but the pattern seems to be every sixty to eighty years or so, it skips generations."

"And prior to your incident, the previous occurrence was?"

"1928. It, or she, was involved with my grandfather Benjamin Pennfield."

"And your incident occurred in 1996, sixty-eight years later, correct?"

"You're being much too careful in your selection of words, Jules," Pennfield answered. "It wasn't an incident; *it was my downright downfall, dammit!!!"*

"And the time before your grandfather Benjamin?" Weisman asked.

"I believe the previous occurrence was in the late 1840s, early 1850s," Pennfield answered.

"Eighty years or so?"

"YES, CORRECT." Pennfield took a deep sip of chardonnay.

"So given the two previous occurrences of the curse prior to yours, of course, the timing of your incident was a little early," Weisman hypothesized.

."Perhaps," Pennfield answered, "but how can you attempt to rationally analyze the irrational?"

"But there is an established history to it."

"Alright, let's hear it."

Weisman quickly clapped his hands. "Let's suppose this *person* who visited you last night, this Jimmy Mashimoto-Pennfield, is the same person who visited little Ship that night in 1963 and stunned him into his catatonic state."

"Isn't that obvious, Jules?" Pennfield barked.

"Maybe," Weisman answered. "Now suppose this Pennfield from the future never interlopes on little Ship that night. Suppose Ship grows up normally, and with his precocious intellect plus Pennfield lineage, he becomes a big success in whatever field he chooses."

"Fair assumption."

"Then when he's in his mid-to-late forties, he becomes the victim of the curse. That would be sometime in the early 2000's somewhere around there, about eighty years after your grandfather."

"That's impossible," Pennfield barked, "*I* was the victim of the curse."

"That is, only if Ship wasn't there to take your place."

"What!"

"Maybe Ship was pre-ordained to be the victim but this Jimmy Mashimoto-Pennfield, by visiting him that night, changed history."

"And I became the substitute?" Pennfield asked, shaking.

"Maybe," Weisman answered. "If Ship hadn't become catatonic and had lived a normal life, he may have been more of an obvious candidate than you given the timing."

"That's awfully humbling. Second choice to be scorned." Pennfield scowled.

"Now, with you becoming the victim, that re-sets the timing of the curse. Correct?"

"I would suppose so." Pennfield answered feebly.

"And this Mashimoto-Pennfield fellow says he's from 2052, fifty-eight years later. Still on the short end of the timing, but still, too close for comfort."

"Presumably," Pennfield answered.

"But if Ship became victim of the curse, let's say sometime in the early 2000s, the earliest it would strike again would be in the 2060s, out of this guy's time frame."

"Yeah," Altieri cut in, "but it could still get this Mashimoto guy, only ten years later."

"True. But maybe for some reason there's something especially critical about the early 2050s. He needs to avoid the curse striking then at all costs."

"Feasible," Altieri responded.

Weisman chuckled. "My friends, I think we have a viable theory here."

"And what would that be?" Pennfield asked cautiously.

"This guy from the future booby-trapped himself."

"Huh?" Pennfield exclaimed.

"By intervening and causing Ship to go catatonic, he placed himself right in the path of the curse…"

"Say that again?" Swann winced, attempting to follow.

"This fellow from the future wants to undo the damage he did to Ship that night in 1963 so that Ship could become the victim instead of Chris."

"But that's preposterous!" Christopher pounced on Weisman's statement.

"Maybe. Maybe not," Weisman answered. "But I think this fellow is trying to change Ship's past to save his own future and he's trying to get *you* to help him by dangling the possibility of undoing the event that was your undoing."

"So this Mashimoto-Pennfield fellow wants Ship to remain normal so that Ship will become the victim of the Pennfield family curse rather than him," Pennfield suggested.

"Or you." Swann nodded towards Pennfield.

"Exactly," said Weisman.

* * *

TIME FRAME: 2053

48

WESTMASS GAB, The Egg, 3:00 AM, January 5, 2053

The night was quiet and still, devoid of any real energy. Nonetheless, the Egg exuded a special charisma as it calmly hovered over the WESTMASS countryside, rising above its superconductor platform. Streaks of intense brightness from the powerful lights above reflected a quiet eeriness across the surrounding grounds.

An entourage of six large military trucks interrupted the ambient silence of the evening, pulling off the access road and heading for the Egg's loading platform. Quietly, their giant tires treaded over the periphery, a constant muffled growl emanating from the engines. Two giant robotic soldiers, each twenty-feet tall and forged of an impenetrable alloy, followed the large tank-like trucks.

Jimmy Mashimoto-Pennfield and several Pennfield Technologies' technicians stood waiting at the platform.

Four human soldiers emerged from the oversized cab of one of the two lead trucks and walked to the door of the other. They stood at attention as a set of stairs unfolded from the truck's side. Ibu Bonne-Saari descended from the stairs, nodding as the soldiers saluted.

"Welcome, Ibu." Jimmy shook Bonne-Saari's hand.

The Prime Minister gazed upwards, scoping out the massive structure. "What a sight, such a large structure rising on its own. Magical, truly magical."

"Yes, just to take precaution, we decided to perform de-levitation maintenance prior to your arrival."

"It's quite a spectacle."

"It's really just the result of pumping water back into the Egg's base and maintaining its optimal temperature of 60-degrees Celsius."

"Amazing."

Together, they watched for several moments as the Egg rose majestically to its "resting place" 300 feet above its platform.

"So I think we're ready." JMP nodded at the Prime Minister.

Bonne-Saari nodded and then snapped his fingers in the direction of the four soldiers.

"Okay, time to unload," one of the soldiers signaled to the driver of a truck in the second row.

The truck peeled off and backed into the Egg's levitation portal. Several more soldiers emerged from the other trucks. As the driver opened the truck's rear doors, they awaited its cargo.

A square, shiny cube, about 10-feet long on each side, was robotically pushed to the end of the van as the soldiers awaited. Lowered to the ground by a pneumatic platform, the cube was immediately surrounded by eight soldiers and placed on a small gurney-type device which followed the lead soldier's voice-commands.

"Forward."

The soldiers flanked the cube, pushing it over to the levi-portal.

"Do they have any idea?" Jimmy whispered to Ibu as they watched.

"No, not at all."

The soldiers carefully moved the large shiny cube from the gurney onto the platform of a levi-jet. Bonne-Saari and Jimmy then joined the cube on the levi-jet as it ascended 500 feet upward to the giant hole in the structure's northeast quadrant, the Egg's only entrance.

Dr. Li-Pin greeted them in the entrance area. "Mr. Prime Minister, finally we meet." He extended his hand to the Prime Minister.

"Your stunning reputation precedes you, Doctor," the Prime Minister responded.

Li-Pin nodded. "Thank you, sir. It is my pleasure to help with this most momentous task."

"We wouldn't trust it to anyone else," Bonne-Saari replied.

"Well, let's get to it," Li-Pin responded. He turned around and signaled for several technicians to help him transport the cube to the hibernation pods.

Solemnly, both JMP and Bonne-Saari watched as the technicians carefully rolled the cube into a large air-avator.

"Think of it, Jimmy," Ibu whispered, "this can lead to one of the most historic events in the history of mankind."

"Without doubt." Jimmy nodded.

Awed, Bonne-Saari surveyed the elegant simplicity of the smooth contours and ergonomic technology inside the Egg.

"Okay," Bonne-Saari raised his voice from a whisper, "now give me that tour you promised me."

* * *

49

NYGAB: Manhattan, Pennfield Technologies Tower, Late afternoon, January 6, 2053

Incessantly, Jimmy Mashimoto-Pennfield tapped his fingers on his desk, his anxiety mounting. Here he was, the owner of what could possibly be the most amazing technology ever created, yet the pressure was enormous, overwhelming. If anything ever happened to the frozen body of Izan Bonne-Saari while in the Egg, he could not even begin to fathom the consequences. Yet, should everything be pulled off flawlessly, his name would go down as one of history's most famous and revered entrepreneur-geniuses.

But even if his cryonics initiative could conquer death, it would all be irrelevant if the Pennfield family curse conquered him.

So what's next? he asked himself. The girl, Robyn: could she be the one who brings him down? Bonne-Saari would have his back, but was that enough? Is the curse so powerful as to overcome the protection of the most powerful leader in the history of civilization? Can Bonne-Saari even be trusted?

Suppose the girl was just a decoy, a diversion, an alluring intoxicant soothing him into a sense of false security?

Perhaps the Pennfield family curse was too powerful, too diabolical. Perhaps it had him just where it wanted him. Perhaps it would snap at him with a vengeance just as he was beginning to think he had evaded its sting.

He gnashed his teeth. He could never risk being complacent. There was far too much at stake. He had to eliminate every possible chance of failure. He had to pull up this Pennfield family curse by its roots. He had to make sure that this Arthur Shipkin Pennfield became his shield, his insulation. He had to assure that Arthur Shipkin Pennfield absorb the ravages of this curse, not he.

His mind churned at light speed. He pointed, summoned a holoscreen and began to draw a diagram.

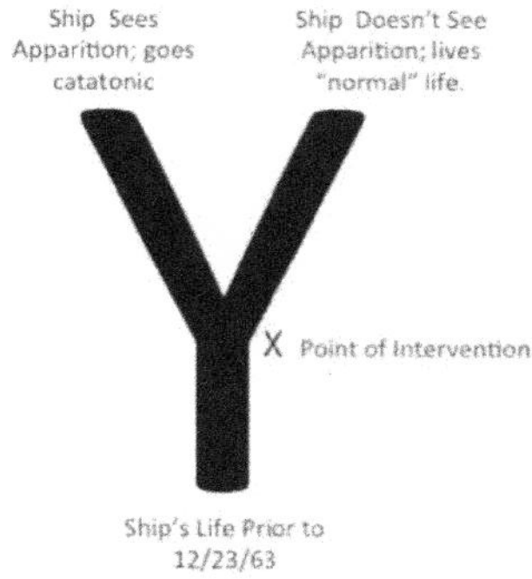

It was a simple proposition, actually. Post-December 1963, there were two possible paths Ship's life could take. If he goes out on the dock and sees the apparition, he goes catatonic. If he somehow doesn't, he leads a "normal" life and with high probability falls victim to the curse, of course, upsetting the timing of the curse and thereby minimizing the probability that he, JMP, would suffer its consequences.

So the question is, how to intervene to cause Ship to bypass the visit to the dock and therefore fall victim to the curse?

It should be do-able, JMP thought. He had made contact with the past numerous times. The very fact that he could communicate with the young Ship and scare him into a catatonic state or have a conversation with his great uncle Christopher across decades provided compelling proof that he could potentially alter the past.

If he could communicate with the right person at the right time and convince them to work on his behalf, a *trans-temporal agent*, so to speak, it might work.

* * *

TIME FRAME: 1963

50

Greenwich, CT, Indian Harbor, Early evening, December 22, 1963

Somberly, Ophelia Pennfield stood at her window as she did every evening about this time. Before the guests arrived, before the joyous chatter and Christmas cheer, before she saw her darling Christopher for the first time in over six months, she needed time with herself, her thoughts, and whomever or whatever the psychic waves might conjure up.

The early evening sky was a rich indigo blue, the half-moon a delicious orange and the snow, mostly frozen, glistened with an alluring, shimmering sheen flirting with the lights from the house and the sky.

Part of her ritual, she lit two candles— one on each side of the window sill — and then dragged deeply on a cigarette. She needed to "talk to the window," converse with the darkness, before she strode down the wide center-staircase to greet family and friends.

She took another drag, closed her eyes tightly for a moment, then opened them, looking out into the twilight. The window panes reflected a blue and orange glow from her twin candles.

Her eyes roamed: the grounds, the snow, the trees. At first, she swept by the strange image, her preoccupied mind causing it to meld with the shapes and hues of the treetops and sky. But when her eyes scanned by again, she recoiled.

She was not easily shocked, but this was eerie.

A naked man, comfortably horizontal, hovered outside against the early evening stars.

It frightened her in a way, yet aroused her in another. She took a deep drag, held it in, and then puffed it out, the nicotine seeping soothingly through her veins.

The naked man was still there. She smiled, growing comfortable with this odd vision. As she watched him, amazed and bewildered, her mind hearkened back to one of her favorite poems during her Wellesley days, by TS Elliot:

Let us go then, you and I,
When the evening is spread out against the sky
Like a patient etherized upon a table...

"You can't let him do it." A deep resonant voice emanated from nowhere, interrupting her moment of reverie.

"Who? Do What?" She answered instinctively.

"Your brother Arthur, you can't let him go out alone to the dock this evening."

"The dock? Why not?"

"I can't say, but bad things will happen. He'll become sick, very sick."

"But wait—"

"Just don't let him go out there, not alone."

The strange, naked man evaporated into the mist leaving only the deep blue sky in his wake. Ophelia took another long drag on her cigarette, allowing the sensation— almost erotic— to seep through her bones.

Ninety minutes later, when Ophelia greeted cousin Christopher in the entryway to the Pennfield's impressive, grand Dutch Colonial, she had almost forgotten her experience at the window earlier that evening.

"So the prodigal son finally returns!"

"Ophie!" Christopher exclaimed the moment he caught a glimpse of little Arthur's older sister.

"Chris, how are you? It's been months!"

"Only six, but who's counting," he responded, kissing her on the cheek.

"You must tell me about Paris."

"Indeed, I will."

"Jonathan! Charles! Lance!" little Shippy exclaimed with glee the

moment he spotted his young cousins. He sprang from Christopher's grasp and darted towards them.

"Well, it has to be the most beautiful city in the world," Christopher continued with Ophelia, "the food is beyond heavenly and, of course, the wines are—"

Shippy barreled into the crowd and tugged at his mother's dress. "Mother, can we go outside and play?"

Bunny Pennfield shook her head. "No, Shippy. It's getting dark and it's viciously cold."

Shippy looked over towards his sister, Ophelia.

Defenseless against the expressive eyes of her spry, freckle-faced brother, Ophie was an easy mark.

At first, she almost spontaneously answered yes. But then, she stopped before uttering a word. *What if there was something to her vision at the window? What if her little brother Shippy was in harm's way?*

"It's getting a bit dark, isn't it, Shippy?" she answered.

"But I hardly ever see my cousins and it's Christmastime and..."

With a barrage of family guests whisking around her, she thought about it once more, but decided to err on the side of caution. "I don't think so, Shippy. It's too dark."

"Don't worry, Ophie. I'll go out with them," Christopher offered.

"You sure?" she asked.

"No problem," he replied, and then looked over at Ship. "Now bundle up, Shippy!"

"Magnifique!" little Shippy exclaimed, showing off his precocious grasp of French.

As Christopher wiggled back into his coat, he whispered into Ophie's ear, "And I'll meet you upstairs afterwards."

"Excellent!" Her eyes sparkled.

* * *

51

Greenwich, Connecticut, Indian Harbor, Shoreline, Evening, December 22, 1963

Followed dutifully by their older chaperone, their cousin Christopher, the four young boys barreled out the front door, caroming off arriving guests and bouncing playfully into the mounds of crusty snow bordering the inlet. The beach was cold and brittle, frothy water brushing back and forth against its thin shoreline.

"Hey, Arthur!" Jonathan Pennfield's voice cast a frosty echo against the slight whistle of the cold December breeze.

"Yeah?" His little cousin Arthur turned around.

"Heads up!" Jonathan lofted a snowball towards Arthur's face.

"Moron!" Arthur scowled, wiping snowflakes from his face.

"Now is that the way to treat your cousin, Jonathan?" Christopher called out, chastising him. "You hardly ever see Shippy and within two minutes you throw a snowball in his face?"

SHIPPY SCOOPED up a pile of snow and ran towards his cousin. Larger and faster, Jonathan easily pulled away from Arthur's chase. Embarrassed, little Shippy walked off towards the dock in a huff.

"Shippy, don't go out on the dock. It's too cold and dark!" Christopher rushed over to him.

"But they're making fun of me. They always make fun of me."

"Listen, Shippy, I want to tell you something." Consoling him, Christopher patted him on the back. "Right now you're smaller and younger than they are, so they pick on you."

"But why?"

"Because that's how kids are."

"But do they have to be like that?"

"Possibly not, but it's just human nature." Leaning over, Christopher looked Shippy right in the eyes. "But listen to me, Shippy. You are tremendously bright and smart for your age. You're going to do great things in your life. Believe me, you're going to do *great* things. Your future is boundless. You understand that, don't you?"

Shippy nodded.

"Now come on," Christopher held out his hand, "let's go inside for some hot chocolate."

Together, they ploughed toward the house.

* * *

TIME FRAME: 1975-1977

THE ALTERNATIVE LIFE OF ARTHUR SHIPKIN PENNFIELD

52

Connecticut / New York/ Yale University / Various locations, April 1975

Arthur Shipkin Pennfield followed his family's legacy to Yale University, where he became a resident of Jonathan Edwards College. During his time at Yale, the frail, bony adolescent matured into a tall, striking young man with a wavy mane of flowing blonde hair. Eschewing his family's proclivity towards economics and finance, Ship set his course towards a career in medicine. He sailed through most of his pre-med courses.

Without doubt, Ship's academic performance at Yale made his father proud. Yet, there were several incidents during the young Pennfield's college career that drew the ire of Percival Pennfield, especially one near the end of his junior year.

"How could you ever do that!" the elder Pennfield barked into the phone.

"We had to," Ship answered defiantly, standing in a cramped hallway of the Washington County, NY jail.

Ship had befriended a group of student activists, led by a leftist political-studies professor, Ira Roth. They had camped out for several days at the front gate of the Hudson Falls General Electric capacitor plant on the banks of the Hudson. For years, the plant had spewed toxic PCBs into the river's water. At the end of the third day, the entire group was arrested for trespassing.

"Do you realize that I've worked on deals with that company?" Percival Pennfield barked on.

"That's not the point, father," Ship responded firmly.

"And that I'm in the Union League Club with their CFO, Art Sunderland?"

"*The Union League Club*, a place where exploited black Americans wait on tables wearing white gloves?" Ship answered flippantly.

"Now stop that! Stop that right now! No one's forcing them to work there," his father retorted.

"Well, gee, how times have changed."

"Cut the sarcasm," his father exclaimed. "Sometimes I really wonder what's going on in that God-damned head of yours."

"What's going on in that God-damned head of mine is that no company has the right to pump poisons into our rivers, no matter how many deals you've worked on with them, no matter who you know."

"Well, sometimes you need to think a bit before you act," Percival Pennfield blurted. "Do you know how many fences I'm going to have to mend?"

"Think before I act? Does it bother you that I have a mind of my own, father? That I realize there's more to life than the Union League Club or the New York Yacht Club or Winged Foot for that matter."

Perhaps it was ingrained in his personality, but Ship reveled at the opportunity to take little jabs at what he considered to be his family's bloated sense of privilege. It wasn't that he would go out of his way to strike at the Pennfield legacy, but if in the normal course of life he happened to come across something or someone that would help him prick a pin into the Pennfield family bubble, it would make the experience that much more enjoyable.

SUCH WAS Ship's romance with Lori Bernstein. She was one year behind him, a freshman in Yale's Samuel Morse residential college— a "Morsel" as they were known around campus. The two had met in Ira Roth's seminar on political activism and then sat next to each other on the long bus ride up to Hudson Falls. Ship had become immediately entranced with her pure, natural, fresh, unaffected beauty. They had little in common except a strident passion for protest and a mutual attraction.

At first, they had an almost unspoken understanding that romance was out of the question. Ship would often ask himself why, but could never come up with a decent answer. In one sense, it was so inanely stupid that he dismissed it. He had an almost clinical, albeit naïve, detachment about it: *she has 23 chromosomes, I have 23 chromosomes. Why can't we get together?*

And then, she was Jewish. He was Presbyterian. Her family migrated to the U.S. from Germany in the 1930s. His family boasted a lineage extending back to the Mayflower. Her family lived in Great Neck, Long Island in a community of affluent Jews. His family lived in Greenwich in a community of affluent WASPs. Each group lived in their own self-indulgent worlds, begrudgingly acknowledging the other's existence, tolerating interaction when the situation warranted, but otherwise staying out of each other's way.

That was how it was.

By fiat, Ship and Lori were destined to some sort of antiseptic platonic friendship.

Yet, with time, fiat proved no match for anxious hormones.

THE INEVITABLE OCCURRED on one of those mid-April Saturdays, when aseasonal warmth conspired with cool, soothing winds and blue azure skies to create a captivating serendipity. Ship imprisoned himself all morning in a small study-carrel in Sterling Library, poring over his molecular biology textbook. Up for a break, he noticed Lori at a nearby table.

He tapped her on the shoulder.

Surprised, she flinched.

"Too nice a day to be studying, don't you think?" he said.

She smiled when she recognized him. "Hey, what's up?"

"Nothing too interesting," he answered. "How many neurotransmitters can you fit on the head of a pin? How 'bout you?"

"Dante," she answered. "Finding signs of political symbolism in the Divine Comedy."

"Would that be in the original Italian or the English translation?"

"Hate to disappoint you, but my Italian is not close to being that good."

"So which translation, Longfellow, Sayers, Ciardi?"

"Looks like someone knows their renaissance lit."

"Lucky guess," he responded.

"I'm impressed."

"Don't be. Hey, it's too nice a day for this stuff. Wanna get out of here?"

"Yeah? Where to?"

"Good question," he answered. "I've heard there's this little gorge up in Cheshire with these beautiful falls."

"Sounds awesome. But..."

"What?"

She nodded towards her book.

"Screw Dante. That book'll always be around. A beautiful day's a perishable commodity. Let's enjoy it while we can."

THE DAY WAS WONDERFUL. Springtime's fresh green leaves filtered the clear blue sky, casting splotchy shadows on the sparkling grass. They nestled underneath a large oak, bathed in its shadows. The constant swishing wind tickled the leaves above providing an undercurrent to the splashing water cascading down the thin, steep gorge.

They spoke for what seemed like hours. The subject matter was irrelevant; it was the resonance of the two of them in this fleeting setting, at this fleeting moment that sealed their bond. As the winds picked up, and the azure sky grayed, they snuggled closer, until it finally happened, their first kiss.

"Did you like that?" Ship asked.

"What's not to like?" Lori answered.

"Just wanted to make sure."

"Why's that?"

"Because I want to do it again." He smiled.

They embraced one another and engaged in an even longer, more smothering kiss as time and space melted away.

She moved into his off-campus apartment that very night.

* * *

GREENWICH, Connecticut
Indian Harbor
Evening
May 23, 1975

WORD of the relationship was not warmly received at Indian Harbor.

"Jesus, Ship, a Jew?" His father blurted across the dinner table one night when he returned home for summer break. "With all the fine young women at Yale— from the best families, the best schools, debutantes even— did you have to choose her?"

"I didn't choose her, we chose each other, father," Ship answered calmly.

"Oh, please, cut the malarkey, will you," the elder Pennfield retorted. "That's nothing more than hippy-dippy pinko talk. Get real."

"Calm down Perce," Ship's mother cut in. "It's just a college fling. He's not marrying her."

"Who says I won't someday?" Ship answered.

Silence. His mother's eyes darted around the table, to Ship, then Ophie, then finally to her husband.

Inside, Percival Pennfield steamed. Then blasted out his words: "I don't know who will say you *won't*, but I damn well know who will say you *can't*."

"Perce, please…" Bunny Pennfield intervened.

"Oh, come on, dad, if we're right for each other and make each other happy, why would you ever want to stand in the way?" Ship said.

"I told you. She's a Jew. You're not."

Ship's sister, Ophelia, remained uncharacteristically silent throughout the exchange, until finally she stood up from the table.

"And what's wrong with you now, Ophie?" her father asked.

"I find your whole attitude reprehensible, father."

With those words, she retreated upstairs to her room.

ABOUT AN HOUR LATER, Ship tapped on Ophie's bedroom door. The pungent odor of marijuana scented the hallway.

He tapped again.

No response.

Carefully, he opened it and slowly tiptoed in.

She was in some sort of trance, gazing out her window.

"She's back." Ophie whispered to the window.

He stepped closer. Entranced, she had no awareness of his presence.

"She'll seduce you."

A pause, as if she was listening to someone or something:

"Jennifer."

After another pause, she spoke slowly and deliberately:

"November 10, 2052."

Ship remained frozen as his sister finished her strange conversation with no one. It took several minutes for Ophie to wind down, her hands on the window sill, her eyes shut, until she abruptly turned away from the window and towards Ship.

"Ship? Have you been watching me?" she asked.

"Only for a minute or so. What were you doing?" he asked.

"Just my little daily ritual. Nothing special."

"I need to talk to you."

"Let me guess," she answered, "father, right?"

"Seems as if things don't change, Ophie, the old man's his same old bigoted self."

He waited for affirmation, but didn't get it.

"You shouldn't marry her, Ship," she said tersely.

"Don't tell me you're turning into someone like him."

"No, I'm not."

"Then what's your problem?"

"Terrible, terrible things will happen if you ever marry her." She wiped her eyes.

"How can you say that?"

Silent, she nodded toward the window.

"Your window thing?"

Calmly, she answered, her eyes moistened. "There's nothing more that I want than your happiness, Shippy. But I see terrible, terrible things."

"Like what?"

She shook her head and whispered, "terrible, terrible things."

* * *

TIME FRAME: 2007

53

Boothbay Harbor, Maine, Evening, May 23, 2007

Tonight, it was Gershwin, a break from *The White Album*. He opened a bottle of Ardmore and pressed *play*. To Christopher Pennfield, *Rhapsody in Blue* oozed New York: not today's New York, but the much grander stylized art-deco New York of the twenties and thirties, a monochrome collage of motion and style. And, of course, it reminded him of Ophelia. If born earlier, she would have thrived not unlike a winged goddess in that mystical world, one of the majestic *beaux arts* figures adorning Manhattan's classic venues. The thought gave Pennfield a sort of rush, that vision of Ophelia and, of course, Gershwin's masterpiece underscoring it all—the melody's vibrant backbone, a stentorian presence, orchestrating the evening's twinkling stars over the quiet harbor.

"So have we wreaked enough havoc yet, Ophie?" Pennfield mused as he sipped from his omnipresent scotch and puffed on a Rothmans.

The light shimmered at the edge of his window, rivaling the twinkling stars. Noticing it, he squinted. Enlivened by the window's glass and Gershwin's rousing flourishes, the shimmering light spoke to him.

Do you suggest we leave well enough alone?

Pennfield's face lit up when he noticed her, but then he shrugged. "Who knows?"

Then what, dear cousin? Tonight, she was celestial; a sparkling transparent presence hovering before his grand windows, beatified by the twinkling stars set against evening's deep blue: *winged goddess, indeed!*

"Damnit! Something's bothering me, but I don't know why." Christopher slapped his hand on his end-table then took a quick gulp of scotch.

Relax... Pennfield's transcendent cousin sat in his lap and slowly grazed the back of her hand against his cheek. *Relax...we'll figure it out.*

"I'm baffled, confused," he whispered after a short pause, staring into the deep blue eyes of a youthful Ophie.

In what way? she asked so smoothly and softly, his skin tingled.

"These damn dreams!" He pounded his fist. "Perhaps it's the alcohol."

Could be.

"I'm concerned about Shippy."

How so?

"I had this dream, it was very vivid." He lit a Rothmans. "We were at Indian Harbor. That same evening, the Christmas party. Instead of allowing Shippy to go out with his two cousins, I volunteered to go with him. He never made it to the dock. And now..." He hesitated.

Now what, my dear. Ophie soothed him.

"And now, I'm just not certain if that was a dream or the way it actually happened. And, if so, if it happened, I mean if Ship grew up normally, did I inadvertently set him up for the curse?"

But if everything happened that way, you wouldn't be here today, living at Boothbay. You'd be in Vermont, presiding over the college, correct?

"Correct," he answered, "but maybe I'm here today as is because somehow I intervened once again, went into my past and undid what was done. Perhaps, I went back somehow, let him go to the dock by himself and allowed events to run their proper course."

Well, if you did, you already did. That's why you're here. You're here today as a result of your cumulative past.

"Yes, that's right." He gazed out his large picture windows and contemplated the universe. "Yes, I must've intervened in the past. But have not yet in the present."

What's that?

"I have not yet taken any action in the present to reverse that past. What happens if I don't take action now?"

But, it's pre-determined. You're here, aren't you?

"Am I? Or is this another dream? I don't know anymore, Ophie, I don't know."

So if you don't do anything, the present version of you will melt away and you'll become some other Christopher Pennfield?

"Perhaps…"

So isn't the answer obvious? She smirked. *Do nothing and all your suffering will melt away into a universe of unrealized possibilities.*

He took a long slow drag on his Rothmans, and then paused, until he finally mustered the courage to say it. He squashed his Rothmans in the ashtray, leaned over and held his head in his hands. Then he whispered:

"I can't."

Why not?

"Damnit!" He pounded the ottoman. "As much as I'd love to relive these past eleven years, live them free from that blasted curse, give myself a second chance, I can never risk allowing my son, my own flesh and blood, to endure the pain that I've endured. I won't do it to him. Even if it means suffering for me. I can't."

Are you sure? Ophie asked.

"And, suppose, just suppose, one day the doctors at Gladwell can actually cure him."

Pennfield turned towards the windows, his eyes following the bright yellow reflections of an arc-light atop a buoy as it rippled its way across the water. "Long odds, granted. But I'd much rather bet on that, than the certainty he'll suffer the ravages of the curse."

That's heroic, Christopher, truly heroic. Ophelia's eyes welled with small, delicate tears. Christopher could see them clearly.

"He's our son, Ophie. How can I allow him to suffer what I've gone through? I have to hope. I have to do it for our son."

54

Spring Lake Heights, NJ, Early morning, May 24, 2007

Ed Swann was stunned when he answered his phone. "Mr. Swann, I'm on my way to New Jersey. Where can I meet the three of you?"

"Chris?"

"Yes, it's me."

"What's going on?" Swann asked.

"I have something of extreme importance to discuss with you and your colleagues. Where should I meet you?"

"Today? Well I'll have to check with Bren and Jules, but..."

"Bullshit! Just give me an address. I'm sure my driver will find it and I'm sure they'll make time for an issue of this magnitude."

"Okay, this better be good, Chris, I guess the best place would be Bren's office in Princeton."

"Fine. So be it. Princeton it is."

* * *

THE FIRST THUNDERCLAPS of a nasty Nor'easter crackled as Pennfield— shielded by an oversized black umbrella— was assisted up Altieri's front steps by his aide. Torrents of rain sprayed against the large bay windows as foreboding black clouds hung over central Jersey. Confused, shocked and dazed in ways he had never been before, Pennfield leaned on his cane as he slowly entered the office.

"Well, you picked a mighty fine day to call a meeting in Jersey, Chris," Swann chortled as he took Pennfield's umbrella.

"To me, weather is never an obstacle when issues of this magnitude bare their ugly heads." Pennfield's hand shook. "May I ask if you have anything to drink, Dr. Altieri? Perhaps a nice port or sauterne?"

"Well I generally don't serve alcohol during office hours, but I'll check upstairs in my hutch."

"This one better be good, Chris," Weisman interjected, "I'm missing my fantasy baseball group."

Pennfield grimaced with disapproval.

"How about scotch?" Altieri asked, returning from a quick trip upstairs. "Best I can do on short notice." She handed him a tumbler.

He sniffed the contents, then sipped. "Adequate. Quite adequate."

"So what is it?" Weisman asked anxiously.

Pennfield set down his scotch, looked up and locked onto their eyes, then whispered:

"It's happened."

"Huh?" Swann answered.

"Jules was correct. This fellow from the future has struck." He took a deep breath then announced softly:

"I need to change the past."

"You— huh?" Swann repeated.

This time he said it with more amplitude: "I need to change the past."

"What happened?"

"I have strong reason to believe, close to certitude, that this Mashimoto-Pennfield fellow might have done something to change the past, something that would prevent Ship from going catatonic."

"So, you see, this proves everything!" Weisman preened like a self-flattering peacock. "This guy from the future, from 2052, the guy Chris saw in his OBE, the one who magically appeared to him in his bedroom, is trying to change history. He wants Ship to grow up normally…"

"So how did you learn about this, Chris?" Altieri questioned him.

"A very, very, vivid dream."

"And you're basing this all on a *dream,* a simple dream?" Altieri responded.

"A dream it was," Pennfield answered, "but simple it was not."

Perplexed, Altieri shook her head. "I can't… I mean… this is way beyond any… way outside the realm of any science I know."

"Maybe. Maybe not." Weisman sprang up, walked across the room and pointed.

WEISMAN BURIED his head between his shoulders, focused on the ground below and paced across the room, flapping his arms, oblivious to his surroundings. "Quantum physics tells us that particles, any particle— quarks, electrons, neutrinos, whatever— don't exist at all until someone or something observes them. So, Schrodinger— the cat guy— writes this equation predicting the location of a given particle at a given time. And then this probability equation would collapse when someone made an observation or measurement. But, Everett said that, *no*, it wasn't a probability wave that collapsed upon observation, it was that the particle *occupied all possible spaces at once*— in many different universes simultaneously and we only *perceived* the particle in the one universe that we're in."

"And this has *what* to do with Chris' dream?" Altieri exclaimed.

"Well," Weisman continued to pace, "if you allow for the existence of parallel universes…"

"Please, don't drag us down *this* road, Jules." Altieri interrupted.

"And five hundred years ago, the intelligentsia thought the sun revolved around the earth, my dear, glad they got dragged down—"

"But," interrupted Pennfield, "if these so-called parallel universes exist, then *where* are they, Jules? Be rigorous, please." Pennfield chastised him.

"*Where* are they?" Weisman repeated his question. "Right here. In between the lines so to speak. Perhaps what we perceive as empty space, the other *us*— the analogues of us— perceived as matter."

"Now you're really off the deep end, Jules."

"C'mon, most of us learned in middle school that atoms are mostly empty space," Weisman answered, still pacing, without even looking up. "So, most objects that we see as solid are virtually nothing. Correct?"

"With the exception of scotch." Pennfield scoffed, taking a long sip from his glass. "I had asked for *rigor*," he added, disdainfully.

Weisman looked up for a moment, shaking himself out of his funk, and posed a question to Pennfield. "Chris, did you ever realize that a dog is partially color blind?"

"Alright. Yes, I think I knew that."

"Well, we see the same scene as the dog, but in a much more vivid spectrum of colors. So what's the true underlying reality? What the dog sees or what we see?"

"But that's a function of the dog's eyes, is it not? The rods and cones and all those sorts of things," Pennfield barked, regaining interest.

"But what if there were, what if God or whatever, created a creature that saw only in infra-red? That creature would only perceive the world in terms of the heat it gives off, differently than either us or the dog, correct?"

"But, yes, again, it's a biological function of the creature, nothing to do with what he's looking at."

"Maybe, but it's still a perspective on the same underlying reality, Chris. Now suppose this God-or-whatever created a creature who could *see between the lines*— see where the other possible positions of the particles exist— a creature who could perceive what exists as empty space in our universe as an alternate version of reality— actually, to him *actual reality*— in his universe."

"And what would that creature be?"

"Us," Weisman answered quietly. "Or creatures like us."

"Creatures?"

"Even though an infinite number of universes might be right here with us now— all part of the same reality— residing in that 'empty space' so to speak, a given human being can only perceive one of them at any given time."

Perplexed, Pennfield asked, "Exactly what do you mean by, *at any given time?"*

"Perhaps our consciousness skips around between universes that are somewhat like ours, but different in subtle ways. Perhaps we pick our own paths."

Pennfield looked toward Altieri, trying to read her reaction. She caught his eyes, took a deep breath and directed a question to Weisman. "But then, Jules, what happens if your consciousness skips around as you say, how does it resolve contradicting histories in different universes?"

"Maybe you only remember the past relevant to the universe you're in."

"So, you're saying we can remember more than one past?" Altieri asked.

"Yeah Bren," Weisman responded, "but only one at any given time."

"Let's say someday some physicist cracks the code on time travel..."

"Highly, highly speculative." Altieri interjected.

"Alright. Could you just suspend disbelief for a moment or two, Bren, and indulge me?" Weisman again paced across the room. "Suppose someone went back in time, oh let's say about forty or fifty years, met his grandfather as a young boy and killed him."

Pennfield grimaced. "Yes, but if he killed his grandfather, how can he ever exist in the future to go back in time to actually kill him."

"Bingo!" Weisman bounced up and pointed at Pennfield. "Many scientists have posited that time travel is impossible and will always be impossible because of exactly that. The time traveler could potentially create a contradic-

tory past, one such that when he returned to the present, he might no longer exist. Ergo, time travel is impossible given simple logic."

"Indeed, this may be a hint of the rigor I had requested, if—"

"Except..." Weisman cut off Pennfield, "if, once our time traveler alters the past, the universe splits in two." He smirked with glee.

"Splits?" Pennfield exclaimed.

"Suppose the time traveler kills his grandfather which, of course, would mean that in that particular universe, a new one, all of his yet to be born relatives, including himself cease to exist. But in his original universe, the one he traveled back in time from, his family lineage is intact."

"Then which of these two universes is he in, Jules?" Pennfield asked.

"Either," he answered, "or both. Wherever his consciousness takes him. In one universe he could have existed only as some sort of temporary doppelganger who killed his grandfather then ceased to exist, yet in another universe he can be as alive and well as ever."

"Well, Jules, you never cease to provoke thought, I'll give you that," Pennfield admitted. "But it still tells me nothing about how I can change the past."

"Yes it does."

"And how would that be?"

"We need look no further than one of the twentieth century's most famous philosophers."

"Camus? Sartre? Chomsky?"

"Nope." Weisman shook his head. "Berra."

"Huh?

"Yogi Berra." Weisman's face lit up cockily. "When you get to a fork in the road, take it."

* * *

55

Princeton, New Jersey, Afternoon, May 24, 2007

W*hap!*

The sharp, swift snap of a thunderbolt obliterated the silence in the room, lighting up the entire street.

At what he believed to be the appropriate moment, Pennfield chimed in, "Is arcanity one of your foibles, Jules? Can we skip this bit about the 'fork?' I am eager for intelligibility."

"Alright, let me explain. *Occupational necessity...*" Weisman began, still pacing. "But hold on, isn't it obvious, Chris? This guy from 2052, he intervened and somehow caused the Chris Pennfield of 1963 to change the past. If we intervene at an appropriate point, we can likewise reverse it."

"Knowing you, perhaps over time your argument may prove brilliant, but *obvious* it is not," Pennfield retorted.

"Anyone got a pad of paper?" Weisman asked abruptly.

Altieri pointed to a credenza across her office. Weisman picked up a pad and pencil and began writing, drawing what appeared to be a large capital letter 'Y.'

"Okay, so here, look at the stem." Weisman held up the pad for all to see. "This is the universe before Ship went out on the dock." With the zeal of a professor mid-lecture, Weisman scribbled something at the letter's stem and then pointed at the figure's upper left branch. "Now this part here is the universe where Ship goes out on the dock, sees the apparition and is shocked into his catatonic stupor, got it?"

They all nodded.

"Now over here," he pointed to the opposite branch of the large letter 'Y,' "this is the universe where per Chris's dream, his younger self accompanies Ship outside and prevents him from ever going to the dock, the universe where Ship goes on to live a normal life, whatever that may be."

He threw down the pad on Pennfield's coffee table for all to examine:

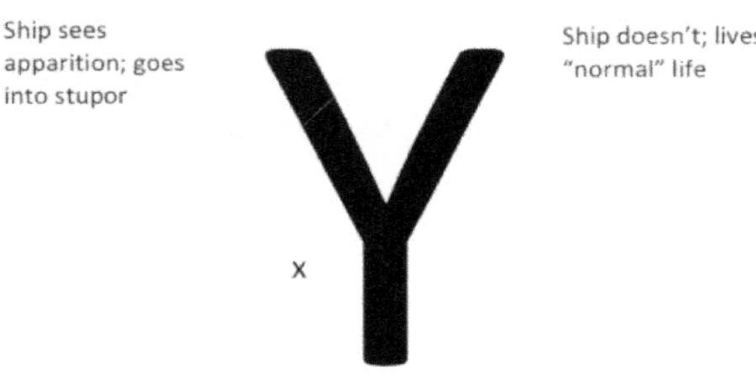

"So if we intervene at a point anywhere around here," he pointed to the middle of the 'Y' where all three branches came together, "we can undo the action of Chris accompanying the young Ship outside that night. So then Ship goes to the dock by himself, sees the apparition and goes into his stupor. The right branch goes away for all intents and purposes, at least to the current 'us'. Ship *may* never be cured, might never lead a normal life, but, consequently, he definitely *won't* fall victim to the curse. So, we're back to where we were."

Pennfield, his nose shriveled and eyes squinting, studied Weisman's chart. "Jules, you're giving me a terrible case of mental indigestion."

"No, I think I get it. It's simple really," Dr. Altieri interjected, "it's a decision tree, only both outcomes exist at once."

"Exactly, Bren."

"Okay?" Swann asked somewhat skeptically. "Makes sense theoretically, but in terms of action… I mean, *how* do we intervene?"

"Good point!" Weisman scooted across the room and sat silently.

"Take your time." said Pennfield sarcastically sipping some scotch.

"Give me a minute. Just give me a minute." Weisman jaunted back across the room, flapping his arms, over-stimulated.

They waited some more.

"Okay," Weisman started as if talking to himself, still pacing around the room, "the only way we've been able to come into contact with the future, the past, other dimensions, whatever the hell we're dealing with here, is through heightened consciousness induced via a Ganzfeld state. So we're at least going to have to use that, a Ganzfeld state."

"But for what?" Pennfield retorted. "Exactly *what is it* that we're going to do with this Ganzfeld state?"

Weisman paced back and forth in silence, his arms flapping as the thunderstorm rattled the house windows and wreaked havoc with the trees outside, slapping them with thunder strikes, spraying them with torrents of streaming rain, and agitating them with swift cross-currents of violent, shifting winds.

Almost simultaneously with a loud crack of thunder, Weisman snapped his fingers:

"I've got it," he looked up at the group and grinned.

"OKAY, so let's say we induce a Ganzfeld state on, like Chris for instance, take advantage of his demonstrated psychic tendencies. Here's where it gets tricky…" Weisman continued.

"Ahhh, a catch." Pennfield commented, smirking.

"We need to have Chris, in his Ganzfeld state, get in touch with someone from the year 1963 who can undo what's been done by this Mashimoto-Pennfield guy."

"Well, shouldn't that person be obvious, Jules?" Pennfield queried.

"Obvious?"

"Yes, me." Pennfield pointed his shaking, bony finger at himself.

Weisman didn't answer. Instead, he fidgeted around the room with a disturbing, inquisitive look across his face. Deep in thought, he motioned awkwardly with his hands, almost oblivious to his colleagues in the room.

Finally, nodding his head, he spoke: "No, can't do it. Feedback."

"Aw come on, are you serious?" Swann responded.

"Yes, feedback," Weisman repeated. "You know that screeching sound you get when you place a microphone too close to a speaker? It's like that paradox I told you about the first day we met— the man whose car was a time machine and kept meeting another one of himself from the past. Potentially, he could get caught in a continuous infinite loop from which he could never escape. Too risky."

"So what do we do?" Altieri asked.

"It's obvious," Weisman answered. "Find someone else."

"Okay, so?" Altieri continued.

Immediately Weisman swiveled towards Swann. "Ed, how old were you in 1963?"

Swann scratched his head. "Let's see… ummm… thirty-six, thirty-seven."

"So that's it!" Weisman snapped his fingers once again. "We'll induce a Ganzfeld state upon Chris and see if his consciousness can contact the 1963 version of Ed Swann who can hopefully help us alter— or in this case, *restore* — the past."

The group stood silent, impressed— and somewhat seduced— by Weisman's ingenuity.

Christopher looked over towards Swann. Surprisingly, the man looked more than a bit apprehensive, not at all intrigued by the possibility of a metaphysical visitation to his former self. *What bothered him so?* Pennfield wondered.

A violent strike of thunder slapped a nearby tree.

* * *

TIME FRAME: 1963

56

Montclair, NJ / Various Other Locations, December 16–22, 1963

"Bless me father for I have sinned." The thirty-seven-year-old Ed Swann, kneeling in a dark confessional at the Church of the Sacred Heart in Montclair, New Jersey, blessed himself as he whispered to the priest across the small square of space carved directly into the polished oak wall between them. *"It has been one week since my last confession."*

"Go on…" Father Benedict Morris yawned.

"It's me, Ed," Swann whispered.

"I know, Ed," Father Morris retorted.

"No new sins this week."

"Good for you. Let's recite the prayer of absolution."

"Except," Swann interrupted.

"What?"

"I need to discuss something, Father," Swann answered sheepishly.

"What's on your mind, Ed?"

"Don't feel real comfortable talking about it, but I've been seeing things," Swann answered timidly.

"Seeing things? What do you mean?"

"Just things. Things that make no sense to me."

"Okay, so tell me…"

"Well, I was asleep the other night and as I turned I woke up. I thought I saw something, just hovering over the bed. It was fuzzy at first, but then it became more clear, you know what I mean?"

"No, I don't know what you mean, Ed."

"Well, I rubbed my eyes and then it just looked like a person, a man floating, all stretched out, he had these things over his eyes, looked like golf balls actually."

"Okay, Ed. Okay. Well, did it, did he… say anything?"

"Good question, Father," Swann answered. "His lips didn't move, but throughout the room, a voice sort of echoed. It said something like, 'I need you to intervene, Ed Swann.'"

"Intervene at what?" the priest asked.

"Here's where it gets spooky. He said something like, 'I need you to help change the past.' Confused the bejesus out of me."

"Edward, I certainly understand the bizarre nature of your experience, but please remember not to take the name of the Lord in vain."

"Oops, sorry Father." Swann blessed himself

"Anything else? Did this voice say anything else?"

"Not sure, Father. It sort of like came in and out."

"Well, I'm sure it's not the work of the Lord. He would never intervene with man's free will."

"So you're saying it's the devil?"

"No, what I'm saying, Ed, is I think you should see a psychiatrist."

"But I'm no looney-toon Father!"

"Hopefully not. For your penance, say three Hail Marys." Father Morris whispered a short prayer, and then shut the little window between them.

"But Father…"

Psychiatrist! Swann huffed as he barreled down Bloomfield Ave, for the moment oblivious to the downtown Montclair Christmastime jubilance. The lamp-posts may have been crowned with twinkling lights, a giant red bow garnished with garland might have hung on the large wall of Hahne's department store and the Salvation Army Santa Claus might have been clanging his bell in front of the Wellmont Theater, but Swann saw none of it.

Was he embarrassed, angry, scared or some combination thereof? He didn't quite know.

Of one thing he was sure, though: He shouldn't have brought it up, never should have at all. But he didn't know where else to turn and so he did. *Damnit! Now Father Morris thinks I'm some sort of kook!* Swann thought, as he continued barreling towards his car, parked across from the YMCA. *A psychiatrist was out of the question,* he thought. *What would happen if word ever got out?* Too big a risk, he quickly surmised.

As he was about to enter his car, he looked up at the deep blue, darkening sky and the twinkling stars over the roof of the Louis Harris Department Store. He paused. *What a magical sight!* Quickly, he transported himself out of his dilemma, relaxed, and drew in a deep refreshing breath. He exhaled a puffy cloud of frosty air.

Then he froze in place, stunned.

Damnit! he moaned. *Why? Why? Why?*

He was seeing it again. The old guy with the golf balls over his eyes. Saw him as clear as could be hovering over the roof of the Louis Harris Department Store.

He squeezed his eyes shut, hoping it would disappear. But it didn't. Even with his eyes shut, he still saw that image of that man floating across the darkness, as if etched directly on his retinas.

Oh God! Swann muttered.

SWANN'S strange encounter with the paranormal persisted throughout the evening. While washing the dishes after dinner, he innocently looked up and stared out the wood-framed window above the kitchen sink. *Lo and Behold.*

There he was again, the same man, now floating in Swann's backyard. *What the hell am I supposed to make of this?* Swann thought as he methodically scrubbed a pot with a Brillo pad, his eyes fixed on the man floating outside.

He called over to his wife in the living room. "Hey Marie,"

"Yes, Ed?"

"Nothing. Nothing, honey. I thought we were out of Brillo pads, but I found one."

He stared and stared, scrubbing rhythmically along as if to trivialize the whole incident. The man was definitely older: a taut, ashen-white face, a frail spindly frame, and those round objects covering his eyes. The strange man floated peacefully, somewhere between the patio and the hedges.

Abruptly, Swann threw down the pot he was scrubbing and impulsively strode towards the door. It was time to take action.

He burst out the door, barreling over to the spot where he saw the man floating.

God damnit! Swann uttered to himself. *What the hell's going on here? Either I'm going crazy or someone's playing a wicked trick on me. Either way, it's not good.*

Sheepishly, he walked back inside.

"Everything okay, Ed?" Marie called to him from the parlor.

"Yeah, thought I saw a deer in the backyard."

"Well, bundle up; it's cold out there."

LATE THAT NIGHT, the figure haunted him once again.

At first, Swann slept peacefully, snoring intermittently, bumping shoulders with Marie now and then. During a lighter phase of sleep, he became very much aware of— and then irritated by— the pings and clanks of the steam radiator at the foot of the bed. He tossed and turned trying to carve the perfect crevice in his pillow.

He looked up.

A frosty sheen coated the windows at the foot of the bed, sustained by a calm whistling breeze. Indeed, all afternoon Swann felt snow in his bones. There was a storm brewing, he was sure. But even the contemplation of a winter wonderland proved impotent in lulling Swann back to sleep.

He shifted again, flipped the pillow and carved another crevice with his fist. As he turned to position his head on the pillow—

Holy Shit!

There he was again. The bony, frail man floating at the foot of his bed with the round things over his eyes.

Swann stared, drinking the image in. It was clear, very clear, most likely the clearest he had seen it.

Swann rubbed his eyes.

"Can you hear me, Mr. Swann?"

Shit! Swann growled, mashing his teeth. He looked over at Marie: fast asleep.

"Yes I can, but what the hell are you doing here?" Swann whispered, hoping and praying not to wake Marie.

"I need your help."

Interesting, Swann thought, how he could see this apparition, or whatever it was, as clear as day, but when it talked, its lips did not seem to move at all.

"Where are you from? Are you a ghost?" Swann asked as forcibly as he could while whispering.

"That's not really important. It'll just get in the way."

"Then how do I know to trust you? How do I even know that you exist?"

"I'm here, aren't I? You see me, don't you? Isn't that proof enough?"

Swann ruminated for a moment, and then shook his head. "No, not enough."

"Jesus, Mr. Swann, you're holding us up! We've got work to do!"

"But, I don't..." Abruptly, he swiveled towards his wife; he thought he heard her stir. *"Shhhhh..."* He shushed the apparition as he looked upon his wife. Fast asleep.

"So why don't we just cut to the chase, I know all about you Mr. Swann. And what I'm asking you to do will cause you absolutely no harm, just some minor inconvenience."

"What is it you know about me?" Swann asked.

"Would you prefer the entire litany or merely the abridged version?"

"Abridged would be fine."

"Okay. Your name is Edward Patrick Swann you were born to Cornelius Denis Swann and Maureen Patricia O'Brien on March 26, 1927 in Jersey City, New Jersey. You graduated from Sacred Heart High School at the top of your class. You played football and baseball. Anything else you'd like to know?"

"Very good," Swann answered. "But that's all stuff you can look up in the public record. Tell me something that only I would know."

"Ummm, let's see... okay, here's one. When you were in college at Columbia, you saw an apparition of your Uncle Arthur on the night before he died."

Swann's heart pounded, his face drained of color. He scratched his head. *How can anybody ever know about that?* he asked himself.

"Impressed, aren't you?"

"How do you know all this stuff?"

"If I told you it would only get in the way. I just need one simple favor."

"Okay", Swann responded. "What is it?"

"Tomorrow I need you to travel into New York and perform a minor task for me..."

SWANN BARELY CONCENTRATED at Sunday mass the next morning, his mind meandering along with his eyes around the stained-glass windows towering above the altar. He almost had convinced himself to give it a try, but then as Father Morris entered through the vestibule— in purple vestments accompanied by two altar boys and the choir regaling *Adeste Fidelis*— a cold hard dose of reality jolted him, perhaps driven by the sternness of the good Father's glance as he passed by Swann: *Might he be committing a sin— a real major sin, a mortal sin— by complying with this voice from above his bed. This person— or whatever— was certainly not a messenger of God. Or was he?*

Didn't Father Morris say something about altering events, that The Lord would never interfere with man's free will?

Swann heard hardly a word of Father Morris's homily, his monotone-tenor drone almost hypnotic. *But how in the name of bejesus,* Swann asked himself, *how could that strange floating man know about his visit from Uncle Arthur all those years ago? And all he was asking him to do was a really, really trivial act?* Oblivious to the collection plate being passed down the aisle, Swann had to be gently elbowed by Marie. He quickly rummaged through his pocket for their weekly envelope. *Yes, but suppose this frail man who has been taunting him was evil, perhaps a messenger of the devil?*

The choir sang a beautiful rendition of *Away in a Manger* as the communicants shuffled back into their pews. Swann continued to struggle with his thoughts even as he walked silently back, his hands folded. *Listen,* he told himself, *there's something there. Gotta be. The apparition knew about Uncle Arthur. That was evidence enough.*

Finally, Father Morris stood triumphantly at the altar, faced his parishioners, spread his arms and recited the final blessing:

"Mass is ended, go in peace, to love and serve the Lord. In the name of the Father and of the Son and of the Holy Ghost—"

Swann swallowed hard. The word *ghost,* the actual use of that word in a serious context jolted him once again, made it way too real. And there was no way he could go anywhere in peace, he had never felt less at ease. He coughed, and looked behind himself, tightening his coat over his chest.

"You okay?" Marie tugged at his coat as Father Morris and the altar boys retreated down the main aisle.

"Sure, sure, honey, just swallowed wrong," he answered.

All the way home, Swann trained his eyes on the road, but his mind was somewhere else altogether. He battled with his conscience: *should he do it or not?* If he didn't, life would just go on as is. *Fine, no problem.* If he did, he might discover something, something unusual, something insightful, something special. *But what if it wasn't special, what if it was evil? What if it was a Pandora's Box?* But, then again, the encounters were so real, so vivid. There must be something there, he thought.

"Something bothering you, Ed?" Marie questioned from the passenger seat.

"Nope," he answered matter-of-factly. "Just thinking about all the things I have to get done by end of day tomorrow. Thank God Christmas only comes once a year."

The compulsion to drive into New York City still pestered him, even after they arrived home at around 11:30. When the phone rang around noon, it gave him an opening.

"Hello?"

"Is Camille there?" a squeaky female voice answered.

"Camille? No, no Camille here. I'm sorry, I'm afraid you have the wrong number."

"Is this 239-8614?" she asked.

"Nope, it's 8615," Swann answered.

"Oops, sorry!" she responded then promptly hung up.

As Swann was about to place the phone down, he froze momentarily. *This is it, the opportunity!* he thought. He leaned over in his easy chair and spotted Marie through the kitchen door, chopping vegetables for Sunday dinner. With a glean in his eyes, he pulled the receiver back to his face and mumbled for several moments before he hung up.

"You'll never believe who that was," he announced to Marie as he strode into the kitchen.

"Yeah?"

"Artie Winfield, my freshman roommate at Columbia."

"Isn't he a doctor or something?"

"Yep, in Dayton."

"Geez, it must be years since you've seen him," Marie answered as she diced a carrot.

"Yeah, but I'm going to see him this afternoon."

"Really?

"He and his wife, Kate, came into the city to see the Christmas decorations and the Radio City show and all that stuff. She wants to go to the Metropolitan this afternoon, but Artie has no patience for art museums— you know him, can't sit still for anything— so he asked me to meet him at PJ Clarkes for a beer or two around four o'clock, just like the olden days."

"But I thought you're really busy. "

"Yeah, I'm busy all right. But isn't Christmas all about being with friends and family?"

This particular Christmas, however, was a bit diluted. Swann ruminated as he drove up Eighth Avenue in Manhattan. It definitely *looked like* it was Christmastime— all the props and accoutrements in place: the people, the stores the decorations— but it seemed everyone was just going through the motions; the energy wasn't there, the spirit lacking, lurking somewhere in the background, hesitant to come out.

He turned right onto 49th Street, transporting himself from the frenetic energy of the panhandlers, porn theaters and masses of humanity on the West Side onward toward the stately elegance of Park Avenue, with its grassy median, the Waldorf and countless apartment buildings with regal awnings and dignified wreaths hanging from their front doors.

What would you expect? Swann mused. It had only been a month since the national tragedy, still hard to believe the shining young President was gone. Although the holiday season might have had the capacity to pull America out of its doldrums, it achieved quite the opposite effect: the odd juxtaposition of Christmas cheer with the lingering sense of loss only made things that much more awkward and sullen.

Swann read the numbers off the townhouses as he slowly rolled down E. 64th Street. Number 235 was about halfway down on the north side. Quite a structure, he thought: About twenty-feet wide, five stories high, an odd shade of Pepto-Bismol pink, with beautiful, high and sweeping, rounded bay-windows jutting out towards the sidewalk on the second through fifth floors.

But that wasn't what he was here to see. The clue he was looking for was much more subtle.

Swann took a deep slow gulp, and then turned his head to search for it.

His first glimpse of it tingled his spine.

Yes, as predicted— *exactly as his ghostly visitor predicted*— it was there. Adjacent to the front steps at the end of a short steep driveway: a garage door, the same shade of pink.

Taxi horns blaring, Swann carefully surveyed the surrounding homes one more time just to be sure. On the entire street, he could count only one other home with its own garage.

Whoever that voice belonged to last night knew that 235 E. 64th St. had a garage. If it were merely a dream, how could his mind have fabricated it with such accuracy? It was more than a coincidence or a dream, definitely more.

SWANN WRESTLED with indecision for seven loops around the block. The eighth time around, he glanced at his watch: nine after four. The visitor instructed him to do it by 4:30; he had very little time to make his decision.

The ninth time around, he did it— impulsively— but he did it. He could not even begin to explain why. There was absolutely no logic to it: this overwhelming feeling— this electrifying sense that *he just had to do it*— took complete control of him, compelling him to pull up parallel to the car parked on the far side of the driveway, throw his Chevy into reverse, cut the wheel all the way to the right, and carefully back his vehicle into the restricted space blocking the driveway.

He sat silent in the car for several moments, tapping his fingers on the wheel, still pondering as he glanced up and down the street, giving himself one last out before the point of no return. Then just as impulsively as his decision to park, he abruptly thrust open the door and walked out. Again, there was no firm conclusion, no closure on the pros and cons he had been assessing over and over again; something just moved him forward, a feeling, an illogical yet absolutely cocksure feeling.

What to do now? he asked himself as he walked down the street toward Third Avenue. He would have to kill a good couple of hours to make sure his deed had been accomplished. *Get some shopping in?* No, he quickly concluded; he had surpassed his holiday budget several days ago. *A movie?* Not in the mood, he shrugged. Then, he cracked a slight smile.

Before he turned down Third Avenue, he stopped for a moment, and for no reason in particular, glanced up. Immediately, his eyes hopped over to a young man, a lone young man walking brusquely toward him amongst a throng of busy New Yorkers. It was as if some sort of magnetism had directed Swann's eyes there. *A privileged chap*— this young fellow— Swann figured, quickly sizing up the lush, double-breasted Burberry coat tapering down his six-foot frame, the bright red cashmere scarf wrapped elegantly around his neck, his full head of light brown hair and his elegant, thin brown moustache.

For an odd fortuitous moment, both Swann and the young man stared at each other, their eyes lingering as if cementing some sort of cosmic bond. That single instant of contact seemed to last an eternity. Then, awkwardly, Swann nodded. "Good afternoon," he uttered in hushed tones, as if somehow he knew the young fellow. The young man— in his mid-twenties— reflexively nodded back. "A good day to you as well," he responded in slightly more than a whisper.

As Swann drifted along Third Avenue, bumping into last-minute shoppers rushing to beat the clock, holiday tourists navigating an intimidating metropolis and convivial New Yorkers getting a head start on their Christmas cheer, he thought about that young man's voice: *For some odd reason it sounded eerily familiar to that voice in his room last night, didn't it?*

* * *

DAMNIT!

Christopher Pennfield's face grew beet red as he approached his family's townhouse midway down E. 64th Street: a blue Chevy with Jersey plates was blocking his parents' driveway. For a moment, he burned his eyes into that ugly vehicle with its odd shade of blue and its grotesque front grille, scoffing at it, then bolted up the front steps.

"Damnit, father, some heathen from Jersey is blocking our driveway!" he shouted as he lunged up to the parlor on the second floor, hastily throwing down his Burberry coat and red cashmere scarf.

"So what?" his father, attorney Richard Pennfield responded, sipping his daily afternoon martini. "Who wants to arrive early anyway? It only means I'll have to tolerate that condescending, windbag big brother of mine that much longer."

"But we'll be *late*," Christopher exclaimed, "It's my only chance to see the family this break. We need to leave for Uncle Perce's and Aunt Bunny's in a half hour. It's Christmas for God's sake!"

His father answered coolly, "Then Christopher, I'm sure if you call the precinct, they'll have it towed promptly. I'm busy."

"Yeah, but…"

The elder Pennfield picked up his pipe, lit it, then quietly quipped, "you must really want to get into Ophie's pants again…"

"Father!"

"WHAT DO you mean you can't get anyone here immediately?" Christopher barked into the phone. "Do you know who we are? *We're the Pennfields damnit!"*

"Oh, sorry, Mr. Pennfield, real sorry, but we're a bit short-staffed this afternoon," the desk officer answered. "You know we're expecting the blizzard-to-end-all-blizzards at two or three in the morning, so we moved most officers' shifts back a few hours to help with the snow."

"Unacceptable! You absolutely must do something, you need to figure it out *now!"* Pennfield barked back. "We have an important family event to attend in Connecticut and I can't believe you'll allow some idiot from New Jersey to deprive us of that right."

"Mr. Pennfield, we'll do the very best we can."

EVEN WITH THE Pennfield name weighing heavily upon its shoulders, it took the NYPD an hour and a half to deploy a tow truck to E. 64th St. The rapid whistling winds, in full pre-blizzard fervor, rattled the townhome's oversized windows as Christopher Pennfield observed them from the second-floor portico, wringing his hands and pacing rapidly as the officers methodically attached the tow truck's hook to the front grille of the interloping Chevy, maybe *too methodically* for Pennfield's liking.

"Can't these dimwits do it any faster?" Pennfield writhed, counting the seconds, one by one, *"Are they getting paid by the hour or something?"*

"Calm down, will you please," his father admonished, stirring another martini.

"But father, the *incompetence...*"

BY THE TIME the police moved Ed Swann's bright blue Chevy from the spot blocking the Pennfields' driveway, Swann was comfortably seated at the bar at PJ Clarke's on E. 53rd St., indulgently sipping a pint of Guinness Stout, dark brown with a frothy mocha head. About halfway through his ritual, Swann stood up from his seat, strode to the payphone on the wall, deposited a few coins, and carefully dialed the number he had scribbled on a jagged scrap of paper.

After three full rings, a familiar voice answered, *"Hello?"*

"Hey Artie, Merry Christmas!" Swann began ebulliently, his cheeks reddening like a pair of ripe apples, "This is Ed. Ed Swann, long time no speak!"

"Hey! Eddie! What's up?"

"Oh, same old stuff. How 'bout you?"

Swann happily gulped his pint, relieved to know he would not be lying when he recounted his evening to his wife later that night. Indeed, he had enjoyed a beer at PJ Clarke's while visiting with his dear college friend, Artie Winfield from Ohio.

* * *

THE WINDS BLUSTERED off the sound as the Manhattan Pennfields motored up I-95. No flakes of snow had yet dropped, but every indication— the brisk winds and chilly moisture in the air— portended an impending storm.

"Can't you drive any faster, father?" Christopher admonished from the back seat.

"Jesus, keep it in your pants, will ya?" His father retorted.

"Richard!" Martha Pennfield slapped her husband's leg as he drove. "Will you please hold your tongue!"

"Yes, dear." His eyes twinkled; he had made his point.

* * *

"THIS JUST ISN'T LIKE CHRISTOPHER," Ophelia interrupted her father in the bustling foyer of their large home, "he's always so punctual."

"Don't worry, I'm sure they'll arrive soon," Percival Pennfield assured his daughter in his whispery, raspy voice as he choreographed his way through a throng of guests, holding a scotch in one hand and offering holiday greetings with the other.

"I just have a feeling," Ophelia pouted, "I have a feeling that something's wrong."

"Oh don't worry yourself needlessly, Ophie," her father interjected as he swiveled from guest to guest, "I'm sure it's weather-related."

OPHELIA PENNFIELD WORRIED, but not without provocation. Shortly before their guests began arriving, she had seen a mysterious apparition through her bedroom window: a naked man hovering horizontally, a resonant voice, detached and hollow, emanating from somewhere beyond, warning her about little Shippy and the dock.

Distant and deep in thought, oblivious to the dozens of guests whirling around her, Ophie surmised that the two incidents *must be* related. It would be too much of coincidence if they were *not*; her heightened sixth sense told her so. She constantly peeked out the front door, hoping to see her Uncle Richard's Lincoln pull up.

"CHARLES! LANCE!" little Arthur exclaimed with glee the moment he spotted his young cousins and then tugged at his mother's dress. "Charles and Lance are here, Mother. Can we go outside and play?"

Bunny Pennfield shook her head. "No, Shippy. It's getting dark and it's viciously cold."

Undeterred, Little Shippy looked over towards his sister, Ophelia, an easy mark. *"Ophie! Ophie!* Can Charles and Lance and I go out and play?"

No response, her eyes trained on the front door windows.

"Ophie!" Little Shippy tugged at her dress.

"Huh?" she answered vacantly.

"Charles and Lance and I, can we—"

"There they are!" Ophie's face brightened and eyes lit up as she pointed towards Uncle Richard's Lincoln making its way along the circular driveway. "Chris! Christopher!" She bolted out the front door, bumping into guests, even forgetting to put on her coat.

Shippy took her lack of response as permission to proceed. He scurried out the door with his cousins and began throwing snowballs near the inlet.

THE NEXT TIME Ophelia would see little Shippy, he would be naked, shivering and catatonic at the end of their rickety old dock.

* * *

TIME FRAME: 2053

57

Manhattan, NYCGAB, Pennfield Technologies Tower, Morning, January 17, 2053

S*hit!* JMP slapped himself on the knee.

How can this be happening? Just when he thought he had outsmarted Weisman *et al* from 2007, they come back at him. Granted, Weisman was a brilliant fellow for his time, but how could he ever outsmart Jimmy Mashimoto-Pennfield, industrialist, innovator, genius?

The situation irked JMP. In his Ganzfeld session the previous evening, he had again visited Indian Harbor. As his consciousness seeped into the festivities of the annual Pennfield Christmas Party, JMP was shocked to observe Ophelia in the hallway fretting over cousin Christopher's tardiness. But that has to be wrong! he thought. Last time he Ganzfelded into that event, JMP had clearly seen Christopher with Ophelia and Ship and then observed as Christopher accompanied his young cousin outside, saving him from his encounter on the dock. *So what changed? Where had Christopher Pennfield gone?*

Mashimoto-Pennfield was so consumed that he almost missed little Shippy tugging at Ophelia's dress, then bursting outside with his cousins as Ophelia ran out to greet Christopher. From there on, everything played out: Shippy's older cousins threw snowballs at him, then ran off, leaving their little cousin to go pout, alone on the dock, where he would see the apparition and be shocked into his catatonic state.

JMP pointed, summoning a holoscreen and pulled up the diagram he had scribbled several days prior. He marked an "x" underneath the left branch:

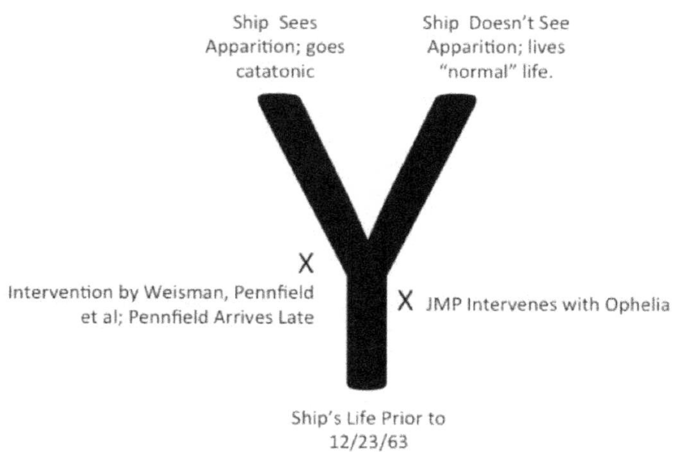

Damn, another event to be unraveled! Somehow, someway, he had to get Ship back on the other branch. He was sure this Julian Weisman was the brains of the operation. Had to be. He was the only one near being a quasi-genius according to the historical record.

He caressed his temples with his thumbs, his elbows lying on his expansive glass desk. Painfully, he squinted. He focused, more and more and more and more intensely.

"The answer should be obvious."

Startled, JMP recoiled and then swiveled around, surveying the room. "Narc, what are you doing here? I didn't summon you."

"It's called anticipation, my dear other," Narc responded, lounging comfortably on a glass table behind JMP's desk.

"You're getting too independent for your own good."

"But you invented me, did you not?" Narc answered.

"Quite right," JMP answered. "And always remember that."

"Surely, dear other." Narc jumped up off the table. "And now to the task at hand."

"So tell me about this so-called *obvious answer* of yours," JMP stated.

"Of course. Let's weave together some simple facts. Number one: our little Shippy circa 1960-something suffers from an incurable condition called Catatonic Schizophrenia, correct?"

JMP nodded.

"And you and this Weisman fellow have been going back and forth, reversing and un-reversing the young boy's fate."

"Tell me something I don't know, Narc!" JMP censured him.

"Well, after Weisman's latest move, the young lad is again stricken with catatonic schizophrenia which means he's back at the Gladwell Institute in the 1960s under the care of Dr. Hazard who is desperately trying to cure him."

"Yeah, so?"

"And now you, in 2053," Narc continued, "have the foremost nano-biologist in the history of humankind in your employ."

Stoically, JMP processed the thought until the hardened lines in his face softened and his lips slowly formed a euphoric grin.

Giggling like a schoolchild, he pounded his fist on his desk, rattling its contents. "Narc, that's brilliant! Fucking brilliant! And so obvious I should have thought of it myself."

"That's why I exist," Narc answered.

Immediately, he pointed upward, summoning Dr. Li-Pin on his holoscreen. As Li-Pin's face appeared, JMP looked over towards his clone. "You can go now, Narc."

Frowning, Narc dematerialized.

"Mr. MP?" Stavros Li-Pin answered from his laboratory.

"Stavros."

"What can I do for you?"

"Question for you: are you familiar with a condition called catatonic schizophrenia?" JMP asked.

"Let's see, it sounds vaguely familiar..." Dr. Li-Pin pulled up a holoscreen and began flipping through its e-files. .

"Ummm... yes, here it is," Li-Pin ceased his virtual flipping, "...Catatonic Schizophrenia: a debilitating condition... would put people into catatonic stupors that could last their entire lifetimes."

"Any idea what causes it?"

Li-Pin peered deeper into his screen. "No, says here it's never been definitively established."

"Any cure?"

He virtually flipped through more e-pages. "Interesting." Li-Pin smiled, "it was one of the first neuro-psychological conditions which responded to a regimen of nano-microorganisms. It says here Dr. Kuama Su-Wil, a Namibian researcher, first tested the protocol in 2024."

"Good." JMP leaned forward and softened his voice. "Now I'm going to ask you a question, a question that is of extreme importance to me personally. And I expect you to keep it confidential and not to question my motive."

"Of course, Mr. MP." Li-Pin looked quizzically at his screen.

"Is there a way— any way possible— that you can retro-fit, so to speak, the curative regimen for catatonic schizophrenia so that it could be implemented by someone using medical technology of, let's say, a hundred years ago?"

"What?"

"I want you to *'dumb it down'* so someone with access to century-old technology could replicate it."

"That would be extremely difficult, Mr. MP."

"*Extremely difficult?*" JMP softly censured him. "The reason I hired you was to do things that are *extremely difficult*, Stavros."

"And, of course, the person implementing the regimen would have to be highly gifted," Li-Pin continued.

"That's not a cause of concern," JMP snapped back.

"But why would you ever want to—"

"I told you not to question my motive."

"Of course. Of course."

"So?" JMP raised an eyebrow.

"Well, I suppose if I put some of our best people on it, including myself of course, there may be a way to retrofit the regimen, but it would—"

"Stop right there." JMP raised his hand.

"Yes, Mr. MP?"

"No *buts*, Stavros, just results."

"No, but what I was saying is that it would take away from our progress on the cryonics imitative. I only have so many resources, Mr. MP."

"I realize that," JMP answered briskly. "And I also realize you're the best in the world at what you do."

"Thank you, Mr. MP." Li-Pin blushed.

"That's why I realize that if you want to earn all the rewards we've discussed, you'll do both. The cryonics initiative *and* my little favor. And do both ASAP." JMP leaned in towards the holoscreen, his furrowed brow framing a menacing grin. "Am I clear, Stavros?"

Dutifully, Li-Pin answered with a whisper. “Yes, of course, Mr. MP.”

SMILING, JMP pulled up his diagram once more and drew a diagonal line connecting the two branches:

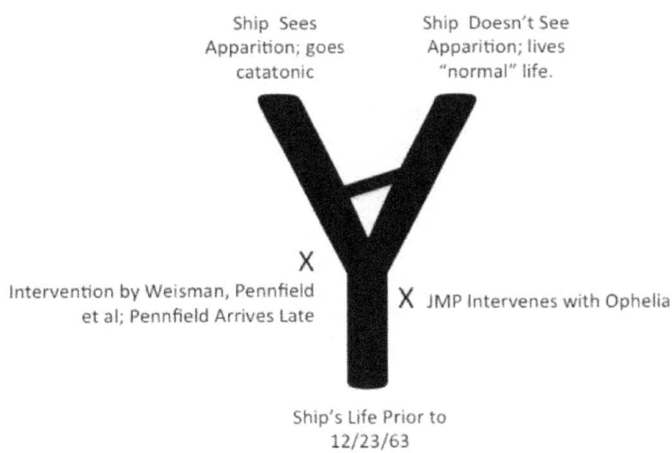

“*Check.*” JMP chuckled. “*Your move, Weisman.*”

* * *

TIME FRAME: 1965 - 1966

58

Lenox, MA, Gladwell Sanitarium, Evening, August 14, 1965

The dark, old basement stank.

The intermittent groans and yelps only accentuated the stench.

Yet, each evening, usually around six, Dr. Emilio Hazard would wobble down the cobweb-draped stairs, deep into the entrails of Gladwell Sanitarium, and check on the progress of his experiments.

The *specimens,* as Dr. Hazard would call them, were chained to their beds by their ankles and wrists, stacked three to a bunk, their urine-soaked plastic mattresses thin and uncomfortable.

In some ways, it bothered him.

But he had a budget, he always reassured himself, and he had to stretch it: the more specimens, the more likely the chance he would find the cure he was looking for. By that logic, he was doing mankind a favor.

Abruptly, he heard something stir.

His eyes jumped over to an emaciated African male in the middle bunk in the third row. The tall, lean body— its large feet dangling over the end of the bunk— shook and rattled.

Hazard darted over.

Eyes wide open, the face vibrated, its teeth chattering and its lips wobbling as if a strong electric current ran through its bones.

"*Dr. Hoq!*" Hazard called up to his assistant.

"Yes, Dr. Hazard." Hoq rushed down the stairs.

"What regimen have we been testing on this specimen?"

"Extremely high ECT. Five hundred joules, I think along with a regimen of several hallucinatory drugs at high dosages," Hoq answered dutifully.

"Five hundred, eh?"

"Yes, five hundred. I am sure."

"Perhaps a bit too aggressive, don't you think?" Hazard raised an eyebrow.

"Perhaps," Hoq answered, "but we were attempting to test the limits."

"Yes. Yes. I know." Hazard nodded. "But perhaps too aggressive. Can you kindly prepare me a sedative?"

"Certainly, Dr. Hazard."

THERE WERE at least fifty of them: victims of catatonic schizophrenia, mostly from Africa and Eastern Europe. When he first received the funding from Percival Pennfield, Hazard had sent his assistants on a worldwide mission to "recruit" victims of this tragic affliction, rewarding their families handsomely —by local standards— and promising a possible cure.

To most families, it was an attractive offer and released them from the burden of providing care for a loved one with a condition they could not even begin to comprehend.

To Dr. Hazard, it was fifty data points— the opportunity to stretch the limits of his experimental regimens in an attempt at everlasting fame, at least within the world of psychiatry. And, of course, if he did discover that elusive cure, the Pennfields, one of America's most powerful families, would be forever indebted to him.

"HERE." Dr. Hoq handed Hazard a syringe filled with a heavy dose of sedatives.

"Thank you." Hazard pulled a surgical mask over his face and punctured the specimen's shoulder with his needle. Within several minutes, the vibrating ceased.

As Hazard pulled off the mask, he gagged loudly— his eyes popping from his reddened face— nauseated by the fecal matter smeared across the mattress.

"Water? Can I get you some water, Dr. Hazard?" Dr. Hoq offered.

Hazard shook his head and waved him off.

ABSORBED AND FOCUSED, Hazard meandered between bunks, checking scribbled notes on the clipboards attached to each. So intent in his concentration, he barely noticed the small mouse scampering across the dank cement floor.

It was somewhat of a menagerie: Hazard's basement laboratory, populated with specimens sharing the same affliction but manifesting it in wildly divergent manners. One old eastern-European woman with a crackled face sitting perfectly silent with both forearms dangling from her outstretched arms; an entranced African pygmy spouting out indecipherable words; a tall Asian woman with a round face and a baldish scalp, her legs contorted around her shoulders.

To anyone but Hazard and Hoq, the scene would be terrifying. To them, it was commonplace, merely experimental subjects being observed and tested in the name of scientific advancement. Hazard proceeded dutifully, bunk to bunk, just as he did each evening at this time; a tiresome, but necessary task.

"Time to try something new, don't you think, Dr. Hazard?"

The voice startled Hazard; he thought Hoq had retreated to his upstairs office several minutes ago.

"Dr. Hoq?" Hazard quickly scanned the room.

No Dr. Hoq.

A thin film of sweat misted Hazard's face.

"Dr. Hoq?" Hazard stiffened. *"Fareed, where are you?"*

Silence.

Again, he scanned the room, squinting to observe every nook and cranny of the basement. He didn't see Dr. Hoq or anyone else for that matter.

"If you concentrate hard enough, you should be able to see me. Or perhaps you're not psychically gifted? A pity if you aren't, you know?"

"And why would that be?" Hazard perspired in beads.

"For a psychiatrist of your stature to have even a tiny bit of psychic sensitivity would be absolutely incredible, don't you think?"

"Of course, hearing strange voices could be a sort of ill-defined psychic gift, but much more simply, it could also be a singular sign of schizophrenia."

"Bravo! Always the esteemed scholar."

"A true irony, eh?" Hazard responded, still perplexed over why he was speaking to some strange, disembodied voice. "A specialist in schizophrenia becoming victim of the very condition he has devoted his life attempting to cure."

"You're much too modest, Dr. Hazard."

"Eh?"

"We all know you're the best in the world."

Hazard grinned. "Some may say that."

Then, Hazard stopped. *This is strange, unreal,* he told himself. *Why is he obliging to the whims of some psychiatric disorder?* He quickly surmised: *the only way to make this odd phenomenon go away is to totally ignore its existence.*

Deliberately, he walked over to his small desk and began updating his notes, concentrating on shutting out any contact with this strange voice from nowhere. He scribbled away fortuitously, paying more attention to what he was avoiding than what he was writing.

"C'mon, quit trying to flush me out of your brain. I'm here for you, my friend."

Hazard grit his teeth, clamped on this pen and forced himself to concentrate on the piece of paper on his desk.

"It's almost flattering, the intensity of your avoidance."

Hazard breathed deep and drilled his eyes so intently into the paper he could see its grainy imperfections.

"You know, I wasn't lying. If you try hard enough, you can see me."

Hazard put down his pen and lifted his eyes from the paper, staring at the painted cement wall before him.

Face down, Hazard began scribbling again.

"Please, don't stop now. We're just beginning to get acquainted."

Hazard forced a harsh cough, and then zeroed in on the paper.

"I can do wonders for you, you know."

Ignoring the voice, Hazard clamped again on his pen and continued writing.

"Please, don't make this too hard."

He forced himself to concentrate on the paper.

"I can make you more famous than you ever imagined."

For a moment, a deep, anticipatory silence.

Then, Hazard put down his pen, looked up, and responded.

"How?"

"There you go. Now we're talking. C'mon. Turn your head. Take a look."

Partially out of curiosity and partially out of self-preservation, Hazard slowly turned his head away from his small desk and glanced over toward the rows of bunks.

"Peek-a-boo!"

Hazard's heart stopped for a moment.

The apparition, naked and horizontal, giggled:

"Now there. Much better, don't you think?"

"Who are you?" Hazard asked, as he gasped to regain his breath.

"Does it really matter?"

"For my sanity, it does."

"Sanity? SANITY? Does that even enter into the equation?

"You're confusing me."

"Would you prefer I slow down for you, Doctor?"

"Not necessary." Hazard grit his teeth. "Now what do you want?"

"I'm here to help you, give you a message, a solution."

"Really?" Hazard's ears piqued. "Tell me more."

"I can help you in ways you would never imagine."

"So, on with it!" Hazard demanded.

"How about a key to unlock the mystery of catatonic schizophrenia?"

Hazard's eyes widened. "Why, of course, I've spent my entire life trying—"

"You needn't tell me. I know all that and more."

"But how can *you* help me?"

"I see you have a pad of paper."

"Of course. Of course."

"Start taking notes. Copiously, please."

* * *

Lenox, MA

Gladwell Institute of Mental Health Sciences

Morning

January 13, 1966

"Emilio! Emilio!" Dr. Hoq bolted through Hazard's door. *"It just came. Front page! Front page!"*

Hazard lifted his eyes from the papers he was studying at his desk, a slight smile brimming. "Really?"

"Yes, right here. Look! Look!" Hoq flipped over *The New York Times* he held and pointed to the article in the lower left-hand corner.

Hazard's slight smile became a slight frown.

"What? What's the matter, Emilio?"

"Below the fold?" Hazard scowled.

"Yes, but it's still the front page, is it not?" Hoq responded. "And such a superb article it is. Here. Read."

Psychiatrist Discovers Cure for Schizophrenia: January 12, 1966 --

Dr. Emilio Hazard (pron. ha-*zaird*) of the Gladwell Institute of Mental Health Sciences in Lenox, Massachusetts announced and documented a cure for an esoteric psychiatric disorder, Catatonic Schizophrenia, in the March 1966 edition of *The Journal of the American Medical Association.* The affliction, rare in North America, but more prevalent in third world countries such as Africa and parts of Eastern Europe, casts a catatonic stupor upon its victims which lasts anywhere from a few minutes to the rest of their lives. Hazard's research, funded by the noted Percival Pennfield family of Greenwich, CT, had been ongoing for three years. The Pennfield family's donation coincided with the rare affliction striking their 7-year-old son, Arthur Shipkin Pennfield, in December 1963. According to Hazard, application of his regimen has already begun on the now 9-year-old Pennfield, and a complete recovery is expected within weeks. So far, ten patients who participated in Dr. Hazard's clinical study have experienced a complete recovery.

"WHAT A SUPERB and fitting tribute to our resident genius and my trusted mentor!" Hoq beamed.

"I suppose…." Hazard muttered.

"*Suppose?* You should be elated. This is just the beginning Emilio. There'll be more. Symposia. Appearances. Television. Celebrity. Maybe a Nobel Prize, perhaps?"

"Yes, yes, I'm sure this will all be very good, very good for the Institute," Hazard practically whispered.

"Emilio, why are you so sullen?" Hoq asked. "This is the beginning of the absolute pinnacle of your career."

Hazard shook his head and shrugged his shoulders. "I don't know. My own form of post-partum depression possibly? Perhaps I'm melancholy because the challenge is over, achieved."

"And triumphantly, indeed!" Hoq responded. "No need to be melancholy, Emilio. Just enjoy."

"That's very difficult, Fareed, very difficult," Hazard answered. "Perhaps I'm struggling to determine what I can possibly do to top this so-called *achievement* of mine."

* * *

LENOX, MA

Gladwell Institute of Mental Health Sciences

Afternoon

February 3, 1966

THEY HAD WAITED three years for this moment.

"Si agréable de vous voir aujourd'hui, le père, la mère, la soeur." The young man greeted them.

"Oh my God!" Percival Pennfield's jaw dropped to the floor.

Ophelia clutched onto her mother, tears pouring from their eyes.

Befuddled, the young man asked, "Why are you all acting so weird? It's me, Ship!"

It was amazing. The nine-year-old Arthur Shipkin Pennfield, stepped into Hazard's office, perfectly groomed, dressed impeccably in a tweed jacket, white shirt and khaki pants, a conservative red and blue necktie, the same boyish face, freckles and all.

Ophelia rushed over and clutched him to her breast. Her mother followed, clutching both of them.

"Why are you crying?" the young boy asked. "What's the matter?"

"Of course, you don't know. You can't. This is such a shock." Ophelia answered, still sobbing. "You've been catatonic for over two years."

"*Huh?*" the young boy did a double take. "Catatonic, what's that?"

"It's like you've been in a coma, asleep," Ophelia answered.

"I have not!" Ship asserted. "Just yesterday you and I took the boat out into the Sound. We had a wonderful time together."

"Poor baby. Poor baby." Ophelia wiped his brow. "It's easy to understand why you're so confused. Everything will be okay. Everything will be fine."

"But I'm not..." Ship shifted his eyes around the room, wondering what was going on, "... *confused*."

"Arthur." Percival Pennfield walked over to him and extended his hand.

"Father?"

"Welcome back." Percival Pennfield vigorously shook Arthur's hand.

"Buh...Buh...Welcome back *to what*?" Arthur asked startlingly.

"Son, you've been through a lot," Percival addressed Ship calmly and assuredly, "everything will become clear to you over time. Don't worry."

As Arthur pummeled his mother and sister with a series of questions, Percival Pennfield pulled Dr. Hazard into a corner of the room.

"Strange, that he thinks nothing ever happened to him," he whispered.

"Yes, but we must realize that he had a very rare affliction and a new form of therapy. We are in an uncharted territory, Mr. Pennfield," Hazard answered.

"Indeed," Pennfield responded snappily, "but how and when do we get him back into *charted* territory?"

"I don't think that will be difficult, not at all," Hazard responded. "We've conducted a battery of tests. His IQ is as high as ever, there's been no neural damage. He's basically as good as new except he hasn't experienced the world for the last two years."

"But what about education?" Pennfield asked.

"You must remember, prior to his affliction, he was a very gifted second grader," Hazard answered. "Actually, our tests indicate that he retained virtually all of his knowledge prior to the incident in 1963 and, in fact, tested at the level of a fifth grader, so he should fit in just fine."

"But he's missed three years of schooling."

"I wouldn't worry, Mr. Pennfield," Hazard responded. "With his retained knowledge, his level of achievement and, of course, his intellectual capacity, and the proper rigorous private tutoring, I'm sure he can cover all that ground in no more than several months and, soon, far surpass his grade level in terms of achievement."

"What makes you so sure?"

"Believe me, Mr. Pennfield. He can do it. I have no doubts whatsoever. Rest assured, in eight years he'll be entering Yale."

* * *

TIME FRAME: 1977-1993

THE ALTERNATIVE LIFE OF ARTHUR SHIPKIN PENNFIELD

59

New Haven, CT, Yale University, March 1977

During the next two school years, Lori Bernstein and Ship Pennfield grew closer by the day, sharing his apartment, studying together, eating together, sleeping together, doing everything together. It was clear to Ship that he never wanted to leave her. Accepted at six medical schools during his senior year, Ship's decision was an easy one: he would attend Yale Medical. He proposed to Lori and they would marry in a year after she graduated from the college. Predictably, the news was not well accepted at Indian Harbor.

"What are you trying to do to me, Ship!" His father screamed into the phone.

"This shouldn't come as a surprise, father," Ship answered calmly.

"You're right," his father answered. "Surprises are supposed to be happy. This is a travesty, damnit!"

"It's *my* life. You have to let me live it on my terms,"

"Bullshit! You're part of this family. We have a reputation. A good one, in fact. And one thing we don't do is go around marrying Jews!"

"Well I *am* doing it. You can't stop me." Ship asked.

"Oh, just watch me. Just you watch me." His father slammed the phone into its cradle.

* * *

New York, NY: 250 Park Ave.
Mid-day
April 6, 1977

THE FRESH SPRING rain sprayed the verdant median running up Park Avenue, polishing the black tar two-way thoroughfare. It was not quite a depressing day, just a bland day, the light gray sky shading the city with a cover of monotonous sameness. The weather had no effect on Percival Pennfield, not even prompting him to wear a hat. He barreled through the Helmsley Building walkway, focused on just one thing: the meeting about to ensue a few blocks away.

By the time he emerged on 47th Street, the rain had softened to a fine spray. He pulled the piece of paper from his inside jacket-pocket and studied it. *250 Park.* His eyes surveyed the tall pre-war office building to his left. After struggling to find the number it finally caught his eye: *250.* Brusquely, he strode across the street, whirled through the building's revolving doors, and drew a beeline for the reception desk. He barely waited for the attendant to look up.

"I'm here to see a Mr. Morris Bernstein," he announced.

A deal-maker by trade, Pennfield was poised to make yet another.

THE OFFICES OF BERNSTEIN, Miller & Shapiro were tastefully decorated, but not at all what Pennfield was used to. The décor of Pennfield's Wall Street offices differed significantly: mahogany and cherry, pristine antique desks, arched windows with leaded panes draped in red velvet overlooking Lower Manhattan, as quiet as a library. These offices were much more contemporary, an underlying buzz of activity and chatter, modern art on the muted tan walls and even a glass-enclosed conference room.

"Percival?" A stocky bald man, a thin crown of white hair framing his bald scalp, emerged in the lobby and extended his hand.

"Mr. Bernstein?" Pennfield stood up and reciprocated.

"Morris Bernstein. But please call me Moe." Bernstein, with no jacket, just a white shirt with an open collar and suspenders holding up his blue pinstripe pants, led him down a hallway past a bank of desks and into his corner office.

The office was large with an expansive kidney-shaped desk of light wood and a small work table off to the side cluttered with papers. A panoramic view of Central Park graced the large window.

"Well, it looks like we're about to become relatives." Bernstein sat back and smiled. He raised his hand. "Mazel-tov."

Pennfield cringed. "Yes. That's why I'm here."

"Of course, at first Beatrice and I were a little concerned about the..."

"As were we," Pennfield answered.

"But you know, life is to too short." Bernstein reached into his desk drawer and pulled out a box. "Cigar?"

"No I don't partake," Pennfield answered tersely.

"You know, there's the whole issue of children and how they'll be brought up."

Pennfield's brow furled.

"But... hell, over time things like that tend to work themselves out, don't you think?" Bernstein continued.

"Over *time*?" Pennfield mumbled.

"So what can I do for you today, Perce. Can I call you that?"

"I prefer Percival."

"Okay, Percival, so what's up?"

"I'm here to discuss the very issue you just mentioned."

Bernstein leaned back in his chair.

"Perhaps in our youth we sometimes make mistakes we regret years later," Pennfield suggested.

"Well, yes, but, that's for them to work out, don't you think?"

"Morris, I'm just not sure we do them any good by allowing them to perpetuate a mistake."

"Oh? What makes you so certain that they're making a mistake?"

"The two... cultures, I mean they just don't..."

"Mix?"

"I wouldn't put it quite that way, but, yes, you can't deny it, there are fundamental differences."

"So what were you thinking?" Bernstein asked.

"I have a suggestion that may help us around this issue. And each for the better."

"Okay. Shoot."

Pennfield reached into his lapel pocket and pulled out an envelope. "Perhaps I can provide a little incentive to assuage any despair your daughter might experience over the possible ramifications of a break-up." He handed Bernstein the envelope.

Baffled, Bernstein accepted the envelope. He looked at it. Nothing written on the outside. For a moment he hesitated, then ripped it open and pulled out its contents. He examined the sheet of paper carefully, and then frowned: a cashier's check made out in the amount of $2 million.

Bernstein caught the cigar that had fallen from his lip, then giggled. "So you're trying to buy me off?"

"I wouldn't put it quite that way."

"You think I come that cheap, do you?"

"Cheap? I would consider my offer substantial."

"Bullshit!" Bernstein's face reddened.

"Morris, we're reasonable men, I'm sure we can—"

"You hoity-toity white-bread types don't want to consort with Jews, do you?" Bernstein blurted. "Right, Pennfield?"

"I wouldn't put it quite that way."

"Let me tell you something, Pennfield. I didn't inherit a dime."

"That's not what this is about…."

"Yeah? We didn't come over on the goddamn Mayflower. We escaped from the Third Reich when I was twelve years old. You know what we had?"

"That's not the point," Pennfield muttered.

"I'll tell you what we had. We had nothing. In Germany, my dad was a university professor. Here he could only get a job as a high school teacher. My mom, she worked as a seamstress. They worked their balls off, paid my way through Penn and then Columbia Law. You see this office?"

"Yes. Yes. Quite impressive," Pennfield muttered some more.

"I didn't inherit this place. I built it. So let me tell *you* the 'point'."

"Morris, I'm only trying to avoid what would be a major mistake for both of our children."

"Here's what I think of you and your type." Bernstein stood up, marched around his desk. He shoved the check into Pennfield's face. "See this?"

Pennfield nodded as he brushed away Bernstein's hand. Then Bernstein ripped the check into pieces and scattered them on the floor.

"Morris, think reasonably. Consider… the *numbers.*"

"You think your God damn inherited money is the solution to every problem?" Bernstein scoffed, gazing down upon the scattered pieces. "I think you've underestimated me, Mr. Pennfield. You know what you can do with your check?"

"Go on, tell me."

"Take those little pieces of excrement on the floor and shove them right up your lily-white ass. Now get the hell out of here."

Pennfield retreated towards the door.

"And don't worry. My daughter will never be part of your family. Ever!"

Walking out, Pennfield grinned.

SHIP NEVER FORGAVE his father for interfering with his marriage to Lori.

Ship attended UCLA Med School, as far away from New Haven as feasibly possible. Lori graduated from Yale and then went onto Cornell Medical School in Manhattan. Although Lori's father had vehemently banned her from ever corresponding with Ship, they sneaked in a few sporadic calls during Ship's first year in Los Angeles. After that, they didn't speak again, their attentions drifting away into their present lives.

60

Los Angeles, California, Various Locations, April–October 1983

Ophelia was a frequent visitor to Los Angeles. She was very protective of her "little brother," never wanting to remain out of touch for too long. She adored the Bel Air Hotel in the hills overlooking the UCLA campus. To her, the place was magical with its pinks and greens, a relic of the "old" Hollywood of Gable, Chaplin, Fairbanks and Pickford.

The lounge and bar area of the hotel did not look Hollywood at all. If anything, it had a New England feeling to it, a large crackling fireplace surrounded by lush upholstered chairs and love seats scattered into islands of three or four each, centered around a mahogany coffee table. A small bar was off to the side. Celebrities were known to frequent the venue, but were treated with a certain detachment, as if not celebrities at all.

"Shippy, you look divine, absolutely divine!" Ophie jumped up from her chair in the lounge and bounded towards Ship.

"Oh I bet you say that to all the guys." He rushed over and hugged her.

"A dear friend of mine is having a party at Malibu on Sunday. You must attend." Ophie segued directly into conversation. "And don't you for one moment give me that look of yours." She pointed her finger at him.

"What? That look that residency is a bitch and 'party' is a word that vanished from my vocabulary the instant I got here?"

"Oh. Phooey. No wonder why doctors are so boring. No fun at all. Well at least have a drink." She motioned for the waitress. "Or has that vanished from your vocabulary as well?"

"No. I have a genetic predisposition for Scotch."

"Here. Here." She clapped her hands.

Although it had only been two months since Ophie's last visit, the two of them could talk for hours. Their conversation ran the gamut, everything and anything was fair game. Politics. Gossip. Movies. And, of course, mutual friends.

"You'll never guess who I bumped into on the Upper East Side last week."

He thought for a moment and then answered teasingly. "I think I can narrow it down to one of three. It was either the Prince of Wales, the Sultan of Brunei or, perhaps, Marlon Brando?"

"All wrong." She teased him back.

"So then who was it?"

"Lori."

His face turned white. "Bernstein?"

"None other."

"Well how is she?" he stuttered. "Is she umm…."

"No, from what I could gather she was not *attached*, if that's what you're poking at. She's going through med school hell just like you. She spent a summer in Ceylon, or was it Sri Lanka, doing volunteer work or something like that."

"How does she look?"

"Fine. As attractive as ever. Although, from experience I can say that medical students do get this laboriously dogged look about them. Comes with the territory I suppose."

"You look like you've taken off some weight. "

"My dear little Shippy," she responded, "are you deliberately trying to change the subject."

"No. Well maybe a bit. But you do look rather thin. You've been dieting?"

"Not really."

"Exercise?"

"Of course. I do a delightful job of flexing my right arm when I reach for my wallet in Saks. And I do so quite frequently."

EVENTUALLY, Ophie was able to twist Ship's arm into attending her friend's Malibu party. The estate of Izzy Archambeau, a third generation French-Iranian billionaire— pure *Eurotrash* as Ophie would refer to him— was, without doubt, palatial, both tall and wide, spreading its wingspan across a large stretch of prime Malibu beachfront. The entrance had a Greek revival tinge to it, tall white columns contrasted by pinkish stucco sides. But it was the back of the estate that really dazzled the guests. The mansion's large third floor living room provided breathtaking views of the Pacific through its expansive wall of solid glass, the doors of which opened to a series of terraced patios with curved stairways eventually leading down to the pool and then the beach.

Clumps of people surrounded the pool, sipping libations, as shapely young women and muscular young men frolicked in the water. There was a long temporary bar, accented by pink and green tablecloths and potted palms, with six bartenders attending to guests' every whim along the beach-side of the pool; its focal point was an ice sculpture of a cherub peeing champagne. He was surrounded by scores of fluted glasses, tempting guests to take a specimen.

"Izzy's parties are so decadent they're adorable, don't you think Ship?" Ophie remarked as she led Ship through the islands of people dotting the estate's grounds.

"I suppose," Ship answered reservedly.

"Oh, please…," she responded, "… don't be so serious all the time. When in Rome…."

"Okay." He shrugged as she dragged him by the hand.

"See over there," she pointed, "that's Marc Laurel, he's up for best director and that young-looking guy over there, Steve Acosta, is an up and comer, this year's flavor." Then she swiveled abruptly. "And there's Eve Sutherland," Ophie pointed to an attractive long-legged brunette and then lowered her voice to a whisper. "They say she's up for the lead in Coppola's next biggie. Of course, she's boinked half the industry."

Underwhelmed by the celebrity of Izzy Archambeau's guest list, Ship interrupted. "Can I get you a drink, Ophie? Scotch?"

Uncharacteristically, Ophie thought for a moment. "Not quite yet. My stomach's been a bit sensitive lately. I'll wait." Then from the corner of her eye, she caught a glimpse of a dark-haired, well-tanned, mustachioed man. She abruptly swiveled and embraced him. "Oh, Izzy, what a delightful party."

Izzy Archambeau nodded at her.

Then she grabbed him by the hand. "You must meet my little brother Shippy."

EVENTUALLY, Ophie and Ship drifted off towards the beach. For Ship it was an escape; the late afternoon sea breeze soothed him, and the golden rays of sunlight calmed him in a way that Izzy Archambeau's party never could. For Ophie, their little stroll was a mere diversion.

"Has the pursuit of a medical career completely robbed you of your personality, Shippy?"

He smiled. "No. Not at all. I just prefer *this* to *that* over there." He pointed over his shoulder towards Izzy Archambeau's estate. "I'd rather be walking along a beautiful calm beach with my beloved sister than mingling with Hollywood's A-list."

"I'll take that as a compliment," she answered.

"As you should."

"So, epidemiology, huh?"

"Yep, that's what I plan to specialize in."

"And I was praying for plastic surgery," she teased him.

"Yeah, right. I'm going to waste a good medical degree on giving boob-jobs to rich women."

"Well, I could try, can't I?"

"I suppose."

Ophie drifted towards the water's edge and dipped her hand in the froth. Approving of the sea's warm temperature, she leaned over to remove her shoes and suddenly winced, clutching her abdomen.

"Something the matter?" Ship asked.

"It's just my damn stomach. It's been acting up lately. I've been bloated and—"

"So you've been taking off weight without trying and your stomach's been sensitive for how long?"

"Oh, a few weeks. Maybe two, perhaps three."

"You sure? I've never seen you turn down a drink before."

"Okay. For the better part of a month. Four, five weeks. That's all."

"That worries me."

"Oh, Jesus, it's just—"

"Don't slough it off, Oph."

"But I've gone through episodes like this before."

"*Episodes*? You need to be checked out," Ship responded. "I'd like you to see a gastroenterologist friend of mine. Gene Karatopitos, he's really good."

"Oh, Shippy, is it really necessary?"

"Yes. When it involves the health of my sister, yes. Very necessary."

OPHIE HATED doctors and hated their "procedures" even more. She was not happy at all when Dr. Karatopitos recommended she undergo a lower GI series. But she dutifully drank her thick, chalky-tasting barium cocktail and then sat like a docile animal, pouting in front of an x-ray machine

"WELL, I don't think you have anything wrong with your GI tract," Karatopitos stated.

"Oh?" Ophie responded, relieved.

"But there's a strong possibility of something going on in the ovaries."

Her face whitened as Ship gripped her hand tightly. It took a long sobering moment before she could respond.

"So what now?" she whispered.

"I want you to see Dr. Greene. Dr. Sheryl Greene. You know her, don't you Ship?"

Ship nodded and glanced towards Ophie. "Yes. She's a gynecological oncologist."

"Exactly," Karatopitos responded. "That's the next step. I'd get an appointment as soon as you can."

DR. GREENE immediately recommended diagnostic surgery. If a tumor were found, she would remove as much of it as she possibly could and then send it to the lab for a biopsy.

The procedure seemed to take hours. Ship stood in the waiting room throughout, anxiously pacing. His eyes remained fixed on the waiting room clock. Each second seemed like a minute and each minute seemed like an hour. About a half hour into the surgery, he ran downstairs and did something he hadn't done in years — he smoked a cigarette.

When Dr. Greene finally emerged from behind the waiting room door and signaled for Ship to come out to the corridor, he sprang into action.

"We removed a medium sized tumor from her ovaries," the doctor stated blandly.

"Yeah, and…"

"We'll send it out for biopsy and see what happens."

"What do you think, Sheryl?"

"It's hard to say." She shrugged. "Let's have the lab do their work and then we'll go from there."

SHIP WAS HARDLY CONSOLED by Dr. Greene's lack of certainty. An advanced student of medicine himself, he realized that was about all she could say without being irresponsible, but as Ophie's brother, he yearned for something to hang onto, he wanted hope.

Five days later, the biopsy results were in. Dr. Greene phoned Ship to give him a heads-up.

"So?" Ship asked hopefully.

"Well, we did find a malignancy," she responded.

He winced. "Yeah, how bad?"

"There's a good chance we got all if not most of it."

"So what's next?"

"At this point, I would recommend a complete hysterectomy and then several rounds of chemo just to be safe."

Ship frowned. "Geeeezzzzzz……"

"I know it's tough, Ship. But that's the best course of action."

"It's just that she doesn't have any children. And she'd be such a good—"

"I know. I know. To be told you can never bear a child is a terrible thing, but, remember, we're trying to save her life."

OPHIE TOOK THE NEWS WELL, much better than Ship would have anticipated. He sighed and smiled, remembering that she had always had grit; her courage, her wit, were in full force now as she calmed him with her wry plans for the future.

"Well I suppose this gives me a great opportunity to assemble a glorious collection of wigs," she mused, "let's see, we can get a Liz Taylor brunette, a Marilyn platinum blonde, a Lucille Ball redhead. This is actually going to be fun."

"Ophie, aren't you being a little cavalier?"

"It's my life, not yours, Ship."

"I get it. But I love you. We all love you. But for you never to be able to—"

"Oh, don't be silly. I have no pressing need to be a mother. I have you to love, don't I?"

"Yeah, but…"

"Don't worry. Everything will work out, Shippy, it'll all work out."

SHIP PREVAILED upon Ophie to rent an apartment in Los Angeles so he could be with her throughout her treatments. She tolerated the surgery and chemotherapy treatments as gracefully as one possibly could. Ship was always there for her: getting her to and fro, spending time at her bedside during her recovery from surgery, and sitting beside her during virtually all of her chemotherapy sessions. He even helped out with drawing blood at times.

It was a long and arduous process, definitely not one for the faint of heart. Instead of being intimidated by it all, Ophie challenged it, conjuring up her inner sassiness to tease the fates into compliance. At the end of three months of chemo, Dr. Greene called them into her office.

"It's gone," she announced.

Ophie and Ship looked at her strangely.

"Wha....?" Ship responded.

"The cancer, it's gone. You're clean, Ophelia."

Ophie said nothing, and then burst into an uncontrollable laugh.

"Holy Freaking God!" Ship exclaimed, squeezing Ophie's hand. "You're clean, Oph. You're free."

"Of course, we'll want to monitor you periodically," the doctor interjected, "but, yes, you're clear now."

THAT EVENING, Ship treated Ophie to dinner at a little French bistro on Sunset in Beverly Hills. They dined on escargots and *coq au vin* at a banquette in a secluded corner.

"Here's to Ophelia Pennfield." Ship raised a glass of vintage champagne. "She's conquered many obstacles in her life, but none more mighty than the big 'C'."

Hesitantly, she half-tipped her glass towards his.

"And why the reluctant toast?" Ship asked.

"It's I who should be toasting you." She grabbed his hand. "You saved my life, Ship."

"I think you're giving me much too much credit. If you continued to have those symptoms for another week or so, you surely would've visited a doctor and he or she would—"

"You saved my life." She interrupted him, a tear running down her cheek. "No matter what you say, you saved my life."

He paused for a moment, his eyes moistening. He started to say something, and then stopped himself. Then he started again. "And you...Oph... you *gave* me life."

Ophie said nothing, her eyes wide and fixed on his.

"I know." He squeezed her hand again. "I've known for a while now."

She blinked, and set down her glass. "How did you find out?"

"I'd always heard rumors. And, then, when I was drawing your blood one day, I took an extra vial and—"

"How dare you." She snapped at him and pulled her hand away.

He took her hand again. "Listen, Oph, I had a right to know. After all the whispered innuendoes over the years, don't you think I had a right? I mean, back then, when I was born, there would have been a stigma. And no way that father... *uh, grandfather...* no way he would have let the world know his teenage daughter had a child out of wedlock. But now, who really cares? If it's possible, I love you even more now that I know."

For Ophie, it was impossible for her to remain angry at Ship. The lines in her face softened, and then she smiled. "I suppose you do have a right to know. I'm proud of you, Ship. You've grown into a fine man. I'm proud of you. Very proud."

"Which begs one other question."

"Oh?"

"Who is he?"

"Your father?" She paused, collected her thoughts, and then answered. "Let's just say this: he's a good man. Perhaps misunderstood, but a good man."

* * *

61

Various Locations, 1985–1993

Upon completion of his residency at Cedars-Sinai, Ship took a fellowship with the World Health Organization. With his specialization in epidemiology, Ship was particularly concerned with how certain lethal viruses were causing virtual genocide in some African countries. The latest was HIV/AIDs, a virus believed to have originated within certain species of chimpanzees and passed on to "bush meat" hunters as the chimps' blood mixed with the water supply. The disease mutated wildly, making it especially difficult to develop a proper therapy and vaccine.

Eventually, Ship was transferred at his own request to Cameroon, in West Africa, where the incidence of the disease was particularly high. His assignment included both treatment of inflicted patients as well as research on possible alternate therapies and, ultimately, a vaccine. Ship was stationed in Yaoundé, the country's capital city, but each week would spend several days in rural areas, treating villagers.

Although he had prepared himself, Ship was shocked by the squalor and unlivable conditions in some of the villages. The conditions were so unsanitary he was surprised that more villagers were not afflicted by malaria, meningitis, or sleeping sickness, or other any endemic disease. And then, there were those who were afflicted by the HIV virus.

There was one day that cast a life-long impression on the young doctor. He was arriving in another small poverty-stricken village. As he jumped off his jeep, a young boy dashed over and tugged at his pant leg.

"Docta man, docta man, my mom, she's sick, very sick. Please come. A cure, please come!" the young boy, about eight or nine, pleaded.

'I'll try as hard as I can," Ship answered.

"But Docta man, you can. She need to live. Then, I live."

"You have to be strong."

"But my mom, Docta man, my mom, she *make me* strong."

The young boy's mom was all but dead when Ship examined her. Her immune system was shot, and she had a very severe case of pneumonia. There was nothing he could do other than make her as comfortable as possible.

"Docta man, docta man, is she OK?" the young boy rushed up to him when Ship walked outside the village clinic.

Ship struggled to find the right words. "She's not suffering anymore."

"She OK? She OK?"

Ship leaned over, took a knee, and looked in the young boy's eyes. "What's your name?"

"Nnamdi."

"Nnamdi, your mom was a very strong woman. But now it's your turn. You have to be strong now. Your mom left us today."

Tears flowed from Nnamdi's eyes. *"She is my strength. She is my strength. She is my strength,"* he howled uncontrollably.

Ship hugged the young boy and let him cry. "No, you can live, you have to be strong, she would want you to be strong," Ship whispered.

"You stay with me, docta man?" Nnamdi whispered, sniffling, into his ear. "Please stay."

SHIP'S ASSIGNMENT in Cameroon ended four months later. He had decided to leave the World Health Organization and move on to a position at the Center for Disease Control in Atlanta where he could do some very intensive research on the HIV virus. Before he left West Africa, he made one more stop at that little village.

"I'm looking for Nnamdi, the young boy whose mother died several months ago," Ship asked a villager.

"That way," the villager pointed, "he live with his uncle."

Ship hiked over to a small hut and poked his head in. Immediately a young boy sprung up from the dirt floor.

"Docta man! Docta man! You bring my mother back? Will you stay?"

For the moment, Ship felt helpless. His lips quivered. He leaned over and looked the young boy in the eyes. "Nnamdi, I'm afraid even doctors can't do that."

"But docta man!" Nnamdi's large forlorn eyes looked up at him. "But when..."

Ship shook his head. "I can't do that, Nnamdi. But there's something I can do. Can I speak with your uncle?"

The young boy nodded.

NNAMDI LED Ship down a dirt path to a very dilapidated chicken coop. Nnamdi's uncle — a heavyset man wearing a sleeveless t-shirt and chewing on a corn-cob type pipe — was tending to his chickens when the young boy interrupted him.

"Uncle Aboubakar! Uncle Aboubakar!"

His uncle bit down on his pipe. "What Nnamdi, I'm busy."

"Docta man wants to talk to you."

"Docta man?"

"Yes, he's the docta man that tried to save mamma."

His uncle looked over at Ship and grunted. "Must not be that good of a docta man."

"I tried," Ship responded. "Sometimes people get so sick, there's nothing we can do."

Nnamdi's uncle raised his eyebrows and went back to checking the coop.

"I want to ask you something," Ship said.

"Talk to me," the uncle answered, not looking up.

"I've arranged for Nnamdi to attend a Christian mission school in Yaoundé."

"What?" Astounded, he turned back towards Ship.

"I would like Nnamdi to attend a school in Yaoundé."

The uncle chewed on his pipe. "Why?" he grunted. "Are you trying to steal him? Sell him to a family?"

"No. I would just like to see the young boy get a good education."

"And who pays?" he asked.

"I do."

"Everything?"

"Yes. Everything," Ship answered. "There's an account in his name at a bank in Yaoundé. The school will be paid from it. Even his transportation there and back."

"But why?" the uncle asked.

Ship hesitated for a moment. "Let's just say he's done more for me than I could ever do for him."

SHIP HAD LEARNED the most important lesson in his life from little Nnamdi. There were those who *had* and those who *had not.* And the disparities weren't minimal; they were monumental. He thought about the way he was brought up in a large home on Indian Harbor overlooking Long Island Sound. He could have anything he wanted, was sent to a fancy boarding school and then onto Yale. Yet, this young Nnamdi, through no fault of his own, was destined to scrape and scrounge for his entire lifetime just because of where and when he was born. *Is that justice?*

Once Ship got settled at the CDC in Atlanta, he made himself a promise. He was going to dedicate himself to doing as much good for as many people as he possibly could. For his remaining life, he would devote himself to serving those who never had the privileges he had enjoyed. *It was only fair.*

Ship had considerable resources to work with. His share of the Pennfield Family Trust was worth close to $75 million, and he planned to spend most of it on helping others. He began a foundation that built housing for the poor in blighted urban neighborhoods in Detroit, Oakland, East St. Louis, Camden, Newark, Memphis and Baltimore; the foundation created cooperative "enclaves" where each capable adult was obligated to put in 20 hours a week working for the betterment of the community, be it in maintenance, daycare, preparing community meals or other tasks. Then he set up free health clinics serving those same enclaves and established training programs to give residents the skills necessary to compete in the marketplace for jobs. The Arthur Shipkin Pennfield Foundation gained a national reputation. Of course, not everyone in the Pennfield family was impressed.

"Yes, I can see it now," Percival Pennfield barked into the phone, "Lenin, Trotsky and Pennfield, the crown princes of communism in the twentieth century. Our ancestors are turning in their graves."

"Do you really believe that, father?" Although Ship had known for some time that Percival Pennfield was not his father, he and Ophelia had made a pact to continue the charade as the lesser of several evils.

"Ship, you're using our hard-earned family money to finance cooperatives in urban areas benefiting people who are functionally un-trainable!"

"So exactly when did you lose your faith in the human spirit, father?"

"Ship, I know you don't want to hear this, but some people are destined to prosper and others are not. Providing artificial means of support for those incapable of doing so for themselves just prolongs their agony."

"And now you're becoming the crown prince of Social Darwinism..."

"Yes, but I have the advantage of being on the correct side of this argument. I thought by the time you fully matured you might outgrow some of this silliness, but I thought wrong."

"And Merry Christmas to you, too, *father*." Ship hung up the phone.

* * *

TIME FRAME: 2053

62

NYGAB: Pennfield Technologies Tower, Late Afternoon, February 5, 2053

JMP galloped down the hallway of the Pennfield Technologies Tower executive floor with a surge of enthusiasm uncommonly witnessed by PT employees. He had received the news which he had awaited for years. And now he was to make the announcement to his most important constituent. He took a sharp turn, up the air-avator, and scooted into his office, shouting through his embedded microphone to his assistant in Tokyo. "Suke, get me Ibu on a v-conf right now, this instant."

"The Prime Minister?"

"Yes, the Prime Minster."

"Of course, sir."

WITHIN MINUTES, Ibu Bonne-Saari appeared across from Jimmy Mashimoto-Pennfield in a v-conf.

"Ibu," JMP beamed a wide smile, "I have great news, wonderful news!"

Straight-faced, Ibu Bonne-Saari responded, "Which is?"

"Yesterday, Dr. Li-Pin and his team finished their last round of clinical trials with their nano-microorganisms. The results surpassed expectations. They just contacted me. Everything's a go."

"Really?" the Prime Minister responded, his eyes widening. "Excellent news!" He hesitated for a moment. "What does it mean for…?"

"Your father?"

"Yes," Bonne-Saari almost whispered.

"It means with your permission, we can have Dr. Li-Pin apply his protocol to your father's remains, or soon to be non-remains," Mashimoto-Pennfield answered. "Of course, you'll probably want to have Apexia medical authorities speak with Li-Pin before we do anything."

"Of course. Of course." Ibu Bonne-Saari nodded.

"And we must decide how to handle the media on this, there's going to be an explosion of coverage."

"I understand."

"Mr. Prime Minister, I'd like your permission to discuss this with my most senior level staff," said JMP. "I would say, given the latest developments, they're in a need-to-know position. They can be quite helpful in planning this all out, they can work with your people. I trust them completely."

Ibu Bonne-Saari contemplated for a moment and replied. "Permission granted." Then his face hardened. "But, of course, you do realize if there are any breaches of confidentiality, the consequences will be dire."

"Understood."

* * *

"THACKLEBERRY HERE!"

Nigel Thackleberry from Pennfield Technologies' London office was the first to appear for the emergency v-conf called by CEO Jimmy Mashimoto-Pennfield.

"Morning, Nigel," JMP nodded, "or should I say good afternoon?"

Thackleberry nodded back.

One-by-one the other participants joined, the virtual conference table elongating as each materialized. Gustav Eggert from Pennfield Technologies Frankfurt, Stavros Li-Pin from his laboratory inside the Egg, Maria Pagnetti from Milan representing Pennfield Technologies Global External Communications, Charlene Miller from Miller-Gold Public Relations in Los Angeles, and Hugh Nisselman from Cryonics Operations at the Egg.

"I have a crucial— a… *thrilling* announcement to make, everyone." JMP stood up as he spoke. "Dr. Li-Pin and his team have accomplished what we've been awaiting for years. They have been able, through their brilliant nanobiotechnology, to revive human life. Death has finally been conquered."

At first, silence. Then after the news soaked in, Thackleberry stood up.

"Here! Here!" Thackleberry pumped his fist in recognition of the company's triumphant achievement.

Vigorously, they all clapped.

"I appreciate your applause," JMP continued. "But it's not time for celebration. Not quite yet. First, we have some work to do. Everyone here knows how important this initiative is to the future of this company, the future of this world, and may I dare say the future of this universe. As I've told Stavros, we are standing on the cusp of immortality…."

When on his game, JMP could impose a riveting, taunting presence, at the same time both inspirational and terrifying.

"…Needless to say, there is no room for error here. The introduction must be carried off flawlessly, do I make myself understood?"

His eyes roamed around the table.

"Stavros? Bryan? Nigel? Gustav? Maria? Charlene? Hugh? You all understand? I'm holding you all personally accountable."

Nervously, they all nodded.

"Shall we start?" JMP glanced over at Li-Pin. "Stavros, can you update the group on your technical breakthroughs?"

"Yes, indeed." Li-Pin stood up. "Over the last several weeks we've optimized the implementation protocol working with our sub-100 test subjects. If you look here…" Li-Pin pointed up, summoning a holoscreen, "…you can see we have determined the best way to administer nano-microorganisms is while the body is still in the canister."

The holoscreen displayed images of technicians in white, sanitized, hooded uniforms removing the top cover of a seven-foot-long, canister and injecting serum into the neck of the partially unfrozen body inside.

"We then gradually increase the temperature as the microbes attack the cells, multiplying exponentially over the next fifteen days. At that point, we restart the heart and place the body in a state of suspended animation for several more weeks in a chemical bath which helps acclimate the skin and muscle tissues. Here you see a sub-100 body being removed from the bath…"

The technicians carefully dried off the body and placed it on a hospital bed.

"…and prepared for a small electric current which will jolt it out of suspended animation."

The attendees gasped as they observed life literally being transfused into the body of an elderly, Asian-looking sub-100.

"Now, the re-activated body is ready to be treated for whatever specific affliction caused the original onset of death…"

The body of the sub-100 was placed on a gurney and wheeled into a nearby operating room.

"…in this case a damaged liver. A new cloned liver was then transplanted into the subject and within days, the subject was restored to normal."

Fully reactivated, the subject walked out from the recovery room alive and well.

They all watched in silent breathtaking awe.

"Phenomenal!" Thackleberry mumbled.

"Jesus effin' Christ!" Charlene Miller gaped in awe.

"Holy Shit!" Nisselman exclaimed.

"Wow!" McPherson stood dumbfounded.

"Amazing, Stavros, amazing." JMP nodded in deference to Li-Pin. "We fully expect the rest of our team to perform as flawlessly as you have." Briefly, he scanned the table looking each one of them in the eyes.

"Now I have another important announcement to make," JMP stated. "Even more important than the last."

Surprised, they all stood in silence.

"This is an announcement that is truly top secret; no one in this room can repeat it to anyone outside of this group. If so, there'd be extreme consequences," JMP said. "It is something monumental, something that may shock you, but you need to know."

Mesmerized by the intrigue in his words, JMP's staff clung to every syllable.

"About a month ago, Ibu Bonne-Saari called me, as some of you may remember. He was curious about the Cryonics Initiative, so I took him through all the specifics. He was quite impressed, actually marvelously impressed. He then disclosed to me that upon his father's death ten years ago, the body was not buried as observed by all in the news coverage. Instead, they buried a very well-crafted wax replica. The real corpse of Supreme Prime Minister Izan Bonne-Saari was secretly frozen. Of course, at the time they did not have the benefit of Dr. Li-Pin's methodology, but their relatively crude technology proved passable, nonetheless.

"Shortly thereafter, under heavy security and utmost secrecy, we transferred the preserved remains of our Supreme Prime Minister to the Egg where Dr. Li-Pin and his team applied their advanced methodologies to its preservation. Since then, it has been stored under tight security within an isolated section of the facility. And now, I'm proud to announce that Izan Bonne-Saari, will be among the first to be restored by Dr. Li-Pin."

They gasped.

Slowly, they turned to each other.

"So how are we going to handle this?" Charlene Miller, the public relations whiz from Los Angeles, brash and flamboyant with a bright red tattoo on her upper right arm, broke the silence after the full impact of JMP's announcement had set in. "I mean we have a real double whammy here."

"I'm not sure exactly what Ibu would prefer," JMP responded.

"So then ask him," Miller retorted.

"We have to think this through carefully. This may cast a very different light on the introductory event," said JMP.

"No shit!" Miller announced. "You have two of the most significant events in the history of our planet happening simultaneously."

"Do they have to?" Maria Pagnetti questioned.

"Have to what?" Nisselman asked.

"Occur simultaneously." Pagnetti responded. "I don't think people could, *should* have to take in both at once. It's dangerous. We can risk an ultra-ultra-big announcement all in one shot, or let them take in two incredibly big announcements spread over time."

"Good point, Maria." JMP paced across the v-conf room.

"What about security, Bryan? Any difference if we make it one or two events?" JMP asked.

"She has a point. The reaction will be huge." McPherson answered. "But, the Egg has the tightest security in the history of the planet. We can handle one. We can handle two. No matter what they do, it's no problem."

"Are you sure the Prime Minister even wants the world to know about the revival of his father?" Nisselman added. "Maybe we should downplay it. Or at least have a plan in place to explain whether and how this matters for current structures of power—"

"*Time Out! Time Out! Time Out!*" Miller stood up from her seat, forming a capital "T" with her hands. "You have the two biggest announcements since the ascent of man and you want to *downplay it*? You want to take a moment to *explain structures?*"

Flustered, Nisselman responded, "It's not that *I* want to. I'm just considering the Prime Minister's wishes."

"No! No! No!" Miller shook her head vigorously. "We have to *guide* the Prime Minister, *lead him* to the solution with the optimum impact. This is a monumentally historical event. Now picture this." She stood up and spread her arms. "First, we have a beautiful state-of-the-art amphitheater set up on

the grounds. Dignitaries from around the world sit back in comfy, levitating seats. The golden glow of the Egg — the most sophisticated, technologically advanced structure in the history of the world — hovers in the background against a blue sky and green, rolling hills. JMP makes a dignified yet simple announcement. A giant holoscreen materializes. Dr. Li-Pin narrates as we observe ten initial clients being revived inside the Egg — *as he speaks, in real time.* Then, twenty minutes later, they walk outside, completely re-activated, greeted by friends and family!"

JMP grinned. "Is that technically possible, Stavros? Can we revive them in real time?"

Li-Pin thought for a moment, then responded, "Umm… if we were to choose clients whose cause of death was something simple, like a cardiac event, where the nano-microbes can repair the cardio scar-tissue damage and revitalize the arteries during the reactivation process, theoretically yes. Of course, the subject would have had to go through the initial fifteen-day process and suspended animation period. But yes, we could do it."

"Okay, but wouldn't that alone be enough for one event?"

"No. Not at all," Miller answered. "Think of the second act… just when we've grabbed the audience by the balls, at the height of total amazement, when they think that's it, the event's over and done with, we spring an even bigger zinger on them: Izan Bonne-Saari, the forefather of our system of government, the most significant individual in the history of this millennium, walks out, alive, completely recovered, having defeated death itself!"

Impressed by Miller's histrionic description of the once-in-a-lifetime event, everyone around the v-conf table clapped.

Except JMP.

He ran his hand across the back of his neck and took a long, deep breath. "That could work, it could be phenomenal, wonderful, Charlene. But we have to take the Prime Minister's wishes into account. If the event is emotional for us, think what it will be like for him."

"JMP— *Sir—* don't forget," Miller broke in, "that this is the very best testament to Apexian Exceptionalism and the PGU system one can ever imagine. It will be a shining example of what the collective efforts of our very best people have accomplished. We've conquered death. *Do you hear me? We've fucking conquered death and in a big fucking way.*"

JMP paced silently, and then looked over towards Pagnetti. "What do you think, Maria?"

She took a moment to process it all, then answered: "I think I'm convinced. Charlene's idea is quite compelling. And if McPherson's right about security, there's no reason to minimize it. Yes, it's an ideal opportunity to display Apexian Exceptionalism. I think you should lead with *that* when you discuss it with the Prime Minister."

Perplexed, JMP again stood silent for several moments. He seemed to almost be breaking a hint of a sweat. He wiped the side of his face with the back of his hand then suddenly spoke: "Yes, you're right. I'll speak with the Prime Minister. I'm sure he can be persuaded."

* * *

63

Location Unknown, February 12, 2053

Robyn Viega woke in her comfortable, oversized bed in her beautiful cottage set upon the sparkling green garden. She yawned, then stretched. The morning sky was bright and blue, the sun just about a quarter of the way up from the eastern horizon. It was that way everyday — bright blue skies, a few clouds, the sun in the exact same place. She walked over to the door to enjoy a big breath of fresh morning air, the same morning air she breathed in day after day after day.

Her stomach panged. She felt hungry, had a yearning for fruit, perhaps pineapple.

Instantly, the front door creaked open.

"Would you like some pineapple, Ms. Robyn?" Pascal stood at the entrance, his smooth tan chest framed by the lapels of his white puffy robe, funneling down to his waist in a perfectly taut "V." He offered a plate with fresh sliced pineapple garnished with almonds and cashews.

"Of course, thank you Pascal. That's quite thoughtful of you," she responded. By now she was not surprised at all upon his immediate appearance whenever she felt hungry or in need of anything for that matter. He had some sort of sixth sense, she figured.

Sitting out on the terrace, she munched pineapple pieces, interspersing tastes of their sweet juiciness with crunchy bites of almonds and cashews. Without doubt, she was bored. She had been that way almost from the very beginning. Everything was too perfect, too pleasant. Every day sunny, the sky always a bright shade of blue, the grass forever sparkling, the flowers aromatic and colorful, the hedges tidy and pristine. Quite a departure, she thought, from the life she knew where every day was a struggle, every obstacle unconquerable, every thirst unquenchable.

She wondered whether Pascal would sense her growing desire to do something, to disrupt the monotony. Lately, she had even been thinking that it was time to venture out, to examine the boundaries of this unreal perfection. As she bit down into the last sweet, ripe cube of fruit, it became clearer than ever: it was better to encounter an unknown adventure, replete with zest and even risk, than the staid predictability of perfection.

She wandered out into the garden, breathing in its fragrances, absorbing its beauty. She was directionless, had no mission, just the pure wanderlust of venturing to somewhere she had never been, savoring the magic of something yet undiscovered. She followed the path to the end of the garden, knowing somehow, someway the end of the path was no wall of finality, but a passageway. Despite her best instincts, she was sure there would be more to her journey; it would not end at the edge of the garden, abruptly halted by the tall green hedges. There was—*had to be*— more to it than that.

Yet, there she stood, her nose poking into the hedges, nowhere left to wander, no way to wiggle out.

She waited for some sort of sign. It would be easy to surrender, turn back, and retreat across her beautiful, uneventful garden back into her perfect little uneventful cottage reaffirming her bland uneventful existence. But she was sure, certain, there was more, had to be.

In defiance, she stood up to those hedges, firmly erect, staring down those green, dense leaves, their sharp branches tickling her nostrils, brushing her eyelids.

At first, nature's divine intervention was hardly noticeable; a subtle wisp of wind tickling her shoulder. Then it grew stronger, a soft breeze caressing her face. Over time, that soft subtle wisp of wind defied her senses; stealthily, almost surreptitiously, growing into something much, much stronger.

The wind swirled behind her— whipping itself into a funnel— stirring up energy, more and more, until it spun so rapidly it could no longer tolerate the sheer power it was inflicting upon itself. In a giant whoosh, the funneling wind breezed behind her jolting her into the hedges, their branches magically parting, allowing her through.

She braced herself to be scraped by the parting branches, but did not feel one prickle upon her skin. It was more like a warm, tingling sensation. She felt comfortable, free, almost as if floating, though she was standing perfectly erect. She walked slowly, not wanting the comfortable feeling and the tingling sensations to end. When she felt she was about to penetrate the other side of the hedge, she winced, unsure of what she might encounter.

What she saw surprised her.

Dark blackness, not pitch black, but splotchy black, random splotches of dark grey transitioning to pure black and then back again, like shapes she might see with her eyes shut. She heard water bristling and smelled the light scent of the sea, but all she saw was the splotchy shades of grey and black.

She did know one thing: she was somewhere else, somewhere unencumbered. Wherever she was, whatever her fate, her instincts told her it was safe, it would not be boring. She relished the chance to see more, discover what might be lurking behind those splotches of black and grey.

You've arrived, I see.

She blanched.

Looking up, she saw her. Small and petite, fair skinned, a white bonnet covering her black hair, a black bodice tied into a bow at the neck, and around her torso a black apron wrapped around her white skirt. She looked like a chambermaid or perhaps a servant.

"Who are you?" Robyn asked.

Many people, I would say. A soft, warm glow emanated from the young woman's very essence.

"What do you mean?" Robyn asked.

I am the one who's scorned, used for evil purposes, a sufferer for others' sins, she said with an uncommon air of placidity.

"I don't understand."

They did it to me. They'll do it to you, she said without an ounce of emotion

"*What?*" Frightened, Robyn winced. "*What* will they do to me?"

Use you. Abuse you. They already have, haven't they.

Nervously, Robyn nodded her head.

"Then why am I here?" Robyn asked.

Simple, the woman answered. *For justice.*

"You're confusing me."

Everything will become clear. You will soon understand.

"Can you tell me? I want to know now!"

Do you understand history? she asked.

"Uhhhhh... I don't know."

There are those who exploit and those who are exploited, she answered. *It's the way things work. It has been that way for centuries, thousands of years.*

"But what does it have to do with me?"

The woman in the bonnet paused for a moment, then spoke: *Many suffer so few will thrive. Don't you?*

"Suffer?" Robyn mumbled, second-guessing herself. "Um…"

Think about it, the young woman entreated her hesitance.

"Well, of course," Robyn answered. "Yeah, I'm 12th PGU. We all suffer. What do you want me to say? What do you want me to do?"

Exact revenge, the woman answered.

"But how can I…"

You doubt yourself, she answered. *That's not uncommon. I doubted myself too.*

Robyn looked up and peered into the woman's eyes as she continued:

You have the power. I have the power.

"How then? What can…?" Robyn paused, gathered her thoughts. "How can I?"

We are one and the same, replied the young woman, maintaining a face devoid of any emotional clue that might help Robyn grasp some meaning, some sense of what to do.

MINUTES LATER— or perhaps hours, she had no way to tell— Robyn Viega woke on her large bed, in her quaint cottage, beside her beautiful garden.

* * *

OBSERVATION BOOTH
Location Unknown
February 12, 2053

THE TECHNICIAN in the observation booth above the small room where Robyn Viega was sequestered flicked on the hovering holosphere. The face of Ibu Bonne-Saari immediately appeared.

"What the hell is going on over there?" Bonne-Saari barked.

The technician shook, having never communicated with the Prime Minister prior to this moment, much less being barked at by him.

"She's fully back under control of the EVR program again, sir" the technician stated.

The room below was a perfect cube, composed of six shiny surfaces, antiseptic and white, its perfectly smooth uniformity compromised only by a flat, knobless door blending in with the wall, and the large glass window of the observation deck fifteen feet above.

"There she is," the technician pointed towards the floor of the bright white room below.

Naked, Robyn Viega stood suspended in a transparent, permeable sheath completely enwrapping her body; in fact, awkwardly extending it about ten inches from the surface of her skin, forming a crude transparent outline of her form. She would move intermittently, apparently going through what appeared to be the activities of a normal everyday existence. She would take a step in one direction, then stop and retreat, put her hand to her face, and even assume a sitting position, the transparent sheath bending with her and providing support.

"And she's been under strict watch since she's been here?" Bonne-Saari asked.

"Twenty-four-seven, sir."

When the drugged Viega was brought into the Bonne-Saari Capital District on the island of Sri Lanka, she was placed in the EVR sheath — or Enhanced Virtual Reality sheath — immediately after semi-permanent contact lenses were fused into her eyes. Small, invisible, microbead-like pellets filled the sheath conforming to every micro-millimeter of her body's surface. In concert with the virtual reality environment, the tiny beads were programmed to collectively simulate the effect of any type of force, sensory experience or object on the human body. The precise programming of the EVR environment directed the beads to clump together as necessary to simulate the sensory impact of a chair or a bed or a garden, complete with natural fragrances, a hand or body part of a virtual companion, even realistically simulate the impact of a bullet.

"And so what happened?" Bonne-Saari asked.

"She just walked over to the edge of the virtual garden, stood before the hedges and —*Poof!*— she temporarily disconnected. She just zoned, stopped responding to the EVR program for about ten minutes or so. We even tried simulating a massive explosion and it didn't…"

He stopped, interrupted by some sounds.

"Yes, Pascal, that would be fine."

They looked down. Robyn Viega was engaged in conversation.

She walked across the white room, completely enwrapped by the sheath, and sat down at an invisible table subjectively generated by the EVR program, the micro-beads in the sheath supporting her while simulating the sensory experience of sitting in a chair.

"Thank you so much, Pascal," she said.

She extended her arm across the virtual table, grabbed something and then brought it to her mouth. She munched on her non-existent food.

"YOU SEE, now she's perfectly fine," the technician commented as Viega navigated through her virtual world in the room below.

"Yes, but what caused the damn break in the protocol? We can't tolerate anything other than complete adherence to the protocol," the Prime Minister blurted.

"If we knew, we'd tell you sir," the technician answered humbly. "We haven't been able to figure it out yet."

"Well that's not good enough!" Bonne-Saari snapped. *"Not good enough at all."*

"I understand sir," the technician answered, visibly shaking.

"Do you realize what could happen if our security is breached?" The Prime Minister's cheeks turned beet-red. He raged on: "this woman is *very* important to us and the future of the Apexian nation, you must figure this out and it must be soon."

The technician nodded.

"Do I make myself clear?" Bonne-Saari barked, looking down upon the young technician, minimizing his existence.

Shaking, the technician responded. "Yessir."

* * *

64

PAWVA GAB: PHA 432B, February 12, 2053

Derek Fane slowly, deliberately pushed himself off the cold steel floor of the excavator bucket where he had been curled up in an emaciated, bony spiral. Straining, he applied extreme effort to fully lift himself. His back still bent, he collected his bearings, his eyes scanning his slimy surroundings. His mouth was dry. He thirsted. Slowly, he dragged his skin and bones across the massive bucket, shaking all along the way, and walked out of its wide mouth. His eyes stung from the sunlight. He struggled to walk the fifty yards or so to the public water fountain half-way down the dirt path; it twisted its way around giant, rusty, industrial wire-spools, abandoned hydroelectric and mining equipment, and sub-100s clumped in small groups, quietly desperate.

Slowly, he leaned over towards the water spout. His back ached as he bent down, his spine crackling. The water quenched his cotton mouth.

"Hey, Dee!"

Slowly, Fane turned his head, looked, then almost whispered, "Shockshaw?"

"Yeah, it's me! Haven't seen you in a dog's life. What's up, man? You OK?"

Fane pushed himself away from the water spout, wincing as he straightened himself out. He took a deep breath. "Went on a deep, deep bender, Shock. Been coming down, withdrawin'."

"Sucks," Shockshaw commented.

Silent, Fane nodded.

"Need somethin'? I mean, I can get—"

"No." Fane raised up his hand. "This time I'm gonna get real."

"You shittin' me!" Shockshaw laughed. "Dee man is gettin' real? Now that's one fer the record."

"Nah, really —"

Suddenly, Fane stopped and covered his temples with his hands. He grit his teeth, writhing in pain. He fidgeted animatedly, shaking his hands rapidly, his eyes wincing, his head pounding.

Shockshaw lunged over and grabbed him, bear-hugging him to quell the shaking. "You okay, man?"

Fane grit his teeth as hard as he could, his eyes locked closed, until the pain subsided. "It's these fuckin' headaches. They come and go."

"Shit! You sure you don't need something?"

"No. I told you. I'm gonna do it. Get real."

"You sure?" asked Shockshaw. "I mean, like nothing's changed, we're still getting screwed, every fucking day. There ain't no way out of a shithole like this. Only thing we can do is say 'fuck you' by gettin' fucked up…"

Fane slowly turned to him and then spoke softly. "Robyn."

"Huh?"

"Robyn's lost. She needs me. I'll never find her fucked up."

"You kiddin' me? When she left your ass she said she's never comin' back. And you know what?"

"What?"

"She was right."

"I don't need her to come back. I need to find her. Help her."

"Help her?" Shockshaw exclaimed. "Hah. My friend, she can help you more than you her."

"I don't care. I owe her."

"You sure you can hold out long enough?"

"I gotta try," Fane answered.

"You *really* sure?"

"I gotta try. I gotta."

* * *

TIME FRAME: 2003-2010

THE ALTERNATIVE LIFE OF ARTHUR
SHIPKIN PENNFIELD

65

Various Locations, 2003–2007

The Arthur Shipkin Pennfield Foundation grew over the years, expanding its reach, providing low-cost heating oil to underprivileged families, establishing schools in the most impoverished villages in Africa, daycare centers in US urban areas, and "booster" learning programs in areas where public school resources were restrained. Eventually, the Foundation became involved in politics, making substantial contributions to progressive candidates and PACs that shared Ship Pennfield's policies.

Ship took extreme caution not to become politically vocal, at least on the broadest scale, until after Percival Pennfield's death. Even Ship wanted nothing to do with the inevitable confrontation— combustible, without a doubt— which he was sure would have ignited had he become outspoken too soon.

Ship's medical career advanced nicely in tandem with his foundation. He accepted a research grant and faculty position at Massachusetts General Hospital in Boston where he would further pursue his research in epidemiology and infectious diseases. Between his teaching, research responsibilities and stewardship of his foundation, Ship had little time for anything else, remaining single despite being named one of the city's most eligible bachelors by Boston Magazine. During his time at Mass General, his political activism grew by the day. He had a deep sense of what he thought was right and wrong and a deep frustration over how world leaders put self-interest and hidden agendas ahead of the welfare of the people. With his highly sensitive political instincts, he was among the first to detect a burgeoning threat which he thought could potentially change the course of civilization.

HIS NAME WAS IZAN BONNE-SAARI.

Bonne-Saari was Chairman of GMFC— Global Millennial Financial Corporation— a multinational bank holding company headquartered in Sri Lanka, a country held hostage by the company's economic stranglehold. Starting with the takeover of a small Sri-Lankan bank, Bonne-Saari's company had been on a relentless acquisition-spree over the past decade-and-a-half, now controlling the largest banking companies in most European countries, Canada, the Mid East and most of Asia. Bonne-Saari, with his metastasizing worldwide network of financial institutions, had more power than most heads of state and he was far from timid about using it.

"The world is suffering from antiquated political institutions and boundaries," Bonne-Saari commented in an interview on CNN. "Money knows no boundaries in today's world. As such, the world demands a political infrastructure which acknowledges this reality and conforms to the trans-global flow of capital."

The interview enraged Ship. He had little use for Bonne-Saari— a slimy, puffed-up little man with a trans-European accent that was impossible to place — but he envied his savvy and cunningness. Ship knew exactly where Bonne-Saari was going with his argument and it would not be good for any of the causes to which Ship had so fervently dedicated himself. Bonne-Saari's ramblings about "antiquated political institutions" were merely a prelude. There was much more to come. Stealthily, the crafty Bonne-Saari was setting the stage.

* * *

BOSTON, MA
Mid-day
June 15, 2007

DESPITE SHIP'S RIGOROUS SCHEDULE, there was one person he could always find time for:

"Ship, I have glorious news!" Ophie announced before he even had a chance to say hello.

"And that would be?" he asked.

"Cousin Chris has just been named the next President of Pennfield College. Isn't that wonderful, Shippy?"

"Took long enough, didn't it," he responded.

"Oh, Shippy, be kind."

"Wasn't it sort of expected?" he asked, nonplussed.

"Yes, it was. But it doesn't happen until it happens. And now it did. What a great testament to all of his contributions."

"He's had an uncanny ability to always stay one step ahead of the posse," Ship quipped.

"Oh, Shippy, let's be charitable at a moment like this. Everyone has a chink in their armor or two, including you, although I must admit, I'm still in search of that one," Ophie responded.

"He's the one, right?" Ship asked.

"The one, what?" Ophie answered, confused.

"My father."

She paused for a moment, and then answered, "And why would you think that?"

"The way your face glows every time you see him."

"Of course, I get excited when I see him. He's one of a kind. Urbane, erudite, charming. An absolute thrill to be around."

"Perhaps true, Oph. But it's more than that."

"Well, you can think whatever you want, Shippy, but this girl," she said, "she'll never tell."

Ship sent "cousin" Chris a congratulatory note and wished him the very best as he embarked upon the presidency of the college funded by their ancestral wealth. After his conversation with Ophie, Ship had absolutely no doubt that Christopher was his father. He was fine with it, inwardly proud of it. Ophie was right: Christopher Pennfield was urbane, erudite, charming and more. In a strange way, his flaws made him more human. Ship concluded he could live with that.

He did often wonder, though, if a cousin mating with another cousin would have some sort of negative long term genetic impact and what it might be.

* * *

66

Various Locations, October 2008–October 2009

Early one morning as he prepared for work, Ship received an email from a colleague, Norman Steinberg, an economist at Harvard. The message simply said, "Read this." Ship quickly downloaded the attachment and began reading. As Ship read on, he became more and more infuriated.

The attachment was a copy of a white paper written by financial analysts at GMFC, Bonne-Saari's multinational banking corporation. The controversial document had been leaked online. It was entitled: *"Global Wealth: The New Standard."* The crux of the paper was that an individual's or a family-unit's net worth was all that mattered in the new economy and that the global political infrastructure should be radically changed to conform to this "new standard" as the paper dubbed it.

The paper suggested that under the new standard, governments should be based upon virtual worldwide communities which transcended geographic boundaries. The thesis: a banker in Hong Kong is more similar to a banker in Paris than he is to a janitor in Hong Kong, and likewise that a janitor in Hong Kong is more similar to a janitor in Paris than he is to the aforementioned Hong Kong banker. "Ever since the emergence of the World Wide Web and various digital social platforms," the paper explained, "the concept of 'community' has changed radically; no longer are communities bound by the strictures of geographic proximity. Today, communities span the globe and should be recognized and formalized as such."

The paper espoused a new hierarchal form of government consisting of "Para-geographic Governmental Units" or PGUs which spanned the globe, composed of people with similar wealth and professional profiles. The old geographic political areas would be replaced by Geographic Administrative Bureaus, or GABs which would provide basic services such as law enforcement, transportation and infrastructure management, health care and the like. However, individual citizens residing in the same GAB would only be bound by laws of their particular PGU.

The media soon dubbed this "radical" system of government as the "spreadsheet society" with the hierarchy of PGUs— the "rows" of this conceptual spreadsheet— traversing across a range of GABS— the "columns" of the spreadsheet. The hierarchy within each GAB—or "column"— would be abundantly transparent. It was regarded by the conventional wisdom as a "Bonne-Saarian Fantasy" which would never pass muster with the masses. However, the conventional wisdom underestimated the basic tenet of Bonne-Saari's philosophy: this new "democracy" was defined by wealth, not people. Indeed, ninety-five percent of the people in the world could be in opposition to this new form of government, but if the five percent who favored it controlled an overwhelming amount of global wealth and resources, the population-advantage of the opposition would be meaningless.

Bonne-Saari's financial empire and his political influence grew rapidly, feeding upon one another. GMFC continued its aggressive acquisition spree, sucking up major financial properties in Australia, India, Saudi Arabia and Germany. Bonne-Saari had become somewhat of an international celebrity: a business titan with a political agenda and a voracious appetite for the spotlight.

Bonne-Saari's political rhetoric, and the swirl of media coverage around it, had been infuriating Ship for years. As he sat staring at this latest e-mail, he could no longer withstand the heinous venom spewed by Bonne-Saari and his advocates. Even more infuriating, he had been observing how this was being accepted as gospel even by those who would not benefit, who would actually be harmed by it. This new world order was being sold to them as a new sense of protection, but Ship saw through it all. He closed out of his e-mail and opened a blank document. He drafted an Op-Ed. It appeared the following week in the New York Times:

"Some people are advancing a philosophy that one's capability to accumulate wealth is the pre-eminent criteria in determining an individual's value to society and, therefore, those that accumulate more should, by definition,

enjoy more privileges and exercise more say over the course of society. I find this logic to not only be flawed, but also the most heinous, hateful view of humankind advanced during the course of modern civilization.

"All I can do is resort to what I call 'natural law.' Somehow, someway, humankind was put on this planet. Regardless whether you believe that our existence on Earth is a result of a deity, a colossal explosion ignited billions of years ago, extra-terrestrial colonization and/or anything else, the fact remains, we are here. Someone, something or some force put us here, or, facilitated our emergence into what we are today. I cannot imagine that whatever or whomever that is would have intended for a small minority of humans to control an exponentially disproportionate share of this Earth's resources. Even if 'it' had no intentions at all, the measure of human flourishing has time and again been shown in our ability to cooperate, coexist, and ensure the mutual flourishing of what sustains us. Thus, I believe humankind is intended, or is at least dependent upon sharing as close to equally as possible in the bounties of this planet. Without doubt, Mr. Bonne-Saari and his followers do not."

* * *

SHIP'S OP-ED caused quite a stir. He was besieged by the media as paparazzi amassed outside Mass General on a daily-basis, waiting to pounce on a photo-op. His following on social media erupted into the millions. He became the de-facto persona of the opposition to Bonne-Saari's movement

It took little time for Bonne-Saari's response to appear in the media: "Dr. Pennfield is nothing but an outdated, self-appointed deity, a minority of '1', attempting to impose his sole will upon the masses as they seek to modernize along with me. I understand Dr. Pennfield is an outstanding epidemiologist. I think he should stick to that rather than his feeble attempt to play the part of an ancient, irrelevant God."

To which Ship Pennfield retorted: "Thank you for your compliment, Mr. Bonne-Saari. As an epidemiologist my job— simply stated— is to find germs and render them incapable of spreading a disease. That's exactly what I'm doing."

The war of words took on a life of its own, extending many months. The media would ask Ship for a response to a quote from Bonne-Saari and then Bonne-Saari would respond to Ship. The words funneled into a tight spiral of rhetoric which whipped itself into a more rapid frenzy with each passing comment. The public ate it up. Evidently, Mr. Bonne-Saari was reaping at least one benefit from Ship Pennfield's assaults. Now he finally had a concrete enemy to attack, a face of the opposition, through which he could reach millions of people and spread his message on a daily basis. Within weeks, the inevitable occurred. CNN asked the two to appear simultaneously in an informal debate. Always a hog for the spotlight, Bonne-Saari accepted immediately. Ship struggled with the opportunity: if he didn't do it, it would be construed as a sign of weakness, if he did, there was considerable risk he could be sand-bagged by the flamboyant and cunning Bonne-Saari. Reluctantly, he agreed.

THE TWO COMBATANTS sat in different parts of the world. Bonne-Saari chose his 103rd floor sanctuary at GMFC's Shanghai office, a brilliant, alluring cityscape scintillating through the glass windows around him. Ship sat in a cramped studio in Boston in front of a green screen, a typical picture of Boston Harbor inserted behind him. The moderator, Lydia Fortunette, was in Manhattan. She walked into the studio about two minutes prior to the broadcast.

"Gentlemen." She nodded, adjusting her mic.

"Good evening," Ship answered.

"Indeed." Bonne-Saari nodded.

Although Ship and Bonne-Saari could see each other in their preview monitors, neither acknowledged the presence of the other.

"Five. Four. Three. Two." The floor manager cued Fortunette.

"Good evening. Tonight we take a departure from our normal program-format to bring you a highly anticipated event, a debate on a topic that has been capturing a lot of attention as of late. We have with us on CNN tonight the two most prominent spokespeople on each side of the issue…"

The back-and-forth between Ship and Bonne-Saari began with civility. Bonne-Saari first set up his concept and the rationale, and Ship went on to explain his objections. This was then followed by series of points and counter-points on rather esoteric economic and financial issues. It wasn't until near the end of the hour that the dialogue grew prickly.

It began with Bonne-Saari explaining the virtues of the privileged class: "If we recognize there is a new concept of community and allow the most privileged and talented among us to have their own self-sufficient strata of government and thereby free and liberal reign over the deployment of capital, it will ultimately be for the good of everyone."

Ship rebutted instantly: "In the 1980s, they called that trickle-down economics. It didn't work then, and it won't work now."

"I think the facts say not, Mr. Pennfield," Bonne-Saari countered. "The combination of generous tax cuts for the job creators combined with restraint in spending led to an unparalleled level of growth."

"Which was financed by excessive deficit-spending that may have been unnecessary without those, as you call them, 'generous tax cuts.'"

For a moment, Bonne-Saari displayed a small hint of frustration. A man of his magnitude and power was not used to being talked back to like that. "I don't think the facts bear that out, Mr. Pennfield."

"They certainly do," Ship responded. "But let's not waste time on that. There is one question I do want to ask you, however: how can any individual with even the slightest sense of humanity tolerate a system that rewards the rich and punishes the poor and middle classes? I don't get it."

"We are neither punishing nor rewarding anyone," Bonne-Saari retorted. "We are merely acknowledging the mechanics, if you will, underlying the economic growth engine and fostering such an environment for the good of everyone."

"And so you're saying it's good, in effect, to create a system of government so that the benefits that would go to the middle and lower economic classes have no source of funding?" Ship asked.

"I'm simply saying," Bonne-Saari responded, "that each strata of government will be self-sufficient. People will be able to determine their own fiscal and entitlement systems within their PGUs."

"They may sound great in theory. But you're de facto creating a system where the very wealthy PGUs would be left with giant surpluses and the middle and lower income PGUs would have virtually no source of funds for social programs."

"And those surpluses generated by the wealthy PGUs will be invested in job-creating businesses that will provide greater sources of funds to the middle and lower income PGUs," Bonne-Saari answered. "We're simply creating a bigger pie for the good of everyone."

"Historical evidence proves otherwise, Mr.Bonne-Saari," said Ship. "Most likely the extra surplus will be hoarded in tax-free trust funds to finance excessive generational wealth or perhaps spent on lavish and extravagant lifestyles."

"I find it a bit ironic, Dr. Pennfield, that you cite 'excessive generational wealth.' Can't the Pennfield family be accused of that *venomous crime*?"

"I've done everything I can to devote whatever generational resources that have been distributed to me to help the poor and underprivileged."

"So what's good for the goose must be good for the gander, correct?"

"Not at all. I've fought against privilege my entire life. What you're actually doing is camouflaging a highly skewed wealth distribution system — one that allows the rich to hoard, and provides the less-fortunate with hardly any funds for development programs — camouflaging it as a new, progressive form of government. I think most people see through your little scam, Mr. Bonne-Saari."

Frustrated, Bonne-Saari responded: "Must I tell you again, Dr. Pennfield? In our suggested form of government, each PGU will have the capability to finance its own social welfare programs as it sees fit."

"Need I say it again?" Ship barked back at him. "Your system will leave all but the very upper echelons of your dream society with practically nothing to live on, so what you suggest would be impossible. There would be *no revenues* for those lower and middle class PGUs and, hence, no entitlements."

"You're forgetting the protection and securi—"

"And what's an entitlement anyway?" Ship cut in. "Is a pension an entitlement? No, it's *earned.* Is healthcare an entitlement? *No, it's humane.* Is education an entitlement*? No*, it's the most sacred investment in our future that humankind can make."

"Are you ready to get off your soapbox, Mr. Pennfield?" Bonne-Saari quipped.

"No. But I'll tell you what an entitlement *really* is," Ship blurted back. "An entitlement is giving economic benefits to a privileged class way beyond — *exponentially beyond* — the value they provide to society. An entitlement is allowing such a disparity of wealth to exist that the very wealthiest among us are cowardly enough to advocate a system of government where they don't have to see or deal with the poverty they've helped create. An entitlement is—"

"It must be fun to be a living deity, Dr. Pennfield," Bonne-Saari cut in.

"If espousing the interests of humankind makes me a deity, then I plead guilty, Mr. Bonne-Saari," Ship countered. "However, you should be very familiar with what it's like to be a deity, sitting in your billion-dollar office overlooking the bright lights of Shanghai while people live in abject poverty just miles away."

Bonne-Saari's face reddened. "Have you no respect for my accomplishments, Dr. Pennfield?"

Ship thought for a moment. "To me, respect is something that must be earned. And no, you have not earned mine just as, apparently, the middle and lower economic classes have not earned yours, even though they are the workers that create the value that funnels billions upon billions of dollars into your banks. Perhaps—"

ZZZZZZZZzzzzzzzzzzzz.....

The image of Bonne-Saari broke up, fizzling into blotchy patches of pixels.

Stunned by the sudden interruption, Ship and Fortunette stood silent, awkwardly waiting.

The screen from Shanghai remained blank.

Fortunette cleared her throat. "Well, we seem to be having some technical difficulties with Mr. Bonne-Saari's feed. But, without doubt, we have just all witnessed a very lively discussion between two opposing viewpoints on the future of global government." She turned towards the monitor displaying Ship Pennfield's feed. "Dr. Pennfield do you have any last words to leave us with?"

"Just three," Ship answered.

"And they are?"

"Don't be Saari." He grinned.

ENRAGED, Bonne-Saari flung a paperweight across his office. "*How dare you cut me off?*" He accosted his communications advisors, shriveled together in the farthest corner of his office. "I would have pummeled that bastard on my rebuttal. And you left him with the last word!"

"We were just thinking damage-control, sir," a strong, young Asian woman responded. "We made a snap decision." She stood with her legs together, her chest puffed, as if she were military. We thought it would be much better for the world to think it was a technical issue rather than—"

"Damage control, my ass!" Bonne-Saari barked. "I'm the one who'll make decisions around here, got it? Now get the fuck out of here, all of you!"

THE PRESS POUNCED on the incident. Absolutely no one bought the story that Bonne-Saari's abrupt cut-off was a technical flaw. As one newscaster stated it, "I can say that if the so-called debate between Mr. Bonne-Saari and Dr. Pennfield was a fight, it would have been stopped. However, Mr. Bonne-Saari's handlers apparently did that for us."

As a result, Ship's celebrity gained momentum. More important to him, though, was that support for Bonne-Saari's view of the future lost significant momentum. Adversaries of Bonne-Saari began a grass-roots movement. A stylized, non-flattering portrait of Bonne-Saari, with Ship's memorable last words from the debate, *Don't Be Saari*, slapped in bold letters right above his face, became a viral meme, and it was printed and plastered on every lamp and wall in highly trafficked urban areas. For several weeks, it permeated the cultural landscape.

THE AFTERMATH INFURIATED Bonne-Saari even more than the actual debate. "I want him followed," Bonne Saari barked to his advisors. "I want to know where he is, what he's doing and even what he's thinking 24/7. Understood?"

A roomful of advisors nervously shook their heads.

"And anything we can get on him, anything that we can use to disrepute that bastard, I want to know about it as soon as you do," Bonne-Saari commanded.

* * *

67

October 28, 2009, Late Afternoon, Massachusetts General Hospital, Boston, MA

For over a month, Ship resented his status as a media darling. Soon, he began turning down almost every interview request, as he focused on his research and teaching. Increasingly, he realized an inner need to pull back, cocoon, refresh, assuring himself he was prepared for whatever lie ahead. One day as he walked down the corridor to his office in Mass General, he saw a tall young black man standing outside his office: he feared the man was a reporter who somehow had snuck in through a service entrance.

"Dr. Pennfield?" Timidly, the young man approached Ship.

"I'm not giving any interviews right now." Ship attempted to dismiss him.

"That's not what I want," the young man answered.

"Then what is it you do want?" Ship asked.

"You don't recognize me…"

"No." Ship peered over his glasses. "Should I?"

"You tried to save my mother in Cameroon."

"What?"

"Remember? The small village. Asking my uncle…"

"Nnamdi?" Ship's face glowed.

The young man smiled. "Yes, that's me."

"Oh my God!" Ship chuckled, and then hugged him. "Wow, you've grown into quite a man."

"Thank you, I will always be thankful for your generosity."

"It was the least…"

"And we now share a trait in common," Nnamdi interrupted.

"Really?"

"I'm a medical doctor as well."

Ship beamed, and then wiped his eye. "That is fantastic, Nnamdi. Come on, come into my office."

The two of them talked for hours. Nnamdi had taken well to academics and graduated with high honors from his Christian School in Yaoundé. From there he earned a full scholarship to the University of Nairobi in nearby Kenya. He never really had to think about choosing his course of study; early in his schooling, he had decided to use his education to do something about the terrible epidemics besieging his homeland, such as the HIV epidemic which took his mother. He would pursue a degree in medicine. Nnamdi went on to earn his MD degree at Nairobi and then returned to Cameroon to practice. The story made Ship proud, tremendously proud.

"So what brings you to the US?" Ship asked.

"Well, um, actually you, Dr. Pennfield."

"Me? You came all the way to see me?"

"As indebted as I am to you, I came to ask another favor," Nnamdi said timidly.

"Okay…"

"The villages near where I live have been stricken with a terrible virus. It has killed many, many people."

"What is it?" Ship asked.

"Ebola."

"Jesus— are you sure?"

"Yes. We need support. Perhaps you can arrange for some of your doctors to come and help in our clinics?"

Ship pondered for a moment. He thought about his early days in Cameroon and today's media storm swirling all around him. "I'll do you one better, Nnamdi."

"Yes?"

"I'll go there myself."

This time it was Nnamdi who beamed.

* * *

68

Hong Kong, China Mid-day November 13, 2009

Izan Bonne-Saari had a plan and the plan required obliterating the influence of Dr. Arthur Shipkin Pennfield and those like him— hell-bent on destroying his concept of a "spreadsheet society," as it came to be known.

By acquisition, Bonne-Saari planned to form the world's largest banking conglomerate, so vast in scope that no one government in today's world would be able to control it. Ultimately, the conglomerate would be the ruling force of society, trumping the power of any other institution. And, ultimately, the conglomerate would use its immense power to form the utopian society Bonne-Saari envisioned.

But he had to do it stealthily, so by the time this conglomerate achieved its maximum power it would be far too late for any one government to challenge it. The game, in effect, would be over before it even began.

Bonne-Saari considered Dr. Pennfield a minor irritant, one that could be easily vanquished, but by necessity *had* to be— lest this minor irritant grow into a major infection— the acclaimed epidemiologist becoming an epidemic himself. Their debate on CNN drove home the point that Pennfield's protestations were the last thing Bonne-Saari needed in pursuit of his vision.

His first step was to develop an obsession over always knowing Pennfield's whereabouts.

"WHERE IS HE? What's he doing?" Bonne-Saari barked to his staff, all nine of them bunched together in his vast office overlooking Hong Kong harbor.

"He seems to be winding down his work hours at Mass General," one of Bonne-Saari's lieutenants answered.

"Not good enough!" Bonne-Saari barked back with bludgeoning thunder, pounding his fist on the table. "I don't want to know merely what he's doing. I want to know what he's thinking. I want to know what he's about to think before he even thinks about it. Do I make myself clear?"

"Yessir," the lieutenant responded.

One of the younger staffers, huddled behind the others, responded meekly, "There's been rumors,"

"What?" Bonne-Saari jumped out of his chair. "Rumors? What kind of rumors? From whom?"

The young man stepped forward. "We've heard he might be going on a trip to Africa. Maybe Cameroon, where he spent some time early in his career. It's unsubstantiated, of course."

"Well, substantiate it! Now!" Bonne-Saari barked. "And if it is true, I want an undercover surveillance team there with him. Got it?"

They all nodded together.

* * *

69

Outside of Yaoundé, Cameroon, Rural Village, January 2–Feb 7, 2010

Nnamdi and Ship looked more like astronauts than doctors as they emerged from the large white tent set up as a clinic at the western edge of Nnamdi's childhood village. Their heads were draped in white, disposable hoods, their eyes shielded by a plastic cover. Respirators covered their mouths and noses while full white gowns draped the contours of their frames. Their thick gloves made it difficult to properly administer a shot or insert an IV.

For a moment, Ship's eyes scanned the village. The dirt roads were the same, small huts strewn around in about the same pattern. The chicken coop where Ship first met Nnamdi's uncle was still there, at least a dozen chickens pecking around. But something was different, much different. There was a deep look of despair in the villagers' faces. He could see it in their glassy-eyed stares, their almost involuntary movements as they plodded along through the mundane motions of life, in their firm jaws and expressionless faces — they were doing what they were doing because it was the only thing they knew, but they realized their efforts would prove fruitless. The terrible virus could take them all.

The small village's make-shift "clinic" impressed Ship. It was the best that could be expected under the circumstances. Those seeking to enter within a fifty-yard periphery of the big white tents were subjected to a quick thermal scan via an instrument that resembled a high-tech radar gun. Anyone with an elevated temperature would be denied entrance. There was one white tent set up solely for the donning of Personal Protective Equipment by doctors and other health care personnel. Putting on the PPE was a laborious process which always required an observer to assure it was donned properly. Likewise, there was a separate tent for the removal of PPE which, again, required an observer.

Ship and Nnamdi watched in silence as the remains of a villager they had cared for over the last several days were carefully removed by two PPE-wearing attendants. The deceased had been taken directly from the hospital bed, enwrapped in his bed sheets with the IV still inserted in his arm. His body was immediately placed in three layers of body bags, the second one heat-sealed. Two attendants took the bags to a contamination free "cold zone" and turned them over to another set of attendants who carried them to a makeshift mortuary at the opposite end of the village where the remains, still encased inside, were placed in a metal coffin.

Ship motioned to Nnamdi and pointed towards the large white tent. Thirteen other victims of the dreaded Ebola virus required attention. The two doctors marched stoically into the tent, poised for another shift.

At all times there were six or seven doctors at the clinic, mostly American and European volunteers who had taken leave from their practices. They came in and out, some staying for a week, others for months. Although they worked in cramped quarters, their bulky protective equipment provided a sort of anonymity; most of them never even got to know each other's names. They were functionaries, working for the greater good, bonded solely by their common purpose and profession.

There was one doctor— Ship thought "she" was a woman underneath all her bulky protective gear— whom he had worked with for several days, assisting each other with IVs and the drawing of blood and the repetitive tasks of caring for the patients. Again, today, she was there, working with him as they examined a small child who was just brought in.

The young child reminded Ship of Nnamdi all those years ago. So cute, so full of potential, much too young and promising to have his life threatened by the wicked Ebola virus. *Damn! Why can't we do more!* Ship asked himself as he and the woman examined the young boy. The shield covering his face masked the tears.

After another three hours with the patients, Ship and Nnamdi entered the "doffing" tent as it was called. For the first time, the other doctor was in the tent with them as they removed their protective clothing. Methodically, under strict supervision, they began removing everything in precise order, disinfecting each layer of protection with an alcohol-based spray before removing the next and then disposing of most of their clothing and equipment into infectious waste containers.

As the woman removed her hood and respirator, a pleasant chill ran up Ship's spine. He looked at her quizzically, trying to fit together pieces of a puzzle. Her eyes were very familiar. So was the shape of her jaw and lips. Her hair was different, though. He didn't remember it being that curly.

As the woman removed her boots, she looked up and their eyes met. Similarly, she seemed to be piecing together a puzzle of her own.

"Ship?" she asked.

"Lori?"

* * *

70

Cameroon, February 8–March 26, 2010

Upon first recognizing each other, Ship and Lori shared an awkward moment of silence. It had been years. They had been formally banned from seeing each other by their families, and now here, in a remote village in the jungles of Cameroon, its people infested with a terrible virus, they met again.

His face flush red, Ship struggled for something to say. "Lori. Wow, this is..."

"Strange?" Lori completed his thought.

"Yeah, it is, don't you think?" he answered. "I mean, I never thought I'd ever see you again and, now here, *here,* shit, what a..."

"Coincidence?"

"I guess."

"Or fate?" For the first time, she smiled at him.

Ship shrugged. "Geez, you must've been here... we must've been working together for several days without knowing it."

"Yeah, that is sort of weird," she responded.

"Where are you staying?" Ship asked.

"I have an apartment at the University in Yaoundé. How about you?"

"Yaoundé. At the Hilton." Ship answered, and then glanced at his wrist-watch. "There's a van leaving for the city in twenty-five minutes. Let's catch a ride."

"Sure."

WHATEVER IT WAS that had attracted Lori and Ship to each other two decades earlier still smoldered. At first, its latency cast a shadow over their actions, resulting in a fair degree of awkwardness. They were cautious as they shared dinner that evening, their words and actions carefully measured. Each wondered if the other could sense their bond emerging from its long hibernation. And each hoped it would occur sooner rather than later.

"Well, this has been great," Ship said as the waiter at the restaurant in the Hilton brought their coffee.

"And completely unexpected," said Lori.

"Yes, how strange things are sometime," Ship mused. "You would think the odds of you and I meeting years later in Cameroon after everything we had been through would be infinitesimal."

"You're right," she answered. "But I guess when you think about it we're both doctors, both humanitarians at heart, aligned with the same causes. That's what worked between us the first time." She had nearly whispered it.

Ship perked his ears and raised his eyebrows. *"The first time?"*

"Well, I didn't mean…"

"But you do, don't you?" He smiled at her.

"You never know." She blushed.

STILL, they were measured. Instinctively, both realized the necessity to re-establish their friendship before rekindling their romance. Their strange environs provided them with the motivation to explore. They were able to coordinate several days off from their grueling schedules to hike Mount Cameroon. It was a true adventure, following the guides through the rainforest and then up the steep terrain, from hut to hut on their way to the summit of the slumbering volcano. They held hands briefly at the summit, saying nothing. At times, when their bodies crossed on the path during the descent, they brushed hands past one another again, sometimes clasping each other's fingers until they needed their own hands to balance across a stream, hold onto to the branch of a tree, catch a fall.

Several weeks later, they visited the waterfalls of Lobé, a series of spunky falls created by multiple streams rushing together through a kilometer-long steeplechase of cascades until finally smashing through the mist into the Atlantic. For hours, Ship and Lori sat on the sandy beach in a small, tranquil cove, watching the torrents of water crash into the sea. It was a narcotic, savoring the awe of nature's wonder: the fresh salty air, the mist flirting with the cascading streams, the relentless sizzle of torrents crashing into the sea. It reminded them both of another moment they shared— that day, many years ago at Yale when they journeyed off to the nearby falls and shared a kiss.

In that tranquil cove, with the panoramic view of the Lobe waterfalls, they did so once again. As they loosened their embrace, he asked her the same question he asked all those years ago:

"Did you like that?"

"What's not to like?" Lori answered with her same words as before.

"Just wanted to make sure."

"Why's that?"

"Because I want to do it again."

WHEN THEY RETURNED TO YAOUNDÉ, they spent the night together, their first in Cameroon. They felt strange awakening next to each other in Ship's hotel room the next morning, an awkward sense of renewal: being intimate once again after so many years. They shared something from way back, but now it was different, something new again, but not quite, something that would still take time. As the alarm buzzed, Ship flipped over and slapped the snooze button.

"What time is it?" Lori asked, rubbing her eyes, her first words of the morning.

"Six-thirty," he answered.

"What time does the van leave?" she asked.

"Eight," he answered.

"This is weird, don't you think?" she said.

"Yeah, I get it. After all these…"

"Weird, but good." She smiled.

"Me too."

"And weird in another way…"

"Yeah?"

"Look. Look around us. We're in a suite in a luxury hotel in Cameroon while not too far away people are living in the worst possible—"

"But that's why we're here." He patted her hair.

"I get it. But it kind of makes me squirm."

After they showered, they dressed for the hour-long van ride out to the village. As usual, a copy of the day's *Financial Times* was slipped under Ship's hotel room door. He picked it up and glanced at the headline: *Bonne-Saari Acquires Australia's Second Largest Bank.*

"Up to his old tricks." Ship mumbled.

"Who's that?" she responded, fixing a towel in her hair.

"Bonne-Saari."

"Oh him." Lori stated matter-of-factly.

Although Ship had become somewhat of a celebrity after his televised debate with Bonne-Saari, Lori and Ship had never really discussed Izan Bonne-Saari since they had become reacquainted in Cameroon.

"What do you think of him?" Ship asked.

"Bonne-Saari?" She winced.

"Yeah."

"What do I think? I think he's a major scumbag."

* * *

71

Sydney, Australia, Mid-day, April 15, 2010

The photographers huddled around the podium as Izan Bonne-Saari stepped up to speak. Amid a flurry of flashes, Bonne-Saari obliged with a smile, waiting for the photographers to finish so their resultant images could be spread worldwide in a matter of minutes; more than anything, Bonne-Saari understood the power of publicity.

Neurotically self-conscious about his height— Bonne-Saari would confide in his friends that he stood 5'4" tall, but it was a generous estimate. He always stood on an 8 to 12-inch riser, concealed neatly behind the podium.

As the last flurry of flashes clicked away, Bonne-Saari sagely adjusted his bow tie. He waited for complete silence and then addressed the members of the press and assorted dignitaries:

"My dear friends, this is truly an historic day for Australia and the worldwide banking system. With the Australian Bank of Commerce now a vital part of GMFC, there is an unprecedented opportunity for capital to flow through our network into real investment in the economy of this most bountiful continent."

Educated at Cambridge, Harvard Business School and the London School of Economics, Bonne-Saari was a financial genius. He understood the forces that shaped economies, the political climates that could either buttress or destroy economic growth, and how the banking system could function within the political economy of today and the future.

Through acquisition, he had already built the world's largest multinational banking network, giving him rampant flexibility to outmaneuver any individual nation's regulatory authority. But his ultimate goal was much more ambitious: to control a major share of the world's banking assets, establish a new global currency and, consequently, a new form of world governance.

Bonne-Saari knew all too well that the financial sector in mature economies had sucked massive amounts of assets away from the working class and siphoned it into the pockets of the most wealthy; indeed, he was one of the foremost perpetrators of the shift. Bonne-Saari understood that this radical transfer of wealth was, under the current political climate, unsustainable. Inevitably, Marx would be proven right, the workers of the world *would unite* in defiance of a set of rules which no longer gave them access to capital, nor provide equal justice under the law.

That was exactly the scenario Bonne-Saari's grand plan was designed to avoid.

By snatching control of a major share of the world's banking assets, GMFC would become a corporation without a country, an overarching entity that would answer to no one. As such, through financial controls, he could shape the course of governments and ultimately establish a revolutionary new system which would make the inevitable middle-class uprising impossible.

IT WAS an idea that came with devastating consequences.

"Mr. Bonne-Saari," a reporter in the crowd asked as Bonne-Saari finished his carefully-prepared statement, "what's your end game?"

"End game?" Bonne-Saari answered. "What exactly do you mean by that?"

"That should be obvious, I would think," the reporter answered. "But what's your vision for GMFC?"

"Well, we're already the largest global banking company; I think that's pretty good, don't you?" Bonne-Saari said with a faux sense of naiveté. "But to answer your question, since we have no one to compete with but ourselves, we don't only want to be the largest, we want to be the *dominant force* in global banking, providing capital for an unparalleled, worldwide, global economic expansion. Industry provides the mechanics, we supply the fuel."

"But what about your 'spreadsheet-government' concept?" another reporter blurted out.

"Good question." Bonne-Saari patronized the reporter by pointing at him. "It's an interesting idea and I support it. But I'm a banker, not a philosopher, nor politician. We'll leave it at that."

A tall reporter in the front row stood up and flipped her tablet open. "Isn't it true you're off to China soon to discuss your plan for GCU's with President Ch'en?" she asked.

"And your name is?" Bonne-Saari gazed at her covetously.

"Katherine Rison, Global Worldwide Network News."

"Well, Ms. Rison, I do believe that ultimately, in the future, a worldwide currency might be in the best interest of all humankind, but right now I have no plans to advance that cause. I have other things to do."

She tucked a piece of her auburn hair behind her ear and swiped the screen of her tablet. "But according to the flight plans your pilot filed at Sydney airport, your next stop is Beijing, is it not?"

"That'll be it for now." Bonne-Saari dismissed her and strode brusquely off.

* * *

72

Various Locations, July 2010

"That bastard!" Ship exclaimed, sipping his morning coffee as he scanned the New York Times in his breakfast nook.

"What happened?" Lori asked, emerging from the bedroom of his Boston apartment, one of his white dress-shirts draped over her naked body.

"Bonne-Saari," Ship answered, pointing to a large picture on the paper's front page, "a fucking liar. Here he is, in Beijing. He's negotiating some sort of deal with the People's Bank of China. Just a month ago, he said he had no plans to do anything with China."

"What do you think he's up to?"

"Who the fuck knows." Ship answered. "But I'm sure whatever it is will advance the cause of Izan Bonne-Saari and no one else."

Ship and Lori had returned from Cameroon a month earlier, their volunteer programs over, but their mission far from complete. Ship had returned to Mass General and Lori to Cornell Medical Center in Manhattan, resulting in the initiation of a long distance relationship. Every weekend one would travel to the other's city. Given their busy schedules during the week, it worked perfectly for them.

"Why let it bother you so much?" Lori asked, fixing herself a coffee. "There's nothing you can really do from here."

"Lori, you should know me pretty well. I'm an idealist, and a stubborn one at that," Ship answered, "and even if the odds are way against me, I'll fight for what I think is right."

"Battling windmills, are you?" she teased him.

"If I have to."

IT DID NOT TAKE LONG for Bonne-Saari to show his hand. After several weeks of intense negotiations in Beijing, Bonne-Saari was set to make a major announcement. The Global Financial News Network was the first to jump on it, interrupting its normal programming to get ahead of the story. The news anchor, a somewhat sullen, late-middle-aged man appeared a bit bewildered as he filtered the information coming in on his teleprompter and through his earpiece:

"This is Dan Testa from the GFN headquarters on Wall Street. Reportedly, Izan Bonne-Saari is about to make a major announcement in Beijing. According to GFN exclusive sources, Bonne-Saari's global financial holding company, GMFC, is about to purchase all of the US debt held by the People's Bank of China, apparently at a deep discount. This, of course, could have enormous consequences on the US economy as well as the worldwide banking system. We have Dr. Megan Cohen, GFN's banking expert and former member of the Federal Reserve via satellite from Lucerne to help explain the effects of this announcement. Dr. Cohen?" He turned towards the giant screen behind him. "At first blush, what does this all mean?"

"Well, we don't want to jump to rash conclusions," Cohen answered, "but in some scenarios, this transaction could have severe consequences."

"How so?" Testa asked from New York.

"It's all still rumor, of course," she responded, "but according to my sources, Bonne-Saari is purchasing the US debt at a thirty-to-thirty five percent discount. That will immediately make all US interest rates jump precipitously, perhaps up to 200 basis points, maybe more if panic sets in. This will force the US government to pay higher rates when it issues its next series of bonds, triple what we're paying now, and that will increase the deficit, everything else being equal, due to increased interest payments alone."

"But one thing still remains unclear for our viewers, I think," Testa broke in, "what's in it for the Chinese?"

"Higher interest rates in the US would make the dollar increase relative to the Yuan which would make Chinese goods more competitive on the world market. But that alone, is certainly not enough incentive for the Chinese to make the deal. There's probably something more, it could be—"

"Excuse me, Dr. Cohen," Testa broke in again, "Thank you for being with us but we now must turn to Mr. Bonne-Saari who, sources tell me, is about to make his announcement." He turned to the large screen behind him which displayed a satellite feed from China. Bonne-Saari and a group of senior officials from the People's Bank were standing before a podium.

THE ANNOUNCEMENT DID NOT GO UNNOTICED by Dr. Ship Pennfield. His face reddened as he watched the replay of the press conference that evening. Bonne-Saari smothered his true motives with subterfuge and a barrage of empty platitudes.

"Can you say any more about your personal motivation for this transaction, Mr. Bonne-Saari?" a reporter asked.

"It's a very simple answer. It's about the good of the global economy," Bonne-Saari answered.

"Can you *elaborate*, though," the reporter followed up. "Can you give us any specifics?"

"China is a bountiful land with billions of enterprising people," Bonne-Saari answered. "This transaction allows them to free themselves from the large portion of US debt they've been holding while also allowing the currency implications to make their goods more competitive on world markets. It's a major boost for a major economy."

Another reporter jumped in: "But is that really enough? Economists say the amount the Chinese are losing on the debt transaction will not be made up with the currency effect on international trade."

"Perhaps the Chinese were losing faith in the US economy and no longer wanted to hold US debt," Bonne Saari said. "You'll have to ask them."

"But that makes no sense," the reporter followed, "the Chinese could have sold that debt for much more than you paid them."

Bonne-Saari smirked. "Maybe there's more to this transaction than meets the eye."

Disgusted, Ship clicked off his TV. He immediately grabbed the phone and dialed Lori's number in New York.

"Did you see it?" he announced without even saying hello.

"Yeah, pretty shitty," she answered. "What comes next?"

"Hard to predict," Ship said, "but long-term he's trying to establish a new world currency which he can control and use as leverage to establish his dream of a global government."

"That's terrible, Ship."

"And the worst part is, it really seems like there's nothing we can do."

After a few moments of silence, Lori whispered, "I'm not so sure."

* * *

TIME FRAME: 2053

73

Location Unknown, White EVR Room, March 2, 2053

The perfection of her surroundings drove Robyn Viega to greater depths of boredom. There were no challenges, no opportunities, nothing to disrupt her cycle of homogenized predictability. She wondered if she would ever break out of her environs, escape back to the real world.

She had no idea how to escape, but at least she knew how to squelch her boredom. And that she would.

Brusquely, she stood up from her lounge chair on her beautiful terrace overlooking her beautiful garden, and strode over towards the hedges. She confronted the tight branches and bristly leaves, right in her face, standing up to them, just as she had done before.

Then she waited.

"SHIT, I think she's zoning again!" exclaimed the technician in the observation deck over the pure white room where Robyn Viega remained encased within her EVR sheath.

"You sure?" his colleague asked.

He pointed up towards the monitors.

"She's standing in the same spot, all metabolic functions are down substantially."

"What should we do, notify the Prime Minister's office?"

"No, not yet. Let it play out."

THIS TIME when Robyn walked through the parting hedges, the young woman was already waiting for her. She radiated like a fine crystal against the absolute blackness of eternity.

I knew you would return, she said to Robyn.

"So did I," she responded, then added, "…I think."

Why did you come? the young woman asked.

"Not sure," Robyn answered.

You know, she responded. *I'm sure you know.*

Robyn stood silent.

Don't be shy. Tell me. Glowing warmly, the young woman emanated a sense of serenity that loosened compunction's grip on Robyn's hesitance.

"Last time I was here you said we were, we are, one and the same. How's that?" Robyn asked, quivering. "And then how can I exact revenge?"

Watch. She turned and motioned for Robyn to follow. *Just watch.*

"ANYTHING NEW?" one of the technicians in the observation deck asked his supervisor as he walked back into the room.

"Nope," the supervisor answered, "her EEG is barely detectable, other metabolic functions in hibernation mode."

"Geez, you sure we shouldn't notify someone?"

"Fine, tell them she's zoning just like last time," the supervisor answered. "My bet is she comes out of it. This is exactly what happened last time."

ROBYN WATCHED.

She watched the deep blackness of her environs part, revealing another, lighter, more textured blackness blending into shifting shades of dark purple. She could smell the salt air of the sea, hear the swishing of water and feel the slow, undulating rhythm of the swells.

You are here to learn the truth, the young woman said.

"The truth?" Robyn repeated her words.

You are here to understand your mission.

"How did you know those were my questions, what I was thinking?" Robyn questioned.

As I said, we are one and the same. The young woman nodded her head and smiled. She pointed farther back into the darkness, summoning some unknown force.

Robyn braced herself.

WHOOOOOOOOSSSSSHHHHHH!!!

The darkness opened. The wind swirled, rain poured in sheets, thunder crackled and lightning spanked the sea below. The maelstrom sucked her in, swirling her around, lifting her above. Her heart fluttered, her face whitened, her body twisted and turned to the whimsy of the rushing winds.

Then, suddenly: silence. An abrupt return to quietude and serenity.

She floated downwards, slowly, peacefully, quietly above a vast ocean. *But where was the woman, her guide?*

Things were different. Stark and calm, the violent storm was now nothing more than a memory. Only the sensations of the sea provided a familiar rhythmic undertone. Robyn surveyed the eerily vacant setting, groping for what might come next.

Slowly, she turned and surveyed the vast ocean, blurring into infinity in all directions. After some time, she noticed a small dot on the horizon. She floated towards it, squinting: it appeared to be in the shape of a ship. She floated closer, testing her judgment, until it became clear and distinct. Tall-masted and deep-bellied, the ship's wooden hull rocked with the ocean's gentle swells. With time-lapse rapidity, the sun dipped below the horizon, bathing the ship in grayish twilight.

Robyn floated above it, swirling around the flapping top-sails, giving her faculties ample opportunity to sense and observe.

THERE WERE a few crewmen on deck, two at the bow, one at the wheel and one at a lookout in the crow's nest. She floated over to the stern, closer and closer until she settled directly above. She saw a lone man gazing out to the sea.

She could sense strongly that the man was perplexed. Something bothered him as he stood out over the stern, his elbow on the railing, mulling over some dilemma or crisis.

Suddenly, an interruption:

"Master Pennfield?"

The man shuddered, his moment of quiet contemplation abruptly shattered.

Slowly, he turned around. He squinted. The woman glowed in the night. As Robyn floated in closer, she could see a luminous highlight around the woman. She was dressed in white and black, the light of the moon silhouetting her with a silver halo.

"It was you," she said to the man.

Robyn gasped. It was the same woman— the serene glowing woman— who had guided her here.

"What?" The man squinted again.

"It was you who did it," the woman said to the man.

"Did what?" he snapped back at her.

"You killed him. You killed my mate. You poisoned him, Charles Pennfield."

"Rubbish!" The man scowled. "Where did you hear such lies?"

"I just know." She shivered as she spoke, yet glowed through the mist of the night.

Anger flamed from the eyes of the man's reddened face. "You know nothing! Now be gone with you!" He glared at her, sweat oozing from his collar. Then, without warning—

WHAAAAPPPP!!!

He slapped her across the face.

The force of his blow slammed her body onto the wooden deck.

He began to walk away, but then stopped abruptly, turned around, looked down upon her and barked:

"Should I ever hear any of this again, I'll tell the Ashfords you were his whore. I'll ruin you. I'll scorn you with everyone, whore!"

With those words ringing in her ears— *I'll ruin you. I'll scorn you with everyone, whore!*— the skies turned pitch black.

What was *that?* Robyn thought as she floated through the blackness.

Anchorless in the pitch-black void, Robyn could no longer gauge her bearings, had no idea where she was, how she could escape. Time had no meaning here. Neither the precise metric of seconds nor the timelessness of infinity mattered. She was just here: unanchored, untethered, her locus immeasurable by any yardstick of space and time.

Then, without warning, without why, with no sense of time or space, the indecipherable blackness parted.

The sky turned sunny and blue. She had no idea how long she had been in her limbo, feeling only joy that somehow, she had been released. She floated over the sea once again, spotting the same tall-masted, deep-bellied ship now with a strip of land off in the distance.

The breeze pushed her closer.

The ship turned on its keel, a slow and laborious movement. Passengers lined the rails, straining to catch a glimpse of the strip of grassy land off to the west. Crewmen manned the sheets and climbed the masts. She could observe the Captain gazing up at the sails, judging the vagaries of the winds. As she listened to the sheets slackening and then being pulled taut, something propelled her to the stern.

A young woman stood there alone, undetected by her preoccupied fellow passengers and crewmen. Robyn quickly recognized her: the young woman, her guide. She was sobbing, tears running down her cheeks. Her face was white and pale.

"Charles Pennfield be damned! The devil take him!" she wailed out loud.

But no one heard her.

"May he and his family rot and perish." She climbed up on the rail, the black wool hem of her skirt billowing over the green fathoms below. *"Forever. For all time."*

She looked straight out over the sea, white breakers all around. She yelled out her final words:

"All mean spirits are doomed to fall."

She spread her arms like a set of wings, drew a breath, then jumped. The fluttering winds lifted her, prolonging her path, extending her arc, until she crashed into the frothing breakers.

Robyn clasped her hands over her heart and gasped as she watched the young woman struggle, shocked, bouncing up and down on the shoals' sandy bottom, battling with the force of the breakers and the pull of the currents. *Had she changed her mind, did she want to go back?*

"Help me! Help me!" the young girl screamed.

Yet no one did. The ship moved farther and farther away as if oblivious to her plight.

Robyn watched as the young woman finally succumbed to the whims of the sea.

As the ship turned and let a patch of sun flank its starboard side, she could clearly read the words painted on the ship's wooden stern:

Mayflower of London.

ONCE MORE, everything turned black. The young woman, her guide, now stood before her.

Now is your time, she said. You are me as I am you.

"My time? My time for what?" Robyn asked.

Justice, the woman answered.

"How?" Robyn asked, confused.

Scorn to the Pennfields. Scorn to them all.

"But how..."

It's your mission, your destiny. Our mission, our destiny, she said.

"But again, how?" Robyn asked.

The young woman bowed her head, squeezing her eyes shut, inducing a trance. As Robyn watched, the woman's face turned blue and white, her teeth rotted, her hair entangled with seaweed and flotsam. A living corpse, she looked up at Robyn and spoke through her blue lips and rotted teeth:

All mean spirits are doomed to fall.

UPON NOTIFICATION of Robyn Viega's condition, about a dozen virtual figures — officials from Apexian Security and P&C— appeared in the observation deck, strictly observing the technicians' procedures.

"Are you prepared to implement reinstatement protocol?" the senior security official asked the supervising technician.

"Yeah, yeah, but I wouldn't make that decision quite—"

"It's not your decision to make," the security official interrupted.

"Understood," the technician answered. "But you don't want to let her out of EVR too abruptly..."

"Prepare for reinstatement protocol," the official ordered, indifferent to the technician's warning.

"Yessir," the technician obediently answered. He began making the necessary adjustments on his control panel.

"Look," the second technician interrupted, pointing to the monitors. "She's coming out of it..."

WITH A THUD, Robyn awakened. She was back in the cottage on her bed. Her face was clammy, and her heart beat rapidly. She looked out to the garden through the French doors.

How could she ever fulfill her mission? she wondered.

* * *

74

TEX-ARK GAB, March 9, 2053

The MagLev flew rapidly on a sheet of air, zooming above its track at 450 miles per hour from the PAWVA station near PHA432B to the TEX-ARK station in what used to be southwestern Arkansas. Derek Fane sat on a long bench in sub-class, squeezed between a fat, blubbery, hairy, tattooed man in a T-shirt and a scrawny little Hispanic-Asian man with a harelip quietly chewing on some green substance he would pull out of a folded square of aluminum foil. The hot, crowded car and the boredom of the trip annoyed Fane, but it was a trip he had to take, an important step in his mission to find his ex, his lover, Robyn Viega.

Unexpectedly, the fat, blubbery man grunted at him:

"Got SMARF-ite?"

"You mean me?" Fane asked, startled by the man's request.

"Yeah, you, who'd you think?"

"Nope," Fane answered.

"Faggot," the man retorted.

After six weeks, Fane felt secure enough in his sobriety to embark upon his journey. Withdrawal from SMARF had taken its toll— a sudden urge had compelled him to break his abstention several times, throbbing him into near-submission, yet each time through pain and anger and clenched teeth, he resisted.

Now it was time to find Robyn.

The two-and-a-half-hour trip seemed like an eternity to Fane. The MagLev's modern exterior— a silver bullet-like horizontal missile speeding along its repulsive magnetic tracks— belied the interior of sub-class. Six long benches without backs, two and a half feet between each, ran the length of the car, barely leaving room to move. A trip to the restroom was an arduous journey, obstructed by countless knees and elbows and smack-talk, as he navigated around anxious, screaming children playing on a urine-soaked floor. The smell in the car was hideous, but nothing compared to that of the rest room.

Although Fane felt a strong urge to pee, he tolerated the heavy burning in his crotch, choosing the lesser of two evils. The burning, swelling sensation made each and every remaining moment of this journey to TEX-ARK an increasingly intolerable challenge. Yet he held out, immediately sprinting for the station's restroom upon arrival.

FANE PICKED up a rental cycle at the station and biked through a forest of thick pine groves; perfectly vertical, the trees stood at attention in row after row, their bright green foliage providing a canopy for the reddish-brown terrain below. Stopping momentarily, he breathed in the pleasant scent and savored the colors and shapes of this fated storybook forest knowing it would soon be razed by powers beyond his control.

PHB718D was a demarcation of sorts, nothing more than a shanty town, squeezed between the verdant pine grove forest to the east and towering industrial steel oil rigs lining the horizon to the west. The haphazardly placed shanties displayed no lack of creativity. Any piece of material which could possibly be turned into part of a shelter was utilized to its maximum utility: one shanty was built entirely of scrap metal, a big scalloped piece providing a flat rusted roof; another was made from an entire stern side of a houseboat, its jagged wooden edges testimony to its being ravaged by some disaster at sea. Then, there was an old mini-van gutted by fire; next, a semi-translucent shelter, cobbled together from discarded glass desk tops, coffee table tops, frosted shower doors, and discarded windows. Fane snapped out his e-let. His notes read *432 Rusted Cottage Lane*, but the scattered nature of the settlement showed no signs of such presumed organization. He finally found Rusted Cottage Lane by asking around. The numbers on each dwelling were so indecipherable, he had to believe it was intentional. He examined each in detail.

THE NUMBER on the off-kilter doorframe of a house half-way down the lane was unreadable as any other. Flaked and weathered, the paint-markings could be reasonably interpreted as one of many combinations of numbers, but Fane convinced himself that the vertical stroke on the left, followed by a roundish segment in the middle, then the horizontal line to the right, could be the decayed remnants of what was originally intended to be the number 432.

Spurred on by that droplet of confidence, he knocked at the door, with its flaked red paint equally weathered. At first, no response. After the third sharp rap, he could hear some sort of activity from inside the small dilapidated structure. Ominous, the sound resembled that of a large animal awakening from a long hibernation, lumbering around to get its bearings.

After a while, the door eventually opened.

"Huh?" an unshaven, bleary-eyed man belched.

"Are you William Viega?" Fane asked.

"Why zat important to yah?" he countered. The man appeared to be in his seventies, but could have been younger Fane thought; traces of his beard were speckled black and gray; his hair tangled and unkempt swirling around his bald crown; his fatty tattooed arms dropping from the shoulders of his slightly-ripped sleeveless T-shirt.

"I need his help."

"Help? What could 'William' ever do fer a rascal like you?" the man retorted.

"My name's Derek, I'm a friend of his daughter Robyn."

"Ain't seen her in months," the man answered, turning back towards the door.

"So you *are* William Viega?" Fane jumped on the man's slip.

"Sheeee-yat!" the man babbled. "Yah got me on that one. Yah caught me in a blur. Got my defenses down. Now go 'way." Again, he turned for the door.

"Mr. Viega?"

"Who?" He turned back.

"I'm talking to you," Fane answered.

"Haven't been called that in years," Viega answered. "Scumbag, buttfum, turdwaste, fatfuck, ecoshit, all sortsa stuff. Never Mr. Viega."

"She might be in trouble."

"Join the fuckin' club. We're all in trouble, aren't we?" Viega paused and eyed Fane's kempt jeans, his button-down shirt, his clean-shaven face and well-groomed hair. "What're you, seventh, eighth?"

"Eleventh."

"Bullshit!" Viega blurted. "You ain't no eleventh. You dress too sharp, look too clean."

"I am what I am," Fane answered. "Maybe I chose to be in the eleventh."

"Sheee-yat!" Viega chortled. "Then you are a lot dumber than you look. You playin' me or somethin'?"

"No," said Fane. "I told you I'm trying to find your daughter Robyn."

"Can't help."

"Nothing, not even a hint of where she is, where she might be?"

"Last I heard — she sent me a damn e-message and it cost me 13 GCUs to get it — she was workin' as a V-way monitor in Scumville."

"Scumville?" Fane asked.

"You know, NYCGAB, New York," Viega answered. "Scumville."

"Why thank you, anything might help," Fane scribbled on his e-let.

Viega called back to him as he walked away. "Hey, smartass?"

"Yeah?" Fane looked back.

"Why do you care so much 'bout what happens to Robyn?"

"You really wanna know?" Fane answered.

"Yeah. Could use a laugh or two."

"Because I loved her," Fane answered.

"Now that's an 'effin joke," Viega answered, "you just loved that tight little ass of 'ers, that's what you loved."

For a moment, Fane stared back at him, then answered:

"And I think she might've loved me, too."

* * *

75

Manhattan, NYCGAB, March 18, 2053

Manhattan was its eclectic self— a simmering cauldron of grand old structures, shiny reflective skyscrapers, dazzling technologies, state-of-the art transportation systems, industrial waste and urban decay tethered together in a state of perpetual disruption. Fane's first stop upon arrival was at the V-way administration office near the southern tip of the island. They did not give him much to go on, but he was able to squeeze a little bit of information out: Robyn Viega's primary station was near East 23rd Street right off the river.

The V-Way towers sprouted up from the remains of the FDR Drive, right on the old meridian. They stood majestically as if a symbol of contemporary civilization's mastery of such antiquated things as land mobility. Stationed every mile or so, these towering structures— built of twisted steel beams wrapped around each other like strands of a heavy cord— rose to a height of 500 feet where the monitoring station sat above like a giant nest. Octagonal-shaped with windows at each surface, the towers provided a dividing line for northbound and southbound traffic and a perfect perch for the V-way monitoring personnel to discern any irregularities.

"Haven't seen her since that night in November, around mid-month, I think it was," Jon Minsk, her former supervisor, told Fane.

"Can you pin it down more precisely," Fane asked.

"Sure, give me a minute." Minsk summoned up a holoscreen, then flipped through employee attendance data. "Ummm… looks like it was November 10th. Clocked out at 6:02PM and never showed the next day. Haven't seen her since."

"Do you know who her friends were, where she used to hang out?" Fane asked.

"I don't, but Kenny may," he mentioned, then called over to one of the V-way monitors sitting behind a bank of holoscreens at one of the station's eight windows. "Hey Kenny, got a sec."

Suspicious, the young man was hesitant to give much information, but finally Fane cajoled a morsel out of him. "I was just friends with her here, at work basically," the young man disclosed, "But I do know she liked to hang out after work at a place in the East Village. Went with her there a few times."

"What's its name?" Fane asked.

"It's called *Undertaker*."

ABSENT OF PATRONS, *Undertaker* displayed all the flaws usually obscured by its crowd of tightly packed bodies, swirls of smothering smoke, and streams of drunken chatter. Nothing more than a glorified basement in a crumbling brownstone, the tavern was indeed a mortuary of sorts; its dank cinderblock walls hastily painted a maudlin shade of purple, cobwebs clinging to every corner, and the thin rug covering the floor smelling wretchedly of stale beer and mouse droppings. The bar was nothing special, formica-topped and about twenty feet long, a few round barstools spaced haphazardly along the way, their faux leather seats marred and scraped.

When Fane walked in, he was greeted by a grumpy middle-aged man with muscular, tattooed arms, a pair of sharp elbows scraping the bar, leather and metal wristbands, a droopy black moustache and a head of long, tangled hair drooping to his shoulders.

"Ain't open yet," the broad-shouldered man grunted as Fane approached.

"I'm not here to drink," Fane answered as he walked over.

"Then what the fuck are you here for?" the man attacked back. "This ain't no charity, not a place to hang."

"I need a little information," Fane said.

"Yeah?" The man behind the bar eyed Fane more carefully. "What kind of information?"

"You ever see this woman here?" Fane pulled out his e-let and flashed an image.

The man shuffled his jaw. "You a cop?"

"Nope, just a friend of hers."

"Yeah, I've seen her. Nice ass, nice pair." The bartender answered. "What's that to you?"

"Like I said, I'm a friend. She's been missing."

"Interesting."

"What do you mean by that?" Fane asked.

"Yah know, so many babes come in and outta this place, it's hard to keep track. Though Bobby G — works Thursdays and Fridays — he had the real hots for 'er. Love at first sight. Wanted to jump her bones, knock knees. Bad, real bad."

"Really?" Fane answered tersely.

"That bother you?" The bartender caught himself. "You been fuckin' her or something?"

"It doesn't surprise me. She's a good-looking woman," said Fane.

"Yeah, well the only reason I bring that up, the Bobby G thing, is that he really had it hot for this girl. What's 'er name, Robyn or something?"

Fane nodded.

"Well, like I said, he had this thing for 'er. The minute she walks in, his eyes are all over 'er, undressing 'er, you know what I mean? Dude could hardly work."

"Yeah, I get it."

"So this one time — and this is why I remember it — this fucking a-hole dude, bald guy, walks in decked out in these tight leather pants, and this tight t-shirt, his biceps bulging. You hardly ever see shit like that around here. Mucho dinero, all the way. Well Bobby's sweatin' bullets here behind the bar cuz it looks like she's comin' onto this guy. Or vice versa. Or both, who knows? After a few minutes, they walk out and Bobby gets all pissed off, thinks he lost her forever." The bartender giggled. "Actually turns out he did."

"Huh?"

"For the last three years or so, the girl's a regular here. Comes in at least two, three times a week. So after that night she leaves with this guy, Bobby keeps waitin' for 'er to come back, but she never does. So he gets pissed, real pissed. I thought the guy was gonna go bonkers he was so pissed off. Figured she shacked up with that high dollar dude and they're into happily-ever-after land. That sick fuck Bobby still ain't over it..."

THE MOMENT FANE jumped on a MagLev back to PHA432B, he pulled out his e-let and began exploring. He was able to track his 20,000 GCU payment that day when he was strung out on SMARF to a Bryan McPherson at Pennfield Technologies, a mammoth global corporation. Soon, he determined that

McPherson was the company's global head of security. He then flipped through scores of files to learn more. One picture stopped him in his tracks, a somewhat attractive middle-aged man, dignified looking, in a business suit. The man had a perfectly shaven bald scalp.

His name: Jimmy Mashimoto-Pennfield, Chairman & CEO.

* * *

76

Manhattan, NYCGAB, Pennfield Technologies Tower, Morning, March 25, 2053

Busy in his office on the 34th floor of the Pennfield Technologies Tower, Bryan McPherson was surprised when he received a call from the lobby security desk.

"There's a man here to see you," the attendant announced.

"Really? I don't have anyone on my schedule," McPherson responded.

"He said you would know him," the attendant said, "his name's Fane, Derek Fane."

Momentarily, McPherson's mind shuffled through his memories while he continued to sort through a stack of files with one hand and sip coffee with the other.

"Ummm, I'm not sure…"

"He says he met you in a PHA, 432B," the attendant stated. "He said you interviewed him."

McPherson stopped for a moment, then put everything down on his desk. "Give him a complete security scan, everything, and then send him up here with a guard immediately."

IT TOOK twenty minutes for Fane to undergo the battery of security checks—

physical, emotional and the verification process— that McPherson ordered. When the guard finally escorted Fane to his office, McPherson was shocked.

He could see a vague resemblance, but this guy looked nothing like that strung out incoherent druggie, his face pale and his arm pierced by IV tubes, mumbling convoluted sentences in the back of a rusty old excavation bucket. This fellow looked downright respectable: dressed casually in a jean jacket and khakis, his face cleanly shaven save for a neatly trimmed goatee and moustache, his moderately long hair perfectly combed. This fellow could pass for a member of the 7th or maybe even the 6th PGU.

"Hello, Mr. Fane," McPherson said when Fane and the escort appeared at his office door. "May I speak with…" McPherson read the attendant's name from a holoscreen, "um… Mr. Albertson for a moment."

Fane stepped outside, and McPherson closed the door.

"So you ran all the tests on this fellow?"

The guard nodded.

"The complete verification battery across all known databases?"

"Yep, it's him, Derek Fane, 11th PGU, definitely verified."

"Okay," said McPherson, "you can go out and let him in. But stay right outside and be on alert."

"So Mr. Fane," McPherson leaned back in his chair, "things are a bit different from when I last saw you."

"Yes, I would say so," Fane answered tersely.

"So what brings you here? What can I do for you?"

"I decided that wasting my life away high on SMARF was not the way to deal with my problems, so I cleaned up my act."

"That's good to hear." McPherson indulged him. "What kind of problems were you trying to avoid, may I ask?"

"Shouldn't that be obvious?"

"The whole Apexinator thing?"

"Of course," Fane answered. "The system of government is corrupt; the rules are corrupt and the people in power are corrupt."

"And you're telling me this because…."

"I'm not sure," Fane said. "I was high off my ass when you came out to the PHA, but there was something about you. You're really not one of them."

"And how would you know that?" McPherson asked.

"As I said, I was real fucked up at the time, so I may be wrong but, still, there was something, something different about you."

"If you think that's going to get you any sympathy, you're wrong, Mr.

Fane," McPherson answered. "My boss is an Apexian, he's personal friends with the Prime Minister and I'm a member of the 5th PGU, soon to be a Diamid, I hope."

"Yeah, that's what you *have* to say, you have to spout the expected bullshit, but I think there's more to you than that."

"Well, you're certainly entitled to think as you like, Mr. Fane, but I'm a little busy, so if that's all…"

"She's dead."

"Huh?" McPherson sat up in his chair.

"Robyn Viega is dead," Fane stated again.

"And how do you know that?" McPherson asked.

"After you visited me, questioned me, I cleaned myself up because I wanted to find her. I've checked with everyone she ever knew, and even some she didn't. There's no trace of her. There's been no trace of her since the day she was seen leaving a tavern with your boss."

"Okay, so if you believe that—"

"I don't believe it. I know it," Fane interrupted him.

"Okay, so if you know that, why didn't you go to the proper authorities, why did you come to me?"

"The proper authorities are bullshit," Fane stated. "The laws say what they say, but there's no real justice for people in the lower PGUs, just lip service. I came to you because of the feeling I had about you."

"Mr. Fane, for some odd reason you're trying to pump smoke up my ass, but this guy's not biting."

"As you wish."

"You know I could probably have you locked up."

"For what?"

"I've been around the block; I can find something."

"Don't you get it?" Fane looked him right in the eyes. "That's what's so fucked up about everything. There's nothing fair in this world unless the Apexians and the Betamils and whoever says it's fair. Those people, they've been so seduced by privilege, they even believe their own bullshit. They've turned right into wrong and wrong into right and make eloquent fucking arguments defending their exploitation and atrocities. But anyone with a dash of common sense knows they're wrong. Don't you?"

"I told you, Mr. Fane, you're barking up the wrong tree," McPherson answered.

"Well, I came in here thinking you might have something most of them don't. And I still think you might. Maybe I'm wrong, but I think you're putting on an act because you're scared of them finding out."

"Finding out what?"

"Like I said, finding out that you have something most of them don't."

"Which is?"

"A conscience."

SEVERAL MOMENTS AFTER FANE LEFT, McPherson summoned up a holoscreen and placed a call to his buddy on the force, Frankie DeVito.

"Bry Mac, what's up?"

"Not much. Same old, same old," McPherson answered. "Can I pick your brain for a sec?"

"Sure. What's left of it," DeVito quipped.

"Okay. Let me give you a hypothetical."

"Shoot."

"Suppose you wanted to make someone go away, but didn't want to whack 'em. How could you hide someone?"

"Well, Bry, the easiest answer is the most obvious. Change their identity. Usually that'll do, although ocular recognition is getting pretty good. Hard to avoid that."

"Okay. But suppose, the person wasn't necessarily a willing accomplice, if you know where I'm going?"

"Sure, sure, I get it." DeVito paused, thinking. "Well, there is this new technology I heard about. I'm not sure if it's being widely used."

"Go on."

* * *

TIME FRAME: 2010-2011

THE ALTERNATIVE LIFE OF ARTHUR SHIPKIN PENNFIELD

77

Various Locations, August 14–November 22, 2010

Bit by bit, Bonne-Saari's plan became evident. The US debt bought by Bonne-Saari's financial network would be sold to shadow banking companies under his control. There, the bonds would be repackaged into a new derivative security denominated in Global Currency Units or GCUs, a currency which would be issued solely by Bonne-Saari's global banking network. The shadow banks would then sell these GCU-denominated derivatives to investors worldwide.

The Chinese would exchange the dollars received from Bonne-Saari one-for-one for GCUs valued at $1.30 in US currency, an exchange rate guaranteed by Boone Saari's financial network and a rate which would make up for the discount at which the Chinese sold the debt. Going forward, China would accept two currencies, the GCU and its own Yuan. And then, anyone wishing to invest in US Treasuries would be forced to buy GCUs to purchase the derivative securities, putting upward pressure on Bonne-Saari's currency and downward pressure on all others, particularly the US dollar.

As a result, the Chinese would enjoy the best of both worlds. The nation's domestic currency, the Yuan, would be free to decline against the US dollar, creating a favorable trade balance for Chinese goods. However, the Chinese could use the higher-valued GCUs to purchase imports at a more favorable price.

* * *

"THE QUESTION IS," Dr. Winston Morgan, MD, former Senator from Massachusetts, asked, "what's his next move?"

"Well Norm, this is right in your wheelhouse. What do you think?" Ship Pennfield addressed Dr. Norman Steinberg, Nobel Laureate in Economics.

They were all assembled in Pennfield's Boston apartment: Steinberg from Harvard, Emilio Rossini, a prominent physicist from MIT, Susan Morgenthau, a highly-regarded sociologist from Boston College, Dr. Morgan and, of course, Lori Bernstein.

"Well, what do you think, Norm?" Dr. Morgan asked.

Steinberg took a long, meandering puff on his pipe. "He has many options. Basically, he has the US by its balls."

"No shit." Ship asked.

"With the Chinese in his back pocket, his own global currency and his financial network in possession of so much US debt, he can wreak havoc on the US economy in many ways."

"There must be something we can do," Lori implored.

"Nothing short of political upheaval," Susan Morgenthau added.

"Is that what it's come to?" Ship lamented.

"My friend," Rossini answered in his thick accent, "I'm afraid if nothing else can rein in Mr. Bonne-Saari, that task will fall to people of good conscience."

Without doubt, Bonne-Saari had spurred this group into a heightened sense of alert.

"He has an end game and it can only be one of several things," Steinberg stated.

"So go on," Ship encouraged him.

"Number one, he's definitely setting the stage to make the GCU the pre-eminent global currency supplanting the dollar. That's a no-brainer."

"Which would mean?" Lori asked.

"In the worst case, he would have control over every country's fiscal policy. They would not be able to act without his involvement or approval."

"But why?" Ship asked. "The guy is already phenomenally wealthy. He can live a million lifetimes and never spend what he has."

"Which leads me to option number two," Steinberg responded. "It's not about wealth. In my estimation, he's out to change the world order. He wants to make himself some sort of supreme world leader."

"But that's impossible," Morgenthau said. "Or is it?"

"In the history of human affairs, stranger things have happened," said Dr. Morgan.

"So what can we do?" Ship asked.

A long pause and then Lori answered:

"Drastic circumstances require drastic measures."

* * *

IT WAS ONLY a matter of weeks until Ship was whammed by the uncharacteristically bold headline on the morning Times: US SENT INTO FINANCIAL TURMOIL AS BONNE-SAARI SHORTS US TREASURIES.

The moment he saw it, he felt nauseous. By the time he fully absorbed the implications, his heart beat so rapidly it rattled his chest.

"Bonne-Saari really outdid himself on this one," Norm Steinberg, the economist, explained to Ship on the phone. "By shorting US Treasuries to the extent he did, he throws US interest rates further up which will send the US economy into a deep recession, perhaps even a depression. The value of the dollar gets bid up versus the Yuan which gives the Chinese an even more favorable balance of trade which then deepens the US recession."

"But can't the Federal Reserve do something?" Ship asked.

"Their only real weapon would be to devalue the dollar which, I suspect, is exactly what Bonne-Saari wants. That will increase the value of the GCU and make even more gains for his derivative investors."

"So what's next?" Ship asked.

"Just the usual," Steinberg answered. "Panic will set in which will make the damage even worse. Just watch."

BY THE END of the day, the Dow Jones Industrial Average had plunged 1500 points, its largest loss ever. The President of the United States addressed the nation at 8pm, basically assuring the US and the world that the government would take all necessary steps to mitigate the disaster, but his words fell largely upon deaf ears. The overnight markets in Asia and Europe only exacerbated the damage begun on Wall Street.

"The man's a tyrant," Lori said to Ship over the phone after the President's address. "My god… he is truly a tyrant, a monster, does he care about *nothing?*"

"Simple answer," Ship said. "He's a fucking bastard. A narcissistic son of a bitch."

"But I can't imagine…"

“Don’t try to,” Ship interrupted her. “You can’t apply rational thought to an irrational mind.”

“So you really think he’s that fucked up?” she asked.

“Oh let me count the ways,” Ship responded. “At very least he’s a sociopath, perhaps a psychopath.”

“So what do we do? Just let a madman have his way with the world?”

Ship gazed outside his large window absorbing the Boston skyline as his mind wandered in many directions.

“Why are you so quiet, Ship?”

“Whenever I think about it, the only possible solution pains me,” Ship lamented.

* * *

78

Boston, MA / Colombo, Sri Lanka, Mid-day – Early Evening. November 23, 2010

Things got worse.

Rapidly, the world economy fell into a deep hole. Unemployment in the US shot up to 12% within two months. The stock market declined by 42%, devastating retirement accounts and pension funds covering tens of millions of families. The US foreclosure rate hit an all-time high and business failures were rampant. Even the Chinese— their economy buttressed by Bonne-Saari's currency manipulations— felt the wrath of the deep worldwide recession.

The weaker economies dropped first. The already high homeless rate in sub-Saharan Africa leapt to over 50%. In Southeast Asia, scores of people were living in the streets, as they were in Panama, Guatemala, Venezuela, Haiti, Ecuador and most of the Caribbean. The industrialized nations felt it as well, perhaps worse, in that they hadn't seen such conditions in nearly a century. The high foreclosure and unemployment rates conspired to create a perfect storm, casting middle class Americans, British, Canadians, Brazilians, Japanese, Germans, French— particularly older ones— into nomadic, commune-like groups, with dozens living in a neighbor's house that had not yet faced foreclosure, and then, once the creditors caught up, moving onto another.

The world demanded an answer, and there was only one person who could give it: Izan Bonne-Saari. Cagily, he waited for the wound to fester to the point where citizens of the world were dreaming of a white knight to swoop in and save them from catastrophe. And the solution was obvious: *who else to play the hero other than he— the global economic titan— and, ironically, the one who caused the damage in the first place?*

Each day Bonne-Saari hesitated brought with it more uncertainty, turmoil and panic. Many large companies were near bankruptcy. The US Treasury needed more cash to pay its obligations, but was being forced to borrow at record-high interest rates, creating an unprecedented deficit.

But still, Bonne-Saari prolonged it all.

Shrewdly, he allowed the misery to build, draining all remaining powers of resistance out of his adversaries, waiting for that precise moment right before the system would snap.

Then he struck.

Bonne-Saari chose the National Museum in GMFC's home city of Colombo, Sri Lanka as the setting for his global TV address. Surrounded by several dozen of his closest advisors—clearly the beginning of his cabinet for a new world government—Bonne-Saari addressed the world.

"My fellow citizens of this great planet," he began, "some may accuse me of causing this worldwide economic crisis. And to those, I must confess, I did. But I assure you it was not out of malice, but merely an acceleration of the natural forces that would have undeniably occurred without my intervention. The process would have been slow and painful, tremendously more painful than what has transpired here. The world has suffered for a mere six months. The alternative would have been six years or perhaps sixty years. The fundamental global economic forces were so out of balance they would have wreaked torrential havoc on us all.

"That is why I come to you today. I come today with a solution. We've accelerated the misery and now we can accelerate the rebirth of our global economy. Alas, nothing is easy. It will take discipline and sacrifice, but I assure you it can be done. Our global economy fell out of equilibrium long ago because we relied upon antiquated forms of government to regulate and control our economies. The relationship between global economies was disjointed and mostly at conflicting purposes. The waste and inefficient utilization of resources was rampant. Now we can address that.

"Today I ask the governments of the world to join me, join me in a new and robust form of government which reflects the realities of the contemporary world. In today's information-intensive economy, it is no longer necessary to define nations of people by geography alone. We live in a virtual world and our government structure should reflect that.

"We must face facts. People are different. They have different beliefs, lifestyles, ethnic backgrounds, professions and financial accomplishments. Yet our archaic form of geographically based governmental entities has forced these dissimilar beings upon one another while their governments remain shackled by the obligation to provide similar services for all despite their inbred differences. In an effort to appease these populations of disparate peoples, our governments have watered down the solution, homogenizing it to the extent that in an attempt to please all, it does service to none.

"I say it's time for that to end.

"So today join me, governments of the world. Join me in a new and bold undertaking. Join me in a movement that, in fact, has already begun. The GCU, our global currency unit, is now the pre-eminent currency in the world. I ask all governments who have until now resisted expiring their domestic currencies in favor of the GCU to wait no longer. Now is the time.

"And it is also time to implement what I, among others, have referred to as the spreadsheet form of government. No longer shall we herd disparate peoples with disparate values and disparate goals into the same box simply due to geographic proximity, forcing them to compromise to the extent that the result is dysfunction. No longer should hard working people, those building our infrastructure and those creating our jobs, be shackled with the burden to provide for their less industrious neighbors. No longer should government reward those who don't reward themselves. Today that all changes.

"This morning, the President of the People's Republic of China informed me that China would be the first sovereign nation to join this new global government. This was followed later in the day by pledges from Mexico, Guatemala, the Philippines, the Ivory Coast, Honduras, Haiti, Indonesia and the Dominican Republic. Today I ask the industrialized nations of the world to join us as well. The great democracies of the world— the United Kingdom, the United States, Germany, France, Japan: I assure you, this new system of government will not compromise your democracies, but, instead, will enhance them. Be bold, be progressive, be responsive to the yearnings of the world.

"Nations of the world, I implore you, it is time to unite."

Ship and Lori clasped hands throughout the address. A death sentence for all democratic ideals they held sacred had just been issued. Bonne-Saari had used his billions and control of the worldwide banking system to impose his will upon planet Earth.

"And it's only going to get worse," Ship muttered. "He's creating economic leper colonies. Anyone born into poverty or even into somewhat reasonable means will never be able to escape their station in life. It's against every concept of equality and opportunity."

"Well there is something we can do…"

"Lori, it bothers me to even think about it."

"But this is for the future of the world, Ship."

"Whatever's truly left of it."

* * *

79

Various Locations, November 27, 2010–February 4, 2011

One by one, countries of the world jumped on the Bonne-Saari bandwagon— India, Pakistan, Vietnam, South Africa, and Australia with more being rumored each day. Plans for his new worldwide government were becoming concrete. Each PGU— or Para-Geographic Governmental Unit— would determine its own fiscal policies, with the GCU serving as a common currency. The world's land-mass would be partitioned into logical geographic areas administered by Geographic Administrative Bureaus or GABs, providing geographic-relevant services such as police, fire, safety, infrastructure and a judicial system. Each GAB would be funded proportionally by the percentage of members of whatever PGUs resided in it. Different sets of laws and levels of services would apply to people from different PGUs although they resided in the same geographic area. Bonne-Saari and his cohorts had already named the "elite" PGUs: Apexia, Betamil, Chrysalix and Diamid.

Bonne-Saari's new governmental order would require a massive transition operation. Everyone in the world would be required to take a special test— named the Quality Algorithm or QA test— on a computer, smartphone or tablet. Based on their QA score, people would be assigned to one of the 15 PGUs— which would make them subject to that government's laws and entitlements. If individuals had no access to digital technology— or were illiterate — they would immediately be assigned to one of the very low PGUs— the

11th through 15th. Those people would be assigned to live in hypothetically "self-sustaining" Public Housing Areas.

"I'M sure they're going to gerrymander the GABs," Norm Steinberg said to the group as they sat in Ship's apartment discussing alternatives. "Monaco, Paris, Manhattan, Cape town, Singapore, Hong Kong will all be small, tight GABs, only affordable to members of the wealthiest PGUs, with maybe a small area for the hired help, and then big expansive parts of Africa and Mexico and Central America— areas with rampant poverty— will be large, unmanageable and grossly under-funded GABs."

"But how are the countries of the world buying his act? They're falling like dominoes, to his... vacuous, stupid... lines!" Ship exclaimed, pacing the room.

"Two reasons," Dr. Madison, the ex-Senator answered. "Most governments are at wit's end. They see it as impossible to reconcile the current extent of economic inequality with the concept of democracy and justice for all. The more affluent classes see this as a way to flee from the problems of the poor, the pensioners, and the social service recipients. And then, in my view, by promising the less-affluent their own self-determination— the ability, or at least the *perceived ability* to get out from under the thumb of governmental restraint— Bonne-Saari's message has struck a chord."

"But that's ridiculous," Ship blurted. "They're acting against their own self-interest."

"True," Steinberg answered. "But they don't think that. Bonne-Saari's whole system is one big canard. Although they've been lured by his promises of autonomy, safety, and self-determination, soon those in the middle-classes will realize the error of their ways. The higher PGUs will have relatively low tax rates and high levels of services because taxes levied on the very wealthy will not be subject to the burden of funding entitlements for the middle and lower classes. The middle PGUs will be forced to levy exorbitantly high tax rates to provide a paucity of services, much less than their citizens would have received in the past. The fiscal mess gets worse as you move down each level of the totem pole. If you ask me, the whole system is one giant time bomb."

"What a... *an a-hole!* There aren't even words to describe... him. *It.*" Ship exclaimed, shaking his head.

"Such is the power of a charismatic world leader." Dr. Morgan took a long puff on his pipe. "And the interesting thing is that although Bonne-Saari has painted a rosy, utopian picture, as Prime Minister of the Apexian government, the sole issuer of the GCU, he'll hold all the cards."

* * *

80

Various Locations, February 5–April 25, 2011

By design, Bonne-Saari had placed the United States government in an economic stranglehold. His global banking network kept on shorting the derivative securities backed by US Treasuries, throwing US interest rates higher every day and driving the US economy into a tailspin.

Each time the US government refused to either accept the GCU as its currency in place of the dollar, or join Bonne-Sari's new global government, he tightened the vice, going so far as to impose an embargo on US goods for all geographies that had joined his new global government. Midtown Manhattan became a shadow of its former self, with scores of homeless people living openly on the streets. Silicon Valley was replaced by Hyderabad and Bangalore in India as the center of global technological innovation. Even Hollywood suffered as the foreign market for American-made entertainment-content dried up.

Washington DC was beset with a horrific schism; there were those who accepted the inevitable and urged the government to immediately comply with Bonne-Saari's invitation to join him before more damage could be inflicted. Alternatively, there were those who were loyal to the core, willing to accept devastation before "surrendering" to Bonne-Saari's ultimatums. The schism grew wider and more rancorous by the day.

"There is a way to stop him, Ship," Lori said as they shared breakfast in his apartment.

"Which is?"

"He has to be eliminated," she answered, cold and stern.

"And what makes you think that will do it? He has thousands of devoted followers. Others will take over."

"You know the old saying, *'Cut off the head... '* "

"Even if we— if *I*— I'm torn, I guess. I'm really torn," he said. "If he succeeds, the world suffers in a way it's never suffered before. If he's, you know, defeated, yeah. What *would* take his place?"

"But if he's defeated, eliminated, that's a start. It destroys the momentum. Eventually, cooler heads will prevail, and this bullshit elitist government of his will go away. I know it. I just know it."

"And who's going to do it?" Ship asked.

"Why, us, of course."

"And what makes us so special?"

"Why not us?" Lori answered. "You were the one to expose him for what he really is. You smoked him in the debate. That would have been enough to stop him, except—"

"Except for the fact he has the world's economy by the balls," Ship completed her thought. "But that's reality. He has all the marbles."

"But does it really have to be?" she implored him. "Think about it: where's his headquarters, Ship?"

"That's easy, Sri Lanka."

"And what about Sri Lanka?" she asked.

"If I recall you spent several months there during med school."

"Yes. I lived in Sri Lanka. I volunteered in Sri Lanka. I know Sri Lanka."

"And why would that be any more than of marginal help?" he asked somberly.

"Because we have you, you're brilliant. We have me, I know Sri Lanka. So who better to do it than us?"

Sullenly, Ship sat silent in deep contemplation. "Very low odds of ever working," he mumbled. "Security would be over the top. You and I, we can't just—"

"Where there's a will, there's a way," she countered.

"And, even if we were successful, with prompt medical attention, there's a strong likelihood he could be saved."

"But there are some toxins which are virtually irreversible."

"Such as?"

"Batrachotoxin."

* * *

THE SEVERITY of Lori's words sent a disturbing signal to Ship. Here, someone as sweet and good-natured as Lori Bernstein, the love of his life, was reduced to contemplating cold-blooded murder. And everything happening was *real.* Not a fantasy, not a bad dream, not some movie, but *real.* Bonne-Saari was fundamentally changing the world order, the way human beings would interact with one another going forward. And it was all for the worse.

The dilemma gnawed at Ship day after day. There did not seem to be a good way out, only the lesser of many evils. It hammered away at his sense of right and wrong. For several days, he straddled a narrow moral pathway, wavering, waiting for clarity.

CLARITY CAME ON A MONDAY AFTERNOON.

"Dr. Ship?" the voice on the other end of the phone stated, distant and muffled.

Ship smiled. "Nnamdi?"

"Yes, it's me," Nnamdi answered from his hospital in Yaoundé.

"How are you?

"Fine, but…" Nnamdi's voice trailed off.

"I know. I know," Ship answered. "Are things any better in Cameroon than here?"

"No, things are not good at all. "

"I'm sorry to hear that."

"The clinic is being closed."

"What!" Ship exclaimed. "I thought that was funded for years into the future."

"No," Nnamdi said. "They took the funds."

"Why?"

"Where we live… everyone is poor… with this new government, there's no money to fund the clinic. They had to use the funds to pay for other things."

"Holy Christ!" Ship exclaimed. "Just what I thought would happen."

"I hate to ask, but is there anything you can do, Dr. Ship?" Nnamdi asked feebly.

"Maybe," Ship answered. "You just hang tight, Nnamdi. We'll figure something out. We have to."

Within seconds of Ship hanging up, the phone rang again. It was Lori.

"What's up?" Ship asked.

"Put the TV on now," she blurted.

"Why?"

"The President is making an announcement. We're joining. The US, I mean, is joining Bonne-Saari's government. The USA is no longer, Ship! The '*grand experiment in democracy*' is over and done with."

Silent, Ship bit his lip, absorbing the full impact of the news. Then he responded:

"And where can we get Batrachotoxin?"

* * *

81

Various Locations, February 5–May, 2011

Extracted from the golden poison-dart frog found in Colombia, batrachotoxin was perhaps the world's most lethal poison, causing irreversible paralysis as well as fatal damage to the heart muscle. The effects of the poison were swift, with death occurring within two to six hours. Once ingested, there was virtually no way to neutralize the poison's effectiveness.

"So how do we deliver it?" Ship asked Lori.

"Nano-molecules," she answered confidently.

"Huh?"

"We embed the batrachotoxin in small molecules which can be aerosolized and then released into the ventilation system of the building."

"So you have this all figured out?" Ship replied.

"Of course. I've been thinking about it ever since it became apparent that that beast would get his way."

"And how about the logistics, have you thought that through?"

"Well, we're going to need some allies. I would hope to get our whole group participating in some way or another."

Immediately, Ship shook his head. "No. Let's not."

"But, they're all very concerned, trustworthy. All very talented in their fields. Isn't there strength in numbers?"

"They're all infinitely talented and trustworthy. But you just never know.

One little leak and the whole idea backfires. We need to keep this small. We need someone who knows what they're doing, with this kind of— *thing*."

"So who do you suggest?" Lori asked.

"I have an idea," Ship answered.

JUSTIN REYNOLDS WAS AN EX-CIA OPERATIVE, having joined the agency after eighteen years in army intelligence, retiring with the rank of Lieutenant Colonel. Having known Reynolds since prep school, Ship suspected his friend wanted nothing to do with Bonne-Saari, but still approached him cautiously, not sure where his present-day loyalties might lie.

"God damn mother*fucker*!" Reynolds blasted out the moment Ship floated Bonne-Saari's name in their initial phone conversation.

"Yeah, you like him that much, huh?" Ship chided him.

"Fucking idiot is out of control. Using his sick wealth to destroy everything we worked for, fought for. Fuck 'em."

"So Justin, can we get together?"

"What's on your mind?" Reynolds asked suspiciously.

"I have an idea I'd like to bounce off you."

REYNOLDS LOOKED MUCH like Ship remembered him. Short and squat and with straight bristly white hair, the ex-CIA operative was a walking Coke machine. Several minutes into their face-to-face in a non-descript New York watering hole, Reynolds declared himself all-in. "The sooner we could put that howling little bitch down, the sooner things can get back to normal," he told Ship. "So what do you got in mind?"

"Ever hear of batrachotoxin?"

Reynolds eyes lit up. "Can you get us any?"

THE BASIC RUDIMENTS of the plan fell quickly into place. Through his sources Reynolds confirmed that Izan Bonne-Saari would usually lunch with his unofficial cabinet of twenty-eight advisors on Monday afternoons on the second floor of the Sri Lanka National Museum, probably the most classically beautiful structure in the entire country; Bonne-Saari had expropriated the upper floors of the structure as the temporary executive offices for his Prime Ministership of the Apexian government as he awaited the building of a new governmental palace. Downstairs, the building remained a museum.

Through contacts in Sri Lanka, Reynolds was able to obtain engineering diagrams of the building's HVAC system. Through an intermediary in Guatemala, Ship found a source of batrachotoxin in Colombia and a lab in Mexico that would embed the poison in small inhalable nano-molecules.

Reynolds devised an intriguing plan to find an operative in Sri Lanka while shielding the identities of himself, Ship and Lori. He would employ a tactic used for decades by organized crime: a chain of multiple contacts, each one only aware of two links in the chain, the person who would feed them the instructions, and then the person to whom they'd pass them on.

Finding people to form this chain of command was not a difficult endeavor.

While Bonne-Saari might have been popular to those assigned to the upper PGUs, he was despised by most assigned to the middle and lower PGUs. To them, his arrogant exploitation of the economic system and his cruel imposition of the QA test was tantamount to the bully child who hoarded all the toys in the sandbox. This vast pool of the disenfranchised provided Reynolds a fertile source of talent recruitment despite the risks involved.

Their first recruit was a Chinese-American in Boston, an acquaintance of Reynolds, who owned a string of restaurants. The restauranteur then recruited an operative in London, a bank clerk and sometimes drug dealer, who recruited another operative in Johannesburg, a landlord who owned a number of small apartment buildings, who then recruited an operative in Islamabad, a woman who owned several salons, who recruited an operative in Sri Lanka. The Sri Lankan, a middle-aged pharmacist with a store near the museum, recruited the most critical link in the entire chain: Fathima Ranatunga, a thirty-three-year-old curator who worked at the National Museum.

No one who knew Ranatunga would ever suspect her of being an insurrectionist. Quiet, studious and demure, she was an Oxford-educated scholar well-versed in the history of her country and southern Asia. Petite with straight dark hair, Fathima Ranatunga was a model employee at the museum where she researched and prepared exhibits, gave lectures on the history of Sri Lanka and, at times, served as an expert spokesperson.

Ranatunga had a particularly deep hatred for Bonne-Saari: in the new governmental order, her grandmother was classified in the Tenth PGU where there were no funds for elder-care for those over ninety. Hence, her grandmother was forced out of her nursing home and now withered away in the home of Ranatunga's parents, bereft of proper medical attention.

Ranatunga's first task was to recruit a person in the museum's maintenance department. In order to maintain proper insulation, she recruited him through a third party, Isuru Perera, a local restaurateur in Colombo. He, likewise, recruited Sahan Liyanage, a twenty-four-year-old custodian in the museum. All communications between Ranatunga and Liyanage would go through Perera. Neither knew the other's identity.

ONCE THE LAB in Mexico embedded the batrachotoxin into the inhalable nano-molecules, the resulting powder was mixed into an aerosol can that could be easily sprayed into a ventilation system. Two fully loaded cans, labeled as a generic brand of hair spray, were shipped to the pharmacist in Sri Lanka via Tokyo and Shanghai.

Upon receipt of the two cans, the pharmacist delivered a text message back through all the links in the chain. Eventually it got to Reynolds.

On Thursday, May 19th, Reynolds delivered the news to Ship. "Elvis is in the house."

Ship put down his phone and addressed Lori. "The cans arrived in Sri Lanka."

"So?"

"Everything else permitting, next Monday, May 23rd is D-Day."

82

Boston, MA/Colombo, Sri Lanka, Late evening, May 22–23, 2011

Late into the night of Sunday, May 22, Ship and Lori kept vigil at Ship's apartment. Half-way around the world, Bonne-Saari would be hosting his weekly luncheon with his twenty-eight closest advisors in several hours; Fathima Ranatunga, the museum curator, anonymous to them, would soon begin her daily walk to work.

Nine and a half hours ahead of Boston, Colombo enjoyed a warm, arid Monday morning. A bright sun peeked over the south-central highlands, brightening the city's maze of streets, thoroughfares, parks and gardens as its citizens awakened to a new work week.

The National Museum watched over Colombo like a tigress protecting her cubs. The building was beautiful, white and pristine, with arched windows and a flat roof. A placid, almost understated presence lounging behind lush lawns was accented by an elegant circle of low hedges surrounding a statue of the museum's founder, Sir William Henry Gregory, the British Governor of the island— then called Ceylon— during the late 1800s.

The placid exterior of the structure belied the cauldron of power boiling inside: the seat of Bonne-Saari's Apexian government. Like the tigress, if anyone threatened his dominion, Bonne-Saari would strike back swiftly and without compunction.

"THE PLANETS ARE ALIGNED," Ship said to Lori, the clock on his cable box reading 10:26 PM. "Should we do it?" He trembled as he spoke.

"Of course," she answered. "This is what we planned for."

"Yeah, I know," he responded hesitantly.

"What's that matter?"

"I guess it's just the finality of it all," he responded. "Once we say 'go' it will change our lives forever."

"That's why we're doing this, isn't it?" She stroked her hand across his cheek. "There's no turning back."

"Okay," he said somberly. "Let's push the button."

The "button" was a text message from Ship to Reynolds who would then contact his Chinese restaurateur friend in downtown Boston who would then contact his intermediary in London. The message would be passed from London to Johannesburg to Islamabad and then to the pharmacist in Colombo. The pharmacist would then place a pre-arranged text-message to Ranatunga: *Your prescription is ready for pick-up.*

When the buzz of her phone signaled the receipt of the text, Ranatunga's hands shook. She took a deep breath and began to walk, her usual path, nothing different from any other day.

When she turned onto Ward Place, her eyes lasered in on the pharmacy. With each step, her heart beat faster. She stopped in front. The image of her grandmother, dying a little bit more each day, stoked the flames of her anger. She wondered how rational people could actually believe Bonne-Saari's bullshit.

Emboldened, she entered the pharmacy.

At first, she lingered around the rows of merchandise as if looking for something. But she saw nothing— none of the numerous, brightly colored products stacked on the shelves, nor the promotion-laden shelf talkers with bold giant letters, nor the interruptive end-aisle displays— her mind, instead, concentrating on what would come next.

She shook.

It was time, she knew it.

She walked cautiously towards the prescription counter.

The pharmacist recognized her immediately. Silently, he nodded. Nodding back, she handed him a piece of paper. He examined the faux prescription, turned around, and picked two plastic bottles of generic decongestant off the shelf behind him. He then turned back towards the counter and placed the prescription bottles in a plastic shopping bag. Next, he deftly reached underneath the front counter and pulled out two aerosol containers, the ones camouflaged as cans of hair spray, and added them to the bag.

Ranatunga nodded silently and handed him her credit card. When he gave her the receipt, she scribbled her signature and, shaking inside, promptly headed for the exit.

SHE CONTINUED along past Viharamahadevi Park. When she arrived at the museum, there were two busloads full of schoolchildren, noisy and full of energy, standing in a haphazard line waiting to get through the security check at the side entrance. Nervous already, her anxiety grew as she waited and waited for what seemed an interminable amount of time. Her sour expression left no doubt she was apprehensive. It was obvious to the co-worker standing beside her.

"It's just another bunch of fascinated schoolchildren." He shrugged at her.

"I guess so." She nodded.

It took the security guards almost ten minutes to get all the kids through the checkpoint. From the way they were dressed and acted, Ranatunga thought they were probably from a school catering to the Sixth or Seventh PGU.

Finally, she reached the front of the line. Brusquely, she placed her purse and plastic shopping bag on the inspection table. The inspector opened the purse and emptied the contents of the bag.

"What's this?" he pointed to one of the cans, not recognizing the brand name.

"Hairspray," she answered.

"Two cans?"

With a nervous chuckle, she shrugged her shoulders. "Bad hair day."

"Me too." He tipped his hat and exposed his shiny bald head.

She giggled.

Smiling, he motioned her through.

ALL MORNING, the plastic shopping bag sitting on the floor next to her desk taunted Ranatunga. She strained to focus on her work, but then would impulsively look over at it. Obsessively, she glanced again and again. She had no idea what the two cans in that bag contained, but certainly understood the consequences of what might happen when she sprayed them into the museum's ventilation system.

At 11:15am, she was scheduled to speak to the visiting students in the museum auditorium. She had a canned presentation complete with slides, on the history of Sri Lanka—from the ancient Anuradhapura Kingdom to the arrival of Buddhism, all the way through the invasions from India, the British colonization, finally to the island's independence. She had given it so many times before she could recite it on autopilot.

Usually, she would never even notice the faces in her audience. Today she did, her eyes drawn to a little girl in the front row with a cute, round face, dark bangs, wide expressive eyes and a smile that expressed sheer wonderment. During the Question and Answer period, the little girl raised her hand.

"And what's your name?" Ranatunga asked her.

"Rashmi," the little girl answered.

"And your question is?"

"Is Sri Lanka still a country?" the little girl asked.

"Well sort of," Ranatunga answered. "We're still one big island. Our people still share the same cultural heritage, but there are different types of governments that crisscross our island."

"Why?" Rashmi asked.

"That's a very difficult question to answer. There are many reasons."

"But it doesn't make any sense," the little girl added.

"Someday it will," Ranatunga answered. "When you're older, you'll understand."

The confused look on the cute young girl's face cast an everlasting imprint in Ranatunga's mind. Any ambivalence she might have had about her intended mission later that day dissipated after focusing on that little girl. She realized what she was about to do would result in a better world for Rashmi and all children like her.

IN A SMALL WORK-ROOM deep in the entrails of the building, Sahan Liyanage, the maintenance worker recruited by the restaurateur, sat impatiently at a small wooden desk. At 12:16, he received the text: *Your reservations for tonight are confirmed.*

Immediately, he proceeded to the HVAC control-room two doors down and rerouted the ventilation system, restricting the airflow from the intake vent where Ranatunga would spray the cans, assuring their contents would only be blown into the room where Bonne-Saari and his advisors were lunching. Then he removed the filter from the air-handler so the contents of the cans would proceed into the system unfiltered. Finally, he set the blowers to their highest setting, then signaled back to the restaurateur.

SEVERAL MINUTES LATER, Ranatunga, back in her office, received a text from the restaurateur: *Thank you for your patronage.*

Shaking, she slowly pushed herself up from her chair and glanced down at the plastic shopping bag that had been taunting her all morning. She took a deep breath, hesitated, and then picked it up. Trembling, she walked out her door and down the corridor for the ladies' room.

It was time for Step Two.

HIS NOSE BURIED in the day's newspaper, Liyanage was startled when his workroom door abruptly opened. He flinched.

His supervisor, Nuwan De Soysa walked in.

"What's up?" Liyanage asked his boss, innocently.

"Gotta adjust the air conditioning," the supervisor answered.

"*Why?*" Liyanage swallowed hard. "I just reset everything."

"Who knows?" De Soysa shrugged. "Someone upstairs wants us to."

"Do they understand what they're doing, how this all works? Liyanage asked.

"Probably not," his supervisor answered. "But if they tell us to adjust it, we'll adjust it. Let's not complicate orders from upstairs with the facts."

"I can do it." Liyanage snapped up from his seat.

"Don't worry. I'll take care of it." De Soysa patted him on the shoulder and walked out of the workroom down to the HVAC room. Once there, the supervisor reset several settings, reversing all the adjustments Liyanage had made only several minutes earlier.

Back in his workroom, Liyanage shuddered, his nerves tingling. Reflexively, he barreled down the hallway towards the HVAC room.

He bumped into De Soysa exiting the room. "What's up?" his supervisor asked.

"I need to go into the HVAC room." Liyanage stuttered his way through his response.

"Why?" De Soysa asked.

Liyanage thought quickly. "Ummmmm… I left my keys there."

"You sure? You're acting sort of strange."

"Yeah, I left my keys there."

"Okay. I'll let you in." De Soysa turned back and unlocked the door and flicked on the light. His eyes quickly scanned the small room. "Doesn't look like they're here."

"They gotta be there." Liyanage bolted in behind De Soysa. Desperate, he looked around, his body shaking. "I'm sure they're here. They gotta be. Let me look, you can go." Liyanage got down on his hands and knees and rummaged around the floor.

"Don't worry, I'll help." De Soysa hovered over him.

With each second, Liyanage felt more desperate. *He needed to get De Soysa out of that room and do it now, lest something terrible might happen.*

The ladies room was empty. The grated intake-vent was about six feet above the floor behind one of the stalls. Gently, Ranatunga opened the stall door and walked in. Breathing heavily, she sat on the toilet, waiting to get up the gumption to spray the cans into the vent.

She reached for the shopping bag.

Just as she was about to swipe the cans out of the bag and jump up to begin spraying, she heard something, or at least she thought she did: the *click, click, click* of footsteps walking down the corridor.

She braced herself, thinking the ladies room door would swing open.

It did not.

She wiped her brow. Now was the time, she convinced herself, as good as any. Standing up from the toilet, she pulled one of the cans out of her bag. She reached up and sprayed the entire contents into the vent, then repeated her actions with the second can.

Immediately, she placed the cans back in her bag and walked out of the ladies room and back to her office.

She was now left with one final task: her signal back to the pharmacist. She texted him a message: *I have a question about one of my prescriptions.* Then he communicated back to his contact in Islamabad who passed the message back through the chain, eventually reaching Ship and Lori in Boston.

"Everything's done," Ship told Lori when he received the text. "Now we just have to wait."

"We did good." Lori squeezed his hand.

Thirty-five minutes elapsed before circumstances at the museum indicated anything out of the ordinary.

At 1:42pm, an urgent request came from the cafeteria for the museum nurse to immediately rush downstairs: one of the visiting schoolchildren was sweating profusely and unable to move the left side of her torso. Her teachers feared she may be suffering from some sort of stroke.

The nurse immediately examined the young child and realized something was terribly wrong; indeed, perhaps a stroke or some sort of cardiac issue. Just as she put in the call for an ambulance, two other children, both boys, began to exhibit similar symptoms.

A teacher screamed.

By the time Ranatunga stepped outside for her usual lunchtime stroll, a flurry of activity, a full-blown commotion, had erupted outside the building's side entrance. Five or six EMS trucks lined the street, while a SWAT team in camouflage suits and gas masks rushed into the building. A screeching siren wailed on and on. Police officers with bullhorns instructed those inside the building to evacuate.

Ranatunga walked across the street and observed from a distance. While she had no knowledge of the contents of those two cans, she realized that whatever was happening in the building was the result of her actions. She felt proud of herself. Usually one of the powerless masses, for once she could actually exercise power, power she hoped would bring down an evil system of government and restore dignity to everyday people.

Her pride soon turned to disbelief, then shock.

She watched as EMS personnel in gas masks wheeled stretcher after stretcher out of the building, each carrying a body, one after another, some of the faces covered with sheets, others not. She tensed up as she realized that most of the bodies appeared to be small, much smaller than adults; certainly not the bodies of Bonne-Saari and his colleagues.

They were the bodies of the children she had just lectured in the auditorium. Someway, somehow, something backfired.

She rushed across the street to get a closer look. Whirling her way through a chaotic swarm of medical personnel, SWAT teams, EMS vehicles, police officers, stretchers and observers, she was suddenly jolted— *socked in the face*— by one of the myriad haphazard visions streaming past her eyes.

Her mind filtered everything else out— the chaotic buzz of all the activity around her: the sirens, the screams, the blur of the crowd— her eyes trained on one haunting image, one particular stretcher, one particular face.

It was Rashmi, the beautiful inquisitive little girl in the front row, the one who had asked such an innocent, but telling, question, now struggling to inhale the very last breaths of a life cut far too short.

Ranatunga screamed: a piercing, screeching scream.

With the flurry of commotion whirling around her, hardly anyone noticed.

Quickly, she caught her breath. Her eyes scanned the horrific panorama of confusion, panic and death. Her mind raced, processing a wide spectrum of conflicting feelings; she had no idea what to do. Flush white, her heart pounding against her chest, sweat pouring down her face, her instincts prompted her to rush, run far, far away.

She bolted off.

Around 4:30am in Boston, Ship and Lori received an initial third-party confirmation that their plan had taken effect. CNN was the first to report it: "We just received word from Colombo, Sri Lanka that apparently some sort of lethal toxin had been released in the National Museum where Apexia Prime Minister Izan Bonne-Saari was lunching with advisors. Witnesses have observed bodies being carted out of the building, but we know nothing more. We will keep you posted as reports continue in."

Sternly, Ship focused on the television screen, biting his lip.

Lori nuzzled up behind him, placing her arm over his shoulder.

"Why such a sour face?" she asked. "Everything's going according to plan."

Silent, he paused and solemnly shook his head.

"Whether or not we achieve our goal," he began, his eyes trained on the screen, "the very fact we had to resort to this in a world that's supposed to be civilized is all the proof you need that we're not."

Ranatunga rushed down Cambridge Place, past the Royal College. She had no idea where she was headed; her rushing adrenaline prompting her to run, run anywhere. *What had she done? Her actions had punished the very people she intended to save.* She rushed on and on, tirelessly, the sheer energy of it muffling her mounting feelings of shame and depression. If she stopped, her emotions would overwhelm her, thrust her into a deep, dark hole from which she might never escape.

She could not allow herself to stop. Not now, not ever.

Ship and Lori kept their eyes on the television, waiting for every fresh bit of news. By now, CNN had a camera crew outside the museum. The on-scene reporter gave an update: "Although not confirmed, it is believed that some sort of toxin was released through the building's ventilation system. Again this is not confirmed, but it is believed the toxin was intended to poison Prime Minister Bonne-Saari and his advisors. However, apparently, the toxin poisoned the air in a downstairs cafeteria where a busload of schoolchildren on a field trip were eating lunch. So far, there have been at least seven fatalities and virtually all of the remaining children, teachers and the cafeteria workers are displaying similar symptoms. We will update our information as soon as we learn of any new developments."

Immediately, the phone rang. It was Reynolds. "Fuck! What happened?"

"We're fucking screwed, we're murdered, that's what happened." Ship's hand was rattling so vigorously he could hardly hold the phone.

"Calm down. Calm down."

"But what happened? You set it all up."

"I don't know. It's hard to tell if it was an accident or if someone booby-trapped us."

"How could someone booby-trap us?" Ship asked.

"Only way would be if there was a mole in our chain. I doubt that would happen, but it's the only way."

"So what do we do now?" Ship interrupted.

"First of all, don't panic. Go about everything like business as usual, okay? Let's not do anything out of the ordinary, at least for a bit. It'll just raise their suspicions."

"We're just gonna stay here like sitting ducks?"

"No. No. I'll figure something out. Just give me a little time."

"How much?"

"A couple of hours."

Ship put down the phone, quivered, then threw up onto the floor.

* * *

RANATUNGA STOPPED BUT ONCE. At Flower Terrace Road, breathing heavily, she tore off her shoes and threw them at the curb. Barefoot, she continued—around a bend, down a thoroughfare, then onto Palm Court. Her chest heaved with every stride, yet she could not stop, she would not stop. She weaved her way towards the shoreline; people, restaurants, stores, office buildings blurring by her. She had done something terrible. She had killed those little children. Running, running forever, was her only option, her only recourse. She had nowhere else to go.

She dashed by a bank, the Post Office, down a short lane, and then swiftly cut right down Colombo Plan Road. She stopped briefly: the city's edge, the sea's crashing breakers sweeping up along the shoreline. In a burst, she dashed off, hugging the coast, bound for nowhere.

Her feet bled. Sweat drenched her dress. Her breathing could not keep up with her buzzing energy, yet she ran on. Forward, forward, onto nowhere. She stopped: the station, a train barreling in.

The whistle blew, the engine roared, the tracks rattled. Her shame, her guilt, her confusion blurred into a swirling enigma. She could not focus, could not process.

Impulsively, she acted.

She leapt onto the tracks.

* * *

83

Colombo, Sri Lanka, Late Afternoon, May 23, 2011

Three hours later, Bonne-Saari addressed the media.

The short, brushy-haired Prime Minister walked up to the make-shift podium, his jaw firm and square, his voice defiant: "We have suffered a great tragedy today. Forty-eight people—children, teachers, cafeteria workers— were mercilessly killed by a toxin released through the National Museum's ventilation system. Without doubt, the toxin was intended for my advisors and I. I am deeply sorry that some misguided peoples' hatred for me resulted in today's tragedy. A wicked, evil museum employee" Bonne Saari looked down at his notes, "...a woman named Fathima Ranatunga, we believe, was the one who perpetrated this terrible crime. We have learned that this insurgent, this Ms. Ranatunga, took her own life only an hour or so after our tragedy..."

The members of the media gasped amidst some awkward muffled clapping.

"In an act of extreme cowardice, she threw herself onto the train tracks at Kollupitiya station." Bonne-Saari paused and looked up, a cold, defiant stare: "*May she forever rot in hell.*" He paused for effect. "We are not naïve. We do not for one moment believe that this tragedy was planned by Ms. Ranatunga alone. She was merely an operative, a pawn. There are many envious of our new governmental system. They are many envious of me. I vow a pledge to you today: we will find whoever planned this wicked tragedy and, once found, they will be brought to swift and permanent justice."

* * *

As each second passed, Ship felt sicker and sicker. His stomach knotted, sweat poured from every duct in his body and he experienced a headache like none he ever had suffered before. Lying on the couch— a compress over his forehead— he watched the events unfold on TV. He blanched when the newscaster stated: "Here's what Apexian Prime Minister Bonne Saari said about the perpetrator, Fathima Ranatunga."

"We have learned that this insurgent, this Ms. Ranatunga, took her own life only an hour or so after our tragedy. In an act of extreme cowardice, she threw herself onto the train tracks at Kollupitiya station. May she forever rot in hell."

"She was just as innocent a victim as all of those kids," Ship whispered to Lori. "She was trying to do good and now— we failed, Lori. We failed miserably…"

"No, we didn't," she responded. "We'll get him. The battle's just begun."

"I'd like to believe that but somehow I can't."

"Well there *must be* something I can do," Lori said.

"Yeah, change the past."

When the phone rang, Ship pushed himself off the couch.

"Justin?"

"Yeah."

"So?"

"Okay, okay." Reynolds' voice was rushed. "I've worked it all out."

"What are we gonna do?" Ship asked, Lori hovering beside him.

"First of all, we're gonna wait 'til tomorrow, tomorrow night."

"You sure?"

"Yeah, I'm sure. I'm gonna have a stolen car parked, clean plates, off Exit 10A on the Mass Pike, near Worcester. I'll give you the address."

"Yeah?"

"You and Lori should get there about 9, 9:30. Any way you can, except not in your own vehicles."

"The train?"

"Yeah, that works. Then take a taxi and get the car, but have 'em drop you off a few blocks away. The key'll be under the floor-mat. Then I'm gonna give you another address, in New York state, near Albany. It's an old warehouse. I'll meet you there in another stolen car."

"Then what?" Ship asked.

"You'll see," Reynolds answered. "Rather not say on the phone."

"Okay. Okay. Got it." Ship clicked off his phone and took a deep breath.

"So what is it? Lori asked anxiously. "What are we doing?"

"Check the train schedule to Worcester."

* * *

84

South Station, Boston, May 24–28, 2011

On weeknights at 7pm, South Station Boston transitioned from its rush-hour hustle-bustle to a much more restrained level of activity. Ship and Lori slipped into the station unnoticed. They strode across the main floor undeterred by the few clumps of commuters scattered around. Instructed by Reynolds not to purchase their tickets at the counter, but rather from the conductor en-route— thereby minimizing detection by surveillance cameras— Ship immediately looked up at the main display, scanning for the 7:40 to Worcester.

"There," Lori pointed. "Gate 7."

Ship grabbed her hand as they proceeded brusquely towards the gate.

EVERYTHING FELT different as they stepped from the platform onto the train. Usually their minds would be preoccupied with anything other than the ride, taking their mode of transportation for granted. Now both were extremely aware of every single detail, their eyes scanning each and every passenger in the car, wondering if this one or that one might be a spy or an informant or, worse yet, one of Bonne-Saari's plain-clothed intelligence agents.

They hardly talked, they barely acknowledged each other during the next hour. The ride itself seemed meaningless, just another leg in a long journey marching them closer to their ultimate fate, whatever that may be.

WHEN THE TRAIN stopped at Worcester station, both remained circumspect. As he strode off the train, Ship discreetly glanced back to assure no one was paying undue attention. Holding hands, Ship and Lori marched forward and spoke without looking at each other, their eyes laser-focused straight ahead.

"See anything?" Lori asked as they walked.

"Not that I can tell," he answered.

"I'm not sure if that's a good thing or bad thing," she said, hardly moving her jaw.

"I hear ya."

The taxi-stand was right across the street from the station. Parked in front, two well-weathered cabs waited for their next fare. The drivers were in the small office with the dispatcher, reading their papers, drinking coffee and shooting the shit.

"Can we get a ride?" Ship stuck his head through the office doorway.

"Sure," the dispatcher answered. "Where to?"

Ship pulled a crumpled piece of paper out of his pocket and squinted at the scribbling. "Ummmm… 419 Canal Street."

"Canal Street?" The dispatcher chuckled. "That ain't no place for a high-dollar pair like you."

Ship shrugged. "Looks can be deceiving, I guess."

CANAL STREET WAS NOT one of Worcester's high-rent districts. The houses appeared as if they had been there for years. A few were abandoned, plywood covering their windows, and several looked as though they hadn't seen a coat of paint since the 1950s. The street lights were hardly helpful, providing scant illumination— just enough to give Ship and Lori a general idea of the area and just little enough to cloud everything in murkiness.

They could hear random chatter from inside some of the houses and saw a bunch of teens sitting on the front stoop of another; the young kids did not even acknowledge Ship and Lori's presence as they walked quietly by. Near the corner of the block, a constant mumble groaned, sometimes escalating to a moderate twang. It was coming from one of the boarded-up houses. A *safe-house*, they presumed, probably heroin addicts.

"How much farther?" Lori asked as they rounded the corner.

"Two blocks that way." Ship pointed down the street.

THE CAR, an old eggshell-blue 2007 Honda Civic, was parked just where Reynolds said it would be— in a small lot abutting a convenience store and gas station. The moment Ship opened the door, the strong odor of cigarette smoke attacked them. He reached under the mat and found the key.

Heading westward on the Mass Pike late at night provided them with a predictable monotony. The static from the radio would buzz into the sounds of music or an announcer and then, just as soon as it came in, would buzz back to static. Lori futzed with the radio tuner, but it didn't change anything.

THEY PULLED up to the warehouse at about 2am. Reynolds had given them a four-digit combination for the padlock on the chain link fence at an obscure back entrance. Ship rolled the barrels on the lock until the numbers aligned and then yanked. It opened. Ship held up the lock and nodded at Lori back in the car.

"Are you really sure we should do this?" she asked as Ship slipped back into the driver's seat. "You sure this isn't some sort of setup?"

"You've hardly talked for the last four hours and now you're questioning all this?" He responded.

"Yeah, I mean…"

"What are our options?" asked Ship.

"How well do you know this guy Reynolds?"

"Fine time to be asking," Ship answered, "but I've known him over thirty years."

"I didn't say how *long*, I said how *well*."

"Don't worry, Lori." Ship shifted the car into Drive. "I trust him."

Lori sat silently as Ship drove the car through the open gate.

SHIP HAD BEEN INSTRUCTED to park the car in a space at the northwest corner of the expansive lot— about a hundred yards from the loading dock— and then to blink his lights twice every five minutes until Reynolds met up with them.

"Where is he?" Lori mumbled after ten minutes had passed.

"Be patient," Ship responded.

The third time Ship blinked his lights, he sensed motion nearby. The sound of tires crushing gravel intensified until a car crunched to a halt right in front of them. It just stood there parked, lights off, for several ominous seconds.

They braced themselves.

The driver's side door creaked open. Lori squeezed Ship's hand. When the man stepped out and turned to them in the murky light, they could make out his face: Reynolds. He motioned for them to step out.

"How was the trip?" he whispered to Ship.

"Good. Good. Nothing out of the ordinary."

"Okay," Reynolds said. "Now let's get out of here."

"WHAT'S NEXT?" Ship asked as they entered Reynolds' car.

"Just watch," Reynolds answered as he drove them over to the loading dock.

They headed towards a lone 18-wheeler being loaded at the far end of the dock. He stopped the car and opened his door.

"Follow me," he ordered.

The three of them walked up onto the loading dock towards the point where the back end of the lone truck was being packed. Reynolds motioned for them to stand back and then, by himself, walked up to a guy at the back of the truck holding a clipboard.

Reynolds and the guy whispered for several seconds, then Reynolds called them over.

"Here's our new home for the next couple of days," Reynolds pointed to the inside of the trailer. Scores of boxes were tightly packed from floor to ceiling, but a narrow alleyway had been left vacant at the right-hand side.

"Follow me." Reynolds walked them over to the alleyway and squeezed himself in, practically walking sideways to allow his squat, thickly built frame to fit. Lori and Ship followed. The tightness of the space and its foreboding darkness made the eighty-foot walk an ominous, if not treacherous, journey.

At the end of the alleyway, surprisingly there was light and a little space set up like a room. There were three cots, electrical outlets, some chairs, a microwave, a refrigerator stocked with food, a port-a-john and even a periscope so they could peer outside.

"All the comforts of home," Reynolds quipped as they entered the small space, no more than several hundred square feet in area.

"So how long are we going to have to stay here?" Lori asked.

"Only a few days," Reynolds answered.

"Then what?" Ship asked.

"In a few hours, this truck is bound for Mexico. I have this old farmhouse in the middle of nowhere where Lori and you can stay."

"And you?" Ship asked.

"I'm gonna hop on another truck and go on to Panama. Keep us separate for now."

"And how long are we going to have to stay there?" Lori asked.
"Can't answer that yet."

A MONOTONOUS ORDEAL, the trip's four days seemed like four weeks. The constant rumbling on the road, the cramped quarters, the paucity of things to do and, of course, the underlying odor from the port-o-john infused them with misery.

About a day and a half into their trek, Reynolds pulled something out of his pocket. "You play cards?" he asked.

"Why not?" Ship nodded over towards Lori.

She shrugged.

A marathon of card games ensued: blackjack, pinochle, all variations of poker, hearts and even go-fish. It lasted hours until the games became monotonous as well. Their cell phones provided some stimulation. They would browse the web for something interesting to read, but the trailer's shaky wi-fi and the sparse cell coverage in some areas made the effort more of an ordeal than a rewarding pastime. And, then, there was always solitaire.

ALTHOUGH THEY KEPT logical track of time on their phones and watches, they found it difficult for their bodies to relate. Time was just a number, there was nothing really to grab onto except the artificial yellow light of their quarters. Sporadic peeks outside through the periscope didn't help. They could certainly see the shades of daylight and nighttime's darkness, but they processed them as pictures, not part of their environment.

On the fourth day they waited with renewed enthusiasm. Each time they heard the transmission growl or the brakes squeeze tight, they prayed it was the final stop, the one that would allow them to escape their captivity.

Finally it came, about five minutes after the truck ground to a grunting halt, several sharp knocks rapped on the side of the truck. They could hear the muffled voice of the driver shouting: "We're here. Time to get out."

Immediately, their spirits lifted. At last, they were free from their mobile prison, they could be part of the real, natural world again, breathe fresh air, absorb pure sunlight. This time when they squeezed through that narrow alleyway leading to the back, they did it with exuberance.

Once through the narrow space, Reynolds pounded his fist on the back panel. "We're here. You can open up."

As the panel rolled upwards, they squinted, their eyes recalibrating to the sun's intense brightness. Once adjusted, though, their eyes stared directly at an unexpected, incongruous sight.

"By order of the Apexian government, you are all under arrest for 48 counts of murder and the attempted assassination of Prime Minister Izan Bonne-Saari."

Seven helmeted soldiers in camouflage gear formed a semi-circle around the rear of the truck, pointing automatic weapons at them.

There was no escape.

* * *

TIME FRAME: 2014/2007

85

Boothbay Harbor, Maine, Morning, June 11, 2014

The morning sun shone brilliantly across Boothbay Harbor, tickling the frothy waters with a healthy morning shimmer, then beaming through the large leaded windows of the Pennfield estate just as it had thousands of mornings before. But this day, things were different; Christopher Pennfield could tell the moment the sun's warm glow caressed his face.

At first, he tossed, tangled in his sheets. He was not a genteel sleeper, never was. He didn't actually sleep on his bed, he wrestled with it. He yawned and stretched, drinking in the air as his eyes slowly focused.

Actually, today he felt a bit better than usual, more vibrant, almost youthful. He didn't have nearly the headache of most mornings; no throbbing in his brain, no pressure beneath his eyes, no cotton in his mouth. He looked over towards the cherry curio next to his easy chair and noticed his collection of spirits and wines was missing. *Had he abstained last evening and forgotten about it? Had someone taken them away? God forbid.*

Abruptly, Pennfield pulled the rope on the side of his bed and summoned his housekeeper.

"Nora? Nora!"

"Coming, Mr. Pennfield," she called up from the parlor.

"Can you bring me a nice eye-opener?" He asked, as she stood in front of his door.

"Of course. Five minutes, sir."

Pennfield sat up on the bed and squinted at the beaming rays of sun. This is funny, he thought. If he had abstained last night, he would remember if someone removed his collection of spirits. But he didn't remember a thing. He could understand having a blackout if he had drank to his usual level. But he probably hadn't. So there was the possibility that he was blacking out in a state of sobriety.

Something is strange, very strange.

"MORNIN', Mr. Pennfield." Nora entered the room carrying a tray with a Bloody Mary and a chaser of vodka on the side.

"And how are you this fine day, my dear?" Pennfield reciprocated.

"Fine, Mr. Pennfield." She placed the tray down on the night table. "Mrs. Pennfield rang earlier."

"Really?" Pennfield answered, stunned. "What would she want?"

"Didn't really leave a message, Mr. Pennfield. But she asked if you could try to get back to her before noon."

"Of course."

"And then the provost called."

"The *Provost?"*

"Yes, she said there was an issue she needed to discuss."

"She?"

"Yes, I told her you'd get back to her as soon as you woke."

"Surely." Pennfield sipped his Bloody Mary, his mind distant and confused, attempting to determine what was happening to him.

"And, of course, remember, Dr. Bilardi will be here at two."

"Wha—?" he answered blank-faced, his mind wandering.

"Dr. Bilardi. He'll be here at two."

"Yes, thanks."

"Just call when you need me," she said, turning towards the door.

"Yes, of course, of course."

THE MOMENT NORA left the room Pennfield gulped the entire Bloody Mary then chased it with the shot of vodka. Still, his nerves pulsed, his mind clamored, his face moistened.

He ran his hand across his cheeks, wiping the sweat away. Something felt different, quite different; things he had taken granted for years just didn't seem right. His usual taut, crackled facial skin, stretched tight across his cheekbones, felt smooth and contoured, full of life. Then for some unexplainable reason, he gazed towards his right leg. Since the instant he awakened, he had ignored it; but now he noticed the incongruence. *Why the hell was the bandage missing?* He always had a bandage on his right foot.

Immediately, he raced across the floor to the bathroom. Surprisingly, he sensed his right leg didn't drag. Everything felt pure and clean: no arthritic jolts of pain, no lazy right foot, bandaged and trailing, no deep, heavy breaths. Effortlessly, he glided across the room.

Egads!

What he saw in the mirror shocked him. Vain by nature, Pennfield would normally be elated if he suddenly appeared ten years younger. Today it terrified him.

Quickly, he decided he needed an anchor, something to unite this horrifically weird incident with reality, at least reality as he knew it.

He looked behind himself, and then stepped out, quickly scanning the entire room. Everything was familiar, but just slightly off kilter. His cherry curio was there, but no liquor. He swerved over towards the windows. *Were the curtains the same?* He couldn't quite tell, but he thought something was just a tad different. The bedspread: he had hardly noticed it. *Was that new?* But it was of little consequence. Nora had always changed them from time to time. Carefully his eyes journeyed around the room until they came back to the curio.

Of course, of course, he should have thought of it instantly. It would provide incontrovertible proof one way or another.

He ripped open the drawer to the curio and pulled it out: the newspaper article, the *dreaded* newspaper article.

As he unfolded it, the shock overwhelmed him.

May 27, 2011 — Pennfield Sentenced to Death — Philanthropist doctor, Arthur Shipkin Pennfield, was sentenced to death without trial for his role in an assassination attempt on Apexian Prime Minister Izan Bonne-Saari which resulted in the inadvertent deaths of 48 innocent people. As a youth, Pennfield suffered from a rare affliction, Catatonic Schizophrenia, which was cured by Nobel Prize winning psychiatrist, Dr. Emilio Hazard…

Pennfield shivered, shaking vigorously, giant drops of sweat pouring from his brow. *So this was it! One of Weisman's cockamamie theories had proven true. That interloper from the future had hijacked Ship's past. Somehow, some-*

way, Ship had been cured of his affliction, but had still become the victim of the curse in place of himself.

INSIDE, Pennfield rattled. It was a combination of both extreme anxiety, and a fear that he may be trapped in some type of weird place— or time, or dimension— from which he could never possibly escape.

He tried to calm himself; he needed to learn more about exactly where he was and how he got there. *Collect facts.* That's all he could do: collect facts. *But how?* He'd have to take a risk and make a call. Quickly, he surmised it should be the provost, had to be. Elizabeth knew too much, would be very hard to fool. And how could he fake not knowing his own "wife's" number? He called down to Nora.

"Nora, can you be a dear and find me the provost's number? I seemed to have misplaced my directory."

"Certainly, Mr. Pennfield," she called up to him.

Within minutes, she returned with a scrap of paper: *Laura Vanderkliff 404-397-8102.*

He tapped out the number on the bedside phone. With each ring, he shook vigorously, fearing what he might discover.

"Hello?"

"Provost Vanderkliff? Chris Pennfield. I'm returning your call."

"President Pennfield, thank God it's you, Chris. Have you seen it yet?"

"Seen what?" *President? He was President?* Another confirming piece of evidence.

"The latest issue of Newsweek. There's an exposé on the college on page 47."

"What does it say?"

"Here's the headline and I quote, *'Northern Alpine College: A College by Any Other Name Does Not Smell as Sweet'*"

"Oh my. Read on…" He grimaced. *Northern Alpine College?*

" *'In 2012, Pennfield College, a highly respected small liberal arts college in Percer, Vermont founded by the Pennfield Foundation, changed its name to Northern Alpine College to disassociate itself from Arthur Shipkin Pennfield, the family scion who had disgraced the family in the 2011 botched assassination attempt on Apexian Prime Minister Izan Bonne-Saari, resulting in the deaths of 48 innocent victims. Today, the college still suffers from the wounds of its past. Applications are down by forty percent and of those admitted, even fewer are choosing to attend. In the past, the college attracted students whose profiles would have placed them in the Diamid and Fifth PGUs, but now the student population is composed mostly of students in the Sixth and Seventh PGUs. As a result, the college has been forced to seek funding in order to support what has been referred to as by far, the highest level of financial need per student by any institution of higher learning in the world.'* It's not sustainable, Chris, this is very serious, it's terrible."

"Indeed. And where did they get the information?"

"We don't know, but we have our suspicions."

"Oh?"

"Parker Whitehurst," she responded. "Ever since we let him go as Admissions Director, he's had an axe to grind."

"And I can assume we've been called by every news organization far and wide?"

"Media Relations has been flooded with calls," the provost answered. "Dan Haverkost thinks you should make a statement."

"Yes, yes indeed. But it has to be well thought-out. Have him draft something, will you? And I'll do the same. Between the two we'll cobble something together."

"Fine. We'll get right on it."

"Yes. Either you or he call me the moment you have something."

"Of course," she paused for a moment, "and Chris…"

"Yes?"

"I can only imagine how much this pains you."

"I appreciate that Laura, I really do."

IMMEDIATELY HE RUSHED over to the laptop on the large antique desk in the corner of the study. He typed in Google.com as the URL. *Damnit, why was this fucking computer so slow? Was this still a dial-up connection?* Finally, he got a response: Sorry. Website Not Found. *No Google? What was the world coming to?*

He scanned the browser, settling on the upper right-hand corner where he was accustomed to finding a search window. Yes, it was there. Except instead of the usual Google logo, all it had was a decorative capital letter "K." He typed in his search phrase anyway: *Pennfield College.* Quickly, the results of his search appeared on the screen. At the top of the page was a splashy logo for something called *KERFUFFLE. What the hell?* He clicked on the first entry of his results page.

A burning pit erupted in Pennfield's gut.

According to KERFUFFLE, or whatever it was, Pennfield College was, of course, funded by his great-grandfather, Alfred Pennfield, and was— or had been— a small, academically prestigious college in Vermont. After Arthur Shipkin Pennfield's assassination attempt, the institution was renamed Northern Alpine College to disassociate the Pennfield name with the college. The Pennfield name, a moniker he had savored like a badge of honor his entire life, was now regarded as a badge of shame.

He felt nauseous, yearning to vomit, but unwilling to force it upon himself.

"Mr. Pennfield?"

He snapped out of it and swiveled his head toward Nora.

"Mrs. Pennfield is on the phone."

"She is?" Confused, Pennfield answered. "I thought I was to call her."

"That's how I understood it, sir, but she seems intent on speaking with you now."

"Ok. Ok."

The words blurted into his ear the moment he picked up. "Don't tell me that woman is there with you!"

"Huh?"

"Don't try to be coy, Christopher, we all know the rules of this game."

"And exactly whom do you think is with me?"

"Oh please. Laura Vanderkliff, that slut. It's bad enough that the whole town of Percer knows about your shenanigans. It's worse when you go cavorting around with her in Maine when you're supposed to be recuperating."

"*Recuperating?* I would hardly—"

"Christopher, as much as you want to deny it, the doctors made it very clear. You were teetering on the edge of a nervous breakdown. You needed rest."

"Well, I suppose that might be correct, but—"

"I don't see how a roll in the hay up in Maine with slut Vanderkliff will help you recuperate."

"Elizabeth, I can assure you she's not here, not anywhere near here. In fact, she just called me from Percer about the *Newsweek* article."

"*Jesus Christ, Christopher!* You know you're not supposed to be working."

"Yes, but I believe this issue would be classified in the *extreme emergency* category."

"Emergency or not, stay away from it. Act as if it never happened."

"But—"

"Are you seeing Dr. Bilardi this afternoon?"

"Yes, I believe he's coming at two."

"Well, Christopher, I am going to have a conversation with him after his visit and if I hear anything about you working or taking phone calls from the college and if there's any hint of that slut being anywhere near the state of Maine, the stress you're experiencing now will be nothing compared to the stress I'll dish out. You'll have hell to pay."

"Yes, Elizabeth," Pennfield answered dutifully, then hung up.

PENNFIELD PACED THE FLOOR, struggling to make sense of this bizarre series of events at this very so-called time and place. *Was he trapped here forever? How could he escape from a life that wasn't really his— or perhaps a weird variant of his?*

His pacing accelerated. Think logically, he told himself. Use your well-polished skills as a consummate professor of philosophy. He closed his eyes and squinched his forehead, concentrating hard, but his efforts yielded nothing but diffuse noise. He tried again. Think; think hard, he told himself. He was presumably President of the College. His unfortunate incident with Jennifer Winston apparently never happened. Ship was somehow cured, but had become the victim in a new sense, botching an assassination attempt on some Prime Minister thereby killing innocent people, and losing his life. But Prime Minister of what? And why the hell was he recuperating in Maine?

He did the only thing he knew how to do. He turned his focus to nature's masterpiece sitting beyond his windows— the one constant in his life. Throughout time, those waters swirled through a range of emotions. They intrigued him and, in an odd way, guided him. From their bright blue mirror-like days, a glassy surface reflecting the sun's fiery exuberance to those other less fortunate days when their dark green thrashing swells bubbled beneath threatening black and silver clouds— there was always a message there for him.

AFTER SEVERAL SILENT MOMENTS, he drifted back to his study, sure of his mission. He went to KERFUFFLE and typed. He attacked the search engine with his queries, accumulating everything he possibly could about the current state of reality. He soon learned that this world—or universe— in which he was held captive was similar enough to be vaguely familiar but undoubtedly different enough to cause him major problems if he ever hoped to keep his cover.

He learned a bevy of interesting facts:

The United States as he knew it was no longer.

A new governmental order, referred to as "spreadsheet" government, traversed the globe.

The governments were apparently virtual and caste-like; they were called Apexia, Betamil, Chrysalix, Diamid and then there were a bunch of governments referred to merely as numbers.

From what he could tell in a few brief articles, this fellow, Izan Bonne-Saari, used his economic might as head of the world's largest banking network, to coerce all the countries of the world to accept his new form of government.

Ship Pennfield was, or had been, a medical doctor and philanthropist, and an adversary of Bonne-Saari's. As a result of masterminding a botched assassination attempt, he was publicly executed.

As he mulled over the implications, a sharp tap rapped the door.

"Yes?" Pennfield called out.

"It's me, Dr. Bilardi," a deep, rich voice answered as the door opened.

Quickly, Christopher checked his watch: 1:37.

"I know. I know, I'm a little early, but I was over at the Harbor House for lunch and Nora said to—."

"No worry. No worry at all, doc."

Bilardi was an interesting looking man, some inexplicable combination of earthy and urbane. About 5'8", he had a broad face with oily black and slightly gray hair combed from right to left, a bushy black unibrow, a lighter tone of olive Mediterranean skin, a thin, wide set of salmon-colored lips and a square physique.

He dropped his black leather medical bag to the floor and took a seat on the sleigh-couch to the left of Christopher's bed.

"So how have you been, Chris?" Bilardi asked with a restrained, probing innocence.

"Well, what do you exactly mean by that, doctor?" Pennfield blurted, searching for clues.

"Nothing one way or the other, it's just an opening pleasantry." Bilardi winked.

"Pleasantry, eh?" Christopher looked at him skeptically. "Let's face it, Dr. Bilardi. You're smart. I'm smart. You're trying to find something wrong with me, aren't you?"

"Wrong? What do you mean by that?"

"You're trying to prove me flawed, aren't you?"

"Where did that come from?" Bilardi asked as he pulled a blood pressure cuff out of his bag. "I'm just here to monitor you, Chris. I don't judge. Besides, Dr. Stanton back in Percer is your psychiatrist."

"So be it, but—"

"Let me take your pressure before we go on, okay?

"If you must," Pennfield obliged pulling up his sleeve.

Bilardi wrapped the cuff around Pennfield's arm and began to pump.

"Has the time away from Northern Alpine helped you relax?" Bilardi asked as he continued to pump.

"Yes and no," Pennfield answered candidly.

"And why's that?"

"I'm still worried about the place, Sam." He opened up to the doctor. "We've changed the name, done everything we could to maintain our academic integrity, but—"

"One seventy over a hundred," Bilardi interrupted as he read the round dial. "Way too high."

"But I'm trying to tell you—"

"Let's not worry about that now. There are more important things than that." Bilardi reached again into his bag, pulled out a small vial, punctured its seal and then drew its contents into a syringe.

"What are you doing?" Pennfield asked pensively.

"You need to relax, Chris. I'm going to give you a little shot of valium."

"Must you?" Pennfield asked.

"One seventy over a hundred," Bilardi answered as he pricked Pennfield's bicep with his needle.

"Really?" Pennfield asked again.

"One seventy over a hundred," Bilardi repeated with a sly wink.

"Yes, but,"

Within minutes, Pennfield was asleep, sprawled across the king-sized mattress of his four-poster bed.

* * *

TIME FRAME: 2007

86

Boothbay Harbor, Maine, Mid-day, June 11, 2007

Pennfield twisted and turned in his bed, wrestling with his sheets more vigorously than usual, a grimace of pain across his face, spewing a stream of unrelated utterances.

Damn you, Dr. Hazard! Damn you!

Northern Alpine. Blasphemy. Blasphemy.

Ship, no! No, Ship!

It must be her! Must be her!

Ophie, help! Ophie?

OOOOpppphhhhhiiiieeee!!!

Then a swift force jolted him.

"Chris? *Chris!* Wake up! Wake up!" Dr. Bilardi shook his arm, then shook his shoulder hard.

"C'mon Christopher..."

Pennfield fought back, as if wrestling some invisible tormentor. After several more shakes by Bilardi, Pennfield sat back on his pillow and rubbed his eyes. Curiously, he scanned the room. At first, a blur— then Dr. Bilardi hovering over him with Nora standing back, just like before.

"Wha?" he whispered.

"Chris, can you hear me?" Bilardi asked

"Uh…huh, why shouldn't I? Is my blood pressure okay?"

"Your blood pressure? I haven't…" Bilardi asked quizzically.

"Has Haverkost called? I owe him my statement."

Bilardi leaned over Pennfield, held him by both shoulders and shook lightly. "Chris, you okay?"

Slowly, Pennfield answered, "I think so."

Bilardi looked him straight in the eyes. "You've just experienced global transient amnesia, sometimes called a delirium episode. You were hallucinating."

"I should say not!" Pennfield barked haughtily. "You were just here, taking my blood pressure. I even remember the reading: one-seventy over one hundred. Nora, you were here. Don't you remember?"

Nora hesitated.

"Well, don't you?"

Shyly, Nora shook her head, her eyes trained on the floor. "No, Mr. Pennfield. I came to wake you and saw you flipping about in the bed, sayin' all sorts of things. Then you sat up and began havin' a chat with people who weren't even here. Finally I rang Dr. Bilardi. I was worried for you, Mr. Pennfield."

"I appreciate it, Nora," Pennfield answered. "But let me make it clear, other than my blood pressure, I am in no need of a doctor."

"Would you care to have me take it now?" Bilardi interrupted.

"Huh?" Pennfield squinted.

"Your blood pressure?"

"Why of course, go right ahead." Pennfield stuck out his arm. "But that's not going to prove anything. You gave me the shot of valium."

"What?" Bilardi asked as he pumped the blood pressure cuff. "Valium? When did I do that?"

"Must I repeat? You came here to check on me after I had just heard about this incriminating article about the college in Newsweek and you…"

"One thirty-eight over eighty-nine." Bilardi interrupted, eyeing the readout. "Not great, but not terrible either."

"To my point!" Pennfield barked, "Your reading means nothing. Obviously, the valium has calmed me."

"Let me take a quick look at you," Bilardi methodically flashed his light in Pennfield's eyes, "and then we can see where to go from there."

"My dear Doctor Bilardi," Pennfield answered as Bilardi tested his reflexes, "there is absolutely no place for us to go."

"Do you have a psychiatrist?" Bilardi asked.

"A psychiatrist?" Pennfield asked.

"If you don't have one, I suggest you get one."

Pennfield paused, ruminating.

"What's up?" Bilardi asked as he packed his medical bag.

"Well, I do have one, sort of."

"What's his name?"

"*Her* name. Brenda Altieri. Dr. Brenda Altieri, she's in New Jersey."

* * *

DR. BILARDI PUT in a call to Altieri as soon as he left Pennfield's bedside. She was not surprised at all that Christopher Pennfield had suffered a delirium episode. She then asked Swann to place a call to Pennfield to get the story straight from his perspective. Chances were, he would open up more to Swann than her.

Swann had a long conversation with Pennfield, listening to the entire bizarre story—about Pennfield waking up in a completely different world where he had never been touched by the curse and, consequently, was President of the college, where the world was now ruled by some sort of global governmental order, where Ship thrived as a humanitarian doctor until somehow, he tried to murder this Izan Bonne-Saari person and it backfired.

That afternoon, Swann met Altieri in Princeton.

"LET'S SEE, now we have delirium, schizophrenia, paranoia, both acute and chronic, substance abuse," Altieri counted on her fingers, "a whole laundry list of psychiatric afflictions to treat."

"So you're telling me this is all BS. That there are no apparitions or overlapping time frames, parallel universes or psychic connections, nothing of the sort. It can all be explained by some highfalutin names, that taken together mean Christopher Pennfield is crazy?" Swann retorted.

"What do you think?" Altieri asked.

WHAM!

Jules Weisman, in sweats and sneakers, flew through the front door. "Bren, Ed, I tried to get here as soon as I could," Weisman said sheepishly. "So what's up?"

"The good doctor here," Swann pointed to Altieri, "believes Christopher Pennfield is crazy and all that we've been through exists only in his warped imagination."

"All because he had a minor delirium episode?" Weisman asked, adjusting his Baltimore Orioles cap. "Well that sorta sucks. C'mon Bren. We all saw what we saw at Indian Harbor, didn't we?"

Altieri shook her head. "Yeah, I suppose some of the things we've been through with Pennfield might possibly be attributed to psychic phenomena, maybe... perhaps, but I thoroughly believe most of what we've been through are the fabrications of a very emotionally-damaged mind."

"So what do you want to do?" Weisman asked.

"Are you asking for my medical opinion?" said Altieri.

"Of course."

"The man needs to be hospitalized."

"Bren I think you're missing the point!" Weisman chided his partner.

"No I'm not, he had a delirium episode, pure and simple, and it was probably triggered by all the other ways he's abused himself," she responded tersely. "From my viewpoint, it's pretty straightforward. Get it in your head, Jules, it was a delirium episode."

"No it wasn't," Weisman snapped back. "Somehow, someway, he either woke up in, or dreamed about, a parallel universe, one in which he never succumbed to the curse."

"Agreed," Altieri grinned, "and, of course, it was a manifestation of a delirium episode. And he may be on the verge of some sort of breakdown."

"It's not that simple, Bren."

"How is it not that simple?"

"This Bonne-Saari person he read about in the newspaper article, the guy really exists, Bren. He's CEO of some banking conglomerate in Asia. I googled him."

"That means almost nothing," she responded.

"How can you write that off so quickly?"

"Easy. Many times dream episodes are built around things or people you've seen or heard about just prior to falling asleep. Suppose he read something about this Bonne-Saari character in a newspaper or saw something about him on CNN or CNBC right before he dozed off?"

"But he hardly knows anything about the guy. Why would he build a dream around him?"

"Ask Freud," she answered curtly.

"He's dead."

"Are you absolutely sure?"

"Very funny, Bren."

"You deserved it."

"But bear with me for a moment." Weisman began pacing across the office. "Let's say we have two universes, at least two. The one we're living in where Christopher Pennfield is a recluse in Maine and the other where Chris is President of the College and Ship is a doctor and, for some reason, tried to kill Bonne-Saari, gets publicly shamed and is, by definition, the victim of the curse."

"No, Jules," she answered. "We have one universe, this one, and then, of course, Chris Pennfield's delirious dream. You know, we're going to look back on this someday and really laugh at ourselves."

"Laugh at ourselves? Why?" He questioned.

"Because we've been reacting to the alleged— or should I say, fantasized — actions of a Pennfield descendent yet to be born, running a giant multinational company in the 2050s and a hypothetical alternate Ship, both of whom are most likely, if not definitely, a product of the dreams and hallucinations of a mentally damaged old man."

"You're hung up on a null hypothesis, hon. Open up a bit," Weisman countered. "Consider the risk of a Type II error?"

"A Type II error, really?" She giggled. "Geez, you scientists, now you're using statistics to try to convince me. Next time I go looking for a boyfriend, remind me not to choose a theoretical physicist."

"You can do a lot worse," Weisman countered.

"Doubt it."

"Any chance you have Ship's date of birth?"

"Why?

"Because on the odd chance that I am right and that was not a delirium episode Chris experienced, then what would that mean, Bren?"

"Who really cares?" she answered, crankily.

"Apparently not you," Weisman responded. "But, FYI, that would mean that this Mashimoto-Pennfield fellow did something to reverse things and now Ship gets stung by the curse. So I have this idea brewing…" He pointed to his brain.

"Oh please no," Altieri answered, half in jest.

"Do you have it?

"His birth-date?" Altieri answered. "Not off the top of my head. I'm sure if you call Gladwell, you can get it from Dr. Shankar. But count me out. My only concern in this whole circus is that Christopher Pennfield gets proper medical care."

"Sure…sure…" Weisman responded, his mind adrift.

Immediately, Weisman pulled out his cell phone, scanned his directory and pulled up Dr. Shankar's number. He dialed. Shankar was as cooperative as could be expected, connecting Weisman to Gladwell's medical records department.

"*May 18th, 1956?*" Weisman repeated to the clerk in the records dept.

"Yessir, that's it," the clerk answered.

"Thank you."

Weisman's mind spun. "May 18th, 1956. That would mean that Arthur Shipkin Pennfield was conceived sometime during… let's see… July, 1955."

* * *

TIME FRAME: 1955

87

Newport, Rhode Island, July, 1955

During her summers in Newport, Ophelia Pennfield's disposition could range from despondency to toleration to joy, depending upon her ever-changing moods, trivial fluctuations in the weather and the quality of her company. She relished those bright summer days as she strolled down Cliff Walk— that wonderful zigzagging path overlooking rolling breakers brushing up against walls of hard, sharp rock— a gentle sea breeze whisking her face and indulging her senses.

Other times, during grey and doleful days, her disposition mirrored the heavy sky. There was a mysterious allure to her despondency. On those somber, wasteful days, alone in her despair, she would wander over to the Rough Point Bridge and seep in the fury of the sea.

The view captivated her: crashing grey breakers, bubbling with foam, pounding against grey rock walls, all blanketed by an umbrella of ominous grey clouds. And it soothed her in an awkward sort of way, encasing her personal melancholia within a cocoon of even greater melancholia, creating a strange, almost mystical bond between self and surroundings.

By far, her most joyous times in Newport occurred when cousin Christopher, an undergrad at Yale, would visit the venerable family cottage for several weeks. The two shared a deep intuitive understanding of one another that far surpassed mere familial ties. Christopher's presence in Newport made even those grey rainy days a joy for his cousin Ophelia.

"Ophie, I have a surprise for you," the young Christopher announced. Sheets of torrential rain and treacherous whistling winds attacked the cottage's great windows.

"Oh, phooey, you do not!" she teased him.

"Oh, yes I do," he assured her. "Follow me."

CHRISTOPHER'S THIRD-FLOOR quarters at the Newport cottage reminded him of his freshman suite at Yale— dignified, yet spartan— a small lounge with a brick fireplace, a comfy Chesterfield and French doors leading to a modest bedroom and private bath. Its tall, classic windows overlooked the Atlantic to the south and Narragansett Bay and Jamestown to the west. On dark rainy days, no one would ever doubt the home's legendary history as a refuge for all types of spirits, ghosts and poltergeists.

A crack of thunder rattled the old windows, jolting a chill up Ophelia's spine.

"It's scary, Chris." Ophie grabbed tightly onto her cousin.

"Oh, please, Ophie. You really don't believe that rubbish about this old place being haunted, do you?" He pulled a small paper bag out of a drawer and poured its contents onto the table.

"What's that?" she asked.

"Don't tell me you don't know!" He answered, surprised. "It's marijuana, silly."

"Really!" Excitedly, her eyes lit up.

"Have you ever tried it?" he asked.

"No." She shook her head.

"Want to?"

She nodded her head. "But what about Mother?"

"How long should she be at her luncheon?" he asked.

"Till three at least, I would guess."

He looked at his watch. "Not to worry. More than enough time!"

"But what about Henrietta?" she asked, referring to the housekeeper.

"Her? That old swatch of leather, she won't have a clue."

HE PULLED a pipe out of his dresser drawer, tapped it on an ashtray to empty its tobacco remnants, and then placed a small screen of fine wire mesh into its bowl followed by a healthy sprinkling of marijuana.

Holding a lighted match over the bowl, he sucked hard as the marijuana fumes seeped into his lungs. Straining, he forced himself to hold it in as long as humanly possible, and then let it out with a long rapturous gasp.

After several moments of quiet self-indulgence, smiling widely, he looked his cousin in the eyes, and exhaled. "That was beyond heavenly, Oph. Wanna try?"

"You sure I should?" she asked hesitantly.

"Why not? It's no different than taking a shot of whiskey, maybe not even as bad for you." He handed her the pipe.

He watched as his fifteen-year-old cousin struggled. Her first inhalation resulted in a barrage of hacking coughs with smoke escaping from her nostrils. On her second attempt, Chris admonished her to take it slow. Although she put in a credible effort, she coughed again upon attempting to inhale, this time not quite as violent a barrage. On her third try, she finally mastered it, slowly allowing the smoke to seep into her lungs, mimicking her cousin's ritual, holding it deep inside for as long as she could endure.

When the pipe dropped out of her mouth, Chris knew cousin Ophie had been successful.

She giggled, and then smiled curiously, still woozily exhaling the last puffs of smoke.

"It's like… it's like… I skipped over several seconds, *like they just went away, gone!* Can I try again?"

"Whoa! Slow down. My turn."

CHRISTOPHER HAD BEEN INFATUATED with Ophie for several years, enraptured by her smooth porcelain skin and rosy-red cheeks, her luscious jet-black hair and irreverent spunk. She carried herself with the sophistication and propriety of a debutante— even at this young age— yet at her very core resided a mischievous, devilish spirit. The contrast overwhelmed him with desire.

Although he had fantasized about how one day their mystical, spiritual bond would evolve into something more, his infatuation was not without a degree of apprehension. She was his first cousin; she was only fifteen. *Was it proper for him to pursue her?* He mulled over it for months, going back and forth, yet no matter how hard he tried to rationalize it, he could not.

Ultimately, rationality proved no match for gushing hormones.

All it took was a soft, sweet caress of her shoulder, and everything else flowed naturally. Spurred along by the pungent scent and disarming quietude of cannabis, the caress soon became a kiss, its passion building to deep, heavy fondling which led to the inevitable. Surprised and aroused that Ophie took it upon herself to disrobe first, Christopher savored her milk-white skin, perfectly shaped breasts, her alluring nipples, her thighs, everything, while the storm outside continued to rage.

* * *

TIME FRAME: 2007

88

Princeton, NJ, Early evening, June 11, 2007

Altieri could not understand the excitement Weisman experienced by the mere act of estimating Ship's date of conception. Perhaps good scientists need to channel their inner child, she thought, perhaps that's the energy that keeps them going, urges them to explore on even when there may be no apparent end in sight. Maybe that's why she was attracted to him.

"Okay, Jules," Altieri chided him. "So now you know Ship's birthdate and approximate date of conception, what are you going to do?"

"Use it to our advantage."

"How?"

"Simple. We'll use it against this Jimmy Mashimoto-Pennfield guy."

"Who may or may not exist."

"Something which, at this point in time, we can neither prove nor disprove."

"Okay. Then what do you propose to do about this possibly existing guy?" Altieri asked.

"On the possibility he does very well exist, which I wholeheartedly believe, we should use his strengths against him. Make him think he's helping himself when he's actually helping us. Didn't he change the course of Ship's life by intervening in 1963? Who says it can't be done again?"

"So let me get this straight. You want to trick some person in the future—

who may or may not exist— to change things in the present to our advantage?"

"Correct," he answered grinning.

"It's not a very elegant solution, is it? You're introducing so many variables, I mean, why do you need to trick him, why do you need to use him against himself? Can't you do it more directly?"

"He has demonstrated rare psychic tendencies."

"But so has Chris."

"Non-starter," he answered reflexively. "Remember that feedback thing I told you all about?"

She thought for a moment. "Okay, got it."

"And besides that," he continued, "we're dealing with so many alternate universes; we have to make sure that we affect the right one."

"Huh?"

"Let's see...," Weisman began, "we have the one where Ship goes catatonic and Chris is struck by the curse, the one where Ship grows up normal and is the prime target for the curse, and then there's another possible one where he's cured by Dr. Hazard at age nine or so which, we think, was the same one Chris landed in during his so-called *delirium* episode."

"Too murky for my taste. Make your conclusion."

Therefore, the only way we could make absolutely sure we're affecting the one proper universe is if we use Mashimoto-Pennfield directly against himself in the very universe we're trying to affect."

"Jules, you've created one big tangled mess. It'll never work. Even if you could untangle it all, it'd be impossible to trick this Mashimoto person."

"And why's that, Bren?"

"Simple. He has the advantage of knowing the past."

"Sure, but we have the advantage of shaping the future."

* * *

TIME FRAME: 2053

89

NY GAB: Manhattan, Pennfield Technologies Tower, Early evening, April 5, 2053

Impulsively, Jimmy Mashimoto-Pennfield swiveled around in his glass chair and pointed deliberately at a spot across his office, summoning up a holoscreen. He had been meaning to do this for over a month, perhaps longer, but between the impending introduction of the Cryonics Initiative, a Trans-Polar MagLev project and negotiations on a restructuring of his company's debt, he simply hadn't had the time. Now he would do it, though; step inside the mind of Drs. Julian Weisman and Brenda Altieri, his trans-temporal adversaries. He searched through hundreds of databases, until he found it: The Nature Journal, May 2019.

Time, Space and Consciousness: A Multi-Dimensional Approach

By Dr. Julian Weisman, PhD, Massachusetts Institute of Technology, & Dr. Brenda Altieri, MD

In his Special Theory of Relativity, Einstein posited that space and time were different facets of the same continuum: elastic and malleable, not fixed and stable as previously presumed….

MASHIMOTO-PENNFIELD YAWNED through the opening few paragraphs, finding them predictable, simplistic. *C'mon Professor Weisman and Dr. Altieri*, JMP chided, *you can do better than a sophomoric review of Einstein, Bohr and Descartes! For this they almost gave you a Nobel Prize?*

But as he read on, JMP became intrigued with some of the paper's insights:

> *...when you overlay the distinct characteristics of the three disciplines and then attempt to unify them into one theory, certain phenomena become abundantly clear: 1) if, indeed, the Copenhagen School's thesis can be applied on a more macro-level, then the entire universe, not just sub-atomic particles, would by definition, be observer-dependent, and 2) this, then, adds an element of subjectivity to the progression of reality, as each individual observer can theoretically create his or her own personal space-time and universe.*

MUCH BETTER, JMP thought, stretching his legs across his desk. *But, still, his conclusions and questions do lead rather obviously from the essential natures of the three disciplines.* He read on:

> *... the obvious implication of this train of thought, of course, would be that there are myriad extant "universes," each being generated by an individual's subjective reality. At times these subjective realities can be intersected or "crisscrossed" by other individuals' subjective realities, creating "collisions of conflicting realities" ...*

NOW IT'S GETTING INTERESTING, JMP thought.

This leads to a critical question: How does human consciousness mediate between one's own subjective version of reality when it comes into direct conflict with someone else's, across space and/or time? Moore, Uberstein and Suh (2018) have hypothesized that a major underlying cause of extreme psychotic or neurotic conditions can possibly be a "space-time" disorientation, i.e, the voices a patient reports hearing, and which typically result in a diagnosis of schizophrenia, may be voices emanating from another person's subjective reality, "overlapping" into the patient's time and space. Furthermore, a hallucinatory "apparition" of a past event could feasibly be explained by an event from a different time (or space) occupying the same space-time as the present-day observer of said apparition.

DIRECTIONALLY, *very good, albeit a bit coarse, but certainly not bad for 2019,* JMP conceded. He skipped ahead:

...in this paper we present a theoretical framework for how this mechanism may be possible, by layering two new dimensions above the conventional 4 space-time dimensions (x, y, z, t). We have named our theoretical fifth dimension "Parallel-Reality." This dimension encompasses all alternate subjective versions of "reality" (which, in itself, is a subjective dimension). Each alternate reality which resides in this dimension is subject to the same physical laws as the lower x, y, z, t dimensions, most significantly, the speed of light "c" remains a constant in this dimension with any given space/time velocity "v" being unable to surpass it ($v < c$).

We have named our theoretical sixth dimension "Entangled Consciousness," the realm where consciousness — both human and non-human (i.e. "particle entanglement") — resides. As a dimension hovering above all alternative universes in the lower fifth dimension, this new dimension allows "travel" across all of these alternative universes. However, physical travel (restricted to the x, y, z, t dimensions) is impossible. Only consciousness (or some as-yet-unknown variation of *"consciousness" which allows entangled particles to communicate) can travel across this dimension and seep into lower-order alternate realities. We theorize that the enabling mechanism underlying this dimension is the violation of the v < c restriction of the lower dimensions. Here, v can exceed c, allowing consciousness to traverse across time — past, present and future — and thus allowing consciousness to violate conventional temporal causality. This results in a negative Lorentz transformation for this dimension:*

$$E = mc^2 / \sqrt{1 - v^2/c^2}$$

where:

$$v > c$$

Therefore:

$$E < 0$$

This, then, translates to the complex number:

$$E = mc^2/i\sqrt{(1 - \frac{v^2}{c^2})}, \text{ given } v > c$$

This would then lead to a variant of the electromagnetic field in this dimension:

$$E = {}^{hc}/_{\lambda}$$

where:

$$E, \lambda < 0$$

For this equation to be true, by definition, one of the elements on the equation's right side must be negative. We would theorize that lambda (or electromagnetic wavelength) is the only possible candidate given that c and h (Planck's constant) are prima facie constants.

Brilliant, JMP thought, *absolutely brilliant.* He was amazed that Weisman's and Altieri's theories predated the great Borzov by at least a decade. Voraciously, he read forward:

We would then theorize that true consciousness (or the "collective consciousness") resides in this sixth dimension in the form of an anti-electromagnetic spectrum residing in the realm of complex numbers, traveling in wavelengths that are negative variants of the standard electromagnetic spectrum and undetectable by conventional contemporary electromagnetic receiving devices. With consciousness being a wave, therefore the human brain acts as a receiver/transmitter within these hypothetical wave fields. Consciousness, therefore, can travel faster than the speed of light, travel backwards in time, travel instantaneously to any other point in space, and "tune-in" on all parallel possibilities of reality residing in our theorized fifth dimension. We would further theorize that this dimension provides the mechanism that allows entangled particles to communicate instantaneously across vast distances (Einstein's "spooky action at a distance").

JMP WAS OVERWHELMED by a combination of enlightenment and envy as he read on, now fully understanding why Weisman and Altieri had proven to be such formidable adversaries.

Thus, each human being is able to "tune-in" to a specific idiosyncratic frequency of this anti-electromagnetic spectrum, providing their "reservoir" of conscious thought. This "tuning-in" to a certain frequency is tantamount to making an "observational choice" which collapses the underlying dimensions into a concrete version of reality (in effect transforming the negative energy and mass of the sixth dimension to positive energy and mass in the underlying dimensions).

Individuals who are more genetically-predisposed for this "tuning in" trait may have the capability to "tune-in" to other people's frequencies across time and space and alternate realties (explaining certain "psychic" phenomena such as clairvoyance, ESP, apparitions, out-of-body experiences, near-death experiences, pre-cognition and past-life regression, among others). Furthermore, certain individuals may exhibit "flaws" in this trait causing them, perhaps, to tune-in to more than one frequency simultaneously or "incorrect" frequencies, resulting in certain psychiatric disorders (schizophrenia, multiple personality disorder, etc.).

NOT SHOCKINGLY INSIGHTFUL, JMP concluded, *but a very straightforward implication supported by rigorous logic.*

The impetus behind this paper was a project we were working on involving a family presenting with generation-crossing psychic phenomena. We hypothesized that these phenomena may be attributed to some of the theories discussed above. We discovered, by inducing a Ganzfeld state on a family member who had a proclivity for "psychic sensitivity," that his consciousness could visit other times and places (potentially through the mechanism described above) even to the extent of interacting with individuals from that time frame (or spatial frame) and directing them to perform small actions that could change the course of history going forward, therefore creating or affecting other alternate realities in the fifth dimension.

JMP SMILED BROADLY. He had been "battling" with Weisman, Altieri and their colleagues over the fate of Arthur Shipkin Pennfield for months. Now he had a glimpse directly into their minds.

Delicious!

A member of this same family suffered from catatonic schizophrenia (CS). While it would be difficult to induce a Ganzfeld state upon this individual, we were able to observe significant trans-temporal and trans-spatial psychic activity during administration of bilateral electro-convulsive shock therapy (ECT).

SO THAT EXPLAINS the set up on the deck with the hospital bed, equipment and medical attendants, JMP surmised.

Based upon many of these Ganzfeld and ECT "experiments" we came to determine that the family member's CS was very likely caused by a psychic "visitation" from another family member from the future during the individual's childhood, shocking him into this condition...

SPOT ON!

JMP had concluded that very fact after his Ganzfeld session at Indian Harbor. Impressive though, how Weisman and Altieri were able to deduce the very same discovery with old technology and outdated scientific theories.

During our experiments, we began to sense — through the psychic sensitivities of one of the contemporary family members — that someone or some force from the future was attempting to reverse the very incident causing the initial onset of CS.

Definitely delicious! JMP wiped his lips. It was as if a military leader was openly sharing his battle plans with the adversary. Excitedly, he read on:

For reasons not relevant to the substance of this paper, those of us in the present (2007) believe we found ourselves in a struggle with the family member from the future (2052/53, as best as we could ascertain). The family member from the future attempted several times through psychic intervention to convince family members in the present to take small actions which appeared insignificant on the surface but, from his perspective from the future, proved monumental in changing the course of events going forward. We went through several rounds of undoing each other's psychic actions until those of us in the present finally prevailed by having our psychically-gifted family member have his consciousness travel back to the year 1956...

"*What!*" JMP jumped up out of his seat.

JMP read that critical sentence once again:

We went through several rounds of undoing each other's psychic actions until those of us in the present finally prevailed by having our psychically-gifted family member have his consciousness travel back to the year 1956....

"PREVAIL? HOW COULD THEY PREVAIL?" He shouted at the empty room.

He pounded his fists, shaking his levitating desk.

"How did they do it? What the *fuck* is going on?"

He banged his desk once again.

"Cocksuckers!"

JMP'S POUNDING fists reverberated throughout his entire office suite.

Under no circumstances could he ever allow that to happen.

Under no circumstances could he ever fall victim to the curse.

Under no circumstances could anything ever occur that would jeopardize the successful completion of the Cryonics Initiative and its triumphant introduction to the world.

He banged his fist on his desk once again, and then yelled.

"Narc!"

"Yes, my dear other. We seem a bit agitated today." Narc materialized across the desk from JMP.

"They're undoing what I've done," JMP lamented.

"Are you surprised?" Narc answered. "You're not the only one with ingenuity and intelligence. So how can I help?"

"I need to strike back. I can't put myself in the path of that damn curse. There's too much at stake."

"Good point," Narc answered.

"So what do I do?" JMP asked.

"Perhaps switch the battle to a different venue," Narc suggested.

"Huh?"

"You've each been struggling to undo and then redo Ship's affliction. Perhaps we should concentrate on someone else?"

"Who?" JMP asked.

"Why, of course, Christopher Pennfield, shouldn't that be obvious?" Narc answered. "Perhaps instead of taking actions to assure that Ship *is* the victim of the curse, you should take actions to assure that your great uncle Christopher *is not* the victim of the curse and allow everything else to fall in place."

JMP smiled. "Very good, Narc. Very good. In fact, that's brilliant."

"That's why I exist, my dear other."

"Yes, okay, so: if we make it impossible for Chris to become the victim, it has just as good a chance of affecting the curse's timing to provide insulation for me."

"Precisely."

"Good. Now, how are we going to do this…" JMP asked.

"I would direct your attention to the article's seventh paragraph."

JMP quickly re-read the paragraph:

This leads to a critical question: How does human consciousness mediate between one's own subjective version of reality when it comes into direct conflict with someone else's, across either space and/or time? Moore, Uberstein and Suh (2018) have hypothesized that a major underlying cause of extreme psychotic or neurotic conditions can possibly be a "space-time" disorientation, i.e. the voices a patient reports hearing, and which typically result in a diagnosis of schizophrenia, may be voices emanating from another person's subjective reality, "overlapping" into the patient's time and space.

JMP FOCUSED and once again absorbed the words of the paragraph. "*Conflicting subjective realities?* Well, that's, of course, what we've been doing. Correct?"

"You're missing the key point," Narc announced.

Frustrated, JMP pointed once again and enlarged the words so he could focus more intently, his eyes burying into each and every one.

"Try the second sentence," Narc suggested.

"What?" JMP snapped. "*Space-time disorientation? Schizophrenia?*"

"Very good."

"But why? How?"

"Let's put a few facts together," Narc chided him. "Number one, you've demonstrated an innate ability to travel psychically through time and space and communicate with family members from the past."

"Correct." JMP nodded.

"Number two, the study cited in the article suggests that schizophrenia could possibly be induced by a space-time disorientation."

"Yeah?"

"And if you studied up, you would discover that in extreme cases of schizophrenia, in the middle of the last century, they applied a barbaric treatment called a pre-frontal lobotomy."

"Which rendered people practically emotionless," JMP continued, smiling, "like zombies, incapable of anything normal."

"Correct my dear other," Narc responded. "So let's hypothesize. If Christopher Pennfield demonstrated symptoms of schizophrenia in his youth and was lobotomized…"

JMP beamed a broad smile. "He would never be sane enough to fall prey to a curse and, therefore, it would significantly reduce the odds that it would strike at me."

"Voila."

"But wait a minute," JMP interjected. "Didn't the paper say that a family member did something in 1956 to undo what we did?"

"Correct," Narc answered. "And, without doubt, that family member must have been Christopher Pennfield."

"For sure."

"So, if we were to intervene with Christopher Pennfield prior to 1956, we would both prevent him from undoing the results of our interventions, and also prevent him from becoming the victim of the curse, a double whammy!"

"Brilliant, Narc!"

* * *

TIME FRAME: 1955

AN ALTERNATIVE LIFE OF PROFESSOR CHRISTOPHER PENNFIELD AS A COLLEGE STUDENT

90

New Haven, Connecticut, Yale University, Mid-morning, March 11, 1955

A *brisk day*, young Christopher Pennfield thought as he darted across Old Campus tucking his exposed chin down close into the collar of his wool coat. A sophomore in Yale's Davenport College, he had forgotten his scarf as he rushed out the door, bound for a psych seminar. It was a busy time for him. He had two papers due the next week and two mid-terms the week after. He was currently carrying a 3.7 GPA and was hell-bent on maintaining it, if not increasing it, so he could pursue his PhD and then a prestigious career in academia.

But as the stiff breeze swooshed cold air down his collar, he was briefly distracted from those ambitions, longing for the heat of summer break. It was then that he would spend four delightful weeks with cousin Ophie at the family's Newport estate, situated on a promontory jutting out from the end of Cliff Walk. Dreaming of the foamy water, the breeze and the jagged coastline soothed him as he rushed onward through the biting-cold remnants of a passing New Haven winter. He tried to return his focus to his studies, but he couldn't deny that what he dreamed of most was Ophie.

Five years his junior, Ophie was innocently seductive, like a young nymph. In his sophomore art history course, he had often been reminded of her by Lefebvre's 1875 portrait, '*Chloé.*' Visions of that masterpiece, of the raven-haired maiden with her soft skin, sustained him throughout his sophomore year.

He and Ophie shared a mutual attraction, an infatuation, a strong psychic bond. Flirts, suggestive glances and salacious inferences always slipped into their conversations, the intensity building over time.

But it hadn't gone anywhere.

Not as of yet.

Until it *did* go somewhere, it was merely a secret fantasy, perhaps one never to be consummated.

"You seem preoccupied," a strange voice interrupted him.

Stunned, Pennfield quickly flicked up his head, searching for the source.

He saw nothing.

"Oh, come on, you can do better than that."

"Better than what?" Pennfield mumbled to himself.

"I do believe I made a comment. Doesn't it deserve a response?"

"It's impossible to respond to someone who isn't here," Pennfield answered.

"Don't sell me short, young man; I'm right here beside you."

"Bullshit," he whispered.

"Would you please be considerate and watch your language."

"I'll say whatever I want to say," Pennfield spoke in a normal tone, looking around to assure that no one would see him talking to himself.

"Big balls for a little man."

Ignoring the voice, Pennfield looked up. He was only several steps from Linsly-Chittenden Hall, where his seminar would meet. He rushed over and strode brusquely through the building's door, ignoring the disembodied voice.

"Don't worry, we'll talk again soon," the voice teased Pennfield as he galloped up the stairs to his seminar.

* * *

91

New Haven, Connecticut, Yale University, Mid-day, March 11, 1955

By the time Pennfield's seminar was over, he had all but forgotten his strange experience on his walk over. He retraced his steps back to his dorm, once again burying his neck inside his coat collar to avoid the cold. Unfortunately, as he proceeded, he soon discovered he was not alone.

"And what was it today, cognition, maybe a little Rogerian behavioral theory or perhaps Maslow or Pavlov?" The voice returned with abandon.

Pennfield buried his neck deeper into his collar and leaned forward; his eyes focused on the footpath crisscrossing Old Campus and trudged on.

"Oh, please! Ignoring me won't make me go away."

"Yes it will," Pennfield mumbled.

"You underestimate me."

"It's hard to underestimate something that doesn't exist."

"Oh, but I very much do."

"No you don't."

"Your mother was a whore, you know."

Pennfield stopped short, turned his head and looked up.

"Ah ha! I got you."

"Those stories aren't true."

"They say she sucked every dick at Harvard and swallowed, to boot." The voice cackled a giggle. *"Just another nice Radcliffe girl, I guess."*

"Go away, okay."

"Well, we all know about sloppy seconds. But your dad, he got sloppy three hundred and forty-seconds, I guess." The voice cackled again, this time louder.

"Fuck you."

"That would be delightful, but we're having so much fun as is!"

"Just get out of here." Pennfield trudged onward.

"I guess I can possibly grant you a brief respite, but I'll be back."

Pennfield stopped again, looked up, swiveling his head as he eyed all the spare, semi-gothic sandstone buildings that made up the Old Campus, and pondered for a moment.

Then he continued on.

* * *

92

New Haven, Connecticut, Yale University, Evening, March 18, 1955

The Davenport College dining hall oozed classic Ivy League. Arching columns, fine wooden moldings, the chandeliers, and two long, parallel dining-tables running lengthwise down the narrow room resembled a cathedral more than a dining hall. Christopher Pennfield usually caught dinner around 6PM, sitting comfortably mid-way down one of the long narrow tables, always a textbook beside his plate, with his suite mates Arch Richmond, Kelly O'Rourke and Tad Wallenbach across and aside from him.

"Did you hear, Arch?" Wallenbach muttered as he munched.

"What?"

"Rumor has it, Delta Phi's bussing in some Vassar babes this weekend."

Richmond's eyes lit up. "Aw that's swell Tad! Can we get in on the action?"

"Yeah, I know Nate Cunningham, he's their social chair," O'Rourke chimed in.

Despite his peers' excitement, the silent Pennfield buried his eyes in his textbook. He was falling behind in his dastardly course on matrix algebra.

Until —

A vigorous shake of his shoulders disturbed him.

"Whaddaya think, Penny?" Wallenbach blurted.

"Huh." Pennfield flicked his head up.

"The chickies from Vassar…."

"Oh yeah, when?" he asked, not having heard their previous back and forth.

"Well, it'll be…" Richmond began, but Chris Pennfield heard none of it.

Instead, a familiar, albeit unwelcomed, voice pierced through:

"More little whores like your mom to feed on…"

Pennfield cringed. *Shit! What the fuck was happening to him?* He tried not to listen.

"Penny? Penny?" Wallenbach shook him once again.

Resilient, Pennfield jolted up, hoping to get himself out of all this. "Yeah, chickies from Vassar. How'r we getting in?"

"You're no better than those Harvard assholes who fucked the shit out of your mom, correct?"

Stunned and angry, Pennfield stared up at the arching windows, in a trance-like state.

"Weren't you listening, Penny?" Wallenbach responded. "Kelly knows Cunningham, their social chair."

Pennfield did not listen. All he could think of was that voice, that terrible, irritating voice.

"Get out of here." Pennfield mumbled through gritted teeth.

"What?" Wallenbach exclaimed, shocking Pennfield out of his trance once again.

Pennfield smiled, covering up. "Get *outta* here." He giggled. "So you think Cunningham can get us in?"

"Yeah, just like those Harvard boys got into your mother," the wicked, taunting voice cackled.

"Good as gold. He owes us one."

"You think you're gonna fuck your little cock off, don't you?"

"Stop!" Pennfield mumbled briskly.

"Stop what, Penny?"

"Yeah, you're acting sort of weird."

"Not as weird as the stuff your mom did with those Harvard boys."

"I'm okay, I just have a lot on my mind," Pennfield answered.

"You know that saying, 'any and every orifice?'"

Pennfield's face reddened as he cracked his knuckles.

"Let's see, there's the obvious place, then the mouth, the earlobes, the nostrils…"

Pennfield pounded his fist on the table, desperately searching for an escape from the inescapable.

"Rumor has it, she even took it up the ass." The voice cackled wickedly.

That was it. Pennfield had had enough.

"SHUT THE FUCK UP!" Penfield stood up, trance-like, and shouted at the top of his lungs.

A sudden deep, stark silence.

All the students in the dining hall looked over towards the red-faced Pennfield.

* * *

93

New Haven, Connecticut, Yale University, Evening, March 18, 1955

The attack on Christopher Pennfield's psyche by the teasing, disembodied voice increased over the next week. Pennfield was someone else, not himself. Usually calm and confident as he strolled around campus or buried himself in a study carrel at the library or attended classes, he had become anxious and circumspect.

The change in personality did not go unnoticed by his suitemates.

"Penny, what the *fuck's* up?" Kelly O'Rourke questioned him as they all sat in the parlor of their suite.

"What do you mean, Kel?" Pennfield answered stoically.

"Last week you shouted out in the dining hall and ever since you've been sort of weird, not yourself."

"Yeah, what's up?" Tad Wallenbach chimed in.

"Nothing."

"C'mon, it's gotta be something."

Pennfield pondered for a moment. "I don't know… maybe I'm feeling pressure, mid-terms coming up, a big paper due, heavy course load…"

"Penny, that's crazy," Arch Richmond interrupted, "you are one of the brightest nerds around. You've been through a lot tougher semesters than this. There's something going on."

"Yeah, you gotta take care of yourself," O'Rourke followed-up.

For a long moment, Pennfield stared at the floor, his forehead resting in his palm.

"Well, yeah, maybe…" he answered, not looking up.

"No, definitely," O'Rourke corrected him.

"Look, we've been talking," O'Rourke began, "and we don't like what we're seeing. There's some very good psychiatrists at the hospital just down the street."

"What!" Pennfield exclaimed. "I'm not going to see a fucking psychiatrist! Only weird, demented people see psychiatrists!"

"Why come on, Penny, no one has to know," Wallenbach responded, "it's for your own good."

"Seeing a shrink doesn't mean you're weird or demented." O'Rourke continued. "For some unexplainable reason, you're just going through a tough time."

"Yeah, you'll get over it," said Richmond. "It'll just be faster if you get a little help."

"Yeah, why suffer more than you have to?" O'Rourke added.

Pennfield's eye stared blankly at the floor.

"So, you gonna do it?" Wallenbach asked.

"What?" Pennfield answered not looking up.

"See the psychiatrist?"

Slowly, Pennfield lifted his head, grit his teeth and looked each of his suitemates in the eyes. Then he mumbled:

"No. I'm not seeing any God-damned shrink. The decision's final."

* * *

94

New Haven, CT, Yale University, Mid-day, March 24, 1955

The psychological torment of the young Christopher Pennfield persisted. Just when he thought the voice had gone away, it would reappear, taunting him with more and more ferocity. It attacked when he was doing his laundry, studying in the library, and lounging on the green on Old Campus. The voice observed no boundaries in its exploitation of Christopher Pennfield's inner psyche.

On Wednesday afternoons, Pennfield attended the esteemed Professor Avril Winnington's class on *Spinoza's Ethics.* The class was held in an old lecture hall in the Hall of Graduate Studies. Professor Winnington's popularity transcended his subject matter; students from every discipline yearned to be admitted to Winnington's lectures. As a philosophy major, Pennfield had been attempting to forge a positive relationship with Winnington and was making decent progress. He hoped that the professor might write him a recommendation for PhD programs during his senior year.

"PLEASE TURN to Spinoza's Proposition Twenty-seven," Winnington began the day's lecture. "Can you read it for us please…, ummm…" Winnington looked down at his seating chart, "yes, Mr. Hobbes."

Hobbes, a diffident sophomore with a nasally voice, read from his text: "A thing which has been conditioned by God to act in a particular way cannot render itself unconditioned."

Pennfield scribbled a note to himself on his pad, anticipating Winnington's question.

"Yeah just like your mom was conditioned to give great head."

Aghast, Pennfield tightened his grip on his pencil, squeezing it. That voice, that scurrilous, obscene voice attacked him once again.

"So what does this say about determinism?" Winnington looked down at his chart "Mr. Stark?"

Winnington loved picking on entitled jocks. Clement Stark, the fullback on the Yale football team, usually lounged on a chair in the back row, paying half-attention to Winnington's words of wisdom.

"They say there's not a dick at Harvard her lips didn't touch."

Pennfield's face reddened.

"Mr. Stark?" Professor Winnington asked again.

"Ummm...yeah..." Stark thumbed through his book, "...well, I think it says that he thought everything is pre-determined. Sorta."

"Sorta right, Mr. Stark," Winnington chided the young man. "Go on."

"Like your mom went on and on and on with every Harvard dick."

Pennfield grit his teeth with such intensity he feared his jaws might pop out of his face.

"I hear she could do marvelous things with her tongue in her day."

"Fuck off," Penfield mumbled under his breath.

"If only I could do that as well as your mom..."

"Anything more Mr. Stark?" Winnington prodded the young jock. "Would you care to elucidate us with your understanding of Spinoza?"

"Well, umm... so if everything is pre-determined, then I would assume he was saying we have no free will."

"Well your mom certainly had free will in sucking cocks."

Pennfield's face reddened. He jabbed his pencil into his notebook.

"*Assume*, Mr. Stark?" Winnington asked haughtily. "Either he said it or he didn't."

"No...No....," Stark began, "....it was just a figure of speech..."

"Have you had a paternity test lately? I think the outcome may be illuminating." The voice giggled mischievously.

Pennfield banged his fist on the desk. The students around him glanced over.

"*Figure of speech*, Mr. Stark?" Winnington continued his assault.

"Yeah," Stark answered, "He definitely said it, I think."

His face red, his teeth gritted, his nostrils flaring, Pennfield found it impossible to concentrate.

"You *think*?" Winnington retorted. "That'll be enough for today Mr. Stark." Winnington paused to again look down at his seating chart.

"Your mother still sucks cocks you know."

The words enraged young Pennfield. He had had enough. He pounded his fist again, more forcefully. A wider periphery of students glanced over.

"Let's see..." Winnington thumbed across the seating chart, "Mr. Pennfield, can you ...*amplify*... Mr. Stark's profound analysis?"

Pennfield hardly heard Winnington's words. He looked up, his face beet-red.

"If you don't believe me, ask your Uncle Percival. She sucks his cock whenever she can."

That was all he could take.

Enraged, his beet-red face oozing sweat, Pennfield stood up and screamed:

"FUCK YOU. FUCK YOU. FUCK YOU. FUCK YOU."

He flung his pencil towards the professor.

The students took a collective gasp, everyone's eyes directed at Pennfield.

Clement Stark, in an attempt to recover from his feeble performance, ran over to Christopher and restrained him.

* * *

TIME FRAME: 2007

95

Booth Bay Harbor, Maine, Early Morning, June 17, 2007

Christopher Pennfield squeezed his goose-down pillow, and then rolled awkwardly around it, hanging on for dear life. He squirmed and stretched with sudden maddening jolts, twisting his covers and sheets into a maze of puzzling entanglements. He finally freed himself, wrestling himself away from his silken cobweb, and sat straight up, sweating.

He breathed rapidly.

His eyes scanned the room, straining in the unrelenting darkness— layered tones of fuzzy gray— and scoped everything out: the classic leaded windows, the regal velvet curtains, the grandfather's clock ticking continuously, his curio, his stash of elixirs on top, examining them all to the minutest detail possible under the night's fuzzy veil of grayness.

Nothing seemed out of the ordinary.

Damnit! He punched his fist into the mattress. *What was becoming of him?*

His mind was fucking with him once again, must be.

In a bold attempt to re-write history, it was trying to convince him that somehow as a youth he was hearing weird voices and going crazy, compromising his undergraduate years.

HE REMEMBERED his college years vividly. He didn't go nuts, didn't hear voices; he was popular, had a slew of friends, Phi Beta Kappa, graduating Summa Cum Laude. From there he went on to bigger and better things.

Until, of course, the curse cut it all short.

Again, he surveyed the room, his heart beating rapidly. He reached over for his scotch and took a large gulp. Slowly, it calmed him, soothing him to a point where he could think reasonably again.

Just to be sure, he checked his foot: bandaged as usual. He pushed himself off the bed, grabbed his walking stick and hobbled over to the bathroom. He flicked on the light and looked in the mirror.

Relief!

He did not look younger, did not appear to be another version of himself. He was the same wretched old man he was when he had retired that evening. Odds were, he had not been transported to another parallel universe; his life had not taken a different path. But again, to be sure, he needed something more.

He hobbled out of the bathroom and towards his curio, his bandaged foot scraping the wooden floor. He yanked open its drawer and grabbed for the newspaper clipping: *UNDERGRADUATE FALLS FOR PROF.*

Yes, it was still there. He was still living his terribly flawed life. Things hadn't changed. For a moment, he pondered the irony. He was actually relieved he was his "normal" self, living his normal, highly-compromised life. His passive resignation to his fate gnawed at him.

He sat still for a moment. Then shouted:

"Ophhhhiiiiiiieeeeee!"

He scoped out the room, searching for any sign of his eternal soul mate.

He summoned her again, this time with less volume: "Ophie, please, don't abandon me now. Please don't abandon me now…"

For several brief moments, the darkness of night pecked away at him, chilling him with an unaccustomed fear.

All this for a nightmare, a little dream?

He swiveled towards the grand windows.

"I thought you'd never arrive," he addressed her.

Perhaps I didn't think a trivial nightmare warranted a visitation, she answered.

"Oh, please," he responded, "I've been so out of sorts lately, you should realize that what might be a *trivial nightmare* to you is a major assault on my sanity to me."

My apologies, she said in an emotionless, unapologetic tone. *But you've checked it out, done your due diligence, haven't you?*

"Yes, it appears as if everything's normal, whatever that is," he lamented.

"But I don't know…everything seems to be getting worse and worse…I'm not sure if I even trust my own instincts anymore."

Poor Christopher. She lightly grazed her hand across his cheek. *My poor, dear Christopher.*

"What if—" he blurted.

What if what? she asked.

"What if my dream, in fact, actually reflected reality?"

But you just told me it did not.

"On the small chance I am wrong…and I have very little trust in my judgment these days…if the dream had even a miniscule element of truth to it, how would the dominoes fall?"

What do you mean?

"If, indeed, I was haunted by strange voices in college, what would have happened? Would I have graduated? Been institutionalized? Perhaps live my expected, normal life?" He paused. "And, of course, the most crucial question…"

And that would be?

"How would it have affected Ship?"

* * *

TIME FRAME: 2011

THE ALTERNATIVE LIFE OF ARTHUR SHIPKIN PENNFIELD

96

Mexico / Sri Lanka, May 28th, 2011

The officers shackled and handcuffed Ship, Lori and Reynolds and rushed them into separate Jeeps, each prisoner's hands bound to the door. They sped them off to a small airport in rural Mexico where they immediately boarded a military jet to Sri Lanka. There they would presumably be tried for conspiracy against the state and for the murders of the victims in the cafeteria. Upon landing, they were rushed under heavy security to a local Sri-Lankan detention facility and segregated from the other prisoners.

BONNE-SAARI WOULD TAKE no chances that anyone other than himself would be the ultimate executioner. He made his intentions quite clear in a meeting with his closest advisors

"It's taken awhile, but we finally have Pennfield exactly where we want him." Gleefully, Izan Bonne-Saari wrung his hands. "Defeated, shamed and destined to be scorned forever. Our operative gave us perfect information. We set the perfect trap."

"Yes, but the children, Izan," an advisor from Australia asked, clearing her throat and taking a small step back as she dared to continue, "was that absolutely necessary?"

"Collateral damage," he answered swiftly. "They will be honored as heroes for as long as our system of government exists. An unfortunate, but necessary, sacrifice."

"And Pennfield?" another advisor asked, "When and where's the trial?"

"There will be no trial," Bonne-Saari responded abruptly, then stood up and paced the room. "Our evidence is concrete and unassailable. A trial would be a superfluous waste of time. He will be declared guilty by executive order."

"And then?" an advisor from Norway asked.

"He will be publicly executed, made an example of, so no one will ever again have the temerity to challenge our system of government."

The room was silent. He looked each advisor in the eyes as he paced the room.

"And why are you all so quiet?" Bonne-Saari asked. "We have a mission, a mission to inject a new system, a new way of living, into this planet. Naturally, there will be detractors, insurrectionists. They need to be flushed out, eliminated, and potential future detractors put on notice. I do not believe in subtleties. The masses lack the acuity to be influenced by subtleties. So let's make it easy for the feeble-minded masses. Let's be bold and decisive."

"What did you have in mind, Izan?" another advisor timidly asked.

Bonne-Saari grinned. "I've been thinking this through for quite some time. *Electrocution?* Effective, shocking, but underwhelming. *Lethal injection?* Far too subtle. I think for this, we will revert to an earlier age. The guillotine, a public beheading. Shameful, bloody, effective of course, and quite, quite memorable."

Bonne-Saari paused and again scanned the faces in the room, gauging the mettle of each individual, and then announced:

"For his crime of insurrection and conspiracy against the state, Dr. Arthur Shipkin Pennfield will be publicly beheaded in the National Museum courtyard, the scene of his horrific crime."

* * *

Colombo, Sri Lanka
Mid-afternoon
May 30th, 2011

Held in solitary cells next to each other, neither Ship nor Lori had any idea what would come next. The guards had separated Reynolds out and imprisoned him in another facility, making Ship suspect that his friend might have been a plant by Bonne-Saari. Several days passed before they heard anything.

On their fourth day of imprisonment, they were brought out of their cells and into a small interrogation room. They were ordered to sit down on a bench behind a cold, metal table. Two guards stood behind them brandishing automatic weapons across their chests.

After several minutes, a middle-aged man in a suit and tie was escorted into the room by two heavily-armed guards.

"Dr. Pennfield? Dr. Bernstein?" The man said with a hint of a British accent.

"Are you our attorney?" Ship asked.

"Not exactly," he responded as he seated himself. "My name is Alan Columb-Barnes, solicitor general of the Apexian government."

"So you work for *him*?" said Ship.

"Yes, and all those fortunate enough to call themselves Apexians."

"So why are you here?"

"Very simple," Columb-Barnes answered. "I'm here to officially inform you, Dr. Pennfield, that you are accused and convicted of conspiracy against the state, and the murder of 48 innocent victims."

"Convicted?" Ship blurted. "What do you mean, convicted? No trial? No justice? Not even a masquerade of justice?"

"The state's evidence is quite compelling," Columb-Barnes cut him off. "We see no need for a trial. It would simply waste time."

"What *evidence*?" Ship exclaimed.

"Would you care to see it?"

"I sure would," Ship answered.

Columb-Barnes pulled a tablet out of his briefcase. He turned it on, placed it on the table and played a video:

It was Ship in his Boston apartment. He was on the phone giving instructions and tapping out text messages, then pacing the room and watching the news and finally expressing extreme distress when he learned of the deaths of the schoolchildren.

"Where did you get that?" Ship sprang up.

The pair of armed guards standing behind him braced themselves.

"We have our methods, Dr. Pennfield," Columb-Barnes responded. "You will be executed on Monday at 1:46pm, exactly one week to the minute after your horrific crime."

"Dr. Bernstein?" Columb-Barnes addressed Lori.

"Yes," she responded.

Ship looked over at her. Something was wrong, something was different.

"You are now free to go."

"Thank you," Lori said, devoid of emotion. One of Columb-Barnes' guards began to remove her handcuffs.

"What?" Alarmed, Ship sprang up once more.

The guards stepped closer.

To Ship, in those few brief moments Lori transformed into someone else. Her appearance was the same, yet her demeanor was 180-degrees off. This was not the girl he fell in love with at Yale, the woman he reunited with in Cameroon. This was someone else.

His mind processed it, but refused to accept it. Yet, it was crystal clear. *Lori was the mole. She had been working for Bonne-Saari all the time.*

He looked at her and whispered, "Lori! *Lori…*"

She stared back at him. Their eyes connected. He peered deep inside: cold and steely, something awry. She began to speak, but in a different tone of voice, a detached monotone, hypnotically-induced.

She nurtured each word:

"All mean spirits are doomed to fall."

"Huh?"

She responded with the words:

"November 10th, 1620."

* * *

TIME FRAME: 2007

97

Lenox, Massachusetts, Gladwell Institute for Mental Health Sciences, Night, June 27, 2007

The room was dark and pale. An irritating fluorescent buzz hummed underneath. Ship Pennfield sat upright, strapped in his hospital bed, staring somewhere but aware of nothing. He had gone days without uttering a word or making a deliberate, considered movement. He was just there, occupying space, filling in the moments between past, present and the ultimate cessation of his existence.

At 10:30pm, he stirred a bit. A wiggle of his finger, a twitch in his face: hard to tell if the movements were deliberate or some neural-muscular reaction to brainwaves uncontrolled.

But he twitched again. And again.

His eyes, usually hazy and undirected, seemed to focus.

His lips strained to move.

Then, he exploded.

"*NO! NO! NO!*" He shouted abruptly, twisting in his bed.

The nurse on duty down the hall looked up at the video monitor.

"DO NOT...DO NOT...DO NOT DO IT!" Ship shook vigorously, his lips struggling to form words.

The nurse watched carefully, grasping for her phone.

NOOOOOOOOOOO!!!

STOP! STOP! STOP!

NOOOOOOoooooooooooooooo!!!!
PLEASE!
NEVER! NEVER!
She had seen enough. Immediately she dialed for Dr. Shankar.

* * *

"We seem to have a problem," Christopher Pennfield spoke after Swann answered his cell phone.

"Gee whiz, Chris, it's eleven-thirty, I hope this is a good one," Swann said sitting on the edge of his bed.

"Dr. Shankar just called me," Pennfield answered. "Ship is having some sort of attack, screaming and spewing out all sorts of words. He fears it may get worse."

"Well what was Ship screaming?" Swann asked.

"All sorts of gibberish. Mostly just repeating the word 'No.'"

"Let me call Bren and I'll get right back to you," Swann said.

* * *

Altieri spoke with Shankar shortly thereafter. Ship's outbursts were definitely out of the ordinary. He had mumbled, coherently and incoherently, many times before, but never in his past forty years residence at Gladwell had he ever shouted out with such amplitude and fury.

"Has he convulsed?" she asked Shankar.

"Yes early this morning. We were able to stop it with valium. But, of course, there's a strong probability it could happen again."

"What do you think's causing it?" she asked.

"It's hard to tell," Shankar answered. "This is unprecedented for him. Something's going on, we just don't know what."

The moment Weisman learned of Ship's condition, he worked himself up into an intellectual frenzy. "This is big. This is something. Something's going on Bren. I know it. I know it. I know it. Damn!" He punched his fist into the air as he paced across Altieri's office.

"Down boy," she chided him.

"The guy does nothing but sit there and sporadically mumble for years. And now he starts screaming and having convulsions. Don't you think he's trying to tell us something? Don't you think it's unusual that it's happening exactly when this Mashimoto-Pennfield guy might be trying to alter Ship's life-path?"

"That would be the Mashimoto-Pennfield guy who may or may not exist?" She raised her eyes above her glasses.

"Bren..."

"And how can you say it's happening exactly when the yet-to-be-born Mashimoto-Pennfield is doing something, if he would be doing it in the future? There's no simultaneity there."

"I just know it," he responded, pacing the room. "I feel it."

"Such academic rigor, professor."

"Bullshit. Sometimes you just gotta go with your gut, Bren," Weisman answered. "So when are we leaving?"

"For where?"

"Gladwell, of course."

"Let's not put the cart—"

"Bren, do you have any question about going to Gladwell? We may lose the guy and then we lose our gateway—"

"And, of course, you're fully taking the patient's well-being into consideration?"

"Yeah, that too."

* * *

TIME FRAME: 2053

98

The Egg, Dr. Li-Pin's Lab, Early Morning, April 8, 2053

Subdued by nighttime's veil, the Egg resembled more of a zeppelin hovering over the sleepy countryside than a shimmering testament to modern technology: the perfect time for Ibu Bonne-Saari to sneak into one of the structure's security pods for his rendezvous with Dr. Li-Pin and the cryonically frozen body of his father.

Now was the time, a time for an act that, quite literally, was biblical in proportions. His father was about to be reinstated into the world of the living.

The room was small, super-insulated on all sides, a small nuclear back-up generator embedded in the wall, a precaution in the event of a power failure. The walls were white with a bluish tinge cast by two powerful overhead lights, nested in a ceiling module along with two shiny capacitor plates.

Four weeks earlier, Dr. Li-Pin had opened the canister containing the body of Izan Bonne-Saari and injected nano-organisms into the neck of the former Prime Minister. The heart was then restarted, sedation was induced, and the body placed in a chemical bath to stimulate the body tissues back to normal. Now it was time to welcome Izan Bonne-Saari back to life.

"What next?" Ibu Bonne-Saari asked, hovering over the tub containing his father.

"We shock him out of sedation and he should be alive and well."

Although Ibu Bonne-Saari was the most powerful man in the world, he stood back, humbled, awed beyond anything he had ever felt, as he processed the notion that his father, Izan Bonne-Saari, deceased for over ten years, would be standing and talking before them at this very time, in this very place.

"APPLY THE JOLT," Li-Pin ordered to his assisting technicians.

The two technicians, sworn to secrecy, methodically focused the two plates hanging overhead at a point on the body's chest.

"Okay, do it!" Li-Pin announced.

Ibu Bonne-Saari braced himself. Suddenly, his father's body lurched slightly, wiggling unnaturally. The technicians looked over to Li-Pin, readying to apply another charge. He shook his head and waved them off.

Slowly, the pale, hopeful pink of Izan Bonne-Saari's skin turned a fuller, more promising shade. Natural color gradually returned to most of his body. Bonne-Saari and Li-Pin could sense slight movement. A twitch in the corner of the eye; a subtle movement of the thumb, and then, what they had been waiting for: a slight expansion of the chest followed by a subtle contraction.

Slowly, deliberately, the expansions and contractions occurred several times in succession. And the eyelids began to quiver slightly. Bonne-Saari, barely able to conceal his slight smile, glanced over towards Li-Pin. Encouragingly, he nodded back.

Almost involuntarily, Izan Bonne-Saari's right hand reached slowly up towards his face, rubbing his quivering eyelids. Within moments, the eyelids opened fully, exposing Bonne-Saari's deep brown eyes. Then he lifted his left hand to his face, somewhat faster. Both hands rubbed his now-opened eyes in unison.

The former Prime Minister rubbed his eyes for several moments, first slowly, then more rapidly, finally returning his hands to his sides. He gazed silently at the ceiling: a confusing disorientation. After several moments, he gasped, shifting his eyes from left to right, slightly turning his head. His son grasped for his hand.

"Huh? Wha?" Izan Bonne-Saari whispered.

"Everything will be fine, father," Ibu responded. "Just relax. Just relax." He patted him on the forehead.

Still prone on the table, Izan Bonne-Saari moved his head around a bit more animatedly, attempting to get a fix on his surroundings. Woozily, he whispered, *"Where...?"*

After several moments of confusion, he attempted to push himself up.

Ibu restrained him. "No father, just stay still for now."

He rubbed his eyes again, this time more briskly, then spoke: "But wha, wha...what's happened?"

"You're alive, father."

Izan Bonne-Saari touched himself, poking several spots on his chest. "But wasn't I…"

"Dying?" his son completed his sentence.

Izan Bonne-Saari nodded, still weak.

Ibu turned to Li-Pin and the two technicians. "Please allow us some privacy."

"Of course. Of course." Li-Pin responded, then led the two technicians out of the treatment room.

"FATHER, you've been dead…or should I say *preserved…*for over ten years. Exactly as you had desired."

"But just a few moments ago…I was…I was…on my deathbed. And now, only a few seconds later, I awaken."

"Believe me, it's been ten years. Over ten."

"Then what's happened since? Are you still Prime Minister? Has our government changed?"

"We'll have ample time to discuss all of that, father, but it's all good. Right now, just relax."

"And who was that man standing over me?

"Dr. Stavros Li-Pin, a genius. He developed the protocol to reconstitute human life."

"And where are we?" Izan asked.

"We're in a facility called the Egg, one of the most technologically-advanced facilities in the world."

"Apexian?"

"Of course, yes. It's a private facility, owned by the company that funded Dr. Li-Pin's research."

"What company?"

"Pennfield Technologies," Ibu answered. "You remember Jimmy Mashimoto-Pennfield, don't you, father?"

Immediately, Izan Bonne-Saari pushed himself up to a sitting position, looked his son directly in the eyes, leaned forward and exclaimed:

"What!"

* * *

99

Manhattan, NYCGAB, Pennfield Technologies Tower, April 10, 2053

JMP leaned back in his levitating glass chair and stretched his legs across his desk as he surveyed the somber nighttime cityscape surrounding his office high atop the Pennfield Technologies Tower. To him, the late-night hours were full of magic, a time to refresh, relax, re-assess and, yes, a time to celebrate his accomplishments. Izan Bonne-Saari had been successfully revived. Ibu Bonne-Saari would insulate him from any flack over that girl. In a few short weeks the world would be dazzled by Pennfield Technologies' Cryonics demonstration and of course, the sting of the Pennfield family curse had been successfully redirected away from him.

"So you've done it," Narc said to JMP across the dark office, "you rendered Christopher Pennfield mentally incompetent. Bravo."

JMP thought for a moment, then said, "No, correction: *we've* done it."

"You're being much too kind, dear other," Narc responded.

"Not at all," JMP answered. "You were the one who planted the seed."

JMP loved this time, loved this place. Perched high and mightily above the fray, sitting in his glass office atop the Pennfield Technologies Tower, he was akin to a king overseeing his kingdom, a kingdom he had rightfully earned in his estimation— *and one he never wanted to give up, one he wanted to last forever.*

"So how do you feel?"

"About what, Christopher Pennfield?" JMP asked.

"Yes."

"Someone had to be scarified, someone had to suffer," he answered. "Look, in this world, there are winners and losers. With progress, comes a cost."

"Are you sure about that?" Narc asked.

"Certainly," JMP answered. "Think of it this way: by inducing schizophrenia on him, we saved Christopher from the shame of the curse."

"And now it's Ship that gets to absorb its wrath," Narc commented.

"Someone had to be the victim. It certainly wasn't going to be me," JMP mused. "So now, the Cryonics Initiative will be—"

"Tremendously successful, I'm sure," Narc finished his thought. "Now that Great Uncle Christopher and that woman are out of the way."

"What makes you think that? We have no idea what happened to that woman. For all we know—"

"Yes, why not take the high road?" Narc suggested. "The girl's out of the way. Christopher's out of the way. Ship will take the brunt of the curse. The pathway is now clear. The Cryonics event will go marvelously, free of the threat of the Pennfield family curse blowing it all up. We should congratulate ourselves, no?"

"Look, that girl, what I did to her, it was..." JMP struggled for the right word.

"A mistake?" Narc finished his thought.

JMP nodded.

"Are you sure of that?" Narc asked.

"We're all entitled to at least one, aren't we?"

"Some more. Some less."

"Think of what I — *we* — can do for the world. Certainly we couldn't let one girl get in the way, c'mon."

"Perhaps you got a bit of a thrill out of the way you— *molested* her."

"Okay. Okay. Alright."

"You really took it out on her, didn't you?"

"You can stop now. I know damn well what I did." JMP's face reddened.

"As do I."

"Look, as I said, the girl had nothing going for herself," JMP said.

"So we're playing God now, are we?" Narc said.

"God is on sabbatical."

"But, if so, who says you're his replacement?"

"We must move on, we cannot let things like that woman, that girl, drag us down."

"Very pragmatic today, aren't we?" Narc commented.

"Perhaps."

"But usually pragmatism comes with a cost, don't you think?"

"What cost?" JMP asked, not quite understanding.

"Your principles," Narc responded. "You're valuing your life way above that girl's. What makes you think your life — our life — is better than hers?"

"Why are you asking me this?" JMP barked. "What difference does it make? We have a mission. We have a universe to save."

"Are you sure of that?"

"C'mon, Narc. We are about to give the world the gift of everlasting life."

"But only to those whom you deem worthy, correct?"

JMP did not respond.

"So then, you do think you're God."

"I never said that," JMP snapped back.

"Sometimes words left unspoken speak the loudest."

"Stop it, Narc. Stop depressing us. Don't let trivial incidents bring us down. Let's feel proud of ourselves," JMP said. "That woman, that aberration of a woman, was mere collateral damage."

"Define *aberration.* Define *collateral,*" Narc responded. "Better yet, define *trivial.*"

JMP wanted no part of it. "Let's get on with it. Let's save the universe."

"Yes, let's."

* * *

100

BSCD GAB: Sri Lanka, Prime Minister's Residence, April 15–30, 2053

Upon reconstitution, Izan Bonne-Saari was transported under utmost secrecy to the Prime Minister's residence in the Bonne-Saari Capital District in Colombo. Only Ibu Bonne-Saari and Dr. Li-Pin, through v-conf, were allowed access to the reconstituted former Prime Minister as he progressed through his recuperation period. Li-Pin set the expectations: for the first several days Bonne-Saari would waver between semi-coherent and semi-comatose, virtually devoid of emotion.

As predicted, with each day Izan Bonne-Saari became stronger and more lucid, his long-term memory falling into more precise alignment. Gradually, his comatose, sedated-state lapsed away, and he transitioned into his old self.

If anything could snap Izan Bonne-Saari back to complete normalcy, it was the mention of Jimmy Mashimoto-Pennfield. As his lucidity improved, he became more and more angered over the impending event where Jimmy Mashimoto-Pennfield would become elevated to the status of a god.

"You must never do anything to heighten the reputation of that scoundrel, Jimmy Mashimoto-Pennfield!" Izan Bonne-Saari barked to his son. "Why that bastard used you, tried to create a scandal around you, tried to bludgeon your reputation and mine as well! He's evil, Ibu, all of them are evil."

Shocked and pleased that his father's temper had returned with such an abrupt vengeance, Ibu Bonne-Saari remained calm. "Believe me, father, it's all been thought through. Your reconstitution is part of a much, much bigger plan."

"Then why haven't you told me!" Izan Bonne-Saari barked once more.

"The time wasn't appropriate. You are one of the very first people ever to experience the trauma of reconstitution," Ibu responded. "Now that your faculties have approached full recovery—"

"Cut the crap, tell me now," his father ordered.

"Pennfield Technologies invested trillions of GCUs in developing the cryonics technology. Normally, we would applaud the effort," Ibu began. "However, it became apparent to us that his financial plans necessitated his company offering this service to those much further down the PGU scale, all the way to…perhaps…the Seventh PGU…"

"What!" Izan-Bonne Saari practically jumped off his bed.

"Yes, of course, father. We couldn't allow him to profit immensely as he brought down the quality of the population. We wouldn't want to perpetuate certain levels of society beyond their natural limits."

"So…"

"When we first learned of his so-called Cryonics Initiative, we put Jimmy Mashimoto-Pennfield under tight surveillance. A network of undetectable gnat-cams followed him everywhere. We knew sooner or later he would compromise himself, he's always been impulsive and profligate. And, of course, he did. Our gnat-cams caught him brutalizing this woman from the Twelfth PGU."

"Yes, but he's protected by Apexian Privilege."

"True, father," Ibu responded, "but we seized the opportunity and abducted the girl before she had a chance to leave the location where he brutalized her. We have her hidden in an EVR environment."

"I see," his father answered, nodding.

"And, of course, there is no Apexian Privilege for murder, now is there?"

Izan Bonne-Saari grinned. "Very interesting."

"So you see, we will take his event— the very event where Jimmy Mashimoto-Pennfield intends to elevate himself to the status of Christ raising the dead— and throw it back in his face. We will use it as a platform to humiliate him for eternity and ultimately take his company away from him," Ibu Bonne-Saari explained to his father.

"And how do you plan to do this?" Intrigued, Izan Bonne-Saari asked.

"Just wait, father, you'll see. Just wait"

* * *

It took only several days for Bonne-Saari's plan to unfold. Somehow a holofile of Jimmy Mashimoto-Pennfield and some anonymous young girl made its way onto the Qnet. It took only several hours for the file to dominate all information outlets.

She tried to grunt out a response, but could not.

"Now listen to me." He stuffed his other hand under her chin and forced her jaw upwards, twisting her neck unnaturally so she could look right into his eyes. "Tell your impoverished cronies to fuck off, fuck off or I will ruin you, do you understand?" She gurgled softly.

He growled. "Your entire life, your whole existence, is meaningless, get it? I will destroy you. I will destroy you if you ever mention one fucking word about this Get it? Get it, you little whore..."

On and on he punished her, his anger whipping him into a barbaric frenzy.

He fucked her once again— rapidly, panting like a dog. Finished, he took his clothes, his jacket, and disappeared, refusing to listen to her last attempt to explain.

Even Apexians, usually indifferent to the plight of those in the lower PGUs, were shocked by JMP's blatant brutality.

The "Jimmy Tape" as it was referred to, became a viral topic of conversation: the world's foremost business executive brutalizing a woman from the 12th PGU. When Ibu Bonne-Saari appeared at a public ceremony at the Apexian Institute shortly thereafter, the press badgered him for his opinion:

"Yes, I am aware of the holofile that's been streaming through the Qnet," he announced to the few members of the press allowed access, all from outlets friendly to the Apexian government.

"Mr. Prime Minister, there's been rumors that an announcement of a major breakthrough by Pennfield Technologies will occur any day. Don't you think the timing of the holofile showing up right before—"

"Stop right there," Bonne-Saari hushed the reporter. "I have no idea how this holofile was obtained and how it got out. But let's put it in perspective. Right now it only shows acts of a sexual nature between a consenting Apexian and a member of the 12th PGU. As brutal as the acts in that file might seem to some, no Apexian laws have been broken."

"Are you absolutely sure it's Mashimoto-Pennfield in that holofile?"

"I have no idea," Bonne-Saari answered abruptly. "Next."

"Do you know if that woman's alive?"

"An investigation's under way. If we find evidence that she was murdered, we will deal with it at the appropriate time."

* * *

JMP WATCHED Bonne-Saari's comments in disbelief. There was something wrong, he could sense it. He was being played and he knew who was behind it; he could sense it from Bonne-Saari's patronizing, non-committal response. He knew that bastard was behind it, knew that Ibu Bonne-Saari and his aberration of a father had something up their sleeve, scheming against him. They were self-flattering, paranoid, hyper-sensitive egomaniacs, unwilling to share the spotlight with anyone.

Immediately, he demanded a v-conf with the Prime Minister.

"What the fuck's happening, Ibu?" JMP barked at the Prime Minister the moment his image appeared.

"Now, Jimmy, is that the way to address your Prime Minister?" Bonne-Saari responded calmly.

"You didn't defend me. You didn't deny it was me. You hung me out to dry."

"Now, now, Jimmy," Bonne-Saari answered. "What's a Prime Minister supposed to say? '*Even if she shows up dead, I have the guy's back.*' That'd never fly, and you know it."

"Tell me you didn't have anything to do with this. Tell me you didn't know about it!" JMP barked once again.

"And why would I do anything to sabotage an announcement that will be such a brilliant tribute to Apexian Exceptionalism and the triumphant resurrection of my esteemed father?"

"I can think of a few reasons."

"My dear friend, why do you underestimate me so?"

"I'm not your dear friend and I don't underestimate you."

"Oh please, that pains me. We do go so far back, don't we?"

"Stop posturing, Ibu. You're as transparent as hell."

"Then what can I do to prove my friendship."

"Make it all go away. Say it's a fake."

A long moment of silence as Bonne-Saari pondered.

BONNE-SAARI ANSWERED SOFTLY,

"But then I'd be telling a lie, wouldn't I?"

WITH THAT, the image of Ibu Bonne-Saari vanished. The v-conf was over.

Stunned, JMP stood alone in the virtual conference room, then yelled:

"NAAAAARRRCCCCCCC!!!!"

"Yes, dear other?" Narc materialized before him.

"The Bonne-Saari's are trying to set me up. If that girl is alive, we need to find her and find her NOW!"

"But isn't McPherson on that case? What could a poor holographic clone like myself do?"

"If you're begging for a compliment," JMP said, "you're not getting one."

"I was only…"

"Go. Just do it," JMP commanded. "NOW!"

As Narc dematerialized JMP asked himself a critical question: *had he been focusing on the wrong nemesis? Instead of focusing on those from the past should he have set his eyes on the present all along?*

* * *

THE COLLAPSE OF THE WAVE

TIME FRAME: 2007

101

Lenox, MA, Gladwell Institute for Mental Health Sciences, Mid-day, June 29, 2007

"Welcome. Welcome." Somewhat tepidly, Dr. Shankar greeted Swann, Weisman, Pennfield and Altieri upon their arrival at Gladwell.

"How is he? Has anything else occurred?" Altieri asked.

"We must be very careful, Dr. Altieri," Shankar responded. "We don't want to over-react, now do we?"

"That's not what it's about," she stated. "It's about doing what's right for Ship."

"Agreed."

"Can we see him?" Weisman blurted.

"Of course, follow me." Shankar led them down the hallway.

PROPPED up in his hospital bed, Ship sat virtually comatose, taking up space, but not experiencing life. His vacant stare projected a haunting, disturbing presence. With his pale skin, his vacant, opened eyes and his expressionless face, he was more a breathing corpse than a living being.

"The waste of it all…" Shaking his head, Christopher Pennfield mumbled through doleful, quivering lips.

Without uttering a word, they all sensed the same feeling: the feeling that within those flesh and bones, there was a human being, one deprived of ever truly experiencing life, one who could have etched his own special imprint on the world if only things had been different.

It stung at them.

Then, suddenly: a grunt.

"FAAAAA—"

They shook...

—THER." This time Ship grunted more loudly, slow and deliberate, his eyes still vacant and unfocused.

"What? What's he saying?" Weisman asked anxiously.

"FAAAA—" He grunted then strained once more. *"—THER!"*

"What? What?" Christopher replied.

"*SAAAAVE...*"

Intensely, they all focused on Ship's straining, quivering lips.

"*MEEEE...*"

"Oh my God!" Christopher's face whitened.

"SAVE…ME…" Ship repeated, more quickly.

"What the fuck?" Weisman's jaw dropped.

"DON'T..." Ship's slow deliberate monotone haunted them.

"LET..." Sucking air, he could hardly get the word out.

"THEM..." He exhaled.

"NEV..." Struggling, he was determined to finish. "*...ER...*"

"LET..." His eyes appeared to expand as he struggled with his words.

THEM..."

"Let them what?" Christopher asked feebly. "What does he want?"

Again, Ship's lips struggled to form a word. He strained, his cheeks lifting slightly, his jaw jutting forward. He took a deep breath, sending the EKG and EEG spiking, then after much effort, turned slightly and slowly raised his finger in Christopher's direction:

"YOOOUUUUUU..." He answered with a hollow, haunting resonance.

KNOOOOOWWWW..." He pointed his shaking finger at his father.

Ship slumped back in his bed, exhausted by the effort.

* * *

"ARE YOU CONVINCED, Bren? Are you convinced?" Weisman attacked Altieri with his words as the four of them convened in a nearby room.

"Slow down…" she admonished him.

"There's something going on inside that brain of his. Definitely something," Weisman snapped back.

"I suggest we all step back and take a deep breath," Swann said.

"I concur," Pennfield added.

"Okay. Okay. I get it," Weisman responded. "But this is highly unusual." He looked over towards Shankar. "Dr. Shankar, has Ship ever before in his fifty odd years here consciously responded to someone's words?"

"We have to be very careful not to jump to conclusions," answered Shankar. "He could just be uttering gibberish which we wrongly attribute to actual responsive dialogue."

"Bren? Bren? What do you think?" Weisman began pacing the room.

"Dr. Shankar makes a point," she answered.

"Oh come on, guys. You saw what I saw. There's something going on. Something very unusual for him. We need to do something now."

"Do what?" Christopher asked.

"We need to figure out what he's thinking, why he's been convulsing and now this, acknowledging the presence of his father and asking for help."

"That's a pretty tall order." Altieri said. "How do you propose we do it?"

"No, it's simple," Weisman answered. "Ganzfelding."

"Great. Maybe we should call in an astrologer and alchemist just for good measure." Altieri chided him.

"Oh, come on, Bren. It's worked before."

"What do you mean by *worked?* We didn't fix or change anything. It all could have been illusory. And, besides, I would never condone administering ECT to Ship when he's at risk for convulsions."

"Maybe we don't need to," Weisman responded. "He's aware of our presence or, at very least, aware of Chris' presence. Maybe if we just induce a Ganzfeld state on Chris, here in the presence of Ship, maybe that will have the same effect."

"You're digging yourself deeper and deeper into the hole of pseudoscience," Altieri stated.

"Say what you want, Bren. But what harm would it cause?"

She stood silent, about to return an answer.

"I'll tell you what harm it would cause," Ship's father announced stridently.

They all looked towards Christopher Pennfield's wheelchair.

"Absolutely none at all," he firmly stated.

* * *

102

Lenox, Massachusetts, Gladwell Institute for Mental Health Sciences, Mid-morning, June 29–30, 2007

They set the time for the next morning, giving them all a chance to rest prior to the event. Throughout the night Pennfield was as cranky — and curious— as ever. Part of him wanted to see exactly what was going on inside his son's mind. Another part of him wanted to be the farthest possible distance away. The conflicting feelings tied him into an emotional knot. By the time he awakened the next morning, he had accepted the inevitable. He *was indeed* going to do it. He *would* confront whatever it was that was attacking Ship's mind, good or bad, benign or catastrophic.

"Ready?" Weisman asked, handing him the eye-covers.

"Not really?" Pennfield answered, "but who's ever ready for a clash with destiny?"

With those words, Pennfield wiggled onto a cot set up near Ship's bed and prepared himself to be sedated by the calming monochrome of bland grayness and the banal monotone of white-noise. Still anxious, Pennfield took longer than usual for his EEG to slow down to theta range.

Quietly, they waited, wondering where and when his mind might take him.

* * *

Colombo, Sri Lanka

Morning
May 30, 2011

DEJECTED by his failure to eradicate the world of Izan Bonne-Saari and devastated by Lori's betrayal, Ship had very little left. There was nothing else he could possibly do. Alone in his cell, he mulled through it again and again, torturing himself, second-guessing himself: *What went wrong? Why did it go wrong? What could he have done differently?*

What an irony, Ship thought: trying to save the world from a tyrant, he would now be regarded as much, much worse, a cold-blooded murderer of innocent children, shamed for eternity.

Mercifully, by his count, today was the day it would all end.

MID-MORNING, Ship heard them coming: a regimented pounding on the stairs leading down to his holding cell.

This was it, he was sure.

Four armed guards marched into the room and stood before his cell. One of them spoke:

"Dr. Pennfield, it's time."

Ship gulped.

They pulled him out of his cell and surrounded him, two guards in back, two in front. They pushed him forward. His ankles shackled, he struggled to keep up. After he fell, they dragged him up the cold, sharp-edged cement stairs, scraping his knees and shins along the way.

They pulled him through the door. The sun shone brightly, and the sky was an inviting shade of blue. A retinue of officials stood waiting. Ship immediately recognized Alan Columb-Barnes, holding some sort of official papers.

Promptly the solicitor-general read from a document:

"Dr. Arthur Shipkin Pennfield: By order of the Apexian government, you are hereby sentenced to death by guillotine on this day of May 30th, 2011."

Defiant, Ship looked straight ahead without emotion.

Then Columb-Barnes added, "And before you lose your head, we're going to give the people of this fine island a chance to say a proper goodbye."

A jeep-like vehicle was parked behind Columb-Barnes and his colleagues. Ship was escorted to it. He would stand up on the vehicle's open-air platform, his feet shackled to braces on its surface.

The vehicle took a long, slow route to the museum, practically traversing every street in the city. Irate crowds lined the motorcade's path. Their shouts came loud and in rapid succession: *Asshole. Killer. Murderer. Child Killer. Fuck You. Up Yours. Fuck Yourself.*

All sorts of projectiles were hurled at him: rocks, mud, feces, rotten tomatoes, rotten eggs. He stood stout. Somehow, someway, he did not feel pain from the objects hurled at him or shame from the peoples' derisive screams.

It was hot, very hot. He longed for that final moment, for his neck to be sliced from his shoulders. It would be over, done with, releasing him from the pain of a terrible, terrible mistake.

A distant crowd roared as the vehicle turned onto Cambridge Place. The roar grew in intensity as the vehicle progressed closer to the museum. There were at least thirty-thousand in the stands set up around the courtyard. A giant video screen was mounted on the museum's roof, capturing every detail in high definition. As they entered the courtyard, Ship noticed a large stone monument with words engraved: *Circle of Heroes.* Indeed, there was a large circle on the well-manicured grounds, about fifty stone platforms marking its circumference, a glass capsule atop each.

The reviewing stand stood at the far end of the circle. Bonne-Saari and his advisors stood there sternly, feigning solemnity. The vehicle took a sharp turn and followed the circle, deliberately driving as close as possible to the glass capsules on the stone platforms. The guards forced Ship to look.

He was shocked. In each of the airtight capsules were the preserved remains of one of the schoolchildren or adults poisoned by the batrachotoxin. The vehicle passed them slowly, one by one. *A cute dark-haired little girl dressed in her school clothes. An adult, a teacher, her hair in a bun. A small little boy, no more than six or seven, wearing a baseball cap.* When Ship tried to look away, the guards would rap him on his back with the butts of their guns, forcing him to stare at each and every corpse, allowing each image to singe his brain.

Ship could not imagine any pain more terrible than this; he yearned more and more for the sharp, swift blade of the guillotine plunging into his neck. After seeing another of the preserved children's corpses— a little girl in a blue dress with shoulder straps— he cracked, screaming:

"NO! NO! NO! NO!"

* * *

LENOX, Massachusetts
Mid-morning
June 30, 2007

"NO! NO! NO! NO!"

Suddenly, unexpectedly, Ship blared out some words.

Stunned, Altieri, Swann, Weisman and Shankar looked over.

"NO! NO! NO! NO!" Ship blared again, wiggling unnaturally in his hospital bed.

Shankar and Altieri rushed over.

Restrained by his straps, Ship squirmed into a pretzel, struggling to free himself.

"Let's not take any chances," Altieri addressed Shankar.

"Agreed. I'll prepare a sedative." Shankar rushed over towards a supply cabinet on the opposite side of the room and pulled out a syringe and a vial.

"Wha...What's going on?" Weisman bolted over towards them.

Altieri looked back at Weisman as Shankar prepared the injection. "Slow down, Jules, slow down..."

"All hell is breaking loose, that's what's going on!"

A strident, resonant voice responded to Weisman's question.

They looked over.

Christopher Pennfield, fully awake, sat straight up on his cot across the room.

"Huh?" Altieri gasped.

"Chris? Chris?" Weisman ran over to him. "What happened?"

"I had a very disturbing dream," Pennfield explained.

"Tell us." Weisman demanded.

"I observed Ship. An older Ship. He was incarcerated in some third world prison. He was about to be executed. I could sense it, sense it strongly."

"Then what happened?"

"The guards were escorting him in a jeep around a circle, a circle of monuments with glass tubes on top. I couldn't quite make out what was in the tubes. But apparently they disturbed Ship, disturbed him very much. Then he screamed: *'NO! NO! NO! NO! NO!'* and that's when I awoke..."

For a moment, silence. Weisman paced the room, his mind spinning at hyper-speed.

"Holy...fucking...shit..." Weisman raised up his arms, celebrating Christopher's revelation.

"Holy fucking shit *what?"* Altieri asked him.

Enlightened, Weisman pointed towards the lifeless body propped up on the hospital bed. "Ship..."

Weisman pointed again, his hand quivering. "Ship."

"Ship *is* Schrodinger's cat." Weisman continued. "I should've figured it out a while ago, a long while ago. It was staring us right in the face."

"What?

"Ship is Schrodinger's cat," Weisman said it again.

"DON'T YOU GET IT? HE'S FUCKING SCHRODINGER'S CAT!" Weisman paced the room, flapping his arms, animate with nervous energy.

"What do you mean?" Swann asked.

"He's living two lives at once, one superimposed over another." Excitedly, Weisman responded. "This is awesome, fucking awesome!" He punched his open hand with his fist. "He's sitting here catatonic, comatose, and he might not even have a clue he's here."

"What?"

"He might have no fucking clue. In his mind, he's living some other life at some other place and probably some other time."

"But that's impossible."

"No it's not." Weisman strode around the room once more, his arms flapping as he walked. "He's in two universes at once. He's here, but he's not. His brain, his mind, whatever, is tuned to two parallel universes simultaneously."

"Which one's real?"

"They both are. Until—"

"Until what?"

"Until the wave collapses and it resolves itself."

"*Resolves?* That's what we want, right? How do we do that?"

"I think we may already have—"

"Have what?" Altieri asked.

"Just wait. Just wait," Weisman answered.

"Oh lord, what do we do in the meantime?" Swann asked.

"Put Christopher back under and let it play out."

THIS TIME when he was subjected to a Ganzfeld state, Christopher's mind ventured into unexpected territory.

* * *

NEW HAVEN, CT

Yale University Hospital

Mid-afternoon

June 7, 1955

RICHARD AND MARTHA PENNFIELD sat in nervous anticipation across from the desk of Dr. Blanton Moscone, head of psychiatry at Yale University hospital. They were flanked by Drs. Allenson and Stein, the Housemaster and Dean of Davenport College.

After his outburst during Dr. Winnington's lecture, Christopher Pennfield had immediately been taken to the University hospital and isolated in a private room. For two weeks he had been treated with a regimen of Insulin Coma Therapy, where he was injected with enough insulin to induce a coma and then revived via the administration of glucose.

"So exactly what are these insulin treatments doing to our son?" Martha Pennfield asked clutching her husband's hand.

"Normally, once the patient awakens from the coma, his recollection of whatever thoughts or anxieties that were bothering him — in this case the voice he's been hearing — are significantly reduced," Moscone answered.

"So Christopher is improving?' his mother continued.

Moscone paused for a moment, biting his lip.

"Unfortunately not," Moscone answered.

"What do you mean?"

"The voices he claims to hear have not gone away," Moscone explained. "In most cases we would expect to see a significant reduction immediately after the patient revives from the coma, but in Christopher's case, we have not. In fact, sometimes the frequency of the episodes increases immediately upon revival."

"So what are our options, how can he get better?" Richard Pennfield asked.

"Well, we could supplement the ICT, the Insulin Coma Therapy, with shock therapy either interspersed between or during the treatments."

"Or....?"

"If that doesn't work and the condition persists for a long while, there's always the option of..." Moscone paused and then whispered, "...lobotomy."

"Oh God!" Dr. Allenson, Ship's Housemaster, covered his mouth.

Martha Pennfield shook visibly, trying to remain composed, as her husband took a seat in the nearest chair and buried his face in his hands.

"But there is this doctor in Massachusetts," Moscone continued, "a Dr. Emilio Hazard, who runs Gladwell Sanitarium. I think it's in Lenox if I remember correctly. He's probably one of the top four or five specialists in schizophrenia in the world."

"So you're suggesting we send Christopher there?" Martha Pennfield asked.

"I think if anyone could help Christopher, it would be Dr. Hazard," Moscone answered.

"And how long would he have to be there?" Richard Pennfield asked.

"Probably about three or four months at the very least."

* * *

LENOX, Massachusetts
Mid-morning
June 30, 2007

RESTING CALMLY, Christopher laid on his cot in a Ganzfeld state, motionless, not even a stir. This time he remained under much longer.

"Maybe we should wake him up," Weisman suggested.

"Really? You sure?" Altieri answered.

"Actually, it might be a good thing. It might improve his recall." He looked up at Altieri. *"Bren?"*

She nodded. "Sure, go ahead."

"Ed, will you do the honors?" Weisman requested.

Swann nodded, tapped Chris on the shoulder, and then shook vigorously.

"Chris? Chris? Do you hear me?"

"Wha? Who?" Stupefied, Pennfield removed his eye coverings, rubbed his eyes for several moments, and then answered: "Of course, I hear you…"

"Do you remember anything? Did you connect with Ship?"

"I'm afraid the Lords of Ganzfeld are not cooperating today," Pennfield said.

"Then what did you see? Anything?" Weisman asked excitedly.

"A very disturbing scene, but unrelated…"

"Go on…"

"I'm a bit fuzzy about this one, but it seems to be a continuation of a dream I had a short time ago. I was at Yale, sophomore year, or at least I think it was. My parents were called into a conference. Apparently, I had had some sort of breakdown, was hearing some kind of voices. It was suggested that my family send me here."

"To Gladwell?" Weisman asked.

"Yes, here, to Gladwell, they wanted to hospitalize me… electroshock therapy, all sorts of mind-numbing procedures, literally. Very, very chilling."

"Anything else?" Altieri asked.

"That's it, all I remember," Pennfield answered.

All three of them of stared down at him.

He shriveled into a corner of the cot, and then asked feebly. "I suppose you want me to do it again, do you?"

They all nodded.

* * *

Greenwich, Connecticut
Indian Harbor
Early evening
June 14, 1955

"Ophelia?" Bunny Pennfield called up the stairway, summoning her daughter into the parlor.

"Come here, sit down." Ophelia's mother pointed to a love seat across from her.

Tentatively, Ophelia walked from the staircase to the love seat. Her mother's tone and demeanor confused her.

"Yes, mother."

"I need to discuss something with you."

"Really?" she responded. "What's going on?"

"It's about your cousin Christopher."

"Is there something wrong?" Ophelia's hand clutched tightly onto the arm of the love seat. "Is he okay?"

"Something happened to him at Yale…"

Ophelia gasped and leaned forward. *"What? What happened?"*

"Perhaps it was stress or whatever, but your cousin has had some sort of a breakdown."

"Oh mother, you had me so scared," she sat back on the love seat, "I thought he might have been in a terrible accident."

Her mother looked her straight in the eyes. "No that's not what happened. But I'm afraid he's very, very sick."

Ophelia's eyes moistened. "What does he have? What's going on?"

"It's called schizophrenia."

"Oh God!" Ophelia gasped. "What does it mean?"

"It may affect him for the rest of his life. We just don't know. He's going to be institutionalized for several months."

"But what about Newport? What about this summer?" Small tears began to flow down her cheeks.

"I'm afraid he won't be with us in Newport this summer."

It took her a moment to absorb it all, until:
"No!" She screamed, sobbing.

* * *

LENOX, Massachusetts
Mid-morning
June 30, 2007

"ANYTHING NEW?" Weisman shook Pennfield out of his Ganzfeld state once again. "How do you feel?" Christopher rolled his weary eyes in silence. "Anything new, Chris?"

Slowly, Christopher Pennfield sat up.

"Where were you? What did you see?" Weisman jabbered away.

After stretching and sorting out his thoughts, he began to answer. "This time I saw Ophelia. She was in her teens. She was being told about my institutionalization at Gladwell. When she realized I wouldn't be spending the summer in Newport with her, she let out a terrible scream."

"And what summer would that be?" Weisman asked.

"Let me think," Pennfield answered. "So if it was the end of my sophomore year, it would have been the summer of 1955."

Instantly, Weisman glowed. "So that motherfucker Mashimoto-Pennfield took the bait. He took the fuckin' bait, Bren!"

"Huh?"

"He took the fuckin' bait and we haven't even set the trap yet."

"How?"

"Think. Think. The summer of 1955. What happened?"

"The summer when Ship was conceived?"

"Bingo!"

"But that's impossible. If Chris didn't make it to Newport, Ship would have never been born. And if he had never been born…"

* * *

COLOMBO, Sri-Lanka
Mid-day
May 30, 2011

THE MUSEUM COURTYARD took on the character and fervor of a modern-day Roman Coliseum: a hyperbolic crowd whipped into a frenzy, society's elite in the reviewing-stand, the inmate in the center ring surrounded by the preserved corpses of his victims, and the instrument of death primed for its mission. All that was lacking was a signal to set the deed in motion.

The deafening announcement blared from the large loudspeakers:

"Dr. Pennfield, it is now time for you to perish for your crimes against humanity."

The crowd roared.

Bonne-Saari watched sternly from the reviewing stand, a slight smirk barely detectable.

The guards marched Pennfield to the guillotine where two tall black-hooded executioners met them. The guards threw Pennfield to the ground.

The crowd roared once more.

The executioners picked him up and dragged their victim to the platform. They secured his neck down and shackled his hands to the braces.

One of the executioners grasped for the rope controlling the blade. He tested its tautness, and then looked up to Bonne-Saari.

The Prime Minister nodded.

The executioner released the blade.

The crowd roared with approval.

The sharp blade came rushing down, accelerating with each instant.

Then —

Everything stopped, frozen in place, forever melting from existence.

* * *

LENOX, Massachusetts
Mid-day
June 30, 2007

THE SUDDENNESS of it shocked them.

For a moment, for a brief expiring instant, a nanosecond, before being swept away by the unforgiving consequences of multiple universes warped out of alignment, Ship sat up, coherent, and looked at them all: Weisman, Swann, Altieri, Shankar and his father, Christopher Pennfield.

He smiled, and then whispered, struggling to form words.

"Thank you."

For a fleeting moment, they absorbed that profound, eternal farewell.

"Jesus, Joseph and Mary." Altieri blessed herself. "You were right, Jules. You were right."

From that moment on, and for an eternity before it, Arthur Shipkin Pennfield ceased to exist as an entity bound by human confines, escaping forever the ravages of the Pennfield family curse, passing it forward to yet another unfortunate Pennfield.

The wave had collapsed, the alignment shifted.

QUICKLY, all memories of that event evaporated, dissipating throughout the multiverse or perhaps, forever hibernating deep within the recesses of its collective consciousness.

* * *

RIPPLE EFFECTS

TIME FRAME: 2053

103

Manhattan, NYCGAB, Pennfield Technologies Tower, Mid-day, May 1, 2053

The announcement was both subtle and profound. Family members of those preserved in the Egg received a simple, somewhat cryptic, invitation:

YOU ARE INVITED
TO
A VERY SPECIAL, EXCLUSIVE EVENT
BY
MR. JIMMY MASHIMOTO-PENNFIELD
CHAIRMAN & CEO, PENNFIELD TECHNOLOGIES INC.
THE EGG
WESTMASS GAB
3PM MAY 15TH 2053

RUMOR HAD it this wasn't just any announcement; there was an enormity to it, a magnitude reserved only for those earth-shattering, game-changing developments that occur once or twice a century. When word slipped out that Apexian

Prime Minister Ibu Bonne-Saari might attend, speculation accelerated. The Pennfield Technologies special event at the Egg soon became the number one topic among almost every news source.

There were many rumors floating around; some thought it might be the announcement of some kind of Vac-Gravity Train that would travel from New York to China in less than an hour while others thought it might be the announcement of some new transportation method to approach a significant fraction of light speed. Despite constant badgering by the press, representatives at Pennfield Technologies remained tight-lipped.

Whatever the event, it was evident that Jimmy Mashimoto-Pennfield stood at the precipice of greatness. Not as evident were the measures he had taken to guarantee his success and, likewise, the measures Ibu and Izan Bonne-Saari were taking to sabotage it.

"Mr. MP, got some news for you, really important stuff!" McPherson blurted as he rushed into JMP's office.

"What? What's that?" JMP looked up from behind his desk.

"Bonne-Saari's gonna declare the girl dead," McPherson announced, catching his breath. "Since no evidence exists to the contrary, he's gonna claim her dead and have you arrested right before the cryonics event."

"And who the fuck is your source?"

"Guys down at the station. World trickles down, you know. Where there's smoke…"

"What a fucking bastard!" JMP slammed his fist on his desk. "He'll never pin anything on me. He'll pay. He'll pay." Then he screamed, *"NAAAARRRRRCCCCC!"*

Immediately, Narc materialized. "Yes, dear other."

"We've got to find that fucking girl," JMP announced. "Both of you. No more fooling around. We've got to find her. Nothing is more important."

"But we still have no more clues than we've had before," Narc responded, "unless the *brilliant* Mr. McPherson has finally come up with one."

"Can't say I have," McPherson answered, ignoring the intended put-down. "Actually though …"

McPherson turned silent for a moment. He remembered his conversation with his buddy Frankie DeVito: *Suppose you wanted to make someone go away, but didn't want to whack 'em*

"Yes, go on…" JMP prodded him.

"Well, we haven't been able to find her by using the usual stuff. There's still always the possibility that Bonne-Saari had her bumped off. But then again, if she's not…"

"If she's not, then what?" JMP demanded.

"So as I said I was thinking," McPherson continued. "My buddy, Frankie D, he told me about this new method they're using called EVR."

"What's that?" JMP demanded

"Enhanced Virtual Reality," McPherson continued. "They enclose a person in a sheath-thing, which, along with all the standard virtual reality-tech stuff simulates all the other senses, you know, like smell, touch, all that stuff. It's like they're in a whole other world. The person in the sheath doesn't even know where they are. Great way to hide someone, even from themselves."

JMP swiveled his head towards Narc. "And you've never heard of this, Narc."

"Not that I can recall, dear other."

"Well maybe you should!" JMP admonished him. "You're fucking virtual yourself, are you not?"

"Of course. Of course." Narc responded sheepishly.

"Then do something about it, damnit!" JMP screamed.

"I'll be right on it, dear other."

"And I'll check up on that Fane fellow," McPherson said. "I think he knows more than he's letting on."

"Yes. Get on it, everything," JMP exclaimed. "And don't come back 'til you find her."

* * *

NARC TOOK JMP's directive as a personal challenge. Immediately, his qubits scattered around the globe at light-speed, infiltrating the QNet. Shifting back and forth between waves and particles, particles and waves, they explored every micro-millimeter of fiber, every wavelength of bandwidth, splitting themselves into entangled clones of one another, discovering more and more micro-tributaries sprouting into even more nano-tributaries sprouting into even more pico-tributaries. The qubits accelerated their splitting until some powerful juncture or security block demanded they recombine to outmuscle it. The qubits flashed on and on, in ever more furious pursuit, circling the QNet again and again, waves and particles, splitting and recombining, searching and exploring, spinning again and again in a rapid fury of pursuit.

* * *

104

EVR Chamber, Location Unknown, May 11, 2053

"*Pascal?"*

Drowsy, Robyn Viega pushed herself off her comfortable, clean mattress and looked over towards the source of the sound. She was sure it was Pascal making one of his unannounced visits, full of hospitality and treats, no doubt.

She could see no sign of him, though.

"Pascal?" she called again.

Definitely, she had heard some rustling, had sensed his presence. She stretched her arms above her head and cautiously approached the cottage's vestibule.

Still nothing. Until—

She heard more rustling, this time from another part of her room, from somewhere behind her. Quickly, she turned.

When she saw him, she screamed— a blaring, piercing scream.

Was it a ghost? she thought. Standing before her was the shape of a human — pure, unnatural white— its body parts resembling a rough draftsman's rendering of a robotic man but without any features. His face was just a plain white oval— no nose, no mouth, no ears, just two small pin-holes for eyes.

Shaking, she looked over at him.

"And how are you today, Robyn?" the creature, the man perhaps, greeted her cordially.

"Wha! Wha! Wha!" Trembling, Viega pointed her finger at the man.

"No need to be scared, my dear."

"But you're...you're..."

"I'm Narc, a holographic clone."

"Huh?" she grunted, bewildered. "Clone? Of what?"

"That's not of importance right now my dear."

"Then why are you here, to take me away?" she asked.

"It's not that simple," Narc answered.

"Why?" she asked, shaking.

"First of all, *here* is not here at all, it's not even real."

"What do you mean?"

"You are living in a virtual world, one created just for you."

"What!" she exclaimed, startled. "You're full of it."

"Reality is merely an illusion, my dear. Not only here, but everywhere."

"But I can *feel* things, I can *touch* things, I can *smell* things..."

"Merely a contrivance of some technological wizardry and the subjective reflexes of your mind. You are encased in a Virtual Reality Sheath. Everything you see is a manufactured interpretation of some false reality."

"But ...why?"

"It was, how should I say this, it was in someone's best interest to keep you sequestered, under wraps. Foreign to the world and estranged from yourself."

"That man, that man who raped me*?"* She shuddered.

"No not him," Narc answered tersely.

"You're confusing me."

"It will all soon become quite clear," Narc said.

"Then how can you possibly be here? Did they put you here? Are you one of them?"

"I can assure you, I'm not," Narc answered. "My own virtual existence allows me to slip into virtual worlds like yours quite readily, quite readily indeed. I'm quite good at it actually."

"Then what are you here for?"

"Well, of course, to get you out of '*here*'."

"But how?"

* * *

EVR Observation Deck

Location Unknown

May 11, 2053

ZZZZZZZZZzzzzzzzzzzzzzzzzz!

A giant spark crackled from the EVR sheath.

An alarm went off in the control room above.

"Shit! What happened?" one of the technicians screamed out loud.

"I don't know, we just got some sort of spontaneous spark," his partner responded.

"How are the vitals?" the first one asked.

"Frozen. Can't read a thing."

"Can you reset everything?"

The technician poked his finger at various buttons on the holocontrol panel, yet none would respond. "We seem to be cut off. Can't get anything to work."

"Is she alive?"

"Looks like it, but can't really tell. Still can't see her vitals."

"Well then go down and take a look."

Rapidly, the technician jumped up from his seat and bounced down the narrow stairway leading to the pure white EVR chamber. He walked up to the gelatinous sheath and examined Viega. Her eyes were open, her skin was reddish, she seemed alive. When he went to touch the sheath…

ZZZZZZZZZzzzzzzzzzzzzzzzz!

Another spark crackled, burning his finger.

"Shit!" The technician bounced up and down, holding his burnt finger. "Water, or get me some ice, *fuck*."

"Yeah but is she alive," his partner called down to him.

"Far as I can tell, but she's sort of… kind of isolated."

"Okay, I'll inform Operations ASAP!"

"WHAT!" Ibu Bonne-Saari exclaimed loudly from his office in the Bonne Saari Capital District. "What the fuck is happening?"

"We're not quite sure sir," a security liaison answered. "There seems to have been some sort of malfunction with the EVR. She's alive. But we've lost all control."

"Get it back," Bonne-Saari shouted. *"GET IT BACK NOW!"*

* * *

105

The Egg, Afternoon, May 13, 2053

"WHERE IS ROBYN? WHERE IS ROBYN? WHERE IS ROBYN?" The protesters chanted in unison as large drums kept the rhythm. There were several hundred of them — mostly in the 8th, 9th, 10th and 11th PGUs — marching in an oval outside the security perimeter of the Egg. Pennfield Technologies security personnel and local law enforcement officials kept constant watch.

McPherson observed it all via holoscreen from the Command Center inside the Egg. He was surprised the protesters had organized so quickly, using the release of the video to ignite another spark in their deep-seated hatred of Apexians and the other privileged PGUs.

The security holoscreen focused on an African man with Asian features and orange dreadlocks, standing on a platform, egging them on:

"*WHAT DO WE WANT?*" He shouted.

"*VIEGA!*" They responded.

"*WHEN DO WE WANT HER?*" He continued.

"*NOW!*" They shouted.

"*NO ROBYN?*" He began,

"*NO PEACE!*" They answered. They continued doggedly shouting their demands.

"*WE WANT ROBYN V.!*" He incited them.

"*AND JAIL FOR JMP!*" They screamed louder.

"ONE MORE TIME!" He cuffed his hand over his ear.
"WE WANT ROBYN V., AND JAIL FOR JMP!"

THE HOLOSCREEN MADE the African-Asian man appear larger than life. McPherson studied every detail of the man's features and then studied the faces of the protesters surrounding him.

"Hey, Bruce, pan over the holoscreen, will ya?" he asked.

"Sure."

The screen surveyed the crowd, slowly swinging by the face of each protester. McPherson stared at each, assaying if he had seen any of them before or if they looked particularly suspicious.

"Stop right there," McPherson directed. "Zoom in."

It was Fane, huddled with several other people in deep discussion. He had some sort of communication device in his hand.

McPherson loosened his collar, pulled off his tie and threw his jacket on a chair. He walked for the door.

"Where you going, Mac?" One of his lieutenants asked.

"I think it's time for me to have a little talk with our protesters."

"You want cover?"

"Nope," McPherson answered. "I'll handle it."

ESCHEWING A COMPANY VEHICLE, McPherson walked across the grounds until he approached the protesters about 200 yards from the Egg's boundary. He slipped into the crowd, swerving between protesters, catching quick glimpses with his trained detective's eye and taking mental notes. He didn't miss a thing.

"McPherson, have you decided to join our movement?" Derek Fane tapped him on the shoulder.

McPherson swiveled around.

"Aaaahhh, Mr. Fane, I had a feeling I'd run into you here."

"Greetings." Fane nodded.

"So let me get right to the point," said McPherson. "What the hell are you doing here?"

"What do you think?" Fane answered. "A woman is missing. I have absolutely no evidence that she might be alive. She was last seen with one of the most powerful Apexians, the man who owns this massive structure, your boss. There's nothing in the law that says an Apexian can get away with murder."

"Why here?" McPherson nodded towards the Egg.

"What better venue than the site for Pennfield Technologies' quote *big event* unquote. I don't even know what this event is all about. But I know it's going to be big. And I'm sure it will be glorifying the accomplishments of Jimmy Mashimoto-Pennfield and the myth of Apexian Exceptionalism."

"You do realize you're putting your neck on the line," said McPherson.

"Not any more than draining my life away high on SMARF. And this is a much more noble cause."

"I see. I see." McPherson nodded.

"You know, it's funny, I've been doing my homework on you."

"I bet you have."

"Actually, I was surprised. You were a college professor before you started draining, correct?"

"Yep, economics."

"You could have been in the 6th PGU, perhaps even the 5th, easily."

"Didn't want it," Fane answered.

"And why's that?"

"Just didn't want it."

"Oh, come on, Fane," McPherson prodded him; "you can give me a better answer than that."

Fane mulled it over for a moment, and then blurted:

"Listen, I don't want status of any kind in a system that I consider to be unjust and bogus. Would you want to be the wealthiest pauper, the healthiest leper? It's an empty title, it means nothing."

"Meaningless, huh?" McPherson said.

"Yep, meaningless. Who would want any status of any kind in a society that glorifies the accomplishments of a man who has no respect for human rights and a system of government that couldn't care less. A man who thought a poor girl from the 11th PGU was his plaything. How would you like it if he brutalized and killed your wife or your daughter, Mr. McPherson?"

"Please, Fane, you have no proof…"

"I really don't need any."

McPherson chuckled.

"Don't laugh," said Fane. "You're an experienced detective. You have a detective's instincts. Let me give you a hypothetical."

"I'm not going along with…"

Fane interrupted him: "Suppose a respected titan of industry, an Apexian, was seen leaving a tavern frequented by the lower PGUs with a beautiful young woman. Suppose this titan of industry had a history of rather lewd sexual behavior. He takes her to an apartment in a bad part of town. Then, about an hour later, he's seen running down the street, alone. After that, the girl goes missing. No one close to her has seen her since. How would an experienced detective like you feel about that?"

"He would feel absolutely fine, I would dare to say."

Blindsided, McPherson quickly scoped the area for the source of the voice "Huh? Wha? What was that?" He looked over to Fane.

Fane shrugged.

Within moments, Narc materialized in generic form, pure white.

"It's only me, coming to your aid once again," Narc replied, addressing McPherson.

Fane and those around him shuddered at the sudden materialization of this pure white figure.

"What the hell?" Fane uttered, dumbfounded.

Others crowded around.

"Don't worry. It's okay," McPherson reassured them signaling for them to stand back.

"What the hell are you here for?" McPherson retorted bitterly.

"I have the young lady."

"*Really!*" Fane's eyes lit up.

"Alive?" McPherson asked.

"Quite."

* * *

IMMEDIATELY, McPherson ordered that they proceed back to a security-protected pod in the Egg. He questioned himself as to whether he should allow Fane to accompany them, but concluded he had no alternative. Should Narc be correct, better that Fane be within eyesight in a secure area than left to his own devices in the throes of a volatile mob. It was not difficult to gain Fane's cooperation: if there was even the most minute chance of Robyn being alive, Fane would want to be part of it.

"Okay, Narc," McPherson began, "tell us what you have. Just facts."

Narc flicked his wrist and pointed above. The face on the holoscreen was familiar to them all.

"Robyn!" Fane exclaimed, elated.

"Derek," she gasped.

"You're alive!" he shouted.

"And you're…"

"Not on SMARF anymore," he answered. "Are you okay?"

She shook her head. "Sort of."

"And where are you?"

She thought for a moment, then replied slowly, "I'm not sure."

"But you're alive?"

Silently, she nodded.

"To answer your question," Narc interjected, "she's in an EVR environment in some undisclosed location."

"She's a prisoner?" Fane asked.

"Not anymore," Narc answered. "For all intents and purposes, the circuitry controlling her environment has been isolated and sequestered."

"But she's still held captive, no?" Fane asked.

"If the bumbling fools who control the QNet could ever decipher my isolation algorithm — which they won't, I can assure you — they'll find themselves victims of a quite virulent strain of hijaxian which will immediately disable their entire network control system."

"Really?" Fane responded, dumbfounded.

'Yes, really." Narc beamed. "Quite frankly, she's untouchable.

"Then what about…" McPherson asked.

"My other?" Narc continued.

McPherson nodded.

"That, my friends, is our next challenge."

* * *

NARC IMMEDIATELY OPENED up a holoscreen to converse with JMP. "We found her, dear other."

"What?" JMP exclaimed.

"We have the girl."

"Where is she?"

"For once your friend McPherson proved to be correct," Narc answered, "she was encased in an EVR."

"Yeah? By who?"

"I can't tell you with a hundred percent accuracy, but I have my very strong suspicions."

"Bonne-Saari?"

"Indeed."

"Bastard." JMP scowled. "So you released her?"

"No, she's still there, but they can't touch her."

"So can we get her to…"

"To answer the question I'm anticipating you are about to ask, no she doesn't know that you and I are one and the same. I chose to approach her incognito for obvious reasons."

"Well, when you gonna tell her?"

"Perhaps we shouldn't."

"No, you have to."

"But I'm sure she despises you."

"Yes, I get it, but I wasn't the one who held her hostage. Bonne-Saari was. We just need her to make a statement, an appearance, tell the world she's alive and Bonne-Saari loses all his leverage."

"Easier said than done, dear other."

"Well, go. Go do it. Whatever it takes."

* * *

JMP IMMEDIATELY SNAPPED INTO ACTION, summoning Bonne-Saari on his holosphere.

"You sonuvabitch!" he screamed into his holosphere. "You've had her sequestered all the time. You've put me through *hell…*"

"What!" Ibu Bonne-Saari exclaimed.

"You have the girl, Robyn Viega. You've had her all along."

"And all for good reason," Ibu Bonne-Saari answered. "If I didn't have her to hold over your head, how do I know you would have reconstituted my father?"

Angrily, JMP responded between gritted teeth, "My word by itself should have been good enough."

"That sounds all well and good, Jimmy, but it's not enough for me."

"And I know what was coming next. You were going to fake evidence that she was dead and have me arrested so you could steal Pennfield Technologies."

"Oh, please, Jimmy, they say you geniuses have heightened imaginations but this one is really to the point of psychosis."

"Really?"

"Yeah, really. But now your plans are foiled. We have her isolated. We can prove she's not dead."

"You do not!"

"Here look."

At that instant, the image on Bonne-Saari's holosphere changed from that of JMP to Robyn Viega alone in her virtual environment.

"She's isolated, sequestered and if any of your goons try to fuck with anything, your whole network will be destroyed."

"You sonuva…"

"See you at the event tomorrow…" JMP chided him.

"Why you...you don't have the balls to show up after your disgraceful holovid."

"Just watch me," said JMP.

"You're full of shit."

"Full of surprises." JMP answered. "Just watch."

* * *

106

WESTMASS GAB, The Egg, Afternoon, May 15, 2053

This was it, the day.

The weather was ideal— a refreshing blue sky with just a few wispy clouds, the sun beaming brilliantly over the rolling green hills, a sparkling, shiny glow off the majestic levitating gold Egg.

A buzz of activity swirled around and above the grounds: Hover-jets carrying members of the press circling above and others carrying guests awaiting their turns to dock at the reception pad; security personnel, in uniform and undercover, infiltrating the crowd and keeping strict watch over the Apexinators protesting on the far-off hill; family members being escorted to the giant Levi-Stand set up across from the Egg.

The day's spectacular weather was an omen, JMP reassured himself, as he gazed out over the venue. Today's historic event may have presented him with many obstacles— some past, some present— but he felt assured the day was bound for greatness; without doubt, this would be the most momentous event in the history of his company— or any company— and the entire Pennfield lineage, or any lineage. But, still, his nerves were tested. Despite every preparation, every precaution, dotting every *i*, crossing every *t*, JMP jittered inside.

Hidden in a security pod deep inside the Egg, McPherson, Narc and Fane were in constant communication with Robyn via holosphere. They were under strict orders from JMP to convince her to make a token appearance, or at very least a statement, to prove to the world that she was alive. Isolated in her EVR sheath, she was nonetheless immune from any interference from Bonne-Saari's security force. To no avail, McPherson pleaded with her to make a statement.

"Just give them an assurance," McPherson said. "It's simple. We'll put you on the giant holosphere and all you have to do is tell them you're alive. That's all. You're not endorsing anything. It's just a fact."

"Jimmy Mashimoto-Pennfield should rot in hell," she answered, devoid of emotion.

"Do it," McPherson pleaded. "He will make it worth your while. He'll issue a statement apologizing. You'll never have to worry about money again."

Fane looked her in the eyes. "Robyn, have you decided?" he asked.

She stood silent, non-committal.

"I don't want his money," she whispered. "I despise his money."

"So then you're siding with Bonne-Saari," said Fane, "someone who has created misery for billions of people. We fought against him, fought so hard against him."

Stoic, she shook her head. "No. No. I'm not doing that."

"Then what are you doing?"

"I don't know," she whispered. "I don't know."

A BLARING, whistling whirr, followed by a deafening thunderous boom, scorched the pleasant mid-day skies. A squadron of supersonic aircraft forming an inverted "V" escorted the Prime Minister's craft into the area. Leaving a trail of vapor, the squadron circled the Egg three times at high altitude before Bonne-Saari's craft broke formation and settled gently in the reception area.

The crowd rewarded the spectacle with a thunderous cheer. The chant began the moment the giant holoscreen displayed a close-up of the Prime Minister and his entourage emerging from his craft.

Forever Bonne-Saari. Bonne-Saari forever.

Forever Bonne-Saari. Bonne-Saari forever.

As Bonne-Saari waved to the crowd, music blared from the loudspeakers: the Apexian anthem, *Apexia Supreme Forever.*

"DON'T you realize the power you have?" Fane walked closer and looked directly into the holosphere, connecting directly with Robyn. "You have the fate of two of the most powerful men in the world in your hands."

"But by attacking one, I strengthen another?"
"Yes, but there's another way."
"And what's that?" she asked.
"Attack them both," Fane answered.
"How?"
"You have the power. Use it."

JIMMY MASHIMOTO-PENNFIELD GREETED Ibu Bonne-Saari with a faux smile as the crowd watched. When they clasped hands and together waved to the crowd, Bonne-Saari whispered his true feelings, "I can't believe you had the balls to show up here."

"Fuck you," JMP whispered back between clenched teeth.

"So where's this threatened surprise of yours." Bonne-Saari gloated.

"Just wait, you bastard," Jimmy responded still shaking his hand. "Just wait."

AFTER THEIR HANDSHAKE and muffled exchange of harsh words, Jimmy Mashimoto-Pennfield stepped up to the podium, wiping a rare bead of sweat from his brow.

"Prime Minister Bonne-Saari, distinguished guests, family members, ladies and gentlemen," he began, "we gather here on an historic day — for the families of those whose bodies are preserved in this structure, for our research team, for all the technicians and employees of Pennfield Technologies, but more so for humankind, itself. What's been rumored is indeed true. Dr. Li-Pin and his superb team have conquered death."

The crowd gasped.

"And today, May fifteenth, in the year two thousand and fifty-three, you will witness here, with your own eyes, the very first revivals of your formerly near-dead loved ones."

The crowd gasped once more, stirring with excitement.

"Let me direct your attention to the holoscreen above," Mashimoto-Pennfield continued, "as I introduce Dr. Stavros Li-Pin live from his laboratory inside the Egg." He pointed upward.

"Thank you, Mr. JMP," Dr. Li-Pin addressed the crowd. "Several weeks ago, we picked one canister randomly to determine the first body to be reconstituted. Please observe."

The holoscreen displayed several technicians in protective gear removing the top of a seven-foot long cylindrical canister and pulling out the head and shoulders of a preserved body.

"You are watching a recording of our technicians injecting the body with nano-organisms about four weeks ago. In the interim period, those nano-organisms have been multiplying exponentially and repairing all cell damage," Li-Pin narrated. "We then restarted the heart and placed the body in a form of suspended animation in a bath of fluids to help reinvigorate its skin and muscle tissues. You will soon see us apply a minor electric charge which will shock the body out of its suspended animation and back to full, independent life."

The attendees watched closely as the technicians pointed the electro-plates hanging overhead to the body's chest. When Dr. Li-Pin gave the signal, a slight burst of electric current was applied. The body jolted momentarily and then settled back to rest.

The crowd gasped, waiting.

Suddenly, the head stirred. The arm moved slightly. The body began to sit up.

The holoscreen cut back to the face of Dr. Li-Pin.

"We will now take several moments to freshen up our very first revived human being before we welcome him back to the world of the living."

After four minutes, the moment came:

"Welcome, back, Richard Norman, former CEO of Norman BioSciences, of the Apexian nation."

The holoscreen now revealed a close up of the entrance-hole in the north-east quadrant of the Egg. A man in a hospital gown emerged from the doorway. He raised his hand acknowledging the crowd.

Thunderous, rapturous applause. Awed, the attendees drove themselves into a wild frenzy. Tears flowed. The levi-stands shook.

One by one, the nine other randomly-selected people were revived by Li-Pin and his colleagues. After the final revival— that of Elizabeth Janreau-Mickleson, an heir to the Mickelson Energy Conglomerate— JMP walked back up to the podium.

"Indeed, this has been a very special day, a glorious day," JMP began, "but it's not over yet. It is now my pleasure to introduce Apexia Prime Minister Ibu Bonne-Saari to make a very special announcement..."

The crowd, already buzzing with electricity, turned raucous.

Forever Bonne-Saari. Bonne-Saari forever.

Forever Bonne-Saari. Bonne-Saari forever.

"ROBYN, LISTEN TO ME!" Fane entreated. "You have the power.

"The power?" she responded.

"Yes. Now use it."

"How?"

"Just use it."

Viega squeezed her eyes shut, crinkling her brow and touching her temples. She squeezed harder, hoping that by so doing she would come to some sort of clarity, see the answer before her. Her mind swirled in the darkness. She saw splotches, odd shapes combining, swirling together, drifting apart. She heard a voice, a hollow voice, far, far off in the distance.

"I'm no gate, leave me alone. I'm Shippy."

The splotches formed the image of a small boy, sitting scared, petrified at the end of a rickety old dock on a dark, cold night. *Where the hell did that come from? What was its relevance?* she asked herself.

Then the splotches came together, obscuring the young boy. Now another image. A man, shackled and defamed, guards dragging him up a flight of concrete stairs, throwing him to the ground in front of some sort of official panel.

"Dr. Arthur Shipkin Pennfield, you are sentenced to death for the murder of 48 innocent people and the attempted murder of Prime Minister Izan Bonne-Saari."

The darkness, the pure black darkness, both consoling and threatening, shielding and exposing. Again, the blackness melded and separated, swirling into odd shapes. She saw strange, disconcerting images.

The woman, the very woman who guided her through the darkness in the garden, jumping again off the back of the deep-bellied wooden ship in 1620.

As she jumped, she cried out the words.

A woman on yet another ship, the skull and crossbones flying from its mast, its timbers ablaze, pushing a young man overboard to his death.

As she pushed, she cried out the words.

A woman leaping to her death inside a large building, her body impaled on the spike of a four-sided clock.

As she descended, she cried out the words.

And then back to the first man — this Ship Pennfield — being dragged to his sentencing. Before he left his cell, a woman's face bore into him, crying out the same few words as those other women:

"All mean spirits are doomed to fall."

Robyn gasped. That final image— the woman in the jail cell, her name was Lori she thought— scorched her brain. *It looked exactly like her.* The more she examined the features — the eyes, the nose, the mouth, the lips— *it was her, herself. But she had never been with that man, in some jail cell, in some unbeknownst location. Or at least she thought...*

"WHAT A WONDERFUL DAY, INDEED," Ibu Bonne-Saari announced to the crowd. "It would be almost impossible to increase the level of joy and exhilaration of such an event. But you know what?"

The crowd gasped in anticipation.

"We will!" Bonne-Saari punched his fist into the air.

"I would like to introduce a special guest, a very special guest. Yes, we have one more revival to talk about. Please direct your attention to the holo-screen, where my father, Izan Bonne-Saari, now revived and alive again, is about to emerge from inside the Egg to once again be with the people he loves."

First, dead silence. Then a long gasp of disbelief.

Not until the Apexian Anthem once again blared from the loudspeakers, did the crowd comprehend the significance. They cheered wildly and raucously.

Forever Bonne-Saari. Bonne-Saari forever.

Forever Bonne-Saari. Bonne-Saari forever.

THE FACE OF THAT WOMAN, that Lori, exactly resembling her own, confounded Robyn, obscuring her ability to dwell upon anything else. *That wasn't her. That couldn't be her. Not in that time. Not in that place.* But as she dwelled upon it, in a strange way, the incident seemed vaguely familiar, something she may have witnessed in a way, but had never lived through.

Then it became clear.

They were her, each and every one, each of those women.

They were her as she was them and together they were one.

She opened her eyes.

"Have you decided?" Fane asked.

"Yes."

"What are you going to do?"

She looked deep into Fane's eyes and slowly whispered, "Derek, I love you."

Then she turned towards Narc. Her eyes lasered in on his. He appeared as if in a trance. She stared intently at his white oval face. A power connected them, some sort of strong, overwhelming power.

"Look at me. Look me in the eyes!" she commanded.

Mesmerized, he did. He absorbed her presence.

THE CROWD'S anticipation built moment by moment. After a brief hiatus, a golden, resonant voice made the announcement:

"And now, once again, the most important and significant person in the history of modern civilization has come back to be with his people. Ladies and gentlemen, please welcome Izan Bonne-Saari, your founder and leader resurrected!"

The Apexian anthem blared once again. The attendees shook with enthusiasm, cheering raucously, rapturously, swooning to an orgasm of pure fervor and exultation.

Forever Bonne-Saari. Bonne-Saari forever.

Forever Bonne-Saari. Bonne-Saari forever.

This was it, as unbelievable as anything— magical, mythical, legendary— they could see him with their own eyes: the same short, slightly pudgy frame, the same memorable face. Their ultimate leader, the pre-eminent icon of modern civilization, Izan Bonne-Saari, was now alive and living once again. As he emerged from the Egg, waving exuberantly, the crowd's exultation reached such an elevated pitch that it was bound to burst in an uncontrollable climax of pure excitement.

Forever Bonne-Saari. Bonne-Saari forever.

Forever Bonne-Saari. Bonne-Saari forever.

A STRAIGHT, sharp laser, leaping from the holosphere, connected Robyn's eyes to the two, small pin-holes in Narc's plain white face. The power overwhelmed them both. *Neurons begat qubits and qubits begat neurons.*

Hyper-focused, she gave Narc his directive:

"You know what must be done."

His face nodded and shook.

"Now go do it."

The force connecting them crescendoed, sparkling and crackling.

ZZZAAAAAAAAPPPPPP!!!

At that instant, that very instant, the powers that haunted the Pennfields for generations coalesced.

At once, all the family's tormentors became one. The poor servant girl on the Mayflower. Betty Jenkinson, the minister's wife in 1920s Newport. Marie De la Croix, the prostitute in 16th Century Martinique. And, of course,

Jennifer Winston, the student who brought down the mighty Professor Christopher Pennfield in 1996.

That spirit, that force, skipped through time and space, piercing them together as a thread weaves through fabric.

At once, they were the same, yet different.

Swiftly, the spirit bonded Robyn Viega and Narc, those destined to defy this generation of Pennfields.

UNCONTROLLABLE, the crowd's enthusiasm continued to build with no peak in sight. Even as Izan Bonne-Saari walked to the podium there was no sign of the crowd's emotional fever climaxing.

Bonne-Saari raised his hands.

The crowd's intensity only increased.

He waved, trying to settle them down.

Another eruption of unadulterated enthusiasm.

It took another twelve minutes for the crowd to cooperate.

Bonne-Saari smiled, then said: "Well this reception almost makes dying worth it!"

The crowd erupted once again.

"My dear people, I appreciate your enthusiastic response, but allow me to speak," Bonne-Saari said. "About two weeks ago, I awakened, or should I say *I was revived.* My last memory was of me on my deathbed, surrounded by family and medical staff. It felt like only an instant before, but I was told it was ten years. The staff here has told me as much as they could about the brilliant technology utilized to enable my revival, my resurrection so to speak. I must admit, I am truly overwhelmed and impressed with this outstanding achievement fueled by Apexian Exceptionalism."

ZZZZZZZZZzzzzzzzzzzzz! ZZZZZZZZZzzzzzzzzzzzz!

The image of Izan Bonne-Saari on the giant holoscreen hovering above the platform wavered, suddenly cubellating. Bright cubes of color popped on and off the screen. A harsh buzzing sound, like static, blared from the speakers.

ZZZZZZZZZzzzzzzzzzzzz! ZZZZZZZZZzzzzzzzzzzzz!

The crowd gasped.

Another loud burst of static — *ZZZZZZZZZzzzzzzzzzzzz!* — then an image appeared. A face, a face of a beautiful woman: a pure, natural, fresh unaffected beauty. The confused crowd buzzed as her face filled the giant screen, then hushed as she began to speak:

"My name is Robyn Viega. I am a member of the 12th PGU."

The crowd gasped.

"I am here today to tell a different side of this story, the ugly side."

From his spot on the podium, Izan whispered over to his son sitting next to him. "Get her the hell off that screen. Tell your guards to take her off."

Even before Ibu could take action, the head of his security detail rushed over and whispered. "We're trying to stop her sir, but we can't find where her message is coming from."

"But can't you cut off the signal?" the Prime Minister asked.

"We're trying, but there's something wrong. Whenever we try to cut it off, it finds another pathway… It's like it has a mind of its own."

Emboldened, Robyn Viega continued: "Jimmy Mashimoto-Pennfield is no hero. He is a brutal, vicious man who will let nothing get in the way of his success. You've all seen the holovid. You've all seen what he did to me."

Immediately, Mashimoto-Pennfield sprinted off the main platform and ran towards the Egg and its control room, seeing if there was any way he could make it all stop.

THE QUBITS DEFINING Narc slithered unimpeded throughout the multi-layered network of networks that shielded the Egg's infrastructure. At lightspeed, they explored.

"YES, I am that woman, the one whom JMP brutalized. I am also the woman whom Ibu Bonne-Saari planned to use as a pawn, so he could stand preeminent and unchallenged. Yet, in this world, those atrocities are not a crime. It's called Apexian Privilege. You should be ashamed. No honor. No decency. And I am the woman who will bring back decency and honor to all people."

The crowd grumbled.

THE QUBITS IGNITED into superpositions of their binary essence, streaming throughout every millimeter of fiber, across all wavelengths of connectivity, every micron of processing power, splitting themselves again and again into sets upon sets of photons, electrons and atoms.

"THERE IS no Apexian Privilege for what that man did to me that night. And there is no Apexian Privilege for anything you do. In fact, Apexian Privilege is a myth."

Flurries of cat-calls and boos emanated from the crowd.

THE QUBITS DANCED A SYNCHRONIZED DANCE — scaling firewalls, deciphering complex keys — spreading throughout the system in multiples, until every qubit in every processing unit in every subsystem had been scoured and analyzed.

"APEXIAN PRIVILEGE and Apexian Exceptionalism are myths begun by evil people, some of whom are sitting right here. Some of whom are you. Yes, you. Apexian Privilege means the few imposing their ways upon the many. Apexian Exceptionalism is an excuse for great riches for the few and pain and suffering for the many. Apexian Exceptionalism and Apexian Privilege are nothing more than sets of words designed to make you feel better, to not feel guilty about what you've done. They're perverse and wicked terms."

The flurries of boos propagated into a wave, the crowd filling the air with insults.

"Shut up whore."

"You're a jealous bitch."

"You slut."

THE QUBITS ENTERED the main control algorithm, deciphering the code, skipping across processors, reprogramming regulators. Then, they did what they set out to do all along. They set the water temperature in the Egg's tanks to its maximum, hyper-boiling, overriding all set parameters.

"IT'S time for the many to strike back against the few. It's time for an end to your selfishness. It's time for a new beginning. It's time to deliver a message that will live on forever. And I'm the one destined to do it."

Currents of steam rushed from the water hyper-boiling to ultra-elevated levels, applying enormous pressure on the tank.

She paused and clutched her eyes, covering them. Momentarily she remained in a deep, eerie trance. She then uncovered them. They sparkled with some weird, mysterious glow. She addressed the crowd:

"All mean spirits are doomed to fall."

The boiling water's steam attacked the tank's encasement with ferocity. The pressure built beyond maximum tolerable intensity. The tank shook and shuttered, small fissures emerging, buckling at its seams, currents of steam escaping.

Then, Robyn Viega whispered her final words:

"November 10th, 1620."

The Egg shook, its golden shimmers blurry and diffuse.

From deep inside: a long, thunderous percussive roll.

BOOOOOoooooooooooommmmmmmm!!!!

The tanks burst.

Intense wobbling. Gushing water. Roaring thunder. Golden remnants flying.

A wall of water enveloped the podium, its sheer power sweeping up Ibu and Izan Bonne-Saari, pummeling their bodies into the ground with an intense, unforgiving current as high-speed shrapnel and hyper-boiling water attacked their bodies.

BOOOOOoooooooooommmmm!!!

The giant wobbling structure struggled to stay aloft, wrestled to maintain levitation.

BOOOOOoooooooooooooommm!!!

A violent thundering roll shook the giant Egg, vibrating the lawns, the hills, the people.

BOOOOOoooooooooooooommm!!!

The golden structure descended.

CRRRRRRRaaaaaaaaassssssssssshhhhhhhhhh!!!

Waves of shock pummeled the platform, the grounds as the once mighty Egg collapsed upon itself. Jagged pieces of debris scattered about. Expanding clouds of dust rose skyward. Flames flickered. Heat scorched.

The fire crackled in wicked, lightning-like strikes.

An orange fireball rose, growing rapidly, leaping upwards, exploding into bright yellows and reds.

BOOOOOOOooooooooooommmmmm!!!

The conflagration raged.

The Egg burned red-hot for hours, slowly disintegrating into mere ashes.

IBU BONNE-SAARI WAS DESTROYED. The revived body of his father, Izan Bonne-Saari, was destroyed. The Egg was destroyed. Jimmy Mashimoto-Pennfield had been shamed, exposed and rendered useless. The spirit had extracted revenge upon yet another generation of Pennfields and by so doing conquered the most de-humanizing regime ever to reign over planet Earth.

THE MISSION of Arthur Shipkin Pennfield was now complete.

* * *

REVISIONIST HISTORY

107

WESTMASS GAB, The Egg, Early Evening, May 15, 2053

Jimmy Mashimoto-Pennfield never intended to run back to the control room. His only intention was to save his own life. Sooty and scorched, he burst through the fiery debris, his mind on overdrive. *What should he do? What could he do?* If there was ever a moment in his life when he needed to think quickly, it was now.

Booooooommmmmmmmmm!! Another exploding burst of flames.

Chaos reigned. Screaming and shouting, attendees scattered about, jumping off the Levi-stand to escape the cascading flames and exploding destruction. In the ruckus, JMP gained momentary anonymity.

He exploited it.

BOOOOOOOoooooooooooommmmmm! Another deafening explosion. The fire crackled.

Cutting against the grain, JMP sprinted toward the devastation as everyone else ran away from it. Squirting through the rushing throng, he dashed over to his hovercraft. Coughing from the smoke, he jumped in, hoping he could navigate through the debris and the confusion.

His eyes watering, he quickly scoped the controls through the blur and the soot. Not even closing the roof, he jolted the vehicle to an abrupt start, rose it straight up, hovered it in place for an instant, and then — *POOOOOOOOOOOWWWWW!!* rocketed it right at the devastation.

That way, this way, that...

Abruptly, he commandeered the vehicle away from the blaze and circumvented it with a series of sharp, nail-biting turns.

Zig-Zag-Zig! Zig-Zag-Zig!

His mind raced. *Did he have enough fuel to make it? How much would the financial loss be?* He frowned. Spinning, his mind calculated the estimated cost of the legal suits that were sure to be initiated by the families.

He quickly realized the Cryonics Initiative was so highly leveraged that the consequences of today would bankrupt both his company and himself—wiping out all corporate cash reserves, shareholder equity and post-career maintenance obligations owed by Pennfield Technologies to tens of thousands of Diamid and 5th and 6th PGU employees— and every single GCU that JMP had ever amassed.

And he would be scorned, scorned forever as a complete and utter failure! He killed Ibu Bonne-Saari and the revived Izan Bonne-Saari and perhaps their whole system of government!

He accelerated, leaving the blazing oranges, yellows and blues and the clouds of black suffocating smoke well behind him.

Shit! Fuck! Piss! JMP uttered a string of random expletives for no reason other than extreme frustration. *What should he do? Should he Ganzfeld into the past and change it all? Should he escape to some undetectable lair where he'll never be discovered?*

Jet-streams stung his sooty face.

God Damnit! She got me. That Goddamned servant girl got me.

FOR THE FIRST time in his life, Jimmy Mashimoto-Pennfield had no idea what to do.

* * *

108

Boothbay Harbor, Maine, Early morning, July 18, 2007

The old grandfather clock read 2:35am. Christopher Pennfield awakened anxious, fretting over the virtual erasure of Ship from existence. *Never was, never is, never will be.*

Yet, if that were the case, why did he remember him, his son, by his dear and precious Ophie? How can he remember so vividly someone that never even existed?

He shook his head, quite overwhelmed by the circumstance. His shaking hand searched for his scotch. After a quick sip, he reached for his Rothmans and lit up.

"Did we do the right thing, Oph? Did we do the boy justice?" he wondered. He exhaled, then took a giant gulp of scotch, settling his eyes on the dark harbor outside his windows.

You philosophers fret way too much.

His face lit up. She was there, sitting playfully on the window's ledge.

"Yes, it's an occupational necessity, I'm afraid." He puffed on his Rothmans.

What would make you think we didn't do right, my dear Christopher? She was young, nubile. Her bright red lips and captivating blue eyes sparkled against her pure white skin.

"Merely the fact that we sat back passively and allowed the elimination of his very existence…"

But what could we have possibly done? she asked.

He shook his head. "I don't know. I don't know. It perplexes me."

Believe me, he still exists, she teased him, and then winked. *We're all part of a collective consciousness, he's with us.*

"But he was wiped out, ka-put"

He'll exist, my love. He'll exist...

As Ophie shimmered away, Christopher called out to her. *"Au Revoir, my dear."*

She stopped shimmering momentarily and winked at him. *Mais, Bonjour mon amour.* She motioned for him to join her.

Effortlessly, Christopher Pennfield floated towards the window, towards his beloved Ophie, leaving what was left of him behind in his large leather chair. They joined hands and journeyed onward, floating somewhere beyond, the burden of the Pennfield family curse forever lifted from his shoulders.

* * *

109

Sea Girt, New Jersey, Boardwalk, Early morning, May 23, 2008

Clammy and cold, Ed Swann, snuggled up in an old grey blanket, sat motionless on his favorite bench on the boardwalk across from where the old Yankee Clipper used to stand on Ocean Road. His eyes wandered aimlessly along the shoreline. A grey fog-soup muffled the horizon, an impotent glow struggling to shine through where the edge of the sea touched the rim of the sky. Intermittently, he sipped coffee from his thermos as the eerie darkness of night slowly lifted its shadow off the misty shoreline.

Unable to sleep, Swann had driven over to *his spot*, as he liked to call it, at 3:30am. Now, it was morning, the sun exerting all of its effort to cast light on a part of the earth that was an unwilling accomplice so early this day.

The misty grey fog and the struggling sun together conspired to create a strange, macabre feeling, much more eerie, in actuality, than the black darkness of night. Swann was not unnerved by it, though. He had bigger issues to ponder.

Each day, more and more of his memory was slipping away. He could remember the far past with vivid detail— the first time he met his dear Marie, his days as an undergrad at Columbia, his construction business, his initial adventures in ghost-hunting. Yet, the near past flummoxed him. Even now he questioned himself: *why was he here? How did he get here? Why was he sitting on a bench on the boardwalk at such an odd time?*

One thing he did remember, though: it had happened almost a year ago, his mental faculties beginning to blunt, but still sharp enough. He had been on a mission with Bren and her new friend Weisman. They had worked with Christopher Pennfield. They had encountered a man, Ship Pennfield, who was catatonic. Yet, there was another Ship Pennfield, too. One that wasn't. And then this other fellow from the future. And they each tried to affect the life of this Ship, so he would or wouldn't be a catatonic vegetable. Beyond that, Swann's memory failed him.

But he wondered:

Was what he had gone through real or just an aging mind playing a wicked trick with his sensibilities?

Truthfully, he could not tell.

He could make a case either way, he thought. Yes, he had seen much of it with his very eyes. And, yes, he and his colleagues did everything they could to intervene, to keep reality intact, not allowing some interloper from the future to hijack history.

Yet, by definition, the very fact that they may have succeeded left no proof of their success. The result of preventing someone from changing history is merely history, the status quo.

At least that's what he thought.

He vaguely remembered Weisman saying something about reality being merely a layering of myriad possible universes, with human consciousness choosing its own path.

Swann struggled to remember, and then shrugged. Impossible to tell, he surmised.

He challenged himself:

So how does it all end? As written or do we have free choice? Can an interloper from the future actually change his past and, thereby, our future? Likewise, can we actually change our future and, thereby, his past? Does the past mutate to fit our current choices?

Swann asked himself why he— an old man with a softening mind— even cared, why this conundrum of past versus future and of consciousness versus fate challenged him so. He was in his early eighties, he had accomplished much, he was generally happy. He was more than willing to let fate have its way.

But it really wasn't about Ed Swann, he surmised. It's about everything we've ever learned about human existence. Perhaps we are just meaningless facades allowing the clock of time to tick away as we navigate through life. Perhaps our memories fade away in our waning years because they were never real to begin with.

Or not.

Swann took a quick sip from his thermos as he gazed at the struggling sun. No, that's impossible, he thought. We aren't facades. We're real. Everything that happened was real. Everything he saw was real. And there are layers upon layers of things we can't really see, but they're there, interacting with us, touching us, acknowledging us.

The amazing thing about reality is it's more real than we ever imagined.

He gazed out and squinted; then a deep, abrupt gasp.

Slowly and gradually, the sea morphed into something else, a different world, a kaleidoscope of colors, shapes, people, creatures. *Was this it? Was he actually seeing it? Was Weisman's wave collapsing right before his eyes?* Indeed, for once, the Almighty allowed him to see clearly between the lines, the other worlds, the other times, embedded beneath, between, over and under our everyday existence— as imperceptible to us as we are to them.

Then, suddenly, a cascade of bright, intense light, blinding him, overwhelming everything.

He squinted, searching, and then gasped in wonderment.

Was this the end, or merely the beginning?

SEVERAL HOURS later as the morning sun cast a silvery pathway across the sea, a teenage boy found an old man, wrapped in a grey blanket, slumped over on the bench at the end of the Sea Girt boardwalk, cold and lifeless.

A joyous smile ran across the old man's ashen white face.

* * *

EPILOGUE

CONFIDENTIAL: EYES ONLY

Stockholm, Sweden
Nobel Committee for Physics
The Royal Swedish Academy of Sciences
April 15, 2021

Dear Committee Members:

While, of course, we understand, by rule, your list of nominees is always kept in strict confidence, it has come to our attention— through the grapevine of *speculation*— that our names may be under consideration as a nominee for the Nobel Prize in Physics primarily on the merits (or lack thereof!) of our paper entitled, *"Time, Space and Consciousness: A Multi-Dimensional Approach."*

Should that be the case, we respectfully request that our names be withdrawn from consideration. In said paper we planted a deliberate falsification that should disqualify us *de facto*.

To explain: In the text, we deliberately falsified some information regarding the specifics of our "experimentation" with Ganzfelding in 2007. The misinformation was planted so that a specific reader in future years would be tricked into taking an action that would work against his interests and in the interests of our subject.

We contact this esteemed committee not out of hubris, but rather out of the deep respect we have for the Institution and, therefore, feel it imperative to prevent the Committee from making a disastrous mistake. The risk of the latter, in our opinion, far outweighs the consequences of any perceived hubris attributed to us.

We thank you for reviewing this letter and trust that you will abide by our wishes.

And if you're curious — Yes, our little trick seemed to work!

Sincerely yours,

Dr. Brenda Altieri, MD
Princeton, NJ

Professor Julian B. Weisman, PhD
Chairperson, Department of Physics
Massachusetts Institute of Technology

CPSIA information can be obtained
at www.ICGtesting.com
Printed in the USA
LVHW012333180720
661024LV00004B/221